Dear Bro. Crieglow,

I hope you enjoy my first fiction novel but based on some truth - I can't wait for you to read "The Cross of the South," April 30, 2017 -

You've always been an inspiration and champion in my life, and I love you -

Dr. Sherman S. Smith   Ps 73: 25, 26
8/2/16

ALSO FROM SHERMAN SMITH

Exploding the Doomsday Money Myths

Lie 2K

Life Under Pressure

Clearfield

Put Your Money Where Your Heart Is

Cross of the South (coming soon)

CHRONICLES *of the* KNOBS

SHERMAN SMITH

HERITAGE BUILDERS PUBLISHING
MONTEREY, CLOVIS CALIFORNIA

HERITAGE BUILDERS PUBLISHING

First Edition 2016

Cover Design, Rae House, Creative Marketing
Interior Book Design, Keith Bennett
Published by Heritage Builders Publishing
Clovis, Monterey California 93619
www.HeritageBuildersPublishing.com 1-888-898-9563

ISBN 978-1-942603-37-5

Printed and bound in the United States of America.

HERITAGE BUILDERS
PUBLISHING

Author's Note: This book contains some mild language that is part of the culture, but not necessarily the language the author is in the habit of using.

DEDICATION

Dedicated to Shirley Ann Shanahan Smith
(my mom)

ACKNOWLEDGEMENTS

I wish to acknowledge the following people who helped formulate this book:

Mr. Steve Reimer, Mr. "B", Mr. Jesse Alerta, Mr. Perry Ramierez, Mr. Mike Hatten, Mr. Vel Rogers, and Mr. Joseph Jardin who read this book. Combined, they have read thousands of books, and their critique was invaluable.

I wish to acknowledge those men, women, boys, and girls whom were an integral part of my upbringing and helped formulate my thinking.

Finally, I acknowledge Mr. Fred Jufer my life long friend and brother-in-law.

INTRODUCTION

The mountains of Eastern Kentucky are part of the Appalachian Chain that runs nearly the length of the Eastern Seaboard of the United States. A little known region of these mountains lies in South Central Kentucky known as "The Knobs." Kentucky is divided into seven geographical areas. The Bluegrass Region in Central Kentucky is famous for Thoroughbred horses, Kentucky Bluegrass, and the horse capital of the world, Lexington. The Cumberland Plateau is where the second largest falls in North America is located on the Cumberland River. The Pennyroyal (pronounced Pennyrile by the locals) is another mountain region as part of the Appalachians in South Eastern Kentucky. The Western Coalfields and the Jackson Purchase Area are in extreme Western Kentucky. The Ohio River Shelf is part of these Kentucky geological phenomena and the Knobs.

The Knobs are a narrow, crescent-shaped band of conical hills that cover approximately two thousand two hundred square miles. They are an irregular strip of hills winding south of the Bluegrass Region. A spine of steep ridges and timber growth of various types characterize them. The beautiful little hills are dissected by a multitude of streambeds, rills, and creeks. The soil is found from fair to poor.

Lincoln County lies in the Southern Region of the Knobs filled with people of Scottish descent and juxtapositioned in the middle of no major highway and hosts a variety of little known communities. The irregular pattern of ridges and narrow valleys forced the early settlers into landlocked positions. The virtual typography of the Knobs forced the farmers to eke out a living on rocky soil with little modern technology. It also forced them into a self-governing way of life as they struggled trying to make a living from the small tobacco crops. No other crop except small acreages of corn and soybeans are grown in the Knobs. Tobacco was the cash crop that sustained the populace along with state and federal food assistance.

In spite of all the adversities, the Knob people are among some of the most colorful in the United States. They are fiercely clannish and deeply religious. Lincoln County was and is the most Republican in a state which is traditionally Democrat in politics, but Lincoln County has been solid Republican since the Civil War.

The Knob people retained their social customs of the eighteenth and nineteenth centuries long into the twentieth century. Language, folklore, and general outlook on life were those of another age to the middle and beyond the central part of the twentieth century. Homes were modest unpainted houses for most of the poor, and many log houses devoid of refinement were typical of the way of life. Roads were gravel or creek rock for most of the last century, and the modernization of life passed them by.

The settlements of Chapel Gap, Ottenheim, Pine Hall,

Broughtontown, Crab Orchard, and the larger city of Stanford were the trade points of the communities, and this is where this story takes place. Although only thirty-five percent of the people living in these areas graduated from high school, the subculture survives by a stubborn folk unwilling to delve into modern society. Years after the time of this story, the Amish culture has found a home in the rural areas of the Knobs.

Nothing was more loved by the people living in the Knobs than their churches. From the churches of various denominations, but mainly Baptists, emanated the social functions of life. This is a tale of that life and the Preacher who served them. This book is fiction although some of the stories are based on evident truth. Some of the characters are real although their names have been changed, and some are completely a figment of my imagination. However, the locations are real, and the reader will have to decide which stories to believe and from which to derive pure entertainment.

Some may find this book offensive. For that, I apologize. This is the story narrated to me verbatim by my cousin, Mr. Sonny Smith.

Sherman Smith, Ph.D.

CHRONICLES
of the
KNOBS

CHAPTER ONE

T he bell rang loudly across the Kentucky hills called the
Knobs. It was Sunday, and my dad hung precariously on
one end of the rope. He was ringing the bell to alert the
members of his new church living on the nearby farms that
it was time to worship. These were strange days for me, and
it seemed only a week had passed since we packed our things
and left our wheat and cattle farm in Kansas.

Things happen quickly, and for no apparent reason, when
you are only eight years old. I was happy living on our farm in
Kansas. On a cool Saturday morning, I walked out of the farmhouse headed for the outhouse. I was surprised to see all our machinery parked in the large barn lot. The sheep and cattle were
penned, and the farm vehicles parked neatly in short rows. I
looked east and west across the rolling plains. You could see forever out there in the wide open spaces, and I saw mounds of dust
boiling up from behind pickup trucks and cars as they followed
one another down the dusty Kansas roads toward our farm.

"What's happening, dad?" I asked nervously.

"We're selling the farm," he answered.

"Why?" I asked somewhat fearfully. "Where we going?"

"We're moving to Kentucky."

"Where's that?"

"It's a long way from here, but you'll like it."

"Have you ever been to Kentucky, dad?"

"No son, I haven't."

"Then, why we going?" I looked in the barn and saw Buck, my horse, and my dog. Bouncy was nipping at Buck's hooves. "Are you selling Buck?"

"I'm selling everything and the farm animals," he explained as the pickups and cars veered into the big yard.

Things were real foggy for me. All I knew was that my dad and mom were drinkers, and my dad was a cusser. In fact, I learned it from him. My grandmother told me one time that I could cuss so vile that it would make cold chills on her. I was mean, too. I hated my sister, Leah. Everything was fine until she came along. I had all the attention, but she ruined that for me, so the only thing I could think of was to kill her.

I lashed my sister in a big tractor tire. She was small enough to fit easily inside the tall wheel. I coaxed her in and tied her with ropes so that she would make it all the way down the big hill I was about to push her over. She would not be able to get out or fall out before she would crash into the tall silo looming so largely at the end of her journey. Maybe I wasn't really trying to murder her so much as teach her a lesson. She wasn't innocent. She did things, bad things, and then blamed them on me, and I took the punishment. I was through with all this.

I watched as she rolled over and over, and the tire picked up speed. My plan was working. Soon she slammed into the silo, the tire bounced back about twenty feet, spun around and around and came to rest on its side with Leah still secure inside. I hurriedly ran down the hill and peered into the tire.

"That was fun," she said grinning at me. "Let's do that again."

This didn't work, so I thought I would try something else when the opportunity came along. It did one day as we were on our way with our mother to Salina, Kansas to buy groceries for the month. We always looked forward to this trip every fourth Saturday. Mom would buy us soda pop and candy, and she would always take us to the Sunset Park for a picnic lunch.

On this particular day, we were riding in my dad's 1941 Ford Sedan. Leah and I were fussing in the back seat, and my mom yelled at us to stop it. She told Leah to crawl over the front seat and sit by her, and this would stop all the nonsense. The windows were open on this hot dusty summer day, and dust was rolling up behind the speeding car. My mom was driving pretty fast, which she always did. My dad said she had a "lead foot".

As Leah was crawling over the seat, I saw my awaited opportunity and gently nudged her toward the window with my foot and out the window she flew. I turned back to see my handiwork and was rather stunned as I watched her bounce as she hit the road behind us.

We continued at breathtaking speeds down the dirt highway and then my mother suddenly realized that there was no noise coming from the back seat and that Leah was not beside her.

"Leah, honey, I thought you were coming up here?" No answer and I was dead silent. "Leah? Come up here, honey."

My mother looked in the rearview mirror trying to find my sister and then suddenly whipped her head around. She slammed on the brakes, and the car slid in the dirt.

"Where's Leah!" She screamed.

"She fell out," I replied very softly as if I were in a state of shock.

My mom did a one eighty in the spongy dirt and then drove faster than I had ever been. In a few minutes, we came upon the scene. My sister, dressed in her blue chiffon dress with pretty ruffles, was sitting beside the road. Mr. McMillan, a neighbor farmer who lived a mile or so from our farm, was combining wheat when he saw my sister fall from the car.

"She's okay, Mrs. Smith. Just a little dusty, and she'll have a bruise or two. Probably will need a new dress." Mr. McMillan explained to my mother who was terrified and in hysterics.

I have to admit this actually scared me, and I resolved to never bother my sister again. Besides, she refused to die. All these thoughts came to me as I watched the yard fill up with folks, and I had the strange sensation I was being punished by God. I didn't know anything about God, but according to my dad, He was the reason I was going to have to move to Kentucky.

A few months earlier our cousin, Albert Smith, visited a church up in Abilene, Kansas. Something called a revival meeting. A Preacher was there from Lexington, Kentucky, a Baptist, and Cousin Albert had been visiting the farms and relatives of our community trying to round up people to come and hear this man preach. Our family farms were in proximity to each other because our grandfathers had inherited and split up the seven thousand acres my great grandfather had homesteaded in Ottawa County in the late 1880's.

Cousin Albert had become "born again." I remember that he visited my dad and asked him if he would come to a meeting at the old Sun Valley Schoolhouse where all us kids went to school. Sun Valley wasn't really a valley; it was more like a depression in the land lying somewhat lower than the surrounding flint hills of Ottawa County.

My dad knew nothing about God or Jesus Christ. He made fun of God as did all my relatives when Albert visited them, and my grandfather was the worse. However, my grandmother, who was the grand matriarch of the family, decided that the whole clan was going to the meeting whether they liked it or not. No too many contradicted my grandmother when she laid down the law, so the family was there the first night of revival and filled up the little building with Smiths.

I don't remember all the details, but my dad got born again and so did my mom, uncles, aunts, and many cousins and most surprising, my grandfather. Then shortly after, Albert announced that he was "called by God to preach the Gospel." He was followed by Sam Smith, our cousin, and believe it or not, my dad.

I remember well when all these people were baptized in the horse tank below the windmill that stood by Sun Valley School. This was a strange time of life. Alcohol disappeared from our house, and my mom and dad were actually getting along. They didn't always practice peace between them. I cowered in the corner of the living room one night after my dad found out that my mom had been dancing with Johnny Fox over in Manchester at a barn dance.

I stood by the wall that night watching her dance, flipping her skirts, and laughing up a storm. My dad was off selling cattle, and I knew if he ever found this out, he would kill her.

He came home drunk the next night, but the news had already reached his ears before the engine was cold. He did nearly kill my mom, and I remember how scared I was. Not any more. We were going to church over at the school on Sundays, and I found myself almost living at the Sun Valley School house. I would spend five days of school there, and a full day on Sunday.

Our farm was being sold, and we were moving with Albert Smith, Sam Smith, and their families to Kentucky so that all three Smith farmers could attend the Bible College where that

Preacher, who preached the revival and all my family out of hell fire, was the President. I couldn't understand this, and I wasn't happy. I do crazy things when I'm not happy. My life had definitely changed, and it was going to change even more.

We made the trip. Each family was pulling a house trailer behind their cars. I remember nothing about the trip except a clutch went out of our car in St. Louis, and the single lane highways were so crowded with traffic that it took forever to get to Kentucky, and I was completely exhausted.

Our first introduction to this new culture was when we pulled into the parking area of an old country store along side the highway. It was hot and very humid, and we needed something cold to drink. I looked out the window and saw more trees than I have ever imagined on the earth. There were more trees than I had ever seen in my entire life all put together.

Old timers were sitting on the wooden porch of the store whittling and spitting some brown looking stuff from their mouths. My dad asked one of them how much cabbage they actually grew in this neck of the woods. We had seen acres and acres of the green stuff growing as far as we could see.

The old timer looked at my dad like he was crazy and then burst out laughing. "You ain't from around h'yere," he said in his Kentucky drawl, which was a strange way to speak, I thought. "Them's not cabbage, them's tobaccer!" He slapped his knees and coughed real loud. "Hey boys, this h'yere feller thinks them plants out thar is cabbage!"

Those hillbillies were still laughing as we fled the scene.

Sam Smith didn't stay long in college. Eventually, after my cousin got killed in a motorcycle accident, he took his family back to Kansas. Albert Smith and my dad graduated from the seminary, and they headed for the hills of Kentucky to begin their individual ministries. Cousin Albert went to Bryantsville, Kentucky, and my dad to Chapel Gap in the Knobs.

They would serve their God among the most backward and homespun people; a strange life that I would learn to love and become a part of while forgetting all about my former life in Kansas. Kentucky was my home, and I was so far away from any memory of my other life that it seemed there never was another life. I became a bonafide hillbilly even though I wasn't born one. I would have adventures city dwellers could only dream about.

The church stood proudly on a little knob overlooking tobacco farms. It had been built in 1861 during the beginning of the Civil War. At the crossroads in Crab Orchard stood the First Baptist Church. The Confederate Army needed the church for a hospital, so the members vacated the church until after the war and built the Evergreen Baptist Church several miles up the hollers at a place called Chapel Gap where they would be safe and out of harm's way to worship God.

A tidy cemetery surrounded the building. The church was a small one-room building, but its greatest feature was a tower, which housed the big bell that could be heard for miles. The members took pride in their little building with the clapboard siding, and it was one of the few structures in the area that was painted. Most of the buildings dotting the landscape whether houses, cribs, or barns were unpainted and remained that way.

The road to the church was built of creek rock. These were large smooth stones that had to be hauled by the farmers periodically from the local creek beds in the vicinity to maintain the drive.

Mr. Sterling Deaton lived in the old log house on the right side of the church, and in a little valley on the left lived the large Turner family.

The inside feature of the church was a large stained glass window placed there in memory of James W. Bishop in 1917, a former pastor. I read that inscription hundreds and hundreds of times while in church.

The seats were solid wood seats that were taken out of the old movie theater in Crab Orchard when the movie house was remodeled in the 1930's. Its most unusual feature was the pot bellied stove sitting in the middle of the floor. Stoves such as this were common in the farmhouses of the community as people burned wood to heat their houses in the sometimes-harsh Kentucky mountain winters.

The first Sunday on the job was in late spring. Daffodils were blooming around the building and along the drive. Their yellow heads were bobbing and dancing in the warm wind, and my sister was picking a bouquet with some of the girls. As my dad pulled the bell, and it rang across the countryside, people were seen walking across the fields and down the gravel road that led from Crab Orchard to a place called Ottenheim.

Along these roads were many farms, and the lanes led deep into the hollows and woods. The Chapel Gap Hill was steep and treacherous and had to be negotiated by most of the congregation each Sunday in order to reach the church for worship. You could hear among the toll of the bell the trucks and cars groaning and spinning gravel trying to climb this famous hill.

As people arrived, it was noticeable that boys and girls were dressed in their best clothes. Some of the more fortunate children had on store bought clothes, but most of the kids wore overalls and handmade dresses. Few had fancy shoes but wore common high-topped work shoes with rows of metal claps around which leather laces were strung.

Most of these kids had shoes but there were many who did not. Their rugged and calloused feet were their shoes. I would need to get used to feed sack shirts. These were shirts and blouses made from the fifty pound sacks of grain or flour that were bagged in brightly colored cloth with various patterns just for this purpose. The mothers would save these sacks for sewing patterns into clothing for boys' shirts and girls' dresses. Girls did not wear pants because their culture and religion did not allow girls to wear "boys clothing" as they explained it just as boys did not wear dresses.

Sally and Junior Barber lived about a mile from the church. Mrs. Barber was making her second trip to the church that morning. She and Junior had walked through those fields so many times that they had made a well worn path that could not grow grass or weeds and could easily be seen winding through the dense brush and trees to the church on the hill.

"Junebug," as the boys called him, and Mrs. Barber had come earlier that morning to clean the church and ready it for the services. Sally had this job for years and took special pride in making sure that each Sunday the church was ready for worship.

It didn't take long before the building was filled with curious members. Church worship in those Lincoln County days was the social event of the week. People came to church to greet their friends and neighbors, to catch up on the latest gossip, and talk about the tobacco crop for the coming year. This morning, however, was the dawning of a new day for the church, and there were many more farmers than usual because they had come to check out the new Preacher who had come all the way from Kansas, had graduated from the Lexington Baptist College, and was beginning his journey as the new Pastor of their little church.

Smoking was not prohibited in this Baptist community. The church was supported almost entirely by tobacco farming, which was the only way these people made money, and they supplemented their diets by large gardens. Each farm had a smokehouse that housed canned vegetables and fruit they would exist on from spring to spring. They used tobacco themselves and a lot of it. Most smoked and some chewed, including the women, and some did both. It was a strange sight watching men light up cigarettes and pipes around the church in order to get their last "fix" before the services began. The women were not allowed to smoke at the Evergreen Baptist Church, but many of them did use snuff, and some of the older ladies during the services. Every now and then, you would see some of them "dipping" beneath the shawls they wore around their shoulders.

There were many young people in the church my age. Every boy I saw was smoking, and even though my dad would eventually thunder from the pulpit the evils of using tobacco, nobody paid any attention. In fact, the idea in the back of my head was that I needed to start smoking myself, which is exactly what I would later do. I couldn't stand the fact that so many men and boys were smoking, and so I would have to try this myself.

The church had two outhouses all the way to the back of the cemetery. On the left of the church was the outhouse for the men and on the right the outhouse for the women. The outhouses were positioned very far apart. The boys that had to sneak to smoke were using the outhouse as a lounge because their parents or the Preacher couldn't see them from the church. That outhouse would eventually become my hideaway when I learned to puff homemade cigarettes.

Our lives began in Kentucky, in the hills of Kentucky with colorful people who talked funny and didn't accept outsiders very well. They lived in these hills on mountainsides, on small cleared patches of ground hewed from forests by their forefathers. They owned farms that had been in their families a hundred years or more, eking out a bare existence on rocky ground, raising their tobacco crops and selling it in the marketplace in the winter of the years. I would learn everything there is to know about farming tobacco. It was hard work, so the use of tobacco just seemed necessary even to a little boy.

There were people living so far back in the woods that the only way to get to their houses was to walk up dry creek beds. They used these paths to walk to the main road and wait on somebody to come along and give them a ride in the beds of their pickups. Kids went to school some of the time although there were many kids who never went to school. There were multitudes of folks who never learned to read and write. Many times in Crab Orchard where people did their business, I have seen farmers sign their names with an "X." The Xes were creative and no two were alike as each person had a distinctive signature. Some Xes were bigger than others, and some were slanted one way or the other. Some had a fancy curve but no two alike. This was how they could legally conduct affairs whether it was to sign a check, put a signature on the credit accounts where they charged their seed to plant crops, or credit given by grocery stores where they did their shopping.

This was a life far from any big city; a place no one ever heard of and few outside visitors came to visit. When someone did wander off the trail running through Crab Orchard and by happenstance turned onto the Chapel Gap Road, everyone living on the road knew miles ahead of the arriving stranger that he was headed into unfamiliar territory. These people had a grapevine that was uncanny. There were few phones, but they were scattered close enough that one call to the "party line" would alert others some strange car was on the way, and the guessing would begin as to whom this vehicle belonged and who this person was going to visit. By the time the stranger came by, people were on their porches or by their fences watching with curiosity at the approaching encroacher.

Phones were important. Although few were privileged,

farmers who owned phones would allow neighbors to use them for important business only. There was no chitchatting on the phones. Phones were known to come in handy in case of emergencies and more than one life was saved after phone lines were strung up the valleys.

Hard crime was pretty much non-existent except for the moonshine stills hidden from all civilization deep in the woods. The well-known "bootleggers" sold whiskey, beer, and moonshine from the trunks of their cars. Most of Kentucky was dry, meaning alcohol could not be bought or sold in the dry country. A stiff jail sentence awaited anyone breaking these laws. Bootleggers risked their lives to travel to Lexington or Louisville and run these long trips along isolated roads; their trunks loaded with booze they would sell in the most discreet parts of the county where there was almost zero chance of being caught.

A sophisticated grapevine would relate to buyers of illegal alcohol when and where one of the bootleggers would arrive, where they would be parked, and the drinkers could seek them out to buy their whiskey and beer.

The bootlegger's car was extremely fast, and in fact, much faster than the police cars that chased them. Their cars had souped up engines that generated a lot of horsepower. They would run very fast through the little towns giving the police little chance to apprehend them and few cops even tried.

Baptists were forbidden to drink and to smoke, but it was widely known that many of the very church people worshipping on the hill at Evergreen Baptist Church had their own stills and made beer in the dark corners of their barns.

An old piano stood in the church but nobody could play it. All the church people sang, and unlike Baptists that I would know in the future who only sang three verses of any song, these people sang all the verses whether there were five or a dozen. They sang slowly, very slow. I always looked forward to "Amazing Grace" because it has short verses.

Thus, the old theater seats were filled that Sunday morning. We cooled ourselves with the fans that Floyd's Funeral Home in Crab Orchard provided for our comfort. The fans were made of cardboard with a handle that looked like the tongue suppressors dentists would use to open your mouth and keep you from swallowing your tongue. Each had a classy picture of Floyd's Funeral Home on the front and a verse of Scripture on the back.

Old women fanned, kids were bored, and the men sat by the windows and spat tobacco juice. You had to be careful walking too close to that old building. More than once someone had their clothes soiled and stained by tobacco juice skillfully spat by one of the chewers worshipping the Lord.

Lost in time was this Preacher, but he would change the world for these folks who lived in the Knobs.

CHAPTER TWO

saw a young boy walking across the field by himself that Sunday morning, our first at the church. It was curious. He was carrying a rifle across one shoulder, and as he neared the church property, he carefully hid it in the weeds of a fencerow. He climbed the fence and proceeded to walk through the cemetery weaving in and out of the many tombstones until he reached the crowd of men talking and fellowshipping with each other near the church house. I wondered about him.

He was small, about my size, and was dressed in bibbed overalls, no shoes, and no shirt. His face, hands, arms, and chest were deeply tanned from working in the sun. He could not have been more than ten years old. I watched him curiously noticing that he didn't greet very many people and seemed to want to avoid those standing around gossiping before the service. I later learned that he made this trip every Sunday morning and had been carrying that same gun since he was seven years old. When his mother heard the bell, she would prompt him to get dressed and head to the church for Sunday school.

Like the other kids, his overalls were clean and neatly pressed. The old irons were heated by every mother on Sunday morning on the common wood stoves and put to good use because no good mother would send her child to Sunday School without pressing the clothes and putting creases in the trouser legs.

I watched as this boy leaned his back against the church building and stood on the grass growing next to the rock foundation. He immediately reached in his pocket on the front of his overalls, took out a pocket watch, looked at the time, and quickly shoved it back in his pocket. He then took out of another pocket a small sack of tobacco that had a string attached which was used to tightly close the sack, preventing any tobacco from spilling. Attached to the small sack of tobacco were cigarette papers, and he deftly pulled one of these out and put two fingers into the paper; one holding the paper, and the other to catch the tobacco in the small trough he had made and held together with his forefinger. He never used the other hand at all, and when he had finished rolling the cigarette, he used his teeth to pull the string taut and put it back into his front pocket without spilling any tobacco, and he never touched the smoke with his other hand. I had viewed many men rolling cigarettes that morning, but I had not seen one person rolling with only one hand. He lit up by striking the match on its head with his thumbnail. This was different. Most of the men would strike the match by a quick action on the seat of their pants, which they drew tightly in order to create the friction needed to light a match using this method. I was jealous. I had to learn to do that.

A blond kid walked by. His name was Buster Kirk, and he obviously was one of the more privileged kids because his clothes gave him away. He wore black store bought pants and shoes. His shirt was the see through nylon type that was very popular with the kids who could afford them. Pink and black was the color that year, and some of the fancy cars we would see now and then like the Ford Hardtops were pink and black. I wished I could have a pink shirt.

"Hey, job," he hailed as he passed.

"Job!" The boy exclaimed. "My name is Job!"

"Okay, job." He mispronounced the boy's name again, and they stood and stared at each other. I sincerely thought a fight was about to begin, but Kirk just shook his head and walked off laughing. These boys had squared off before because of the mispronunciation of Fran Job's name.

It took courage to meet this boy who seemed aloof at the presence of other kids. I walked over to him.

"Hey, my name is Sonny; I'm the Preacher's kid."

"I know who you are," he replied. "What do you want?"

"Nothin. I was just wondering what kind of rifle that was you hid in the weeds down by the fence?"

"None of your business," he replied rather nastily.

Stan Kirk, Buster's older brother, saw this happening.

"Fran's an okay guy," he explained to me, "He's just not too friendly."

Stan was a tall kid, polite and obviously very smart. I liked him from the first moment I saw him. He was nice to me.

"Hey, come on, I'll show you around," Stan said.

There wasn't much to see around this little building with all the people gathering for the service. Stan put his big hand on my shoulder. He was three years older than me, and I learned that he was tough and nobody messed with him.

"You come in here and sit with me," Stan demanded. Something told me I better obey. We entered the building and looked for a seat.

"There's one right there," Stan said, and we sat next to Fran. Fran was slinked down so far that he was almost sitting on his shoulders.

"Sit up, Fran," Stan said sternly. "This is church not the movie house!"

Fran's eyes met Stan's, and he immediately sat up straight. Stan pointed to Fran and told me to take the seat on his left, and Stan sat on his right. Fran didn't like this, and you could tell by the expression on his face that he was less than pleased. However, this was Stan Kirk, so he couldn't do anything about it.

"This here's Smith," Stan said as we took our seats. "Shake hands with him." Unbelievably, Fran stuck out his hand.

"I'm Fran," he said, "Fran Job. Like Job in the Bible. Don't call me job like something you do."

Thus began an introduction via Stan Kirk and a friendship bond between me and Fran Job that would last a lifetime.

After church that morning as the people were pouring out of the building and shaking hands with my dad at the door, Fran said to me:

"Want to come home with me?"

"What?" I asked trying to figure out what caused this big change.

"Where's your home?"

"Across that field there about a mile. Want to come?"

"I'll have to ask my dad," I replied nervously.

A custom I would have to get used to was the invitation of members after church on Sundays for our family to have Sunday dinner with different families of the church. Dinner was their name for "lunch." They loved taking care of the Preacher because his salary was low, so they fixed dinner for the Preacher on Sundays and took turns bringing fresh vegetables for him in the summer months and canned fruit and vegetables in the winter. These people could cook. They made bread from big sacks of Robin Hood Flour, which was bagged in patterned cloth, and made clothes from the fifty-pound sacks. The women made everything from scratch including killing a chicken or two for the Preacher's dinner. Preachers love fried chicken. In this way, the people got to know the Preacher. They also used this time to gossip about the neighborhood and told the Preacher who he needed to look out for. Many times those tips amounted to nothing but gossip, but sometimes there was validity to what they were saying. We were going to find out about that on our first Sunday night.

I pulled on my dad's pant leg as he was ushering people out the door. April May, an old lady who drove a 1950 Chevrolet pickup and married to Henry May (she refused to allow Henry to drive anything but his tractor) was telling my dad her life story. I pulled harder.

"What do you want?" He finally asked.

"That boy over there wants me to go home with him." I pointed to Fran who was nervously waiting and smoking a roll-your-own. Stan was standing nearby.

"Then go," my dad said rather hurriedly.

I couldn't believe it. My dad was actually going to let me go home with Fran.

"Hey Fran," my dad called. "Do you go to church on Sunday nights?"

Fran nodded the affirmative. Actually, everybody went to church on Sunday and Wednesday nights. No good Christian would do anything else.

I bounded out the door before my dad could change his mind. Fran took off running, and I quickly followed. It was clear he wasn't going to wait for me and expected me to keep up. So, I did.

"Fran will your mom care if I come home with you?"

"My mom don't care," Fran said as he was picking up the rifle from the weeds by the fence. "She don't care."

"How about your dad?"

"Daddy don't care about nothin."

Fran didn't say much as we lumbered along across the hay field. The hay had been freshly cut, and the shocks of hay were neatly placed at attention as if they were royal soldiers.

"That's my house," Fran pointed.

It was a small house with two front windows and no porch. There was a big rock laid in front of the door, which without any mortar or cement was uneven. The rock was the only step into the front room of the house. The house was never painted, at least from what I could tell, so this family was poor. Beside the house was an old dilapidated garage. Fran's dad was the community mechanic. He fixed up old cars with problems, worked on tractors, and welded plows, discs, and other machinery. The farmers used Fran's dad, Abe, when they had minor repairs to make and mostly for emergencies. Otherwise, they took their equipment to Crab Orchard or Stanford, Kentucky, the County Seat of Lincoln County.

We walked into the front room. The customary potbellied stove was in the middle of the room with a pile of wood beside it. Fran's mom, Mandy, came in to meet us.

"Well, who's this?" She asked. She was nice and friendly.

"The Preacher's kid," Fran said tongue in cheek. "We're going to hunt elephants."

Fran sat the rifle in one corner of the living room as his mother explained that she would fix something for us to eat. Fran had a very attractive older sister. Her name was June, and she sat silently in the corner. She was a teenager, but I thought, *She's a very pretty girl.* She was. She had crystal blue eyes and blond hair. I wasn't too interested in girls at this time, in fact,

I didn't like them at all because my sister was a girl, but I had the notion if I did like girls, she would be the one.

Mandy led us into the kitchen. I had never seen a kitchen like this before. The other three rooms of the little house had wood plank unfinished floors, but the kitchen had no floor; it was dirt.

Many of the people living in the Chapel Gap area had dirt floors in their houses. It was rather odd because they kept the floors clean. How do you keep a dirt floor clean? They would sweep them and put water on the floors to harden the clay. They put many coats of wax on the floors, and after months of waxing, the floors looked as if they were shiny concrete.

Sitting on the handmade cabinet was a bucket for drinking water. Everyone drank out of the same bucket, and the dipper was a hollowed gourd. Gourds were grown in every garden and had many uses, including dippers.

I could see through the back door, which was open, and a screen door framed from raw pine was closed with a metal latch. This door let in air and kept the flies out of the house. I could see the rusty pump covering the well from which water was drawn for the needs of the family for drinking and an occasional bath.

Every room had a kerosene lamp. This house, as most in Chapel Gap, had no electricity, so the lamps provided the dim light needed before bedtime which was generally just after dark. I wasn't shocked to see the outhouse in back of the yard because the only time I had ever used an inside toilet was when we lived in our trailer in Lexington where my dad went to college.

"Your dad won't be joining us," Mandy said sadly. We sat down at the table to a meal of cornbread, soup beans, and green-stemmed onions.

"He never joins us," Fran said sadly. June never said a word.

"I'm so tired of this!" June suddenly screamed as she ran from the room crying.

"She'll be fine," Mandy softly commented as we quietly finished our meal.

I was puzzled by these actions by June, but I would soon learned that Abe was an alcoholic, and he drank up almost all the money that he made from his little shop, which wasn't much, and the family was left to exist on their garden, milk from one cow, and the free cheese the government provided once a month, which they received at the Chapel Gap School House. They also had a few hens from which they gathered eggs.

Fran and I left the house after dinner, and we could hear Abe moaning as he was lying in the back seat of an old rusting car that had been left there for years.

"Are there elephants around here, Fran?"

"Yep, big ones," he explained as he picked up the rifle and sighted down the barrel. "We're going to find one and kill it. Ever been hunting, Smith?"

Smith, he called me Smith. It was funny, but when these people didn't know you, they would call you by your first name, but when you became friends, they would call you by your last name.

"I used to go with my dad to hunt pheasants and rabbits," I replied.

"What's a pheasant?" There have never been pheasants in Kentucky, so he knew nothing about them.

"It's a big bird," I explained. I put my arms out as wide as they could go and tried to show him just how big the bird was.

"Big as a turkey?" He asked.

"Bigger," I exaggerated, "A lot bigger, and they have a white ring around their necks and fly very, very fast, and you can eat them, too."

Fran looked at me. I think to him elephants in Kentucky weren't so strange after all. Just like everybody else living in that world, spinning yarns was all part of the culture. Nobody thought these stories were lies. Good entertaining tales were told down through the ages although the kids believed them all.

Fran had this little vehicle. It was a funny looking thing. It was long, sat low to the ground, and had four wheels. It had handlebars and pedals were on the front wheel. It had two single seats, one on the front for the driver, and one in the rear for the passenger. The odd vehicle was about four feet long.

"Hop on," Fran said. "Hold my rifle."

Did this rifle have live ammunition in it? It was a 22 single shot, and he did keep the chamber loaded. Man, was that neat, having your own gun. Fran was strong; small and skinny, but strong. He pumped us down a path that led to the woods behind his house.

"I spotted one here one time," he explained as we sat at the edge of some very deep and dark woods.

"You take my rifle, and I'll drive. If we see one, you shoot it."

We were having so much fun; Fran was my best friend, now.

"I don't know how to shoot a gun very well. I've only done it twice."

"What?" He asked rather shocked. "You can't shoot?"

I was embarrassed. I wanted to cry. "I never learned how."

"All right. Hold the gun like this," and he showed me how to aim the rifle. "See that knot on the tree? Shut your left eye and look down the barrel. When you have a bead on it, squeeze the trigger."

This seemed easy enough, so I aimed, took my time and squeezed the trigger ever so carefully. I missed the whole tree.

"Wow!" He yelled, "I've never seen anybody shoot that bad." I was even more embarrassed. "Try it with the other eye."

I aimed using my left eye and squeezed the trigger. I hit the knot dead center.

"I'll be a suck egged mule!" He squealed, "You're left eyed!"

Fran patted me on the back and taught me how to load the gun and shoot. We roamed around in the woods for the rest of the afternoon, but we never did see an elephant. I had more fun with Fran than I ever had with anyone in my life.

We had our evening sandwich at supper. Mandy and June dressed for church. Mandy and June went to church on Sunday and Wednesday nights because they worked for one of Abe Job's brothers in his fields on Sunday mornings to make extra money. The Job boys, three brothers, settled in Chapel Gap area years ago when they came from Germany to America. Hans and Frans had nice farms and homes, but Abe Job was poor.

Fran and I ran ahead. We walked down the gravel road to the church because the ladies didn't want to get their feet wet walking across the fields that in the evenings were covered with heavy dew.

There's gonna be trouble," June said. "I heard about it this morning from Joe Brown. He said the boys from Broughton-town are coming after the Preacher."

CHAPTER THREE

The road was dark as we walked along toward the church. A few cars passed us, and we ate their dust. Each time a pickup or car passed, we would get as close to the side of the road as we could and wait for the dust to clear before we continued on. No one complained because this was a normal part of life. I was wondering what June was talking about when she said there was going to be trouble, and someone was coming after my dad. Who was someone? We could hear the bell ring as my dad sounded the alarm-calling folks to worship.

The vehicles were arriving, and we had joined Sally Barber and Junebug as they emerged from the path they took from their farm across the woods. The cars' headlights shone brightly against the brilliant white building reflecting and illuminating the entire parking lot. The church had a single light that hung over the doors at the entrance of the church. One bulb was all there was, so very little light broke the darkness as the cars and trucks parked and shut off their lights.

Before the service began, I needed to go to the outhouse. I walked back there and surprised two boys who were drinking some homemade brew one of them had stolen from his dad's stash.

"Get the hell out of here!" One of the boys yelled as I opened the door to the outhouse. I had no idea anyone was in there, but the smell of beer was prevalent.

"You better not tell on us. We're warning you. We'll beat the crap out of you!"

"Sorry," I apologized as I backed quickly out the door. I peed beside the outhouse being cautious so that none of the girls could see me from the outhouse across the cemetery. There were several girls waiting their turns and straining to see what I was doing beside the Sycamore tree.

I ran down the cemetery path, entered the church, and took my seat beside Stan Kirk and Fran. The Sunday morning crowd was all there, and the singing was just as slow and methodical as it was in the morning service. There was no one playing the piano, and it looked like it had never been played, but this was not so. I learned that Babs Kirk, who owned a little store near the church, had been sick, and she was the pianist. She wasn't very good. She could only play in the key of "C," so some of the songs were way too high, and some were very low, but she rocked back and forth when she played as if she were a concert pianist.

April May had a strong alto voice. As we were singing "Face to Face," she carried the notes after "sky" singing loudly after everyone was finished with that part of the song. "Sky, yi, yi, yi, yi," she sang all by herself, and everyone waited until she was finished with the melodious notes that echoed off the wood slat ceiling and wooden plank floor.

"Let's hear from the Booster Choir," my dad called out as he stepped behind the big pulpit enclosed on three sides and painted the same color as the walls.

Stan Kirk rose to his feet and motioned to all us kids sitting in the section where all the many kids who came to the church sat. No one hesitated except Fran and me.

Stan stared us down. He was the leader of the Evergreen Baptist Booster Choir. The group was made up of virtually every kid in the church fourteen years old down to six years old.

"Let's go," Fran said. I didn't want to go. I knew nothing about this, and I was thinking trouble was about to happen, or supposed to happen, and I wanted to be in a position to help my dad.

The church had a few rows of seats that were perpendicular to the rest of the congregation and faced the pulpit from the side. Stan stood tall up there in front of the kids with his bibbed overalls and high-topped shoes. He could have, but didn't, dress like his brother, Buster, who was in the choir with his pink and black outfit. Stan started off and the kids followed singing at the top of their lungs and mostly off key. They sang with enthusiasm, and the choir was designed to fire up the congregation before my dad's sermon. Stan waved his arms in rhythmic time:

"Evergreen Baptist Booster Choir, Evergreen Baptist Booster Choir,
Ready now for service with your hearts on fire,
Evergreen Baptist Booster Choir!"

The song was short, so Stan made us sing through the chorus six times and by the time we had sung the third verse, I had memorized the tune and the words and was trying to out sing everyone. June Job and her friend, Jean Hackman, gave me some dirty looks. The older kids left the choir section to return to their seats but us kids ten years and younger had to stay put through the whole service. That way all the older folks could keep an eye on us to make sure we were paying attention and not goofing off.

No one clapped in church back then; that would be considered sacrilege, but the mothers and grandmothers nodded their heads in approval just as if they had heard this song for the very first time. Kids had been singing in the choir for generations.

My dad stepped into the pulpit for the second time that day. He welcomed everyone and then proceeded to tell him or her that the night's service would be a little different than what they were used to. He wasn't going to preach; he was going to outline his doctrinal positions, the new government of the church, and told us a lot of changes were going to be made. One thing we learned after this sermon was that people in this place did not like changes, and they would not accept them readily.

After he had spoken for a few minutes, and all seemed perfectly normal, we could hear gravel from the main road beating against the underside of some vehicle apparently in a slide. Although the men and women were straining their necks to see out the front door, which was always open, and to discover what was happening outside, my dad kept on preaching.

Soon, an old Ford car was speeding up the church driveway very fast and kicking up creek rocks and a lot of dust. When the car came to a stop, it slid sideways pushing the dust into the building. It took a few moments to clear, and my dad didn't flinch; he kept on preaching. Soon, there was loud talking heard from the car as four men were bellowing above the radio that was playing a Hank Williams song, "Cold, Cold, Heart." The men were doing more screaming than singing which made it very difficult to hear what the Preacher was preaching.

After a few minutes of disturbance, which had the congregation of farmers buzzing and whispering to each other, we heard the clang of a beer can hitting the parking lot rocks. We knew it was a beer can because pop came in bottles back then. A couple more cans hit the rocks, and the noise from the car grew louder.

"Hey there Preacher man," a voice called out from the darkness. "What you think now? There's beer on your precious parking lot." A huge roar of laughter came from the car as the men jeered and whistled.

Evel Martin was driving the car, and his low life friends from up in Broughtontown, a village up a gravel road in the middle of nowhere were in the car with him.

Evel Martin was a punk. He was a green-toothed man of twenty years and hadn't brushed his teeth in his life. He had long bushy bright red hair and freckles. He was a lanky guy but wiry and tough. He hated Preachers for no apparent reason, and he thought that churchgoers were a bunch of hypocrites, which some of them were, no doubt.

"Whatcha gonna do, Preacher?" Evel yelled as he tossed another beer can out the window; this one landing closer to the open door of the church.

Every eye was on my dad, and there was obvious fear for his safety. Homer Shanks was there that night with his thirteen kids. Homer was six feet nine inches tall, so he said, but he looked taller than that to me. Homer married Willow House when she was twelve years old, and by the time she was in her early thirties, she had thirteen children. Homer was twenty years older than Willow.

"You want to take care of this Preacher?" Homer Shanks said as his tree tall frame rose above the congregation.

"I'll handle it," my dad said quietly. Everyone gasped when he said this. *He'll get himself killed* was the thought in all their heads. Another good man in the church, who would later become Sheriff, was Houston Crane. Mr. Crane called out:

"I'll go for help." My dad said nothing, but Homer Shanks held up his hand as if to stop anyone else who might have an aspiration to interfere with the Preacher's business.

"Excuse me," my dad said as he walked out of the pulpit and down the aisle toward the front doors of the church. My dad was five feet seven inches tall and weighed about one hundred fifty pounds. He was an old farm boy who grew up during the hard depression, working with his hands to help eke out a living for his mom, dad, and six siblings. He grew up fighting his brothers and his cousins. I saw him pin one of his brothers one day for goofing off in the hay field. He made him scream for mercy as he wrapped his unusually long arms around his brother's chest and bear hugged him into submission. I saw him take a big old boy to his knees, who was twice the size of my dad. That day, he was just playing around. People said that my dad had the strongest grip and arms anyone had ever seen back in Ottawa County, Kansas.

My dad went off to the Navy, became a flyer, saw his share of killing, and was a Navy champion boxer, a farmer, and a Preacher. I wasn't worried; I feared more for that dumb hillbilly throwing beer cans from his car than my dad's safety.

Darkness was as black as ebony, and Martin couldn't see my dad as he approached his car, so he was surprised when he suddenly realized my dad was standing outside the driver's window where heathen Evel Martin was about to toss another empty beer can.

"What's going on boys?" My dad could be heard clear as if he were standing behind his pulpit. No one was moving, whispering, or talking in the church. I am sure they thought my dad was going to try and talk these boys down and end the whole thing. But, they know Evel Martin. He was trouble from the get-go, and this wasn't the first time he disturbed one of their services. He beat up a Preacher at another church he was terrorizing when he found him cowering behind the pulpit after one of his beer can throwing tirades.

"Drinking a little beer or maybe a whole lot," Martin jostled while the man in the front seat and the two in the backseat were roaring with laughter. "What you think about that, Preacher man?"

"I think you better get out of the car and pick up all these beer cans, that's what I think," my dad said with authority.

Martin and his cronies couldn't believe their ears and the audacity of this little man. They laughed even louder. They were bent over with laughter and tears were running out of Evel's eyes. He wiped them.

"PPPPPick up what?" He stuttered on purpose.

"Pick up the cans," my dad ordered, "And don't show your faces around here again."

This made Martin mad, really mad. He was so mad he shut up his mouth and clenched his teeth. He gave my dad an ugly gesture with his middle finger and said: "Screw you Preacher, and your congregation of do-gooders sitting in there scared to death. Screw you all!"

Martin reached for my dad from the window of his car. Dad had inched up closer and closer trying to see what was in the car, a gun or something that he needed to be aware of before he taught these boys a lesson.

As Martin pitched his arm toward my dad trying to take a swing, my dad grabbed his arm and pulled him toward the window. This hurt Martin, and his eyes welled up as the pain racked down his arm to his chest. Martin was helpless as my dad pulled him through the window and scraped Martin's head on top of the doorframe as he yanked him out. One of my dad's hands was on Martin's head pulling him through the window by his hair.

"You S-O-B," Martin cried, "I'll kill you, you bastard."

"I don't think so," my dad exclaimed while slamming the hick to the rocks beside his own car.

Martin jumped to his feet quick as a cat. The entrance of the church was teeming with people pushing and shoving to get a view of what was going on. Homer Shanks was head and shoulders above the tallest man, so he was keeping an eye on the situation as was Mr. Crane.

Martin took a wild swing at my dad, which was blocked with my dad's left arm. With his right fist, he hit Martin square between his eyes in the middle of his forehead. Martin's eyes crossed when the blow struck him like a twenty-pound sledge-hammer. He had never been hit this hard in his punk life. He flinched a couple of times, shook it off, and ran wobbling at my dad. This guy didn't know how to fight, and he was throwing haymakers while charging with all his might. Dad wasn't going to throw any more punches. He knew that if he hit Martin again with all his power, he would knock him out and spoil all the fun he was about to have.

The Preacher pulled Martin off the ground and looked into his eyes. They were blackening and swelling shut from the powerful punch to Martin's forehead. He pulled Martin by the hair, and Martin tried lunging at him another time. My dad stepped out of the way, and Martin stumbled and fell. Again, my dad with his hands full of greasy, unwashed red hair pulled Martin from the ground and raised him to his full height. He was taller than my dad by four or five inches, but that didn't matter. It just made it easier for my dad to do what he was about to do.

Dad slid his long arms around Martin's skinny waist. He pulled hard enough to let Martin know what he was in for. My dad slid his arms quietly around Martin's chest and squeezed harder. The air gushed out of Martin's lungs, and his eyes bugged from his head as he looked at my dad in disbelief.

Martin made a feeble attempt to poke at my dad's eyes, a maneuver that might break a bear hug. He was too weak; my dad applied more pressure. Soon, Martin was unable to breathe and then slid between my dad's arms, landed on his knees, and held onto dad's legs.

Dad gave him a second or two and again pulled him upright to his feet by his hair. He then let go and caught Martin quickly before he fell and brought his strong grip around his chest once more and squeezed every breath of air out of the young man as his eyes rolled back into his head as he was falling once again.

Three more times my dad did this until Martin was completely helpless and had defecated in his own breeches. Dad then picked Martin up and placed him gently behind the car's steering wheel and placed his hands on the wheel as if he were getting ready to drive off down the road.

"Now, you two there, pick up these cans," my dad ordered forcefully with a commanding voice.

Two men remained in the car. The third man was seen high tailing it down the lane as fast as his legs would carry him. Then, a real big man got out of the backseat. He rose to his feet.

"Go to hell," he quipped, and then laughed. "You're a piece of crap!" He yelled at my dad.

As he took his turn swinging at my dad's face, my dad blocked the punch of his fat forearm and hit him so hard with an uppercut that he went on his tiptoes. Dad then came back with a right cross to the jaw with such force that the man's eyes showed only the whites as he fell to the ground as hard as a tree falling in the forest blown down by a cyclone wind.

The Preacher turned around and looked for the other guy

and then spotted him picking up cans and throwing them into the backseat of Evel's Ford. He then helped his buddy, who was waking up, into the car.

When the last can was cleared from the yard, my dad walked into the church and into his pulpit as calmly as if nothing had ever happened.

"So," he concluded, "This Wednesday evening, you all think about who you want to elect as officers of the church, and the new Sunday School teachers. This Sunday, we are going to have Sunday School a solid hour before the regular church service."

We sang "O Why Not Tonight" and filed out of the church. People were shaking hands and heads as they greeted the Pastor. Not one person said one thing about the incident which news would spread like wildfire throughout the countryside and define my dad's persona as the Preacher at Evergreen Baptist Church. My dad was never messed with again by anybody at any time. He was known as the "fighting Preacher" although he never had another fight. It was also a warning that you should never, ever, cuss at him.

We exited the parking area that first Sunday night of my dad's ministry, and as we filed by Evel Martin's Ford, he was sitting at the wheel of his car disoriented and obviously trying to figure out what went wrong.

CHAPTER FOUR

My first rifle was given to me by my dad for my tenth birthday. I had been using the old single shot Mossberg 22 that was given to my dad by my grandfather when he was a boy, and he passed it on to me. After shooting some 22 shorts and target practicing, I came into the front room of the old trailer house where we lived. I had meandered down to the spring that was a half-mile from our house carrying a bucket of water for drinking. I made the trip twice, and sometimes I had to carry water three or four times a day. The two gallon galvanized bucket was too heavy for me to carry this distance, so I would fill it a little more than halfway full and lug it back to the house.

The spring was at least a hundred years old, but the water was pure and tasted good. Years before, some farmers hollowed out a deep well where the spring water ran from the ground, and several farmers living in the area that didn't have a cistern or well, used this spring. From time to time, the spring had to be cleaned, which was a tedious job, but the murky water caused by the stirring mud cleared itself quickly.

This particular day, I was in a hurry and had sloshed water over the side leaving only about a gallon or so in the bucket. This was my second trip in a row because my dad made me go back and get another bucket. I was more careful this time because I knew that my only birthday present was waiting for me.

As I entered the room and put the bucket on the kitchen sink, Fran walked in.

"Hey, Bud, did you get what you wanted?" "Bud" was Fran's new favorite word. He was referring to my birthday present.

"Sonny, ready?" There was great anticipation as my dad walked from the bedroom to the open living room. He had something wrapped in a blanket.

"Happy birthday," he said as he handed the wrap to me. I knew it was a gun, but I didn't know what kind. I unwrapped the blanket that was tied by a cord.

"HOLY COW!" I screamed. Fran was smiling.

There were two guns wrapped in the blanket. I held up the JC Higgins 22 automatic rifle and a 12 gauge JC Higgins pump shotgun. I was overwhelmed by my dad's generosity, but he explained:

"The rifle's for your birthday, and the shotgun is for Christmas." Christmas was eight months away. "I don't want you to miss rabbit season this year."

Fran and I didn't wait. We grabbed our guns and headed for the woods. There were deep woods all around us, and the Knobs could be tiresome as we would climb many times to our secret places. Our parents trusted us with guns, and I thought over the years that kids I would one day know and meet could never be trusted with weapons so dangerous.

Fran and I had our favorite places to shoot, so we headed

quickly to our secret lair where we had sometimes camped out for two or three days at a time.

"Let me shoot that rifle," Fran said as I loaded a couple of Remington shells into the shotgun chamber.

Fran put some rocks on a fallen moss covered log, and we began target practice. After Fran shot off a few rocks, he had a smile on his face.

"This thing's pretty good, but it don't shoot as straight as my gun."

Fran fired about ten shots in a row. He had never used an automatic rifle before, and this was one of the few automatics in that part of the county. His comment about my gun would become a point of contention between us, and the only time when I actually ever wanted to jump him since we had become friends. I held myself back; restraining because Fran was so poor that he could only dream of having a gun like this. He didn't have his own shotgun, either. Abe let him borrow his old 16 gauge double barrel, which was ancient enough to have been on Noah's Ark.

I pointed my shotgun at a bird high in a tree, took aim, squeezed the trigger, and the kick was so strong that it knocked me flat on my butt, and it hurt my shoulder. Fran roared with laughter.

"Don't shoot at birds," Fran warned, "They eat insects that damage our tobacco crops."

I felt terrible, so I took a glance at the top of the tall Hickory tree, and the bird was still singing away as if nothing happened. I would need to learn to shoot that gun.

Towards the middle of the afternoon, and after we had shot one box of shotgun shells and two boxes of 22 long rifles, we were sitting down in the shade of a big Walnut tree. Black hulls were all around us, and Fran was trying to break one open with a couple of rocks. Out of nowhere, the bark flew off the tree just above Fran's head and then we heard the loud noise echoing through the hollows.

"What the......?" Fran yelled.

Another piece of bark flew off inches from his head, and the bark landed several feet away from us. The crack of the gunshot again echoed for what seemed like miles. Someone was firing at us.

Whoever this was wasn't shooting a 22 rifle. The reverberating sounds through the hills and valleys were much too loud for an ordinary gun. We heard someone laughing not more than one hundred yards from us.

"Benji McDuff," Fran mumbled.

Benji was a kid about fourteen years old and like so many kids living in the Knobs had red hair and freckles. He didn't live in Lincoln County; he lived in Cincinnati, Ohio. His grandparents, the Hanovers, owned a grocery store as part of their farm in the deeper hills toward Chestnut Ridge. Benji would travel from Cincinnati and spend the summers, but this particular weekend, he was down for spring break from school in the big city.

I was scared to death. I had heard about Benji, and he didn't come to church. He hated hillbilly kids, hated farms, hated the farmers, hated everything. His parents sent him to Chapel Gap for the summers to keep him out of reform school. His grandparents spoiled him, letting him get away with murder, and had bought him a Winchester 30-30, a powerful rifle that used expensive shells. Benji wanted to hunt deer, and this gun would kill one easily.

Benji was never required to work like the rest of us boys, and I hated him. I hated his red hair. I have never seen so many people with red hair. My dad tried to explain to me one time that these people were all of Scottish descent even though most did not have Scottish names. Their ancestors had settled in that part of the country when they came across the Cumberland Mountains after Daniel Boone had blazed the trail west to Kentucky. I did not like Benji McDuff.

Benji took another aim, and Fran pushed me to the ground just as another bullet ripped the tree we were leaning against.

"I'm not shooting at you," Benji yelled, "If I was, you'd be dead." He laughed some more.

"This here's my granddaddy's land, and I'm warning you two to stay off it because the next time I catch you on our property, I will kill you." Benji yelled from his perch on a knoll some twenty feet high above our position. He had a good view from where he was, but it was difficult for us to see him. We didn't know if he was going to kill us or what.

As quickly as Benji had come, he was gone.

"Should we tell dad about this?" I asked Fran who was breathing rapidly.

"No, Bud," he explained, "If we do, Benji will hurt us bad."

"So, what do we do?" I asked while shaking.

"Tell Riley Pat," Fran answered quietly.

"Who's Riley Pat?"

"He's Benji's best friend, but he won't like this. He's the only guy around here Benji will have anything to do with."

Fran always had a plan. He had a unique ability to figure things out. He explained to me on the way home that Benji was always upset that he crossed a little bitty portion of his grandfather's land on the way to church. He once told Fran that he would beat him up if he caught him climbing one of their fences.

"Fran, is that why you carry your rifle?" It suddenly dawned on me that I never asked exactly why Fran felt the need to carry his gun to church and hide it in the fencerow before he climbed over the fence and into the cemetery.

"Yep. I started carrying my gun when I was seven years old. Benji saw me one day crossing the field and chased me down.

He caught me and beat me up. I had Mr. Hanover's permission to walk that way, but Benji didn't care. He wanted to stop me because he didn't like it. I was bleeding pretty badly after that beating.

"So, why didn't you tell Mr. Hanover?"

"Wouldn't do any good. Benji tells them what to do, and when he is in trouble, he tells them everybody else is lying, and they believe him. Nope. I decided if he ever touched me again, or tried to; I'd just shoot him down and be done with it."

Fran was tough and meant business. "Never bothered me again as long as I had my rifle," Fran said.

We were just kids, but this was serious business. These clannish people learned at an early age to protect themselves. There were feuds that got started just this simply and carried on for a hundred years. I learned from Fran where I could go, and where I couldn't, who I could trust, and who I couldn't. His wisdom beyond his years would save me many times as we were growing up in Chapel Gap.

Riley Pat was Haley Pat's son. His dad was dead, and he and his two sisters, Jane and Maggie, were raised without a dad. Haley was a large woman, and probably weighed four hundred pounds. Maybe she didn't, but she was the biggest woman I'd ever seen. She came to church, but she had to rely on someone to come and give her a ride while her kids walked the mile and a half to the services. I wondered many times how Mrs. Pat could get into that little seat at church. She certainly did take all of it, and many times looked uncomfortable but never complained.

Maggie Pat was my Sunday School teacher, and I was in love with her one time. I didn't love many teachers; especially, schoolteachers, but I did love her. She was nice to me, but Fran was her favorite although he didn't seem to want to have much to do with her. "Can't trust fat women," he would say.

Jane Pat was a couple of years older than us, and she used to cuss at me when I pulled her hair during church. This was one of my favorite things to do. I would pull her hair and then run from the church before she could catch up with me, and she would cuss from a distance. It was fun.

Riley Pat was fifteen years old. He was a handsome boy and didn't carry the same genes that his sisters had inherited from their mother. Riley was tall and thin with blond hair, as blond as corn silk. In fact, some of the boys had named him, "Silk." He was more than all this. He was smart. In fact, I overheard one of the ladies in the church telling my dad, "I hope that boy goes to college, he doesn't know how smart he is."

This was one of the reasons I think Benji McDuff liked Riley Pat. When Benji would talk all his nonsense, Riley would blow him away by talking about history or math, or something like that. Benji looked at him as being smarter than all us other hillbillies.

The next morning at church, I saw Fran standing with Riley. Riley had his hand on Fran's shoulder, and it appeared they were in deep conversation.

"I'll handle it." This was all I heard of the conversation, but I knew that Riley was talking about Benji.

After the bell rang, and before church started, I saw Fran heading toward the fence. He climbed over and grabbed his gun. I yelled at him, but he didn't turn back and notice me. I watched him disappear over the hill. Riley was nowhere to be found, and when I asked about him, I was told that he took off.

"What's that little fart doing here?" Benji asked Riley as he pointed to Fran.

Riley and Fran hooked up at the "Y" which was where the road forked; one road led to Chestnut Ridge, and the other down a narrow lane that led to Hanover's farm and store. Riley told Fran to meet him, and they would go over to the Hanover's place and look up Benji.

"I hear you been doing some shooting," Riley said.

"What you talking about?" Benji replied.

"This here boy told me you shot at him and Sonny Smith yesterday, and they weren't doing nothing bad."

"They was on my granddaddy's property."

"So? What was that hurting?"

"I warned the little fart that he better never step one foot on this land, or I would hurt him," Benji explained.

"I'll tell you what, Benji, Fran's been coming that way for a long time, and your grandpa said it was okay. I'm telling you that if you lay one finger on this boy, I'll hurt you."

Benji could hardly stand what he was hearing. Riley was his friend. One time they even cut their fingers and bled into each other's blood. Now, Riley was taking up for this little freak kid.

"Then you'll have to hurt me," Benji sniped.

"You took a big dangerous gun you shouldn't have in the first place and almost killed those little boys. What're you thinking?"

"I'm thinking I warned them to stay off the property," Benji replied.

"Benji, Fran is going to church tonight, and guess what? He'll be moving right across your granddaddy's field just like always."

"Then I'll shoot him!" Benji screamed.

These boys were about the same height and build, but Riley looked stronger. Riley took a step toward Benji.

"Give me that gun," Riley demanded.

"You're crazy, Riley, and if you take one more step closer, I'm going to shoot you."

Fran cringed, and he feared for Riley's life. This guy was

crazy enough to kill them both, and he almost fainted when he saw Benji raise the gun and aim it at Riley.

"Stop!" Benji cried. "Stop or I'll shoot you right between your eyes!"

"You can't shoot that good," Riley taunted. "You better make your first shot count."

Benji cocked the lever actions, which inserted a bullet in the chamber. Riley kept coming at him.

"I'll shoot you; I mean it!"

As quick as lightning, Riley came at Benji with a kick. I had heard many times that when Riley was in a fight, he had that kick. One time, he kicked a guy so hard that the cloth of his shirt was embedded in the guy's chest and had to be peeled off.

Riley kicked the gun from underneath the stock, and the rifle flew straight up. As it did, Benji pulled the trigger. The sound was so deafening that you could hear it for a mile. He hit nothing but air. Fran stood in total shock, unable to move.

"Grab the gun!" Riley yelled, but Fran was unable to move. The gun flew out of Benji's hands and hit the ground ten feet or so from Fran. Fran didn't move.

"Grab the damn gun!" Riley screamed one more time.

Fran realized this was an important moment. If he didn't grab the gun and Benji won this fight, he was going to be shot. He dived for it as Benji tried to push Riley off him and get to the gun himself. Fran jumped to his feet but had no idea what to do.

"Get out of here, fast. Take the gun to the Preacher's house!"

Fran said nothing, but he knew this was a good idea. Without the gun, Benji couldn't shoot Riley even if he did win the fight. Fran took off through the woods as fast as he could go. He knew the way, and he knew all the shortcuts. He had made his way many times over here squirrel hunting and coming to the Hanover's store to buy pop and peanuts whenever he could get a little extra money.

Fran made the trip of five miles to get to the church, and he sighed relief when he saw the bell tower looming in the distance. Several times he looked over his shoulder to see if anybody was chasing him.

"Here," the fast runner said as he stumbled into the trailer scared out of his wits.

My mother, Shirlee Ann Shanahan Smith, a five feet tall little Irish woman, was sitting on the couch in the living room. My father used to say that her temper was so bad that sometimes when she was angry and spit on the ground, it would sizzle.

My mom didn't like where she was, and it would take a long time for her to adjust to Chapel Gap life, if she ever did. She had auburn hair, and I was always thankful that she didn't have the flaming red hair of these people including Benji McDuff and Evel Martin. I associated red hair with evil because one time Maggie Pat told us in Sunday School that Esau was redheaded, and he was out trying to kill his brother, Jacob.

"What's the matter, Fran?" My mother asked curiously. "Where'd you get that gun? That's not your gun."

My mother knew nothing about guns, but she had seen Fran's gun many times. He was hardly without it and carried it most of the time when he came to see me. He said one time that you never know when we would take off and go hunting somewhere. We had gone from chasing imaginary elephants to killing real rabbits and squirrels.

"Where's the Preacher?" Fran asked exasperatedly.

"He's in the study over at the church. What's wrong?"

Fran never answered but ran very quickly to find my dad.

"Fran, what's the matter?" My dad asked with concern in his voice. He thought Fran was in a state of shock. "Where's Sonny?"

My dad feared that there had been an accident, and Fran was coming to try and tell him what had happened, but then he remembered that I was off to the spring to fetch water.

"BBBBBBenji might have killed Riley Pat!" Fran blurted.

"What?"

Fran then told the story and related how Benji had shot at us the day before.

"Get in the car," my dad yelled at Fran, and they took off toward the "Y."

On the way, Fran explained in detail what had happened, and my dad was barreling down the road at some sixty miles per hour, an extremely unsafe speed on these roads. We passed Chet Cullen, who lived next to the Hanovers, and as he was looking to see who was driving my dad's car, he noticed the intensity on my dad's face. Mr. Cullen was going the opposite direction and Fran turned just in time to see Chet whirling his pickup in a slide. It looked as if he might fly off the road in the cornfield, but he didn't. He was in hot pursuit of my dad; fighting to see through the thick dust and gravel we were kicking up that hit the front of his truck and threatened to break his windshield.

Chet and my dad arrived at the Hanover's farm and jumped out of their vehicles. Mr. Hanover, who heard the commotion, came out of his store. Mrs. Hanover followed.

"What're you doing way out here on Sunday, Preacher?" Mr. Hanover asked.

"Where's Benji?" My dad asked sternly.

"He's down in the woods hunting. We heard him take a couple of shots a little while ago," Mrs. Hanover explained with no noticeable nervousness in her voice.

"Which way, Fran?" My dad asked yelling.

Fran took off, and Chet, who was overweight tried to keep up with Fran and my dad running at full speed.

Fran hit the path that the cows used to travel from the back pastures through the woods to answer milking call. Fran jumped the creek and raced toward the place where he last saw his friend Riley Pat and Benji McDuff.

"I'm sorry," Riley said as he stood over the body. Fear and tension were gripping Riley, and the tears were streaming down his face.

Benji lie in a position with one arm underneath him, and the other arm and hand covering the wound and blood that flowed out of his head. The bullet from the gun fired at close range had nearly taken his head off his shoulders. Fran turned away when he peeked at some of Benji's brains lying on the ground where they had spilled from the wound in his head. The bullet had gone clean through taking his right eyeball and left ear.

It was not long before the Hanovers arrived, and Mrs. Hanover fainted when she saw Benji lying on the ground covered in blood. Chet Cullen got her revived and took her by the arm and led she and her husband back to the store.

"It, it was an accident," Riley exclaimed. He could barely get the words out of his mouth.

Houston Crane, the Sheriff, who was a Deacon in our church, soon arrived at the scene. It was church time, and my dad was nowhere to be found. When he asked where my dad was, my mother told him that my dad took off in a big hurry with Fran, and they were on the way to the Hanover farm.

Other people were coming, too. The Hanovers had a phone, which was one of the rare ones in the Chapel Gap Community. They had the phone installed mainly for the benefit of Benji, who used to call the neighbors and relentlessly harass them. Mr. Hanover refused to disconnect the phone when neighbors complained because he wanted Benji's parents to be able to communicate with him from Cincinnati. All the phones in that part of the country were party lines. This meant there were perhaps twenty or more families sharing the same line. Whenever someone made a call, there would be a little jingle on the phone in each house, and the neighbors would listen in on the conversations.

Today, everyone must have been listening because it wasn't long before a large crowd had gathered in the woods. Some of these people were from the church.

Mr. Crane had his pad and pencil and was taking notes. He looked real official as he passed through the crowd of onlookers. He approached Fran.

"What happened, Fran?" Mr. Crane asked.

"I don't know, Sheriff Crane. I told Riley Pat about Benji shooting at me and Sonny yesterday, and he told me this morning at church to come with him. We came and talked with Benji, and they got into a fight. The gun flew out of Benji's hands and landed in front of me, and Riley yelled at me to get the gun and run to the church and give it to the Preacher."

"Did you give it to the Preacher?"

No sir, I dropped it on the way, and I don't remember where."

"One of you guys take Fran and retrace his steps back to the church. We've got to find the murder weapon." The Sheriff screamed at Homer Shanks and a couple of other guys. They grabbed Fran and disappeared into the woods.

"Whoa, whoa," my dad said. "Who said anything about a murder? You haven't even talked to Riley Pat, yet.

Mr. Crane, who was dressed in his Sunday overalls and blue denim shirt, bent over the body. He had pinned his badge on the strap that held up the bib on his overalls. He squatted down and studied Benji's face and head. He squinted and made some marks on his paper.

"Murder," the Sheriff claimed.

When major crimes were committed, the State Police assigned to the county where the crime was perpetrated were called to the scene. In Kentucky, there were two State policemen assigned to the rural counties. We all knew Tip Tuck. In fact, he was dating June Job, Fran's sister. He started dating her when she was thirteen years old. Fran and I had seen them many times riding in the police cruiser, which was a 1955 Ford with a souped up V8 engine.

Tip was just pulling in the parking area in front of the little store as everyone emerged from the woods. The Sheriff and three other men were carrying Benji, who was wrapped in a tarp taken from the corn-husking machine sitting in a nearby cornfield. Blood had oozed through the tarp, and it was a gruesome scene.

"What happened?" Tip asked the Sheriff Crane.

Mr. Crane related what Fran had told him and said that he had sent Fran to lead a couple of the men through the woods to find the gun.

"Hmm," Tip mused, "why did Fran have the gun?"

This was all too much for my dad, and he had already sent word back to the church to have Preacher Roberts take care of the service. There had never been a time in Evergreen Baptist Church history that services were cancelled on a Sunday. People waded through snow many times, so they wouldn't miss a service even if the Preacher wasn't there. Such was their dedication and belief.

"What's the charge?" Tip asked.

"Murder," the Sheriff replied.

"Hold on!" My dad screamed as he heard the exchange between the two cops. "What about the boy?"

"What boy?" Tip Tuck asked.

"Riley Pat. What about him? You haven't even spoken to him."

Riley was sitting in Houston Crane's pickup in a complete state of shock. He knew nothing about any charges at this point, but he was fearful of the State Police.

"We'll talk to him when we get him to headquarters in Stanford."

"What?" My dad said in disbelief. "You can't do that!"

Preachers had a lot of influence back in the day, and in fact, in some cases out in the community, more than a judge.

"What basis do you have for this?" My dad inquired angrily.

"We are going to assume that Fran knows more than he is telling us, and that he disposed of the murder weapon under Riley's orders." Tip was explaining the rationale for keeping Riley penned in the truck.

"We'll take him down to Stanford and get his side of the story. In the meantime, he is under arrest for premeditated murder in the first degree."

CHAPTER FIVE

It was dark by the time Homer Shanks and Shirley Johnson arrived with Fran at the church. Shirley was one of the Johnson boys living down in the hollow below the Hanover's store. He could hear the commotion through the woods and came up to the scene. His name was Shirley, and so was my mom's. She spelled her name, Shirlee, which I guess made the difference between a boy's name and a girl's name. This was always curious to me. Many of the hill people named their boy's girls' names. Shirley Johnson, June Barber, Francis Ethridge, Carol Mealey, and Chris Stevens, are just a few examples of boys with girls' names.

As Shanks and Johnson approached the Evergreen Baptist Church, there was no gun in their hands.

"What happened? What's going on?" People asked as they filed out of the church and either headed for their cars or for the footpaths to their farms.

"Benji McDuff is dead, and Riley Pat killed him. It was

murder," Homer Shanks yelled back as he climbed into John Shea's pickup for a ride back to the Hanover place. Shirley and Fran hopped in the back.

Fran's face was as white as a sheet. He never heard the word "murder" before except on the radio. What were these people saying? They didn't find a gun, and they had looked everywhere along the path Fran took back to the church. Soon, they passed State Trooper Tuck and Houston Crane driving fast coming from the opposite direction. Fran's eyes met Riley's as the cars slowed to make the narrow passage, and you could barely stick your hand between the two cars.

"What's going on?" Homer Shanks addressed Tip Tuck.

"We're taking Riley down to Stanford for questioning. He's been arrested for murder."

Fran could see Riley in the back of the cruiser from his vantage point in the higher pickup cab. Fran was horrified to see Riley's hands cuffed behind his back, and he looked uncomfortable. It was then that one of the most horrific things would happen to Fran in his young life.

"Fran, hop out and get in the back of the cruiser." Tip requested.

"Why?" Fran nervously asked. He's been in Tip's car before, and many times he looked in the back seat, which had no window cranks or door handles.

"You gonna handcuff me, Tip?"

"No, Fran, we just want to hear your side of the story so get in."

"Where's the body?" Homer asked.

"It's on the way down to Floyd's Funeral Home in Crab Orchard. We called out Floyd, and he is picking up the body."

Floyd had a big black 1949 Packard Hearse with a big swan on the hood. While they were side by side talking, the Packard drove up, and my dad was in the front seat with Floyd. My dad had asked Floyd if he would drop him off at Haley Pat's house so that he could tell her what was happening to Riley. By then, there was a long dust procession of cars and trucks coming behind the hearse as people were going home to either get on the phone or walk to a neighbor's house and spread the news.

I was standing by the road when the cruiser and hearse drove by. I saw Fran and Riley Pat in the back seat, and Fran looked at me like, "You gotta save my life!"

My dad motioned for Floyd to stop. He got out of the car and walked over to me.

"Riley Pat and Fran are in a lot of trouble, Sonny. The Sheriff and Trooper Tuck are going to charge Riley with murder and maybe Fran, too."

"Fran didn't kill nobody and neither did Riley," I said as tears were streaming down my dusty face and making a trail down my cheeks.

"I know, I know," my dad replied, "it will all get sorted out."

"But what if it don't? Will they put Fran in the electric chair?"

Kentucky put murderers to death by electrocution, and I often heard about how horrible a death it was with eyes popping out of a person's head, and shaking, and I even heard that people crapped their pants when they were electrocuted. That would be the ultimate embarrassment if it happened to Fran.

I was crying uncontrollably now. They couldn't kill Fran. He was my best friend. He didn't hurt nobody; they couldn't kill him!

"You go along to the church and stay with mom. Tell her I'll be home late. I'm going to see Haley Pat," my dad instructed as the hearse slowly drove off and disappeared over the hill.

Haley Pat, Maggie (who I loved), and Jane were screaming and yelling as my dad tried to comfort them.

"Oh God, no! God please! My boy, no!" Haley was crying

and wailing so loudly that Babs Kirk, who owned the store a few houses up the road from their house, heard the noise and came down.

"I heard the news on the phone," Babs explained. "How bad is it?"

"Pretty bad," was all that my dad would say.

CHAPTER SIX

D r. Sinclair was an old man. For fifty years, after graduating from the University of Kentucky's Medical School in Lexington, he moved to establish his roots in Crab Orchard. His office was a little building in the middle of town on Route 150 that ran through town and was also Main Street. Dr. Sinclair had been in the same office all those years, so he knew every kid in the area and was now so old that he had buried most of his earlier patients and was taking care of their great grandchildren.

Dr. Sinclair was also the resident veterinarian. My dad used to say that you never knew which needle Doc was using on you; the one he used on the horse, or the one he used on the guy who just walked out.

I do remember my first shot by the Doc. My mom had taken me to him for a Tetanus shot one time when I stepped on a rusty nail sticking through a board in the barn. The Doctor took out a big syringe with a monstrous needle. It looked rusty and well used. I wondered if it had ever been cleaned. He blew the dust off his desk, which rarely was clean, and stuck the needle in my arm. Man did that hurt! I cried and screamed, and as soon as the hurt and pain from the nail and needle healed, I was fine.

Floyd contacted Dr. Sinclair as he drove toward Stanford. The Doc didn't drive anymore, so if you needed him to work on your cow or deliver a baby; you had to go get him.

Floyd stopped by the Doc's office, picked him up, and told him about the murder. The Doc was the local Medical Examiner, so every time there was a death, he was called in to examine the scene and then the corpse. Of course, there never had been a murder in Chapel Gap, so this was the first time that the Doc had been called on a murder case.

My dad came back to the trailer, and my mother was sitting on the couch reading one of her soap opera books, as my dad called them.

"What happened?" My mother quizzed.

"Benji McDuff is dead, and Riley Pat is in jail."

"What!" My mother cried.

My dad then explained what had happened and why Fran Job was involved.

"Fran dropped this gun off here, but it's not his gun," my mother exclaimed. "He just ran in here and threw the gun on the floor and took off to find you."

My dad examined the gun and had a weird look on his face.

"You're right, this isn't Fran's gun, and it ain't Benji McDuff's either. Fran told the Sheriff that he dropped the gun on the way to the church and didn't know where it was. Homer Shanks and Shirley Johnson couldn't find it, either."

My dad realized that this was a curious situation. Fran dropped the gun, but this gun wasn't his, and it wasn't Benji's. This was a shotgun. My dad decided to take the gun to the police in Stanford and while there, he would see Fran and try to see Riley Pat if he could.

Dad hopped in his 1953 Mercury Hardtop and drove down the lane. He found a parking place on the street in front of the Courthouse. This was Sunday night and very late, so there was no activity in Stanford.

Stanford is the County Seat of Lincoln County. Although it was only twenty miles from Chapel Gap, it seemed much longer because of the gravel roads, which made traveling much slower than the hardtop highways. Stanford was a small town but much larger than Crab Orchard. The Crab Orchard stores and shops sold most of what everyone needed but when you needed to make a bigger shopping trip or go to a meat locker, you went to Stanford.

The City had a long main street on which most of the business activity took place, and like a lot of Kentucky towns, the courthouse was positioned in the central part of the town.

The Stanford Courthouse was a small but attractive building. Kentuckians took great pride in their courthouses because all legal activities took place there. Driver's licenses, license plates, marriage certificates, and all other civilian stuff required a trip to Stanford. Also in the courthouse was the sheriff's office and the offices of the local police.

My dad carried the gun into the large front foyer of the courthouse. As he did, he noticed that all the lights were burning on the second floor, so he bounded up the stairs taking the steps two and three at a time.

He walked into the Sheriff's office. Houston Crane hardly ever used this office that was designated for the Sheriff. He lived at Chapel Gap, so he did most of his sheriffing business from his farm. He had a two-way radio and phone in his house.

Fran was sitting behind a table drinking an RC Cola. He

seemed all right because Tip Tuck sat next to him dressed in his sharp gray and blue state trooper's uniform.

"Is Fran okay?" My dad asked gently.

"Fran's fine," Tip Tuck said, "he's a little shaken up, but he'll be okay."

Fran nodded in agreement while sipping his cola and chomping on a Moon Pie.

"Can I talk to you, Tip?" My dad asked.

"Sure." The Trooper replied.

"Can we go outside?"

My dad and Tip walked outside the little office while Houston Crane kept an eye on Fran.

My dad reached for the gun he had leaned up against the wall outside the door.

"What's with that?" Tip acted surprised. Tip had the feeling this may be the murder weapon because slugs fired from a shotgun could do the damage Benji had to his head.

"When Fran came running out of the field and into the trailer, he threw this gun at Shirlee."

"Fran carries a gun all the time, so?"

"So, take a look at the gun, Tip. This is not Fran's gun; Fran has a single shot rifle, and it isn't Benji McDuff's gun, either. Benji has a Marlin 30-30. This is a shotgun for crying out loud."

Tip examined the gun again.

"Fran said he dropped Benji's gun on the way to the church and didn't know where. Homer Shanks couldn't find it." Tip raised the shotgun to his shoulder and sighted down the barrel. "So, where did Fran come up with this gun? I think we better talk to the boy again."

Tip and my dad walked back into the room. It was midnight now, and the huge clock on the courthouse tower chimed its twelve-ring cycle. When Fran saw the gun, he slinked down in his chair to his shoulders. This was a familiar position for him especially at church when a sermon was making him feel guilty.

"Where'd you get this shotgun, Fran?" Tip looked directly in Fran's eyes while Houston Crane looked over the weapon.

Fran didn't want to answer and stared out the window.

"The answer ain't out there, Fran, where'd you get the gun?"

"I want my lawyer." Fran said easily.

"You ain't got no lawyer, and you've been watching too much television."

"Let me talk to him," my dad said.

"Okay, we'll leave the room," Tip said while motioning to the door.

After some time of sitting and staring, my dad leaned over to Fran and almost touched his nose.

"Fran, something is going on here, and Riley Pat is sitting across the street behind bars in jail. If he gets convicted for murder, they will electrocute him."

Fran never, ever, cried. Not this time, though. A tiny trickle of tears were easing their way out of Fran's eyes, and one fell on his nose and dripped to the table. Soon, there was quite a puddle, and it was evident to my dad that Fran was very afraid of something.

Tip Tuck and Houston Crane decided that it may take a while for my dad to get Fran's story, if he ever did, so since they hadn't taken Riley Pat's statement as yet, they walked across the street to the County Jail.

The Jailer opened the main doors, which were only a step or two from the main office. Most of the prisoners kept in the jail were picked off the street for being drunk, and the place smelled of vomit. There were eight cells in this complex indicating that Lincoln County didn't have very many crimes where the perpetrators were caught. They used to fill up the cells every weekend with bootleggers they caught running booze into the hills, but the booze peddlers had graduated into such fast cars and were so fast they just let them race on through town and didn't bother them. Moonshine stills were everywhere back in the woods, but the Sheriff's gout problem kept him from hiking and climbing steep hills. He said it was too dangerous tracking those people down as they could easily draw a bead on him and shoot him. and no one would ever find out who did it. Moonshiners were known to shoot trespassers, find a hollow tree, and that was the end of a perpetrator. It happened many times to law enforcement officers but never in Lincoln County, and he wasn't going to be the first.

Riley Pat sat on the bunk in the cell staring at the floor.

Houston and Tip took chairs they grabbed from the office and sat facing Riley.

"Tell us what happened, Riley," Houston demanded.

"I didn't kill Benji," Riley said lugubriously.

"He didn't kill himself," Tip answered.

Riley nervously wriggled back and forth on the bunk. He put his hand to his forehead and rubbed it many times as well as tucked his leg underneath him and placed it back on the floor. He did this ritual several times before he had the nerve to speak.

"I don't know what happened," Riley explained, "Benji and I were fighting, and a shot was fired, and the next thing I know, Benji fell on the ground, and blood was gushing from his head."

"How'd that fight start?" Tip investigated.

"Benji fired some shots at Fran and Sonny in the woods on Saturday afternoon. Fran told me about it on Sunday, so I grabbed him, and we took off to find Benji. I was going to tell him that he better not bother these boys again."

"Oh, yeah, Benji's been mad about Fran crossing his grandpa's fields on the way to church. I never thought much about it," Houston commented.

"When Fran and I got there, Benji asked us to come down in the woods, so we followed him down. A few words were exchanged, and things got heated up. Benji pointed the gun at me and said he would kill me if I touched him."

"Then what happened?" Tip asked obviously listening and taking notes.

"Benji cocked the gun and pointed it at my head. He's crazy. He was going to shoot me. I kicked the gun on the stock with my left foot. The gun went flying, but before it did, Benji fired a shot, but I don't think he hit anything. I was too scared to notice, and I was afraid that he would get the gun and kill me and Fran."

"How did Fran get the gun?" Tip asked.

"I screamed at Fran to the get the gun and run to the church."

"Did he do that?" Houston asked.

"Yeah, I saw him grab it, and I knew I was safe and that I could kick the crap out of Benji."

"Did you and Benji actually enter into any physical contact?" Houston asked.

"Big time. Benji knew he couldn't take me, or at least I thought he knew that. He grabbed a stick and started swinging it at me, and he actually hit me."

Riley pulled up his shirt and showed the wide bruises where the thick limb had landed on his right side. Houston and Tip leaned hard to get a good look.

"I grabbed the tree limb and held it while I hit him in the mouth."

"Did you knock him down?" Tip asked.

"I didn't have the chance to. I was about to throw him down. I had him in a headlock, and the next thing I knew, blood was spurting all over me. I heard the shot and looked up, but there was no one there. I carried Benji off the rocks and laid him down. I knew he was dead."

"Did Fran pull that trigger?" Sheriff Crane asked.

"What? You think Fran shot Benji?" Riley screamed.

"No, we think you shot Benji." Tip made this explicit because there was no way that he was going to put some ideas in Riley's head for a later defense.

The cops left Riley sitting in the darkness in deep despair and were making their way across the street to the Courthouse.

"Tip, do you really think Riley Pat killed Benji McDuff?" The Sheriff asked.

"I hate to think so, but I think Fran Job knows more than he is telling us, and we have to get the story out of him. Things aren't adding up. First of all, the Preacher came over with a shotgun that Fran dropped off at the trailer. Where did it come from? Riley says he saw Fran taking off with Benji's rifle. The gun isn't there, and Fran said he lost it. Doesn't make sense. Fran did have time to turn and shoot Benji. Fran could have had a vantage point that didn't allow Riley or Benji to see him. Then, he shows up with a gun no one knows who it belongs to. Fran shot him."

"Lord, I hope not," the Sheriff replied.

CHAPTER SEVEN

F ran and my dad were still talking when Sheriff Crane and Trooper Tuck walked into the interrogation room on the second floor of the Courthouse. Fran was sticking to his story, and he would not tell anyone how he got the shotgun or where the other gun was.

"How's he doing?" Tip asked.

"I'm fine," Fran interrupted, "take me home."

Tip glanced at the clock on the wall. It was 1:00 AM. He rubbed his head because he was feeling tired himself. He had felt this way many times after laborious investigations of accidents where people were killed. He knew one thing: The longer that they kept Fran there, the more likely he would tell them the truth. Tip was going to force Fran to tell the story whether it would be a confession or the truth. Tip was going to force Fran to tell the story and clear the air that made this whole affair confusing. Tip sat down across from Fran and turned the chair's seat toward him and leaned his arms over the back of the chair. The Sheriff and my dad sat on the sides of the table and Fran at the end.

Benji's body lay on the gurney in the Floyd Funeral Home basement. Doc Sinclair was peering over the body paying particular attention to the hole in the head where the fatal shot was injected. Floyd stood with him assisting when needed.

"What do you make of this, Doc?" Floyd looked puzzled.

"This wound wasn't made by a 30-30," the Doc mused. "This was a shotgun slug that went through the victim's head. There's way too much tissue missing for a rifle to have done this. I've had game wardens come into my office with a deer that survived a shotgun slug, and this wound looks just like that. Yep. This is a slug wound."

At this point, neither the Doc nor Floyd had any information that the gun Fran was carrying back to the church was indeed a shotgun. They discussed the issue for a few minutes.

"Floyd, why don't you run over to Stanford and see if the Sheriff is still there? I'm going to bed; the victim ain't going anywhere. We'll visit this situation in the morning."

"Fran, is that Abe Job's shotgun?" Tip asked.

Fran knew they were getting at something. His dad did have a double barrel shotgun, and Fran was seen with it many times. "There are lots of shotguns like my dad's in Lincoln County," he quipped.

"Then where did you get it?" You and Riley Pat both said that you left the scene with Benji's 30-30." Tip's patience was running thin.

"We know that if you left with Benji's rifle, and if you didn't arrive at the Preacher's trailer with Benji's gun; you arrived at the house with a shotgun just like your dad's, you must have done something with the other gun. Now what's going on here, and where is Benji McDuff's gun?" Sheriff Crane demanded.

A car was heard stopping down on the street, and my dad looked out the window. Floyd got out of his hearse. "Never know when something might happen," he explained when asked why he always drove his hearse when he had a perfectly good pickup in his garage. It was true that he made Chapel Gap folks nervous when they would see Floyd cruising the countryside like a vulture looking for something dead.

Soon, Floyd was making his way up the stairs and into the room where the tired and frustrated team of interrogators were sitting.

"What's up?" The Sheriff asked. He knew Floyd wasn't over there in the wee hours of the morning for nothing.

"Doc Sinclair says the murder weapon wasn't Benji's 30-30. It was a shotgun slug that went through his head."

"How'd he know that?" Tip Tuck asked.

"It's too complicated," Floyd replied.

Everyone immediately stared at Fran. Sheriff Crane rose to his feet and walked over to Fran's chair, and Tip followed. Both of these tall imposing cops were standing on opposite sides of him.

"Did you kill him, Fran?" Tip questioned sternly.

"No, I didn't do that," Fran somberly and quietly answered with his head and eyes facing the floor.

"Then who did?" Tip asked.

"I don't know. It wasn't me, and it wasn't Riley. I know that for sure."

There was some reservation in Tip's mind that Fran could be telling the truth and that he really didn't know who killed Benji McDuff. He knew that Fran was a good enough shot to have done it himself, and he was creative enough to make up this story.

"Sheriff, swear out a warrant for Abe Job and go pick him up!" Tip yelled at the Sheriff.

Fran looked at the Trooper in disbelief. "No!" He cried. "My dad didn't do nothin!"

"Then you better tell us right now where you got that shotgun and what happened to Benji's rifle." Tip demanded.

Fran choked back the tears. His tanned face made his green eyes especially bright, but the tears clogged his vision. He couldn't let Riley Pat die, and he feared his dad might go to the electric chair.

"If I tell you, will you let me go home?" Fran sobbed.

"Tell the truth, and you will go home," my dad interrupted and ignored the authority of either the Sheriff or the State Trooper. Tip and Houston nodded in agreement.

How articulate could a little kid be? Fran knew he was in a battle, in big time trouble, and a lot was on the line. This was a huge burden to carry on his small shoulders, but he's the one who told Riley Pat about him and me. He thought about how many times Benji had threatened him and about the time he beat him up for crossing the fences on his grand-dad's farm. Benji had taunted and bullied him, but killing? No matter what, he didn't deserve that. He just wanted Riley to beat Benji up or keep away before there was an accident and somebody did get hurt. Somebody was hurt, now. Benji was dead, and Fran felt guilty. He knew Riley didn't kill Benji, and he knew he didn't either nor his dad. He honestly wasn't sure who did. This wasn't his dad's shotgun that was placed strate-gically in his view so that he wouldn't forget where he got it.

"Fran you okay?" My dad asked as Fran was seriously con-templating his situation.

Fran fidgeted with his little Barlow knife that he always carried. No farm boy was without his Barlow or Case knife if he could afford one.

"I watched Benji threaten Riley," Fran began, "and the next thing I know, Riley is screaming at me to pick up the rifle and run to the Preacher's and give it to him. I grabbed the rifle and took off as fast as I could. When you're scared, you run faster," Fran inserted the idea. He hesitated a moment, caught his breath, and went on. "I just ran over the creek, and Sweet John Adams was standing there looking at me."

Sweet John Adams was a recluse living in a cabin deep in the woods. He was hardly ever seen, and when he was, it was just for a moment. He got his supplies from the Hanover's Store. Near a creek in approximation to the Hanover Store was a large Oak tree that had a hollow place in the trunk. Mr. Hanover would find a note from Sweet John and then bring the stuff he ordered and put it in the hollow of the tree. Sweet John would leave money there for bacon, salt, sugar, flour, and shotgun shells he needed from time to time that would be used to kill the meat he ate for his diet. Mr. Hanover always swore that Sweet John stole milk from his cows. Most of the time when Sweet John was spotted, he had wandered out of the woods and would be seen standing in a field where he had chased a rabbit, deer, or quail.

Sweet John Adams was nearly forty years old the best anyone could tell. He was short, stocky and had a very bald head. In fact, there wasn't a hair on his head. His half-brother, Brandon Stevens, lived in the area, but they had fallen out many years ago. The story goes that Sweet John was a queer. When this was explained to me, it was the strangest thing I had ever heard. A man actually loved another man romantically and kissed him? It was worse than this. So it was told that Sweet John didn't love men; he loved boys, and one day Brandon caught him molesting his son, Brady, and they got into a fight. Sweet John left his brother, Brandon, to die on the dusty floor of an old tobacco barn. Brandon survived, but Sweet John was rarely seen again as he took up residence in a cabin he built with his own hands deep in the forest.

"What did Sweet John Adams want?" Tip asked as the three other men leaned way over to catch every word.

"He told me to wait and not move. I had the 30-30, but he had the shotgun." He pointed at the shotgun lying on the table. "He took off running toward where Benji and Riley Pat were."

"You want another RC, Fran?" My dad sensed that Fran's mouth was getting dry.

"Yep."

My dad came back with a ten ounce RC Cola with the bottle cap removed and handed it to Fran. Fran took a big gulp. The room filled with suspense.

"Where do you think Sweet John went, Fran?" Houston Crane asked.

"I don't know, but I heard the shot."

"How many shots?" Tip asked.

"Just one, and in a few minutes, Sweet John came back."

"You were still standing there?" Tip acted surprised. "Why didn't you take off running and get out of there?"

"I was too scared, and besides, he would run me down sooner or later. He's a queer, but he can run real fast. That's what I've heard."

"Weren't you afraid he would hurt you?" Tip asked.

"I had Benji's gun, and I would have used it if he tried to hurt me. Ain't no queer gonna touch me!"

"Okay, Fran, this sounds good, but how did you get the shotgun and what happened to Benji's rifle?" The Sheriff asked.

"Sweet John pointed the shotgun at me and told me to give him the rifle, and just like that," Fran snapped his fingers, "he was no where to be seen."

"Which direction did he go?" One of the men asked.

"He went toward the church, so I was afraid he was going

to go over there and hurt somebody. I took off for the church, but I hadn't run too far, and I saw Sweet John's shotgun leaning against a tree. I don't know why, but I grabbed the gun and took off for the church. That's all I know until the Preacher and me got to the Hanover's."

Fran was completely drained, so my dad told Tip and the Sheriff that he was taking him home, and he could stay the night at the trailer. Floyd told Tip that he would have a complete autopsy report for him by noon the next day.

This was a bizarre story, and Fran could have made it all up, but Fran wasn't known to tell lies except when he was trying to cover my butt for something or other. *No, Tip thought, even Fran can't make up a story like that.*

"Sheriff, get the Judge up and get a warrant for the arrest of Sweet John Adams."

CHAPTER EIGHT

E arly the next morning while the farmers were calling their cows and sometime before dawn, the entire community already knew the particulars of the tragedy between Riley Pat and Benji McDuff. The phone lines were burning up all night as the neighbors reflected on the events of the previous day. Daphni and Garrard Anderson were sitting on their front porch.

"This is big news," Daphni commented as she wrote on a pad with a pencil. Daphni was the Chapel Gap Reporter for the Lincoln County Newspaper. She wrote a column every week reporting on the events of Chapel Gap. Most all the time, the news consisted of who visited who that week, and my dad was always in the paper because she would report: "Pastor Smith, Shirlee Smith, and their children were the guests of Mr. and Mrs. Vernon Daily on Sunday afternoon", or whoever we had visited for Sunday dinner. The big news was always when "Chuck May was the guest of Henry and April

May." Chuck traveled down to Chapel Gap from Cincinnati every weekend.

Dephi was the daughter of John Frazier. Mr. Frazier was old and told us kids stories about walking all the way from Pennsylvania as a young lad to Chapel Gap behind a covered wagon.

Daphni was a crippled lady and walked with a distinct limp. She lived with her husband, Garrard, who she married after being single until she was fifty-nine years old, and they lived on the same farm owned by her dad and mom. She had been there all her life. She married Garrard Anderson, a colorful fellow, who loved to spin yarns and could tell some whoppers. One of my favorite stories he told was about how "tight" Daphni was with her money, and she would hardly let him have a dime. He said they went to Crab Orchard shopping one time, and he asked his wife for a dime to buy some candy, and she told him that if she "let him have a dime this week, he would just want another one next week."

Dust was flying from behind the long procession of cop cars, and Houston Crane had rounded up his posse of farmers he had deputized after they volunteered in case an event such as this ever took place at Chapel Gap.

"I remember one time way back when my brother got shot."

"Shut up, Garrard," said as she was writing away trying to describe the scene unfolding in front of her.

Getting down to Sweet John Adam's place wouldn't be easy. The posse and state police pulled into their designated meeting place, which was at the "Y." Houston Crane was surrounded by his posse that was dressed in customary bibbed overalls and had left their barns after milking time and answered the call.

"We'll set up perimeter," Houston explained, "we'll go in from around a big circle."

The posse looked at him as if they didn't understand what a "perimeter" was or connect it with a "big circle." My dad came driving up, got out of his Mercury, and walked up to where the Sheriff and his posse were standing.

"Hey Preacher, I think it's too dangerous for you to be here." My dad looked around; they weren't within a mile of Sweet John Adam's place. It didn't look dangerous to him.

"I know Sweet John," my dad explained, "and I want to be the first to talk to him before one of these nervous trigger happy critters shoots him."

Tip came over and asked my dad to come with him to the other side of the "Y" where seven or eight cops were meeting.

"Preacher, we want you to stick with us. I know you know Sweet John, and he'll probably respect you and won't try anything stupid."

My dad knew Sweet John, knew that he was queer, and knew that he had tried to molest his nephew, Brady, and he knew more than that. He also knew that Sweet John was "foxy," and that he wouldn't be easy to catch. He reasoned that Sweet John had seen them coming and would be taking his position deeper in the woods. Besides, Sweet John knew every inch of these woods and hollows and every place to hide.

Upon Sheriff Crane's order, the posse rushed for their pickups and fell in behind the state cops leading the way. Some went right at the "Y," and the others took the left fork, and by no more than a few minutes, everyone was on his way.

The search began for part of the group at the Hanover Store. The Hanover's had been taken for their own protection over to the Messer farm; the richest people at Chapel Gap. The Messers were two brothers that had married two sisters and after living years together in the same house, they swapped wives. They were still sharing the same house and farming the same farm. The Hanovers would be safe there.

The other group had a long climb, and a long treacherous path along a ridge that they had to negotiate by moving single file. Sweet John could have sat there and picked them off one by one, but that idea had not crossed their minds.

The groups moved very slowly; the first group being the Sheriff and his posse, and the second group was the state troopers. The Sheriff's bunch arrived at Sweet John's cabin first. By the time Tip Tuck's group arrived, huffing and puffing from the long climb, the situation was secure. Sweet John was nowhere to be found.

Sweet John was a queer all right, but he was also a "neat freak." His little one room cabin was clean as a pin and once inside, the cops found his bed made, and his clothes hung washed and neatly pressed and hanging on a rod Sweet John has hewn from Hickory. All the furniture was made from Hickory and Poplar, and he had carefully painted or stained each piece. The kitchen was orderly, and you would have thought an all American Christian lived there.

My dad noticed how curious that Sweet John must have been reading his Bible that morning since it was still on the chair and opened to Psalm 100. "Make a joyful noise unto the Lord all ye lands . . ."

"He's around here somewhere," Tip exclaimed, "the coffee's still warm, and the cooking stove is still putting off quite a bit of heat."

CHAPTER NINE

S weet John Adams stared Fran face to face. He knew the boy would be scared; even though, he had a 30-30 in his hands. Earlier that morning, Benji McDuff had come to see him as he had done many times before. In fact, he had been visiting Sweet John since he was a boy. Sweet John gave him candy and particularly his favorite, a Zagnut, and took care of him. He was also doing something else to him. He was molesting Benji. Benji kept this horrible stuff a secret because Sweet John promised he would kill him if he ever told what he was doing. Sweet John had also molested Riley Pat and David Cullen, Chet and Naomi Cullen's boy.

"Come on in, boy," Sweet John said as Benji stood at the front door.

"I can't come in," Benji said after which Sweet John opened the door and pulled him into the room.

"What'd mean you can't come in? You're in."

"Yeah, but I ain't doin nothin," Benji cried. "I, I came here to tell you I am not letting you do these things to me anymore."

"Take your clothes off, boy. I'm ready for you. Come over here and let Sweet John give you a hug."

As Sweet John reached to take Benji's pants off, Benji pushed him off balance and made for the door.

"Come here, you little bastard, or I'll beat the hell out of you."

Benji raised his 30-30 and pointed it at Sweet John. "If you touch me, I'll shoot you, and I mean it!" Sweet John knew Benji McDuff was brave enough to pull the trigger.

"What's the matter? You don't love me anymore?"

While Benjibacked away toward the front door, he said, "I came here to tell you that you are a queer, and I am going to tell Preacher Smith what you been doing to me since I was a little boy."

Benji was running back to the Hanover's Store when he met up with Riley Pat and Fran Job. Sweet John had followed close behind, trying to catch the kid, but he stopped short when he saw Riley confront Benji. He stood in the woods listening to the argument and watching the ensuing fight. He saw Fran pick up the gun and start running through the woods, so he cut around the bend in the creek, waded it for a little bit, and caught up with Fran.

He made Fran wait for him while he went to take care of some business. He arrived in a few minutes; Riley Pat and Benji McDuff were locked in battle with Benji's head being held in a headlock by Riley. Riley was shaking Benji back and forth trying to throw Benji on the ground. Sweet John carefully loaded a shotgun slug in the left barrel of the double-barreled shotgun. He wasn't afraid of being heard because the boys were making too much noise cussing each other.

Shotgun slugs weren't like shooting buckshot. You had to

aim as carefully as if you were shooting a rifle, and Sweet John Adams was known to be an excellent marksman.

When Riley swung Benji around, Sweet John fired the gun, and the slug tore through Benji's head. Sweet John watched the horror and shock on Riley's face as Benji's blood poured all over him, and then Riley carefully laid the limp, lifeless body on the ground. He never looked around him, and it wouldn't matter anyway because Sweet John had already disappeared.

"Give me that rifle, boy," Sweet John said to Fran. Fran handed it to him. Sweet John was enraptured with the beautiful feel of the gun. He picked up his shotgun and ran toward his cabin.

Sweet John took an alternate route and ran towards the church. He wanted to make Fran think he was going to the Preacher and blame Fran for the shooting. He stopped to relieve himself against a Beech tree of the several cups of coffee he had that morning. He laid the shotgun against the tree while holding the Winchester under his arm. When he buttoned his fly, he took off without the shotgun.

Fran was running fast and almost skipping across the bends in the creek. He had to wade one crossing of the creek and then he caught a glimpse of Sweet John running off with his shotgun leaning against a tree. He could smell the foul odor of urine, and he noticed the tree was wet with some of the pee leaking toward the ground. It was then that Fran's sixth sense took over his dull headedness at the moment, and his quick brain told him to pick up the gun, although he knew no reason why.

Sweet John Adams arrived at his cabin somewhat out of breath. He doubted he had ever made the trip from the creek to his house that fast. He took a minute to catch his breath and then reasoned that he better find a place in the woods in order to see what was happening at the scene of the killing.

Sweet John climbed a Sycamore tree and hid behind its

huge leaves, so he could see and not be seen. He watched as Houston Crane, Fran, and my dad came running from the Hanover's Store and then found Riley standing over Benji's dead body. He listened for any sign that Fran would tell them that he had met up with Sweet John Adams. He figured that would come out sooner or later, but he felt he had good alibis since no one had actually witnessed the murder. If it did come out, he better figure a way out of there. He had no car, truck, horse, or mule, but he did have his feet, and he knew the woods better than anyone, but he forgot about Fran and then he thought about Fran. How he wished he had shot that boy while he had the chance, and he would be long gone before they figured it all out. Next, he thought about his shotgun. What did he do with the thing? The thought troubled him greatly as he remembered that he left it by the tree where he relieved himself. He scurried down the tree and ran to the Beech tree where he left his shotgun, but it wasn't there.

Sweet John hurried back to his cabin. He noticed the warm stove still smoldering, and the coffee pot on the cast iron burner was still hot. No time to take care of this. He grabbed some bread from the cupboard and took off. He had spent the night at his cabin figuring it was safe to do that, plus he needed time to think and formulate a plan. He had just been over to the edge of the Messer fields, and he saw the cops gathering at the "Y." *They've figured it out,* he thought.

The search started from the cabin, and by this time, at least thirty men had joined up. The forest was thick and dark, but passable. Late in the afternoon, the darkness in the woods prohibited any more searching, and Tip ordered the men out of the woods to reconvene the next morning.

"We'll find the S-O-B," Tip said.

CHAPTER TEN

I didn't want him to die," Fran sorrowfully complained. "I didn't like him, but I didn't want him to die; it's my fault."

Fran and I were down in the woods where we went so often. We were sitting on the fallen moss covered log near where Benji had shot at us.

"It's not your fault, Fran," I explained. "Riley Pat was trying to help, and he had no idea that things would turn out this way. Benji was a mean dude, and he just might have killed you both."

"They think I killed him," Fran said. "I'm upset with Tip because he might think that, too."

"Tip doesn't think that and neither does Sheriff Crane." I was trying to comfort Fran. "Sweet John Adams killed Benji. I know that for a fact."

"How do you know that?"

"I heard Brady Stevens say one day that if Benji didn't kill Sweet John, he was going to. He said that in front of Sweet

John when I was in the Stevens barn helping them pile up tobacco sticks. Sweet John said he would kill Benji, first. Brady
told me one time that Sweet John tried to kiss him and that
Benji kissed him all the time."

Fran looked at me strangely.

"Did Sweet John ever bother you, Fran? I mean in that
way?"

"If that queer ever touched me, I'd cut his throat."

Such were the secrets of men and boys. My dad wasn't
the only one who knew about Sweet John Adams. There were
many in Chapel Gap Community who had experiences with
Sweet John one way or another. If he hadn't kept to himself
after Brandon Stevens ran him off, he would have died a long,
long time ago.

Tip Tuck drove up in his State Police cruiser and found
Sheriff Crane drinking some coffee from a thermos and talking to the men Tip had left to guard the roads leading out of
the hills where they were searching for Sweet John.

"See anything last night?" Tip asked.

"Naw, Harold and Louise Randall went out. They said they
were going to Stanford for the night. Said it was too dangerous
out there with all those farmers with guns."

Louise Randall was a schoolteacher. She taught at the
Broughtontown School where most of the kids in Chapel Gap
attended. She was my favorite teacher. Harold Randall worked
at the glass factory in Danville, and they were one of the few
families who lived back there that were not natives and hadn't
been born in Lincoln County. They moved to the back Knobs
to "get away from the big city," as Mr. Randall would explain.

Sweet John Adams had run as far as he could and still feel
safe. He deftly avoided the posse. Toward the end of the day,
he barely escaped by hiding behind a tree as several of the
searchers passed by. He could have reached out and touched

them. He also could have shot them because he had Benji's 30-30 in his hands. There was only one bullet in the gun, so he knew better than to shoot; he couldn't take on them all. Sweet John did not know that Fran found the shotgun, and there would be no proof that the 30-30 killed Benji McDuff.

Early in the morning around 2:00 AM or so, Sweet John fumbled his way to a sinkhole in a remote part of the woods. It was a common sight in Kentucky because of the many caves that permeated the landscape throughout that part of Kentucky. Sinkholes would open in the ground and usually where there were limestone indentations. This particular hole was located on the side of a steep slope below some limestone cliffs. He was sure that this was the opening of a cave, but he could never get past the eight or ten feet depth of the sinkhole. It was easy to crawl in and out because of the limestone shale that exposed makeshift steps. The opening of the hole was no more than three feet across but opened up to the width of a good-sized room. This would be a good hiding place since the darkness of the woods, and the narrowness of the opening made it impossible to see down there. He knew, however, that some of the men would be carrying flashlights, and that they would certainly check out all the sinkholes they found while searching for him. With this thought, he took out the bread that he brought with him and began to feed the spiders.

All day the men searched; they checked every sinkhole and every hollow tree, but there was no sign of Sweet John Adams. He had simply disappeared.

Fran and I were sitting in the trailer when Tip Tuck drove up in his cruiser. Fran nervously walked out. He didn't really want to see Tip.

"Howdy, boys," Tip greeted us as he waved out the window of the cruiser.

"You okay, Fran?"

Fran didn't answer, and Tip sensed that his feelings might be hurt because he made him go down to the Courthouse in Stanford and put him through all this.

"Hey boy, let me talk to you."

"You didn't trust me, Tip. You thought I killed Benji."

"Naw, Fran, we knew there was more to the story, and we knew you were scared. I knew that if you did kill Benji, it would have been in self-defense, or it would have been to save Riley Pat's life. Sweet John Adams killed Benji, and we now know from the Preacher what would motivate him. We can't catch him, though."

"Why not?" Fran asked with disappointment in his voice.

"We searched the whole woods, Fran, and couldn't find hide nor hair of him."

"Check the sinkholes?" Fran asked.

"We checked every one we could find that was open enough for a man to crawl into, and I think that was about all of them in the area."

"Check the one up by the limestone cliffs where the mountain tea grows?"

Mountain Tea is a plant that grows in the Knob areas in very remote parts of the forest in damp wet places. Fran and I used to find Mountain Tea and bring it home to Fran's mom, Mandy Job, and she would make home brewed tea from the dark green leaves that had a wonderful flavor. Sometimes when we found a patch of the tea, we would eat it raw. Fran knew where every mountain patch of tea was in that part of the country.

"I checked that one myself, Fran. He wasn't in there; the spiders' webs weren't broken, so he couldn't have been down there."

"That's where he is," Fran said.

"How do you know that?"

Fran's answer was prolific. "If you chase a fox or a squirrel into a sinkhole, one or the other will break the webs when it goes in. You know it is in the hole, and the fox knows you are waiting him out, so he stays in the hole where it is safe. After a while, you can then watch the spiders weave their webs across the hole where the fox did its damage. If you leave and come back the next day, you will never believe the fox is still down there."

Sweet John Adams knew this, too. He fed the spiders so that a larger and thicker web would be woven, making it impossible for him to be down there. He heard Tip's comments to the other men when he came up to the sinkhole where he hid. "Nobody in there," Tip explained, "the web's not broken."

Tip reached for the microphone of his two-way radio.

"Attention all troopers in the Chapel Gap Area; return immediately to the crime scene below the Hanover's store. Immediately."

This message was also relayed by the station where the Troopers resided in Stanford.

Garrard and Daphni Anderson were sitting on their front porch as the State Police cars sped by kicking dust that blew into their faces and house.

"They found Sweet John Adams," Garrard said.

It didn't take long for the troopers and Sheriff Crane to reach the sinkhole where Fran said Sweet John was hiding. Margot Crane was baking some of her delicious bread when she spotted the cruisers speeding by her farm. She hurried out to the barn and told Houston Crane that the troopers were speeding in a hurry toward Chapel Gap Hill. It didn't take Houston more than a few minutes to arrive at the sinkhole.

"Come out of there, Sweet John; we know you're in there, now throw out your gun." Tip yelled loudly into the sinkhole through the unbroken spider webs. The webs worked against

Sweet John this time. If he had broken the webs, they would think he wasn't in there, but he didn't think about that because no one in the whole world could figure out that feeding spiders would make a man safe.

The troopers stood with guns drawn and ready to shoot, and one trooper had a shotgun. They stood away from the entrance to the sinkhole so that Sweet John couldn't get a direct shot at them.

DAMN! Sweet John thought. *How did they ever figure this out?*

He made the decision to stay in the sinkhole one more day, and when they tired of the search and had given up; he would take the ridge to Buck Creek, hitch a ride to Tennessee, and be long gone.

"Come out, or we'll start firing!" Tip yelled.

No more than a few seconds after he said this, a shot was heard from inside the hole. The troopers and Sheriff Crane dived for cover, but that was it. One single shot, and Sweet John Adams was dead. There was only one bullet in Benji McDuff's gun; Sweet John had no need for 30-30 caliber shells, so with this one bullet, he ended his life.

"The Lord giveth, and the Lord taketh away," my dad sermonized, "blessed be the name of the Lord."

The church was packed for the funeral of Benji McDuff. Most of the people attending the funeral were there to support the Hanovers rather than mourn for Benji McDuff. Benji McDuff never went to church, but his grandparents attended and were members of Evergreen Baptist. Benji's parents, his mother a Hanover, wanted him buried in the church cemetery because a long line of ancestors had been buried there. All the historical families had plots of ground where every tombstone bore the family name. Someday, Christiana McDuff would be buried beside her son and her parents.

Riley Pat wasn't there for the funeral. Riley was so traumatized from being in jail for four days, and the memories of Benji's head being blown apart in his very arms, that a funeral was too much for him. Floyd would not allow the casket to be opened because the sight would be too gruesome, and with all Floyd's undertaking skills, "the body wouldn't look natural," Floyd explained.

Fran and I stood near the gravesites and listened as the family, and others, who never knew the Hanovers or Benji McDuff, cry and wail. The visiting mourners made special efforts at these funerals to cry and wail more than the families did at the funeral and burial they had last attended. It was a big deal, these funerals, because the louder the mourns, the more successful the funeral.

"Dust to dust, ashes to ashes," my dad said as he slowly and methodically poured dirt from his hand onto the casket below. He was skilled at milking every mourner's cry out of the grieving crowd gathered so solemnly between the gravestones, some of which had been there more than one hundred years.

CHAPTER ELEVEN

F red and I doubled on the big tractor tire that was too heavy and awkward for us to pick up by ourselves and threw it on the pile of wood and other tires we had gathered for burning Abe's tobacco bed.

Tobacco beds, where the tiny seeds were planted, were burned in the spring of the year. We were eleven years old now, so it was time to go do some serious work. We could see beds burning, and the black smoke rising into the blue sky as farmers all over the area were doing the same chore in order to get ready to plant their tobacco crops.

Each farm had a tobacco base. The base was land set aside out of the acreage of their farms controlled and strictly enforced by the government. Agents monitored these bases and every year, they could be seen measuring tobacco fields. If you were over your base limit, they would cut down plants in excess of the base and destroy them. Abe was allowed only one tenth of an acre to grow tobacco on his little farm.

The plants were bedded after the burning by planting the seeds and then covering the bed with tobacco cloth, which was a thin sheet of porous cloth like cheese cloth and would keep moisture in which was vital to the well being of the plants.

At the beginning of summer, the plants were pulled and set in the base that had been plowed and disked and made ready for the year's crop. Most of the farmers had tobacco setters, which were machines pulled by a tractor or mule. On each side of the machine were two seats. As you passed up the rows, you would set the tobacco plants by dropping it into a small hole made by the setter. A shot of water would then flow into the hole from tanks that set on each side of the machine. Someone would follow the setter on foot and carefully nudge the wet dirt around the plant to keep it from falling over. The machines were crude but very effective.

Abe couldn't afford a setter, so he, Mandy, June, and Fran would peg the tobacco by hand. The peg was a crude stick made from wood with a small handle. After pouring water from a can, you would jab the stick into the wet dirt and make a hole and then carefully put a plant into the hole. This was back breaking work, but one that Fran and I learned to do very effectively. We weren't paid for this work, and I volunteered to help because in the spring the fish made their way up the creeks, and we wanted to be finished early enough on Friday to go gigging.

During this time of year, the creeks were full of fish lying on the riffles of water flowing over the shallow slate rock beds. The eddies of swirling water provided pockets of sand and gravel for the fish to spawn, and after the eggs were hatched, the fish would make their ways back to the main rivers and streams until spawning time the next year.

Fran and I loved to gig, and in fact, we lived for it. We couldn't wait until the creeks were full from the spring rains because gigging season was about to begin. We walked deep in the woods and found places that we thought were ripe for harvesting fish.

This particular day, we worked with anticipation, and looked forward to quitting time so that we could head for the woods and wait for darkness to come. We had already prepared for the new season. We made gig poles from Hickory sticks and had sharpened the ends and fitted our gigs. We drove nails in the holes on the gig's sides into the stick to prevent the gig from slipping off when we nailed a fish.

The gig was a trident with very sharp barbs that stuck into the fish and fixated it so that the fish could not swim away once the gig had plunged into its body. Three pronged gigs were used for gigging frogs because they wouldn't tear up the meat. To gig fish, you needed a bigger weapon with four or five prongs, which came in various sizes. Large gigs were used for fish weighing three to ten pounds and smaller ones for the fish that were big enough to eat up to that weight. Once in a while, we would come upon a garfish, which could weigh up to twenty pounds, or more. When we came across one of these fish, we would let it alone since we weren't strong enough to fight it. If a gar got loose, it could tear you up attacking you with its long, sharp teeth. More than one gigger had lost fingers, a hand, or arm trying to pull a twenty-pound gar from the water. In order to gig these large and dangerous fish, the giggers made their gigs from pitchforks, which were heavy and strong. We weren't ready for the big fish, yet.

Gigging required a fishing license, which we could buy at Babs Kirks's store. It didn't cost much, but if the game warden ever caught you without a fishing license in Lincoln County, there would be big trouble including a hefty fine. It seemed that gigging without a license was a stiffer penalty than getting caught with a moonshine still.

There were limits on the amounts of fish you could gig. You couldn't gig game fish such as: bass (large or small-mouth), rock bass, bluegill, crappie, and gigging these fish carried large fines or a jail sentence or both if you were caught. Fran and I never paid much attention to these laws because gigging game fish was like mining gold. We loved to see a nice three to five pound bass laying on a riffle, and we filled our bags with enough game fish over the years to get a life sentence. Fran always said to not worry about it. "Game Wardens are too lazy to hike all the way back here," he reasoned. "Game Wardens will wait at your car if they thought you were in the creeks gigging. The smart giggers hide their game fish in the brush and show up with the rough fish and then retrieve their prize catches the next morning." Fran had everything figured out.

You could gig all the rough fish you wanted. Rough fish consisted of catfish, suckers, and basically any fish classified as "bottom fish" and not classified as "game."

Gunnysacks were used to carry the fish you gigged. Fran and I would use binding twine, which was a cord used to bind hay bales, and make a loop through the sack, tie the string so that we could throw the sack over our shoulders secured with the twine, and then let the sack drag in the water behind us to distribute the weight of the fish we had caught.

Gigging fish was an art, and it isn't easily mastered. First, you have to be careful to not scare the fish when you come upon them. Second, you have to take precise aim allowing for the flow of water and the movement of the fish fighting that flowing water. When you gigged the fish, you would bring the gig to your hand, pull the fish off the gig through the barbs sticking into the fish, and throw the fish in the sack. Sometimes, we would have so many fish we could barely carry the bags home.

Mandy and June loved gigging season because they would fry fresh fish for dinner and supper. Sometimes, Mandy would fix fish for breakfast. The Job family ate well during gigging season.

Abe loved gigging most of all. Although he never went gigging, the next morning after he would wake up, which was always early, he would yell out, and we could hear him from the back porch: "Those boys got a whale of a catch last night!" By the time Fran and I would get up for breakfast, fresh fish would already be frying on the stove because Abe had cleaned every one of them. Fran and I never cleaned a fish we gigged or caught.

Flashlights were a bad idea for gigging, and the batteries that didn't last very long in those days, were expensive. We used carbide lanterns. These were neat little pieces of equipment. Carbide lanterns were mainly used in Eastern Kentucky by coal miners, but Lincoln County had no coal, so the lanterns were used for gigging.

Each lantern had a small round container on the bottom, and carbide was put into these containers. Carbide came boxed in small pieces about half the size of a sugar cube. Behind the large reflector was a small tank of water.

The reflector was made of polished tin and shaped into a concave mirror. A line ran from the carbide container up to the center of the reflector. When you turned on the small water valve, the liquid would drip slowly into the container of carbide. The chemical reaction caused by water mixed with carbide put off gas that fed through a line and out the tiny nozzle in the middle of the reflector. Each reflector had a lighter that was a wheel like a cigarette lighter you turned on a flint, and the spark lit the gas. The fire from the nozzle reflected off the shiny surface of the reflector that would send a bright beam of light reaching some forty or fifty feet. The whole assembly weighed less than a pound, so it never tired you from holding it.

Occasionally, a line would stop up, so all giggers carried a thin piece of copper wire to unstop the line when necessary. The little carbide container would burn for hours before the carbide needed replenishing. Fire from the carbide light mesmerized the fish much better than a flashlight could. A fish would not budge when the firelight shone in its eyes. The fish would lie there waiting for the slaughter. Once your gig was positioned carefully aimed at the fish's back, you would plunge your gig with a forceful push through the fish and then pull it from the water and dump it into your gunnysack.

Abe announced that it was time to quit for the day. "Suppertime," he said. Mandy had already left the tobacco patch and was making our meal. We weren't through setting the tobacco that afternoon, so Abe told us we would be back in the patch at daylight. "You boys make sure you quit gigging in time to get some sleep," he warned. We would work the patch every day until the whole base was set, and the only exception was on Sunday. Although Abe never darkened the door of a church, his brothers were members of the small Lutheran Church at Ottenheim. but he had no interest. He did, however, make sure that his family was not interfered with at church time.

This was the night I had been waiting for all winter and spring. I had begun my gigging experience, and Fran and I would gig every Friday and Saturday nights for a full month and then begin the summer gigging huge bullfrogs lining the banks of the many local ponds on the farms we could get permission to gig. Sometimes, we gigged those ponds whether we had permission or not.

We hurried and washed our hands and took turns pumping the iron handle that brought water from the well beneath and flowed into the washbasin. I looked at the gunnysacks, the carbide lights, and the gigs Fran and I had made. They lay invitingly on the back porch, and I couldn't wait to get going to the creeks.

After a supper of fried chicken, mashed potatoes and gravy, biscuits, and homemade butter and jam, Fran and I headed for the woods. Some giggers wore rubber waders over their clothes, but that wasn't an option for us. Waders were big, cumbersome, and cost a lot of money we didn't have. We wore our tennis shoes and waded the water in blue jeans. The water from the spring rains was chilly and sometimes down-right cold, but we never minded.

We walked about two miles, and the woods were familiar territory to both of us. We had scouted our destination dur-ing the winter, and we were excited with anticipation of this important day.

"This is the spot," Fran claimed. The creek bank was slant-ed so that easy access was available into the water. The creek had a slate bottom, but if we followed it a mile or so, the bot-tom would turn into creek rock as its bed. On this night, the water was especially clear.

One of the things that would disappoint and ruin a gigging night was heavy rains a day or two before your planned event. Many a gigger was disappointed when he came to his gigging place only to find that the water was so muddy and murky he couldn't see the bottom and the spawning fish.

"We'll wade in here," Fran said, "then we'll get out down by the bridge."

The bridge he was talking about was nothing more than logs over the creek that the farmer, Mr. Burns who owned the land, had placed there in order to get his tractor and wagon across the creek and access to his back pastures.

My feet went to the bottom of the creek. It was deeper than it looked, and the cold, icy water that filled my shoes sent a chill up my spine. The real cold part was yet to come. I cringed as the water soaked my jeans at my rear end. The icy water nearly chilled me to death, but I dared not say a word. Fran didn't seem to mind.

"You'll get used to it," Fran said sensing my discomfort and shock. Although this was the first time since gigging with Tip Tuck the year before, he acted as if he didn't feel the cold at all. He was right. After an hour or so of wading the creek, I was having so much fun that I didn't notice how numb my legs and backside were.

Fran had demonstrated many times how to gig a fish, so I was not unfamiliar with the process. As I waded along, I was amazed how the carbide light allowed me to see every rock that lay along the bed of the creek. I saw a few fish sitting in the creek rock unable to move and terrified by the sudden fire in their eyes. I approached one of these fish and raised my gig. As I was ready to plunge it through like some jungle native, Fran said: "Not that fish. It's too little; your gig will tear it up."

It was pretty small, so I backed away. About the time I did, Fran was in his crouch. When he spotted a fish, he would bend at the waist and hump his back like he was doing a war dance. To me, this seemed totally unnecessary, but he told me that was his style, and I would develop my own. He did demonstrate how quick he was for a little guy. The fish never knew what hit it as Fran let his gig slide deftly through his hands and hit the fish dead center. Fran carefully lifted the flopping fish to his gunnysack and pulled the fish off his gig. I would have to get used to blood and fish guts saturating my hands. "E pluribus Unum," he commented nonchalantly.

Did he just quote the Kentucky motto, "One out of many?" I was impressed he remembered this from school and more impressed he used it in this context.

I got my first fish, and it was a beauty. The catfish lay in a bed of gravel, and the light blinded it so that it neither turned right nor left. I approached the fish, which was lying in water deeper than I thought, and I could see its whiskers swaying in the current.

"Easy," Fran instructed, "make sure you get over the fish and bring your gig down to about six inches from its back." I did this and held my position while waiting further instructions. "Now, stick it!"

The fish jerked as the four prongs ripped through it skin; it cringed and shook as if in shock, which it probably was as four barbs suddenly and unexpectedly pierced its back. I felt a little sorry for it, but I could feel the excitement rising in me as I felt its weight pulling against the gig and trying to break free, so I grabbed it. Big mistake. One of its barbs, or horns, sharp as a freshly honed knife, stuck in the side of my hand. That hurt, and I screamed in pain.

Fran was on his way. The fish was stuck to my gig, and I was stuck to the fish. Fran carefully put his hands around the fish's head, making sure that he was behind the sharp horns of the catfish. He then put the fish into the sack and wrapped some of the burlap around its body so that it wouldn't stick him, too.

"This is a good one," Fran said, "about four pounds."

I waded out of the creek and took a look at my hand. It was swelling quickly, and when I told Fran this, he said, "Want to go?"

I could hear the disappointment in his voice, and I didn't want to ruin our much longed for trip, so I said, "naw, lets keep going."

I was having so much fun that I ignored the pain from the hardest fish to gig in the creeks, and the next catfish I gigged, I knew exactly what to do.

Our sacks were full of fish in about three hours; we had

made it to the bridge, and when I pulled my sack out of the water, it was heavy. I tugged it and finally got it clear of the creek. Fran sensed my trouble, so he handed me his carbide light and lifted the sack over his shoulders and let it hang down his back. He grabbed his bag and threw it over the opposite shoulder. Fran was strong, that's all I know, and with both lights and gigs in my hands, we made our way back to the house.

Fran laid the bags on the back porch and put a heavy wooden box over the top securing it further with a rock so that some animal such as a dog wouldn't come along and steal the fish. We stripped our soggy clothes and hung them over the porch rail to dry.

Fran slept in the attic of his humble house. The entire area was open, and the ceiling joists were exposed showing the bottom side of the tin roof. It was hot up there in the summer and very cold in the winter. He slept in an old cast iron bed with two feather mattresses. On cold nights such as this, Fran covered up with one of the mattresses. It was impossible to be cold with those downy feathers shielding you from the chill. Both of us crawled into bed and pulled the big mattress over us. We slept this way many times careful not to touch each other and tonight the feather bed was soft and warm.

"That was so much fun," I said to Fran as he was lying there with his hands behind his head, "but I'm never going to let you carry the fish again."

I learned something else about Fran that night. Every so often, a car or pickup would pass the house. All the vehicles passing in front of the Job house had to slow down drastically because a sharp curve lay treacherously waiting to claim any victim that dared to take the curve too quickly. Cars needed to come almost to a full stop before negotiating the curve, and the demon had claimed so many cars and trucks and turned them into twisted piles of junk that the local folks had named the curve "People's Corner."

Many times the driver of a car or pickup would come speeding down the road, fail to slow down, miss the curve, and slide into Abe Job's garage. There were many boards patching up the holes made by these incoming missiles.

As cars slowed down, Fran would say, "1950 Buick flathead six," or "1954 Chevrolet pickup." This was amazing to me. Fran knew the sound of every car and truck and every engine. He knew the make and model by the sound of the engine and mufflers as the vehicles slowed down using a lower gear in order to make People's Corner safely.

I decided to challenge him so after we waited for some time, we could hear the gravel kicking up and bouncing off the fenders of an on coming vehicle.

"Okay, Fran, what kind of car is that?"

"It's not a car, Bud, it's a 1952 International pickup, and it belongs to Homer Shanks. He's coming home from Crab Orchard."

I looked through the open spaces between the eaves and the rafters of the roof. Facia board had never been nailed to the outside along the overhang of the ceiling joists. The vehicle slowed down, and I could see that it was indeed Homer Shank's International pickup.

I never challenged Fran again, but I did have fun every time I stayed with him listening to him name off each car and truck that would pass in front of his house during the night. He put himself to sleep this way, and he had been doing it for years.

We were pretty tired the next morning as Mandy called for breakfast. Abe was on the back porch cleaning fish.

"Let me see that hand," Mandy said.

My hand was swollen and throbbed a lot. I gently lifted it so she could take a look. By now, Fran, Abe, and June were peering over my shoulder. The hand was bruised and swelled more than I thought.

"I'll get some salt," Mandy said.

I soaked my hand most of the day. Abe forbade me working with the peg to plant the tobacco. That would have been painful. I had one thing on my mind and that was to not allow this pain to ruin my gigging plans. In spite of the pain, the hand was getting less and less swollen. Mandy checked me often and heated up water as the day wore on. My absence from the tobacco patch had slowed down progress, although Fran was working twice as hard to get the day's work done. Abe was afraid it was going to rain, and he intended to work his crew until dark. I sure hoped it wouldn't rain because Fran and I were going to take some serious fish that night from the creek.

"You boys did good," Abe smiled, "four catfish, twelve suckers, and a couple of nice bass. Twenty two pounds." Abe weighed the fish on a scale in his garage. "I reckon you all boys want to go out again tonight." Fran nodded while sticking another plant in the hole he had just made for it and poured some water in the hole from the can he was carrying.

Fran never asked his parents if he could do anything. He seemed to never need permission from a higher power, and I never heard him ask for it. I liked this kind of supervision. My dad was pretty strict, and I had to let him know everything I did. He never turned down permission for me to be with Fran; I guess everybody trusted Fran.

I was much better by that evening. The chores were done, so Fran and I put on our gigging jeans, which were still wet from the night before, and our wet shoes. It was cool in the evening, and I was already chilled before we even started toward the bridge where we pulled out the night before.

We stepped into the cold water that was deeper here than

further up the creek. We had to make sure that we didn't step into water over our heads and lose our fish and equipment. Carbide lights made the water look much shallower than in the daylight; it was deceptive, and you had to be careful.

My bag was about full when I spotted a stick lying on the bottom of the creek. I decided to stick it with my gig and throw it on the bank. The stick also blocked my way to a fish that lay nearby. I jabbed the stick with one prong of the gig and when I did, I received the shock of my life. The stick moved and thrashed, writhing, and striking the gig under water!

I pulled the gig up, and the huge Cottonmouth snake that I had gigged struck at me, missing my face by only inches. I was yelling, and Fran was yelling at me to drop my gig. I was paralyzed as the mouth opened showing its long fangs, and inside its mouth was as white as cotton.

"Drop the gig!" Fran screamed. "If that snake bites you, you're gonna die."

I couldn't drop it, but instead let the gig release in my hands so that the snake wasn't too close to me. This was one mad creature, and he was trying to take me out, fast. I also realized that if he came off that prong in the middle of a strike, he would nail me between the eyes.

Fran finally made his way across the creek, and as he approached me, he sneaked up behind the snake. The Cottonmouth was in striking position, and I could see its evil eyes staring at me, poised for one final attempt.

"Hold real still," Fran said as he eased his hand up the coiled body. "Don't move."

Move? I wasn't going to move. I was completely frozen, mesmerized as the snake and me stared each other down.

Quick as a flash, and before the snake knew what hit it, Fran had grabbed the back of its head, pinching its neck between his thumb and forefinger.

"Grab its tail," Fran instructed loudly as the snake stiffened out.

I hate snakes. I have been terrified of them ever since I was sitting in the outhouse before we left Kansas, and a big rattlesnake slithered across the floor below my feet. The only reason I didn't get bit that time was because my feet wouldn't reach the floor. I had to climb upon the seat in order to sit on the hole.

Somehow, I made myself grab hold of that slimy slithering creature. I grasped it with my free hand while holding the gig and carbide light in the other. The Cottonmouth was not afraid of us, and its thick body strained against our efforts to hold him.

Fran jerked the snake very hard, and as he did, the barb of the gig popped out of the snake's back. At the same time, I let go, and the Cottonmouth and Fran were now in battle.

Fran threw the snake on the creek bank, but this wasn't the end of it. The furious reptile whipped around and attacked us in the water. It hit the water with a splash as it struck with all its might. Poisonous snakes don't sink, they float, and this snake was coming at us uninhibited by the wound in its back; it was free to do whatever it pleased.

We back peddled but not fast enough and before we could react, the huge fangs were showing in full length, and the pure white cotton in its mouth shone brilliantly in the light of our carbide lamps. Fran was going to feel its wrath first, and I had crawled out on the bank. Fran was moving backwards, and it was clear that the creature was going to sink its needles into Fran's flesh.

I could think of nothing to do, so I raised my gig and like an expert spearman, I launched the gig at the snake. The weapon whizzed by Fran's ear barely missing him, and he was surprised as the gig passed his head. Later he would tell me that I could have hit him in the head with the gig and killed him.

The big gig struck the snake dead center of its opened mouth. All four prongs sunk into the cotton, and the snake fell backwards from it striking position with the gig in its mouth. I instinctively jumped in the water, and Fran was already jabbing his gig into the body of the snake. I stepped on it bravely now and pulled the gig out of its mouth. Fran and I poked the reptile until there was nothing left but skin, bones, and white meat floating down the ripples of flowing water.

"That's enough," Fran said, "We've got plenty of fish."

We walked along. I carried my own sack of fish, which was not as full as the night before, and I had gigged a nice Smallmouth bass and a couple of catfish. Fran's sack was a little heavier.

"Cottonmouths are the only snake that will bite you under water," Fran commented out of the silence, "don't gig any more sticks."

We weren't done with our gigging ventures that weekend. We washed early Sunday morning and were clean and ready for church. We took off and traveled across the Hanover's field. Fran didn't carry his gun anymore now that the threat from Benji McDuff no longer existed. We crossed the fence and walked across the cemetery toward the church. I began looking for dad.

I found him behind the church talking to one of the deacons about the Lord's Supper he was presenting that night. He asked Jewel Vance to make some unleavened bread and to bring some unsweetened grape juice. The Lord's Supper was a big event, and I knew the church would be crowded.

I told my dad about my gigging experience and about the angry snake. He listened to every word.

"Tell Abe to send some fish home with you this afternoon,"

he said. My dad was cool. As long as I had permission, he would let me do most anything except go to the picture show down in Crab Orchard. Baptists weren't supposed to go to movies. My dad preached that they were evil, but he would let me go to the Barbers on Saturday night and watch television. I never quite understood this, and I desperately wanted to go to a picture show with my friends.

Fran and I sang in the Booster Choir that Sunday morning because Stan Kirk wouldn't have it any other way. Fran and I tried to sleep during the service while my dad preached on the evils of tobacco, whiskey, dancing, movies, and women wearing pants and shorts. We got it all in there that morning because this was the Lord's Supper night coming. When he gave his altar call, the sinners who had been committing all these sins had to rededicate their lives, or they couldn't have the Supper. The altar was full of weeping mourners so sorry for their sins. Every time Fran and I nodded off, my mother or sister, Leah, who always seemed to be sitting behind us in the services of Evergreen Baptist Church, poked us in the back of the head.

When I returned to church that afternoon, Abe loaded me down with freshly cleaned fish. I felt good hauling my catch for the family, and my career as a bona fide fish gigger had begun. Fran and I would wade the creeks of Lincoln County the whole time we were growing up. It was said that we took more fish out of the streams than any other pair of giggers. After the snake episode, our gigging experiences were pretty much trouble free except one time when Fran and me were gigging in the Cedar Creek.

We always felt blessed when we would come upon a riffle of spawning fish. The creek flowed swiftly over slick and shallow slate beds of rock. Pockets, or holes, were indented in these slate rock beds, and the flowing water would deposit creek gravel being carried by the swift current. These holes were favorite spawning sites for the game fish. As we approached one of these riffles, we could hear and see some large fish flopping in the water laying their eggs.

As we approached the riffle, we noticed one particularly large bass. It was so big that the fish's back fins stuck out of the water. Fran guessed it easily weighed eight pounds or more. Truly one of the biggest fish in that part of the world. It certainly would be the biggest bass we had ever gigged or seen. We lusted after the fish and allowed the other spawning fish to jump the riffle and escape to deeper water.

We sneaked upon the fish that was blinded by our lights. In order to get the monster, we would have to be very careful not to spook it, so we began our slow, methodical approach. I had the best position behind the fish's body, so I let my gig go. I missed. The fish instinctively sensed danger, and it jumped sideways as my gig plunged for it.

Fran did not by any stretch of the imagination want this fish to get away, so he made a move to step on the fish and stop its progress. I thought the same thing as I reloaded and struck again. Unfortunately, Fran's foot stepped on the fish a split second before my gig made its journey through my hand toward the fish. My gig made it into the fish, but it also made it by entering and piercing through Fran's foot, tennis shoe and all.

We caught the fish, but my mother had to take Fran to old Doc Sinclair to dig the gig out of his foot. He never forgave me for this, and every time we had a serious discussion, the incident raised its ugly head. "You did that on purpose," he said, but I knew he didn't mean it.

There was another time when Fran and I forgot how far we had waded the creeks. We were way too far from home. It was a cold night, and there were icicles hanging from the rocks and freezing in the moisture spraying up from the creeks. We were very cold; the fish had taken to warmer and deeper water. These pools were so deep that we couldn't get to the fish.

We were hiking back to the house, and suddenly we were lost. We had wandered over the ridges and waded some of the creeks upstream. We had forgotten which creek was which and lost our way. Deep in the woods, Fran began to complain about how cold he was.

We came across an old dump where a farmer dumped the family garbage. All the farms had dumps somewhere on the land where the farmers could dispose of their trash without annoying anyone or themselves with the smell. We tried to find some old bedding in the dump so that we could spend the night out there and keep warm.

We were also hungry, and Fran found an old pot that miraculously didn't have any holes in it. We had gigged a couple of frogs, so we skinned them and put the legs into the water and boiled them over a fire we had started. We failed to find any bedding or anything we could use to keep warm, so we burned all the dry wood we could find and hunkered down by the fire, which was about to burn out. The boiled frog legs tasted terrible, but we ate them anyway.

"We're going to freeze to death," Fran said as his teeth chattered. I had never seen Fran panic or be scared of anything, but he had a fear of freezing to death for some reason or other. Maybe this wasn't so odd because that night we had every chance in the world of that happening to us.

The fire burned out, and Fran reacted by taking off his coat and throwing it on the fire.

"What are you doing?" I screamed at him.

"I ain't freezing to death," he screamed at me.

The coat burned up fast, and Fran was almost standing in the fire. I had heard of people doing strange things when they had something called "hypothermia," and I reasoned this was happening to Fran causing him to lose his mind. Fran was thin, wiry, and tough, but I was determined to save his life. I grabbed him and threw him on the ground covering him with my body.

I took off my coat. "Now take off your shirt," I demanded while I was unbuttoning mine.

"Do what?"

"Take off your shirt." When he refused to do this, I took it off for him, surprising him of the strength I never used on another human being. We had worked in the tobacco patches and hay fields until we were as lean and strong as two boys could be.

I put the coat over the top of us as our naked torsos exuded the warmth that would keep us from freezing to death through the long night. We had survived a snake or two, a gigged foot, some treacherous deep water in which both of us almost drowned, but that cold night in March was the closest he and I ever came to dying on a gigging trek up the flowing streams.

CHAPTER TWELVE

The Kirk farm was one of the largest in the Chapel Gap Community. Fran and I had hired on that summer to help in the tobacco crop and making hay. I was getting stronger, and I loved to flex those new found muscles caused by hefting the large alfalfa bales, which weighed nearly one hundred pounds onto the wagons for trucks used to haul the hay to the barns. Fran and I couldn't lift the large heavy bales by ourselves, so we doubled up in order to do our share of the work. It wouldn't be long before we could hoist one the weighty cubes of grass onto the wagon by ourselves.

Gib Kirk owned the farm. He had married Loretta Leach when she was sixteen years old, and he was forty. They had four kids, Stan, who led the Booster Choir, Alex, who they nicknamed, Buster, Jim, and Star. This family resembled our own except for Stan, who was older than me.

The Kirk family had a large house and clearly one of the nicer homes in the community. The house was two stories and painted white with green trim. They always kept the house up year by year. They also had a television. One of the reasons I loved working for Gib Kirk was that he and I would watch "wrasslin" on Friday nights after our workday, and if I wasn't spending the night with Fran, I stayed at the Kirk place.

Gib was a tall wiry man. He wore a straw hat with a green visor molded into the hat. He dressed in bibbed overalls and wore the familiar high-topped work shoes. I don't remember his ever dressing any other way. He farmed more than five hundred acres and raised several crops including: corn, tobacco, alfalfa, fescue, and soybeans. His farm was in the backcountry out of the way of other civilization of Chapel Gap. Getting to his farm required a trip down a single lane creek rock road for nearly two miles. The only other family living on the road was Gib's brother, Curt, who was a known bootlegger. The Kirks' lived at the end of the road, and while driving or walking up the lane, you would think that you were at the end of the world. The lane wandered through thick woods, and just as you thought you would drop off a mountain, a beautiful scene opened in front of you. The New England styled farm with its neatly painted silos with green roofs, and the two-story house with green shutters and roof, made a lovely picture with the green fields and neatly trimmed fences in the background. I often thought that this was the most beautiful farm in the entire world, and especially in the autumn of the year when Kentucky is a blaze of gorgeous color.

In the house was a great room where the family ate their formal meals, relaxed while playing board games, and watched Channel 3 out of Louisville. There was only one station available in that part of the world, and without the tall antenna rising from the side of the house, the television reception would have been so fuzzy no one could see the picture. Gib and I had our favorite wrestlers, and we cheered for them with fervor. We loved to watch Don Eagle and The Great Scot pulverize some helpless defender.

The house had a large kitchen where Loretta cooked and served the dinners and suppers on regular weekdays. The house also had one of the few inside bathrooms in Lincoln County but only the family was allowed to use it. Outside the house was a common dinner bell, which every farm had hanging outside the kitchen. When dinner or supper was served, Loretta would ring the bell, and the workers would come from the fields. No one working for Gib brought his or her own dinner. He insisted that each man present himself at the long table in Loretta's kitchen.

Stan Kirk was my friend, and he took care of me from the moment he introduced me to Fran that day when our family came to the Evergreen Baptist Church. One of the reasons I loved Stan was because when Gib was in another field supervising his farm laborers, Stan would let me drive the truck or tractor, and I wouldn't have to lift the heavy bales of hay. Stan taught me to drive slow between the hay rows and close enough so that the workers didn't have to do extra work carrying the bales too far. I paid strict attention to this teaching, and I was so diligent about it that the workers would ask Gib to let me drive the truck or tractor each time we baled hay.

Stan taught me everything about farming, and many times he let me pull the plows and disk the fields. I stayed as close to Stan as I possibly could.

Buster Kirk was the opposite of Stan. He was the same age as Fran and me. He was a toe head boy who was spoiled and took advantage of everyone he could. When Fran and I stayed at the Kirks, Buster always made sure that we didn't get the good beds to sleep on. The Kirk boys slept in a large room, and there were four or five beds in there that Gib required in

case some of his workers coming from longer distances needed to stay the nights while working on the farm. Gib never,
ever made a worker sleep in the barn, which was the custom
of other farmers using migrant workers.

Buster was tall like Stan, and he was strong. He liked his
advantage, and I often thought how much he reminded me of
Benji McDuff. When Stan was around, Buster never messed
with Fran or me, but one day he did.

I had not started smoking yet but that had always been my
plan. Fran didn't want me to smoke because he said, "it will
stunt your growth." He also said it would make me sick, so for
the time being, I stayed away from tobacco.

On a hot summer day, we were in the fields putting up
hay. Stan had instructed Buster that Fran was to drive the big
Chevrolet truck, and I was to drive the Allis Chambler tractor. The Kirks had several tractors, but the Allis Chambler was
their favorite. Buster didn't mind when I drove the smaller
Farmall or the John Deere, but he hated anyone touching the
Allis Chambler with the diesel engine. Diesel engines were
rare in that part of the State because of the expense of owning
one of these powerful machines that could easily exceed twice
as much as a tractor with a gasoline engine.

I was driving without my shirt as all us boys did while
working in the hot summertime. The boys never wore shorts
for two reasons: First, my dad preached against nakedness
as being ungodly, and second the boys thought shorts were
for sissies. No respectable boy living in Chapel Gap would be
caught dead in a pair of shorts. One time the Plummer boy
wore shorts to church, and the boys threw rotten eggs at him
that humiliated him.

In mid-afternoon, it was hot and Buster strolled up to the
tractor.

"Here," he said, "have a chew."

"I don't think so," I replied, "Fran said chewing tobacco would make me sick."

"Fran chews, and he don't get sick," Buster commented. "Have one."

I looked at the big black plug of tobacco Buster was offering me. He had a wad in his mouth that would choke a horse and was spitting on the tire where he was leaning and tempting me to chew.

"Buck, buck, buck," he called making the sound of a chicken. You never allowed anyone to call you a chicken.

"Give it to me," I demanded.

Buster took out his Case knife with the bone handle and sliced off a nice plug of the juicy treat. "Here," he said, "chew this." He had a big grin on his face and was obviously enjoying himself.

I took the tobacco and placed it delicately between my tongue and cheek as I had seen these tobacco farmers do so many times. After a couple of minutes, I spat out some juice. This was a wonderful experience, and I felt manly.

I resumed my driving position on the wide seat of the Allis Chambler and was puttering along and watching to make sure I did everything the laborers wanted. I was also skillfully spitting over the tractor tire onto the freshly cut hay.

In the summertime, there are little tiny bees you can barely see called "sweat bees." These tiny creatures carry a lot of venom for their size, and when you get stung, a large welt will rise on your skin, and it hurts almost as much as a larger bee sting. There are thousands of these in the hay fields, and they will land on your body and drink the sweat to satisfy their thirsts. Normally, they won't bother you except when they are pinched for some reason. Many times one or two will fall into your pants or shirt and sting the devil out of you before you either get them out or smash them.

I was a little dizzy with this first chew, but I felt like I could handle it. Before too long, I felt a sweat bee sting me on the back. This happened several times and irritated me. I couldn't figure it out because there was no back on my seat, but I kept feeling the stings as if I were leaning on the little demons.

Buster was punching these creatures with the end of his pitchfork handle. When he touched them, they would sting and when they would sting, I would swallow a little tobacco juice or "amber" as they called it on the farms. Buster was jumping for joy and beside himself every time one of the bees stung me. Before I could figure any of this out, I began to feel a rumble in my stomach. I had heard that if you swallow tobacco juice, it will make you deathly ill. I swallowed a lot and was getting sicker by the minute. Soon, I was so sickly nauseated that I could no longer drive. I climbed down off the tractor and told Buster to take over. He smiled from ear to ear. Buster was calculating, and he knew exactly what was happening.

I wretched in that field until I thought I would vomit up my intestines. I had never been that sick in my life, and I thought I would die. Stan saw me throwing up, and he walked over to the trailer where I was sitting.

"Are you okay?" Stan asked with concern. I nodded my head that I wasn't.

Stan looked at Buster, who now acted like a possum that was just caught eating your berries. As my world spun round and round, Stan asked Buster what had happened. He figured Buster pulled the old sweat bee trick that had made men who chewed tobacco all their lives, ill.

"He begged me for a chew," Buster explained, "and I told him it would make him sick, but he wouldn't listen, so I gave him a plug."

"What are those welts on his back?" Stan asked. My back was festered with puffy bee stings - there were so many.

CHRONICLES OF THE KNOBS · 113

Buster glanced at Stan, put the tractor in gear, and drove on. Meanwhile, I was out of commission for the day, so Stan took me back to the house.

"Don't worry," Stan comforted, "I'll beat the crap out of Buster when I'm finished but don't chew tobacco." Stan said this as he spit tobacco juice out the window of the truck.

I never did put another chew in my mouth, and after work, Stan beat the crap out of Buster. He came in the kitchen for supper with a big knot in the middle of his forehead. When Loretta asked what had happened, he said that he had run into the barn door while trying to get the cows out.

"Please don't tell my dad, Loretta," I pleaded. "He'll whip me for sure."

"I would never tell your dad, Sonny."

Loretta Kirk was the biggest gossip in Lincoln County. She had a phone, so she was always intercepting phone calls to her neighbors. She occupied herself during the long winters and in the evenings when everyone had settled down. I saw her run to the phone many times when she would hear the longs and shorts of a ring and the quick beep of the bell when someone answered on the other end. She would stand there listening to every word; her facial expressions gave away the news on the other end. Sometimes, she would wince, which meant that the news was good and at other times, she would let her mouth fly open that meant the news was bad. She truly enjoyed this pastime and often times she would repeat the gossip at the supper table that she heard passing up and down the hollows.

Loretta was a tall woman, fairly attractive, but she had one prominent feature. She was cockeyed. She always made me nervous because I could never tell which direction she was looking. She had blue eyes, and Fran, who didn't like Loretta Kirk at all, said that she did have blue eyes. "One blew east, and one blew west," he said.

The Kirks had asked my dad if he would come to dinner after church. Loretta had been "born again" as had Buster and Stan under my dad's preaching. He had baptized them one cold day in March in the Cedar Creek that ran through the Lord farm. My mom and Loretta were good friends, and I think it was because she loved to gossip as much as Loretta did. Loretta was full of it. Loretta also smoked. One day my dad told her she should quit smoking because it was a sin. He reasoned with her that tobacco contained Nicotine and that hurt the "Temple of the Holy Spirit" which is your body.

Loretta reasoned back to my dad that he drank coffee and that was just as bad because coffee had caffeine and that hurt the Holy Spirit as well. Being in a conundrum with logic, my dad said, "If you will quit smoking, I will quit drinking coffee."

To this day and until my dad died, Loretta Kirk never smoked, and my dad never drank another cup of coffee. To replace their habits, my dad drank Postum that has no caffeine, and Loretta chewed gum.

It was Loretta who one time told a terrible tale on my dad. She had "heard" that he was messing around with the Vance woman, who at that time was single, and had been restored to the church by my dad after she divorced her husband, Omer. It was strictly forbidden for anyone to divorce while being a member of the Evergreen Baptist Church, and when you did, you were excommunicated or excluded and became an outcast in the community. Jewel Vance did that, and the church kicked her out. When she came and told my dad she repented, he let her back into the church. The old timers were really upset about this, and so was Loretta Kirk even though she wasn't a Christian at the time or a member of the church. She carried the gossip after hearing Lilly Masterson gossip on the phone to her sister in Ohio.

Poor Jewel had been dragged in front of the church and

CHRONICLES OF THE KNOBS · 115

was admonished for her sins and voted out unanimously by the membership. After her repentance, my dad brought her up before the church again, and a "majority vote" let her back in as a member in good standing. She barely made the two-thirds required to pass a referendum. The gossip went on for months and was doing damage to the Preacher's credibility.

Loretta never did like Jewel Vance, and Fran told me it was because Jewel was such a pretty woman, and she had beautiful daughters who wouldn't have anything to do with the Kirk boys. Patricia and Nancy Vance were two of the most sought after brides-to-be in Lincoln County.

Loretta had spread the rumor that my dad was meeting Jewel on the side in secret places. Nothing could have been farther from the truth because my dad was a good man, and even though my mother didn't always behave herself like a pastor's wife by gossiping and such, he dearly loved her. He wouldn't do anything to jeopardize his ministry at Evergreen Baptist Church. Loretta had done this suddenly; suggesting that something was wrong in his marriage and the gossipers took it from there. The rumor was so widespread that the publicity was affecting the church.

One Sunday morning, Bro. Lord as we called him, and Preacher Roberts, who had a beautiful and intelligent daughter; a girl that couldn't be touched by any boy living in Chapel Gap and looking for a girlfriend or wife, rose to their feet after my dad has quit preaching and asked that everybody be seated. We had just finished singing the invitation song, "If A Man Goes To Hell, Who Cares?"

Bro. Lord hated to tell the congregation what he was about to tell them.

"Members," he addressed, "there is so much gossip about our Preacher that I feel we should ask him to resign."

The shock of this statement disengaged the entire congregation from the morning's sermon, "Judge not lest ye be judged." My dad had something on his mind that morning. He delivered a powerful message on the evils of gossip.

"I second that," Preacher Roberts said although this whole motion business was completely out of whack with Robert's Rules of Orders; a standard of business meeting rules the church strictly adhered to.

My dad stood inside his pulpit and gritted his teeth.

"I make a motion that we have a vote right now," Bro. Lord said. He was a good man, and we all loved him, but he had yielded to the constant barrage from his wife, who was quite a gossip herself that the church needed to do something about this.

I knew my dad was in big trouble. My first thoughts were, *how could the church survive without my dad as the Preacher?* This was serious business.

"I second that motion," Mr. Messer said. He had to interrupt Junior Cullen, who hated my dad for not cooperating with the Southern Baptist Association Missionary. The Missionary tried to schedule himself once a month in our church to preach. In this way, he received a special offering from the churches he visited which supplemented his salary that my dad said was already excessive. My dad refused, which made Junior Cullen upset.

"Under Robert's Rules of Order," my dad explained, "a motion is on the floor to dismiss the Pastor. Any discussion? The church had a debate on the floor after the motions were made before a vote could be taken. Sometimes, voting on the simplest matters could take hours, and the church that had its business meetings on Wednesday nights once per month, could be there until midnight. The kids loved the business meetings because there was no preaching, and the kids would make fun of April May, the Church Clerk, who would read the minutes of the last meeting. This was no trivial vote this time; my dad's future was on the line.

Mr. Henry May stood to his feet. "I don't believe a word of this," he said, "where is the proof that the Preacher is messing around with another woman?" Henry May knew the gossip although his wife, April, didn't gossip and both were strong supporters of my dad. One by one, people spoke of the goodness of the Pastor, and it looked like if the vote was taken, my dad would survive. Many of the people who spoke in favor of my dad said: "I will leave the church if you vote out our Preacher."

Junior Cullen, the fat red faced, redheaded brat testified that the church wouldn't survive if we kept dad in the pulpit. With tears streaming down his fat cheeks, he exclaimed, "Do you want weeds to grow up in front of the church because nobody is here? Do you want your families to continue going to the church where they grew up? This church is going to die; it will never be the same. Please (and he choked up while wiping his eyes with a handkerchief that his mother Naomi Cullen had handed him to him) please, please don't let this happen to us." He sat down as some of the people nodded their heads in recognition that this may be the greatest speech given since Patrick Henry said, "Give me liberty or give me death!" Things didn't look so good for my dad at the moment.

"I recommend we kick those people out of the church who want to throw the Preacher out!" Reuben Pat, Riley Pat's uncle, screamed from his seat and not bothering to rise.

The vote was about to be taken after two hours of arguments. Chicken dinners were waiting at home, but this was much too important to worry about food. Loretta Kirk had a curious expression on her face. Fran noticed this and whispered to me that she was about to break down. When I asked how he knew this, he explained, "her hair is getting greasy; she gets that way when she's really upset." He was right; her hair looked like she had just stuck her head in a five-gallon bucket of lard.

Loretta Kirk stood up. The congregation gasped. Women were forbidden to speak in a mixed church service. "Let the women remain in silence, let them learn at home with all subjection and not usurp authority over the men in the church," my dad would explain the Scripture. Women weren't allowed to make motions in the church business meetings or discuss the business. "Let them ask their husbands at home and learn from them," my dad preached. Of course, all the women wanted to speak in the business meeting, make motions, or testify in the mixed assemblies.

My dad made a sudden move to stop Loretta Kirk from speaking, but it was already too late. She ignored him and the cries from some of the men who were telling her she was out of order and to sit down and shut up. Some of the men were kept from objecting verbally by their wives shoving a sharp elbow into their sides and warning them they better not interrupt this historic event.

Loretta began to speak, and as she did, she could barely get the words out behind her sobbing.

"I caused all this," she sobbed, "I told a little white lie on the Preacher that became a big black one, and I'm so sorry. It was never true, and I don't know why I did it. Please forgive me and don't fire the Preacher."

Loretta wasn't a bad person and many times I have seen her be more than fair. She had saved me many times from getting whippings for things she knew my dad did not approve of, but when she was in the gossiping mode, nothing or anyone could stop her.

Some other ladies began to weep, and one by one, they stood and confessed that they had spread the gossip also and sometimes adding to the tale. Even people, men and women, who had nothing to do with the situation, were weeping. Heck, even Fran and me were crying.

"Well," my dad said, "we have a confession. Does anyone want to withdraw their motions?"

"I withdraw," Bro. Lord said, "and make the motion we accept Mrs. Kirk's confession with no disciplinary action."

"Any discussion?" My dad asked the sorrowful group of members.

Junior Cullen was about to object in argument, but his girlfriend, Carolyn Crane, grabbed him by the belt and dragged him back into the seat.

"All in favor raise your hands," my dad requested. Every member raised his or her hands except Junior Cullen.

"Any opposed by the same sign." No hands were raised. Junior Cullen would have been the only one, but he knew better than to place himself in danger by angry church members who might harm him.

My dad followed Robert's Rules of Order to the tee. "Now, any discussion about accepting Mrs. Kirk's plea for forgiveness? Okay, no discussion. All in favor show by the lifting up of hands." Many hands were raised, and they were counted by Henry May.

"All those opposed to accepting her plea for forgiveness vote by the same sign."

Mr. May counted these hands as well, and there were many who did not want to accept her apology and forgiveness including Fran Job. Loretta Kirk had survived and so had all the other guilty parties.

My dad was standing at the door in his familiar spot shaking hands with each and every member of the Evergreen Baptist Church. Many hugged him and told him how sorry they were for all this trouble. Even though my dad would never be challenged again in this manner, he never forgot what happened that day, and neither did anyone else. He was always aware of how quickly friends could join the enemy against good people.

As Loretta was leaving the church and waiting her turn to speak with my dad, she said to him: "Pastor, I am so sorry. Will you please forgive me and how can I make this up to you?"

"I forgive you, Sister Kirk," my dad replied, "but there is only one way you can make this up to me."

"How? I'll do whatever you ask," she replied lugubriously.

"This afternoon, I want you to go to your hen house. I want you take a pillow slip and fill it with feathers."

"Why?" She asked.

"Because I want you to bring the feathers back here to the church tonight and scatter them on the church yard and cemetery."

"What?"

"Then, I want you to pick every last one of them up and put them back in your sack."

"That's impossible. The wind will blow them away; I can't possibly do that," she cried incredulously.

"It is impossible," my dad explained, "but you asked and that is exactly what you have done to my life."

Loretta had already told everyone in Chapel Gap and Evergreen Baptist Church about my chewing experience and getting sick. She and Buster thought it was the funniest thing. My mom knew about it because Loretta told her about it at church on Sunday morning. We were sitting at the table when Loretta could no longer contain herself.

Fran kicked me under the table. Fran always went with me on Sundays no matter where we were going, but his least favorite place to visit with us was the Kirk's house.

"She's getting ready to tell on you," Fran whispered, but his voice was drowned out by the chatter.

"How do you know that?" I quizzed.

"Her right eye is twitching, and her left eye is all the way over on the other side of her head."

Fran later told me that when Loretta was about to gossip, she would have this look in her eyes. Her eyes would twitch, and one of them would run clean to the opposite side of her face; she had to strain to look straight at someone in order to tell her story.

Fran was right again. Loretta's eye was on the other side of her head as she jokingly told my dad that I got sick chewing tobacco.

"Yep," she joked, "ole Sonny there was sicker than a dog; he was throwing up all over the place. I tell you that boy was green with nicotine," she roared.

Everyone laughed except my dad, Fran, and me. Fran had fear in his eyes because he knew that my dad didn't think this was very funny.

"Come with me," my dad instructed while looking at me straight across the table. He got up.

"Now, Preacher," Loretta pleaded, "He didn't mean no harm."

My dad took me to the barn, and after explaining in a sermon, which he always had prepared for these moments complete with Scriptures about "honoring your father and your mother so that your days would be long on the earth." He whipped the day lights out of me for disobeying him and chewing tobacco. I danced around and around as he flogged me with his belt half killing me for this sin, and I promised over and over that I would never chew tobacco again the rest of my natural life. This promise wouldn't be that hard to keep, and I knew I would never be punished for chomping down on a plug of tobacco, ever.

When my dad was convinced that all the sin and degradation was purged from my soul, he stopped whipping me with the belt. He used the belt most of the time to whip me because it didn't hurt as much as a switch. He later explained the reason for his "softer" decision to use a belt sans a switch was because I got sick which was part of my punishment.

My pride was more hurt than anything else. I had to walk with my dad back to the house and sit to finish my dinner while I looked at the smirking expression of Buster Kirk, who had won on two occasions. He got me sick, and he got me whipped.

CHAPTER THIRTEEN

W|e always looked forward to the days in the fields when we were baling straw. The straw bales were very light, and Fran and I could easily lift the bales onto the wagon or the big truck by ourselves. The days seemed shorter; even though, the hours were the same. The O'Conner boys had been hired by Gib Kirk to help get the straw in the barn.

Frank O'Conner had married Alice Hanover when she was twelve years old. By the time she was thirty-five, she had birthed sixteen kids with no multiple births. There were seven boys, nine girls, and the family was poor. It was common in the Knobs Area for the families to be large, young girls to be married to older men, and the couples raised a bunch of kids to help with the farm labor.

Frank was a tall man and had a mean temper. He was almost a recluse and socialized with no one and kept his family reigned in. The O'Conner children went to church at Evergreen Baptist, and several of them had been baptized. Rhoda, the oldest child, married Johnson Carlisle and was the first marriage my dad performed in his ministry.

The O'Conner boys were all redheaded, or slightly so, and Carey, the oldest, had flaming red hair. Frank O'Conner had instilled in the boys the necessity to work hard, and they were hard workers. They were as mean as their dad and very few of them went to school, but the ones who did had a reputation. Most of the boys on the school grounds at Broughtontown School stayed away from them.

One of our favorite things to do was go swimming after a long day in the hay fields. Gib Kirk had several ponds, and the favorite was one he called the "lake" although it didn't look big enough to be a lake to me. Unlike the other ponds on the farm, the lake was spring fed, so the water was clean and clear. The other ponds were muddy from the cows wading in to cool themselves on the hot, humid summer days.

On this particular day after we had put the last bale of straw in the barn, Stan Kirk said: "Let's got to the lake and go swimming." On this command, we left the pitch forks stuck in the straw bales and ran as fast as we could to the lake. We had done this often, and it was a game we played to see who could get in the water first. The Kirks had a little boat docked and tied to a willow tree. The boat was actually four wooden barrels cut in half and tied together with bailing wire. It was fun to get into the makeshift craft and paddle around with the oars Gib Kirk made for his boys. The first one of us to reach the lake could pick three others from the group and have the use of the boat for the rest of the evening.

All the boys working in the fields wore blue jeans and no shirt, and we were all well tanned above the waist. Most of us didn't wear a hat except for Buster Kirk. He was proud of his collection of hats and wouldn't let anyone touch them. One time he beat up his little brother for wearing one of his hats.

We didn't wear bathing trunks either, which explained why below the waist, we were whiter than a new born baby's butt. The only time we saw swimsuits was in the Sears and Roebuck Catalogue that came twice a year. Sissies wore swim trunks. We all stripped to the bone except for Buster who usually left on his underwear. There were five O'Conner boys, Stan Kirk, Buster Kirk, Fran and myself racing for the boat.

Carey O'Conner easily won the race. Fran and I had no chance, so we had to rely on the winner to pick us for the ride. We knew our time would come when we could out run any of those boys who were beating us now.

Carey picked his brothers, Steve, Shane, and Ronnie to ride with him in the boat. The Kirk brothers didn't like to see other people working their boat made of tubs but trying to out run the long, swift legs of the O'Conner boys was futile. It seemed that every time we were working the fields with the O'Conner boys, they dominated the boat.

On both ends of the lake, there were steep slopes of wet and slimy mud caused from the constant dripping of the springs coming out of the rocks above the water that fed the lake. We were all stark naked except Buster, of course, as we parted and swam to opposite ends of the lake. The O'Conner boys were positioned on one end of the lake with the boat and us on the other.

For some unknown reason, Carey grabbed a handful of mud and slung it across the lake. The mud skipped on the glassy mirror and hit Stan Kirk in the back. This did not hurt him of course, but it did make a mess of slick dripping mud that slid down to his waist. Stan turned around and saw all the O'Conner boys grinning. Shane cupped his hands and dipped into the soft mud. He raised his hand from the water and slowly, methodically formed a mud ball that he quickly threw at Buster. He missed. Stan Kirk formed his own mud ball and threw it skillfully toward Carey O'Conner. The missile skipped off the water picking up speed as it went and hit Carey square in the face, plastering him from one side of his head to the other with black oozing mud. Carey grinned from beneath his murky mask and looked like the black man I had seen sleeping with snakes at the Dog Patch Zoo over in London, Kentucky. Carey's teeth showed white as snow through the dark drapery of slime; even though only a few of the boys in Chapel Gap ever brushed their teeth.

We stood and stared at each other for a moment, and no one moved. However, each of us knew what the other was thinking. The fight started with Ronnie O'Conner slinging a clump of wet mud across the pond and hitting Fran square in his chest. Our team was outnumbered, but we had played a lot of baseball at school, and our throwing arms were very strong and accurate. Soon, mud was flying everywhere. You could scarcely get your hands in the water and make a mud ball before someone had hit a target with a well-placed aim.

Our team was winning the battle because the O'Conner boys didn't play baseball at school. The O'Conner boys were covered with mud from the tops of their heads down to their waists. They couldn't dip in the water fast enough to keep the mud out of their eyes. I had turned back looking for more ammunition when I was struck in the back between the shoulder blades with something very hard, and it hurt. I was stung like a bee.

I turned around and Ronnie O'Conner was hurling another missile at me. Before I had time to duck, the sailing ball hit me in the forehead, and a drip of blood mixed with murky water trickled off my nose. He hit me again on the arm.

"What're you doing?" I screamed. He grinned and threw another, and this one hit Fran on the nose.

"Rocks!" Fran yelled. "He's putting rocks in the mud balls."

Indeed he was. He was feeling rocks in the bottom of the lake and squishing them into the middle of the mud balls. When they hit, they carried the weight of the rocks, and the splat of mud caused the ooze to separate a hard stone to land on its target.

All the O'Conner boys were doing this, and Stan Kirk screamed for them to stop but to no avail.

"Throw another, and we're going to whip your butts," Stan yelled.

He watched as Ronnie, a boy of my size and age, molded his ammo and made another throw. The aim was at me, but I ducked in time for it to fly over my head, but it hit Fran for the second time and the gash it made drew blood.

Stan Kirk led the charge. We followed him as he started swimming across the lake. We were very good swimmers having spent many hours in the ponds and lakes of the farms where we worked. The O'Conners stood their ground and kept firing at us as we were swimming but doing very little damage.

Before they could react, we were on top of them. We reached the shallow water where we could finally stand up. The lake was very deep in the middle, some twenty feet or so, and the banks gently sloped on that side of the pool.

As we stood, no one spoke a word, and we just stood there looking at each other knowing something really graphic was about to happen. The O'Conners taunted us and after the cussing, Stan invited them up the bank.

Stark naked, we stood facing one another in the hay field that had been baled the week before. This particular hay field was rough. There were briars, and the stubble from the coarse stalks of fescue was hardened and sharp.

We charged each other like the 5th Cavalry advancing into battle with the Indians. Six of them and five of us. Although outnumbered, one of the O'Conner boys, a weak fellow ran to the creek made by the water flowing from the lake's spillway. He cowered there and watched the ensuing battle. The odds were now even.

Shane O'Conner was my friend. He was a tough kid, and Fran and I liked him a lot. In fact, he was the only O'Conner boy we did like. Shane and I had spent many days with Fran hunting and fishing in the ponds the O'Conners owned on their farm. Frank O'Conner didn't allow his boys to go any-where but church, so we had to visit Shane at his place if we wanted to hang out with him.

Shane looked at me. That would be the battle most likely to be fair, and as our eyes met, we ran into each other. Shane "patted" me with a soft punch. I flinched as though it hurt just to let his brothers know that Shane and I were engaged in a raging conflict. I knew from the softness of the blow that he didn't intend to fight me. Instead, he turned his attention to Fran, and even though Fran was not a fighter, they went at it slugging wildly but hitting nothing.

I took a blow to the back of my head. I turned and faced Ronnie O'Conner and could see in his eyes that he was going to kick the Devil and all out of me.

Ronnie was a pudgy guy. In fact, he was the only pudgy O'Conner of the girls and boys. Frank had accused Alice one time of having an affair with Jack Rivers, who was a tenant farmer for the Kirks. "That kid ain't like the rest of em," he complained.

Ronnie looked like a Brazilian native from the Amazon River. He had black hair just like Jack Rivers. His skin was nat-urally dark brown; the other O'Conner boys were all fair com-plexioned. His mother, or one of his sisters, had given him a fresh haircut. I could easily see where they placed a bowl over his head and cut around it. With his bronze skin and dark brown eyes, the trim did make him look like the pictures we had seen in books at school about the Amazon natives.

For some reason, as Ronnie and I faced off, the rest of the boys had quit fighting. Most of these boys were friends having grown up together, got baptized together, and worked the farms with each other in the summers. I glanced around and noticed that no one was fighting. They were staring at Ronnie and me. I couldn't see any damage to any of the other boys other than Fran's nose that had trickled some blood and dried on his chest. The tempers that had flared up had now cooled down. Fran and Shane were talking with each other when Fran glanced over at Ronnie and me.

"The fight's over," Fran said, "let's get to the house."

"Shut up, Fran," Ronnie replied. "I'm going to kick the crap out of this Preacher's kid."

Ronnie hated me, and I never knew why. Someone had told me one time it was because when Fran and I came over to see Shane, Ronnie would get jealous. I supposed that to be true because he had that look in his eye of resolve to tear me from limb to limb. I also believed he could do it.

This was my first serious confrontation since the time that Fran and I were up a Sycamore tree that we had climbed over at the Anderson place after a Sunday dinner. We had never been there before and Fran wanted to stake out the place to find fishing holes and gigging spots.

I was above Fran in the tree, and I had a habit of spitting all the time; even though, I didn't chew tobacco. I was spitting from high in the tree to see how far the saliva would fly out of my mouth through the split in my front teeth. Some of the spit fell on Fran.

"Hey, Bud, don't spit on me again," Fran warned.

I spit again.

"I said don't spit on me."

Finally, Fran having taken all of this he was going to and pressed seriously to put a stop to it said, "Get down out of the tree, so I can kick your butt."

I was pretty strong and lean now. My adolescent muscles had grown as I was going through puberty. I didn't believe Fran could take me, so I climbed down out of the tree and stood in front of him. I knew as I faced Ronnie O'Conner how painful it would be if we rolled around in the hay field. Fran and I fought for about a half hour and then we both started laughing. How could two boys who were brothers and loved each other have a fight?

I stared at his body, then mine. We both had briars and stubble embedded in our skin where we had fought with our shirts off, and we had abrasion after abrasion from our heads to our waists. I could feel the burning sensation of that day a few weeks before as I faced punishment by Ronnie O'Conner.

I saw the look in Ronnie's black eyes, and my first thought was to back away and run as far as I could. I saw the fear in Shane O'Conner's face as he watched the rage filling his brother. Those two boys didn't get along. One time they tried to kill each other.

The two O'Conner boys were in Frank's barn, which had a corncrib, and were arguing about something that probably didn't make any sense. They were cussing at each other and threatening to seriously hurt one another which is exactly what they proceeded to do.

Ronnie threw a full ear of corn at Shane hitting him in the face and causing a cut that needed stitches should they have been in the habit of going to a doctor when one of these injuries happened. Shane still carried the deep scar.

The boys threw corn at each other as hard as they could trying to knock each other out. Finally, an ear hit Shane in the head and did just that; it knocked him out. Then, Ronnie took a pitchfork and was about to thrust it through Shane, who lay defenseless on the ground. Suddenly Shane came to and horror filled his eyes as he could see the resolve his brother had to plunge the fork into his body.

Carey O'Conner was on the way to the barn and had heard the commotion. He quickly ran and flung open the passage door that was part of the large hinged barn doors. He arrived just in time to tackle Ronnie from behind. He drove his body hard into Ronnie's back hitting him squarely above the hips and brought him down. The bigger and older more experienced Carey held Ronnie on the ground until he had cooled down.

"You better not tell Frank on me, Carey," Ronnie yelled.

Even though Frank was their father, the O'Conner kids had a habit of calling their parents by their first names. My dad said it was because Alice was so young when the first children were born.

All of these things I knew about Ronnie O'Conner flashed through my brain as I stood waiting on him to make the first move and hit me. The O'Conner boys were on one side, and the Kirks and Fran on the other. Fran called a "timeout" and walked over to me to say something.

It was the unwritten code of ethics we had adopted from football, baseball, and basketball games we played at school. When a timeout was called, you can't go hitting on the guy until he was ready. Not only was this better as far as keeping tempers under control, but it let the fighters have more time to plan their fight strategy. Ronnie held up and let Fran come over and talk to me. He knew that he better do this because even his own brothers would have stopped him if he didn't honor the rule. I also knew that if we were anywhere else, Ronnie would never have honored this code.

"He's strong, Sonny, but he can't fight. Don't let him get

hold of you and remember what your Uncle Willis taught you," Fran instructed.

Uncle Willis was my uncle and a criminal. He had a life of crime starting with robbing egg money from the grocery stores in Longford, Kansas. His first stint that got him caught was when he robbed one of these stores in Longford.

One afternoon, the Sheriff of Ottawa County, Kansas came to my grandfather's farm. It was a cold day in December, and the Sheriff accused Uncle Willis of robbing the store. Willis was wearing a genuine camel hair overcoat that he most likely stole from somebody. The Sheriff searched the coat, found the money on him, and arrested him.

Willis was sentenced to juvenile prison up in Abilene, Kansas and when the war broke out, he was allowed to enlist at seventeen years of age. He chose the Navy because my dad and my Uncle Bud, his older brothers, were already fighting in the war. Uncle Bud was on a ship somewhere in the South Pacific, and my dad was a Navy flyer patrolling the Aleutian Islands in a dive-bomber.

Uncle Willis entered the war and fought on the USS Alabama, and fought bravely. He was medically discharged after taking a direct hit in the face after a heated battle with the Japanese that lasted for three days. After his partner was killed, he manned the Pom Pom gun by himself loading and firing and brought down several Japanese Zeroes before being wounded himself.

After a couple years of surgery to reconstruct the left side of his face, he began another life of crime. He had won a boxing title in the Navy as a middleweight fighter, and many claimed that he could have gone on and won a national title as a professional boxer. His first stint of crookery after his discharge from the Navy resulted in his being thrown in prison for robbing a grocery store in Beloit, Kansas. They caught him after he had bored a hole in the roof and lowered himself down to the safe containing the store's cash. He spent his time for that crime in Lansing Prison.

While in prison he accomplished two things: He boxed and won a title, and he learned safe cracking skills from a cell-mate. It was said that there was no finer touch in the United States when it came to opening safes and picking locks than my uncle. After his release, he robbed many safes and buried the cash in a field outside of Russell, Kansas. He would return there when he needed money, and he started a legitimate business that carried his cover while on his sprees of theft.

He showed up one afternoon out of the clear blue driving a 1949 Mercury. Uncle Willis knew no one would find him all the way up in Chapel Gap where his older brother was a pastor. He could hide out there for a long time. His story to convince my dad that he had changed his life was that he had been "born again" in prison in the State of Texas and that he wanted to learn from my dad an understanding of the Scriptures. His piousness knew no bounds, and we thought he was the best Christian convert there ever was. He quoted Scripture and even taught a Sunday School class.

My uncle taught Fran and me how to fight. We worked with him for hours on a makeshift punching bag he made from canvas tarp and stuffed with rags. We didn't have boxing gloves, so we wore two pairs of brown jersey gloves that kept our hands from blistering and knuckles from being damaged as we worked the bag.

Fran was telling me how to protect myself. He was wise enough to realize that I was about to get whipped.

Ronnie cussed and then charged me like a bull. He hit me in the chest with such force that I thought my breath that whooshed out of my lungs would never return. He jumped at me while I was lying on my back, but I had enough presence of mind to roll over at the moment he would have crushed me again, and he hit the dirt instead of landing on top of me. I knew that if he did land on me, it would be all over.

Ronnie jumped to his feet quickly and charged me again. He had his head down like a bull charging a matador's cape. He hit me again, and this time he managed to roll on top of me. He put his strong arms around me and rolled me over and over in the stubble of the hay field. I felt the sharp barbs enter my flesh. The dread of three or four weeks of barely sleeping, and my clothes irritating me all day because of the festered sores and pain from rolling naked in a hay field, slipped through my mind. I could feel the stickers and briars make abrasions on my skin and drive into my flesh. The pain was almost unbearable and would have agonized me into submission if I had not decided to get on my feet and fight.

Somehow, I was able to slither from under Ronnie's sweating body and jump to my feet. I was facing him upright, and he was really mad because his plan was to end this melee quickly. When that didn't happen, and I was still in one piece, his embarrassment drove his resolve to hurt me further. His nostrils flared as he cussed and threatened.

Instead of charging me, and I believe it was because he'd had enough of the briars and hard sticks sticking him, and he didn't want any more of that, he came at me swinging. His "haymakers" were missing badly, but I could still feel the wind from his flying fists as they whizzed over my head. There was no doubt in my mind that if one of those heavy punches hit me, I would be a goner.

"Step in and block the punch!" Fran screamed instructions at me.

Boxing is a game of opposites and instead of backing away from a punch, you step into it and through it. At least this is what my Uncle Willis had taught me. I also knew that if I lost this fight, everyone would challenge me after seeing my defeat, and I would never have any peace. Besides, my uncle was no longer around to help me out. The Kroger Store in Stanford had been robbed, and tourists spending the night in the only motel in Stanford reported cameras and such missing from their cars. Polaroid cameras were popular at that time, a novelty, and my uncle gave my dad one as a gift. When my dad heard the news after receiving the camera he was proud of, he told my uncle to hightail it, or he would call the cops himself. At any rate, the trunk load of cash that Uncle Willis had shown Fran and me was from the heist in Stanford, and he had other money from a bank in West Texas.

Uncle Willis left the country and to this day no one has heard from him. He did get away with the safe he stole from the Kroger Store. He had actually backed a pickup down the aisle of the store after cutting out the plate glass window. He managed to get the safe into the back of the pickup. Two years later, the safe was found in McMillan's pond near Ottenheim. Mr. McMillan and his boys found the safe while seining the pond for catfish. When Sheriff Crane opened the safe, soggy cash and the remains of the farmer's checks were still intact. Uncle Willis dumped the safe in the pond, and we all knew that someday he planned to return and retrieve his cache.

Ronnie O'Conner swung at me with all the force and strength he could throw behind it. His punch was meant to hit me on the side of my head and thus end the fight.

I stepped into his punch following the instructions of Fran as he coached me, and the shock on Ronnie O'Conner's face said it all. No one stepped into a punch. The Kirk boys were horrified, and the O'Conner boys looked in amazement. Fran nodded his head in agreement with this tactic.

As I stepped in, I threw my right arm up to catch the blow. Ronnie was firing with both fists, and he would never expect a punch to come from a left hand. He never expected a punch to come at all. He was figuring on a wrestling match in which he would pin me and pummel me with his fists until I was a bloody pulp.

I blocked the punch that was so hard I could feel the inside of my arm bruise. There would be one chance. I swung my left fist in a straight uppercut that he was totally unaware was coming and caught him squarely under the chin. This drove his teeth into his tongue and blood immediately ran out of his mouth. His head snapped backwards knocking him off balance. Before he could recover, my right hand was on the way.

I hit Ronnie O'Conner on the jaw. All those hours of working the heavy punching bag paid off. Ronnie never saw it coming. The punch lifted him to his toes; his head flew sideways, and his face was contorted awry. His eyes rolled to the back of his eyelids, and he hit the ground like a tree that just got felled in the forest.

Ronnie lay there on his stomach unable to move. We were standing around him, and he finally caught his breath and looked up at the circle of faces surrounding him and peering down. He shook his head and then pushed himself up slowly. He cussed and made a gesture that indicated he was going after me again. When he did this, Carey said, "Hang it up, Ronnie. If you try to fight him again, he'll kill you."

The O'Conner boys were last seen by us as they disappeared into the woods that would take them down the path to their farm. Just as they entered the forest, Shane O'Conner turned around and gave me the thumbs up.

"You were good, Sonny. Ole Ronnie will never bother you again and not too many other boys will either." Fran told me as he patted my shoulder.

We all knew we could never tell the Preacher that I was fighting.

CHAPTER FOURTEEN

The fall of the year in Kentucky makes the state one of the most beautiful in the Appalachian mountain range. We worked all the tobacco crops we could, and the cool autumn weather was a welcome relief from the hot and humid summer. Fran and I had helped with the cutting of the tobacco, but what we looked forward to more than anything was hanging the long green stalks in the barn.

Tobacco barns were filled with open space from floor to roof only broken by the many levels of tier rails where the tobacco would be hung to cure. These tier rails were either round or square depending on the wants of the farmer. The first rail was ten feet off the barn floor rising to the top rail some forty feet above the ground. Wagons were loaded in the fields with freshly cut tobacco stalks that had been speared onto a thin hickory stick that was sharpened on one end. Once the wagon or truck was in the barn, a man would stand on the huge stack of stalks and leaves and hand the stalks to the man on the first tier. This man would hand it to the man above him and so on until the tobacco stalks reached the top rail. Slowly this process continued until the barn was filled from the top rail to the bottom rail. It was quite a sight seeing a big barn completely filled with tobacco.

Fran and I had the job of hanging on the top rail because we were small and agile. We loved this job because we were high in the barn, and we only had to handle the sticks once. We spread our legs as wide as we could and carefully balanced ourselves while we stretched between the rails. The first time I had climbed to the top rail to hang, I looked down between my legs. It seemed like a mile down there, and nothing prevented or broke a fall if you slipped off the rail. You would either hit the wagon or the ground after you had bounced off the rails below on the way down. It could kill you or severely injure you if you fell forty feet. It was common during tobacco season for a hanger to lose his balance and fall. Many times backs and limbs were broken by this treacherous job, and some had died. Fran and I worked the top rail for two dollars a day and worked long hours.

Fran and I could scamper up to the top of the barns and balance ourselves as easily as monkeys hanging from the limbs of trees. Fran taught me to hang barefooted; especially, on the top round rails because the round rails didn't hurt your feet as the edges on the square rails would. Fran was fast, and I would never be able to keep up with him. He was clearly the best top rail hanger in the county, and the farmers paid him extra money sometimes when the job required someone to climb who was fearless. No barn had a rail high enough that he would not climb.

Tobacco hangs and dries during the fall of the year and when it comes into "case," that was the day when the dried leaves were no longer brittle and could be taken down from the rails without damaging the leaves. On a cold, damp foggy morning and after a farmer had been to his barn and felt the texture of the leaves, he would call his crew to take the crop from its rails. I loved taking the tobacco from the barn more than any other job in the crop. The sticks, which weighed more than sixty pounds when we hung them, were now very light and easy to handle. The tobacco sticks came down the same way we hanged them; one rail at a time passing from the workers on each tier down to the man on the truck until the entire truck or wagon was loaded with the dark brown tobacco leaves.

When the barn was completely empty, the stalks of curing tobacco were taken to the stripping room, which was usually built on the side of the barn. Women were common strippers of tobacco. They took the stalk and stripped the leaves. After a stalk had been stripped, they discarded the remainder of the stalk that was used for silage to fertilize other crops. The remaining leaves were stripped of their veins that ran down the center of each leaf. The women and girls would then tie the leaves in a small bundle using the stripped vein to secure the leaves they had stripped and bundled. A sixty-pound stalk of tobacco now weighed less than a pound.

Tobacco warehouses where tobacco was sold were huge. Sometimes the farmers from Chapel Gap would take their tobacco to Lexington; the largest tobacco market in the world because they would get a better price than the local warehouses such as the closer small cities of Lancaster, Danville, Harrodsburg, or Somerset, Kentucky.

The Penn Brothers Warehouse in Lexington is the largest tobacco warehouse in the world. Its one huge floor covers a vast amount of acreage. Farmers pulled into the warehouses with their crops, and the auctioneers started their bidding after the graders from the different tobacco companies had smelled, tasted, and handled a random selection of bundled leaves.

Farmers who came to these auctions would sometimes be with their trucks all night and the next day waiting for the auctioneer to bid on their crops. It only took a few minutes for the entire crop to be sold once the truck pulled on the block and then a check would be waiting when the farmers checked out. Thus, these farmers sold their crops and lived on the money for the entire year unless they had farms big enough like Gib Kirk who could farm other crops and raised livestock such as cattle, chickens, and hogs. Most of the folks living in the Knobs only had a small tobacco crop, which was their only means of living, chickens for eggs, a cow or two for milk, and some had a few pigs.

I loved the autumn of the year because Fran and I anxiously awaited squirrel-hunting season. Sometimes we would be in the woods for two or three days shooting squirrels, skinning them, and bringing them back to be fried on the old cook stoves. Fran learned to hunt from his dad and old Willy Turner.

Willy was an old man with palsy. He was also humpbacked and lived by himself in an old log house his daddy had built up a creek in the woods. In spite of his handicap, Willy killed more squirrels than anyone in Lincoln County every year. He skinned his kill and put them in glass jars filled with water and many times brought them to church and gave one or two to the Preacher. The squirrels were fat from eating a diet of Hickory nuts and Walnuts that grow wild in the hills of the Knobs.

Willy took Fran and I hunting one time, and I could barely believe that he could hold a gun much less shoot it. He always walked with his right hand shaking and resting on his back as he was seriously bent over from arthritis. It was quite a sight watching him work in the woods.

Willy had a single barrel shotgun, so if he missed, the squirrel would be gone before he could sink another shell in the barrel. He would hold the stock of the gun with his chin and raise his shaky hand to steady the gun while he put his finger on the trigger with his good hand. Willy would take aim after sitting for a long time as still as he could and then squeeze the trigger while his hand held steady for only a moment. He never missed a shot, and the squirrels fell from the trees to the ground. I have seen Willy Turner kill twenty squirrels in a single day and never waste one bullet.

Willy Turner taught Fran how to stalk squirrels. Long before you would see one, the squirrel could be heard running through the dry leaves as it gathered its quarry from under a nut tree and then with the goods to its nest in a tree. He taught Fran how to take quiet steps through dry leaves, and Fran was so good at it that you would think he was an American Indian. He never snapped a twig or caused the sound of a broken dry leaf while sneaking up on squirrels. On the other hand, I was like a bull in a china shop trying to make my way through the woods. "There won't be a squirrel left in the entire Knob area if you keep scaring them," he would say.

Fran learned from Willy how to find a squirrel. He taught him to wait until the squirrel took to his nest with his nut and then wait by a tree with the best view to spot the squirrel as it returned from its nest to do more hunting. Squirrel hunting was definitely a sport of patience. To Willy, squirrel hunting was not a sport but a necessary way to supplement his diet of cheese, butter, and powdered milk he got for free from the county assistance program that distributed these items to the poor people living at Chapel Gap. He lived by himself, and he had been doing this for many, many years. Willy Turner shared his bounty; it was his only means of giving to the church.

Fran taught me all that he had learned from Willy, and

both of us were good squirrel hunters. I started smoking during one of these hunts. I watched Fran as he leaned up against a tree waiting patiently for his prey. He would always roll his own cigarette with one hand, and he had been doing that ever since I had known him.

"Fran, can I have a cigarette?" I asked meekly.

"I guess so," he said, "you just scared off my squirrel, so you might as well choke on some tobacco."

I was quite surprised that Fran was this easy. Every other time I tried to smoke, he would tell me I was too young. I suppose that day he figured I was old enough because he moved from his comfortable spot and rolled me a cigarette.

"I'll roll you this one, but you'll need to roll your own from now on," he explained. "You'll need to buy your own stuff and do you know what will happen to you if the Preacher finds out you're smoking?"

The first puff on the homemade fire stick filled my mouth. I rolled the smoke around and blew it out. The second puff I inhaled and as the fog filled my lungs, I began choking and some of the smoke blowing out my nostrils was an awful feeling. Fran was on the ground laughing so hard he could barely stand it.

The cigarette was so strong and distasteful that I remember thinking, *Why would anyone do this to themselves?* I was determined. I was dizzy, so I braced myself against a tree to keep from falling over and took another puff. By the time the day was over, I had learned to roll my own smoke. Fran gave me a sack of tobacco and papers with the instructions that I would pay him back. Even though my first rolls were crude, and I lost some of the tobacco, I soon would be as skilled as the next boy including rolling a cigarette with one hand.

I did think about my dad and how he had warned that I better not smoke. He would be disappointed and besides, he would whip the day lights out of me if he caught me doing it. He must never, ever know.

"Better never let Loretta Kirk know you smoke," Fran said casually as he drew a puff and blew it out his nose.

We rattled around in the woods getting deeper and deeper. We sat under the shade of a huge Maple tree that was in its most explicit foliage of red and orange hues. The entire woods were ablaze of glorious color. I had just taken a puff when Fran heard a sound. He motioned for me to be perfectly still and put his forefinger to his lips to make sure I would be quiet. Fran had ears like the elephants he used to hunt and a nose like a wolf.

"Hear that?" He whispered, "squirrel cutting on the ridge."

I could hear the faint sounds the creature was making after a moment but they seemed miles away. It was true. A squirrel gnawed on a hickory nut, using its long sharp teeth and powerful jaws to hack away at the hard hull in order to be rewarded by a delicious and juicy nut. The sound was similar to a lumberjack hacking on a tree.

"He's a big one," Fran commented.

"How far away?"

"A half mile more or less," he replied. "It's on the other side of that ridge just over the crest of the hill."

Stealthily, Fran and I crept up the hill. I was careful not to make a sound and followed quietly in Fran's footsteps until we had almost reached the crest. The Hickory trees were huge; rising fifty feet or more in the air and towering over the lesser Maple and Beech trees. The ground underneath our feet was littered with ripe Hickory nuts and a squirrel's paradise. We could see the large Fox squirrel sitting upright with its big bushy tail dangling over the log where it was cutting and enjoying its meal.

We crouched behind a tree and waited. We were out of

shotgun range, and we knew this kill would be special because Fox squirrels were rarely seen. We were in for another treat.

I heard of Flying squirrels, but I had never had seen one and only half way believed they existed, but Fran had seen one, so I didn't question the matter with him. I figured Flying squirrels were in the same woods with the elephants we used to track.

Suddenly, we heard the leaves above us rustling and something jumped. It startled us and then we caught a glimpse of a squirrel flying through the air. The webbing beneath its legs and arms were spread wide as it glided down the ridge. It was a magnificent sight, and I drew my gun to my shoulder and sighted. Fran put his hand over the barrel and downward.

"Can't eat that thing, Bud," he whispered, "let it go."

I put my gun down and watched the squirrel land with a crash in the trees far below us. Away from us, we could still see the Fox squirrel busy with its chores preparing for the winter.

"We've got to get closer," Fran whispered careful not to spook the squirrel. I followed him as we slowly and methodically sneaked from tree to tree ducking under heavy branches hanging almost to the ground and careful not to make a sound. As we were about to blow the squirrel off its perch, we heard voices. The Fox squirrel bounded off through the dead leaves of the dense forest floor. This was disappointing because I wanted that huge red tail to hang on the bicycle I was planning on buying with the money I had saved for the past two years working on the farms.

I understood Fran's concerns. Why would people be way out here and so far back in these woods? We thought we were miles from civilization, and these voices weren't from hunters because they were making too much noise.

Fran sniffed the air. "Smell that?" He was very close to my ear. "Mash," he said.

"What's mash?" I asked quietly.

"Still, that's a still we smell. Someone's making moonshine."

We should have turned and fled but curiosity got the best of us, and we were kids who couldn't feel danger. We heard about what happens when you accidentally stumble on a moonshine still, but we were anxious to feel the adventure of spying and that was too much for either of us.

We laid down our guns realizing the Fox squirrel would have to wait for another day to be killed. We crept to the top of the ridge and peered over.

Down the slope and sitting on a clear stream of water flowing over large rocks, were several barrels with coiled copper tubing protruding from the tops. We could see clear liquid dripping one drop at a time into some large glass jugs at the end of the coils. Shocks of corn were piled near the barrels.

The smell of fermentation was very strong now, and we could see two men standing and smoking nearby.

"Curt Kirk and Evel Martin," Fran said quietly.

It was the freckled red head my dad ran off from the church on his first night as Pastor of Evergreen Baptist Church. I had never seen Curt Kirk, but he looked just like his brother, Gib. I could barely tell the difference between these twins. I thought it might be Gib, but Fran knew the difference. He explained to me that Gib was bald on the front of his head, and Curt on the crown. Otherwise, these brothers were identical.

We were afraid to move. We decided that we better backtrack slowly down the ridge behind us and get out of there as fast as we possible could. I had taken my first step when I saw the end of a double-barreled shotgun resting on Fran's neck. Fran quivered as he felt the cold steel and the two barrels. I couldn't move.

"What do we have here?" Leroy Hildebrand said.

He was a squatty, stout fellow with yellow teeth. Tobacco juice was always running down the corners of his mouth and crusty from years not washing the stains from his face. He smelled badly because he never took a bath. The red hair of his chest protruded from the suspenders of his bibbed overalls, and he wore no shirt even though it was cool fall weather.

Curt Kirk and Evel Martin were startled and looked up the ridge. Fran and I were in big trouble. I had heard about people who had stumbled upon stills and were never heard of again, but I paid no attention to these tales until now. People vanishing in thin air happened every now and then in Lincoln County. The year before, one of the Messer boys had gone hunting and never came back. No amount of searching could find him, and it was determined that he ran away from home. Fran said no way he did that. "He's tied up a holler tree somewhere," he reasoned. There were thousands of hollow trees in that part of the county. Fran said that the Messer kid had to have come upon a still and got himself killed. From that time on, I was always frightened that Fran and I would someday meet the same fate, and at this moment, it looked like someday had come.

Leroy Hildebrand marched us down the hill to the still. I looked around and could see that there were at least one hundred one gallon jugs full of "white lightening" sitting in rows upon wooden planks they carried back into the forest. This was a monumental task for sure. We had no idea how far we were from anybody's farm or house, but we knew we were far enough that no one would be able to track us easily. Only Willy Turner knew what general direction we took, and we had changed that a dozen times.

"Fran Job" (he pronounced Fran's name wrong to irritate him) Evel Martin taunted. He knew how much Fran hated to be called Job like a job, and he would have corrected him except for the circumstances. "You little creep, you. And guess what else the Good Lord has brought to us? It's the Preacher man's boy!"

I knew what he meant by this. Evel had made it perfectly clear in the entire Chapel Gap Community that someday he would punish the Preacher's children's children. It would hurt the Preacher real bad if something happened to his eldest son.

Evel Martin took out the huge hawkbill knife he was famous for carrying. He shaved off a piece of Hickory bark, and the hard wood split and fell to the ground as easily as cutting butter on a hot summer day.

"I'm going to send you back in pieces, boy, in a nice little package," Evel said. "As for you and Fran job, I'm going to cut you up slowly for causing the murder of my friend Benji McDuff." A bit of tear eased out of Evel's eye and fell to the ground. He flicked the blade back and forth, and the fire from the burning logs reflected off its shiny steel blade that made it even more threatening.

These men had been in the woods for a while. They had made lean-tos out of Maple branches, and their bedding was inside each one where they had been sleeping. They also had a lot of supplies, and the ground was littered with Spam cans, sardine cans, and empty cracker boxes. They had killed squirrels, and their hides and tails were hanging from wires stretched between the trees.

They knew we were in the vicinity long before we came on the still. Moonshiners had elaborate security systems. I could see the cowbells I had heard about hanging around a couple of trees and over some limbs so that they could ring freely. Every now and then, the bells would clank and clatter when a gust of wind would blow through the valley. The moonshiners knew the difference between wind blowing their cowbells, and someone tripping over a wire that would set off the alarm.

Moonshiners put a very thin wire around the perimeter of their still sights that was difficult to detect. The wires were high enough off the ground that small animals wouldn't trip them, but humans would. A wildcat or fox could scurry underneath the wires without setting off the alarm. A larger animal tripping an alarm would require emergency efforts to protect the moonshine makers.

Either Fran or I had tripped a wire that we had not noticed. This wasn't hard to do because you could trip a wire and never know it because you couldn't feel the pressure as you accidentally stumbled over it.

Fran didn't say much, and we knew better than to offer up any threats. We both thought for sure we were going to die, and no one would ever find us. It was completely dark in the woods, and we could see the last fading light of sun as it set in the west and turned the sky brilliant colors of red. It wasn't unusual for Fran and me to be gone overnight although we would always tell Mandy and Abe where we were going for the day, and my dad knew we would be gone because I had to ask permission. Most of the time permission was granted for me to stay with Fran for a few days and no log of activity was recorded after that. I did tell my dad that Fran and me were going over to Willy Turner's place and hunt squirrels there. I knew that when we didn't come home, they would decide that we were sleeping in the woods. I thought that my dad would realize we hadn't taken our bedrolls, and he would come looking.

Curt Kirk, Evel Martin, and Leroy Hildebrand were talking by the fire. They positioned Fran and me close by, so they could keep an eye on us. We reasoned they were talking about what they were going to do with us. We could barely hear them, and we strained to pick up the conversation.

"The Preacher don't know crap from Shinola," Evel

screamed, "Before they could find these boys, they'll be eaten by the wildcats."

Curt seemed to ponder the situation. He was much older than the other two men and wiser.

"I'll take the boys back to the farm and talk to them. I believe the threat will be enough to keep them from telling anyone what happened here. Fran Job's pretty street smart," and after Curt put that big chew in his mouth, we could hardly make out what he was saying. "Keep the boys here for a couple of days; let the Sheriff and company look for them and then take them to the farm and let them go from there. I'm not for any killing. After that deal with the Benji McDuff murder, I don't think he will be in any mood to cause him more trouble. Abe buys moonshine from me, and the Smith boy will do whatever the Job boy says."

Evel Martin's face was as red as his hair. "'What's wrong with you two? Don't you remember when Job coughed up that information that led to Sweet John Adam's death?"

"Yeah, but that's different," Curt said, "Sweet John needed to die for what he'd done to them boys."

"Then I'll kill them myself," Evel yelled, "I'll cut the little farts in a million pieces!"

We were really afraid after hearing these words. Even if they did decide to take us to Curt Kirk's farm, Evel would never let it happen. He would kill us in the night while we slept if we could sleep.

"We gotta find a way out of here," Fran whispered softly, "Evel's scary crazy, and he hates your dad so much that they won't be able to stop him."

Curt came over and motioned for us to come with him. My heart sank, and I had trouble breathing. We got up and followed him to his shelter. He had decided to place us in his lean-to and keep us out of harm's way. We gladly crawled in because we didn't believe that Curt would hurt us; at least not after his opinion about what they should do to us. Curt was not violent as far as we knew, and he was the leader of this moonshine operation. Without him and his connections and the safety of the underground boozing community, Evel Martin and Leroy Hildebrand would never make a dime moonshining.

When we didn't return by noon the next day, Mandy walked to the church and told my dad we weren't at her house. She was really trying to find out if we were at the trailer. It was then that my dad realized that our bedrolls were where we always kept them, in the corner by the couch. We left our stuff at the trailer because my mother had a washing machine, and she could keep the bedding clean for us easier than Mandy could do the wash by hand.

"I think they were going over to Willy Turner's place and hunt there," my dad said, "but they had no plans to spend the night. Their bedrolls are still here, and they didn't take enough shells to hunt for a couple of days."

There were dangers in the woods. There were steep slopes that could carry a person over the edge of a cliff. Falling off one of those would be certain death. There were sinkholes that opened up into caverns of caves so common in Kentucky, and more than one child had been lost after falling into one of these deep holes. The Knobs of Chapel Gap were too far west for bears although they were seen in the higher mountains of Eastern Kentucky. There was not much danger from animals in these woods in the fall of the year except maybe a bobcat or rabid fox, and the bobcats were not known to have attacked any human in recent history. Garrard Anderson did tell us one time that he had been attacked by a wildcat and barely survived, but most of us blew that off as one of his big whoppers.

"Did you see Fran and Sonny come this way?" My dad asked Willy as he met them coming up the dry creek bed toward his house.

"I seen them yesterday morning," Willy replied. "They were going to hunt some squirrels up on the ridge. I told them to stay out of my territory," he volunteered.

"Did they come back?"

"Nope. They didn't come back this way, or I would have seen them."

"What if they came after dark, Mr. Turner, would you have seen them then?" My dad asked.

"Nope. Couldn't have done that either. Old Patch over there would have heard them and barked like he treed a coon."

Old Patch was Willy's prize Blue Tick Hound. Even though the hound slept in the bed with Willy, he would have heard us long before we could reach the cabin, and Patch would have been up like a flash warning his master of impending danger.

"Then they still have to be back there or come out some-where else," my dad reasoned. "Where does this creek go?"

"Don't know," Willy said curtly, "never been back to see."

Willy was now bent over at the waist, and his hand shook behind his back. My dad knew this was upsetting Willy, the questions and all, and he didn't want Willy to think he thought he had something to do with our disappearance.

"Shirlee called us," Sheriff Crane said as he and Homer Shanks came into the yard with Jack Clink trailing behind them. Jack Clink owned the woods that Willy hunted in and the land around Willy's place. He let Willy stay in the old cab-in for years after Willy's wife died at a young age because he had no where to go.

It was late in the day now, and they knew there would be no use trying to negotiate the woods at night. They knew that Fran and I were so good at not stepping on twigs and such that we wouldn't leave a trail anyone but an expert tracker could follow.

"Let's check with the neighbors on our way back and see if any of them have seen the boys," my dad commanded.

On the way down the dry creek bed, my dad questioned Jack Clink to see if he knew how deep the woods would go before you came to a road of some kind or other. Mr. Clink informed him that he had no idea how far the mountains reached. He had no occasion to ever go in there, and from what he reckoned, no one had explored that deeply although he had lived on his farm all his life.

Evel Martin glared at us all day and taunted us, scaring the wits out of us. Curt Kirk kept a close eye on Evel. He knew how crazy the boy could be. Curt sent Leroy Hildebrand up on the ridge to find the place where Fran and I had broken the wire that gave away our presence. Soon, he came down the hill shuffling his feet on the steep grade and trying not to fall. As he did, he kicked up hickory nuts and walnuts that were tumbling ahead of him and down into the camp.

The men were busy making moonshine. Fran leaned over to me, and I leaned closer to him. He was careful that Curt didn't see us talking.

"The Preacher will be looking for us by now," Fran whispered, "these guys will have to do something with us, so we need to get out of here."

I agreed of course, but how? The woods were thick, and the going would be slow if we could get out, and I doubted whether two boys twelve years old could stay ahead of grown men. Besides that, we would trip the wire as soon as we left; they would hear the cowbells and be on us before we knew what happened.

We saw a plane fly over and when I said it was a search plane, Fran looked at me like I was crazy. "They ain't going to call no search plane," he said. "That plane belongs to Rich Jameson, and he flies over here all the time." He was right, and I had forgotten that.

"Maybe he'll see the moonshine still," I commented.

"He ain't even looking," Fran replied, "he's taking his girlfriend for a ride. Besides look above you; you can only hear the plane and catch one little glimpse of it now and then. From up there, these woods look like a solid mass of trees with no way to see anything, they are so thick."

I don't know how Fran knew all these things because I knew for sure and a fact he'd never seen a plane much less ridden in one. He did have a point because the men around the still never looked up toward the plane one time.

Rich Jameson was a very wealthy man. He lived over on the other side of Lincoln County, but he owned land everywhere. It was well known that he had this little plane, and he flew high above the land to survey his vast holdings of timber and farmland from the air. He wasn't looking for us.

The plane was gone quickly, and Curt said, "That's it." He doused the fire under the still with creek water and turned off the tap. After he had nearly filled a jug of moonshine and caught the clear liquid dripping from the copper tube, he wiped his hands with the bandana he kept in the back pocket of his overalls. All farmers carried handkerchiefs. These were large roomy bandanas that had several functions. The popular red or blue cloth with white snow flake designs was used by the hillbilly farmers to wipe sweat on hot days, blow their noses, and most important and its main use, wipe their hands. "If we don't get these boys out of here, they're liable to find our still. How would you boys like to spend twenty years in jail? I did five, and it ain't no fun. The law's tougher now boys than it was back in my day," Curt Kirk was philosophizing to the two partners. "If we don't kill them, we'll be going to jail anyway,"

Evel commented. "I ain't going to jail for no murder," Leroy cried, "no way."

"Who said anything about murder?" Evel said as the other two looked at him curiously. "Why does there have to be a murder?"

CHAPTER FIFTEEN

E vel Martin wanted to kill us. He laid out an elaborate plan
to drop us both from high in a tree. "These boys climb all
the time," he explained, "one fell and hit the other, and
they both tumbled to their deaths."

This was way too smart, and Fran and I cringed. Curt
looked at Evel like he was a nut. "How you gonna get those
boys up in the tree, and if you do, what if one of them kicks
your ass and you fall?" That was exactly what I was thinking.

Evel was deep in thought when Curt Kirk gave the orders.

"We'll take our chances with them. They'll never tell. Evel
you take Leroy and pack up a few jugs of this here lightning,
and I'll handle the boys."

Apparently, they weren't going to kill us at the still, so we
followed in single file behind Curt up the steep trail that lead
to wherever it was going to take us. Soon we reached the ridge,
and we knew this was going to be a long hike. You could see
nothing but trees and knobs in front of us. I wondered how

they ever got all the stuff back there, and I figured it must have been with sure-footed mules. It was no wonder that Curt Kirk had been successful moonshining since his release from prison a few years before. Evel pushed on Fran's back, and Fran turned to him as if he were going to try to do something. I held my breath.

Fran stopped abruptly. "Mr. Kirk, do you mind if I walk behind Evel, and Sonny, too?"

Curt must have sensed Fran's anxiety. "Get to the front, Evel, I'll take the rear," he commanded.

I have said, "Fran always has a plan," but this was going to have to be a good one, his plan. I knew from Fran's expression what he had on his mind. The kid was mulling over a plan of action in that brain of his. He had probably been thinking this over all day and the night before, for that matter. If I knew him, and I did, he was planning from the moment Evel Martin walked behind us with the shotgun and stuck it on Fran's neck. I also knew what Mr. Kirk knew, and that was Fran was afraid that Evel would kick us off one of the sheer cliffs we were walking along. We barely had room to walk along some of the cliffs, and the fall was more than two hundred feet to the crevices below on some of these ridges.

There was a strange quirk behind Fran's stare. When he was thinking, Fran's eyes darted back and forth. He was taking in everything he saw, and now and then, I would see his head nod in agreement with himself. It took me awhile, but I figured it out. *Fran's been in this part of the woods before,* I thought. He looked at every tree, every branch, and marked all the spots he'd seen before. The farther we traveled, the more his head bobbed up and down as he confirmed his own reasoning.

The woods are funny. Once in there, unless you are Daniel Boone, it is easy to get lost. You can wander around in circles for days and end up back where you started. Although my instincts were above average, and my dad used to say it was uncanny how I knew my way out of places I'd never been before, Fran was much, much better. He knew where he was all the time, and no matter how confused I may get and argue with him about the direction home, he was always right. We spent many times in the woods wandering around lost.

I noticed Fran looking up the ridge and fixating his eyes for a moment. I glanced with him and saw what he was looking at. I could hardly contain my excitement! Fran's mark stood out to those who knew it well, and in these woods, I knew his mark best of all. Fran marked his squirrel trees. Every time he killed, he would cut a notch exactly the height of his head no matter what year it was. In this way, he could tell approximately how long it was since he had hunted that tree. His mark was always the same. It was a triangle that he notched out so that the entire design showed nothing but bare bark. There would be one in a thousand chances that anyone else would find these marks because there were thousands of acres of trees in these hills. Fran knew the vicinity of where his trees were, and I decided that, yep, Fran had been here before.

Evel Martin complained about a blister on his foot. The men were wearing work shoes unsuited for long hikes. We were climbing a steep path to the top of the ridge when I looked down into a gully below and could see the creek flowing swiftly over some rocks. I was surprised by what I saw.

That's our waterfall! I'd been here, too! I knew exactly where we were at this moment. We were in the woods behind the O'Conner farm, and this was the creek where Shane O'Conner, Fran, and me would come in the spring when the creeks were swollen. Shane showed us this waterfall, which was only a few feet in height, but one of the few found in this area of the Knobs. We had played there many times after Sunday dinner at the O'Conner house.

As soon as Fran saw that I recognized where we were, he smiled and had that gleam in his eye. He was about to put his plan into action although I don't know how many times he had changed his plan over the course of our hike out of the forest where the moonshine lay.

Fran made a gesture with his hands in the shape of something tumbling. He looked at me and did it again. I got it. Fran was reminding me of the time that we tried to jump from this cliff into the eddy of water below formed by the swirling creek beneath the falls and resulting in a deep pool. The water was deep, and the jump about twenty-five feet, so that day we took the plunge. We knew something else about the pool that those kidnappers didn't know. It was impossible to climb back up the sheer cliff from the pool. It would take a hike of almost a mile to find a location slanted enough to make a safe climb back to the trail.

Fran knew this because we left our guns that day of the jump lying beside Fran's notched tree. We had also left our shoes there, so we knew how far it was out of the creek and back to the tree where we had retrieved our guns and then hike up the trail to the exact spot where we were now standing and had left our shoes.

Evel Martin took off his shoe and rubbed the blister on his foot. He sat in some cool moss below an overhang of the path. He cussed at his foot and distracted the other two men. Curt was already taking a look at the hideous blister, and Leroy Hildebrand was lighting his pipe.

Fran went first, and as soon as I jumped, I nearly caught him in the air. We both landed in the middle of the cold water and plunged all the way to the bottom which was ten or twelve feet in depth.

Evel Martin was pointing his shotgun at us when we surfaced. Fran dove down again to avoid the buckshot, and I dog-paddled under a ledge where he couldn't get a shot at me. I looked in the pool and could see Fran come up to me swimming under water. Another blast went off, and the buckshot sprayed water in a spout that splashed several feet in the air. One little bb actually hit Fran on the back but didn't hurt him; its damage was a slight trickle of blood as the buckshot grazed his body.

Evel screamed at the top of his lungs, and he was cussing Curt. "You idiot," Curt yelled, "Frank O'Conner's more than likely heard that shot and will be wondering who's on his land. It was a "well known factor," as some of the old timers called it that Frank O'Conner would shoot anyone who hunted his land or trespassed. "You've hung us for sure, you piece of maggot crap," Curt screamed at Evel.

Curt Kirk was no longer concerned with us. He yelled down and told us he would kill us if we ever told what happened. He was no man to mess with because he was familiar with all the scuzzy riffraff in the hills who would do us in for little money or some moonshine from one of Curt's stills.

Evel Martin hobbled back into his shoe, and Fran and I crept down the creek bank out of sight; we could hear him cussing. Feeling safer, Fran decided that Evel Martin would be the only one who would want to chase us, but because his foot was so sore, that wasn't likely, and he couldn't run us down anyway. We had too much head start.

We climbed the hill leading up to Fran's marked tree. We stayed out of sight and from our vantage point high above the cliffs, we could see Curt and the other men making their way toward the back pasture of the O'Conner farm. We also noticed that Curt had left our guns leaning against the cliff's sheer embankment, and we were happy for that; we thought we had lost them for sure.

It was late when we walked into the churchyard towards the trailer. My mom came out as soon as she saw us.

"Well, ain't you boys a sight for sore eyes. Do you know the Preacher is out hunting for you?"

Sheriff Crane, Homer Shanks, Jack Clank, and my dad smelled the mash from the still long before they found it. The six foot eight inch tall Homer Shanks saw it first. The fire was smoldering, and the many gallons of moonshine were sitting on their log racks.

"Those boys are in trouble or maybe dead," Houston Crane commented.

"That's Curt Kirk's still," Jack Clank said. He should know. He had bought many gallons of moonshine from Curt Kirk, so he knew exactly the kind of jugs he used to catch the clear liquid, and he sold the juice in the same jars. He knew the smell as well, but he forbade himself from tasting some because the Preacher stood by wondering how one of his church members knew so much about Curt Kirk's moonshine.

My dad was riding with Sheriff Crane when they pulled into his barn lot. Curt Kirk came out in his long underwear underneath his bibbed overalls.

"Evening, Sheriff," he casually greeted. "What brings you out here?" Curt knew that he was not in immediate danger because Trooper Tip Tuck of the Kentucky State Police would have been accompanying the Sheriff if there was going to be an arrest. He relaxed.

"Been making moonshine, Curt?" The Sheriff quizzed.

"Quit doing that a long time ago, Sheriff, after that stint in the state penitentiary. Don't want no more of that." Curt answered as he wiped his forehead with his bandana. "What makes you ask?"

"Fran Job and the Preacher's boy got lost somewhere in the woods near Willy Turner's place, and we went looking for them. Seems we stumbled on a still. Could be yours," the Sheriff said.

"Can't be mine, I don't have none," Curt lied.

"Know anything about the whereabouts of these boys? Seen them around anywhere?"

"If you hurt one of them, I'll. . . ," my dad was about to say, "kill you," but the Sheriff put up his hand and stopped him. He wanted nothing to do with Curt Kirk, and he knew he was lying through his teeth. He also noticed that Evel Martin's car was parked in the yard.

"Where's Evel Martin?" The Sheriff asked.

"Ah, him and Leroy Hildebrand are back at the pond fishing."

The Sheriff knew they wouldn't be fishing in the pond this time of year, but he let it go.

"Tell you what. If you see those boys, tell them to get their butts back home."

"Sure do it," Sheriff Curt Kirk knew we didn't tell on him because he hadn't found us yet. But would we? That was haunting him. Maybe he should have drowned us or let Evel Martin push us out of a tree.

"Where have you boys been?" My dad questioned as we sat on the couch eating some of mom's home made pie. She had fixed us a sandwich for we were extremely hungry after not eating for two days. I looked out and saw the Sheriff's car drive up. I just knew we were going to be questioned and would have to confess all and then be killed by Curt Kirk.

"Well, well," the Sheriff exclaimed as he walked in. "If it isn't the long lost prodigal sons returned home. You boys know anything about a moonshine still?"

I was terrified, and I looked at the calm, collected face of Fran. He'd been in this situation before, so he would do all the talking.

"Naw, me and Bud here were hunting and got lost. We ended all the way down by Crab Orchard. Had to walk home, couldn't hitch a ride."

Mr. Crane nodded his head. My dad and he both knew that in order to get to Crab Orchard from Willy Turner's place, we would have to eventually pass through the Sheriff's land, and his coon dogs would have noticed us.

"Well, I'm glad you boys are all right," the Sheriff said and then left the trailer and drove away. My dad grabbed a roll of toilet paper and headed for the outhouse.

Curt Kirk, Evel Martin, and Leroy Hildebrand survived. They never went back to their still behind Frank O'Conner's farm because Sheriff Crane and Deputy Shanks went there and destroyed the whole thing complete with dumping the moonshine in the creek and breaking all the jars. They axed the still in a thousand pieces. Homer Shanks licked his lips as they did this deed, throwing the moonshine in the creek, and it nearly broke his heart to see it happen; even though Sheriff Crane would never believe in a million years that his deputy would touch the stuff.

Curt found another spot and kept on doing his business of making moonshine and selling it to the farmers, some of them members of Evergreen Baptist Church, until one fine day, he got caught.

Curt was bravely dealing out of the back of his pickup one evening in Crab Orchard. John Sherman Cooper, one of Kentucky's most famous Senators, was campaigning in Lincoln County. Lincoln County was one of the few solid Republican Counties in the state. Senator Cooper was unrecognizable by most as he dressed in bibbed overalls and a denim shirt with a large red bandana hanging out of his back pocket. He always dressed this way when visiting Crab Orchard.

Curt Kirk made a fatal mistake. John Sherman Cooper saw

him selling his moonshine and walked up to him. Normally, Kirk knew all the folks living in Crab Orchard, had regular customers, including old Doc Sinclair, so there was never any danger. He didn't even notice the Senator, and when the politician asked for a jug and how much, Curt Kirk sold it to him.

Soon, the State Police had barricaded the roads, and not even Kirk's lookouts had a chance to warn him. They arrested Curt and shipped him off to the Kentucky State Penitentiary at Eddyville, Kentucky for twenty years.

Fran and I never told a soul about the moonshine still and have kept it a secret until this very day. Curt Kirk would never bother us again, but we hadn't heard the last of Evel Martin.

CHAPTER SIXTEEN

Halloween was one of our most favorite times of the year. Although the kids in Chapel Gap didn't Trick or Treat like millions of other kids were doing on the night of witches and goblins, we did love to dress up.

This was the night of pranks and many of the farmers dreaded Halloween. They knew that mailboxes would be blown up with half sticks of dynamite used by the older pranksters, and their farms would be the brunt of tricks by the little hobo demons.

Fran and I dressed like hobos. We put on ragged clothes, and Fran stuffed a pillow in his cotton pants that he borrowed from his dad, Abe. June blackened our faces with coal from the bucket that sat by the potbellied stove. She carefully put cold cream on our faces as a base so that the coal dust would wash off easily. I had a strange sensation that night as she blackened my face and hands. It was the first time that I realized how soft and warm a girl's hands could be. As she rubbed her pale hands with her long fingernails over my face, I thought, *Man, what's wrong with me?* Her skin was soft and creamy like a delicate rose, and her blue eyes were shining like a clear lake in the warm sunshine. I studied her face while she performed this delicate duty, and she caught my stare and looked at me strangely. Her cheeks flushed with a bit of rosy red, and she quickly finished her job.

Fran looked funny with his fat belly and Abe's red bandana tied around his neck. He had picked up a tobacco stick and tied it with a bandana filled with old rags and threw it across his shoulder. He did look like Red Skelton's famous character, "Freddie the Freeloader." We left the house just after dark and hobbled up the road. We hid out in grader ditches as the cars passed because Fran said it would be bad if anyone saw us.

I don't think we were recognizable, but Fran had other things on his mind.

We decided to head to the church first. My mother had taken the little kids and my big sister, Leah, down to Crab Orchard to "find" some candy and other goodies. Crab Orchard folks were known to store up lots of good candy and fruit for the Supermen and Cinderella's who would ring their doorbells after sunset.

My dad was in his customary place in the back Sunday School room of the church. His small study, which doubled as a classroom, facied the rear portion of the cemetery. In fact, tombstones were close enough beyond his window to reach out and touch. I never went back there after dark because it was too creepy. There were no curtains on the large window that illuminated the tombstones directly behind the church.

I inched my way back there and crept ever so slowly, crouching so that the light from the window would not give away my position. I raised myself to the height of the window and gently put my face on the glass and opened my eyes real wide fixing my mouth in the position of a scream.

Suddenly, my dad realized something or someone was there, and he looked up from his Bible. I did not smile or give any other expression. It was really a brilliant acting job. My dad's eyes opened wide in fright and in that moment, all the lectures he had given me about how there was nothing to be afraid of in the cemetery after dark went completely out the window. He was startled, and this clearly scared him. He fell back in his chair and was heading for the door when he caught himself. He turned around very slowly and looked at me, curiously. He wasn't sure who it was behind that mask of black coal dust and cold cream. He looked at me with both an expression of relief and embarrassment. He had been had, and he knew it. Still not smiling so as to not give away his pleasure that his eldest son had scared the devil out of him, he stood and looked down at me through the window as my shadow reflected on the large tombstone behind me. I was literally standing on someone's grave. All of a sudden, his eyes grew wide, and an expression of fright permeated his entire face. He was looking beyond me, behind me, at the tombstones in the cemetery. He then screamed at me and said, "Look out! Don't move!" I could feel the clammy, cold, bony fingers of the corpse rising from the tomb and clamping themselves around my ankles.

I fell back in terror and desperately tried to run, but the skeleton had my being in its grasp, and I froze, terrified because I couldn't move. I fell back on the grave that scared me even more, and then I heard my dad roaring with laughter, and so was Fran as he released his grip on my shins.

My dad laughed so hard he could barely contain himself. Fran was beside himself with glee. He rolled over and over on the grave, his body shaking all over, as he imitated my fright and fall to certain perdition.

"I hate you!" I screamed, but Fran laughed even louder.

"Bud, that was a good one," Fran exclaimed, "you should have seen your face!"

"I almost crapped my pants," I told him, but now I was smiling with him but not totally loving being the brunt of my own joke.

"Come on boys," my dad invited, "Sonny's mom made some apple cider before she went to town with the little kids and Leah."

We did love my mom's apple cider, and we drank a lot of it. She also made some of her famous popcorn balls, which were a divine treat. We left my dad at the church and skipped on down the road not totally sure what adventures we would get ourselves into. As we walked down the gravel road, still being careful to hide ourselves in the ditch and protecting ourselves from detection, Fran came up with a brilliant idea.

Bob and Barbara Jones lived down the lane past the Barber's farm. They had two small boys, Terry and Eric. Fran knew that Bob would be bringing the family home from gathering candy in Crab Orchard at any time. The private lane was not kept up by the county, and the replacement of creek gravel was usually done by the residents on the road.

As many lanes in the Knobs, this one crossed a creek about half way to where the Barber's lived. The creek wasn't swollen this time of year, but it was still deep enough for the water to flow over the hubcaps of the pickups as they forded the stream.

Fran and I exited the Ottenheim Road and started walking down the Barber Lane. As we moseyed along, we came to the creek, and our second diabolical deed was about to unfold. We stood looking at the creek, which was about one hundred feet across and less than fifty wide. We knew we couldn't cross here on foot, and it was a long walk around the creek to find the road on the other side. Engel Barber had made a style of steps, which he placed over his fence so that people could climb the steps and walk along the creek on the upper side.

Fran was thinking, and so was I. Before I could react, Fran took off his shoes and rolled up his pant's legs.

"What are you doing?" I asked.

"Shut up and get your shoes off. We're going in."

Soon, we were both standing in the middle of the creek in the cold spring water that ran from the hill and formed this barricade that had to be forded by any vehicle driving down the lane. There were no cars owned by the folks living on Barber Lane because in high water time, the cars were too low to the ground and would "drown out" as the water gushed into the front radiators and over the engine. The distributors would get soaked as well as the spark plugs, and the engine would die in the middle of the creek. This was annoying but fun when it happened to the tobacco assayers who were coming to destroy a crop. More than one of these inspectors found himself stuck in the middle of this predicament, and Engel Barber nor anyone else would come and rescue them. They would sit in the middle of the creek until their plugs and points had dried so that they could continue their journey. Coming back from their dastardly deeds, the same torture awaited them.

"Help me lift this big rock," Fran said.

There were some boulders lying beside the road that were left there when Engel Barber and Bob Jones dug out the spring where they carried water. We hoisted the rock to the front edge of the creek and sat it squarely in the middle of the lane. We then waded the creek and put a rock on the other side where the road continued from the creek. We carefully placed the big stone so that the driver couldn't move the rock without stepping up to his knees in the water.

"Put some logs behind it," I said as I better understood

the inventive prank, "so that the driver can't see the rock." I thought this was an ingenious idea.

"That's a great idea," Fran answered and we quickly hustled up some tree limbs from the woods nearby to hide the rocks.

"Help me with this style," Fran said.

"That thing must weigh a ton," I replied to his demand.

"We'll grab it from the other side of the fence and heave it over and then drag it to the middle of the creek," Fran shouted.

We crossed the fence on the style and shoved one end of the steps over the fence. Thank God we had been lifting tobacco stalks and hay bales, or we would never have gotten this job done. After we had securely ridded the fence of the heavy steps, we forced with all our might and dragged the weighty structure into the middle of the creek. We waited and caught our breaths.

"Cut the fence wire from the top strand," Fran instructed. I looked at him wandering what he was thinking.

We cut about seventy-five feet off Engel Barber's fence and stretched it to the style on each side.

"Now tie the end to the fence on your side, and I will tie the other side," Fran instructed.

Fran's plan was to place the style in the middle of the creek and tie it so that it would be nearly impossible, or would at least take a long time to unhook the wires and push the style aside far enough to allow room for a vehicle to pass. I was glad Fran was my friend and not an enemy although I was delighting in this devious operation.

After we had finished the work, we waded back out of the creek, put our shoes on, and headed for the woods. We knew of a limestone hangover where we could hide and watch the action. With much anticipation, we heard the truck turn off the Chapel Gap/Ottenheim Road and onto Barber Lane. The truck was making its way down the road, and its headlights shined and illuminated the sparkling creek rocks lying in the bed of the creek.

My heart pumped as the pickup approached the logs in front of the big rock blocking the entrance to the creek. Bob Jones' truck, as many in that part of the country, had a six-volt battery system that would not allow the headlights to shine very far in front of the vehicle. Bob loved Dodge trucks even though there were few in the county. Homer Shanks had one and many times the two tried to compare the power of one against the other. Bob slid to a stop just inches away from hitting the log dead in the center of his front bumper.

He sat there for a moment with the engine idling and then he emerged from the truck. He looked around as if there would be someone standing by to rescue him. He bent over and dragged the limbs away to the side of the lane. As he brushed off his hands and wiped them on his handkerchief, he was startled as he saw the big rock. Like Gibraltar, it sat squarely in the middle of the road.

His feet were not wet because Fran and me placed the barricade just far enough from the water so that it could be moved without stepping in.

"Get out and help me," Bob said to his wife, Barbara. She stepped on the running board of the truck, climbed down, and walked to the front of the pickup.

By-this time, Fran was shaking so hard from giggling that he could hardly stand it. I put my arm around his head and told him to be quiet because if Bob heard us, we would die.

"Who in the world would do a thing like this?" Mrs. Jones cried, and so did little Eric sitting in the front seat of the pickup.

The two struggled, pushing and heaving, and the rock finally rolled away from the truck. Fran and I were laughing so hard now that I thought we would surely give ourselves away. Mr. Jones hadn't seen the steps in the middle of the creek, yet.

As the Dodge pickup approached the style, which was securely fastened and tied expertly by the wire from Engle Barber's fence, the front door of the pickup slammed against the front fender as Bob flung it open, hard. He plunged into the creek, and the water came up over his shoe tops and halfway to his knees. He stood there in the dim headlights and looked at our masterpiece.

"You damn boys. When I catch you, I'll beat you half to death," he yelled. Mr. Jones didn't know who did this and then Barbara rolled down her window.

"Who did this, Bob?" She asked fearfully.

"I know!" He screamed. He took a flashlight and shined it up in the woods. Fran and I ducked away as the beam of light flew over the tops of our heads.

"It was Junebug Barber and that Messer boy, I know that for sure." He called back over the noise of the engine.

Fran hit my arm, and I hit him back. Although Junebug was our friend, and we didn't want him to get into trouble, this was his daddy's land, and Engle Barber owned the lane.

"How will we get out of here?" Mrs. Jones asked her frustrated husband.

"Only one way," Bob replied.

He got back into his Dodge and put the truck in "bull dog," the lowest of gears on the floor shift. He then eased toward the steps and barely nudged up against them. The Dodge strained, and the six-cylinder engine tried to flood out. It backfired, and Bob gave it more power. The style popped and creaked as the wire held its breach. From the power of the pickup, one wire broke and then the other. The style was moving but not before the front grill had caved into the radiator.

Mr. Jones finally got the steps pushed over to the side far enough so that he could pass and revved the engine for his final exit from the creek and to his warm secure house.

As he gunned the engine and ran forward, he gripped the steering wheel with white knuckles because directly in front of him was more logs. He stopped and put his head on the steering wheel. The pickup had been idling for more than forty-five minutes, and steam boiled out of the radiator, rising up like a cloud in a storm and blocking our view of the truck. We could smell the radiator's foul odor as the stink filled the woods.

Mr. Jones stepped out, but this time he calmly waded the water and stepped onto the road running out of the creek. Mrs. Jones opened her door, and Bob told her to stay in the truck, but she didn't listen.

"Let me help you," she said, "you can't push that rock out of the way by yourself." We could hear her say this clearly, as she was soon standing in water nearly to her knees and wading toward the limbs and big rock where her husband stood. He had cleared the brush out of the way and was trying to push the rock.

Barbara Jones had bad knees; she had this problem and condition from many years of riding a tobacco setter, stripping tobacco in the winter, and gardening. Doc Sinclair told her years ago that she would eventually have to have operations on both knees, but she had stubbornly put this off. She struggled to move the rock. We could see her wet nylons clinging to her legs. He shoes were now ruined, so she kicked them off, and we watched them land over the fence. Mr. Jones never cussed or made any remarks.

He was a beaten man, but we knew that if he ever caught the persons who did this treacherous thing to his family, those people would never live. He was an expert shot with a bow and a gun and could shoot a turkey out of the air in mid-flight.

Fran and I watched the pickup move up the road with steam boiling from under the hood. We could see Mr. Jones pull into Engel Barber's drive and walk to the farmhouse.

Quickly, Bob was standing at the door and banging and yelling for someone to answer.

Sally Barber, the church janitor, stirred in her bed. The Barbers went to bed very early after sunset. This was their habit except on Saturdays when it was television night. Sally always said that Engle went to bed with the chickens and got up with the chickens. They were one farm family whose alarm was really a rooster. She punched Engel and told him to answer the door. Uncle T stirred in his bed as well. Uncle T was Engel Barber's blind brother. He had lived with Sally and Engel since they were married. Engel was committed to taking care of his brother and preventing him to be put in some kind of home where he would be unhappy. Unlike his older brother, who was tall, Uncle T was no more than four feet three inches in height although he did claim to be five feet. Uncle T'S bed was in the same room with the Barbers.

When Uncle T heard the ruckus, he immediately reached under his feather mattress where he kept his stash of large peppermint stick candy he loved so much. He guarded his candy like gold in Fort Knox and for good reason. Many times Fran, Junebug, and me would slip into the bedroom and break off a piece of his peppermint stick and suck on the delicious juice it made as it melted in our mouths. Later, Uncle T would cry out that someone had been in his candy. One time, we were too close to Uncle T when we slipped under the feather mattress to steal from him. He grabbed a broom handle and swung wildly. It barely missed me, but it hit Junebug squarely in the side of the head placing a knot on his skull beneath his flaming red hair.

When Engel Barber opened the door, he was still pulling up the straps on his overalls and dressed in long johns that he slept in every night no matter how cold or hot it would be. He carried a kerosene lamp although the family had electricity.

He said a lamp was safer when someone came to your house late in the night. He opened the door and peered outside at the figure standing on the porch. He recognized him.

"Where's Junior?" Mr. Jones asked. "Where is the little criminal?"

"What are you talking about, Bob? He's in his bed. What do you want him for?"

"The hog brained little idiot destroyed the front end of my truck!"

"What? How?"

"He and that peckerwood Messer boy, that's who!"

Engel kept his cool for the time being although his blood pressure was rising from the vile things Mr. Jones was saying about his son. He didn't care about the Messer boy; he agreed with his assessment of him.

Fran and I crept up the Barber Lane until we were situated in the woods across the road from the Barber farmhouse. We couldn't see Mr. Barber and Mr. Jones clearly, but we could see the glow of the lantern, and we could hear every word that was being said as if they were standing and talking right next to us.

"Bob you stop cussing my son. He couldn't have done this. He's been here at the house all day. And as far as the Messer boy, he hasn't been in the house since I ran him off for stealing all my chicken eggs and throwing them against the barn last spring."

"Then who dunnit if Junebug didn't?" Bob Jones asked.

"I don't know, but let's go ask Junebug."

Junebug slept in a rough, unfinished room on the back of the house and behind the common entrance to the kitchen from a back porch that was enclosed. This porch is where the workers and anyone entering the kitchen would shake off dust and clean muddy shoes. Junebug's room, which was juxtapositioned to this porch, remained unfinished for several years, but Engel was "working on it."

Engel didn't knock on the door, he barged in. As he did, Junebug was startled and quickly grabbed the pint of redeye whiskey he had been sipping and shoved it under his pillow.

"Smells like whiskey in here," Engel said while sniffing the air. "Junebug, you been drinking again?"

"Nope, pop," he said. He knew Engel wouldn't press this because he had never whipped him or disciplined him in his life. His mom had that chore. Junebug was the youngest boy. Don Barber, his older brother, had gone off to join the Air Force years before during the Korean War and had never returned. They hadn't seen him for years. Sally Barber was convinced that because her son was in the Air Force, that he was a pilot. So every time she would hear a jet fly over her house, she would say, "Yep. That's Don." She would wipe her hands on her apron, run out of the house and into the yard, and wave wildly as the jet flew over the house. Many times she would say, "He tipped his wings at me, that Don. I love that boy." She was convinced that Don was flying every plane, and no one could tell her different. The truth was that he got killed in the War being the recipient of "friendly fire," and she was never told what happened. Mr. Barber buried his son without a family funeral. Only Engel Barber, Junebug, and his other brother, Stanley, stood over the grave as the workmen filled in the hole. She had spoiled Junebug, and he was allowed to do just about anything he pleased. The only thing she required of him was that he be in church and that he help her clean the church twice a week. It was for these reasons that Bob Jones was convinced it was Junebug who had a hand in this prank.

"I didn't have nothin to do with this Pop. I swear."

"Then who did?" Bob questioned as Engel put his hand on the bib of Bob's overalls and held him back from saying another word.

"How should I know?" Junebug lamented. "But it weren't me for sure."

We soon heard the commotion stop, and the truck door slammed as Mr. Jones scooted behind the wheel. We then heard the slow grind of the starter. The starter drug laboriously and gave up. The Dodge truck had a six-volt battery that was charged by a slow generator that couldn't keep up the charge with the truck idling for so long, and the headlamps draining all the energy the generator could produce. The battery was dead. Bob pushed in the clutch and let the truck roll backwards down the drive. He popped the clutch several times, and the rear tires skidded in the gravel in reverse of the way the truck was moving. He did this several times to no avail, and didn't realize how close he was to the woods on the other side of the road.

The truck flew backwards, and when Mr. Jones pushed on the brakes, they didn't stop the truck picking up speed. The brakes were wet and the brake drums slid effortlessly over the drum with no friction to slow the truck down. The rear end of the pickup dropped 'over the edge of the steep slope and fell off the road heading fast into the woods. The pickup finally came to an abrupt halt as it slammed into a hickory tree. As it did, hickory nuts bounced from the limbs crashing to the ground. The radiator steamed and the front end was damaged from pushing the steps we placed in the center of the creek, and the pickup's tailgate was demolished.

After a minute or so, we saw Barbara Jones and Mr. Jones open the doors of the truck. Bob carried Terry, his oldest son, and Barbara carried Eric, who was rubbing his eyes, in her arms. They climbed their way out of the woods, found the Barber Lane, and headed for the comfort of their modest home.

Fran and I watched as Engel Barber extinguished the lamp he was carrying, and the house grew dark. We slipped from our temporary lair and walked across the field toward People's Corner where Fran Job lived. We were quiet as we walked and neither of us said anything to the other. When we reached the Ottenhiem/Chapel Gap Road with its three quarter crushed gravel paving, we grabbed a handful of the gravel and began throwing them on old man Burns' roof.

The rocks hit the steep slope and rolled over the edge and made loud noises as they tumbled down the corrugated tin roof. We didn't even laugh about this. Mr. Burns soon lighted his kerosene lamp and came out on the porch. He fired both barrels of the shotgun he held into the air and exhaled a few forbidden expletives and made threats at us.

"I'll shoot you boys with this buckshot; blister your hides so bad that you won't be able to sit down for a month!"

He screamed this and then retreated to his front room, blew out his lamp, and went to bed. This was all over in a matter of minutes, and Mr. Burns didn't care, he expected it. In fact, he wondered to his wife why it was taking so long for the rocks to run down his roof. Fran had been doing this gig for years. As always, on Sunday morning at church, he would tell Fran and I how much noise the rocks made rolling down the roof. "Not as good as last year," he would say even though he never knew for sure who rocked his roof on Halloween night year after year.

June washed the coal off our faces, and once again, I had those funny feelings I couldn't explain.

"I've waited for you guys," she said. "Where've you been?"

"Scaring the Preacher," Fran replied.

"Did you rock the Burns' roof again?" She asked tongue in cheek.

"Somebody did," Fran answered.

Later that night, I saw a flicker of light in June's bedroom, so I sneaked quietly down the steps from the attic where Fran and I slept and was careful that she didn't see or hear me. She did flinch once and lifted her head to look at the staircase as she shaved her leg. The blood rushed to my brain, and I for sure thought she saw me lurking in the shadows. I shrank back as far as I could and then she returned to her sponge bath she was taking out of a washbasin she had carried into her bedroom.

June dipped the sponge in the water and gently rubbed the soap along her face and neck, working her way down to her arms and legs. She was bathing wearing only her bra and panties, and I had never seen a girl this naked before. Once again the blood rushed to my face and head, and my breathing was short and gasping. She bathed her whole body this way and then put on a nightgown. After she had dried herself and moved the washbasin to the kitchen, I could hear her throw the water out the back door and the swoosh as it hit the ground. I could smell the sweet talc she dumped on her chest and arms fragrantly floating in the night air.

When I did get my breath, I eased back up the stairs where Fran had already fallen asleep and pulled the covers over me.

"Fran," I whispered, and he stirred.

"What? I'm trying to sleep." He could get cranky when he was awakened from his sleep.

"Did we do the right thing tonight with those rocks and stuff we left in the creek?"

"No, Bud, we didn't. I didn't think things would turn out like that." Apparently this was bothering him as well.

"Do you think we should repent at the church on Sunday?"

"Are you kidding? You stupid or something? They'd never forgive us for that, and they would kick us out of the church just like they did Jewel Vance when she got divorced."

"I feel terrible," I cried.

"The Preacher always says that Jesus is faithful and just to forgive all your sins when you ask Him," he explained, "ask Him."

I lay there for a long time until I was sure that Jesus forgave my sins, all of them. I confessed every one of my sins including watching June take a bath, and I woke up the next morning feeling much better as I listened to the rain beat softly on the tin roof.

June and I were in the kitchen by ourselves. Fran was in the outhouse taking care of morning business; Mandy and Abe were digging potatoes in the garden, so she could fry them for breakfast.

June caught me staring into her soft blue eyes. *She's the most beautiful girl I've ever seen,* I thought.

"The next time I catch you watching me take a bath, I'm going to screw your beanie little head clean off your shoulders, you little creep." June calmly said while leaning over to me so that no one could hear.

Holy cow that hurt! I flinched like I was stuck with one of Doc Sinclair's needles. I felt terribly guilty all that day, but I had to admit that I liked those feelings I had. I was falling in love.

CHAPTER SEVENTEEN

June Job had broken up with State Trooper Tip Tuck.
No one knew the reason, and now she was dating a guy
named Steve Green. She was sixteen and at thirteen years
old, I decided she would never wait for me. Steve Green worked
in Cincinnati, Ohio and like many of the boys who left their
farms where they grew up and moved up there to work, he
came back to Chapel Gap every weekend. Steve was a heavyset
blond guy. He was medium height contrasted with Tip Tuck
who was tall and muscular. Steve actually had blubber hanging over his belt, and he wore his pants like he was proud of it.
We couldn't reason for the life of us why she would date a guy
like that unless it was his car. He was nineteen years old, and
he bought the car from money his dad left his mother who he
convinced to turn loose of enough so that he could purchase
his car. He bought a 1956 Ford Thunderbird Convertible with
a hard top. It was pink and black, and it was my most favorite car in the world. I gave up. All I could offer June was my

1959 Schwinn bicycle that I had bought for ninety-two dollars I had saved from my farm money. It was sharp, though. It had chrome fenders, white wall tires, a horn in the tank, a light and generator fastened to the front wheel and three gears. It was clearly the nicest bike in Chapel Gap, and I was the envy of a lot of teenagers. It was also the most expensive bicycle you could buy at that time, but it couldn't match the Thunderbird Convertible that Steve Green used to win over June Job.

Fran and I spent many days riding that bike all over the knobs of Crab Orchard, Kentucky. We rode most of the time with Fran or me sitting on the tank or handlebars. We were strong and could easily pump the hills from the valleys below except for one; Chapel Gap Hill.

The main feature of the hill was a winding road that rose from the valley floor to the upper land where farms were strung along the lazy highway that led to the little burg of Ottenheim. Cars and trucks would speed toward the hill and try to pull it in high gear. This could not be done with the six cylinder engines that most of the vehicles had in those days. However my dad's new Edsel could pull the hill easily in high gear with its 460 horsepower engine.

One of the great feats for the boys in the area was to be able to pump a bicycle up the hill without stopping. Fran and I could pump the hill riding double, which was an accomplishment that no other duo in the Chapel Gap Area could do. Another example of strength and will was to let the bike go at the top of the hill and ride all the way down to the bottom without touching the brakes. Many boys failed trying this and would sometimes plunge over the cliff and injure themselves as they went flying bike and all down into the ravine below the ridge. It truly took guts, and no one had ever been successful. One rider died trying this stunt. Fran and I sat on the bike at the top of the steep, winding road and contemplated the evil that may swallow us up if we did what we were thinking. We stared at the first most treacherous curve, and we knew that when we hit the snake, we would be going faster than anyone had ever gone on a bike because we were riding double.

"If we can make that curve without flying off the mountain, we have only one more curve to make, and it is flatter," Fran explained as he pointed out the danger of such a risk.

My bike had a speedometer, and I knew that Fran would be paying close attention to the register so that we could later brag, if we survived, that we went faster than any car or truck. Most vehicles crept down the hill, negotiating the treacherous gravel based curves at less than twenty miles per hour.

We debated about who would be the best to handle the bike. "You drive Bud; it's your bike, and I don't want to be responsible in case something happens." Fran said this even though the whole shebang was his idea.

So it was set. I would do the steering, and Fran would sit on the handlebars with his feet resting on the front fender. Fran gripped the bars as we headed over the ridge. Before we could say, "scat," the bike's speedometer needle registered 35 MPH. The needle on the speedometer shook as we hit bump after bump, and we did not expect the chuckholes to bounce us around. There were many more than we thought, and the holes littered the road like the face of the moon. Fran was hanging on with his knuckles turned white."Hit the brakes," he said, "we're not going to make the curve; we'll be killed!"

I had unfailing determination. We were moving so fast that if I did hit the brakes, the bike would slide in the gravel as if on a patch of ice, and we would surely fly off the mountain and land in the treetops far below us. The speedometer registered 44 MPH as we approached the curve.

I put my feet down from the pedals to try and catch us if we went into a slide. The curve lurked ahead like a cobra with its hood up, coiled and ready to strike. I prayed, *Dear God help us, we're just kids, and we don't know what we're doing.*

Fran screamed. Both of us screamed as the bike's back tire started sliding toward the cliff. We had gotten caught in a thick ridge of soft gravel made by the graders, which maintained the road. The center of the road had loose gravel deposited there, about six inches high, and was not tamped down like the tracks where the cars straddled the center line. We rode in the tracks, but I was going to have to cross this ridge to the other tire track in order to make the curve. This wasn't our only problem. We hoped and prayed that we didn't meet another car coming around the corner because if we did, it would mean instant death.

My bike was going over the ridge, and Fran was sliding sideways off the handlebars. My eyes watered from the speed and the cool air blasting my face. I'm not sure what Fran's eyes were doing, but I would bet they were closed. How could I get around this curve when I couldn't see? Fran acted like he was going to jump off and leave me with the problem, but he didn't.

The bike slid at a speed of 50 MPH and headed for the cliff. Our young lives flashed before our eyes. Suddenly, the front tire hit one of the round rocks that was sunken beside the road and partially embedded by the tires of the huge graders running over it. These rocks were common in the Knobs. They were perfectly round, and when broken, the insides were full of brilliant quartz. We spent many days busting open rocks and looking to see how clear the quartz was and then decorating our porches and yards with them. We had no idea that one day one of these rocks would save our lives in the most unusual way.

The tire bounced off the rock and set the sliding bicycle upright. Fran flew completely off but held himself as he gripped the handlebars with his strong fingers. The sinew in his arms bulged as he held to the bike in a deathlike grip.

We were halfway around the curve, and it looked like we were going to make it. There was no slowing the bike down now because we were coming to the steepest part of the hill. Bouncing wildly, I balanced us until we were on the other side of the curve. We made it, and as we did, Steve Green and his T-Bird came flying up the hill throwing gravel everywhere as he floored the car trying to make it up the mountain in high gear. He passed us like a rocket, but we were going faster than he was. He looked at us with surprise on his face, seeing the trail of dust the narrow tires were making behind us. We both thought that five seconds or less sooner, and we would have smashed into Steve Green's T-Bird.

The last curve was not as dangerous, but we were going very fast. The curve was a slight bend, and many cars had gone off the road here trying to take it too fast and landing in the front yard of Jesse and Beth Oaks, who were brother and sister who had never married and lived with each other.

We could see safety ahead of us, but I would not touch the brakes. I wanted to see how fast we could get the bike and how far we could coast after the road flattened out to the valley below. Besides, I felt that God had answered my prayer, or we would be lying in the gully down the hill bleeding to death.

"Yee, haw!" Fran screamed, "we've done it!"

I glanced at the speedometer, and we were doing 56 MPH, and I barely held the bike on the road, but I was in the safe track on the right side, and the road had smoothed out considerably as we left the lunar chuckholes of the steep hill.

We passed a car that was moseying along as a lot of farmers do when they are driving unhurried to get anywhere. The 'Sunday drivers' looked at us like we were crazy, and I guess we were.

We flew by April May's pickup. She was driving as usual, and Henry May sat in the passenger seat, familiar territory for him, with his arm hanging out the window. We passed her so fast that when she saw the blur of two boys on a bicycle passing her like she was standing still, she almost ran off the road and into the grader ditch. She bore down on the horn.

We weren't picking up speed now, and the speedometer showed that we had lost a couple of miles per hour. We passed another car. The red light flashed in the windshield as the car sped up to catch us. Sheriff Crane always carried a spare light that he plugged into the cigarette lighter in order to catch speeders endangering the Chapel Gap population. My heart jumped into my throat, and beads of sweat popped out on my forehead as I glanced into the bike' s mirror and saw the cop pursuing us. We had coasted more than two miles, and the Sheriff spotted us from his vantage point while waiting on speeders. Today was his day to chase racing cars. He pulled us over as we slowed down automatically when we reached the slight grade in front of us. We were trying to make that grade without pumping the bike and coast over the hill and down to the next. If we could keep this up, we may coast all the way to Crab Orchard, but it was not to be.

The Sheriff put on his cap as he got out of his vehicle. All the cops did this, and I never knew why. He strode up to the bike.

"Never stopped a speeding bike before," he said with a serious look on his face. "You boys know how fast you were going?"

Yes sir," Fran exclaimed. Fran took over, but I thought I should have controlled the situation since I was a much better liar than Fran. "We got out of control coming down Chapel Gap Hill, but Bud here did a good job keeping us on the road. We just wanted to see how far we could coast, that's all." Fran told the Sheriff the truth, and I cringed because now the Sheriff had a confession that we were speeding on purpose.

"Hmm," the Sheriff mused. "You know I'm going to have to give you a citation for speeding?"

This scared me to death. "Sonny, step back by the car and put your hands on the hood," the Sheriff ordered.

I stood there in prone position as the Sheriff frisked me down. I didn't like being violated in this way very much. He emptied my pockets and placed the contents on the hood. I held a pocketknife, some matches, my sack of tobacco, my wallet, and a firecracker. While he did this, a strange car drove by, obviously someone who got on the wrong road down at Crab Orchard. The old man and woman looked as if they were going to slow down and perhaps seek directions from the Sheriff, but they moved on while looking confused as to why the Sheriff would be taking two boys on a bicycle into custody.

"Where did this firecracker come from? Do you realize this is contraband; strictly against the law in Kentucky and can carry a big bad penalty? Preacher know you smoke?" He said these things while looking over the firecracker and sack of roll your owns. He then reached around his waist and pulled off his handcuffs. "Put your hands behind your back," he demanded.

"No sir, he doesn't, he'd kill me if he knew," I answered his query with a high-pitched and choking voice.

Sheriff Crane was a deacon in the Evergreen Baptist Church, and we saw him every Sunday and Wednesday nights if he wasn't on a "call" somewhere chasing crooks.

"I may have to speak to your dad about this, and I know he won't be too happy. He may throw you out of the church."

Now, this scared me more than facing a judge and jury. Getting excluded from your church was the unpardonable sin.

After the Sheriff wrote out the ticket, he took off the cuffs and handed me the official piece of paper. It said that I would have to appear in court before Judge Wilston the first Monday of the next month. Fear gripped me like a pair of heavy duty pliers clamped down by a strong man because Judge Wilston was known in these parts as the hanging judge; he never let anyone out of a traffic ticket.

"Why did you have to handcuff me, Sheriff Crane?" I asked lugubriously.

"My own protection. Don't ever let me catch you boys doing anything this stupid again because if you do, I'll throw you both in jail. Fran," he said, "you've been in trouble before, and you should know better."

As the Sheriff drove off, Fran yelled, "Let me see that thing. Wow! You got a ticket, wow, Bud!"

As we pushed the bike up Chapel Gap Hill, we were way too tired to try and pump it to the top. I told Fran I was more worried about the smoking part and being charged with having an illegal firecracker in my possession than I was about the speeding ticket. Firecrackers were against the law in Kentucky, and smoking was against my dad's law. I didn't know which was worse. "He'll take away my bike for the summer and confine me to suffer," I told Fran. "He'll whip me, too."

The loud noise almost blew the fender off my bike. The back tire blew out. The tires had become thin from all the riding that Fran and me did. This thought didn't cross our minds as we dared to challenge the Chapel Gap Hill. If that tire had blown out while we raced down the mountain, we would have died for certain. We began pushing the bike up the road toward Fran's house.

It was getting dark, and we heard a car approaching us from behind. It was Steve Green and June Job riding with the radio on full blast, the top down, and we could hear Elvis crooning, "Love Me Tender." I watched as the couple rode past;

their hair blowing in the wind, and Steve had his arm around June, and as she was snuggled up real close, she glared at me as they passed. Steve didn't even glance our way but continued on blowing up billows of dust in our faces that made us choke. I hated fat Steve Green.

Who did he think he was? He was raised up near Broughtontown down a creek. His dad had died in a car wreck and left his family the unpainted small house they lived in. His mother, Meggie Green, supported the family on the modest insurance settlement and subsistence provided by the county. Steve had two sisters. Nancy was the youngest and Simone, who was the same age as Fran and me. She was a very pretty girl. Steve was the oldest, and when he decided to move up to Cincinnati, instead of helping his mother financially, who had no car, truck, or tractor, he bought himself a fancy car and waltzed June Job right out of mine and Tip Tuck's lives.

Meggie and the girls did all the farming, raising a small patch of tobacco, and a garden. When Steve would come home from Cincinnati on the weekends, he wouldn't lift a finger to help them. Yet, Meggie Green idolized him as did his sisters. "He's a fine boy," Meggie would say. To me, he wasn't fine at all; he was fat, ugly, and he ran around with my best friend's sister.

When Steve Green passed us on the hill, he didn't even slow down although he had to know that we were in real peril and maybe could have perished as we flew down the steep hill. He didn't care. All he cared about was dating June.

It was dark as Fran and me pushed the bike into his yard and leaned it against Abe's old garage. June and Steve were in the T-Bird listening to music. He reached over and pulled her to him. I watched in horror as their mouths came together in a long passionate kiss. I never had these feelings before, but I wanted to kill him; pull that tongue out of his mouth.

"Do you think they're French kissing, Fran?"

"Probably," he said seemingly unconcerned that his sister was in danger.

She struggled a little bit and then I heard her say, "Stop!" I could only imagine what Steve was doing to force out this cry from June. Whatever it was, Steve dropped the grip on her mouth and started the car.

"We're going to the drive-in," she shouted as they pulled away. Steve Green was ruining June. Going to the picture show and drive-in movies was strictly forbidden by the rules of Evergreen Baptist Church. Whenever we went to the movies, we had to sneak, and we did that more than I want to admit. June didn't seem to care who knew she was going to these dens of iniquity; especially, with a boy. Since Mandy and Abe never require permission for Fran and June to do anything, June seemed out of control in taking all these advantages of their good parents. She was doing what she wanted, when she wanted, for as long as she wanted, and with who she wanted.

Fran and I headed over to the Barbers. The Barbers had a brand new television, and many of the neighbors had congregated at their house to watch a new show that had come on the air that year, "Bonanza."

As we approached the house, Sally Barber was standing in the front yard. She had heard a plane going over, so she ran out and waved at Don flying overhead.

"You boys is just in time," she said, "Hoss Cartwright's coming on."

I don't know why she never said "Bonanza" since we all knew the cast of players. The farmers loved Hoss Cartwright, and they spoke of him as if he were their next-door neighbor or closest kin.

We could barely find a place to sit there were so many folks crowded into the living room. My mom was there with the little kids, Val Mark and Nila. Leah usually stayed with my dad when mom took the little kids somewhere.

"Them ain't real horses," Uncle T said as he could hear but not see the action on TV.

"Yes they are, too." Bob Jones said and then explained that they weren't nor could be men dressed up in horse costumes like Uncle T claimed.

Uncle T was mad, so he headed for the bedroom and his peppermint candy. This happened every Saturday night during the Bonanza show. He and Bob Jones would get into the same argument about the horses. We could hear Uncle T making fun of Mr. Jones from the other room that had no door but was enclosed by a curtain. "Stupid people," he mumbled, "real horses on television, how dumb."

Hoss shot the cattle rustler that night and saved the ranch. Little Joe faced down a dangerous gunslinger who threatened Virginia City, Adam fell in love with some girl who arrived on a stage coast from back east, and Ben sipped his coffee while he expounded to his boys and Hop Sing, their cook, the need to run off the sheepherders squatting on his fifty thousand acres.

The group broke up after the Lawrence Welk Show and headed home. Fran and I neared People's Corner when we saw Steve Green leaving the front yard of the Job property. We heard June and him having kind of an argument, and reasoned he was trying to do the same thing with her he had tried earlier in the evening before they went driving off. The crud.

Fran and I crouched down in a fencerow where we always crossed when coming from the Barbers. We were watching Steve coming toward us, and we didn't want to eat his dust. His car slowed down, and we sank lower in the ditch making sure that his car's lights didn't shine on us and give away our position.

"He saw us," Fran whispered, and I thought we should bolt

back across-the fence and run for our lives. I don't know why, but Fran and I were slightly afraid of him. I think I was more afraid of him than Fran because I was sure that June had told him about my watching her take a bath in her brassiere and panties. I felt like he was out to get me sometimes, and it made my skin crawl.

Steve slowed to a stop and got out of the car. Goose pimples ran up and down our arms and spine. We were trapped. The car was sitting and blocking our path to the road, and he would be on top of us before we could ever rush across the fence and save ourselves.

Steve Green walked to the back of his car and looked around. Had he seen us? What was he going to do? He looked up at the stars and then looked straight down into the ditch directly at Fran and me. Fran pushed me lower, but it was clear he didn't see us. The large taillights, which were burning, obscured his vision. We lay motionless.

To our surprise, Steve Green wasn't looking for us at all. He had not seen us, and we didn't want him to, so we didn't move a muscle. Steve unzipped his pants, and we could clearly see that he was going to relieve himself. He whipped it out and started peeing. A big stream of pee shot out from his fingers, and we could see the reflection of the urine as it sprayed and turned a bright red in the glow of the taillights.

It seemed that Steve Green would never finish. I have never seen anyone pee that much. Only had I seen a mule urinate with that kind of reservoir. There was so much pee that the stream ran down the road and into the grader ditch where we lay hiding. Fran was shaking all over, trying to suppress the sounds that would give us away. We were both hysterical, so I pushed Fran's face in the mud to drown out his uncontrollable giggling.

We watched as Steve zipped up his pants, gave a sigh of

relief, and climbed back into his pink and black T-Bird. As he sped off throwing gravel that we had to dodge to keep from being decapitated, we rushed out of the ditch.

"Did you ever see anything like that?" I asked.

"He pisses like a mule," Fran said, and we both roared with laughter, holding our sides from the pain of laughing so hard. With tears streaming down our faces, we were laughing even harder because Fran said "piss" which was considered a forbidden cuss word at the Evergreen Baptist Church. Later that night, we were lying in bed not saying anything and then one of us would burst out laughing, and we would hold our sides as we were both thinking the same thing.

Fran and I heard the bell ringing, and we weren't even out of bed. We scrambled to our feet and rushed down the steps. June had just finished fastening her blouse when we ran by her. The stairs to the attic were in her room, so we had to cross her path to get to the other three rooms of the house. As we passed, she glared at me, her blue eyes burning a hole clear to the back of my head.

The church bell was still ringing as we headed toward the Hanover's field. We crossed the fence into the cemetery. There were many cars and trucks in the parking area, and Preacher Roberts was having car trouble, so we saw him driving his Farmall tractor up the lane with his wife, Alta, sitting on the fender.

I saw my dad and Sheriff Crane talking outside the building. I was in deep trouble; I felt it. They didn't see me, but there was a serious look on my dad's face. *I'm going to be dragged in front of the church this morning and all my dark secrets are going to be revealed before the whole congregation, and they're going to kick me out of the church* were my thoughts. Fear and dread increased my blood pressure, and I could feel the blood oozing into my cheeks.

All of a sudden, my dad and Houston Crane burst out laughing. The Sheriff slapped my dad on the back, and they laughed some more. The Sheriff did tell my dad about writing that bogus ticket and handcuffing me, but he never mentioned finding tobacco in my shirt pocket or the firecracker. He took that from me anyway. All the members of Evergreen Baptist Church knew I smoked, sneaked off to the movies, but not one of them, even the worse gossips, ever told on me.

CHAPTER EIGHTEEN

A fter church on Sunday morning, our family was invited to have Sunday dinner with the Cullens. Chet and Naomi Cullen lived near the old Hanover Store. They had a large farm and were one of the more wealthy families in the Chapel Gap Area. Chet was a deacon at Evergreen Baptist Church and had taken the opposite side of his middle son, Junior, who had lobbied to get my dad thrown out of the church. We liked this family and David Cullen was a friend of both Fran and me, and we had lots of fun riding mules and exploring the woods on the Cullen farm.

This was our thirteenth summer, and this particular day was David's thirteenth birthday, so Naomi Cullen had invited our family and several of David's friends to celebrate his day. David was also a cousin of Benji McDuff and had some of the same streaks of meanness in him that ran in the relatives of redheads.

Buster Kirk, Ray Lord, David Cullen, Ray Denny, Shane

O'Conner, Fran Job, and me were all thirteen years old and had formed a pact and bond of kinship as pals. Naomi had invited all these boys to the event. Naomi was a medium built woman, solid as many of the farmwomen were, and very articulate. She had been educated at the University of Kentucky where her oldest son, Mack was attending college. She was also a perfectionist and was famous for her cooking. I always loved to go to the Cullens for meals, and this day was no different. She had put out a spread like none other you would ever see, anywhere. The table was filled with fried chicken, mashed potatoes and gravy, delicious gravy, brown with cracklings of the chicken that gave it a redolence that made your mouth water. She had a secret recipe for cornbread, which had won many awards at the county fairs, and she made her own scrumptious white bread loaves. She served everything straight from the oven and piping hot. Her corn on the cob with real butter, that she churned herself and lightly salted, was a compliment to the other wonderfully delectable vegetables she had special homemade recipes for making. Her meals were a chef's delight. She decorated the table with pies and cakes for which she was also famous. In fact, Daphni Anderson, the reporter for the paper, had said: "Naomi Cullen's desserts are unmatched in Chapel Gap history going back one hundred and fifty years. She has won more blue ribbons for cooking than any other woman in Kentucky except Barbara Fain from Rockcastle County." My dad bought some of Barbara Fain's deviled eggs and brought them home from a bizarre when Bible Baptist Church of Mount Vernon, Kentucky where Mrs. Fain was a member, had a sale to raise money for summer youth camp. It was said that no one could ever beat her in a cook off, not even Naomi Cullen.

On the farm next to the Cullens, lived the Messers. They were also invited and were easily as wealthy if not more so than the Cullens. The Messer brothers, Earl and Estill, had married two sisters, Opal and Olive. After many years living in the same house together, they swapped wives. Earl had one arm and so did Estill.

One day Fran and I were working in the cornfields with the Messer farmers. Our job was to drive the tractor and trailer to the storage bins after the corn picker had filled the wagons with the golden grain.

About lunchtime or "dinner time," Estill was in the field and the picker got hung up with an ear of corn jammed in the gears. Estill left the conveyor running and tried to pry the ear out of the gear with his right hand. The picker seized his shirt and pulled his hand into the sharp cogs that stripped the corn from the cob. It severed his arm above the elbow and ground the flesh into mincemeat and spit the crushed bones, blood and flesh, into the wagon being filled with kernels of corn.

Estill barely made his way back to the house where we were eating. Blood was all over his clothes where the picker had severed his arm. Olive, his wife, rushed him to the hospital in Stanford and he barely survived. Estill was tougher than his brother.

That same afternoon, there was a threat of rain, so Earl Messer had to finish getting the crop from the field, or it may be some time before the field was dry enough to get the machinery in there and pick the corn before it rotted and was lost.

After a heated debate between Earl and Opal Messer about whether Earl should go to the hospital and be with his brother or go pick the corn, it was decided that Earl could do nothing for him, and that "it's what Estill would want us to do."

Earl said, "he would want me to finish getting the corn in the granary."

Earl instructed Fran to drive the truck back to the field

after it as emptied of the load that Estill started. I climbed on the tractor with Earl and headed to the two hundred acres of corn where nearly a third of it still needed picking. The day was balmy and humid and Earl's khaki shirt was soaked with sweat.

We arrived, and the corn picker was still hooked up to the tractor.

"I wonder who turned off the tractor?" Earl asked curiously. We later found out that Estill realized the tractor would run out of fuel, or perhaps overheat, and that would make it impossible to finish harvesting the crop if the tractor broke down. He crawled up on the tractor with one arm, and the stub where the other arm used to be spurted out blood from the exposed veins where it was severed. Somehow, Estill shut off the engine. When Earl climbed up on the tractor, blood was all over the seat and dashboard, so he obviously had done this.

Mr. Messer started the engine and engaged the power take off. The conveyor would not engage because the corn was still jammed in the rotator wheels that stripped the corn from the cob and carried the kernels up the conveyor and deposited them in the wagon following the picker.

"Damn," Deacon Earl swore, "the picker's still jammed."

Fran drove up in the Chevrolet two-ton truck.

"Better turn off the tractor," Fran instructed Earl. Fran had a sixth sense.

Earl looked at Fran and said nothing. What did a twelve years old kid know about farming equipment? While he was looking at Fran and me, he stuck his hand in the picker and tried to un-jam the ear of corn stopping up the works.

We watched in horror as Earl's sleeve was pulled into the machine. It happened so fast that we could do nothing. Earl pulled with all his might, but the picker continued to slowly drag his sleeve into the cogs of the treacherous spiked wheel. The sleeve was now completely engulfed, and Earl kept pulling his arm back until the shoulder of his shirt was at his wrist. His arm was free, but he couldn't get out of his shirt fast enough, and it was a ghastly sight for two kids to watch a helpless man unable to help himself.

Fran and I grabbed him from behind and pulled, but it was too late. The wheel of spikes that shelled the hard corn was now tearing his arm up like a lion tearing flesh off a freshly killed antelope. I glanced up and could see the blood and flesh being spewed into the wagon from the large spout in a long stream of red and yellow. Earl fell back, but his arm had been chewed to his shoulder. He screamed in agony and begging for mercy as he fell silent and hit the hard packed ground. I had never seen or heard anything like this. I had never seen anyone faint except my sister, Leah, when she was climbing the narrow steep steps to the Sunday School Class for us junior kids, which was in the attic of the Evergreen Baptist Church.

Fran thought Earl was dead and so did I as he lay there bleeding from the exposed arteries pumping blood and squirting streams of the red liquid all over the wheels of the corn picker. Fran dropped to his knees and bent over Earl. He put his ear to Earl's heart, and I said a prayer.

"We've got to stop the bleeding, Bud, he's still alive."

Fran grabbed some rags from the truck, and I took off my shirt. We stuffed and tied these rags over the stump that throbbed and pulsated like a fish flopping on the bank.

"Grab his legs," Fran screamed.

I did, and we carried him to the tailgate of the big truck. We could hardly lift him up that high, so Fran stood on the bed of the truck, and we pushed and pulled Earl into the bed and laid him down.

Earl was still unconscious when Fran drove into the barnyard and started screaming for help. We couldn't get the truck down to the house because of the white picket fence that surrounded the large yard. I looked at Earl, who was colorless, and thought that he was surely gone. The bleeding had slowed down some, and the bandages Fran had fixed to the severed stump were soaked, and the excess of blood ran down the bed of the truck and onto the ground.

Opal heard Fran scream and hung up the phone. She was talking to Olive, who was with her husband, Estill, while he was on the operating table as the doctors were sewing up his injuries.

Opal screamed when she saw Earl and quickly instructed me to get to the barn and drive the pickup down to the house. She jumped in the front seat of the big truck, shoved the gears into place, and drove toward the house entering it from the front on the Hanover road.

I kicked the starter on the floor of the pickup. The starter was dragging like Bob Jones' Dodge did that night in the creek, and I thought, *Please God. Let this truck get going.* God answered my prayer as quickly as He did when Fran and I were about to run off Chapel Gap Hill on my bike. I took off out of the barn so fast that I almost ran off into the grader ditch on the other side of the road.

"You boys help me get him in the pickup," Opal ordered. We did this, and all three of us handled him gently while laying him on some quilts Opal had laid in the bed for his comfort.

Earl moaned, so we breathed a sigh of relief.

"Don't die, honey," Opal softly said, "I'm right here, and we are going to get you some help."

"What about the corn?" Earl whispered.

Opal drove as fast as she could to the church. She slid the pickup sideways in the church parking area sending up chunks of creek gravel and hitting some of the tombstones down in the cemetery. My dad ran from his study to see who in the world made the racket. As soon as he saw Fran and me in the back of the pickup and Opal Messer driving, he knew something was terribly wrong.

"Preacher, please drive the truck, Earl's hurt real bad, and I don't think I can get him to the hospital before he dies!" Opal cried loudly.

My dad took one glance at the floor of the pickup's bed and jumped in the front seat. Opal jumped in the passenger seat and dad yelled at us out the window as he sped down the church driveway.

"Don't let him move," he yelled, "keep him from sliding around."

This was easier said than done because this was the wildest ride I had ever taken in a vehicle of any kind. Fran and I watched as the dust rose in a great cloud of gray and settled over the houses along the way which were too close to the road.

When we reached Chapel Gap Hill, we were going way too fast, but my dad didn't even slow up as we almost went air born over the first hump of the long hill. He flew around the S curve, and the pickup slid sideways, but my dad could drive. He counter steered the wheel and pulled the truck in place for the next part of this treacherous curve.

When we got past, Fran and I looked at each other and quickly checked Mr. Messer. He hadn't moved; our grip was so tight, and we had braced our feet against the sides of the pickup bed and held on.

The speedometer was broken on the 1949 Studebaker truck and had been for years. Fran guessed by the dust that was boiling up behind us that dad was doing at least sixty miles per hour as we hit the long straightaway taking us toward Crab Orchard and on to Stanford.

As we passed, some farmwomen were already standing in the yards waiting for us. Birdie Wells was listening in on the conversation Opal was having with Olive Messer about Estill's condition in the hospital. She had called several women on the road. When she called Janice Clausen, she said, "I've already heard."

When we arrived at the hospital in Stanford, the doctors took Earl immediately to the operating room and worked on his arm. Later, we had some supper and went back to the hospital. Earl and Estill were in the same room. Estill without his right arm and Earl without his left.

They greeted my dad and thanked him for driving Earl to the hospital, and he mentioned the bravery of Fran and me as well. Earl lamented the fact that the corn crop was lost.

"We lost it all, Estill," Earl said sorrowfully.

"Not yet!" My dad said as he left the room in a hurry.

This was truly one of the oddest things that happened in Chapel Gap history. Oh! The crop was saved because the men of Evergreen Baptist Church went to the Messer farm with their own equipment and had the entire crop in the granary in one single afternoon.

After dinner, all the boys who had been invited to the party met in the Cullen tobacco barn. We were milling around in there trying to decide what to do for the afternoon. There, seven of us debated how we would spend our leisure time. All the boys knew that we must time our activity in order to be done in time for church that Sunday evening. Our parents, except for Mandy and Abe Job, forbade us from missing Sunday night services at the church. "Let's go to the creek and go swimming," David Cullen said. It was his birthday, so no one argued the point. Besides, we all loved swimming in the creek that ran through the Cullen farm. Chet and Junior Cullen had dammed the creek a couple of years before, and the pool below the log dam was deep and cool.

The woods leading to the swimming hole were so dense

that we had to walk single file along the path made by the Cullen boys and others who came to the farm to swim in the creek.

The Cullens had constructed a swing using rope and a milking stool and tied it to a Sycamore tree that hung over the hole. We had a lot of fun climbing into the swing and jumping off the limb. You had to be careful though because the length of the rope and the fifteen feet or so drop would swing far over the pool and well over the bank on the other side. You had to time yourself perfectly in order to not drop too soon and fall into the rocks on the other side of the creek.

One time, Riley Pat was swinging at the pool and let go too soon. He fell into the rocks and broke his leg. He was in a cast for several months and every time we went to the creek, the thought was in our minds. We were having fun running toward the creek. David Cullen led the way, and I followed Fran at the rear.

It was dry that time of the year, and we had to cross a dry creek bed that had filled with dry leaves. One after the other, each boy stepped in the same spot while crossing the creek bed. David led the way across and soon disappeared into the dark forest and as he did, each boy followed him. Fran was nearly across when I stepped in some leaves.

I heard a buzzing sound that I couldn't figure out. Suddenly, a yellow bumblebee flew past my head. Its fat body, neatly decorated with yellow and black stripes, whizzed past my ear and turned to land on my face. The bumblebees were large in that part of the country, so I could easily feel the weight of its body as it slammed its stinger into my cheek. That hurt like a hypodermic needle, and I slapped at it, knocking it on the ground and stepped on the bee smashing out its life.

Before I knew what was happening and felt the burning of the sting, there were other bees swarming around my head. I was swinging wildly at them. Fran and Ray Lord turned to see what I was screaming about.

"Don't frighten them," Fran warned, "stand still, and I'll pull you out."

Fran started down into the creek bed as Ray ran off in the woods. There was no way Ray was going to get stung by one of these powerful bees. I froze in place and as Fran started toward me, the bees attacked him. Before he got more than the couple of stings he received, he retreated out of the creek. Immediately the bees gave up the chase and turned their attention to me.

There must have been hundreds of bees swarming all over me. I was successful in knocking some of them silly, but there were too many. I was stung so many times on my face that I buried it in my hands. I had still not moved from the place where Fran told me to stand. However, I was positioned squarely in the middle of their nest.

The bees attacked me and covered my face, arms, and back. They were stinging the back of my neck. When I flinched at each dagger that pierced my skin and swatted the back of my neck, another bee would sting me in the face. There were stings on my eyelids.

The bees were on top of each other and were successful in stinging through my pants aided by the weight of their brothers. They were stinging me all over to the point that I could no longer feel where the aches of the stings were coming from. I was barefooted so from the top of my head to my bare feet, bees were trying to sting me to death in a wild and viciously evil attack.

I looked through my fingers and saw Fran coming. He had chased down one of the boys who had a match and had lighted the dry leaves. He had made a torch by tying his tee shirt and fastened it to the stick he had in his hand. The leaves were slowly burning making a white smoke.

Soon, the other boys were gazing in amazement as the yellow and black bees swarmed my body. Fran ran into the dry creek and started torching the nest that was soon burning, and the bees still in the nest were fleeing up the creek and out of sight. He stuck the smoking log next to my head, telling me not to move, and waved it around until the smoke surrounded me.

The bees were gone, but my entire body burned and ached. Fran grabbed my arm and dragged me out of the creek bed. When safely out, I collapsed on the bank. The boys were in a circle surrounding me and staring down.

"Is he dead?" One of them asked.

"No, he's not dead," Fran answered, "but he soon will be if we don't get him to the hospital."

We were deep in the woods, and it didn't seem that they had time to get back to the house to summon help, so they carried me to the swimming hole over the ridge.

"Throw him in," Buster Kirk exclaimed, "the cold water will cut down the swelling."

The boys pitched me in the creek, and I felt the cool water surround me. I sunk like a rock to the bottom. They watched for me, and when I didn't surface, they became afraid.

"You idiots!" Fran screamed, "He's gonna drown!"

Buster Kirk and Ray Denney were the taller boys, so they waded in and found me lying on the bottom and fished me out. They laid me on the creek bank still not sure what they should do.

Buster Kirk was wrong. The cold water made the swelling come faster, and my face was so swollen I couldn't see out of my eyes. My eyelids swelled shut making me blind. Also, I was having a difficult time breathing. The many stings on my neck were causing my throat to swell shut and then I heard the rustling of leaves. Someone was running through the woods.

"What happened?" My dad yelled at the boys as he noticed me lying on the ground. "We heard Sonny screaming all the way to the house!"

He examined me closer and then he knew. There were bees clinging to my clothes where I had smashed them. "At least you boys weren't stupid enough to throw him in the creek," my dad commented. "That would have killed him for sure." Everyone looked at Buster but said nothing.

"Get him up and carry him," my dad instructed. "Fran, you hurry to the house and tell Chet to get some blankets and make a bed in the back of his pickup."

When we arrived at the Cullen's house, I was unconscious. My dad ran along side of me while the boys hustled through the dense forest and into Cullen's' yard.

"Oh my word," Naomi Cullen exclaimed as she looked at my limp body. "These are the worst stings I have ever seen!"

My arms, face, neck, back, and legs were now black and blue. I had passed out from the pain and from the toxic venom the bees had inflicted on me. Naomi Cullen called Doc Sinclair, and the Doc decided that we didn't have time to get me to the hospital in Stanford if we had any more time at all. "Meet me with Sonny at Floyd's Funeral Home," he said.

Floyd had a gurney and plenty of needles and stuff down in his basement where he worked on dead bodies preparing them for burial. Of course I didn't understand what the Doc's plans were, or I would have protested wildly about entering a place where dead people had been.

"I'm driving," my dad told Chet Cullen, and Chet relented.

The 1956 Ford pickup V8 was much faster than the six cylinder Chevys most of the farmers owned. The pickup was known to be able to climb Chapel Gap Hill in high gear.

We sped toward Crab Orchard, and after scaring Chet Cullen half to death as my dad slid around the S curve on the steep hill, we slid the pickup into the parking lot of Floyd's Funeral Home.

"Get him to the basement, quick like," the Doc ordered.

Doc Sinclair and Floyd were standing and looking at me on the gurney, and Floyd's expression and concentration was as if he were ready to deliver a body upstairs to the chapel for viewing.

"Look at those stings. Every one of them has bruised this poor boy; he is so full of venom that I don't think we can do anything for him." Floyd said this to the Doc as he shook his head back and forth.

"What?" My dad asked. "You told us to bring Sonny here and by God you better know what to do, or I'm going to burn this place to the ground with both of you in it!" This was the first time anyone had ever heard my dad cuss since he was converted at the Sun Valley School House back in Kansas during the revival meeting, and their mouths flew open at the shock of this blasphemous language.

Floyd and the Doc looked at each other as did Chet Cullen, but they dared not say a word.

"Grab my bag," the Doe told Floyd, "and get some penicillin and hurry!"

I didn't feel the horse needle the Doc injected into my butt, so I couldn't scream.

"Rub some alcohol on those stings," the Doc said and Floyd quickly brought a bottle of rubbing alcohol and some cotton swabs while looking at my dad out of the corner of his eye, making sure that he would not be attacked by this angry father and preacher.

When I woke, I screamed in horror. There was no one near me, and all I could see were coffins surrounding me. I thought I had died and gone to the devil's hell. The Doc and my dad came running down the steps.

"Easy little feller," Doc Sinclair said as he gently placed his old and wrinkled hand on my forehead and moved the compress from my brow that he had put there earlier.

"Am I going to die?" I asked tearfully and afraid. I was hurting so badly as my arms and legs wouldn't move.

"We've counted one hundred and thirty seven stings, son, you're lucky to be alive." The Doc explained.

I didn't know this until later, but I had woken out of my subconscious state earlier that night and started vomiting. The Doc pumped my stomach, and nearby there was a pail full of putrid looking liquid. The Doc's maneuver had saved my life. How did the Doc know how to treat this many bee stings? It turned out that the only time he ever experienced so many stings was when his dog, a coon dog, got stung in a dry creek bed and nearly died. The Doc saved its life by using the same treatment on it as he had done on me.

I was black and blue for weeks. School had started, and I had to go to school with my arms bruised and swollen. The yellow swirl caused by heavy bruises could easily be seen on my arms, hands, and face.

From that point on, I had to be very careful to never come in contact with a bee of any kind, and when Fran and I were in the woods, he made sure no bee got near me. In fact, from then on the farmer's wives, who were going to have us over for Sunday dinner, cleaned the "waspers" and the "mud-daubers" out of the eaves of their houses to prevent my being stung. I was now deathly allergic to bee stings, and I would carry that problem the rest of my life.

CHAPTER NINETEEN

hated revival meetings at the Evergreen Baptist Church. These meetings went on every night for two weeks and sometimes three if the Spirit was moving in the Chapel Gap Community. That wasn't the bad part. My dad scheduled "Cottage Prayer Meeting" each night one week prior to the revivals, so we could have a month of preaching, and he scheduled these events twice a year. It seemed sometimes that I was spending my entire life in church.

Cottage Prayer Meetings were something my dad invented, I think. Different church folks would volunteer their homes in the evenings of the prayer week, and all church members would meet in the homes and pray for the revival, special speaker, and each other. The revival speaker was usually someone my dad had gone to the Bible College with in Lexington, Kentucky. We prayed diligently for the evangelist and that his messages would result in the salvation of the wicked farmers in the Chapel Gap Community who had still not repented of their sins, been baptized. and became a member of the church.

Fran and I got converted during one of these long meetings, and like a couple dozen of the other kids who got "born again" during the meetings, we were baptized in the Cedar Creek by the bridge.

Most of the preachers my dad had come for revivals were good men, and some of them could preach the very fires of hell from far beneath the earth, and you could feel the flames licking at your heels. When these preachers had preached for fourteen consecutive nights and an extraordinary amount of people had gotten saved, one of the men would call to order a "special business meeting" on the last night of the revival, make a motion that the church would extend the services for another week, and the church would vote on it. Of course, all the Spiritual neighbors would say "Amen," and we would be stuck for another seven days.

Those revivalists got attached to the people of Evergreen Baptist Church, and the church reciprocated. On the last night of one of these revivals, and it was sure not to go for more days, the evangelist stood in front of the church while the congregation filed out of the seats to form a long line. They would shake hands with the gentleman and tell him goodbye. This was the most emotional time of the entire meeting, and it took forever. Sometimes I didn't think we would ever get the meeting over with.

The reason for the lengthy goodbyes was mainly because of the women. They would hug the evangelist and linger while wailing and crying. There would be rivers of tears, and you would think the folks would never see the evangelist the rest of their lives. That was never true because my dad would invite the same evangelist for the next year's meetings, and we would go through the same line of hugging and wailing and then do it again the next year. Fran and I did some major weeping standing in those lines; especially, if the guy was someone we really liked.

When we met at one of these farms for a week of prayer and supplication before the Lord, the church did not pray in mixed company. Baptists believed and practiced for centuries that women were not to "pray in public because that would be usurping authority over the men." Thus, never did a woman speak out in a public church assembly and never, ever, prayed out loud in the Evergreen Baptist Church.

The women and men were kept separate when it came time to pray. They all met in a common meeting, crowding in the large living room's, for a general exhortation from God' s Holy Word, and instructions as to what my dad thought should be shared with each of them before prayer time.

There was a large group of people gathered for the prayer service at the Frazier farm the night I committed my one and only theft. There were so many in attendance at the Frazier farm that my dad had to separate the men and boys, women and girls.

The men sat around the living room floor, and some of them leaned up against the walls as they sat on the floor. The women went to a large bedroom and did their praying there. Stan Kirk, the leader of the "Booster Choir," was chosen to lead the boys in prayer and keep order. Shirlee Messer, a teenage girl and best friend of my sister, Leah, was chosen to lead the girls in prayer although I can't remember that she had ever prayed in her life.

The customary way these meetings took place was that each person was given the opportunity to make a special request. You were required to remember all these requests and make them known during your own prayer. Only a few actually made spoken requests, but to avoid embarrassment for not being in tune Spiritually when it was your turn to request, you simply said "unspoken" and the others would say, "Amen." In this way, you were off the hook, and the idea behind the shadows of unspoken requests was that there were so many dastardly things you knew needed to be prayed about that you could never speak about them in public. These prayer meetings lasted a long, long time. As the men prayed, they would pray about everything out loud, and the more grunts and groans of supplication that came from the prayers, the longer the meeting lasted. We boys used to amuse ourselves at these prayer meetings by playing an organized game called, "Cottage Prayer Meeting Olympics." We actually timed the prayers with our pocket watches and kept a record of the lengths of the prayers each night to see who would win the prayer gold medal contest.

No one, not even the Reverend Billy Graham, could out pray Preacher Roundtree. His prayers were not only lengthy, but also full of emotion. He used to pray in such fervency that even the angels in heaven must have surrounded him. He would suck air while he prayed: "And Lord, uh, I just want to thank you for your blessings, uh, I pray for this here revival meeting coming up, uh, Lord, uh. Ohooooo thank you blessed Lord, uh, for giving us this fine day, uh, we don't deserve it Lord, uh, we deserve clouds and fog, uh, but not sunshine, uh, we have sinned O God, uh, and we have transgressed thy laws, uh, we have sunk into the debts of despair and sin, uh, but we know, uh, you will forgive us O Lord, uh, because you said in your Word, uh, I can't think where it is exactly, uh, but it's somewhere in there, uh, that if we confess our sins, uh, you are faithful and just, uh, to forgive us our sins, uh, and cleanse us, uh, from all unrighteousness, uh, (my dad interjected the correct Scripture as being 1 John 1: 8,9), Oh God bless those women praying, uh . . ." This went on for a long time, and by the time Preacher Roundtree was finished, the sweat was dripping off his brow, and he had to take his big handkerchief and wipe himself off while he wheezed and coughed because he was out of breath.

The women never prayed as long as the men and my dad used to get aggravated because after they had finished their supplications, they sat and gossiped, and we could hear every word they were saying. He wanted them to remain quiet until the men had finished praying, but that was a request that was destined for failure before it had begun. Stan Kirk encouraged all us boys to pray, and he could pray, I have to admit that. He could speak in flowery language, and he seemed to know who he was talking to with respect. We all made an attempt to follow his example.

Fran was praying that night, and he had waited until all the others had prayed before his gave up his fear and burst into "Our Heavenly Father."

While the boys were taking their turns praying, I looked on the dresser that I sat next to on the floor. We were praying in the back bedroom where Meg and John Frazier slept. Lying precariously and tempting on the dresser was a shiny half dollar. I kept staring at it. Fifty cents in that day would buy you a lot of stuff at Babs Kirk's store. I reached up and slid the coin off the dresser into my palm and closed my hand tightly around it, making sure that all the boys had their eyes closed and were deep in prayer. I knew they weren't and most of them were asleep.

I quickly stuffed the half dollar into my sock. Fran ended his prayer, and Stan Kirk announced that our part of the Cottage Prayer Service was over, but he cautioned us to remain quiet even though we could hear the women and girls gossiping from the other rooms.

Finally, after a year it seemed, the men had finished, and

we could hear Daphni Anderson and her mother, Meg Frazier, in the kitchen preparing the desserts that we always had after the prayer service each night.

We followed Stan into the front room and moved carefully so as not to get in front of him lest we usurp his authority as the leader of the prayer group. I felt the coin slip deep into my sock.

We were fellowshipping with one another as we were commanded to do in the Scripture when we heard Meg Frazier cry out.

"My half-dollar is gone!" She cried. "I left it right here on the bureau, and it's gone!"

My mom and Daphni ran into the room and began searching under the dresser, under the bed, and in every corner of the room. When it was determined that the coin had been stolen, Meg came into the front room and looked directly at me. I shrunk my shoulders knowing that my secret was revealed by the Lord.

"Which one of you boys stole my money?" She declared.

"Now wait a minute," my dad said, "no one would steal money at a prayer meeting."

I felt like every eye in the room was on me, but they weren't really; every one was looking at Rob Turner's boy. They stared at him and every one got quiet.

Jerry Turner was a known thief. His reputation got tainted when Babs Kirk, who was Gib Kirk's former wife before he divorced her and married Loretta Kirk, had told several women at church that she knew Jerry Turner stole from her every time he came into the store. That may or may not have been true, but Jerry was marked for life.

"I didn't do it," the ten year old little kid exclaimed as tears flowed down his cheeks, "I didn't do it."

Oh, how horrible I felt. The pangs of guilt and shame gripped my soul. I had stolen this money from these poor people, who needed it for bread, and now poor Jerry Turner was going to receive the blame, and I liked the little kid, a lot. His dad was a nice man and always had his brood in church. He helped get his kids ready for church services every week that included Sunday morning, Sunday night, and Wednesday night. His wife was sickly, and when she couldn't go to church, Rob would dress the kids himself and bring them. He had them off their afternoon chores and ready for the Cottage Prayer Meeting each night and sat with them every night of the revival meetings.

Sweat was popping in huge beads on my forehead, and I could feel the coin burning the Liberty Bell into my bare leg. I felt like the guy did in one of Edgar Allen Poe's short stories I read in school, who had killed a man and buried him in the floor. No one could possibly know he did it, but when the Sheriff came, his rocking chair was sitting on top of the planks in the floor where the cut up body lie. He was in such duress that he confessed the murder.

The coin now burned a hole in my leg. I had to do something. Little Jerry Turner was still weeping when his dad, who was very angry, escorted him out the house and to his pickup.

In the confusion as people were debating whether or not Jerry Turner had the coin in his possession, I begged excuse to go to the outhouse. Most of the people were standing on the front lawn saying goodbye, and telling John and Meg Frazier how much they had enjoyed the prayer meeting and the dessert, and then added how sorry they were that the meeting ended up with some wicked thief stealing Meg's half-dollar.

I slipped in the back door after going to the outhouse and retrieving the coin from my sock and made a detour to the bedroom. I quickly placed the coin on the dresser where I knew that Meg would find it later, and slipped out the back door again and came around the house to the front disguising my actions as if I had just walked from the outhouse in the backyard. Tom Messer agreed to give Fran a ride in his pickup to Fran's house. Fran sat in the back and Mandy Job sat in the front. June Job rode with Steve Green in his T-Bird.

"What's wrong with you?" Fran asked while studying my face.

Fran knew something was wrong because I was staring off in space and worrying about Jerry Turner.

"I'm under conviction, Fran," I replied lugubriously.

"What for? You've already been saved and baptized in the creek."

I never kept anything from Fran although I knew he didn't tell me everything going on with him.

"I'm the one who took the money," I said ashamedly.

"Holy crap!" He said, and this made me feel worse.

"I put it back, Fran."

"That's the right thing to do. " Fran told me about the time he took some candy from Babs Kirk and that made me feel better.

"What am I going to do, Fran?" I felt terrible.

"Just what I did when I stole," he counseled.

"What's that?"

"You've got to rededicate your life."

Rededications were huge during revival services at Evergreen Baptist church. The altar was full of people every night as they stepped forward and took my dad's hand as he stood at the front of the church while people were singing invitation hymns such as, "Lord I'm coming Home."

The rededicators would whisper something in my dad's ear and then take a seat on the front row to he called up later in front of the congregation. No one actually told my dad what their sin was, but they would tell him they were "rededicating my life to the Lord."

After the invitation was over, which could last for an hour or more, my dad would instruct the congregation to be seated. One by one, he would bring the folks who had come forward that night for rededication and salvation and would ask them to stand and face the congregation. He would then tell the folks why that particular person had come forward.

"John's coming for salvation, Susan wants to be baptized, Mr. and Mrs. Bartlett want to move their membership from another church of like order and faith."

After he had asked the church to vote for baptism or church letter of those folks standing, and a motion had been made by one of the men and seconded by another, the church would raise their hands for approval and by the same sign for disapproval. No one in the history of the Evergreen Baptist church had ever voted against a new convert for baptism or anyone who was coming for church membership from another church by letter.

After this ceremonious rite was done to perfection and all were satisfied, the rededicators would be called to join the line of folks stretched out across the front of the church. He would take each repenter by the hand and tell the congregation that person was rededicating their life to the Lord.

"Special Prayer." This meant the person had done something really bad they needed to repent of.

"Did you rededicate after you stole from Babs Kirk?" I asked Fran.

I had seen Fran up front rededicating his life a couple of times, but I had no idea of what evils he may have been guilty.

"Sure did, Bud. Went right up there and did it."

I was the first one out of my seat on the very first night of revival. The Preacher had preached on "Go Thy Way and Steal No More." I debated whether or not I should so quickly step forward for rededication; especially, since the evangelist

preaching the revival meeting had just preached about stealing, but I did it anyway.

This was the first time I had been in front of the church for
rededication, so I was nervous not being as experienced as so
many others. My dad took me by the hand and asked me why
I was coming.

"I sinned, dad, and I'm sorry," I said, repenting with tears.
Fran had given me 101 instructions on how to properly repent,
and I knew if I didn't do this complete with tears of sorrow, he
would never forgive me much less God.

"I know you stole that money from Meg Frazier," my dad
whispered in my ear, "but I'm proud of you for putting it back."

My sister, Leah, and her friend, Darla Jenkins, were coming back from the outhouse the women used at the Frazier's
and caught a glimpse of me laying the coin back on the bureau. She immediately reported my sin to my dad, but it was
Darla who convinced him I was acting in good faith by returning the coin.

"Am I going to be whipped, dad?" I asked tearfully.

He never gave me an answer until my shirt was wet with
the tears of the folks who hugged me and cried and told me
how much they would pray for me.

"Naw, not this time," my dad said as I was walking out the
door after the service and after I had waited while April May
told my dad her life story.

CHAPTER TWENTY

It was a beautiful warm Sunday night; one of those nights where the Kentucky sky was as clear as could be, and you could see millions of stars so bright it seemed you could reach out and touch them.

I was standing in the church parking lot with my dad and staring up at the sky. He pointed out the Little and Big Dippers.

"Over there is the Seven Sisters," he said.

We saw a pickup heading over the hill below the church, and the driver was going very fast but slowed as he turned into the church drive and sped toward us.

"That's Bobby Gastner's truck," my dad commented. "I wonder what he's up to?"

Bobby Gastner slid to a stop near us and shouted out his window.

"Preacher, my dad is dying, and he is calling for you. Can you come to the house?"

"I didn't know he was sick," my dad answered. "He was just here in church tonight."

"He went down on the floor about an hour ago, and all he can do is whisper, but he said to get you."

It was about 9:00 PM when my dad arrived at the Gastner home. Simon Gastner was a good man. He was very sentimental and often you would see him wipe his eyes with his big handkerchief while my dad expounded the meaning of the Cross of Jesus Christ from the pulpit. He would always tell him at the door, his eyes still dripping tears, "I get all choked up," he explained, "every time I hear about the Blessed Lord's death."

Mr. Gastner had never been sick a day in his life, but this night, the front yard of his little house by the road was full of people, all of who were his kids and grandkids. A couple of neighbors heard Simon Gastner's coon dog braying and that could mean only one thing.

A coon dog was as close to his master as his children, and my dad used to explain that sometimes the coon dogs the tobacco farmers owned were more loyal and more loved by the coon hunters than their own kin. The dogs were faithful, and many nights they would spend together in quiet solitude. You could see farmers in the evenings rocking on their front porches with their arms over their coon dog's necks as they rested before a hunt.

I knew coon dogs, but I didn't own one. I had even been hunting with Fran and Simon Gastner. He had invited us out to his farm on several occasions, and we enjoyed following him and his dog out to the isolated ridges where the coons were known to be.

We sat on the ridge one night, and Mr. Gastner let the dog run.

"Hear that sweet music?" He commented with his soft

sentimental voice about the braying of his dog. "The sweetest music this side of heaven."

I strained my ears every time we went coon hunting, and I was disappointed in myself for not being able to appreciate the "music" of a coon dog barking. It was a fact that most of the coon hunters weren't interested in the raccoons; they were interested in sitting for hours and listening to the dogs bray; their horn like barks echoing for miles in the hills. Mr. Gastner would build a fire and then pull some "sweet taters" from his pocket. "Nothin like roasted sweet taters on a coon hunt," he would say.

The dogs rarely ever caught a coon, and coons could be dangerous when cornered by a dog before they could run up a tree. Many a coon dog had been severely maimed or killed after a fight with a raccoon. The critters were vicious. If the hunter was looking for a coon and found the dog had treed one; the dog jumping four or five feet in the air trying to get up the tree, the hunter would shoot the coon and bring it down, but only for eating.

Yes, I have sat at a table of coon, and the meat when prepared correctly tastes like roast beef. However, most of the coon hunters when they found their dogs reined them in, cooled them down and left the coon safe in the tree.

My dad walked into the front room of the Gastner house and found Mr. Gastner lying on a bed. His family was gathered around him. His dog lay isolated in the front yard and brayed a long, lonesome howl that was eerie as anything you have ever heard. Neighbors and more family soon arrived as the word spread by the gossips on the phones that Mr. Gastner was going to die.

The children, a couple who were in their fifties, and their wives were wailing around the head of Mr. Gastner. "Oh, daddy, please don't die, daddy please don't die." Soon, there was a chorus of wailing that drowned out the dog.

"Mr. Gastner, can you hear me?" My dad asked with his mouth close to the dying man's ear.

Simon Gastner nodded his head that he could hear.

"Are you sure that you have trusted the Lord Jesus as your Savior?"

He nodded his head again in agreement that he knew his Master and was ready to meet Him in the air. The children let out a simultaneous chorus of wailing that would send chills up and down the spine. They bathed themselves in tears and hugged each neighbor as he or she would come through the front door.

Around midnight, I was awakened by a car pulling into the front yard of our house. I stirred and then fell back to sleep. *Mr. Gastner wasn't dying,* I thought, and this is my dad coming back from another false alarm that happened on so many nights. This angered me because it seemed that my dad was constantly being called out in the middle of the night to tend to the sure death of one the church members of Evergreen Baptist Church or one of their unredeemed family members or friends. More times than not these were false alarms, and the sick one was miraculously well by the time my dad arrived with his Bible in hand.

"Sonny, get up!" My dad cried as he shook me. "There's something out here you have to see."

"What?" I asked curiously wondering what could be so important as to wake me in the middle of the night.

"Look at that," he exclaimed as he pointed to the northern sky.

The far sky was turning colors on the horizon, and the night was as bright as if the sun had arisen. The lights danced across the sky in rhythmic time changing to every color of the rainbow. It was the strangest but most beautiful event I have ever seen. It was as if God Himself was taking a paintbrush and moving it across the horizon with deliberate strokes. I knew that many farmers would be out of their houses after being called and told that this was the Second Coming of the Lord Jesus Christ.

"The Northern Lights," my dad said as he pointed to the brilliant, colors,

"Aurora Borealis."

"I wonder if Fran knows about the Northern Lights?" I said aloud not daring to try to pronounce the other name my dad called them.

"I don't know," my dad answered after he yelled for my mother to get up and come out. She didn't seem too interested although she had never seen this event in her life. We lived in the south, and it is far away from the North Pole and the ice cap. None of us knew how rare an event this was to see this light show so far away as Kentucky. For this reason, many of the farmers feared the end of the world was near.

"I have to get back to the Gastner's house," my dad said.

"What for?" I was sure the crisis was over.

"Simon's dying. Hop in the car and come with me."

I felt terrible that I thought this was a hoax and Simon wasn't dying.

We had to pass Fran's house on the way, and we saw Fran and Abe standing in the front yard and looking at the sky. I wondered, *Do only men enjoy these sorts of things?*

My dad drove slowly around People's Corner, and as he did, he yelled at Fran.

"Fran, you want to come with me and Sonny?"

"Sure," he said immediately and climbed in the back seat of my dad's Edsel.

Floyd was already there with his hearse when we pulled into the lane and parked with one wheel hanging over the ditch.

"He's going fast," Floyd told my dad.

"Where's Doc Sinclair? Shouldn't he be here before an undertaker? How soon?"

"A few minutes," Floyd answered quietly.

Fran and I stood in the front yard. We could hear the crying and weeping going on inside as the kids screamed out to God to please save their daddy's life. Mr. Gastner's coon dog was lying by itself next to a fence that separated the yard from a cornfield. It never made a sound.

Suddenly, the dog's ears perked up on its long head. It came to its haunches and raised its mouth toward the light show that was now fading very quickly. The Northern Lights turned off as if God flipped a switch and were gone. The dog let out a howl that sent my spine tingling, and then he brayed. This was a different howl than I had ever heard from any dog, and inside, it grew very quiet. Simon Gastner was gone. I wondered if at that moment Simon's old dog howled, did he somehow see his master winging his way toward heaven?

"Simon Gastner went to be with the Lord," my dad said as he stood over the casket in the Evergreen Baptist church.

Mr. Gastner's dad, "old man Gastner" as we knew him and was at least a hundred years old, had just finished singing "I'll Be A Friend To Jesus." He sang the song without music, slow and deliberate making sure all the mourners gathered in the Evergreen Baptist church for his son's funeral could hear each melodious note. He sucked air after each word or two just like Preacher Roundtree prayed, but the very old man could still carry a tune.

"Simon Gastner's dog, Brown, saw the spirit of his master rise to the heavens. Simon Gastner is now walking the streets of gold with his Savior. Amen."

My dad concluded his hour-long message, prepared the congregation for the following graveside devotion, and answered my question about Simon Gastner's dog.

Doc Sinclair, who was very old, determined that Simon Gastner had died of "Congestive Heart Failure" although it was known that autopsies were only conducted in the big cities. When the Doc was challenged on this he said, "I've been taking care of Simon Gastner since he was a baby. I know what he died from."

For months, the lonely bray of the coon dog, Brown, rang in my ears. When I asked about the "howl" I was told it was the "death howl" and every coon dog who'd been around for a few years and loved his master knew the exact moment the man gave up the ghost, and they had heard the "death howl" many times through the years.

I was saddened by all this. I would miss Simon Gastner; I would miss coon hunting with him and old Brown. The good and faithful coon dog died within two weeks of Mr. Gastner's passing. Brown died of starvation and grief.

CHAPTER TWENTY-ONE

One of the rare occasions that Fran did not go with our family for Sunday dinner happened in the fall of my thirteenth year. We were eating that day with the O'Conner family and crowded around the large table. Frank O'Conner required that every kid of his large brood be present at the table for every meal. After we had said Grace and eaten, Shane O'Conner and I decided that we would head for the woods and find the waterfall where Fran and I had jumped in order to save ourselves from being killed by Evel Martin or Curt Kirk.

We sat on the ridge above the falls, and I related the entire story of our free fall jump into the water below and how we had escaped sure death. Shane was fascinated by all this adventure, listened to every word, hanging on it just as we did when Mrs. Brewer read a story for us from a great classic over at Broughtontown School.

The fall of the year brought dry weather to Kentucky, and

the woods were dry and brittle. The day before, a storm blew in briefly that contained lightning which had struck somewhere in the forest and ignited these decaying leaves. The woods were burning. Almost every year, the dead leaves the trees shed from their summer canopy would burn somewhere in Lincoln County. Most of the time, the fires were caused by lightning bolts igniting a tree that immediately burst into a fury of fiery flames. Sometimes, the farmers claimed the fires were deliberately set since fires would start, and the sky was clear. There were no known arsonists in that neck of the country, but there were boys and men mean enough to start fires in order to get revenge on a family they may have been feuding for over a century.

Shane and I were on the safe side from the burning flames engulfing the trees across the gorge from where we sat. We could smell the burning barks of trees, and we watched the flames jump from tree to tree and leap high to the sky. The wind was blowing down the valley away from our position, and Shane said that when the fire reached the valley floor, it would burn itself out.

Fran told me one time that you should never try and walk in the woods that had been burned because even though there were no visible flames, you had to be careful of "ground fire." The ground would smolder underneath the thick layers of leaves that had been there piling up for centuries, and while you were walking along, suddenly the flames could leap from their hiding places and burn you to a crisp. He told me that before our family moved to Chapel Gap, old man Oaks was walking in the woods behind his house, and ground fire leaped up and burned him dead. They found his body charred and unrecognizable except for his pocket watch that had somehow survived. His son, Jesse Oaks, still carried the watch, and the burn marks could still be seen as a result of the scorching heat.

Shane and I avoided the charred woods, waded in the clear pool below the falls for a few minutes, and headed back to the house.

Frank O'Conner had a mean Black Angus bull that he had not as yet dehorned.

The bull was afraid of the large Frank O'Conner but of no one else.

"We've got to avoid the bull," Shane said as we crossed the field back to the house. We could have avoided this field if the woods weren't smoldering, and we didn't want to risk "ground fire."

"I didn't see the bull on the way over here," I said.

"He was in the other pasture, but this time of day my dad keeps him away from the cows because of milking time."

As we stepped out of the woods and crossed the barbed wire fence that kept the cows from wandering into the woods and becoming lost, I snagged my arm on one of the barbs causing it to bleed. I paid no mind because that happened all the time. We crossed barbed wire fences dozens of times a day.

Shane and I had picked up tobacco sticks, and we were sparring with the sticks like a sword fight. I kept nervously watching to make sure the bull was nowhere around me and looking for an escape route in case it came.

We were in the middle of the field, and we could see the silo rising into the air like a tower in New York City that stood by Frank O'Conner's barn.

We felt a rumble beneath our feet like the earthquakes I heard about in California. The ground shook, and then with horror, we saw the big black two ton bull charging across the field. It was a black blur as it gained speed and quickly came toward us. We dropped our sticks and took off running as fast as we could.

Shane and I were both fast runners, but I was faster than Shane.

"Don't look back," he yelled, "you'll lose time."

I couldn't help it. There was a monster after me for crying out loud, so I glanced back to see what my fate was going to be. There was no way we were going to make it to the fence according to my calculations; the bull was almost on top of us, and we still had a hundred yards to go. Shane put on a burst of speed, eking out every ounce of energy he had left in his body. I caught up and passed him. I had never run this fast in my life.

I reached the wire fence before Shane, and as I did, I jumped.

My jumping ability was something I really never tested although the boys playing basketball with me at school gave me the reputation for being the highest jumper in the eighth grade. It was said that I could jump as high as my head, and I was about to find out. That leap would later earn me some blue ribbons while part of the track and field team at Crab Orchard High School. Mr. Phillips, our gym teacher at Broughtontown, had taught us boys how to high jump. I found out that I could jump higher than my head although I never thought that jumping was very important for a farm boy. Not this time. The jump I made that day was the leap of my life and would have won a gold medal. I reached the fence, which was a cyclone fence unlike barbed wire. The fence surrounded the tobacco field; it had a mesh texture which was made of wire fashioned with six inch holes the length and breadth of the fence. The fence stood much higher than my head, so I quickly looked for another way out. I knew I couldn't go through the fence, but maybe there was a hole in it close by that I could crawl through. Too late; I had to do something, so as I approached the barrier of impossibility, I leaped. I instinctively put my body in the position of a "roll" as I had been taught by Mr. Phillips.

I rolled over the top and made it to the ground on the other side, and I saw Shane just as I landed. He didn't make it. The bull had caught up with him while he was trying to force his way through a six-inch hole. Shane's jacket hanged on the fence, but he pulled his arms out leaving the coat hanging in the wire. He ran along the fencerow trying desperately to find a way over. I ran along with him on the other side trying to grab his hand and somehow bring his body over the fence. The fence was so high that we couldn't connect.

Shane thought he could fake the bull and stopped dead in his tracks. This maneuver did cause the bull to hesitate, but it was uncanny how agile this mountain of flesh could be. The bull slid past him and fainted out of position on the other side of Shane, and Shane ran. Shane ran toward the other corner of the field where there was a round wooden cross tie that held the corners of the fence securely together. If he could make it there, he could spring off the brace and vault himself over the fence.

I now ran the opposite direction and to keep up with Shane, who was running out of breath. I yelled at him, encouraging him to keep running, but he breathed hard and slowed down. He panted hard taking deep rasping gasps of air into his lungs. Less than fifty feet to go, and the bull caught up with him. Its long horns beamed in the sunlight sending off a reflection like a diamond in a jeweler's lamp. The bull caught Shane in his side and tossed him in the air like a rag doll. He must have gone at least ten feet in the air and was screaming at the top of his lungs as he landed on the hard ground.

Shane bounced once, and the bull deftly stuck his horn underneath him and tossed him again. This time Shane went over the bull's back, and I thought that if the toss didn't kill him, the fall to the ground would. I was absolutely as helpless as when those bees attacked me in the creek. I watched in horror as the bull was now playing with Shane on the ground. It teased him with its horns rolling him over and over as Shane tried to scrunch up into a ball and protect himself.

The bull soon tired of his game, snorted twice, pawed the ground, and rammed his left horn into Shane's side. The puncture was deep and then it tossed Shane into the air once again. As he flew upward, I gasped, "Oh, my God!"

Shane had been ripped from below his heart all the way to his groin. Some of his entrails were coming out, and the blood shot all over the bull's face nearly blinding its eyes. I could think of nothing to do, so I took off running as hard as I could, leaping two more fences as I ran to the house.

The folks were sitting at the table eating afternoon desserts as was their custom being too full from the huge dinner we had eaten earlier. My dad saw my face.

"What's wrong?" He asked.

I couldn't get the words out, so I opened my mouth trying to speak, but nothing came out except a tiny bit of air as I tried to form my words. I was in a state of shock, but finally I was able to mouth the words silently, "Shane, bull."

Frank O'Conner and my dad ran out of the house in the direction of my pointed finger. Several of the O'Conner boys ran with us.

The bull was standing over Shane as we approached him lying on his back. Soon, my mom and Alice O'Conner, Shane's mother, reached the scene. Frank came toward the bull, and it took off running as fast as he had chased us across the field. The bull galloped wildly, lowering its head as it ran.

Alice kneeled beside Shane who was unconscious, and fortunately his intestines were not severed. She gently took the slimy, wet entrails in her hands and carefully laid them back into the gaping, bloody wound.

"He's lost a lot of blood," she said sorrowfully.

Shane was still breathing, and you could see the bottom of his right lung as it flexed with each breath of air. Steve O'Conner had opened all the gates and had the pickup idling in the field where Shane lay.

"Pick him up gently and slowly," my dad instructed. "Keep his body stiff."

The boys picked up Shane and laid him in the bed of the pickup. Alice climbed in and wiped the blood with her apron which was so soaked that it didn't seem another drop could penetrate the cloth.

Frank and my dad were in the front seat; Frank was driving. He slowly drove over the rough creek rock road until he could reach the smoother gravel on Chapel Gap Road. Frank knew that if he did not move carefully and jarred Shane too much, he would have no chance of survival.

As we passed Daphni and Garrard Anderson's house, my dad yelled at Daphni.

"Call Doc Sinclair and tell him to meet us at Floyd's. Hurry!"

We made our way toward Crab Orchard and some of the women who had intercepted the phone call from Daphni Anderson to Doc Sinclair were standing in their yards yelling, "What happened?"

A familiar place was this basement of the funeral home where the gurneys were. I saw a dead body lying on one of the gurneys, uncovered, and sliced open as Floyd was doing an examination. Homer Shanks had shot some stranger he caught trying to rob the Jameson Drugstore, and Floyd was trying to find the bullet.

"He won't make it," Floyd said.

He always said this every time there was an injured body lying on his gurney. My dad glared at him, and Floyd shrank back as if he would be disappointed that Shane wouldn't die and rob him of the funeral money.

Doc Sinclair had delivered Shane at birth as he had all the O'Conner children born in their farmhouse. He also had looked after the bull Frank owned.

"You better get rid of that thing before it kills somebody," Doc told Frank once when the bull had pink eye. The bull tried to gore Doc Sinclair and would have if Frank weren't nearby. Now, that warning was fresh in his mind again, but he didn't say anything to Frank during this crisis.

After some quick and temporary surgery by the Doc, they moved Shane down to the hospital in Stanford. We followed Floyd's hearse as he poked along the paved highway leading to the town. This made my dad angry. "What's he thinking?" My dad complained. "He's driving like he's on the way to the cemetery to bury the boy."

Doc Sinclair never went to the hospital in Stanford. "Those baby faced so called doctors over there think they know everything." He griped. "I've treated more patients than they will the rest of their lives if they do it every day." And he had.

Doe Sinclair got burned one time when he gave some doctor kid advice on how to suture after an appendectomy. The young doctor didn't listen, and the stitches broke loose while the guy was coon hunting one night, and he bled to death. From that time on, he knew they wouldn't listen because they thought he was too old to know anything, his methods were out of date, and he was a Veterinarian.

After several hours of surgery, the doctor operating on Shane came to the waiting room.

"Shane will make it," he said, "he's one lucky boy."

Doc Sinclair got out of Sheriff Crane's police pickup. The Doc had called the Sheriff and told him they needed to pay Frank O'Conner a visit. He and the Sheriff walked slowly across the barnyard where they saw Frank and his boys loading a manure spreader.

"Howdy Sheriff, Doc," Frank greeted cordially. "What brings you out here in the middle of the day?"

"We need to talk," the Sheriff said. "Is there somewhere we could be alone?"

Frank knew that if Doc Sinclair was with the Sheriff, this call wasn't casual visit.

"Frank, you need to get rid of that bull," the Sheriff said as Doc Sinclair nodded his head in agreement, "Shane's lucky to be alive, and somebody else, perhaps one of your girls or boys, or yourself will get killed."

The Sheriff was going to hand Frank a court order signed by the Judge in Stanford, which instructed Frank to rid the farm of the evil and dangerous bull. Before he could do that, he noticed some horns, white with bloodstains and moist with the blood lying beside the corncrib.

"Dehorning the bull ain't enough, Frank," The Sheriff said while handing Frank the court order.

"The bull's dead," Frank answered.

The bull was dead. Frank had waited all night in the hospital, and the next morning when he was reassured that Shane was going to survive, he returned to his farm to attend the milk cows and help his boys shuck corn to feed the chickens. This was usually Alice's job but there was no way he could pry her away from the hospital.

Frank went to the field where Shane was almost killed and herded the bull to the barn. He drove the bull in backwards into a stall, which is a very difficult thing to do to a cow or a bull. He then took a heavy oak milking stool and beat the bull between the eyes, swinging his large, strong arms violently into the bull's face until the bull's eyes crossed, and its tongue eased out of its mouth, and the vile creature fell over dead.

CHAPTER TWENTY-TWO

Where's my son?" My dad paused in the middle of his sermon when he noticed that Fran and I weren't sitting in our normal seats in the congregation.

The church was as quiet as the gravestones in the cemetery. This had happened before, so everyone held their breaths. Earlier that year, my dad thundered from the pulpit on the sins of smoking and chewing tobacco. "Your body is the temple of the Holy Spirit," he preached.

It had always been hard for me to understand how the entire church budget including his salary, was supported by raising tobacco. He never mentioned in all the years the evils of "raising tobacco," but the use of the substance was strictly against God's law. I was missing this particular Sunday night as well. I don't know what I was thinking, but I needed a cigarette. I slipped out unnoticed except for everyone seated and listening to his message that turned his or her heads as I sneaked out the front door of the church.

My dad was engrossed in his own preaching. The congregation was as sleepy as they had been many times because of uninspiring sermons. Sometimes he labored in his preaching, but when he preached against moonshining, smoking, chewing, and the sin of women speaking out in church, the congregation was wide awake.

He stopped his preaching and asked, "Where's my son?" The entire group of listeners shrugged their shoulders as if on cue.

I was standing behind the church when this happened. I peed against the tombstone where Reuben Click's great grandfather was turning to dust deep beneath the cold sod.

I rolled a cigarette and was enjoying the smooth flavor as it passed into my young lungs. It was cool that night, and one of the things I enjoyed about smoking on a cold evening was the smoke mixed with the fog of my breath that passed from my lips like the smoke stack blowing out coal smoke at the electric company in Stanford. I took care with each exhale of smoke and watched it shoot into the air magnified ten times by the reflection of the light from the back room windows.

I had just taken a big draw and was ready to exhale. I saw a pant leg step around the corner. It was my dad who had come looking for me. I froze with horror, and the smoke was still in my lungs. I knew if I exhaled, he would know I was smoking, and it would be my death.

I hid my cigarette in my right hand behind my back and fanned away the smoke with my left. I had still not blown out the smoke. I didn't care.

"What're you doing?" My dad questioned.

I couldn't answer because the smoke was trying to get out through my mouth and nose. I had tightened up every passage and avenue from which smoke could pass through the dark chambers of my body to the freedom of space. All I could do was shake my head and shrug letting him know that I was up to nothing important. I pointed to the wet tombstone, but this was a mistake.

"If you had to use the bathroom, why didn't you go to the outhouse?" He asked as I was about to pass out from holding my breath. He knew exactly what he was doing. I shrugged again.

"You smoking?"

I shook my head violently as if the question had disappointed me, and fanned away at the smoke sliding around my body. He glanced at the smoke.

He always wore a suit and tie when he preached. He took off his jacket and hung it over the tombstone carefully so as to not touch the yellow liquid that dripped to the ground.

"Follow me," he commanded.

He went back toward the front of the church, and I threw away the cigarette that now burned my fingers. I flipped it with my forefinger and watched it fly sparks and all into the cemetery. I breathed a sigh of relief to get rid of it, and I took a breath of sweet lovely air. No smoke escaped, but I felt a little dizzy.

Step for step, I followed my dad to the front entrance of the church. He stopped near the front and took off his belt. I was in big trouble, and the sweat beaded on my forehead.

"You're going to get a whipping for two things," he lectured. "One is for smoking, and the second is for desecrating the grave of the deceased."

The church inside was quiet, and he had left the door wide open as all the saints of God were aware of this impending example of how to correct a wayward child was about to take place. "I am ashamed of you," he said to me. He had walked out of the church in the middle of his sermon to track me down. There was not a sound from the membership waiting inside.

He flogged me. He held my arm as he always did and wailed the whip with the other, striking securely and firmly on the buttocks and legs. I danced and screamed as if he was flogging me before Crucifixion. It stung, and I screamed some more.

"I won't do it again, dad," I yelled, "I repent of my sin, dad, I'll never do it again!"

After a few well-placed hits, he stopped abruptly and started threading his belt through the loops of his pants.

"Let that be a lesson," he said, "you've disappointed the Lord and all these good Christian brothers and sisters as well as me and your mother."

For my dad to say he was ashamed of me hurt me worse than the whipping. I was struck to the bottom core of my heart. It hurt worse than offending the Holy Spirit. I started to cry long after the whipping stopped hurting.

Every eye followed me as I walked down the center aisle on my way to the front row seats. My dad instructed me to sit on the front row while he finished his message. I glanced at Fran, and he put his head down and refused to look at me. Instead, he just shook his head because he refused to leave the church and go smoke with me. "I told you so," he mouthed silently.

I took my seat, and my face was as red as a beet that grew in the gardens. My face was hot with embarrassment, and all the people knew what I did because they could clearly hear his lecture before he beat me with the belt. He purposely raised his voice to his preaching volume while he preached to me about puffing and violating the rights of the dead.

I was the first one out of my seat as the congregation slowly sang "Careless Soul while will you linger wandering from the fold of God. Hear you not the Invitation Oh Prepare to Meet Thy God."

I couldn't take anymore, so I took my dad by the hand and

whispered in his ear that I was rededicating my life. Rededication fixed everything at Evergreen Baptist Church. They were instructed during the sermons to "forgive seventy times seven," and I think murder would have no place for judgment if the perpetrator of the crime rededicated his or her life during an invitation at Evergreen Baptist Church.

"What are you coming for, son?" He asked as if he didn't know.

"I'm rededicating my life to the Lord," I said, "and I think the Lord Jesus is calling me to preach the Gospel."

Man, did I come up with a good one there. I don't where that came from, but it was brilliant. My dad grabbed me and hugged and then kissed me on the cheek. The congregation gasped as no one had ever seen him affectionate at church, not even with my mother.

Others had followed my example having been emotionally disturbed by the outpouring of love my dad expressed with the kiss. I was the Prodigal Son returning home from wallowing with the hogs, and he had just killed the fatted calf, so they were going to rejoice with him.

My dad approached me as the last one in the line he had not spoken to and told the congregation to pray for the respective rededicator. He was making sure that the blessings he would share were at the climax of emotion. He had said many times in his messages, "I pray that my sons will follow in my footsteps and preach the gospel of Jesus Christ."

"Sonny is coming for rededication of his life to the Lord Jesus," he explained as he held me by the hand. "And, Hallelujah, Praise the Lord, he's surrendering his life to preach the Gospel!"

I heard several snickers coming from the youth section in the congregation and some dry coughs from the older members of the church. There were no decisions for baptism or the moving of church letters that night. All the decisions were for the rededication of lives.

As the crowd filed around the front hugging and shaking hands with the repenters, Janie Pat, with tears in her eyes, apologized to me.

"I'm sorry I called you a fart sucker," she cried.

"I'm sorry I called you a turd knocker," I replied, and we hugged.

This wasn't the only time I would stand in front of the church and repent of my sins.

My dad stared at the congregation sitting as silent as they could be. "Where is my son?" He asked.

Fran and I had slipped out from behind the standing congregation as they were singing the last hymn before the message, "An Old Account Was Settled Long Ago." We could still hear the accapella voices as we crossed the fence into Sterling Deaton's gourd patch.

Every farmer had a gourd patch. The funny shaped vegetable with the hard shell ripened in the fall of the year long after everything else had been picked, canned, and put up in the smoke houses for winter. After cleaning out the gourds, careful not to destroy them, they ate the delicious and tasty fruit they had taken from the insides. Many a delectable casserole was set on the tables of the homes in the Knobs made from the tasty gourds.

Gourds shells were preserved for many uses by drying them naturally. The gourds were popular as drinking dippers, and they virtually sat on every kitchen cabinet by a drinking pale in the homes of the farmers. Fran and I intended on stealing these gourds from Mr. Deaton and making dippers to sell after we had decorated them with various colors of paint. Some of the hardware stores in the towns sold these hand made crafts as water dippers.

Sterling Deaton was a widower. He was old and lived by himself in the ancient log house in the ravine by the church. He lived simply. He had no electricity, and when the church had installed its electric lights, he was given the chance to run a line down to his house, but the refused. He maintained that lanterns in his house worked just fine, weren't dangerous, and all these modern conveniences would ruin his relationship with the Lord.

Mr. Deaton had an old mule he used to plow his garden, but he was too old to raise tobacco by himself, so he "farmed out" his tobacco base and allowed another farmer to split the crop with him when it was sold at one of the tobacco auctions.

Sterling had two funny quirks. He had an interesting way to say "wonderful."

We kids thought it was funny when he told us about falling off his mule on the road to Babs Kirk's store. He had no car or truck, had never learned how to drive, so he rode his old mule everywhere he needed to travel, which wasn't very far or very often.

"I hit the gravel when that old mule bucked as Evel Martin driving at break neck speed scared my mule. "That boy is going to get somebody killed someday," he explained and then pulled up his sleeve and showed the wounds and scabs on his arm.

"It hurt wonderful," he said as the kids snickered.

We would make fun of him every time we saw him but not to his face. If one of the kids was hurt, he would say, "Did it hurt wonderful?" We would almost die laughing.

His other quirk was even stranger. A weird sound came out of his voice when he finished a sentence or answering a question. It was "eenk" on the end of his words. If you called him, he would answer "EENK" real loudly.

"I was working my mule, EENK, and ran over one of the

hardheaded rocks, EENK. It busted my plow, EENK, so I had to run up to Abe Job's and get it fixed, EENK."

Mr. Deaton wore the same clothes for years. I don't believe he ever washed them, and even in the summer, he had a coat on over his dirty overalls. My mom said one time that my dad shouldn't allow him in the church. She said, "He stinks, and you can hardly stand to sit in the church with him; especially on a hot day."

Some people thought he had a lot of money stashed in the house. This was a widespread rumor. "What's he doing with all those checks he gets from the government? He's certainly ain't spending them or his tobacco crop money." So the gossip went about Sterling Deaton. He was never bothered though because he slept with a loaded double-barreled shotgun, and his coon dog, a sure alarm in the face of danger.

The rumor had foundations and was proven several years after Fran and me left Chapel Gap. Sally and Junebug Barber were cleaning the church one day when Junebug spotted someone lying by one of the tombstones. It was Sterling Deaton dressed in his old clothes lying with a tobacco stick in his hand. Junebug would never touch a dead body or come too close, so he had the Preacher call Floyd's Funeral Home. When Floyd examined the body, he found one hundred dollar bills stuffed inside the lining of Mr. Deaton's jacket that totaled thousands of dollars. It was no wonder he looked fat. Later, when Sheriff Crane searched his house, he found many thousands of dollars in various places. Mr. Deaton had stuffed behind wallpaper made of newspaper, in little nooks and crannies of the logs, and in tin cans found in the smoke house. For years, the people who would visit his farm for one reason or another would make a trip through his house trying to find the money everyone knew was still missing.

Mr. Deaton had no heirs. Many of the gravesites in the

cemetery were unknown to the people of Chapel Gap, or they had forgotten them because no formal record was kept, or had been lost of the folks buried in the ground surrounding the Evergreen Baptist Church.

The best Sheriff Crane and Floyd could determine was that Sterling Deaton had crawled from his house to the gravesite where he was found, dead. His arm was holding onto an unmarked tombstone. That marker had been there for years, and since it was estimated that Sterling was in his late nineties, perhaps no one could remember anyone he had been kin to. The speculation was, and could be true, that Mr. Deaton died that day in the hot sun clinging to the grave of his sweetheart.

The congregation quit singing, and my dad was into his sermon. We could hear him expounding his message, raising his voice to make points, and lowering it when he had driven the message home. Fran and I were over the fence and into the gourd patch.

The sky was overcast that night, and the moon was just a sliver hiding somewhere behind the dense clouds making it a perfect night to steal gourds.

We knew the coon dog would bark, and the mule in the paddock next to the gourd patch would soon give us away, so we had to work fast. We got down on our hands and knees and crawled inch by inch while each of us cut a gourd to be picked up on our way out and probably running for our lives.

We heard the dog barking in the house, but we figured that we had plenty of time. The mule in the paddock never made a sound, and perhaps it knew the dog had everything under control.

Fran cut a gourd vine, and we heard: "I HEAR YOU BOYS, EENK! YOU'RE STEALING MY GOURDS, EENK!"

Mr. Deaton made his way up the row of gourds, and we had another problem.

My dad was just about through preaching, and we would have to be up there in time to slip between the seats during the invitation song, "My Faith Looks Up To Thee."

Our real problems began when we could see the dark shadow of the man moving. In his hands, he had a pitchfork. The three-pronged monster was as sharp as a needle. The faint light from the windows of the church shone off the steel tines as Mr. Deaton jabbed the pitchfork in the ground with all his strength as he moved up the rows. He was going to kill us!

I heard Fran rolling away from him, and the gourd vines pricking his skin as he turned. I had no way to go.

"DAMN YOU BOYS, EENK!" He screamed in his shrill voice pitched higher than a comb raked over a mirror as he stuck the fork in another vine of gourds.

Mr. Deaton's foot was no more than just that, a foot away from my head. I shivered as he came down with a mighty blow that stuck clean through the gourd that I was lying beside. The gourd burst open, and Mr. Deaton had a slight hesitation as the fork stuck into the ground beneath the gourd he had just killed. I just had enough time to jump and run, and as I did, he flung the fork at me, barely missing my head.

I jumped the fence using my hands as a spring to catapult me over as Fran had done before me. As I ran full blast through the cemetery, Sterling cussed me from behind; I saw Fran tossing four gourds in the back of Reuben Click's pickup.

Thank God for the singing because the din drowned out the noise we were making and Sterling Deaton's screaming. We slipped into the church unnoticed except by Jane Pat who looked at me and mouthed the words, "fart sucker;" even though, she promised never to call me that again.

People were happy on the way out of the church, hugging one another and fellowshipping as brothers and sisters in Christ. The last member shook my dad's hand as we heard

Reuben Click yelling that someone had put gourds in the back of his pickup. *Now why did he have to go and do that,* I thought.

"Them's my gourds, EENK," Sterling Deaton said as he huffed and puffed his way to the truck.

"How so?" Reuben asked.

"How so, EENK? They were just stolen, EENK, from my gourd patch, EENK!"

"Who?" Reuben asked.

"The Preacher's boy and that Job kid, EENK."

"They were in church," one of our buddies interrupted, "they didn't steal no gourds."

Oh crap! I thought as I saw Jane Pat standing by the truck. *She's going to tell them she saw me and Fran sneaking back into the church,* but she didn't. She stood there and glanced over at me and Fran trying to find our way out of there, quick.

"All right, all right, what's all the fuss?" My dad asked as he saw the commotion.

"Them boys, EENK, stole my gourds, EENK."

"Them boys who?" My dad questioned.

"Fran Job and Sonny Smith, EENK. That's who, EENK!"

This was the really weird part. Sterling Deaton was in church that night as he always was being a good Christian and all; even though, he cussed like a drunken sailor. Fran and I had felt safe because Sterling wasn't home. He was in church.

Sterling Deaton peered over his ancient specs and caught a glimpse of Fran and me sneaking out. Faking the need to go to the outhouse, he followed us. So that he couldn't be seen, he crossed over the fence down by the Ottenheim Road that ran in front of the church and then doubled back over the far side of the patch where we couldn't see him in the dark and grabbed a pitchfork.

As if he were in court, my dad listened as Mr. Deaton related all this important information. People were standing around their cars and trucks because there was no way they were going home. Stealing was bad.

Dad called Fran over to the pickup, and for some reason, he left me where I was. I was happy about this although I knew the Judgment of God Himself would come later in the form of a switch that would rip the flesh off my back and legs.

"What about this, Fran?" My dad asked as every ear was tuned in. "Are these Bro. Deaton's gourds?"

We were caught, and we knew it. Nobody was going to believe two thirteen-year-old boys over the word of a man like Sterling Deaton. He was baptized in the Evergreen Baptist Church when he was a boy and was the oldest living member of the church some eighty-two years. His great grandfather helped build the church with his own hands before the Civil War.

Fran had this way about him when he was thinking; especially, if he was in trouble. He shifted back and forth between one foot and then the other and crossed his hands behind him. He then would put his left hand in his rear pocket and then reverse the hands and the pockets. He repeated this movement several times.

"Weren't like stealing," Fran mused, "more like borrowing." Man was he good.

"How so?" My dad asked concerning this logic.

"Elijah told the widow to borrow the pots and go sell oil he would fill the pots with." That's all Fran knew about the Bible story, but it was brilliant thinking, and it was from the Bible.

My dad looked into Fran's green eyes, or maybe they were hazel, but they were unique to the color of brown the redheads had or the blue of the blonds.

Reuben Click, the long ago spoiled son of Mason Click, had married Jenny Click. It was not uncommon for the Knob folks to marry cousins, so Jenny's name was Click before she married Reuben.

"Them boys needs a good whippin," Reuben cried as his bright red hair stood on end. "Teach them a lesson, and they should be disciplined from the church." He offered this advice although he had never been whipped in his life, nor had one of his kids no matter what they had done, including shoving their dad over a hill while he sat in the outhouse.

I caught a glimpse of Mandy and June Job walking down the church lane toward home. Mandy was shaking her head.

"Take your gourds," my dad told Sterling Deaton. He knew Mr. Deaton wasn't lying so now he had to turn his attention to Fran and me.

"So, Fran, you were borrowing the gourds. Is that right? What did you intend to do with them?"

"Well, me and Bud here can't pick gourds at my house because they ain't ripe yet. We have this school project due next week, and we decided to do some artwork made of gourds, but we don't have none. Me and Bud are making real good grades and don't want to fail."

He told the truth about the school project due the next week, but this was the first time that I heard our project was going to be made with gourds. Fran could think faster than a fox running from hounds.

"That's all good, Fran, but stealing is stealing no matter what the reason," my dad explained.

"How about killing?" Fran asked.

"What do you mean?"

"Mr. Deaton was going to kill us with a pitch fork. He missed Bud's head by inches, or he would be lying over there in that gourd patch deader than dead. Thou shalt not kill is one of the Ten Commandments, too."

"Hmmm," my dad reasoned as the farmers and their

daughters, one of whom was secretly sweet on Fran, leaned in to hear the outcome of this masterpiece being constructed by one of Chapel Gap's own geniuses.

My dad was almost laughing although he didn't want the folks to think he was light on discipline.

"Tell you what," he said, "I think murder kind of offsets stealing, and both parties are guilty of breaking God's laws, you and Sonny for stealing and Bro. Deaton for committing murder in his heart."

This was beautiful, and even old redheaded Reuben Click and his cousin wife, Jenny, nodded their heads in agreement with this Solomon like wisdom.

I thought I would never steal again after that half-dollar incident at the cottage prayer meeting, and we had justified ourselves by agreeing that when we picked the gourds out of Abe Job's garden, we would replace each one that we took from Mr. Deaton.

Fran and I pondered this situation in our minds and discussed it on the school ground at Broughtontown all that week. Fran felt it was absolutely necessary for everyone concerned that we rededicate our lives, so the next Sunday night, we stepped out together as the old women saw us walking the aisle side by side, began to weep.

CHAPTER TWENTY-THREE

R
ay Hampton was a quiet kid who lived on the Ottenheim Road. He was a smart guy; didn't have much to do with anyone but Fran and me. His dad bought him a 1941 Chevy Coupe even though he was only fourteen years old. Ray was cruising by himself one day, and he stopped by the Lord house. Our good friend and pal, Ray Lord, was finishing his chores on the hot Saturday afternoon.

"Hey Ray" Ray Hampton called. "Let's take a run over to Chestnut Ridge."

"I don't think my dad will let me," Ray Lord replied.

Mr. James Lord was a Godly man, and a deacon in the Evergreen Baptist Church. He and my dad were close friends, and Bro. Lord supported anything my dad wanted to do in the church because he trusted him. He emulated my dad in many things. There was the brief time my dad was influenced by some of the legalists teaching in a Baptist college in Lexington where he had graduated. The influence consisted in a belief that Christmas was a pagan holiday started by the Catholics, and good Bible believing Christians should have nothing to do with it. Gone were the Christmas trees, decorations of the house, and basically the entire Christmas celebration. This was a sad time because most of the members of the Evergreen Baptist Church didn't buy presents for Christmas; a time every kid looks forward to, Catholic holiday or not.

It was widely known that some of the members of the church were secretly celebrating Christmas that year, and the invitations that normally came from the membership for our family to come to Sunday dinner ceased because they were ashamed that the preacher would find a Christmas tree in their front living rooms.

Around Christmas time, our houses seemed like a morgue. On Christmas Day, my dad preached on some Bible subject completely foreign and unrelated to the normal Christmas story other ministers were telling from their pulpits around the nation and world. He did give us kids presents, though. We each got one gift a few days after the Christmas season was over. My sister, Leah, would sneak into the pantry and take the Christmas candy my grandmother Cassell would send to us for Christmas, but we were not allowed to have until after Christmas. My Mom tried to sneak in a fake tree, but my dad found it and destroyed the tree and removed all temptation from the house. Mr. Lord bought nothing for his kids that year in order to preserve the sanctity of not being pagan.

I hated this even though I wasn't thinking about marriage and kids. I thought, "If I ever get my own children, I will never stop celebrating Christmas."

My dad finally repented of this belief and stopped preaching against the pagan holiday. His change of heart came one day when he received a letter from Mrs. Ralston, my eighth grade teacher.

"What did you get for Christmas, Fran?" Mrs. Ralston asked as she was asking the kids in the class to share with others the joy of Christmas celebration and the receiving and giving of gifts.

"Nothin," Fran replied, and she looked at him as though puzzled by this curt answer. Her first thought was that the Job family was too poor.

"How about you?" She asked Jane Pat.

"Nothin," she said.

"Did you get something for Christmas?" She directed this question to Darla Jenkins sitting in the back of the room.

"No," Darla replied.

Two thirds of the kids sitting in the eighth grade class at Broughtontown School attended the Evergreen Baptist Church, and she made her way with the question from seat to seat, and there was no difference in the replies. I dreaded her asking me because I was ashamed of my dad.

"Sonny, did you get something for Christmas?"

I hung my head in shame and answered, "nothing."

Buster Kirk was the only kid in the class besides three or four others that admitted getting anything for Christmas. Each of those kids quietly named one or two things they received from their parents and were careful to not upset the rest of us although we all knew they got much more than they claimed. Some of them were wearing those gifts to school that day. Dennis Wiggington wouldn't play with his new softball glove at our games in the schoolyard because he was so sensitive.

"I got a new bow and arrow, a new baseball glove, lots of clothes, and a brand new pair of black loafers, the kind with the buckle." Buster Kirk blurted out and volunteered even though Mrs. Ralston skipped asking him about Christmas. Loretta Kirk, Buster's mother with the funny eyes, wouldn't buy the "bunk" of no Christmas and refused getting under conviction about it. She had showered her children with gifts in spite of what the Preacher preached.

As I left the classroom after the school bell, Mr. Lassiter, the Principal, was walking up the hallway ringing a bell announcing that school was over for the day.

"Come here, Sonny," my teacher motioned. "I want to talk with you."

"Why are all these kids from Evergreen Baptist Church telling me they got nothing for Christmas? This has never happened before," she commented deliberately.

"My dad don't believe in Christmas," I was embarrassed to say.

"What! Your dad doesn't believe in Christmas?"

"He preached against it all year."

"Now wait a minute," she demanded, "the church families had no trees, cards, or presents?"

"No, Maam. They didn't want to sin against the Lord God Almighty."

My dad opened the letter from Mrs. Ralston. She wisely did not oppose our beliefs to us kids because she loved her job. Evergreen Baptist Church had so many kids attending the school, and Bro. Lord and Nathan Smith were members of the school board, so she took up her issues privately with my dad.

Dear Pastor Smith,

It has come to my attention that the members of Evergreen Baptist Church no longer believe in Christmas. I found this out this afternoon by asking each of the children to tell the class what they received for Christmas. All the teachers at Broughtontown School customarily do this.

I was shocked to learn that each of your young members

got nothing for Christmas. Sonny was especially embarrassed as I asked him privately what was going on.

I'm not a Catholic, Pastor Smith, but I am a Christian having been brought up in the Methodist Church over in Brodhead. I attend every Sunday. I have never heard of a Christian not celebrating Christmas except the Jehovah's Witnesses. Their cult doesn't do a lot of things like salute the American Flag, either.

So what if Christmas is a Catholic holiday? Everything the Catholics do isn't wrong, is it? Don't you believe that there should be a time that the whole world honors the Lord Jesus? The whole story of his birth and the giving of gifts is right there in the Holy Scripture, isn't it?

Pastor Smith, even wars cease in honor of our Savior on Christmas Day. Think about that. Would you rather join the fellowship of those that stop killing each other and pause for a reflection of good will rather than line your whole congregation with the Jehovah Witnesses, who have pledged their non-belief in Jesus Christ as the only begotten Son of God and One and the same with God? What about the Atheists and Agnostics? You have aligned yourself with cults and non-believers in God, and I am quite disappointed that you can't reason better than this.

Sincerely,

Mrs. Ralston

This letter had a huge impact on my dad. He rarely ever admitted that the teachers of his old college were wrong, and then he thought: *Dr. Clarence Walker celebrates Christmas in the Ashland Avenue Baptist Church.* Doctor Walker was a great man, and a huge influence in the Southern Baptist Convention, but when the great split came in the Convention, he started his own college. He kept the college separate from the church.

My dad wrestled with his decision. If he celebrated Christmas, then he would offend the Brian Station Baptist Church, the second oldest church in Kentucky, and the preacher there who had started all this nonsense in the first place.

It was the "Jehovah Witness" part of the letter that got him the most. The cult had infiltrated Lincoln County and had established a congregation near Brodhead. Cathy Kirk, Gib Kirk's daughter-in-law from his previous marriage to Babs Kirk, left the Evergreen Baptist Church and threw herself in with the Jehovah's Witnesses. When that happened, it sent my dad on a tirade of preaching to keep others from slipping in the "dangerous den of poisonous snakes" as he called them.

One day a Jehovah's Witness called on him as he stood in the Babs Kirk Store drinking a Royal Crown Cola and eating a Moon Pie. He got in a heated argument and told the Jehovah's Witness that "I would rather line up my congregation and drink poison than subject them to your damnable heresies." This almost got him into a fight with the Jehovah's Witness. My dad was already mad because he could see the farm where Cathy Kirk lived from the store, and he saw the Jehovah's Witness talking with her and smiling. He knew the man was influencing Cathy to join up with them. My dad had an uncanny jealously over his church members.

The Atheist part got him, too. They didn't believe in God, and here he was joining up with their Godlessness. My dad crumpled the letter in his strong hands, not because he was upset with Mrs. Ralston, but because he was upset with himself for falling for such stupidity. He knew he would have to right his indiscretion, but he also knew that he had convinced many of his membership to follow this teaching, so he would have to undo the wrong very slowly. The following Christmas, all was back to normal, the church was happy, and Bro. Lord became the very best Santa Claus in Lincoln County.

Bro. Lord kept a tight rein on his boys, all four of them. Ray Lord had two younger brothers nearly the same age as my little brother, Val Mark. His older brother, Goose, we called him, missed most of his teenage years. He had Tuberculerosis and spent his days lying in a hospital bed in the front room of the Lord house. I felt really sorry for Goose because he couldn't do the things the other boys had fun doing. I saw the pain on his face many times when Bro. Lord would take Ray, Fran, and me to his pond in the back pasture to go swimming.

Bro. Lord taught Ray, Fran, and me how to swim. He coaxed us off the pond bank one day and into an inner tube he had floating in the middle of the muddy pond. After guiding us into the middle of the pond, he shoved up off the inner tube. It was literally sink or swim, and we three swam for our lives and soon reached the safety of the shallow water where we could stand on the thick mud that had been settling on the bottom of the pond for years. We thought we were going to drown, and no matter how much we screamed and took in water, Bro. Lord wouldn't help us. We swam all day unafraid of the depth of the pool.

James Lord was a disciple of strict discipline. "Spare the rod and spoil the child," was his motto and every time my dad preached to us and confirmed Bro. Lord s personal conviction, we kids would cringe. Bro. Lord didn't use a rod or switch although there was a large willow tree by their well, he whipped his boys with a tobacco stick. No one could say his boys were ever spoiled, and they had a healthy respect for him.

"Come back after I do my chores," Charles Ray Lord told Ray Hampton.

Ray didn't bother asking his dad if he could go "riding around" with Ray Hampton. He sneaked away from the barn after milking the cows. I felt as sorry for Ray as I did for Goose but for different reasons. Ray Lord had to do most of the chores by himself. His little brothers were too young to do the heavy work, but they did feed the chickens or carry milk pails from the barn to the house twice a day after milking time.

Milking was hard work. Fran taught me how to milk cows; he taught me how to hold the utters and squeeze firmly in order to make the utter give up a stream of milk which shot into a bucket. Fran's hands were strong from this exercise as were all the farm boys in the Chapel Gap Community. The cows were milked every morning before school. The boys would rise before daylight and bring the cows from the pasture and into the barn. These boys also knew they would face the same arduous task before their supper in the evening time after school.

Milking cows was part of life and there was no reprieve for holidays and vacations were unheard of. No farm had electric milkers except the Messer Brothers, Earl and Estill. I liked working for the Messers. The milking was easy because all you would have to do is stick the milker nipple on the utter, and the whoosh caused by the suction took hold of the utter and did all the work.

Ray Lord stood by the fork of the Pine Hall Road when Ray Hampton came by. Ray crawled into the front seat and took one glance back toward the Lord house to make sure that Bro. Lord didn't see him get into the car.

Sixteen was the driver's license age in Kentucky, but no one actually enforced this law up in the Knobs. Kids thirteen and fourteen years old or younger were commonly seen driving on the gravel roads. The Sheriff and his deputy didn't seem to mind as long as one of the kids wasn't driving on the paved roads in Crab Orchard. Sheriff Crane justified this permissiveness by saying, "The boys need to help with the farm deliveries, hay, milk, and such, so they need to be on the road." I believe he relaxed the minimum driving age because his boys, Harvey and Wilson, much below the driving age, were seen many times driving their dad's pickup miles from their farm.

We all knew how to drive, even the girls. Learning to drive was necessary in order to help get the hay trucks from the fields to the barns. The boys and girls had this job before they were big enough to handle the heavy hay bails and large tobacco stalks.

Ray and Ray decided to swing by Junebug Barber's house and see if he wanted to ride with them. Soon , there were three in the car rolling toward Fran' s.

The four boys planned to go to the picture show in Crab Orchard. Of course, this was a forbidden place for the members of the Evergreen Baptist Church to be, and severe penalties were doled out to those who disobeyed, including a stinging sermon on the evils of the movie theater when it was found out the members were going there.

Fran and I sneaked off one time and went to the show. We hitched a ride in a pickup and were enjoying the movie, "The Shaggy Dog" with Fred Murray of "My Three Sons" fame. I was eating my popcorn when I was shocked to see my sister standing beside my seat. "Dad said to come home," Leah related, "You're in big trouble."

Fran wouldn't stay and finish watching the movie, so he and I nervously walked out the front entrance of the theater. My dad had sent my mom on this errand just to make me sweat. She sat in our 1959 Ford Station Wagon waiting on us to come out of the show.

"You're dad's not too happy with either of you boys," she said. I knew my mother well. She didn't agree with any of this stuff, and she would have broken every rule at the Evergreen Baptist Church if she could get away with it.

"I'd help you boys out if I could," she said, "but the Preacher's waiting for Sonny at the church."

"It was my fault," Fran said, "I shouldn't have talked him into it. He said it wasn't the right thing to do." He was explaining to my dad the reasons he shouldn't whip me. Of course, it was the other way around. I begged Fran to go with me even when he exhorted me, "You're gonna get caught."

My dad beat the daylights out of me for watching the "Shaggy Dog."

"There's nothing wrong with the movie," he explained as he flogged me with the switch. I was dancing to keep out of the way. "It's the atmosphere and fellowshipping with the world that's wrong."

It was for this reason that Fran didn't have Ray Hampton and the other boys pick me up. He knew that Loretta Kirk had taken Buster to the movies that night, and she would see me there.

A fourteen year old boy wasn't supposed to drive into Crab Orchard; especially, with three other people in the car. Ray Hampton could barely reach the pedals on the floor as he scrunched down and strained to look over the steering wheel. He moseyed on into town as the boys smoked their cigarettes and hollered at the girls.

The four boys sat behind Loretta and Buster Kirk. Stan Kirk wasn't there because he was the leader of the "Booster Choir" and had to set an example as a leader of the church even though he was only seventeen years old.

Loretta Kirk looked around as the boys sat down behind her trying to see if the Preacher's kid was among the group. About half way through the movie, Ray Lord asked Buster if he wanted to finish his coke. "Sure," Buster said and reached behind him to grab the cup. Buster took a big gulp and immediately spit the juice all over the white sweater of the lady sitting in front of him. He soaked her entire back with the thick brown slime.

The boys were roaring with laughter because there wasn't coke in the cup. Ray Lord was chewing tobacco and spitting the ambeer in the coke cup. It was warm and stinking, but Buster took the bait.

Looking at the ruined sweater hanging loosely on the lady who was the recipient of this prank, Loretta Kirk said, "When I get my hands on you boys, you'll wish you'd never been born." She offered to pay for the sweater that Buster spat on causing the poor woman to have to leave the theater.

"Your dad knows you're at the picture show?" Buster Kirk asked Ray Lord while his mother smiled at his brilliance.

"Holy crap!" Ray Lord answered. "They'll stop right on the way home and tell my dad I was at the show, and that I am chewing tobacco. I told my dad I was going over to Dennis Wiggington's house to play ROOK with his dad and him. "Holy crap!"

Ray was a very nervous boy when they pulled into the farmyard of the Lord's. Loretta Kirk's car was in the front drive and Ray's being at the show, chewing tobacco, offering Buster that cup of tobacco juice he spit out of his mouth and ruined the good lady's sweater, wasn't all she told Bro. Lord. She had seen the boys leave the theater in Ray Hampton's car.

This was a low blow to Ray Lord; even more so than lying to his dad about where he was going. Loretta Kirk knew how Sissie Lord, Ray's mother, protected her boys. She worried about them out loud while she gossiped on the phone, and Loretta Kirk couldn't stand it. Sissie already had one boy lying in the front room with TB, and now she had to worry about Ray getting killed riding around in a car driven by an irresponsible fourteen-year-old child!

The last Fran and Junebug saw of Ray Lord for several weeks was at church, and he wasn't allowed to talk to them.

Ray came to church the Sunday morning after the incident hobbling around very sorely from the whipping he took from Bro. Lord's favorite tobacco stick.

Ray Hampton, Fran, and Junebug Barber were now in the car. Ray Hampton didn't even allow the car to come to a complete stop at the Lord farm, and Ray Lord jumped from the moving automobile. There was no way these boys were going to take a chance of meeting the wrath of Bro. Lord head on. The deacon would be mad enough to kill them all, not excluding his own son.

The boys decided to cruise back to Crab Orchard and see if they could pick up a girl. That wasn't going to happen, and they knew it, but it was fun talking about the girls and their newly discovered sexuality made them think more of these unusual things.

The boys were spitting tobacco juice out the windows, and the radio blared loudly. Fran sat in the front seat between Junebug and Ray Hampton because Junebug was bigger and Ray was driving. The back seat of the '41 Chevy was empty because no girls they asked seemed to want to ride.

A red light flashed and Ray looked into his rear view mirror. Homer Shanks had placed his emergency light on the top of his International pickup that was laden with kids inside and out. He had taken his older brood of children to the picture show to see the "Shaggy Dog." As he was returning home, he noticed a kid peering over the dashboard with two other boys in the front seat. Homer recognized the car as belonging to Frank Hampton, Ray's dad.

There was nervousness and fidgeting in the front seat of the Chevy as the tall Deputy Shanks walked up to the car. The Deputy's kids, who were in the pickup, were standing in the bed and watching over the cab at their dad making this arrest.

"Ray Hampton, what are you doing in your dad's car? You

know you're too young to drive," the Deputy said as he sniffed inside the car for signs of alcohol.

Homer Shanks was so tall that he had to almost get on his hands and knees to talk to the boys through the driver's window.

"I'm afraid I'm going to have to tow in your car," he said. This meant that he would have to hook a rope to the front bumper and tow the car himself with his pickup.

"You'll have to catch a ride home, and Monday, you'll have to appear in court with your dad and pay the fines."

Deputy Shanks took out his ticket pad although he wouldn't write on it. He would have to get one of his kids to fill out the information for him because Mr. Shanks, the Deputy Sheriff, couldn't read or write, and he didn't think there was a soul in Lincoln County who knew this.

"Mmmm," the Deputy mused as he looked over the driver's license he was surprised that Ray Hampton possessed. "I was sure you was too young to drive. You are the youngest Hampton boy, ain't you?"

"All right boys," he said after a few minutes of looking over the driver's license, "carry on, but slow down, or I'll have to give you a fine." He said this even though Ray Hampton was driving through town so slowly that the tires were barely rolling.

The driver's licenses that year in Kentucky were blue. There was no such thing as plastic driver's licenses; they were two sheets of folded paper and filled out by hand or typed if the clerk could type, and you received them at the Courthouse in Stanford. That same year Kentucky had a major gaffe. The fishing licenses were the same color blue as the driver's licenses. They were the same size and printed on the same paper.

Quick thinking Fran had handed Ray Hampton his fishing license because he knew Deputy Shanks well, and he knew he couldn't read and write. In spite of the fact that neither Ray or Junebug were aware of this information, and they couldn't comprehend what Fran was up to, Ray took the fishing license and handed it to Homer Shanks. The Deputy turned it over and over. He knew something wasn't quite right, but he didn't want to risk letting the boys know he couldn't read and write, so he handed the paper back to Ray not realizing he had given himself away, anyway.

The boys were laughing about this as they made their way toward the Chapel Gap Hill where Ray would have to shift down because the six cylinder flathead engine wouldn't pull the '41 Chevy up the hill in high gear.

"That was the smartest thing I've ever seen," Junebug congratulated Fran on his quick thinking.

I was coming out of the outhouse when I saw Ray Hampton's car speeding by the church. The dust rose behind the car higher than I had ever seen, and I knew Ray must be doing at least eighty miles per hour. I also knew that Fran was in the car and probably Junebug because Sally Barber had told me earlier as she was cleaning the church for Sunday services that Ray Hampton, Fran, Junebug, and Ray Lord were going to the show. I didn't believe that Ray Lord was in the car because I didn't believe his dad would let him go to the show being a deacon and all.

I heard the impact a few minutes later, and I knew that Ray Hampton had wrecked the car. I ran as fast as I could from the outhouse and woke my dad.

As we arrived at the Job house, we saw the Chevy smashed into the tree which protected Abe Job's garage. Steam gushed from the radiator, and my dad rushed from our car. Fear and dread gripped me, and I knew that Fran was dead and maybe the other boys as well.

Fran was standing by Abe, so he was okay, and I breathed a

sigh of relief. Junebug was lying on the grass by the garage, but Ray was in the car with his head on the steering wheel.

The boys had tried to do what no other driver in Chapel Gap history had done, and that was to take People's Corner at eighty miles per hour.

"You boys are lucky to be alive," my dad said solemnly, "God is watching over your stupidity," and Mandy nodded her head.

"Dumbest thing I've ever seen," June said as she put in her two cents worth.

The Chevy was demolished never to be driven again, but the boys were okay except for some cuts and bruises. Ray Hampton did have five stitches in his forehead as a result of the accident where his face smashed into the steering wheel. Fran would dig glass from the broken windshield out of his forehead for years to come.

I would have many days rambling the hills with Junebug and Fran, but it was the last time any of us at Evergreen Baptist Church ever saw Ray Hampton or the Hampton family.

CHAPTER TWENTY-FOUR

The news traveled fast that a man named Bunch had purchased an old building over in Halls Gap, Kentucky. Halls Gap used to be a thriving hub of activity because it was on State Highway 27 that crossed the United States from Canada in the north and south to the Gulf Coast. After running through Lexington, Kentucky, the route went through Stanford and then to Somerset, Kentucky.

The highway was popular being the main artery from Cincinnati, Ohio to the large Lake Cumberland area famous for fishing, boating, and vacationing families. For years, Highway 27 wound its way through Halls Gap bringing vacationers through the scenic views of the vista that lay in the rolling hills of South Central Kentucky. Down the curvy mountain road, sightseers could pull off at a scenic view area complete with telescopes that cost a nickel to look through and enjoy the views up close giving a nice panorama of the valley below. The little restaurant at the Gap was always crowded and offered good food.

The state decided to by-pass the crooked and scenic route of Halls Gap, which caused an increased amount of traffic problems as the Lake Cumberland area grew in popularity. There were many accidents on the road that caused long traffic delays. They built a new highway through the limestone hills, a straight away which included passing lanes and opened up the barrier of the slower route through Halls Gap.

Long ago, Halls Gap became isolated, and since the tourists no longer had need to travel to the old highway, the souvenir enterprises dried up as well. Large crocheted bedspreads, most featuring a large peacock in the center with various colors, plaster statues of many designs, and an assortment of other junk sold by the locals to the tourists stopping at the vista could be seen all through the spring and summer months. The fall of the year was the most popular as folks visited the area to enjoy the beautiful foliage in the Kentucky autumns. Halls Gap became neglected, and only a morsel of memory exists of its hey day. The telescopes were removed, the restaurant closed and deteriorated to nothing, and weeds grew over the vista area that was left unattended for years and no longer maintained by the state.

At the bottom of this windy road, Mr. Bunch had purchased some cheap land and turned an old barn on the property into a roller skating rink. He concreted the floor and covered it with black tar paper. The surface was a little rough, but skatable. Many people thought he was nuts to build an enterprise like this out in the middle of nowhere.

I learned to skate when I was nine years old because my Auntie Butch in Kansas bought me some skates; the kind you clip on your shoes, and I learned the sport on the sidewalks of Abilene, Kansas when I went to spend the night with my Uncle Eldon and her. Skating was never in my mind after that until Fran and I heard about the grand opening of the rink.

Every Friday and Saturday night, my mother would drive Fran and me to the Halls Gap and Bunch Skating Rink; a distance of some fourteen miles.

My mom was a pretty good skater, and even though she was only thirty-three years old, she was the oldest person on the skating floor. She was thin and pretty and moved gracefully as she weaved in and out passing the younger skaters. I was truly proud of her. Fran and I were good skaters, but skating was one thing I was better at than him. I was the first to learn to skate backwards and could do it skillfully. I mastered some wooden matchstick in my mouth, holding it securely between my teeth, and skated tricks on the skating floor. One of these was a fine trick that no one else could do. I skated in a big circle. As I did this feat, I gradually narrowed the circle and raised one leg off the floor and kept shortening the circle while skating on one leg. I then bent lower and lower, stretching my body until my face and mouth were only a few inches off the floor and struck the match I held between my teeth. Every time I was at the skating rink, the crowd cried for me to do the trick before Mr. Bunch closed for the evening. I enjoyed showing off to my audience.

"One of these times you're going to burn your hair," Fran warned.

There were lots of girls at the skating rink, and every weekend Fran and I would see a blond blue-eyed girl there who was the prettiest girl we had ever seen. Her name was Suzanne Stevens, and we knew nothing about her except that she was beautiful. Her father dropped her off at the rink in his pickup and then he would return to retrieve her exactly one hour before the rink closed.

My mom tired of driving us to the rink twice per week after a couple of months. "You boys will have to skip skating this weekend, I have too much to do," she excused herself.

This was okay because we gigged during the summer or fished, but what would we do in the fall and winter? This was a dilemma that we solved as our fishing and gigging season ended. We would walk and hitchhike every weekend to one of our favorite pastimes. That is exactly what we did. Most of the time, we could get a ride in the back of a pickup, but there were many times we walked the entire fourteen miles going and coming.

Suzanne Stevens was skating when Fran and me returned to the rink. We rented our skates as only the most fortunate had enough to buy their own, and from the money we earned working on the tobacco farms, we could skate, buy some pop, and sometimes we had enough money left over to buy a hotdog from the broiler Mrs. Bunch installed in the arena.

We watched Suzanne's slender yet toned body glide around the floor. Never in my whole life did I think my mind would be on girls, but of late, Fran and I had feelings that to me were somewhat uncomfortable. Fran was the first to announce his desires while we were roasting hotdogs by the fire we had built after we had gigged some frogs. I was shocked at the revelation he gave me.

"Bud, I'm in trouble," he said.

"What kind of trouble?"

"I'm in love."

"How do you know this?" I quizzed with dismay that my best friend was talking like this.

"I get these funny feelings in my stomach when I see her, and I am thinking some pretty bad stuff."

"What kind of bad stuff ?"

"Like I want to explore or something."

"Fran, I don't think Suzanne Stevens will go out with you because she is two years older, and you got no car."

"Who said anything about Suzanne? Goofball."

"Then who you talking about?"

"Your sister."

"Which one, Nila or Leah?" I said this sarcastically; this was hilarious.

"Leah, idiot, Nila's three years old."

"What? Leah?"

"Yep, Leah. I think she's the prettiest girl I've ever seen."

"You got to be kidding me, Fran. She's only eleven years old, and she's my sister for crying out loud. You can't love my sister!"

"Why not?"

I could think of nothing to say. I was horrified. I had seen Stan Kirk fall for Cindy Skinner, Roscoe Barber fall for Carrie Crane, Ernest Jenkins for Diane Smith, Wendell Petrey for Ruth Petrey, and the girls ruined them all. You hardly ever saw them anymore. This was not good; it was going to ruin Fran.

"When did this happen?" I asked.

"A couple of months ago," Fran answered as he stirred the ashes of the fire.

"Okay, so that's why you haven't been yourself all summer?"

"I guess so," Fran said as he began kicking out the remaining ashes and poured water on the fire from the frog bucket.

Fran was lovesick for my sister, and he wasted no time making his moves.

He started sitting with my sister in church, and that was noticed by all the gossips in the Chapel Gap Community. "Little Leah isn't allowed to hold hands or be seen as growing up," they told one another.

My dad was okay with Leah sitting in church with Fran, but they were not anywhere with each other. My dad knew the affinity the boys in the Knobs had for young girls, and marrying one of them at her age was not only possible, it could easily happen. He maintained a tight rein on her, and the pressure on me was horrific.

"I'll be glad when Leah can go skating with me," Fran said one day as were walking toward Halls Gap.

By now, I had gotten used to them being together, and because she couldn't be around Fran except at church, I wasn't bothered by the relationship as much as I thought I would be. Fran spent more and more time at my house, and we spent less and less time at his.

I was the only kid with blond hair and blue eyes. Leah and the little kids had brown eyes like my dad, and his darker complexion. I took after my mom. Leah was trim and neat, and she always dressed fit to kill no matter where she was going or what she was doing. She had good manners, but she and I weren't the best of friends; especially after she intruded into the life of my best friend.

I began to understand more and more about the love business. There were a couple of girls at the church chasing me, who like Leah, wanted to sit with a boy. Sitting with a girl made the sermons go faster, and in fact, you didn't want them to end. It was interesting how my dad's sermon contained more information about being "chaste" than before Fran started sitting with Leah. He thundered from the pulpit the evils of lusting in your heart after the opposite sex. "You have committed adultery in your heart already if you lust after a woman," he preached. He taught that there should be no kissing between two people until marriage. That sermon was like preaching against tobacco in a smoke and chewing infested environment. The boys and girls growing up were kissing all over the place, hiding in secret lairs, even at church, and some were fondling one another.

My first encounter with any kind of sexual experience came one day at church.

"Would you like to see me naked?" The redheaded thirteen year old said with a lascivious look in her eyes. "I'll show you behind the girl's outhouse if you want to come and see."

Somehow I escaped her grasp, and I felt guilty later as I sat in church. I had been tempted to accept her offer. My mind flew back to the night I sneaked and watched June Job bathe, and I had those same feelings, only stronger. I liked it, and I didn't like it; a most stressing emotion.

"Hey Fran, did you ever want to see a girl naked?" I asked as we continued along the road to the skating rink.

"Better get those thoughts out of your head, Bud."

"No, seriously, have you?"

"Yeah. Every time I hold Leah's hand," he confessed and the thought gave me the creepies.

We confessed our innermost feelings and as esoteric as talking about sex was supposed to be, we shared with each other our most secretive thoughts.

"Do you know that Lassie Crump offered to let me see her naked behind the girl's outhouse at church?"

"You didn't do it, did you, Bud?"

"Nope, but I felt guilty about thinking how much I would like to."

"Ain't no sin in temptation, Bud, just make sure you don't do it. That would be sin."

As usual, Fran had the right answer for everything, and he made me feel better. I could have all these feelings and fantasies I wanted as long as I don't act upon them.

"Fran, I think I'm in love with Suzanne Stevens."

"You're crazy, you don't even know her. Have you ever spoken to her?"

"No, but as soon as we get there, I'm going to ask her to skate with me during the couple's moonlight dance."

"She's at least sixteen years old, Bud, she ain't gonna skate with you. Besides, you ain't allowed to dance, the Preacher would kill you."

Dancing was forbidden at Evergreen Baptist Church; but was skating the moonlight skate really dancing? Oh well, I didn't care; I would risk it anyway.

I was standing outside the skating rink when Suzanne Stevens stepped out of the pickup. None of the girls wore blue jeans or pants in the farm communities. They worked, played, and went to church in their dresses. Suzanne was wearing a skirt and sweater. I noticed for the first time as she stepped to the gravel that she was "full" and her dress kind of slipped above her knees so that you could see her thighs. I was sweating.

Before I asked Suzanne to skate with me, I did my match gig. Normally, I would wait until the end of skating time and then do the trick. People got out of my way, forming a huge circle of bodies on the skating rink floor, as I skated in a circle with a match in my mouth. Suzanne was standing nearby, and my eye caught her inquisitive look as she noticed me. I was easily the best skater that glided around the tarpaper floor of the Bunch Skating Arena. There was one other guy I had my eye on, though. He was a redheaded boy from Stanford and had been showing up lately. He was a couple of years older, and he obviously wasn't from the farm community because his arms were white, and he didn't have the muscles all us farm boys had.

After I finished lighting the match I held in my mouth and the cheers rang out, we were distracted by the Stanford kid skating around the floor at a very fast pace. In fact, he was skating faster than anyone I had ever seen since coming to the rink. Mr. and Mrs. Bunch stood watching him. Normally, Mr. Bunch would rip your skates off and send you packing for speeding that fast on his floor, but since no one else was skating at the time, Mr. Bunch let him go.

As the kid picked up speed, he suddenly leaped in the air and did a full flip, easily landing on his feet and glided into his next move. He nicely made his turn backwards and leaped again; this time flipping and landing on his feet like a butterfly on a delicate flower. He did all kinds of spins and turns and effortlessly performed like ice skaters on TV. He ended the whole show by leaping very high and landing with his legs in a split.

After watching this, I decided I would never do the match trick again; especially, after the expert showoff lit four matches in his mouth emulating and improving the trick I had patented at the rink.

"He can skate better than you, Bud," Fran pointed out as he noticed the envy in my eyes. "Better get used to that; he'll be down here every Saturday night."

"Yeah," I replied, "but I won't."

What did I care if I was upstaged? I don't know, but it sure bothered me. I enjoyed being the center of attention and that was something I had never been before. All I really cared about was getting attention from my dad and Fran, but this was a different day and things definitely were changing.

"Ask her," Fran urged, "get over there and ask her."

"All right, all right," I replied, "give me a couple of seconds."

I was trying to get up my courage to ask Suzanne Stevens to skate with me, but it was hard. I was tough and afraid of no one except my dad, but I was terrified around that girl. The announcement had been made by Mr. Bunch that the "moonlight skate, couples only," was about to begin. He turned the lights down, and the bright shiny ball hanging from the ceiling began to turn and shattered bits of light reflected all over the skating rink floor; I had to hurry.

I inched my way over to Suzanne, who looked like a princess in all her regal glory as the lights danced around her blond hair and fair skin. I put the brakes on by jumping on my toes and dragging the front rubber bumpers on my skates coming to a nice easy abrupt stop.

"Would you like to skate with me?" I asked softly.

"Get away from me you little piece of hog crap!"

She cussed! I was shaking the cobwebs from my mind as she startled me when Showoff from Stanford skated up and took Suzanne by the arm. He didn't ask, and she didn't resist. They glided together in one motion as they promenaded into the center of the dance floor. Soon, Showoff was skating backwards and holding Suzanne very close. I watched this with green envy, and my mind filled with hatred. *I'll beat the crap out of him,* I thought.

We were done an hour early. Usually, Fran and I waited until the last possible second, trying to get around the floor for one last time before Mr. Bunch ran everybody off. Not tonight. I was so devastated that I told Fran I wanted to leave. "Get over it," he advised, but there was no soothing the hurt deep within.

"I told you she wouldn't skate with you," Fran confirmed, and I told him to shut-up.

"Why did you tell me to skate with her, Fran, after you told me not to be falling in love with every girl I see?"

"You needed to learn a lesson. Don't go around falling in love with girls older than you are and especially when you've never met them."

Mr. Stevens passed us as we walked along the road. He was on his way to pick up his daughter and take her home. It wasn't long before he passed us on his return trip. It was dark, but we could see Suzanne turn around and look at us. Mr. Stevens made no effort to stop and offer a ride.

The dust had long settled from Mr. Stevens' truck as he blew past us, and now the road was deserted. Farmers went to bed early, so we knew we wouldn't get a ride, and like always, we would walk the fourteen miles to Fran's house.

We meandered along talking, and at times we were silent as we thought about nothing in particular, when we saw the reflection of light coming from the farmhouse window ahead of us. We had passed this way many times, but usually an hour later, and we had never seen the lights on in this house. The house had electricity, so that made it especially easy to see as the lights illuminated the white gravel on the road. We had no idea who lived there.

As we approached the light, we could see someone's shadow on the road.

We stopped and looked at the light shining from the upstairs dormer windows. Someone was moving around' up there, so Fran and I sneaked closer and got the shock of our lives.

"Suzanne!" Fran whispered.

It was Suzanne, and she was washing herself and standing a ways back from the window. Her thought of anyone being out there would never cross her mind, and it was obvious as she carelessly sponged herself from the basin in front of her.

"Dang," I said as I saw naked breasts for the first time in my life. They weren't small, either. We stood in the shadows dripping with desire to see more. We could easily see her breasts, but that was all. Every time she reached down toward her legs with the cloth she had in her hands, our imaginations ran wild. I climbed the trellis that led to the roof beside her house. The vines were gone, so the climbing was easy. Fran did not follow me. He already felt guilty because of Leah. Not me though.

I inched my way from the trellis and put my foot on the roof. I could still see Suzanne's shadow on the road, so I knew that she wasn't finished with her bath. I could hear her softly singing as I approached the window ledge where I could pull myself up and peer over. "I am going to a city where the roses never fade," she sang somewhat off key. I peered over the ledge carefully as I could so as not to give away my position.

I could not believe my eyes. She was beautiful. Her figure was tight and full, and I stared at her as every imagination I had ever had in my life about the female body came true before my very eyes. I looked down to the road for Fran, but he was nowhere to be seen.

Suzanne turned off the light, and I could hear her crawl into bed. I retraced my steps and eased my way back down the ladder. There was no coon dog at this farm because we learned later that Mr. Stevens had been attacked by a raccoon, and because his dog didn't protect him, he sold the dog and quit coon hunting. A coon dog would have spoiled my erotic adventure.

I described to Fran what she looked like after he begged me for an hour, and we looked forward to coming that way the next night. I thought about Suzanne all the way back to Fran's house and all that night. My hormones raged, but I knew I wasn't in love with her. It was something else going on with me, something unspeakable.

There were many nights afterwards that Fran and I would watch Suzanne Stevens in her bedroom window at the top of the house, but neither of us ever crawled up the lattice that led to the roof and to the dormer window. We never invaded her privacy no matter how tempted we were.

CHAPTER TWENTY-FIVE

n our fifteenth year, Fran and I had our girls. He was still sitting with Leah in church and still forbidden by my dad to have any contact with her except at church. There were a couple of other boys who were trying to beat Fran's time, but they knew he would beat the crap out of them if they came near her. My dad told Fran that Leah could "double date" when she turned fifteen, and that was a couple of years away. I tried to talk some sense into his head to give her up because he was going to have to wait until he was seventeen to have a car date.

I told Fran he should try and date Simone Green, Steve Green's sister. She was much prettier than my sister, I reasoned, but I doubt if any boys ever thought their sisters were beautiful. At least Fran never mentioned June being beautiful even though I thought she was. I finally gave up the Green girl idea after I mentioned that he could date Simone Green and sit with my sister at the same time. Fran squashed that idea also and told me that the Preacher would never go for it. He would have to make up his mind which girl he wanted.

I sat in church with Darla Jenkins. She was Leah's best friend but one year older. She was a quiet, pretty girl and totally in love with me. I liked her a lot, enjoyed her company, and had somebody to sit with in church. She had a cute little sister named Betty, but she was too young for me to wait on. I respected Darla, but I knew our relationship would probably not last. I had my eye on a young girl named Kathy Friday. She lived with her family over at Copper Creek, and she was the smartest girl in our grade. It would take me a long time to ease up and approach her since I was still smarting from being rejected by Suzanne Stevens at the skating rink.

We were in high school now. Kathy Friday didn't go to Evergreen Baptist Church; she lived too far away, but she did go to Crab Orchard High. The grade school and junior high schools were located in very rural and backward parts of the counties in mountainous Kentucky, and the high schools were much larger because of the consolidation of all those schools when the lower grades graduated and emptied into the centrally located high schools of their respective communities. We went to church and school with the same kids for eight years, and then we found ourselves in a completely different world. The first thing Fran and I did was join the Future Farmers of America, mainly because Stan Kirk, who was now a junior in high school, impressed upon us the need to do so. He enticed us with his blue corduroy jacket with the nice golden shield that was the symbol of the FFA. He showed us the neat way your full name was stitched in gold below the shield, and we envied him. Stan pressed us until we decided to join the group and get our jackets, although neither of us ever intended on farming another day in our lives after high school. It was fun driving tractors the farmers lent us, so we could learn to paint. I think the FFA boys that year painted every tractor in the Chapel Gap Area, and my favorite was the Farmalls that were painted my favorite color, bright red.

Kathy Friday was a popular student at Crab Orchard High, and the thing I liked most about her was that she wasn't sickenly stuck up like the cheerleaders were. She was fair complexioned, deep blue eyes, and golden blonde hair. For some reason, my mind was made up that I would always be a blonde and blue eyes lover; even though, it was said that blondes were sort of looney, I never found it that way with Kathy Friday. She had no "suitors" that I knew about, and I don't believe she seemed to want any. One of her friends told Fran while we were checking Kathy Friday out, that she wasn't interested in dating boys, or "liking" boys and going steady, because her dad said she was too young to be running around with boys. I had time; I knew that if I could keep all those other boys away from her, that I would not only date her and go steady, but I would marry her one day. I also knew while my eye was on Kathy Friday that I was sitting in church with Darla Jenkins, and in order to consider Kathy Friday my girlfriend, I would have to break up with Darla Jenkins, and I just wasn't ready.

Fran and I spent a lot of time during our class breaks at the Crab Orchard Pool Hall. This was a forbidden place for members of Evergreen Baptist Church and good Christian people in general. It was located in the middle of the small town on main street about a ten-minute walk or less from the school. On our lunch breaks, we would walk with several of the other students down the street to play pool. I was careful to skip pool playing on the days I knew my dad would be in town.

The entrance to the pool hall was through a common door that had a screen.

Inside, it was dusty and filled with smoke. There was no liquor in Lincoln County, but it was known that if you wanted a beer, you could get it from Delbert Blanchard, who owned the hall. There were four tables in the room, and they were kept in real good shape so that Delbert could keep his patrons from running down to the pool hall in Stanford, which was much nicer.

One particular day, Fran and I were playing pool. We had walked down there and were surprised when we entered the establishment to find Evel Martin poking his stick at a cue ball. The ashes fell from Martin's cigarette as he leaned over the table to make a bank shot, which missed. He cussed and then looked at Fran.

"What're you grinning at you piece of hog crap?"

Fran wasn't grinning at all; he was expressionless.

Fran stood his ground because he was not the least bit afraid of Evel Martin although Martin was a few years older than Fran and me. Fran irritated Martin for some reason, and I believe it was because he instinctively knew that Fran wasn't impressed by him. I think this was expressly true when he thought about Fran and me breaking away from Curt Kirk and him in the woods. We never told on him, but every time he came in contact with Fran, he tried to intimidate him. Fran never acknowledged him as more than a missing link. "Worthless human being" was Fran's opinion ever since he tried to break up the church services that night several years ago when our family came to Chapel Gap. Evel was used to "ooh" and "ahs" when he made a good shot, but Fran never once let him know that he appreciated his skills.

Evel Martin cleaned up the table and set the rack for another break. He collected money from Robert Quatrell and looked around the room.

"Who wants to take me now?" He said as he examined the room full of high school students.

"I will," Fran said.

I hustled to Fran. "What are your doing? You don't have money to play him."

"Come on you little chicken crap," Evel said.

Fran strolled over to the table like he was in an international pool championship.

Martin had never seen Fran play pool, but many of us had, and we knew Fran was good, but as good as Martin? The bets hit the table as Fran cued up.

The two guys lagged the ball and Martin won the break. Evel let Fran choose the game, which was a mistake, so Fran chose bank pool that easily was the most difficult game of pool in the sport. I had never seen Fran play bank pool, and I don't believe he ever saw himself play it either. This bothered me greatly because Fran had no money.

Evel took his first shot and banked the ball on a forty-five degree angle. Evel made the shot in the side pocket and cued again. He made three other shots, and as I began to perspire heavily; he missed his fifth.

Fran calmly took his stick in hand and aimed down the shaft eyeing a ball lying in the corner, which was going to have to be banked in the fore pocket and brought the length of the table. It was the only shot that Fran had. He squeezed the trigger and let the cue stick slide between his fingers. The ball banked at a sixty-degree angle off the upper rail and headed across the table and struck the nine ball. The cue backed up almost to the opposite corner as the ball slid from its position and headed cross corner to the other end of the table.

"It's a miss," Martin cried because the ball could not possibly be banked at that angle and hit any pocket, much less the one Fran called.

The nine ball rolled nicely and evenly as it banked three times on its journey to the exact center of the end pocket below where Fran held his cue stick. Fran ran the table on Evel

Martin, and I have never seen, nor has anyone else seen in that pool hall bank pool played so expertly.

Evel Martin never finished the eighth grade at Broughton-town School. He was uneducated and could barely read and write. He was one of the worse troublemakers at the school, and had been expelled so many times that the Principal kicked him out.

Fran on the other hand was very good at geometry. He had that an un-natural gift to figure angles, an acute ability. He didn't look at a pool table full of balls sitting in various positions, he saw angles like invisible wires crisscrossing the table and showing him where every shot could be made. Martin didn't have a chance.

Homer Shanks walked in during this match and was standing nearby. The Deputy was making his rounds ensuring that all the students at Crab Orchard High returned for class, and also to make sure there was no gambling in the pool hall. Gambling was prohibited in Kentucky except at the various racetracks scattered around the state where famous horses ran. However, the Deputy had never arrested one person for gambling in Delbert Blanchard's pool hail even though pay-offs were made right under his nose.

"That's some kind of fancy shooting, Fran," the Deputy commented, "how much did you make?"

"Nothin," Fran replied, "we're playing for fun."

Evel Martin looked at Fran not realizing nor appreciating that Fran was taking no chances of being caught gambling although he knew that the Deputy had never issued one citation or made one attempt to arrest anyone for gambling.

For no reason, and out of the clear blue, Martin hit Fran across the head with his cue stick. Fran hit the floor as the blow knocked him down. Evel came at him with his stick raised and was going to smash Fran's head again, which may have killed him, but as he did, Homer Shanks, who was ten feet tall and strong, grabbed his stick and held Martin's hand pinning it behind his head as Evel's pool cue fell to the floor.

Homer held Martin until he was sure there would be no more incidents, and I knelt down to Fran to make sure he was okay. Except for a knot that was quickly rising from the side of his face, Fran was all right.

"Now pay him off," Deputy Shanks ordered Martin.

"Screw him, he's a damn little cheater," Martin cried and then he bolted out the door. The screen door slammed behind him as two of Martin's buddies followed him to the street.

"You okay, Fran?" The Deputy asked.

"Yep, Deputy, I'm fine, Deputy.

Mr. Shanks seemed impressed that this was the first time Fran had ever addressed him as Deputy."

"How much does he owe you?" Homer asked.

"Nothin," Fran reiterated.

"It's something. Evel don't play for nothing. Now how much is it?"

"TEN DOLLARS!" I screamed.

"Hmmm," Homer mused, "that's a lot of money."

Deputy Shanks had every intention of collecting this money for Fran even though it was illegal.

"DUCK!" The cry came from one of the boys in the crowd. Some onlookers had seen the action through the screen door of the pool hall and at this moment the room was crowded. We turned our heads toward the door at this command and saw a green 1949 Chevrolet Coupe idling on the street in front of the pool hall. A .25 caliber pistol was in Martin's hand and aimed at the door. We all hit the floor, and some of us rolled under the tables.

Pow, pow, pow, the shots rang out, and all three missed everyone, Evel fired again, and this time, a bullet hit Larry

Dishon's arm. He was a boy we all knew very well and a Future Farmer. Blood began to ooze through the sleeve of his FFA jacket staining the royal blue with his blood. I had never seen anyone shot before. Another bullet hit the table beside Deputy Shanks, and another penetrated the back wall near Delbert Blanchard's office.

The Chevy scratched off leaving a trail of black rubber and smoke from the spinning tires. Shanks ran out of the pool hall with his .38 caliber pistol and took aim at the rear end of the getaway car. We couldn't see him, but we heard the loud shots as he emptied his gun in the rear of the speeding Chevy putting six well-placed holes in the trunk. It was later thought that if Deputy Homer Shanks wanted to kill those men, he could have. It was not known by many that Homer could hit a coin tossed into the air dead center with his pistol. After this, the respect Fran and I had for the Deputy took a giant leap in spite of his illiteracy.

There was no pursuit of the law in those days to speak of, so Martin got away with his crime.

"Pay Fran his ten dollars," Homer Shanks directed Delbert Blanchard.

"What? It wasn't my bet," he protested.

Deputy Shanks towered over the smaller Blanchard. "The crime was committed in your place of establishment," the Deputy said eloquently, "you are aiding and contributing to the delinquency of a minor, a major offense of the law."

Delbert looked at the Deputy in disbelief but made no attempt to challenge the Deputy. He shelled out ten dollars and handed the bills to Fran.

A whole group of us boys walked back to the school, Fran in the middle of the pack as he counted the ten one dollar bills one bill at a time and smiled.

CHAPTER TWENTY-SIX

D arla Jenkins sat on the steps of the church on a Saturday afternoon. My sister, Leah, had her arms wrapped
around her comforting her as she wept uncontrollably.
This was her birthday, January 2, and I had delivered the message to her a couple of hours before.

"I will never get over him," she sobbed, "I will love him for
the rest of my life."

"He's a creep," Leah replied, "I hope he rots in hell."

So, I wasn't too popular at the moment. My dad told me I
could not take Kathy Friday to the Crab Orchard High School
basketball game until I broke up with Darla Jenkins. "You have
to do the wrong things the right way," he advised. He loved
Darla Jenkins and had pronounced her as one of the best
Christian girls in Evergreen Baptist Church, and she was. One
thing my dad didn't do was interfere with his kid's love lives as
long as we obeyed the rules of Christian behavior.

I broke up with Darla on the pretense of asking Kathy Friday to sit with me at the ball game although I hadn't asked her yet and had no idea if she would accept. Fran and I didn't have the same rules about girls. I tried to hold onto Darla while I tried to get Kathy Friday just in case Kathy Friday turned me down, and I would be stuck with no girl. This strategy didn't work because I had my dad and Fran Job in the way.

"Look, Bud, you know what the preacher says. You don't even know Kathy Friday. She is pretty, but so is Darla. You know Darla. She goes to church, and is a good Christian and Baptist. You're supposed to marry a Baptist. You know that."

Fran believed this and was adamant about it; I knew that I better find out if Kathy Friday was a Baptist before I approached her. I didn't even know if she knew my name. I also watched a couple of "jocks" on the basketball team, one of which was Buster Kirk, trying to impress her. Buster was only a freshman, but he had already distinguished himself as a respected ball player. He was tall, handsome, although not as good looking as he thought. He could barely pass a mirror without admiring himself. He had his eye on Kathy Friday and this infuriated me. I had already made up my mind that I was going to marry her.

I was a little short for my age, and I hated that. I would grow some more, but at that time I thought I would be the same size the rest of my life. Fran was thin and wiry, and even though I wasn't fat, and in fact, didn't have an ounce of fat on me, I had broad shoulders and was strong for my size. One of the boys at school, Albert Payne who was a good sized kid in his own right, said that he would mess with about anybody except the Preacher's kid. "He'll fool you," he said. My dad commented one day as we walked together from the spring carrying water, "your shoulders are broad, but you better do something about those legs."

My legs were skinny, and I couldn't do anything about that, but they were strong and for that reason, there wasn't a kid in the high school who could outrun me. I trained myself with Fran. Many days we would run into the weeds carrying our bedrolls and guns. All those days pumping each other up and down the hills on my bike didn't hurt, either. I was also becoming a noted baseball player, and the coach told me I would make the varsity team the next year. He had been watching me during our schoolyard pick-up games and noticed how quickly I could attack a ball and throw with authority to first base. Every player knew that if I hit a single, it would be automatic to second base. "Two steps and a cloud of dust, and he's on second," Fran would tell the others, "don't even think about trying to throw him out."

Fran wasn't an athlete, and this would define the differences in our interests as the days quickly passed. We were both good students, and we carried A averages in school. I loved English and hated math, and Fran was the opposite, so we helped each other all the way through school. We found something else about ourselves. We could both sing. Fred's voice had dropped drastically, and he loved to sing the bass part with some of the older men in the church. You could hear Fran in church distinctly singing the bass lead on the song, "Life's Evening Sun."

Fran and I loved singing while we were fishing or camping out. I could sing harmony, and we made quite a duo. My dad even asked us to sing in church, once.

Mandy Job had an old organ in her front room given to her by her mother before she died. It was an old pump organ with those pull stops to alter the sound from the bellows as you played the keys and pumped the huge foot pedals to produce air. I fooled around with it and found another talent hidden so secretly that I didn't know it existed. I instinctively figured out how the key structure worked and played with one finger, "The Old Rugged Cross."

My dad decided that I would learn to play for church. Babs Kirk wouldn't be around forever, and the church needed another piano player. I had zero ambition for this, so he contacted a music teacher down in Stanford, Mrs. Lail, and forced me to enroll in piano school and made sure that my mom delivered me at the teacher's house every Thursday evening.

I hated piano school with all the passion I could hate, but my dad made me go. My mom didn't help. She decided that she would learn to play also, and that would be the deciding factor for my dad to purchase the piano she had always wanted. "What?" He said, "what do you want with a piano, you can't play. So, she picked me up every Thursday after school and drove me kicking and screaming all the way to Stanford. No good solid boy wants his mother to pick him up at school. It put us in the same category as the "sissies" whose mothers drove them to and from school because they were afraid their kids would get beaten up on the school bus. So every time my mom would pick me up, I would sneak to the car and slip in the back and duck all the way to the floor board so as not to be seen.

I flew through piano school, and it wasn't long before I was playing better than my teacher. She finally let me go. "He's gone as far as I can take him," she told my mother one day after a lesson. Music would eventually have more impact on my life than sports could ever do. I was the only kid in school who could play an instrument. We had no band because the farm kids had no time for such frivolous activities such as music; there was work to be done on every farm in the evenings after, and the mornings before, school. "The devil has guitars and such in the bars," my dad would preach.

I invited no one to my first recital. My mom and dad attended, and my dad beamed at how deftly I could negotiate the keys. I never played the music exactly like it was written, but instead, developed my own style. This drove my music teacher nuts. She constantly got on me about "adding to the music," and she slapped my hands every time I departed from the music scene and lashed out into my own interpretation. "Play what's written," Mrs. Lail instructed, and this was the reason she no longer wanted to teach me. After the recital, she said to my parents, "The only thing played during that recital piece was the melody. I don't know where the rest of it came from. It was beautiful and full, though."

I became more and more jealous as I watched the boys flirt around with Kathy Friday. She attracted boys like a light brings in the bugs on a warm summer's night. Jealousy was a new emotion for me, and I didn't handle it very well. I was so distant from her that in my mind there was no way I could ever get close to her much less ask her for a date. She was in a few of my classes, and there was no doubt that she was also very intelligent and could answer all the questions and did her homework. She was smart in addition to her incomprehensible beauty. All this was driving me out of my mind.

It would be music that would be the break through to meeting Kathy Friday. The school had an old piano on the stage in the assembly hall. One of the teachers, Mrs. Brewer who was married to Mr. Brewer, one of the other teachers we had in school, played the piano for the assemblies. She wasn't very good but did her best. Fran and I were in the hall one day by ourselves, Fran said, "Bud, you should get up there and show these people what that piano really sounds likes." Fran was proud of my accomplishment. In fact, Fran was so proud that he bought himself a harmonica and learned to play it so that he and I would have more in common than we already had. He taught himself even though he knew he would never be able to play it in the Evergreen Baptist Church.

I looked around to make sure that nobody saw me sitting on the piano bench. I started to play "Starlight Waltz," one of my favorite pieces. It wasn't long before a couple of girls came in who were passing by in the hallway. They heard the music and made their way to the stage. I didn't notice them until I was startled when one of them asked, "can you play The Pearly White City?" I turned to see who was standing behind me. It was Kathy Friday!

I could feel my heart skipping beats. I wasn't ready to meet Kathy Friday, not like this! Of course I wanted to meet Kathy Friday and she asked me to play a song, "The Pearly White City?" I couldn't remember my first name much less that song. I couldn't remember if I had ever heard it before, but I knew I had. I was discombobulated. My heart was in my throat and pulsating wildly. "Pearly White City," I thought as panic was beginning to creep up on me. I knew this might be my one and only chance. She specifically asked for a special song, not "can you play something for me?" I knew that I better come up with that tune real fast.

"How do you know that song?" I asked, my voice irregular.

"Church," she replied. "I learned it in church; it's my favorite."

Her favorite? Oh, no! "What church?" I asked hesitantly and afraid her answer would end all hope of ever asking her for a date.

"Copper Creek Baptist, Preacher Roberts knows."

"Preacher Roberts? You know Preacher Roberts?"

"He used to be a pastor when I was a little girl and then he moved on up to the farm at Chapel Gap when he retired. You know him."

I thought Preacher Roberts was always at Evergreen Baptist Church. So that's why they called him "Preacher," he really was a preacher!

Fran was walking around in a circle while every now and

then staring up at the ceiling showing the whites of his eyes. I don't know what he was looking at up there, but he didn't seem happy. He may have secretly wished Kathy Friday was a Methodist or something, but we had our answer, she is a Baptist!

I fumbled for the keyboard and then the tune burst forth. I played as fancifully as I could doing arpeggios, difficult runs up and down the piano forwards and backwards, my fingers moving rapidly on all eighty eight keys so as not to lose time, a feat not too many pianists can do. I brought the song to its conclusion like a concert pianist. I made a long run up the keyboard, hand over hand, and then let my pinkie finger pound a deep bass note to put the finishing touches to the song, and then lifted my hands off the keys and up in the air, while I released the loud pedal.

"I've never heard "The Pearly White City" played on an instrument before," she commented. "it was beautiful."

"It was beautiful" rang in my head and bounced around a thousand times. It was beautiful, I thought as I sat there in a trance and then shook the cobwebs out of my head. I turned to thank her, but she was gone. I caught a glimpse of her as she walked with her friend through the assembly hall door and into the schoolyard.

"She's a Baptist, Fran."

"Yeah, Bud, but you don't know how good a one she is."

No I didn't, but that didn't matter, not now. My dad only required that my girlfriends be Baptists; he never said they had to be good ones. Besides, he preached, "Judge not lest you be judged" many times from his pulpit at the Evergreen Baptist Church.

Fran didn't like this, and I think he was influenced by my sister.

"Darla is a pretty girl." This was the only comment he made to me the rest of the day.

I dreamed about Kathy Friday that night and many nights thereafter. I couldn't get her out of my mind. She actually spoke to me first. She knew who I was. I plotted and planned. The most difficult decision I would make about Kathy Friday was to keep my dad out of it. I wouldn't tell him I was courting Kathy Friday, and I would send him a message by not sitting with Darla Jenkins in church no matter how much she cried.

I passed up a couple of chances to ask Kathy Friday for a date. The coast was not clear. My dad had a sixth sense, and his sermon one Sunday morning was filled with advice that I am sure puzzled the rest of the congregation. He often did this. He made points to his children of his approval and disapproval of their behavior subtly in sermons.

"You should never let yourself fall in love with the opposite gender," he preached. He never said "sex" in the pulpit. That would have caused a few heart attacks in the older folks. "Never, ever date a person you don't intend to marry," and when he made this point, he brought his fist down on the pulpit very hard to emphasize the Biblical teaching.

I was doing okay during this exegesis that I knew was for my benefit, and so far he hadn't given any good reason to cause me to abandon my quest. Then, it happened as quickly as a bolt of lightening out of a clear blue sky.

"Make double sure you know the person you are going to marry, more than one marriage has broken up, even Christian marriages, because of a lack of faithfulness by the partner. It is one thing to be a Baptist; it is another to live a consecrated Christian life!" He thundered this point home by driving his fist with a heavier blow to the pulpit. He shook his hand to ward off the pain of the delivery. There was a rousing "Amen" by the congregation, men only, and the women nodded and bobbed their heads in approval.

By the time the sermon was finished, I wondered how any

Baptist could ever get married. I looked around at the girls sitting in church. Some of them were younger than I was, sitting with their husbands. Of those that remained unattached, if I was going to pick one girl besides Darla Jenkins, the rest of them would fail this litmus test my dad fired at his young congregation.

It was too risky to ask Kathy Friday out at this juncture, so I bypassed the opportunity. I had another occasion to meet her when she came into the assembly room and asked me to play "The Pearly White City" again. I chickened out.

I was losing the race, and I felt heartsick as I watched Buster Kirk sitting with Kathy Friday at the basketball game one Friday night. He wasn't playing as a freshman on the varsity team, but he sat directly behind the varsity bench. During the game, he would whisper something to her and then point out an error or mistake that he surely would not have made had he been dressed and on the floor.. Each time he said something, she leaned to him and her soft hair fell slightly on his shoulder; he smelled deeply at the blond strands of golden lace that I was sure smelled like heaven. The idiot was suited up, so the hair touched his naked shoulder and neck. Her blue eyes sparkled with delight, and her smile of pearl white teeth showed how much she enjoyed the attention he was giving her.

I had no idea after the game, as I sat there and watched the last person leave the gym, what the score was or who won. Maybe Buster Kirk won. I had no Kathy Friday and no Darla Jenkins.

CHAPTER TWENTY-SEVEN

Whenever Fran was invited to spend the night with one of our friends, I was always included, and he was part of my invitations. Fran and I were inseparable. Our friendship and kinship would not be like so many relationships with people you grow up with; ours was there for life, and everyone knew that. People didn't think of us as individuals; they thought of us as one person. It was uncanny. We were seldom separated, and it had been that way for several years.

Fran and I were sleeping in Junebug's bedroom. We went to bed late that night after Junebug, Fran, and me had played Rook, our favorite card game. Junebug's dad, Engle Barber, always played with us.

After midnight, the door to the room burst open, and Engle yelled for us to get up.

"What's wrong?" Junebug asked sleepily.

"The Guernsey is having her calf. I need help," Engle emphasized.

298 · SHERMAN SMITH

"Fran, you and Sonny come on and help, too," Engle instructed.

Most of the time, cows giving birth to calves happened in the night when the cow was in the field or in a stall in the barn. A farmer would find the cow and calf the next morning; the afterbirth already cleaned up by the good mother, and the calf standing by on wobbly legs or drinking from the sweet fountain of nourishment from the cow's utters.

Sometimes, the cow needed assistance, and that is how we found Beauty, one of the Barber's prize milk cows. I had milked her several times because she was so gentle. This particular night the cow was in a lot of pain.

Before we reached the barn, we could hear Beauty bellowing a long, lonesome, and painful cry. The cow was in labor, and we found her lying on her side breathing very hard, and with each agonizing breath, her eyes stood wide open as if in a state of terror, while her tongue hung loosely from her mouth. We could see no signs of blood coming from the cow's uterus, and her belly was bloated nearly twice its size as the calf struggled from within trying to escape the den that was dark and wet.

"The calf's breach," Engle said, "Stan, you get over to Crab Orchard and get Doc Sinclair."

Stanley Barber was Junebug's brother and lived on the farm next to Engle and Sally Barber. Stan quickly jumped in the pickup, and he and Jerry Barber, his son, would make the run for the Doc. Stan spun gravel as he drove from the barnyard throwing rock behind, some of it hitting the barn.

"Where's momma?" Doc Sinclair asked. The Doc was dressed in a suit and tie.

"I've delivered lots of babies," he said. "Engle, you get an IV started, and I will scrub and get ready for delivery."

We all stared at Doc Sinclair dressed in his fancy suit as if he were ready for church.

"Old timers," Engle commented.

"You mean Alzheimer's?" I questioned. I had learned about this disease that struck old people erasing their memories of present things and sending them back in time to another place in life.

"Old timers," Engle corrected, "he's got old timers."

Doc Sinclair was taking his time, which made us all nervous.

"What's his name going to be, Jack?" Who was Jack? "Name him Billy," the Doc suggested.

The Doc kneeled down behind the cow in the light of the kerosene lanterns Fran and I were holding. He didn't bother to take off his suit jacket as he stuck his whole arm inside the cow. The cow bellowed loudly and tried to get up, but Engle and Stan had their knees on the cow holding her down.

Doc Sinclair pulled his arm from the cow, and the sleeve of his jacket was soaked with blood and afterbirth. I thought I was going to throw up.

"Take the baby to the nursery and call the father," the Doc said matter of factly. He wiped himself off and headed for the truck.

"Doc, Doc, this is Engle Barber and that is Beauty. You remember her; you've been taking care of her since she was a calf."

"Oh, yeah, where is the cow?" The Doc prepared to start all over.

He walked back into the barn, and the cow mooed even louder. She was straining to give birth, but couldn't. Doc Sinclair stuck his arm back into the cow after taking his jacket off.

"How'd my jacket get so bloody?" He asked and then turned his attention to his patient.

"The calf's breach," the Doc said shaking his head as if he didn't know what to do. "Engle, get a log chain."

"What for?" Engle asked.

"Get the chain."

While Stan retrieved the log chain from another building, the Doc kept trying to pry out the calf by hand but to no avail. The Doc pushed the chain into the cow and with Engle holding open her uterus so the Doc could work, he tied the chain around the calf.

"We're going to lose the calf," the Doc said glancing behind him at the others. "Get the tractor," he instructed, "drive it outside the barn. We'll use the barn for leverage to pull the cow out. It's the only chance Beauty has."

One end of the chain was inside the cow, and the other now stuck through the barn boards forming the high walls of the tobacco barn. Doc Sinclair tied the chain to the tractor and instructed Stan Barber to slowly pull the chain taut and ease the calf from the cow.

Beauty's rear end was all the way against the barn, and the tractor was straining to pull the calf from its hiding place. Blood gushed out of the cow, and she cried and screamed in pain. *Why don't they just kill the cow,* I thought to myself, *and get her out of her misery?*

The others watched the Doc work as if this was a normal event, but they knew it wasn't. No one had ever seen a calf delivered like this before.

"Pull harder, Jack," the Doc yelled at Stan. The tractor groaned, but he realized it was a futile attempt. "Stop!" The Doc screamed, "you're going to kill the cow! What are you trying to do anyway? Jack, I've told you a thousand times to never hook a chain to a cow and try to drag out the calf, you'll kill them both!"

The Doc walked out of the barn leaving poor Beauty in misery and approached the tractor.

"Get off the tractor and get to the house, Jack. You've got no business out here!"

Stan got off the tractor and looked at his dad. "What are we going to do now?" He asked.

"Junebug, get my knife off my dresser and bring it up here," Engle demanded.

Doc Sinclair hadn't given up. "Give me your knife, Engle," the Doc commanded as calmly as a surgeon instructing a nurse during a delicate operation.

"I'm going to have to cut up the calf in order to save your cow."

Junebug handed the Doc Engle's big hawk billed Case knife, which was as sharp as a razor having been honed to shave a man's beard in the leisure time as Engle relaxed with the whet stone in his hands.

Soon, the Doc's strong arm was in the cow as he gently but firmly started cutting up the calf. The first slice of surgery made the calf kick wildly inside the cow. Both were now in so much pain and misery it was difficult to watch. The first piece came out mingled with afterbirth and blood. It was the calf's left leg, but inside the calf was still struggling.

"That's it," the Doc explained while still holding the leg in his hands. "It's a girl." He wiped his hands and cleaned off the mess. "I'll wash up and go talk to the father."

"Give me the knife, Doc," Engle yelled. "Get him back to Crab Orchard!"

I could barely see the taillights through the cracks in the walls as Stan Barber sped down the lane. Engle reached deep inside the cow and started doing what he was going to do in the first place when he told Junebug to fetch his knife.

The calf was silent and Beauty barely breathed as the pain and shock reverberated through her whole body. The ordeal had taken its toll. Engle pulled out the other calf's leg, which was a front leg, and made it easier to work inside the cow. Piece by piece a pile of body parts rose from the dusty barn floor.

Engle had trouble with the head. "Look at the size of that head. No wonder she couldn't get the calf out of her. It must be twice the size of a normal head." When Engle turned the calf's head over and puzzled by the enormity of it; it was then that we were all shocked into disbelief as the calf did not have one large head, but two. This abnormality was known to happen but never on the Barber farm. There was a two-headed calf one year at the Brodhead Fair. Engle stared at the freaky looking phenomena. "It would never have lived anyway."

The next morning, I got up early before breakfast, and I could smell the biscuits, bacon, and sausage cooking in the kitchen. I walked out to the barn to check on the cow. I had been bothered all night about Beauty's suffering. I thought about the weird calf and then about Doc and his crazy talk. He had Alzheimer's Disease; there was no question about it. This disease had apparently been around a long time because Engle Barber knew exactly what was wrong with the old man. I also thought about how I would never, ever think about being a doctor or a veterinarian.

Beauty was still breathing hard from the nightmare she had suffered. She'd given birth plenty of times, but this one wasn't supposed to happen this way. Tied to a tractor, her baby cut up brutally from inside her, and she looked at me with big brown eyes, the eyelashes long and curly, as if there could be no more sorrow she could stand. I noticed trickles of tears rolling off her long eyelids as she pulled her head up and stared at me. She never made a sudden move like she would later when Engle Barber walked in.He had hurt her, and I hadn't.

"What'd you think, Bud?" Fran said as he walked up and patted Beauty on the head and felt her ears. He rubbed her face and patted some more. The pile of calf hide and bones sitting not far from her head had begun to smell.

"I've got to get this mess cleaned up, so Mr. Barber doesn't have to fool with it," Fran said.

"I feel sorry for this cow, Fran. When we were littler, I used to think that cows and other animals went to heaven, but dad says that ain't so."

"Ain't no cows in heaven, Bud."

For days, Beauty would barely eat and drink and then slowly her strength returned, and she was soon giving that rich milk she was famous for. Engle Barber would never let a bull near that cow again.

"Doc Sinclair is sick, Preacher, he's asking for you." This message was delivered by Sheriff Crane a few weeks after Stan Barber had taken old Doc back to Crab Orchard that night after the cow affair.

Doc was ninety-five years old and had been in that part of the country practicing medicine on people and animals for nearly seventy years. He outlived everyone from the day he opened up his office in Crab Orchard, including several generations of animals.

Floyd had taken the Doc down to Stanford to the hospital. My dad and Fran walked into the room where the old man was dying. As it often happened these days, my dad would take Fran with him to make some of these visits instead of me. Fran was trying to walk the straight and narrow so as not to upset his relationship with my dad, which could bother his relationship with my sister, Leah. I think my dad thought I was heading into a life of sin.

We had an incident a few days before at the trailer by the church. My mom needed to go to the outhouse in a hurry, so she grabbed my coat instead of taking her own. I thought nothing of it.

I watched my mom leisurely stroll on the path to the ladies' restroom and reach in my pockets to warm her hands.

It suddenly dawned on me that my pack of Lucky Strikes was in the pocket. Fran and I had enough money at this time to afford the luxury of store bought cigarettes, at least once in a while we could enjoy a pack. Fran purchased the pack for me at the Babs Kirk Store.

Sure enough, within two seconds, the pack was in my mother's hand. She looked at it, turned it over and over, and then took a quick glance over her shoulder looking back at the trailer. Cold chills ran all over me as I watched her discover my best-kept secret. I would be caught directly with possession of the substance and that would be real bad. My mother came back from doing her duty and looked at me sitting on the couch nervously fidgeting with my fingernails. In fact, I had bitten them nearly off.

"I'll have to tell your dad," she said, "I hate to, but I'll have to do it."

My mom never told on me for a single bad thing I did except for smoking. She once told my dad she was sure I was smoking. "He smells like a walking cigarette," she said. Fran said it was hard for my dad to smell tobacco smoke on me because he was in the barns all day visiting the farmers, and their cigarette smoke was on him. "Your mom tells on you because she wants to smoke herself," Fran reasoned. I don't know how he knew this or why he came up with this opinion. He also told me that Loretta Kirk and my mom were sneaking and smoking when my mom visited Loretta at her farm. That was never proven, but I did hear it from a couple of other people.

Fran had smoked since he was seven years old, and neither his parents nor my dad ever said a word about it. He was sitting with my sister in church, and he seemed immune from prosecution. "It's because you're the Preacher's kid, Bud, you have to set an example. If I ever marry Leah, which I will, I won't smoke. It would be bad for the Preacher's testimony."

I saw Fran walking up the church lane. He and I had planned on going rabbit hunting that afternoon. I hurried out of the trailer and all I had time to do was say one thing to him.

"Tell them they're yours," I whispered rapidly.

"What?"

I could say no more. There wasn't time because my dad was walking toward us and followed us into the trailer. He had taken a break from his studies.

"Jerry, Sonny's smoking. I know this for a fact," my mom told him.

Holy crap! I thought, *I'm as good as dead and buried!*

"How do you know that?" My dad asked as he looked at me with that expression on his face that I hated because I knew I was in deep stuff.

My mom pulled out the shiny pack of read and white Lucky Strikes, and the bright red bulls-eye in the center of the pack looked like a target on my forehead where an arrow would soon pierce dead center.

"I found these in his pocket as I was walking to the out-house."

My dad glared at me, his deep brown eyes growing darker.

"I thought I left my pack of cigarettes somewhere," Fran said out of the blue. My mom and dad looked at him. "I put Bud's jacket on this morning and took a smoke. I knew I left them somewhere," Fran cheerfully said acting as if he were more than pleased to find the missing pack. My mom handed the cigarettes to him, and I thought she looked relieved.

Fran used to smoke Lucky Strikes, and that was the reason I smoked them. I think just for an instant, my dad could taste the fine cigarette he used to love smoking while drinking his coffee in the morning on the farm in Kansas. This was a close call because they all knew Fran smoked Pall Malls.

"Doesn't Fran smoke Pall Malls?" My mother asked my dad as Fran and I were walking down the lane.

My dad took Doc's hand and held it.

"Hello, Jack," the Doc said. "How's your mother?"

The Doc never married after his wife died of Tuberculosis thirty years before.

"Is that Jimmy? Come here, Jimmy, and let grandpa take a look at you. My, my, you've grown, boy."

Jimmy was the Doc's grandson who was tragically killed when a tractor rolled over on him while plowing a field where they raised tobacco. Jimmie was thirty-eight years old when that happened.

"You okay, Doc?" My dad asked.

"Preacher. Where'd you come from? Did you see Jack?"

"He and Jimmy went to the cafeteria to get some coffee," my dad told him.

"Jimmy's too young to be drinking coffee," the Doc replied.

Fran had never seen a man die except the night of the Northern Lights, but he actually didn't see Mr. Petrie die. There was no calling the family because the Doc didn't have any. Jack Sinclair died from a heart attack when he was sixty-five years old and had never married. Doc outlived all his other family, so my dad was his next best kin and that is why he asked for him.

"There's a nice surprise for you, Preacher; I left something for you in my office."

He whispered the combination to the safe in my dad's ear and then took a deep and long sigh.

"See the angels?" He cried, "I hear music. See the light? Okay, I'm ready," and then he was gone.

Fran had heard about these deathbed scenes. He had heard about angels, and he had heard that some people go kicking a screaming that they see the devil and can feel the heat from the flames. He described what he had heard the moment Doc Sinclair passed away, and he was shaken by it all.

The Doc released the grip he had on my dad's hand, and Fran said, "I think I saw the angels."

CHAPTER TWENTY-EIGHT

We buried old Doc Sinclair in the Crab Orchard Cemetery. Hundreds of people stood on the little rise that overlooked the Dix River. Many folks had come from miles around and most of them had been long forgotten who had moved from the area in Lincoln County years ago. Old faces were recognized, and as was the custom after a burial, food was brought by the farm community women and put on wagons that had been pulled to the funeral by pickups and tractors. It seemed by mid-afternoon that all these people who had been birthed by Doc Sinclair had forgotten about the funeral, and the occasion seemed more like a huge family reunion. Often years would go by before those who had left Chapel Gap returned from other places. Funerals drew them back together so many were related. Older women would exclaim their wonderment when they recognized one of the boys or girls who had grown up there; especially, in the Evergreen Baptist Church. Most of them were adults and had their own families. The laborious and detailed introductions took a long time.

After my dad had made his rounds and filled his belly, listened to the comments such as, "Pastor Smith that was the most beautiful service I've ever heard," my dad said his good-byes and left the cemetery by himself.

"Where's my dad going?" I asked my mom who was busy gossiping with the women.

"He'll be back," she replied barely looking my direction, "he has to take care of some business."

I had no idea what "business" my dad was attending because Fran never said a word about Doc Sinclair giving my dad the combination to his safe.

"Hey Fran," I called to him while he ate some gooseberry pie. "where's my dad going?"

Fran choked, and I knew that he knew. Fran and I shared every secret we ever had, and I was not going to let him keep this one.

"What didn't you tell me, Fran? I know you're keeping a secret, so lets have it."

"Meet me behind the tent by the grave," Fran said discreetly while covering his mouth so that no one could read his lips, and I knew this was a doozy.

"When Doc went to the hospital, he whispered the combination to his safe in the Preacher's ear and told him to go to his office."

"That's it? Why didn't you tell me?"

"The Preacher made me promise."

"Did you promise, Fran?"

"I had my fingers crossed."

It was the unwritten rule that if you promised something, and had your fingers crossed when you made the promise, you wouldn't have to keep the promise unless of course, the person you made the promise to asked if you had your fingers crossed, and then to show your hands and make the promise again. One time I had my toes crossed, but that didn't count. Fran told me everything, and I am sure that my dad didn't know this rule.

"Let's go," I said.

"Go where?"

"To Doc Sinclair's office."

"Bud, if I go with you over there the Preacher will know that I broke my promise. No way. You better not go either because he will wonder how you knew he has the safe's combination."

"I swear I will tell him I watched him drive away and then noticed that he pulled into Doc's office. That's the truth anyway."

If you looked hard, you could see Floyd's Funeral Home and down the street a little ways, you could see the front entrance of Doc's place.

"You swear you won't get me into trouble?" Fran pleaded.

"I swear."

"Let me see your hands."

My dad didn't have a key to the office, but he knew where one was. Many times my dad had to wake the Doc up who lived in the back rooms of the building. The Doc told him where to find the key that was hidden under the shutter on the left window as you faced the building. It could be that other people knew where the key was as well.

My dad opened the door as several cars passed him that had been at the funeral and were now carrying unvehicled passengers back to their homes. He waved and went on in.

The Doc must have known he was going to die because the place was clean. He had never seen anything in order or organized in the Doc's office. For years, dust had collected on the desk and furniture. The backs of the Doc's shelves had been cleaned and some looked brand new, though dusty. His desk was arranged, but my dad noticed a curiosity. There was a fresh piece of paper pinned to the long spike on the Doc's desk where he kept his most recent billing orders.

My dad unfolded the note, which would have been unseen by anyone except the person who was familiar with the Doc's record keeping. My dad spent many hours sitting across from the Doc visiting him and talking while my mom was shopping at the Rich Jameson store for groceries. He knew the Doc's habits like his own; he looked at the unusually clean desk and knew instantly that the piece of paper lying on top of the spiked bills was out of place.

"Preacher, look behind the book in my library, 'Hie To The Hunters,' and you will find instructions concerning my death."

"Hie To The Hunters" was a book by Jesse Stewart, my favorite author. I had read the book because Doc Sinclair let me take it home with me one time when I was there with my dad, and I noticed the book. I was fiddling with it when the Doc told me to take it home and read it. Perhaps that was the reason he chose that particular book to leave his instructions.

My dad pulled the book from the shelf and noticed immediately that there was paper folded and neatly placed where no one could find it unless they were looking for it.

The papers contained Doc's simple one page will he had scribbled out by hand, and it looked as if he waited until he knew that death was imminent because the writing was scrawled and difficult to read. He had clearly signed it and dated it the day before his death.

"This office building is to be given to a doctor who will commit to this practice and forever it shall remain a doctor's office. A doctor shall use it for as long as he serves the Crab Orchard Area. If for any reason he leaves his practice, the building shall be preserved for another doctor as long as this world shall be. I place the deed of this building in the safekeeping of the Evergreen Baptist church."

The other request by the Doc was strange.

I leave all my cash to the Evergreen Baptist Church to be divided up between the church and Pastor Jerry S. Smith.

Doc Sinclair didn't have a pastor and as close as he ever came to admitting there was a Spiritual advisor in his life was when he told one of his patients one day, "The Preacher at Crab Orchard Baptist is a wimp; the Preacher at Evergreen Baptist, now that's a real man." He never attended the church one time that anyone ever remembered, and he never, ever attended a funeral even though his friend, Floyd, had tried on several occasions to enlist his help with a funeral or two.

Taped to the will was a note written on scrap paper. "Preacher, you will find further instructions in the "Thread.""

There were no instructions about how to pay for the funeral because long ago, Doc Sinclair gave Floyd the money and instructions for his funeral. My dad went to the back room that Doc used for sewing and repairing his clothes. He inspected the old Singer sewing machine and looked for Doc's case of thread.

After searching for an hour, my dad didn't find a note of any kind, or any hint of what the Doc meant by the "Thread."

"What are you doing here?" My dad said as I slid into the building. He had heard me coming in and seemed irritated. "You've got no business here, now what do you want?"

"I, I just wanted to see if you are all right; you left in a hurry."

My dad realized that he had been short with me. "Did Fran speak to you about Doc Sinclair, tell you anything important?"

"Nope," I lied to protect my friend and had my fingers crossed.

314 · SHERMAN SMITH

"Stay here and guard this place while I run over to the bank." I sat down on the Doc's couch and waited.

The Crab Orchard Bank was a small bank that wasn't very secure and had been robbed several times. One of its biggest claims to fame was that Jesse James robbed the bank. There was a large mural covering much of the wall behind the two tellers that depicted the James gang shooting it out with the cops as they rode away with the bank's money. I often wondered how people felt when they were making their deposits while looking at the mural.

Jim Goodnight was the bank's Vice President although he did much more in the bank than be an officer. He was one of four employees. My dad sat down at Mr. Goodnight's desk. They knew each other well because Evergreen Baptist Church and my dad did their banking there and most of the church for that matter.

"Jimmy, I have a very private question, and I have to confide in you. You have to promise that you'll never breathe a word of what I am about to tell you." My dad said this as he watched Loretta Kirk eyeballing him from the teller booth where she was waiting to do banking business.

"Go ahead," Vice President Goodnight said, "I won't tell anyone."

My dad didn't ask to see his fingers but showed the papers to the VP he had retrieved from the bookshelf per Doc Sinclair's instructions.

"Hmm," he mused. He had particularly noticed the paragraph about the Doc's cash.

"He's got no money here to speak of. He has a small checking account he uses to pay some bills and buy medical supplies, but that's it. We've tried for years to get Doc to put his money in this bank, but he always told us, "You've been robbed too much." So, I don't know what to tell you. I suppose his money is in a bank in Lexington or Louisville. When Jack Sinclair was alive, he used to take some of the Doc's money up there, but that would be like looking for a needle in a hay stack, finding that money and all."

My dad did not show Mr. Goodnight the note that said to look in the "Thread."

"Thanks Jimmy. This is in God's hands now, and if he wants the church to have the money, He'll bring it to us."

"Oh, Preacher, as soon as we see a Death Certificate assuring us that the Doc is dead, we'll give you the money in his account here." My dad stared at him and walked out the door.

After my dad retrieved me during a good nap on the Doc's couch, we drove back to the cemetery. The farmers were hitching up their wagons and leaving. Left over food was being divided and shared with different families. There was enough food left over to feed Cox's Army, and much of the food was given to the known poorer families who attended every funeral whether they knew the deceased or not, and some of the food was given to feed other hungry families. My mother enlisted my dad, Fran, and me to help carry dishes of delicious recipes the Preacher always received at funerals. We loaded the trunk of the car.

My dad was silent as we drove through Crab Orchard. He glanced at Doc Sinclair's office as we drove by and then turned onto the Chapel Gap Road. He waved at Odin McGrevey and his wife as we crossed the railroad track before speeding up toward Chapel Gap Hill.

"Did Doc Sinclair ever mention a bank account?" My dad asked my mom. Fran and I were in the back seat.

"The Doc never talked to me," my mom answered.

"I was thinking that Loretta Kirk might have mentioned it. She knows everything that goes on around here."

"Never mentioned it to me," my mom said, "not once. I

doubt if the Doc would tell her anything like that about his personal business. He didn't like her anyway; made her take her kids to Stanford to the doctor; said she should pay more attention to her own business than sticking her nose in everybody else's. Where'd you go when you left the cemetery?"

My dad thought for a minute and then for some reason or other, he showed my mom the note that the Doc left concerning cash that would be given to the Evergreen Baptist Church and to him.

"I looked in his sewing room. I went through everything but there was no sign of any message." He explained.

"Why did you look in the sewing room?" Fran asked.

"The note was in a book, *Hie To The Hunters* by Jesse Stewart. It said to look it in the "Thread."

"The Thread That Runs So True," Fran said quietly.

"What?"

"THE THREAD THAT RUNS SO TRUE," Fran repeated louder, "the will was behind *Hie To The Hunters*, Jesse Stewart's book, and he also wrote the *Thread That Runs So True.*

CHAPTER TWENTY-NINE

We were speeding as fast as my dad could safely drive with four passengers in the station wagon. We were almost up the Chapel Gap Hill when Fran revealed that my dad would find another note in Jesse Stewart's other book in the Doc's library.

"There it is," Fran pointed to the top shelf. "The Thread That Runs So True."

My dad grabbed a small stepladder that Doc Sinclair used to get to the top shelves of his many bookcases. He pulled with anticipation the book by Jesse Stewart from the shelf and opened the cover.

"To Doc Sinclair," the inscription began, "Our lives have many parallels. I've taught school in the most remote places of Eastern Kentucky where education would have been non-existent had I not gone there with little money and no guaranteed salary. You have done the same thing. You have treated folks and their animals when those Knob people would have suffered without. You did it with no pay and little pay. May there be blessings from God and prosperity for the rest of your life." Signed, Jesse Stewart.

I couldn't believe that I was looking at the signature of the most famous Kentucky Folk Author of all time, and it was right there in there in the Doc's office, and I never knew it.

"Can I have a look, dad?"

"I don't think the Doc would mind at all," he said as he handed me the signed copy.

"Preacher, you will find the safe in the basement. Walk six steps from the right wall, and you will see an old bureau. Behind the bureau is a hole in the dirt. You will see the safe there." These were the Doc's instructions.

The basement was entirely made of dirt. There were no concrete or block walls. The basement had been dug by hand years after the building was built. The foundation of the building was easily seen as the diggers left a few feet of solid dirt for the building to stand on. It was dark down there; so dark you couldn't see your hand at your face. It smelled of musty dirt and molded paper as we crept down the rickety stairs.

My dad picked up Doc Sinclair's flashlight lying on the steps, but it barely had a beam, and my dad cautioned us to watch our step. We stood on the dirt floor. Stacks and stacks of papers lay in disarray all over the place. Old newspapers from almost a century ago, medical records he kept of his patients, and more books than we could count.

The bureau stood exactly where it probably sat since the Doc built the basement. It had ornate glass doors and beautifully carved drawers with fancy glass handles.

"That thing must be worth a fortune," my dad commented as he shined the light on the dusty glass that reflected back towards us. "You guys give me a hand."

We pushed the heavy piece of furniture away from the wall

and found the hole that Doc Sinclair had dug in the side of the basement wall to hide the safe. The pile of dirt still lay in the same place where he had thrown it and never cleaned it up.

My dad noticed something shiny on the floor below the hole. He reached down and picked it up. In his hand, was the combination lock to the safe. It was beaten by something very hard because my dad couldn't turn the face as he fiddled with it. He flashed the light into the hole, and the safe was there. One would wonder how the Doc got the heavy piece of equipment down there much less hoist it up into the deep pocket.

"Someone beat us here," my dad said as we saw the safe's door hanging open. You could smell the musty odor of old money coming from the inside. My dad looked for secret compartments and such, but the safe had been completely cleaned out.

"Don't touch anything; don't taint the crime scene," Sheriff Crane ordered as he examined the things we had already touched. "There may be fingerprints."

Yes there were fingerprints, ours, but we obeyed without incident as the Sheriff told us to leave the premises while his investigation was going forward.

He took a few pictures of the crime scene with his old Brownie Kodak Camera with the huge flashbulbs. Floyd came down to the office when he saw the lights of Sheriff Crane's pickup blocking the street in front of the Doc's office. The Sheriff had ordered the road blocked off at each intersection, and the line of traffic coming from Highway 150 towards Brodhead and Mount Vernon, Kentucky was backed up for a couple of miles. Trooper Tip Tuck was stuck in the traffic unable to get into town.

Tip turned on his big red light and eased past the traffic toward Crab Orchard. He radioed that he was investigating a large traffic jam outside Crab Orchard and asked the dispatcher at the station in Stanford if there had been any reports of an accident. He feared the worse.

"10-4," Tip Tuck said as he was informed that there had been no reports of anything happening in Crab Orchard.

Tip noticed that Sheriff Crane's pickup with the emergency lights blinking on top of the cab was blocking the highway. The Sheriff had instructed Bobby Kidd, who stood in the middle of the road at the only traffic light, not to allow anyone to pass. Tip yelled at the kid and told him to get out of the way and go down to the other end of the street and tell the idiot there to stop blocking traffic and let the cars pass through.

"Sheriff's orders," Bobby Kidd said as though Tip wouldn't have jurisdiction over the state route that ran through the town.

"What the hell is he doing?" Tip asked himself as he saw the crowd outside Doc Phillip's office.

Tip got in Sheriff Crane's pickup and moved it to the side of the road himself. He turned off the flashing lights and took the keys.

"What are you doing?" State Trooper Tip Tuck asked the Sheriff. "Why wasn't I called?"

"This is not your business, Tip," the Sheriff answered as if that was the only explanation needed for blocking traffic for miles.

"It is my business if you are going to shut down the traffic flow on a state highway. You know to notify the State Police when you are going to do that."

"Uh, well, uh, sorry, Tip, but we got ourselves a real crime here. I wasn't thinking about protocol."

The Sheriff explained that he believed the Doc's safe, that nobody in the whole universe knew about until Fran had unraveled the clues, was robbed.

"Well, that's pretty obvious," Tip mused, "being locks don't beat themselves with sledge hammers and then empty the safe."

"Give me the lock," Tip said, "and I'll run fingerprints at the lab and see if we can come up with something."

All the fingerprints on the lock were my dad's, and they knew he wasn't the perpetrator. The money was his anyway, so the mystery was going to take a while to solve, if it ever was. Besides, whoever had the cash would be long gone by now, and it sadly looked as if the church would have no money. If there was a chance at all, God would have to reveal the thief very quickly and that is just what the Evergreen Baptist Church was praying about that next Sunday.

"Brothers and sisters in Christ," my dad explained from the pulpit, "We have been praying for the funds to build a new Sunday School building. We have no more room for our kids because the church has grown so much. Unless God brings us a miracle, it could be years before we ever have enough money for a new Sunday School Building."

The church never went into debt and didn't believe in it, although there were those who thought it would make sense since inflation was going to make the building cost more in the future than they would pay for interest at the bank for a short-term loan. This issue was debated hotly in the business meetings on Wednesday nights once a month at the church.

"When I saw that Bro. Doc Sinclair," people stirred at the mention of "Bro. Doc," they hadn't heard him called that before, "had left the church his money, I knew the will of God in all this. Bro. Sinclair would never have left the church money if God wasn't working out His will for us. I was also going to give the money he left to me personally to the church." My mother sat straight up when she heard this because she was already looking at a new car and house.

Eyes also pierced Loretta Kirk and her gossiping buddies

because they had been on the phone telling the rest of the gossips that the only reason my dad was so concerned about the money was because of the part he was getting. "He didn't have any money anyway," Loretta Kirk reasoned.

"Brothers and sisters in Christ, we've got to pray and pray hard that whoever did this terrible thing against the Lord's true New Testament Church and the saints of God will be brought to justice."

There was an "Amen" from the men and some weeping by the women. An unusually long line of rededicators stood in front of the congregation during invitation time that Sunday morning.

Evel Martin flashed an old musty one hundred dollar bill at Lester Bishop. Martin was up in Broughtontown at the Bishop Store trying to buy some bootlegged firecrackers.

Firecrackers were illegal in Kentucky, so some of the more enterprising farmers would make a trip to Jellico, Tennessee where underage kids ran off and got married, and brought firecrackers they smuggled into Kentucky to sell for twice the amount they had paid for them to certain store owners, who would then mark them up again. Lester Bishop was a known firecracker bootlegger.

Jellico, Tennessee was the marriage capital for Eastern Kentucky and the Knobs. It was the Las Vegas of the hill country because you could legally get married in Tennessee at fourteen years old without parental consent. Lester had just bought a load, and the word got out that he had some powerful cherry bombs, the favorite explosive of the kids living in the Knobs.

"Where'd you get that kind of money, Evel?" Lester Bishop asked.

"I don't think that's any of your damned business, Lester. Now give me those cherry bombs."

Martin left Doc Sinclair's office with two gunney sacks

full of cash. He had parked his car at 2:00 AM in the morning behind the Crab Orchard Baptist Church where he knew no one would be looking at that hour in the morning. The only thing he had to be concerned about would be a State Trooper on duty and driving his rounds patrolling the roads for drunk drivers, bootleggers, and checking the Crab Orchard Bank. He exited the back door of the office and used the shadows of the large maple trees to hide as he hoisted the cash sacks and made his way back to the church.

He drove carefully using the back streets of the small town to make his way to the Chapel Gap/Ottenheim Road. No one was awake at that hour, and the little houses in the village were dark. He met no cars or trucks, and as soon as he was safely out of town, he made his way quickly to his farm on Pine Hall Road.

Evel's dad, Vel Martin, had passed away from too much drinking when Evel was only eight years old. He and his mother farmed the land for a living.

Evel pulled into the old farm barnyard. He wasn't worried about waking his mother, Ethel, because she was used to Evel coming in at all hours of the morning, and many times he didn't come into the house because he was too drunk.

Martin carried the heavy sacks of money into the barn and took his flashlight and laid it on the floor of his barn's loft. After he had counted several thousand dollars, he hadn't made a dent in the stacks of bills.

His mind flashed back to that day when he was with his dad at old Doc Sinclair's office. His father was a basement digger and was hired many times to dig and dispose of dirt by some of the townspeople wishing to add storage space to their small homes.

He watched for weeks as Vel Martin dug out the hard dirt with a pick and then carried the dirt in five gallon buckets and dumped them in the back of his pickup. His dad worked hard digging a ramp down to where he would be digging under the Doc's house. The ramp made it easier to dispose of the dirt since he would not have to carry all the buckets through the house. He did all the digging by hand without another person helping him. At the end of the day, he would take his truckload of dirt and dump it on his farm and then begin the process all over the next day. He did this laborious job day after day until he had finished digging the basement under Doc Sinclair's office and home.

"Can you dig a hole in the wall over there?" The Doc asked Vel. "Make it about three feet by three feet."

Vel Martin did this very quickly, and then the Doc paid him in cash. Evel was thinking about this and how he had wondered all those years what the Doc needed that hole for. He remembered this as if it were yesterday. He also told Vel to leave the dirt on the floor and that he would clean it up himself.

When the news hit Pine Hall, Chapel Gap, and Broughtontown that Doc Sinclair had died, Evel Martin plotted about how he would go over to the Doc's office and find out what was in that hole his dad had dug in the wall so many years ago.

Evel was on a curiosity mission, and when he discovered the big black safe in Doc Sinclair's basement, he felt as if he had won the Irish Sweepstakes. He went to his farm that same night and brought with him a twenty pound sledge hammer and beat the lock off the old safe that the Doc had bought from the Crab Orchard Bank when they installed more modern equipment to keep their stores secure.

"He's got nobody to leave the money to," Evel thought as he scraped out the heaps of money from the safe, "so what's the big deal?" He couldn't possibly in his wildest imaginations know that his life long enemy, Preacher Smith was involved.

CHAPTER THIRTY

Hands up!" Sheriff Crane ordered Lester Bishop. "Now stand over there, Homer, you watch him while I search the back storage room."

Barry Wilmott was playing with some cherry bombs behind the Broughtontown School, which was only a half-mile or so from the Bishop Store. The explosion was heard by some of the kids playing in their yards next to the school, and Barry came running from behind the building screaming that his fingers were gone. Three of them were missing from his left hand where the quick fuse had surprised him before he could drop the explosive. Sheriff Crane and Deputy Shanks had wretched a confession out of nine-year-old Barry Wilmott that Lester Bishop had sold him the powerful firecrackers.

The Sheriff knew that Lester Bishop was selling or bootlegging firecrackers, and neither he nor Homer Shanks thought there was really any thing wrong with it, so they didn't harass Bishop. Besides, they were both related to the Bishops through distant cousins.

Selling a little kid a cherry bomb couldn't be overlooked, and they knew the community would be outraged. Members of the Friendship Baptist Church where the Wilmotts were members demanded that Lester Bishop's store be shut down. Firecrackers weren't the only thing he was bootlegging, and men of the little village's dwellers had told the Sheriff that their kids came home drunk from the beer and redeye whiskey Bishop sold them.

"The law's the law," the Deputy stated as he held his .38 revolver near Bishop's head. Bishop was protesting wildly that they couldn't search his store because they didn't have a warrant.

"You've been watching too much television," Homer Shanks commented.

"Now shut up and don't move, or I'll blow your acne infested head off."

The Sheriff found all kinds of firecrackers in the storehouse. *There's enough powder in here to blow up the whole town,* he thought.

The rumors were true that Lester Bishop was bootlegging. Stacks and stacks of beer bottles were found by the Sheriff stored out of the way behind the feed and grain sacks.

"Selling firecrackers is a misdemeanor, Lester, so I'm going to give you notice to appear in court and pay a fine. The judge will decide if there is criminal activity for the loss of Barry Wilmott's fingers."

The Sheriff said nothing about the beer in the storeroom. Lester Bishop could have all the beer he wanted for his own use, and there was no proof that anybody had ever bought beer or whiskey from him.

"I'm taking all the cherry bombs and firecrackers," the Sheriff said.

"You can't do that you S.O.B.'s!" Lester screamed.

Homer Shanks towered over Bishop. "You cuss the Sheriff one more time and disrespect him again, and I'll beat the crap out of you so badly they won't recognize who you are."

Lester was still screaming and cussing as the pickups pulled away completely loaded with contraband.

Homer Shanks was tall and illiterate, but he wasn't dumb. "Sheriff, while you were searching the storeroom, Lizzie McIntyre bought some bread. When Lester opened the cash drawer, I noticed a hundred dollar bill lying on the side. It looked very old, and the strange thing is, I could smell it," the Deputy said keying his mike and then hanging it back on the dashboard.

The Sheriff whipped his truck to the side of the road and slid around, fishtailing in the gravel and headed back to the store. Lester Bishop wiped his face with his bandana.

"Did Evel Martin buy firecrackers from you, Lester?" The Sheriff asked.

"I don't sell firecrackers," Lester said, "they're illegal."

"You don't give them away."

"I have a big family."

A couple of days later, Sheriff Crane was in the pool room digging out one of the bullets Martin had shot into the door jam of the pool hall. He bought an RC and some peanuts and paid for them with a twenty. Delbert Blanchard gave him change. Sheriff Crane had almost stuck the money in his wallet and moved on, but a strange smell stopped him. He fingered the ten-dollar bill in his hands, feeling the musty residue between his fingers, and then put the bill to his nose and sniffed.

"Delbert, has Evel Martin been in here?" The Sheriff quizzed as he poured the salty peanuts into the neck of the Royal Crown Cola.

"Yeah, this morning."

"Did he buy anything?"

"Yeah, he paid for a couple of games of pool."

"Did you give him change?"

"I think so. I don't believe he paid with exact change."

"Did he give you this ten dollar bill?"

"Lots of people pay me with tens, Sheriff, I don't know who."

The Sheriff paused his fingering of the bill and took a swig of RC, and the peanuts ran into his mouth with his swallow. Delbert could smell the mustiness of the ten.

"Wait," he said, "when he handed me his money, I smelled something strange."

"Like this?" The Sheriff put the bill under Delbert Blanchard's nose.

"Yeah, that's it. I thought when I put the money in the cash box that it had a strong odor. Why?"

"Just curious," the Sheriff commented as he walked out of the poolroom.

The Sheriff stopped by Doc Sinclair's office and went through the front door. He found the steps to the basement and grabbed his flashlight and walked down. The old bureau that hid the hole in the wall sat cockeyed revealing the safe that still had its door hanging by the hinges after it took a beating from Evel Martin's twenty-pound sledgehammer.

Sheriff Crane walked over to the safe and stuck his head inside and took a deep breath. The smell was very strong, and there was no mistaking the odor. It was the same smell he smelled up in Broughtontown a few days before, and the same odor he had smelled in the pool hall a few minutes ago.

Evel Martin spent several days counting the money. He was in his barn loft behind a wall of straw bales he had set up to hide himself and the money. After counting, he cleverly concealed the cash into the bales and restacked them the same way the workers had when they were put into the barn.

When Evel had hit the two hundred fifty thousand dollar mark, he stopped counting and then estimated the rest. "There must be three hundred thousand dollars here," he thought although he had no conception of what three hundred thousand dollars really meant.

Martin had no idea what he was going to do with all this money. He did know that he was rich for the moment. He had never been anywhere, didn't know anything about the world outside of Broughtontown, Crab Orchard, Pine Hall, and Chapel Gap. He could buy a farm, but he was too smart for that. Everyone would be curious as to where he got the money. There would be an investigation, and he would be caught.

No, he thought to himself, *the best thing to do is sit on this cash, spend a little of it at a time, have some fun, and wait until Sheriff Crane goes up for election, and I will buy the votes with some of the money and put a more "friendly" Sheriff in office.*

He smiled to himself as he pondered how that he had enough money to head up to Louisville, a place he'd never been, and invest his money in whiskey and beer. Forget moonshining. He could house his beer much easier and wouldn't have to fool with a still. Besides, he could buy moonshine from one of the stills, buy it in volume, and resell it for a nice profit. He could control moonshining and bootlegging in Lincoln County. Evel Martin wasn't original in his thinking, but was he smart enough to pull it off? His reasoning came from listening to Curt Kirk think out loud about how he was going to enterprise the alcohol market. The more that Evel thought about this, the more confused he became. Martin's ears perked up as he heard a car coming up the dirt drive to his house. He got up on his feet and walked over to the wall and peered through the cracks. "Crap!" It's Sheriff Crane. "What the hell does he want?"

Martin quickly ran back to the hay and to the money. He stuffed the bills into a couple of bales and ran across the loft. He didn't want the Sheriff to see him coming from the barn, so he ran out the back of the barn and took a trail to the woods.

"Where's Evel?" The Sheriff asked Evel's mom who was dressed in a skimpy housedress that he could see all the way through.

Ethel Martin stood noticing the Sheriff's eyes glancing down quickly and then up. She shuffled her hair with her hand and eased further into the light coming from the kitchen window. The Sheriff looked away as he realized she had no underwear beneath the thin cotton dress.

"He's somewhere around. Probably checking his fish traps in the pond," Ethel answered.

The Sheriff had never realized how shapely Ethel was. She was full and round at the top, and her hips were firm below the flat belly. If only she had all her teeth, she would be a beautiful woman, but he wasn't looking at her teeth.

"Want some coffee?" She asked casually, "come on in and sit for awhile." Never had Sheriff Crane been so tempted, and the sweat oozied from beneath his cop's hat. Ethel looked down at him, which made matters all the worse. He was feeling so uncomfortable that he realized that he better end this conversation right then and there. He had a wife and kids, who he loved and protected, and his reputation was impeccable. He'd better get his business done and get out of there. "Hey, Sheriff," Evel said as he looked at his mom standing in the doorway.

The Sheriff walked to his pickup and opened the door. He reached inside. "Here, Evel, I want you to read this."

Evel took the piece of paper in his hand and looked it over not understanding one single thing it said. He handed it back to the Sheriff and then asked, "what's up with this?"

"Nothing," the Sheriff replied, "I just wanted everyone to

know that I'm running for reelection; you know, visiting all the farms, drumming up votes and all."

"You can count on us," Evel said, and the Sheriff nodded.

"What was that all about?" Ethel asked Evel.

"No, what was that all about? You standing in the doorway with the Sheriff gawking through your dress!"

"Oh, crap," Ethel cussed as she felt between her legs, "I forgot to put on my slip and panties!"

The Sheriff put the bill he had just received in the mail from the Crab Orchard Feed Store in his pocket after he had folded it carefully. He then picked up the microphone and keyed the switch.

"Sheriff to base," he called, "Sheriff to base."

"Base," came the reply from Priscilla Crane at the farm.

"Would you give Tip Tuck a call and ask him to meet me at the junction by Crab Orchard Baptist Church?"

"10-4. Base out."

In a few minutes, Priscilla Crane confirmed that Tip was on his way from Stanford and would meet her husband.

"Tip," the Sheriff said as the two vehicles were juxtaposition to the other so the cops could talk from their car windows. "I want you to have the lab up in Lexington run fingerprints off this paper. There are probably three sets there. Jack Brown's at the feed store, mine, and Evel Martin's."

The Sheriff handed Tip the ten-dollar bill that he had borrowed from Delbert Blanchard at the pool hall. "I want to know if Evel Martin's prints are on this bill; if they match the prints on the feed bill."

"Okay, Sheriff, but you know it will take over a month to get the results unless I have a reason to hurry it up."

"I have reason all right. I think Evel Martin stole the Doc's money. Besides, you know how much the Preacher needs this money for the new building at the church."

"That's reasons enough. I'll drive up there and see if I can get them to check the prints for a match while I'm there. They owe me a couple of favors, anyway."

The next morning, Sheriff Houston Crane was driving toward his farm on Chapel Gap Road, and he passed the cutoff to Pine Hall where the Martins live. He slowed down and pondered making a turn and going back to the Martins to have a look around. *I need to do this,* he thought, *just to keep the pressure on.*

Temptation showed its head in his groin, and he thought better of it. He'd been offered sex many times by some of the looser women in the Chapel Gap Area in exchange for tearing up a ticket or not making one of them spend the night in jail after stopping them for driving under the influence. He was never slightly tempted but did his job. Now, he was tempted beyond anything he thought possible; he was dripping with it. The others, they were unattractive whores, and he wouldn't touch them with a ten foot pole. But, Ethel was a Christian and attended his church, and except for her teeth, a pretty woman.

The Preacher had just greeted all the folks coming into the church after ringing the bell. I doused my cigarette in the outhouse well and Fran and I headed through the cemetery to the evening service.

This was business-meeting night so there wouldn't be any preaching. This could be a long night though because they were going to debate putting the church into debt for the new building project and to borrow the money from the Crab Orchard Bank. We looked forward to the meeting because it had been predicted that a fight would break out between the "fers" and the "agains."

There was an air of tension as the members of Evergreen Baptist Church found their seats. On this business meeting night, many of the worshippers were out of their normal seat-ing arrangements because the "ayes" sat on one side of the aisle and the "nays" on the other.

After a few songs that took forever to sing, my dad called the meeting to order.

"Let's have the reading of the last minutes," he commanded.

April May, the Church Clerk, stood to her feet. Women had been forbidden to speak in the church for any reason except for the reading of the minutes. The church had decided that a woman could be church clerk and could read the minutes in a mixed assembly. April had been giving the minutes to her husband, Henry, who had in the past read them for her. Henry's eyes got bad, and he took almost an hour to read fifteen minutes of April's report. This irritated a lot of people, but they wouldn't fire April because she had been taking the minutes of the church for over forty years. So, they compromised their long held beliefs and reelected April May to her job, and in the same motion, modified their standard allowing her to publicly address the congregation. The one stipulation of the new rule was that she could make no comment on the minutes after or while she read them.

My dad said the church should make the language of the motion to include "any woman" because Mrs. May wouldn't live forever, and he didn't want confusion for the future generations if the Lord didn't return in the eastern sky. That motion carried as well.

There was a ruckus, and that business meeting was something else. Kids were allowed to vote in the business meetings, and the boys could make motions, but not the girls. If you were a member of Evergreen Baptist Church through Scriptural Baptism and were a male, then you could not only vote, but you could make motions no matter how young.

"Praise the Lord," my dad said that night. "Do I hear a motion that the church allow the women clerks to read the minutes of the meetings?"

Everyone was quiet, and we sat there in silence for a long time. The men of the church knew this was a touchy subject. My dad had taught that women could never speak out in church during a worship service, but it had never been qualified if a business meeting was a worship service.

We had the discussion under Roberts Rules of Order, an instruction rule book my dad paid close attention to.

"If the church is assembled, then it is a church service no matter what you do." This was the main argument, and it did look like a fight would break out. My dad pounded the pulpit and got the shouting match ended and the meeting back to order.

"No more discussion," he said, "discussion is over, finished. Now do I, or do I not, have a motion to allow women clerks in the church to read the minutes?"

Everyone was quiet again, and then suddenly out of the still silence that was so thick you could slice it with a knife, a squeaky voice said, "I make the motion."

All the heads turned in unison and looked at Elmo Kidd, who was a redheaded boy, seven years old, and fat. He had a very round face, which reminded me of the face on the Kool-Aid pitchers. He had a serious look through his dark brown eyes, and his freckles looked like a leopard's spots against his fair skin. He was so short we could barely see him although he was standing.

"Motion made," my dad said as the people whispered to each other. No one that young had ever dared make a motion even though it wasn't wrong to do in the church. Elmo had challenged the rules.

"Do I have a second?"

"Second, second, second, second, second, second, second,

second, second, second," and twenty more than this as every kid in the church under ten years old seconded the motion made by Elmo Kidd.

"Okay, okay," my dad yelled trying to get the seconds stopped. "We have our second," and he pointed, "by Darrell Shoemaker."

My dad picked him out as he was the first to leap to his feet that the Preacher saw. Darrell was eight years old and Elmo Kidd's best friend.

"All in favor?" The ayes lifted their hands and Bro. Lord counted them.

"Any opposed by the same sign?" The nays lifted their hands and were counted.

"What's the church's decision?" My dad asked Bro. Lord.

"Motion carries," he said.

In Evergreen Baptist Church there was no majority two-thirds vote, or three fourths. It was a simple majority, and many times one of the kids in the church made the difference if the vote carried or not. This practice set the church for a split right down the middle, but Evergreen Baptist Church had been doing it this way for over a hundred years and wasn't about to change. The only reason the church didn't split was because of the strong family ties, and the people buried in the cemetery that were their ancestors. No one wanted to go to a church nearby and sit there and worship while his ancestors were buried at the church where he grew up.

The Chestnut Ridge Baptist Church had split and had to change this rule, and many other Baptist churches followed, but not the Evergreen Baptist Church. Simple majority rule was going to stay.

There was a lot of discussion concerning borrowing money for a building. The debate was heated and clearly some of the members were very upset. The arguments went on for an hour or so and maybe longer than that. I got lost in time. My dad was ready to call for the vote. He wanted this to pass badly, and he had told the church that our future may depend on being able to take care of the Sunday School. "Build the Sunday School, and you will build the church," was his motto. The Sunday School was so large that the members' kids were meeting under trees around the building and one Sunday School class was in the living room of our trailer house.

"Do I hear a motion that the church borrow five thousand dollars to build the new building?"

"Motion!" The kid screamed, and I looked in disbelief as Fran was standing to his feet right beside me and making this motion.

"Motion made," my dad said, "do I hear a second?"

"Second, second, second," and my dad held up his hand and stopped the seconds.

"Motion made by Fran Job and seconded by Bro. Lord." Bro. Lord anticipated the barrage of motions and got to his feet first before the kids began their motion echoes across the room. "All in favor by the uplifted hand," he waited, "any opposed by the same sign."

Bro. Lord had to count the vote again. This didn't happen too often in the church because most of the time, there were no opposing votes to count, or it was so obvious that the motion was carrying that there was no need to count. But on certain occasions like this one, the church perched on the precipice of self-destruction.

"What's the total?" My dad asked Bro. Lord.

"Fifty/fifty," he replied.

This was the first time this had ever happened in Evergreen Baptist Church, and we were all curious as to how this was going to be handled. Do you table the motion and start again, or what? My dad tabled the motion. He asked for another vote, and then another, but the results were always the same.

It was almost midnight, now. "I cast my vote for the debt," my dad said to an exhausted congregation.

"What?" Junior Cullen said as he came to his feet. He opposed every motion ever made in the Evergreen Baptist Church business meetings. "You can't do that."

"According to the Roberts Rules of Order, I can," my dad replied.

"Bro. Lord, come up here and act as moderator. How did you vote?"

"I voted 'for' he said."

"Let it stand that Bro. Lord voted for."

Junior Cullen and a couple of others were in the front of the church looking through the Roberts's Rules of Orders Manual, turning the pages rapidly, trying to find the rule that said that my dad could step down as a moderator, appoint another in his place, and then cast his vote.

When it was realized that my dad had hung the vote on a technicality, they sat down.

"All in favor of borrowing money for a new Sunday School building, raise your hands." Bro. Lord was enjoying the power of his new position.

"All opposed by the same sign," he carefully and slowly worded his demand, "Pastor Smith, what is the count?"

"Fifty/fifty," my dad said.

Junior Cullen didn't say anything because he had counted the votes with my dad.

"Fifty/fifty, and my vote already taken, makes a majority," Bro. Lord proclaimed. "This motion carries, and I turn the meeting over to the Pastor to close as he sees fit." Bro. Lord stepped from the platform and looked over the crowd; he had performed his duty well. He grabbed his belt loops and raised his pants over his shoes and sat down.

"Is there a motion that we adjourn?" My dad inquired of the sleepy crowd.

"Motion, motion, motion," about fifty of these came from men and boys, and I think a girl or two chimed in. My dad didn't bother with a second. "All in favor?" Every hand in the building was up. "Motion carries that we dismiss the business meeting," my dad said this without even asking Bro. Lord to make the count, which was technically against the rules, but he knew no one would challenge the opportunity to get out of there and go home, not even Junior Cullen. In fact, the only time Junior did vote with the church was to dismiss a business meeting.

"Why'd you make that motion, Fran?" I asked as were walking toward his house where I would spend the night and go to school the next morning.

"Because no one was going to make it, no man that is, and I didn't want Elmo Kidd doing it."

"Yeah but why?"

"If Elmo made that motion, the church would split, and I think that is exactly what's going to happen anyway."

CHAPTER THIRTY-ONE

The church fled the building and headed for their parked vehicles. Milking time would come early in the morning. Sheriff Crane shook hands with my dad and came out of the building. Ethel Martin was standing by, and when she saw that Mr. Crane and my dad were finished talking, she waited for the Sheriff by her car. Ethel Martin, as was customary for all the members, had not yet shaken the Sheriff's hand. No one would leave a service at the church without greeting one another and comment on how good the message was that night even though they may have slept most of the way through it.

Mr. Crane stuck out his hand, and when he did, Ethel Martin placed a small tightly folded piece of paper in his palm and closed his fingers over the paper and quickly departed. He put the paper in his shirt pocket.

Sheriff Crane unfolded the little note under the light of the brooder in his chicken house. He had gone out there to make sure all the newly hatched chicks were doing well and that he had enough food for the chickens sitting on the nests.

He curiously unfolded the note and read: "Sheriff, I saw the way you looked at me the other day. We need to talk about Evel. Why don't you meet me at my house tomorrow morning about 10:00 AM? I'll fix some coffee, and we can talk."

Houston Crane could feel the blood circulating in his heart and the rapid beat. Emotions that he had not had for a very long time were overcoming him; he felt he would faint. He destroyed the note by tearing it to shreds and depositing it in the manure bin that he used when he cleaned out the chicken house. He made his way to the large porch where Priscilla Crane did her washing, and his mind was running wild.

Priscilla had already gone to bed but was still awake. "What have you been doing?" She asked.

"Just checking on the chickens," he nervously replied, and she could hear it in his voice.

"You've been gone a long time."

She yawned and rolled over as Mr. Crane put his arms around her. "I love you, Prissy."

Priscilla was startled because she couldn't remember the last time Houston had said that to her. She smiled and took hold of his arms and pulled them around her bosom. "I love you," she said smiling from ear to ear while raking his bare leg with her foot.

The Sheriff lay there a long time staring at the dark ceiling. He could see shadows of blue as the new security light he had installed on his silo shone through the window; the blue lines danced on the ceiling as the wind gently blew the curtains.

He dozed off but awoke soon as images of adultery and the consequences ran through his dreams. Evil demons tormented him as he found himself caught in the shame. Priscilla had been devastated, and his boys would have nothing to do with him. Cold sweat popped out on his forehead as the Preacher pronounced him guilty, and he was excluded from the Evergreen Baptist Church. He lost the election, and the image of Ethel Martin's missing teeth haunted him as he tried to have a relationship with her. First, the stress of meeting her secretly, hiding out in the back roads of perdition, second the truth that came out about the illicit affair and the guilt of facing his wife each night as he left the woman he thought he loved alone at home. He didn't want the other woman, he missed his family, and every thing he had built in a lifetime of community and Christian service was now down the tubes.

He startled and sat straight up in the bed waking Priscilla as he cried, "Oh, God, what have I done? Please God, what have I done?"

Priscilla woke frightened of her husband's nightmare. "What's the matter, honey?" She asked trying to calm his wild gyrations.

"I'm in trouble, Prissy," he cried, "big trouble."

"What in the world is wrong with you? It's only a dream." She patted his hand trying to wake him up all the way. "I'll fix you some warm milk; that will make you feel better and let you sleep."

Mrs. Crane came back in a few minutes, and the milk steamed in the cup. Houston was sitting up in bed, and she knew he was troubled beyond a nightmare.

"What's the matter? Please talk to me."

Houston had never lied to Priscilla in his life. They had loved each other since they were kids growing up on the same farms they combined and now farmed themselves. They married at a young age and had eked out a living through some tough times. They had survived the depression and Houston's stint in the armed forces during World War 2. Houston had won election as Sheriff on his first try and had run unopposed in the last three elections, and it seemed that he could remain Sheriff for the rest of his life. He loved the job, dearly. He had been ordained as a Deacon in the Evergreen Baptist Church and was a highly respected man throughout Lincoln County and Chapel Gap where he lived. All these thoughts slipped through his mind as he sipped his milk.

"You've been good to me, Prissy," he said softly.

"And you to me," she replied.

"I have to tell you something and please listen to me before you say anything, all right?"

"Okay, but I can't imagine what is so important."

Priscilla Crane listened as her husband told the shocking story of how Ethel Martin had tried to seduce him at the farm. He spared no detail about her nakedness as she enticed him. He explained the guilt and shame he carried for even giving this woman a second thought. He cried. He told his wife about the note Ethel gave him at church and what he was really doing in the chicken house that night.

Priscilla Crane wept as her husband related how Ethel wanted the Sheriff to come to her house and see her. "Well," Priscilla said as she nearly fainted, "I am going to make it very clear to you that you are never to step foot on that woman's property again, ever shake her hand or speak to her at church."

"I have to," he replied, "I'm investigating Evel Martin, and I have to find the money. I can't do that without going over there."

"Let me ask you something, Houston. Did you enjoy what you saw? Is that the problem? No wonder you're having nightmares. Am I not good enough for you any more that you have to go lusting after another woman?"

Never in their entire marriage did Priscilla Crane challenge her husband about anything, so this accusation set him back.

"I've asked God to forgive me for the temptation, and I'm

asking you. I've never been confronted by any other woman standing in front of me nearly naked. I need your forgiveness."

Priscilla turned her back to her husband and rolled out of bed. "I'll tell you in the morning," she said, "I need to think." She walked out of the room and slammed the door behind her.

Ethel Martin peered from behind the drape on the front door of her house as she saw the Sheriff drive up in the yard at precisely 9:59 AM. *He's not a minute late, he's on time,* she thought. *I knew he'd come.*

The Sheriff strolled upon the porch and knocked on the door's window. He waited a few moments and then saw the shadow and figure of someone standing near the door.

"Come in," she said not opening the door for him, "the door's unlocked."

The Sheriff turned the knob and walked into the room. He looked around the room, noticing its tidiness, and then saw Ethel Martin standing beside the door facing him. He was not ready for this surprise. Ethel was bare breasted and only fishnet panties covered her privates, and the Sheriff had no trouble making out all the details.

"Why'd you come?" Ethel asked. "Do you like what you see? Would you like to have this?"

The figure burst through the door catching Ethel by surprise. She had not seen Priscilla Crane lying over on the seat of the pickup and out of sight as the Sheriff drove into the yard. Her eyes popped open wide, and she grabbed her breasts trying to cover herself and put her elbows down between her legs.

"He don't want none!" Priscilla screamed. "What he wants is right here!" She pointed to herself and mocked the lewdness of Ethel Martin's seduction, swaying back and forth in lascivious motion.

Ethel tried to escape the scene, but Priscilla caught her. She was larger than Ethel and strong from all the farm work she had done all her life. Houston was watching the chain of events before him, helpless to do anything.

"Houston! Get in the truck!" Priscilla shouted, "Now! Dammit!"

The Sheriff had never heard his wife cuss in his life, so he made a beeline for the door and was soon sitting in the truck listening to the screaming and cussing from inside the house. He thought that maybe he should rush in there and make sure that his wife was okay, but he thought better of it. *She'll think I want to see more of Ethel Martin,* he thought. He soon heard things being broken in the house, so he did run in.

Priscilla had thrown a quilt over Ethel, who was lying naked underneath. Priscilla had torn off the risqué bikini Ethel was wearing, and Houston could see it hanging on the kitchen sink. Ethel was bleeding from the nose and mouth, and she was missing two more teeth that he could clearly see as Ethel wiped the blood from her mouth and face.

Priscilla had gone into a rage and pounded the daylights out of the seductive female. She pulled wads of hair from Ethel's blonde head, and strands were sticking out of Priscilla's clenched fists. Priscilla breathed heavily as she stood over Ethel. She had every intention of killing this lady with a poker she had in her hand had the Sheriff not jumped between the two fighting ladies and grabbed Priscilla's arm as she came down with it, saving Ethel Martin's life.

"Attempted murder!" Ethel screamed. "You'll pay for this!"

"Shut the (expletive deleted) up!" Priscilla yelled which startled Houston Crane that such vile and filthy language could come out of his wife's mouth.

"I don't think so," Houston said. "You're the one's going to pay."

"You looked at me. You caused all this! There's no crime to pay when there's no crime. It's not against the law for me to be dressed in whatever I want even if it's nothing in my own house. You came into my house, Mister Sheriff!"

There was silence for a minute or two as these words reverberated through the avenues of thought and decipher ship of Houston and Priscilla Crane's brains. His first thought was of exclusion of Ethel Martin from the church and the disgrace it would cause. Not since Jewel Vance had divorced Herman Vance would there have been such a scandal. They would be rid of Ethel Martin once and for all.

Priscilla thoughts were of how she should have finished the job, or maybe she would come back and kill her later. Then, Evel Martin walked in.

"What the hell is going on here?" He asked as he knelt beside his mother's bloody body still covered with the quilt. He looked at Priscilla. "You did all this? Or did the Sheriff?" Evel said to Priscilla.

"The Sheriff tried to seduce me," Ethel said from the floor through bloody teeth," and this bitch jumped me from behind and hit me with a poker trying to kill me. She caught me off guard; otherwise, I would have beaten the crap out of her. I'm pressing charges against the Sheriff and his crazy wife!"

"You're doing no such thing, momma. Now get up and get some clothes on."

"I'm sorry, Sheriff, Mrs. Crane, my momma ain't been herself lately. Lots of stress since daddy ran off with that woman from Brennel Ridge. Now let's all be Christian adults and forget this whole thing."

The Sheriff and Priscilla were almost home before either one said a word.

"I didn't know you could fight like that," Houston mused. "You beat her half to death."

"You better be glad it wasn't you," Priscilla said dramatically, and the Sheriff flinched, nervously.

The Sheriff knew that this event was going to make the investigation much more difficult. There would be no exclusion of Ethel Martin from the church because it would expose his wife and him. Ethel telling what Priscilla had called her, cussing and all, would be bad enough much less his part of the affair being aired out in front of the whole church. He reasoned that Evel Martin wasn't as stupid as he looked. Evel had diffused the entire situation knowing that the Sheriff would more than likely never come back to his farm again, and if he did, his mother would most definitely file assault and battery charges against his wife, and that would make his being elected impossible. Martin had leverage now, and it would be a nice life for him.

CHAPTER THIRTY-TWO

F ran and I weren't stopping by Suzanne Stevens' house any more to watch her in the upstairs window on our way home from skating. My dad let us drive my mom's 1950 Ford Coupe just about anywhere we wanted to go except the blacktop roads. The cops wouldn't bother us on the gravel roads, but Deputy Shanks was ready with tickets in hand if he caught one of us on a blacktop road he patrolled. Kentucky had different colors for hunting and fishing licenses, so the old trick that Fran had pulled on Homer Shanks that night before he and the boys had failed to negotiate People's Corner wouldn't work anymore. As long as we paid for the gas, we could drive the car to and from our farm work, and use the car on Friday and Saturday nights to run to the skating rink. We tried stopping in front of Suzanne Stevens' house one night, but she heard the car slow to a stop and turned off her bedroom lamp. Thus, one our favorite esoteric events was permanently shut down.

Neither of us could car date yet, and in fact, it would be some time before Leah would grow to the age of car dating. I wouldn't wait around for Fran and Leah. We spent our days riding around smoking, swimming, and skating with the pals we had. At age fifteen, we were very hard workers and knew tobacco backwards and forwards. It was never a problem for either of us to get work doing anything required in raising and harvesting tobacco. We spent our money running around, and we did frequent forbidden places for my mom's car to be.

Fran's first test and temptation to step out on my sister and lose his patience in waiting for her to get old enough to car date him came one night after skating. We were down in Hall's Cap by ourselves. Usually, Ray Hampton or Ray Lord would be with us but that particular night we were alone.

I stood around watching Fran skate by himself during the "moonlight skate." I don't know why he insisted on doing this. He was the only single person on the floor while the lights sparkled from the chandelier hanging in the middle of the ceiling making rays of twilight. Nevertheless, every time I told him he was embarrassing himself, he ignored me.

"Want to skate with me?"

I turned to see who was talking to me from behind, and a nice petite looking girl with brown hair and eyes had skated up to me. Her hair hung loosely on her shoulders, and she had on ruby red lipstick. Her skirt was very short; its colors maroon and white, and her sweater had a large maroon "LHS" against the white background.

I thought for a second before I answered. I was thinking about the fact that if I skated with this girl, I would not be loyal to Kathy Friday. I didn't even know Kathy Friday yet, and she had no idea that I was in love with her. What the heck, I reasoned. "This girl has brown eyes and brown hair, so she's no threat to Kathy Friday and my relationship with her that didn't exist."

"Sure," I agreed.

She took my hand, and we skated to the floor, barely missing Fran who looked at me with surprise.

"Why did you want to skate with me?" I asked.

"Because you're a good skater. I've been watching you for a long time, for the past few weeks. That match trick you do is a hoot. How old are you anyway?"

"Seventeen," I lied.

"Wow! Far out! I'm seventeen. Where do you go to school?"

"Crab Orchard High, you?"

"Lancaster High. Far out, we're both juniors!"

"I'm a senior. I skipped a grade, and I'm going to college next year at Western Kentucky University."

"Far out. You must be smart to do that and all. Far out."

"I guess so, but I'm a better football player than student."

"You play football? Far out. What position?"

"Quarterback. In fact, Western offered me a full scholarship on scholastics and football."

"Far out!"

"Far out," "daddio," and "cool" hadn't entered our vocabularies up in the Chapel Gap Area, and I thought this girl strange. She was strange? I just told a million lies, and I don't even know why, and she's strange?

"What's your name?" She asked.

"Stan Kirk," I said. Stan was the quarterback at Crab Orchard High, and he was going to Western Kentucky University in Bowling Green, Kentucky on a scholarship.

"Oh.My.Gosh! I'm skating with Stan Kirk, this is too cool."

"By the way, what's your name?" I asked as we sped faster with excitement.

"Ming Morgan, Stan."

"That's a real pretty name, Ming, and you skate good, too."

I skated backwards effortlessly now as we glided in and out of the lovers on the floor. We passed Fran at least ten times. He always did skate slowly. He looked at me real hard as if he wanted to talk to me.

The music stopped, the lights went bright, and the announcement came, "ALL SKATE," so Ming skated off somewhere thanking me for the good time as she got lost in the crowded arena.

"What are you doing?" Fran asked. "I guess Kathy Friday is no longer a consideration?"

"What? The girl asked me to skate, so I did. That's all."

"Hey Stan!" Ming said as she skated up to Fran and me. There was a very nice girl dressed just like Ming skating with her. I confirmed my suspicion; they were both cheerleaders. Fran looked around for Stan.

"Ming, this is Fran." Fran stuck out his hand and shook Ming's.

"Stan, this is Judy." Fran stood looking at me and wondering what in the world was going on.

"Hey, Ming," Fran called, "why did you call him ST?" I put my hand over his mouth, like I was halfway kidding or something, and didn't let him spell it out.

"Judy, you won' t believe this, but this is Stan Kirk the quarterback we've been reading about in the Lancaster paper!"

"He's small for a quarterback, and he looks fifteen instead of eighteen." Judy replied insensitive to any hurt feelings I may have had from the snide remark.

"He's seventeen, Judy. He skipped a grade because he's so smart." Ming made sure Judy understood who was meeting her.

"Far out," Judy said.

Fran skated around in a circle while were talking and looking up at the ceiling.

"You girls have a way home?" I asked.

"Yeah," Ming replied, "my mom will come and pick us up when I call her."

"Hey, Ming, we could call her and tell her we have a ride home with Stan Kirk," Judy suggested.

"Far out."

The girls skated off to ask Mr. Bunch if they could use his phone.

"What the heck are you doing?" Fran asked disgustingly. "You told that girl you are Stan Kirk, and you're seventeen and skipped a grade? What are you thinking?"

"I didn't know what to say when she said that she is seventeen," I tried to explain the reason.

"Well you sure as heck have yourself in a bind now, Bud. First of all they're going to find out who you really are, and second, you are going to get the crap kicked out of you by the real Stan Kirk."

This all happened too fast. I was sweating, now.

"Hey guys! My mom says it's okay for Stan and Fran to take us home. She said my dad loves football and sometimes attends the games over in Crab Orchard just to watch Stan play. He's excited to meet him. They did say to come straight home, though," Ming informed the group.

"What are we going to do?" I exclaimed.

"What do you mean, we, Bud? It's your mess, not mine."

"You gotta help me, Fran, please?"

I skated with Ming a couple of times before Mr. Bunch announced the rink closing. Judy stood and talked with Fran; I guess she was waiting for him to ask her to skate, but he wasn't going to.

We turned our rented skates over to the small kid who worked behind the rental counter, while the girls packed their skates in nice carrying cases and headed for the car. When we got to the Ford, the girls looked at it like, "What the heck is this?" The Ford was a little dirty, and inside the floorboard had rusted through, so Fran and I threw some cardboard over the holes to keep the dust from the gravel roads from choking us to death inside the car. So, the car was a little dusty. Ming noticed this when she climbed in the back seat, and the dust flew up and soiled her white cheerleader's skirt.

"Who's driving?" Ming asked as she fanned the dust from around her head.

"I am," Fran answered deliberately. Actually, I had planned on driving. Fran had this all figured out. If he didn't drive, he would have to sit in the back seat with one of the girls, and that would be considered "stepping out" on Leah, an affair.

"Me and Stan can sit in the back, and Judy and Fran in the front," Ming instructed.

"I can't do that," Fran said, and the girls stared at him.

"Why not?" Judy asked.

"I have a girl friend, and that would be cheating."

"Fran, I'm not going to get engaged to you or even go steady. We want a ride home, that's all. I'm not going to kiss you or anything."

Fran stood by the driver's door and refused to get in the car as long as Judy was in the front seat. I ducked out the passenger's side door and pulled him over out of the way.

"What's wrong with YOU?" I demanded.

"I'm not getting in the car if that girl is in the front seat. You got us into this mess."

"Judy, sit back here with Ming and me," I said as I crawled into the back seat and taking my place in the middle where I could be comfortable between the two girls.

"Is he mentally retarded or something?" Judy said as she crept in trying to keep the dust billowing off the upholstery to a minimum. "This car is dirty, you guys ever wash it?"

"Is he weird?" Ming asked quietly.

"A little," I replied.

We drove along the gravel road, and we were all relieved when we hit the blacktop on Highway 27 and turned toward Stanford. The girls were shaking the dust out of their hair. The breeze blew through the open windows and finally cleared the dust so we could relax.

We were moving along with Fran driving by himself in the front seat. This would not be the last time Fran would escort me with more than one girl in the back seat. From that first moment this event happened, Fran never once looked at another girl. I couldn't make him do it even when I begged and pleaded with him and told him my sister wasn't worth it. He passed his test. Whoever he married someday would never have to worry about him.

The girls were giggly, and Ming was close to me with her arms wrapped around my neck. Judy was snuggled up on the other side. If any guy had ever died and gone to heaven, I surely had. Fran watched all this in the rearview mirror.

The girls took turns kissing me on the lips, giggling and saying, "Far out" every time they did it. They had been around, and it wasn't everyday a girl could have a jock like Stan Kirk in the back seat. I glanced up every now and then only to see Fran's eyes firmly fixated on the images reflecting behind him.

Fran had never driven on a major highway like US 27, so he drove very slowly. A big semi rolled up behind us speeding as he came down the long grade of the new road at Hall's Gap. The truckers could make up time on this long stretch of straight road that took them into Stanford. Fran was in the way of the truck. He blew his air horn and almost scared the life out of us as he passed like we were sitting still. The wind whipped up from the draft of the rig and nearly blew us off the road. Fran fought like the devil to keep us from going off the mountain.

The girls never flinched when this happened, and Ming was trying to stick her tongue in my mouth. This was the first time I had kissed a girl like this. I liked kissing Darla Jenkins, but she wouldn't allow this kind of behavior from me. I was learning the ways of the world.

I was in big trouble, and I knew it. From this point on, I didn't know what would happen, or if I could control it. I knew one thing for sure, I liked what was happening, and I like it a lot. I liked it too much.

"Like this," Ming said as she instructed me how to open my mouth and let her kiss me the same way, and then Judy took her turn. There was not an ounce of difference in the way the two girls kissed.

Tip Tuck had just lighted a cigarette and blew the smoke out the window and then tossed his match when he saw the black Ford being passed by the big truck. He thought he recognized the car and wondered what my mother would be doing at that hour of the night all the way over toward Stanford. He eased the cruiser into gear and spun out on the highway. His first thought was to chase down the big rig and cite it for speeding, but it was late, and he had already reached his quota for the night. He was more interested in the black Ford.

Judy was turned toward me with her head slightly slanted toward the rear window, so she was the first one to notice the red light on top of the State Police cruiser. She quickly let go of my neck and straightened up.

"A cop's behind us," she said.

Fran's first reaction as he saw the lights was to step on the brake, and that's exactly what he did. The three of us hit the back of the front seat knocking Fran into the steering wheel. Trooper Tuck almost rear-ended us before Fran let off the brake and coasted to the side of the road.

"Won't no fishing license get us out of this one," Fran said, and the girls looked puzzled at this comment. We had no idea that Tip Tuck was on duty that night.

I knew who was driving the cruiser as soon as I saw Tip's six feet four inch frame step out of the car and put on his trooper's helmet. He reached inside the car and turned on his spotlight and shined it through the Ford's rear window, but all he could see was Fran and the girls in the back seat. I was in the floor hiding between the girls' legs.

Tip put his long arms on top of the car bracing himself with his hands and leaned into the window on Fran's side. Fran had his head on the steering wheel refusing to look at Tip. He gripped the wheel so tightly that his fingers turned white, but not as white as his face.

"How old are you girls?" Tip Tuck asked.

"Seventeen," they both said in unison, and then Ming said, "we'll be eighteen in a couple of months."

I was in a position where Tip couldn't see me scrunched up tightly in a fetal position hiding between the girls.

"What're you doing, Fran?" The Trooper asked.

"Far out!" The girls cried. "The Trooper knows Fran!"

"Get up Stan, it's okay, the Trooper knows Fran!"

"Stan who?" Tip questioned as he looked through the rear window on the passenger's side. He could see me now, but not my face.

"Stan Kirk!" Ming exclaimed, "the famous football player."

"Come on up, Stan," Tip instructed, and I rose slowly from the floor of the Ford to where he could see who I was.

"Well, it's Stan Kirk. I didn't know you ran around with Fran, Mr. Kirk. It's usually that stupid looking Preacher's kid Fran runs around with."

The shame of it all was all I could think about as Tip Tuck put Fran and me in the back seat of his cruiser.

"Well boys, what am I going to do? You better start explaining yourselves." Tip said.

Fran told Tip the whole story and how he'd gone along with it even though I had begged him not to. He also threw in the part about how sorry he was that his sister, June, had broken up with him, and that he hated the faggot faced Steve Green. I started throwing my two cents worth in, but the Trooper told me to shut up.

"Sonny's just pulling a joke and things got out of hand," Fran explained, "he meant no harm."

"It looks like he meant a whole lot of harm," Tip said as he looked at the ruby red lipstick plastered all over my face.

"You boys better pray till the day you die that these girls never find out you're only fifteen years old. And what's with that Stan Kirk deal? Do you know what he'll do when he finds out you embarrassed him like that? What are you going to do the next time you're at the skating rink and these loose girls are there? Uh? What? Uh?"

I didn't plan on being there a next time.

Tip thought a little while making us sweat, and we could see the girls looking at us often with expressions of concern on their faces.

"All right," he finally said, "you boys get in the Ford. You can pull over there in that turn-around and wait. I'm going to let the Preacher handle this one, and I'll give the girls a lift home."

"Oh, my, God!" I thought as the fear rushed through me.

"Well girls," Tip Tuck said as he opened the door of the black Ford. "The car's not doing well, so I am going to take you home. I hope you don't mind."

Fran and I watched the girls slide into the back seat of the cruiser. Their hair was all messed up and dusty from the Ford, and you couldn't tell the color of their skirts and sweaters. We watched as Tip pulled away.

Tip Tuck had no intention of coming back to get us. After he dropped the girls off and told their parents everything was okay, and that Fran Job's car had a little "trouble," he headed toward his post in Stanford.

"I wanted to meet Stan Kirk!" Ming's dad cried out after him.

Tip stopped in Stanford and called my dad from his office. In fact, the call was one of the first my parents had received on their newly installed phone, so it was no trouble hearing the ring at this hour. They tried to beat each other to the phone in the living room and answer it.

Tip explained to my dad where the car was, and that it would be best if my dad would come and get us since he was on duty and couldn't afford the time unless he was going to arrest Fran for driving without a license.

I can never remember one night that Fran and me spent together that we didn't talk. Neither one of us said a word the whole night. I could see Fran now and then shaking his head in total disbelief that I had gotten us in such a predicament.

My dad went back to bed. He wasn't going to fool with us on Friday night, and he was tired. His decision was to handle it in the morning, so he left us sitting, waiting, sweating, stressed, and hoping that Jesus would return and save us from being murdered.

The big blue boat my dad drove pulled in behind the Ford. My dad stood by the car and looked up and down the highway as my mom bobbed her head back and forth in the passenger's seat. He brought her along to drive the huge 1960 Mercury Station Wagon and return to the church. Fran and I looked at my dad curiously as he stood there. I don't know what he was thinking, but I knew it wasn't good. He slid behind the wheel of the black Ford as Fran and me instinctively put our bodies in the back seat.

My mom made a U turn and headed toward Hall's Gap, but my father drove straight ahead toward Stanford. He reached up and turned on the radio, pushing the buttons until the found the station he wanted to listen to. Fran and I stared at each other as my dad got lost in the volume of Patti Page and "Mockingbird Hill." Dad never listened to country music or anything else on the radio. When we were in the car, he always made us turn the radio off. "Peace and quiet," he would say.

Fear and trepidation gripped our souls as the Preacher pulled into the State Police Quarters on the outskirts of the city. Tip Tuck's cruiser sat in front of the post; its nose pointed toward the highway in case he needed a quick get-away.

The Preacher had still not said a word as we watched him walk in the front door and disappear. Soon, he was walking toward the car, and we had no idea what he was doing, and we weren't going to ask.

"We're in a lot of trouble, Bud," Fran said to me while my dad was in the State Police Office.

"What's he thinking, Fran?" I asked lugubriously. "You know him better than anyone."

"I don't know, Bud, but whatever it is, it isn't good. He's mad as hellfire. When was the last time you heard him listen to the radio?"

My dad drove the Ford out of the parking lot and onto Highway 27 and drove toward Lancaster. We weren't "joy riding." We passed the old Lancaster Stockyards down below the square. Lancaster was one of the many towns in Kentucky where the courthouses were in the middle of a square that was actually an island in the middle of the downtown areas. The traffic flowed all the way around the courthouse from four directions.

One time my family was parked in the square waiting for a traffic light to turn. We were shopping in Lancaster, a colorful little town. We had just dropped off some sheep at the Stock-yards when we felt the rumble of an explosion and then saw black smoke rising in the air.

Soon, there were animals, their hair on fire, running wildly up the middle of the street. Burning hair and flesh permeated the air as the poor helpless animals burned to death in front of our faces. We could see flames leaping high in the sky above the buildings, and the smoke filled the downtown area so thick it looked as if a black cloud had dropped from the sky and enveloped the whole downtown.

A gas station was next to the stockyards and was very popular because the fuel there was a few cents cheaper than you could buy it anywhere else, and the station gave away free gifts with so many gallons of gasoline purchased. My mom's complete dish cabinet and linen closet were filled with dish-towels, washcloths, and bath towels she had collected from one of these stations. Whenever my dad would take his cattle and other farm animals to sell, he would bring back the goods whether it be towels or dishes.

A tanker was there filling up the underground reservoirs which held the fuel. Someone accidentally threw a cigarette, the best the fire chief could determine, and it fell into the storage tank and immediately caused the explosion. The Stock-yards had been there for fifty years or more and had never been remodeled. The old wood caught fire like paper and burned, raging for two whole days. Very few animals escaped, and most of those that could find their ways out of the inferno, burned to death in the streets of Lancaster. Many hundreds of other animals, sheep, cattle, horses, mules, and hogs lay in the ashes of smoldering meat. The smell of this disaster lingered in Lancaster for months.

These images flashed through my mind as we turned beside the new Stockyards onto the Preachersville Road and headed toward Paint Lick. I wished that I had burned up in the fire with the pigs. We passed the cemetery where upscale homes of the wealthy businessmen, doctors, and lawyers of Lancaster lived. We turned down a plush side street, and I admired the large but beautiful brick mansions lining the streets.

My dad knocked on the door of the house as the black Ford sat in the circular driveway of the huge home. The entryway of the mansion looked as if you could drive a car through it. I had never seen a front door so big. The landscaping around the house was immaculately trimmed to perfection, and it was obvious that someone spent a great deal of time to make the shrubs and flower beds so beautiful. Someone very rich lived in this grand house.

I saw a person pull the curtains back from an upstairs window and look down at us. I recognized her immediately. After all, she had been all over my face.

"So that's what he was doing at Tip's station," I said to Fran who stared at the floorboard squinting his eyes. "He was getting directions to Ming's house."

"Stan Kirk's here!" We could hear Ming shouting as her father opened the front door. "I'll call Judy!"

"Preacher, what a pleasant surprise. What brings you over here in Lancaster?" Mr. Morgan greeted my dad.

Doug Morgan was a lawyer who defended Curt Kirk in the moonshine trial over at Stanford. My dad had been called as a character witness for the defense, but it turned around on Doug Morgan when my dad decided that there was no way he could attest to the good character of Curt Kirk and testify on Curt's behalf. He turned witness for the prosecution. The papers were filled with the trial news as it progressed each day, and Curt Kirk had vowed that he would someday kill my dad. The Preacher was as surprised to see the attorney as the lawyer was to see the Preacher.

Fran and I sat in the car watching as Judy left her house next door and walked up the sidewalk.

"Hello, Stan, hello, Fran," she said as she waved to us.

Ming met Judy at the door, and they both giggled as they stood in the massive entryway smiling and ogling to us. We watched the girls disappear into the house and then froze in fright as my dad motioned for us to come in the mansion.

We heard voices as we walked in the marble entry foyer. We were amazed at the large crystal chandelier hanging from the ceiling and setting off the curved cherry staircase that wound its way to the second floor.

"We're in the library, Stan," Ming called.

The grand piano made a fitting backdrop to the Picasso painting above the fireplace. I couldn't remember when I had seen a more stupid looking picture. You couldn't tell what the thing was.

"Where's Stan?" Mr. Morgan asked.

"Right there," Ming answered as my dad sat solemn faced in the wingback chair with the soft floral design. "There," she said as she pointed to me.

"That's not Stan Kirk," Mr. Morgan said with a puzzled look on his face.

"I'm afraid, Mr. Morgan, that my son has committed a crime against your daughter." He never mentioned Fran, who sat beside my dad on the arm of the big chair.

The girls' mouths flew open, and their eyes widened as my dad began the explanation as to why Fran and me were sitting in Mr. Morgan's den.

"How old are you, Sonny?" My dad point blank asked me.

I could barely get the words out as I gulped hard. "Fifteen," I said, "but".

"But nothing. Tell her your name. Tell her."

"Sonny Smith," I whispered not able to find enough breath to get the words clear from my lips.

"You raped me!" Ming cried as this caught the full attention of every one in the room.

"What!" Her dad screamed.

"What!" My dad yelled.

"I can't believe this; I just can't believe it," Ming cried.

Mr. Morgan and my dad were racing each other for my throat.

"Wait!" Fran said as he inched his way to the middle of the room. "He didn't rape her. They made out a little, that's all."

"Same thing!" Ming. screamed as Judy took Ming's hand.

"Is that true, Judy?" Mr. Morgan asked as he loosened his grip on my shirt.

Judy looked at Ming and dropped her eyes. "Yes," she said quietly.

"You did it, too!" Ming yelled at Judy.

"Where's Stan Kirk?" Mr. Morgan asked, "what does he have to do with this?"

"Nothin," Fran said, "Bud here told the girls he was Stan Kirk last night at the skating rink, so he could get a date with Ming."

"I made out with a fifteen year old boy," Ming sobbed and wiped her eyes and smeared her make-up, "so did Judy."

There was silence for a few moments as everyone sat and pondered the situation.

"He told you he was Stan Kirk, and you bought it?" Mr. Morgan said almost laughing. My dad wasn't laughing.

"You did put my daughter and her friend at risk driving on the highway without a license," he said now looking much more serious. "What will we do about that?" Mr. Morgan asked.

Judy rushed out the front door, leaving her girlfriend with the problem.

"He'll be punished," my dad said, "oh, yeah, he'll be punished."

"Okay, Preacher," Mr. Morgan said as he slapped my dad on the back as we were being led out of the mansion. "He better stay away from my daughter," and then let out a big roar of laughs as he went into his house.

"You'll never have to worry about that," my dad commented, but Mr. Morgan didn't hear him.

There was silence as my dad drove Fran and me. The closest route back to Crab Orchard was through Preachersville, a town that was five miles long but only had five houses, all of which were parsonages next to the five churches of various denominations. The expected boom of the 1890's didn't happen, and they never changed the town's parameters. It always did puzzle me as to how that many churches operated so far away from anything down an unknown road.

We crossed the Dix River, and Fran was eyeing some gigging spots. He told me that someday we would gig the Dix River flowing through Lincoln County. "The gars weigh fifty pounds," he said.

As were making our way up Toll Gate Hill that led into Crab Orchard, my dad broke the silence.

"Boys, this is Toll Gate Hill. It got its name because years and years ago, the town of Crab Orchard charged the wagons a toll to come into their city, which was the only way the farmers could get there from this direction. They had a big gate and a gate keeper, and he opened the gate to let the wagons through in order to sell their harvest at the Crab Orchard markets."

Fran and I looked strangely at each other after hearing this piece of history. We breathed a sigh at the same moment and relaxed against the back seat.

"You won't get the car I promised you for your birthday

next year, Sonny, and you won't get your driver's license, either." He still did not mention Fran. Then it came. "You'll have to depend on Fran to drive you around. No car dating, either. In fact, no dating period or sitting in church with a girl."

The Crab Orchard High School football team was practicing as we exited the main road and drove up to the field. Stan Kirk came running over with his football pads jumping beneath his practice jersey that had no number. My dad had called Stan after Tip Tuck told him what was going on, and because of this, Stan's mom, Loretta Kirk, had gossiped all over the Chapel Gap Area that I was impersonating her son. She made it look as though I had stolen his identity and Stan would never be the same.

Stan leaned into the passenger window and peered at Fran and me in the backseat.

"What are you trying to do guys, ruin me?"

"It was my fault, Stan, I should never have allowed Bud to do what he did," Fran explained.

"It's okay, Sonny, but I'm disappointed in you. You won't be able to come with me to the football game this Friday over in Lancaster like I promised."

Now I was hurt. Everybody was punishing me, and I just wanted to run away right then and never come back. I idolized Stan Kirk. I looked up to him, and he always took care of Fran and me no matter what, and now he was punishing me. This hurt me almost as much as disappointing my dad.

As we left the field, some of the girls standing around and watching the boys practice glared at me with snarls and leers, and I shrank down so they couldn't see me.

We were silent as we plowed up the Chapel Gap Hill shifting into second gear to make the climb. I mulled over and over my losses in my mind. I lost my car, I lost my dating privileges, I lost my ability to sit with a girl in church, I disappointed my idol, and my dad now hated me. It was more than I could bear. There was only one thing I could do.

There was zero crying as the line filed past me in the re-dedication line at the church on Sunday. The people courteously shook my hand, but they refused to hug me. Loretta Kirk passed me by and hugged the next rededicator but gave no acknowledgement that I was even in the line. Her eyes were so far apart I couldn't believe she could see where she was going. Stan came by and shook my hand and then shook his head.

The Knob people had strange ways of dealing with sinners. Everyone in Lincoln County knew what I had done. It was hard for me to go out in public, much less face the entire church body of the Evergreen Baptist Church. If it was known what your sin was, they treated you different than if they did not know what your sin had been. They would more or less shun you if your transgression was open, and hugged and wailed on you if it was not, and forgave.

I stood thinking this was the longest day of my whole life, and that my life as I had known it, would be no more.

CHAPTER THIRTY-THREE

The bank has decided not to loan the money to the church," Mr. Goodnight said as my dad sat across the desk fumbling with the pen in his hand. This news irritated him.

"But, the church needs this building," my dad exclaimed. "We are busting out at the seams. Tell me why in heaven's name you won't do this?"

The banker eased back in his chair and pondered his answer. "Banks don't like loaning churches money. If we have to foreclose on the church, it makes us look bad in the community, like we're the bad guys."

"How many churches has this bank foreclosed on in the history of the bank?" My dad asked sarcastically. "Furthermore, how many church loans does the bank have now?"

The banker knew my dad was irritated, and the loan committee had anticipated some rebuttal from the Preacher, but Goodnight was surprised by the intelligent questions my dad was grilling him with.

Where did this Preacher get banking experience? Goodnight thought as he prepared his justification for turning down the church loan. "We have several church loans and have loaned to churches in the past, but we have changed our policy."

"That's not good enough, Jimmy. Evergreen Baptist Church has had its bank account here since this bank was opened in the 1880's. Many of the members have their bank accounts here, and so do I. This doesn't make any sense. By the way, how many churches are right now in default on their loans?"

"As of today, none."

"None?" How much does your bank charge off on loans each year, Jimmy?"

Goodnight fidgeted in his seat not wanting to answer the question; no one in his recent memory had ever asked the bank a question like this. "That's not the point, Jerry. It's the bank policy now."

"How many loans default in the bank each year, Jimmy? Do you want me to contact the State Banking Commission and find out?"

Jimmy Goodnight shuffled papers on his desk, picked up the phone and dialed upstairs to bookkeeping. "Excuse me," he said as he left the office and the Preacher sitting by himself. In a few minutes he came back with a long sheet of paper. "Six percent," he said quietly.

"What's that?"

"Six, uh, six percent."

"Let's see," my dad started, "the bank loans X amount of money to X amount of people each year. Six percent of those people default on their loans and the bank gets holes in the bag and loses the money. I'm not even going to ask you how much money that amounts to Jimmy because I personally don't want to worry about my own money or the church's, but

I'll bet a dollar to a doughnut that many of those loans are for money other than any church has borrowed, right?" The banker couldn't keep his body from showing anxiety. "None. Six percent of those deadbeats charged off their loans, but not one church in ninety years has defaulted. It seems to me, Jimmy, that church loans are the best and safest loans you ever made. Oh, one more thing. I understand from the good pastor down the street at the Crab Orchard Baptist Church that you charge churches more interest than you do on other loans. Is that true?"

Goodnight ran his hands through his hair and swerved and rocked the wooden swivel banker's chair nervously. Sweat beads dripped from his face, and he wiped them with his handkerchief.

"We'll revisit this Preacher. Get back to me next month."

"Next month? Next month? Then what? You want to waste another month of my time just to tell me you took this to the board and come up with some other stupid and feeble excuse?"

"I'll try my best, but no guarantees," Goodnight answered and then tried to look terribly busy by shuffling through more papers.

"Yeah, of course. You have no authority, Jimmy, did you even take the loan request to the committee? Wait, of course you did, and they laughed at you, right?"

My dad had experience with underling bankers who acted like big shots when taking loan applications, and on the day of the board meeting, got thrown out of the loan committee because of the stupid way they presented the loan to the board.

"Tell you what, Jimboy, close out the church account right now, and my personal account. I would imagine several hundred other bank accounts would be closed from the Evergreen Baptist Church not counting all the other churches in the community. You're a Catholic, aren't you, Jimmy?"

"That has nothing to do with it, Preacher," the banker said with anger in his voice.

"Oh, yeah? Well it seems to me it does, and I guarantee you, your religion will be a factor by the time I get through explaining this stupid decision to the Southern Baptist Association. I'm sure they would love to hear that Crab Orchard Bank by a decision of its prudent and wise bankers has decided that church loans, which have never been in default, are worthless. Furthermore gentlemen, they've loaned hundreds of thousands to moonshiners."

"You don't know that," Goodnight claimed.

"Really? Who loaned Curt Kirk the money for his farm? I believe he is in jail for moonshining and didn't you sell his farm at Potter's Auction a few months back?"

Goodnight flinched at these words. This was going to be harder than he imagined. He knew that Lincoln County was almost ninety percent Baptist, and if they withdrew their money, it would break the bank.

"Okay, $3,000.00."

"We need five."

"Excuse me Jerry," Mr. Goodnight said as he rose from his chair and walked into another office. My dad could see him talking to the Mr. Enrico Francioni, President of the bank. Now and then, Mr. Francioni would glance in my dad's direction, and the Catholic President was in deep thought, especially when Goodnight told him my dad suspected prejudice by the Catholics.

"Okay, Bro. Smith, we'll loan the church the money but only for a year, and we want personal guarantees plus a mortgage on the property," Goodnight explained, "and ten percent interest."

"Forget it!" My dad raged and walked out of the Vice President's office.

"Wait!" Goodnight cried , but the Preacher was already out

the door. Loretta Kirk was fooling around as if she were busy, her ear tuned to everything she could pick up in the confrontation.

We've got to find that money that Doc Sinclair left the church, he thought, *and we have to find it quickly.*

My dad turned onto the Pine Hall road and drove toward the Martin farm. When he got there, Evel Martin's car was sitting near the barn. He thought he saw Martin peering through the barn's wall planks in the loft. Martin was up there all right, trying to count the money.

As my dad approached the ladder that led to the loft, Martin felt the jiggle of the ladder vibrating on the loft's floor. He screamed, "What do you want?"

"I want to talk with you," my dad answered as he climbed the ladder, and Martin quickly shoved the cash into its hiding place.

"Get out of here, you've no business here. You're trespassing!" Martin yelled, and my dad kept coming.

"So, sue me," my dad said.

Evel Martin wasn't going to mess with the Preacher. His jaw still ached on cold mornings from the Preacher's punch that night of the disturbance Evel caused at the church.

Martin picked up a pitchfork and guarded the bales where the money was stashed. "If you come closer Preacher man, I'll run you through."

My dad stopped. He knew Martin could rage, and this was not the time to challenge Evel because he hated him so badly that he could do some very stupid things.

"I know you stole the money, you piece of hog dung."

"You don' t know nothin!"

"Yeah, I do, and sooner or later you're gonna make a mistake, and I'll be right there. I just wanted you to know that, that's all."

As the Preacher got into his car, he noticed Ethel Martin

372 · SHERMAN SMITH

flip the curtain to the front window of her house where she had been watching. My dad knew Martin stole the money although he couldn't prove it. Martin had been spending the musty cash all over the county.

Bro. Lord was counting the church's money with Harold Brown and Sheriff Crane in the back room of the church. Evergreen Baptist Church required that three men count the money although there never was more than a hundred dollars in the offering plate. Evergreen Baptist Church collected money by passing a plate through the congregation, and as the offering was taken, people noticed who gave and who didn't. Many times blank scraps of paper were placed in the offering so that someone would not be embarrassed by the plate passing and not allowing the scrutiny of the interested parties deciding whether or not that person was tithing.

My dad hated the fact that the deacons who counted the money did it during his morning message, and sometimes the count took so long that the deacons never made it to the preaching service. This irritated the pastor because he could do nothing about it; they had been doing this since the church was founded.

"Look at this," Bro. Lord casually commented. He was mulling over a fifty-dollar bill that smelled musty. "Somebody really got blessed this week."

"Lets see that," Sheriff Crane instructed. He took the bill and smelled it. The smell was familiar.

"Look at this mark," Bro. Lord said.

The Sheriff held the bill up to the light and noticed that there was a tiny "S" strategically placed in the bottom corner of the fifty. He noted his observation audibly, and all at the same time, the three deacons exclaimed, "Doc Sinclair!"

The crowd exited the church, but the Sheriff and Bro. Lord hung back and waited for the Preacher to quit shaking hands.

"Look at this, Bro. Smith," Bro. Lord said.

My dad took the bill and turned it over but didn't see anything unusual.

"Look at the extreme bottom right corner of the bill," the Sheriff pointed, and my dad turned the bill over. "Hold it up to the light."

"Praise the Lord!" My dad praised, "Who put all this money in the offering this morning?" The Sheriff then pointed to the "S." The Preacher figured it out.

Sheriff Crane was on the phone all afternoon trying to find out which member gave so much money.

"Why don't you call Mike Hatten?" Loretta Kirk said. "I believe that he sold Evel Martin his squirrel gun." Loretta had listened to a phone call made to Elsie Dishon, and she said that Mike, her brother, had sold his gun to Evel Martin. The gossip was juicy because the gun had been in the family for generations, and the clan was upset; otherwise, it would never have been noticed.

Sheriff Crane hung up the phone and drove to the Hatten house that was at the bottom of the Chapel Gap Hill. As he drove into the yard, he could see a newly replaced fence where Mike had replaced it after one of the teenage boys failed to negotiate the last curve at the bottom of the hill.

"Mike, did you put a fifty dollar bill in the offering plate this morning at church?"

"That's between me and God," Mike Hatten answered.

The Sheriff knew he was right. Giving was a private matter, and that is the reason no record had been kept at the church of who gave what. The church resisted the popular "tithing envelopes" that was accepted and used by most of the denominational churches in Lincoln County. Evergreen Baptist didn't believe the excuse that a record was needed for the IRS as being a legitimate reason to breach the privacy of offering givers.

They reasoned instead, that controllers of the church wanted to know who the big givers were, and who gave nothing. The church also felt the disclosure of giving would ruin the church because the people would favor the larger donators to God's cause, and those givers would run the churches. This was a stern but simple belief that had more truth to it than met the eye.

"Okay, Bro. Hatten, do you know anyone who did put that much money in the offering this morning?"

Mike Hatten rustled his pocket on the bib of his overalls and took out his sack of tobacco. "Yeah, a friend of mine sold all his guns, and this was his tithe money, but I can't tell you his name."

"Do you recognize this bill?" The Sheriff asked as he handed it to Mike.

"I know the smell because my friend asked me if I thought the bill smelled funny. Why? What's going on?"

The Sheriff took the bill from Mr. Hatten's hand and fled toward his pickup. He never answered the question. He knew that Evel Martin had bought the guns because Loretta Kirk never missed a juicy piece of gossip of any kind that was going on around Chapel Gap.

The Sheriff drove toward Broughtontown as far as the gravel road would allow. He found himself speeding around corners and sliding before he made the climb up the hill to Broughtontown. As he did, he almost slid into a creek. Dust boiled up around the pickup and engulfed the flashing light on top of the truck as the Sheriff slid into the parking area of the Bishop Store in the mid section of Broughtontown. It only took a minute or two before the townspeople were gathering around the store. "Finally," someone said from the tiny crowd, "this bootlegging den of iniquity is going to be shut down once and for all." Heads nodded in agreement.

The Sheriff wasn't interested in illegal fireworks or boot-legged alcohol. Not on this day, anyway.

"Do you still have that hundred dollar bill that Evel Martin gave you a while back?" The Sheriff asked Lester Bishop as he stepped from behind the old Underwood adding machine.

"What makes you think Evel Martin ever gave me a hundred dollar bill?" Bishop asked.

There was no proof of this, but the Sheriff pressed the issue. "All right, Lester, do you want me to go back in the store and shake out all your bootlegged firecrackers again? How 'bout I take an axe and open every cotton pickin' container of booze you have in that storage room you been selling underage kids?" "Probable Cause" meant that the Sheriff would "probably" do whatever he wanted.

Bishop thought for a minute and then decided that the Sheriff wasn't up there to harass him. He had replaced all the fireworks that the Sheriff and Deputy confiscated, and didn't want that to happen again, and besides, the Sheriff may not be as easy as he was the time he raided the store; maybe even arrest him. He went to the cash drawer and dug out the bill that was stuck underneath a pile of papers.

"I saved it;" he said, "I don't even know why."

"Can I see it?" The Sheriff asked.. He knew why Bishop saved that bill. He was curious as to where Martin could get so much money to casually throw around. He might need a bargaining chip someday.

Bishop curiously handed over the bill, watching the Sheriff's facial expressions, and the musty smell was immediate. It was very clear now that the smell of the bill at the Crab Orchard Pool Hall, the smell at the church, and the odor now rising into the Sheriff's nostrils was of the same stack of cash, and Martin had been in all three places spending the money.

Sheriff Crane held the bill in the air and peered at the bottom right corner on the reverse side of the bill. The sun's rays through the screen door showed clearly that the "S" was there, and now it was confirmed in the Sheriff's mind what he already knew; old Doc Sinclair had marked every single bill he had hidden in his safe in the basement of his office.

"Sheriff to base," Sheriff Crane called as he keyed his mike.

"Base," Nancy answered as she manned the station at the Courthouse in Stanford.

"Put a notice out to all the banks in the county, and to all the merchants to be on the lookout for musty smelling bills of all denominations. Tell them to check their reserves they have taken in the last few days. Tell them to look in the bottom right hand corner of the bills on the reverse side. If there is a "S" in that corner, pull those bills aside and hold them and contact the Sheriff's office immediately. Call Trooper Tip Tuck at the State Police Quarters and tell him to meet me in Crab Orchard at the Crab Orchard Baptist Church."

"10-4," Nancy said and hurriedly began making phone calls.

An hour passed before Tip Tuck arrived at the Baptist Church. The Sheriff had already received some feedback from the calls Nancy had made, and there were several bills at the bank in Stanford that had been deposited by several merchants from places where Evel Martin was on a shopping spree. Loretta Kirk had called and said that Babs Kirk had one of the bills in her store. She had heard Babs talking about it to her boyfriend over in Paint Lick.

"We can't arrest him on this evidence," Trooper Tuck explained. "We have no proof that the "S" is Doc Sinclair's mark."

The Sheriff looked down at the rocks on the church's parking area, and they both knew this was too much of a coincidence. Martin had passed all the bills, and they were all marked the same.

"Are we just going to let him keep spending the church's

money, Tip, or are we going to do something about it?" The Sheriff asked.

"Collect all those bills and tell everyone to keep their mouths shut including Loretta Kirk. Tell her if she opens her mouth to anyone about all this that I'm going to arrest her for interfering with a police investigation. Sooner or later, Martin will make a fatal mistake."

CHAPTER THIRTY-FOUR

Babs Kirk was divorced from Gib Kirk, and as part of the settlement, Gib had given her money to open a little store on the corner of Broughtontown and Chapel Gap Roads. Her trade was good because the farmers coming from three directions would often stop and buy refreshments or tobacco at her place. There were always a couple of old timers sitting on the porch and spitting tobacco juice into the gravel.

One of these old men was Uncle T, Engel Barber's brother. Although blind, he was a fantastic whittler. He made things from wood and sold them at the store for a little money to buy his favorite peppermint candy sticks or chewing tobacco he forever had in his mouth. I know for sure he slept with a wad of tobacco, and I think he ate with the wad. There was no evidence that he ever spit out his used chewing tobacco without putting another plug in, and many times, I have seen him put a fresh chew between his cheek and gums before expunging himself of the other.

Uncle T fashioned a neat toy; his famous "dancing man." He whittled the figure from wood and made a thin flexible paddle. A string was attached to the head of the wooden dancer that had moving arms, legs, and head. The paddle was made so that you sat on the thicker part, held the man with a string above the paddle so that his feet barely touched the protruding "dance floor," and then you hit the paddle with your palmed fist, making the dancing man dance. Uncle T sat on the store's front porch as he merrily pounded his fist to make the man dance.

"Hey T," Lane Miller called as he left his parked 1952 Chevrolet Coupe and walked onto the porch.

"Yep," Uncle T answered although nothing significant was attached to this greeting.

Lane Miller lived in Paint Lick, Kentucky and had been courting Babs Kirk for more than twenty years. Babs was a regular attendee at the Evergreen Baptist Church, but she was never allowed to become a member by baptism because Lane was a married man. This situation existed long before my dad started preaching at the church. When Babs challenged him one time that denying her baptism was condemning her soul to hell, he told her that baptism had nothing to do with her salvation, and that she should get her life straightened up. He told her this in spite of the fact that she was the third biggest contributor to the offering at the church on Sunday mornings.

Lane Miller always visited Babs on Saturday afternoons and a rare Sunday, sometimes. Many times his car would be seen parked beside the store in the late hours of the evening. The affair was part of the folklore and gossip of the community for a long time, and each time one of the gossips would pass by Babs' store and see Lane's car there, the gossip would ring throughout the neighborhood as if it was the very first time anyone had ever noticed.

Tobacco was being cut and housed in the barns, so the traffic was light up and down the road in the late afternoon. The news on the phone that day was that Donnie Ballard had fallen from the top rail of his dad's tobacco barn and broke his tailbone. He hit a wagon below, which was almost empty, so there was nothing to break his fall. Babs and Lane were discussing the Ballard boy with Uncle T when Evil Martin drove up. He slid to a stop almost running into the porch on the front of the Bab's Kirk Store.

Evel walked in and looked around.

"What can I do for you, Evel?" Babs asked casually.

"Give me a Nephi orange and one of them Zero candy bars," he said.

"I'm all out of Zeroes, but I have a Clark bar. You've liked those since you were a little kid."

"Yeah, give me one," he replied.

Martin took a swig of his pop and asked how much he owed although he knew it would be thirty cents. Any combination of candy, peanuts, potato chips, and pop was thirty cents no matter how much Babs had to pay for the items she stocked in her store.

"Thirty cents," she said.

Evel reached in his jeans pocket and pulled out a twenty-dollar bill. Babs looked curiously at it.

"What's with the smell?" Lane asked.

"Do you have anything smaller than this?" Babs asked, "I'm running out of change."

"No." Evel remarked.

"Then sign this," Babs instructed as she pulled out a pad with carbon paper between the sheets. "You can pay the next time you're in the store." She gave him a copy of his scrawled signature among many who owed her money.

A curious thing happened then. A memory flashed through

her mind. She never was one to pay attention to gossip and pretty much didn't allow it in her store if it was vicious. She remembered a few days before that Uncle T was talking to Annie Pat who lived a couple of houses down the road from the Kirk Store. Annie said that she heard Loretta Kirk talking about some money that Evel Martin was passing around that might be tied to the inheritance the church was receiving from the Doc Sinclair estate that had been stolen.

"Wait," Babs said, "I have change in the back room." She soon returned with it and counted out nineteen dollars and seventy cents and put it into Martin's hand while taking the twenty-dollar bill from him. She placed the money in the cash drawer.

As Martin made his way back to his farm up the Pine Hall Road, he resurrected the mental note he made when Babs Kirk went to the back room of her store to make change. *She's got money back there,* he thought, *and there's no telling how much.*

Babs always closed her store after dark. Winter, spring, summer, and fall, she did this. It aggravated the farmers because the store would be closed at 4:30 PM in the afternoon in the wintertime, and this made it hard for them to refresh themselves after a hard day of work on their farms. They often met at the store after work and discussed the upcoming prices they expected for their tobacco crops. The store hours were always in contention, and no matter how much they complained, Babs Kirk stuck to her rules.

The store was closed as Martin drove slowly towards it. He passed by and tucked neatly into an opening in a cornfield where the car would not be seen from the road. He walked up to the store and peered through the window where Babs lived in the back. He could see that Lane's arm was around her as they sat on the sofa, and the television was loud enough to be heard a half mile away.

Babs never locked her store because in thirty years of proprietorship, she never lost a dime except an occasional farm brat stealing a candy bar or two. Martin eased into the front door and carefully reached up to the top of the door and caught the bell that rang when anyone entered or exited the establishment. He could hear Lane talking loudly because the old man was hard of hearing, and Babs answered him with equal loudness.

He foraged around in the dark and opened the door where Babs had gone for the money to make change. She had been careless that day, and his eye focused on a gleam of reflected light coming from the living room where Babs and Lane Miller sat screaming at each other. He reached down and found a wooden box about the size of a shoebox. The box was positioned behind a sack of fescue seed. The wooden box was fashioned by Uncle T, and Evel could appreciate the quality. He opened the box and started stuffing the money inside his pockets and underwear.

"I'LL CHECK IT OUT," Babs yelled to Lane. They had been talking about the twenty-dollar bill that Martin had given her earlier in the afternoon.

"I GOTTA LEAVE. BIRDIE WILL THINK I'M HAVING AN AFFAIR," Lane yelled as he walked toward the door. Martin slinked into the shadows as Babs and Lane walked passed him. He could have easily touched either of them. They casually eased through the store and stood at the front door. Evel could see the outlines of their bodies as they said goodbyes.

"I LOVE YOU," Lane called.

Babs mouthed something and then Lane was gone. She wouldn't let Lane kiss her until they could get married because it "wouldn't be right." She closed the screen door and the main door and walked toward the back room that stood between her neatly kept store and where she lived.

Evel Martin stood still in the shadows as he watched Ms. Kirk's silhouette in the backdrop of the porch light shining through the windows. Her figure was remarkably shapely for a woman of her age, probably in her late fifties or early sixties. Martin could feel himself arouse at the sight of her form being revealed through her cotton dress.

When Jack Brown wired the store for electricity a few years before, he did not wire the storage room. Babs kept a flashlight, and the main reason she closed her place after dark was that she didn't want to fool with a flashlight burdening her while she foraged through the storeroom to dig out things the customers were buying. The sun shining through the windows on each side of the room gave plenty of light during the day. It was unusually dark this night; the moon being at its thinnest sliver and hidden by gray clouds. She reached for her flashlight instinctively and thought something was strange in there but not overly alarmed. She would check it out.

The flashlight had been left in her front room earlier that evening when she made a trip to the outhouse while Lane waited patiently on the sofa in the living room. When she turned on the switch, the batteries were dead, and she knew she must have left it on earlier. However, she had an old kerosene lamp sitting on some boxes in the corner of the storeroom that had been there for many years. She had forgotten what was in those boxes; and most likely, it was out dated inventory or unpopular items she could no longer sell. Babs walked into her store and took a matchstick out of a new box on one of the shelves. She held the lamp as she flicked the match with her fingernail, igniting it, and the glow of the match pierced the darkness. The kerosene lamp burned freely even though it had not been lighted for a few years. She had blown the dust out of the chimney and wiped away the cobwebs before setting the wick to flame.

Immediately she noticed the long shadow of Evel Martin's bushy red hair which rose in the darkness like a giant bust of some great dignitary as its black outline fastened to the wooden walls. Babs almost dropped her lantern when she screamed, "Who's there? What do you want?"

Evel Martin stepped out of the shadows and took a few steps toward her. He was almost standing face to face, and his six-foot frame towered over the small woman.

Ms. Kirk held the lamp up so that she could make out Evel Martin's face and then relaxed when she saw who it was. "Evel Martin, what are you doing in my store? I'm closed for the night, and you're not supposed to be back here anyway."

Babs could smell alcohol as strongly as if it were poured all over the room. "You're drunk, Evel, now get on out of here, I don't allow no drunks in my place."

Babs trembled as Evel reached up and took the lantern out of her hands and placed it on the box beside her. "I saw you and Lane Miller sitting on the couch in your front room," he said, "Lane may never have gotten a piece of you, but I will."

"What do you mean?" She cried.

"It's been a long time, ain't it, Ms. Kirk?"

Babs moved backwards, but there was no place to go. Evel moved in and pinned her against the wall not four feet from where she had lit the lamp.

"What, what, are you doing? Don't touch me!"

Evel placed his freckled hands on her shoulders and gently moved her sleeves over her elbows. "Nice," he commented, "let's see what else we can discover."

Babs struggled and fought as much as her strength would allow, but Martin was too strong. He easily held her hands from scratching his face although she did manage to swipe her fingernails across his cheek drawing a trickle of blood.

Evel Martin ripped Babs' dress completely off her, and she stood in her slip.

"Please don't hurt me, take anything you want. I'll give you all my money!" She screamed but no one could hear her. Neighbors were too far away and most of the community was asleep by the 10:00 PM hour.

Evel lustfully looked Ms. Kirk up and down. He ran his fingers over her skin and noticed how smooth she was. He drew himself to her and tried to kiss her, but she was wiry and resisted touching her mouth to his rancid breath and dirty green teeth. He slobbered on her, making her gag.

"I'll die before I'll let you have me," she cried.

"Then you'll die," he replied with a distinct deliberation in his voice that made it clear that he intended to finish what he had started.

Martin ripped off Babs' slip and underwear with one swipe, and she stood naked in the soft glow of the lamplight, and then he took her. A drop of blood dripped on her face near her eye as the wound in Evel's cheek seeped and mingled with his sweat, but this did not deter him.

Martin took his hand off Babs' mouth when he had finished and warned her not to scream. Ms. Kirk jumped to her feet and ran past him as he fastened his jeans. In her haste, she accidentally knocked over the lantern, and the fluid spilled on the boxes and wooden floor. The dried wood exploded in an instant and flames flew up catching the boxes on fire. Evel Martin ran to Babs and hit her on the back of the head with such a blow that it knocked her unconscious. He stepped over the limp and lifeless body and grabbed the wooden shoebox of money and fled out the door. He made no attempt to try and douse the flames or fight the fire, which now burned to such a degree that he could barely get out of the store without catching himself on fire. His bushy red hair singed, and he felt the heat of the raging inferno.

The starter dragged slowly and instant panic hit Martin.

If this damn car don't start, I'm a dead man, he thought, but the engine caught and whirred, and he quickly backed out his hiding place. He was careful not to turn on the headlights or use the brake until he was well beyond the glow of the burning store he could see in his rearview mirror. He parked below the chapel Gap Hill on the Bill Click farm. He placed one hand on the box and emptied its contents on his front seat and started counting the cash.

Dust boiled as pickups flew past him toward Babs Kirk's store. Evel rolled up his window to keep from choking on the dust engulfing his car. He was waiting on the fire truck as Sheriff Crane passed with the red light flashing on his pickup, but the fire truck with its body of volunteer firemen never passed. It was later learned that the volunteer firefighters down in Crab Orchard couldn't get the old vehicle started, and by the time they found the old crank, the fire had burned out of control.

Engel Barber was in the outhouse when he saw the pink glow through the slats in the outhouse door. He had awakened that night with a pounding headache. "Fire," he said to himself out loud and then jumped from his seat and ran to his house. He roused Junebug and told him to get the pickup from the barn.

There was a flurry of activity as farmers and their boys were carrying buckets of water from Babs Kirk's well, trying their best to douse out the flames. The small two gallon buckets didn't make a dent in the fire, so they stood helpless as they wiped the sweat with their huge bandanas and watched the store burn to the ground.

"Has anyone seen Ms. Kirk?" Sheriff Crane questioned Deputy Shanks, who was still in his nightshirt.

"Her car is here, but no one has seen her," the Deputy replied to the inquiry.

The Sheriff shook his head slowly as if he already knew that Babs Kirk was in that fire.

"She's gone," he said softly as others were silent after the realization that Ms. Kirk could have indeed burned up in her own bed.

After finding more than two hundred dollars in the Babs Kirk's cash box, Martin crushed his cigarette in his ashtray and started his car. No vehicles had passed for some time, so he reckoned that he should get out of his hiding place and get to his farm on Pine Hall Road. He eased out on the road and drove the mile and a half from where he hid and turned toward Pine Hall. He neither met nor passed a pickup or a car.

CHAPTER THIRTY-FIVE

The entire community of tiny Chapel Gap and surrounding villages ware in a state of shock. Fran, my dad, Tip Tuck, Sheriff Crane, Deputy Shanks, and I were looking at the smoldering ruins of Babs Kirk's store. Nothing was there but Trooper Tuck had roped off the area and warned everyone that he or the Sheriff would arrest him or her if they came near the scene. Onlookers stood by, and the traffic was heavy as the phone lines burned with gossip about the fire. Babs Kirk was still missing, and phone calls were being made to relatives asking if she had somehow been with them, but no one had seen her.

"We will wait until this afternoon when the heat has died down, and we'll try and find out what happened," Tip Tuck said to the other officers.

Fran had been there most of the night and looked worn as he had been carrying many buckets of water and taking his turn at the well pump. I was also tired from the hard labor. This was the first burning building I had seen since the day the Lancaster Stockyards burned, and the destruction was horrible. We were all saddened by this, and no one could imagine why it happened.

The Sheriff and Trooper Tuck had questioned everyone they could think of who may have been the last person to see Babs Kirk alive. So far, no one came forward who had seen anything.

Late that afternoon, the Sheriff and Tip Tuck decided to wade through the rubble and try to find anything that would give them a clue. They were also apprehensive about finding Babs Kirk's body, and some of the women wiped their eyes as they saw Tip and Homer Crane walk into the ruins of what used to be the main store.

Tip kicked over some broken, charred bottles and a few burnt cans.

"This was a very hot fire," he explained, "worse one I've seen."

Deputy Shanks was foraging through the ashes of the storeroom when his boot kicked something heavy in the waste. He swung his leg back and forth, digging with his boot in the soot.

"Look at this!" He yelled.

"What is it?" Tip Tuck asked as he ran through the rubbish toward the Deputy.

"Oh, no!" Tip hollered.

The body was lying face up. Most of it was reduced to a charred unrecognizable form. One leg was attached to the body, but the arms were completely burned off. Some fingers of Babs Kirk's hands were black from the hot inferno, but still recognizable. All the hair was burned from her head, and the eyes had melted out of their sockets. Although it was inconclusive that this was the body of Babs Kirk, the officers staring at the corpse knew it was.

Floyd arrived in his big hearse. He was driving his used 1956 Cadillac that he had bought when the Florence Funeral Home down in Beaver Dam, Kentucky went bankrupt. He sold the Packard Hearse to the Evergreen Baptist Church who used it for picking up a family in a remote area of the Knobs and transporting them to Sunday School. The sun beamed off the black limousine as Floyd slammed the door and walked over to Sheriff Crane and Trooper Tuck.

"The body's in the storeroom, Floyd. We don't know for sure that it's her," the Sheriff said.

Floyd walked to where the body lay and ordered his new Assistant Undertaker, Stanley Huff to bring a gunnysack that Floyd would use for a body bag. He lifted the charred pieces and carefully placed them in the sack.

"It's Babs," he said as he lifted one of the fingers.

"How do you know that so quickly?" Tip Tuck asked the Undertaker.

"Her wedding ring that Gib Kirk gave her is on her finger. I don't know how the thing survived in this heat."

Everyone who had ever done business with Babs Kirk knew she wore that ring. She was having an affair, but she would never relinquish wearing her wedding band with the tiny garnet stone in a delicate setting. Many of the women who saw the ring wondered why a person would wear a wedding ring after being divorced for so many years. She was never judged by the church for being divorced because she had "Scriptural grounds" according to the Bible. Gib Kirk got Loretta Kirk pregnant while he was still married to Babs. According to the belief of the church, she had a right to leave her husband and marry another because of infidelity. This religious law was also upheld by the courts of Kentucky. She was judged, however, for her long affair with a married man.

What's she doing in the storeroom? Tip wondered, *but that wouldn't be so unusual,* he thought. He noticed the kerosene lamp's chimney that was broken but still partially attached to the metal base of the lamp.

Looks like she dropped the lamp he thought as he bent down and peered over the remains. *Probably caught fire so fast that she couldn't get out.* He mentioned this to the Sheriff standing nearby.

"That doesn't make sense," the Sheriff said. "This part of the store room is clear; she would have plenty of time to get away."

"Yeah," Tip agreed, "but what if her clothes caught fire, and she was trying to put it out, but couldn't?"

It was then that all three of the officers and Floyd noticed that there was not a shred of clothing on her body. When a fully clothed body burns, no matter how raging the fire, there is always some of the cloth that survives the fire. There were no buttons, zippers, or any remains of cloth on Babs Kirk's grilled flesh.

"Normally, you would find at least some clothing underneath the body where the fire had been sheltered from the heat," Floyd confirmed what the others were thinking. Floyd was miraculously knowledgeable even though he had never investigated a fire where a burned body had been found.

Fran followed my dad into the store ruins after asking the Sheriff if he could look around. Fran had a broomstick that somehow did not perish and was poking around near the outside ruins of what used to be a wall. He raised his stick and stuck to it were the remains of a cotton dress.

"Something's bad wrong," the Trooper said as he stirred up the ashes and found Bab's brassier. The metal clasp and cup stays were partially in place. Her clothing was nearly ten feet from her body.

"Why would she be naked in her storeroom and drop her clothes so far from her body? This is foul play," the Sheriff explained while others were listening and mouthing to each other with surprise, "foul play."

Sophia Lord was with her husband, Bro. Lord, praying over the situation, and she quickly made the excuse that she needed to go home. She felt sick. When Bro. Lord dropped her off and was out of sight, she ran to the phone as fast as she could and called Loretta Kirk.

"Murder," she said. Tip Tuck said that Babs was murdered and the gossip rang up and down the valleys and hills like wildfire. Dephi Anderson had heard the news and was writing as fast as she could to get her column in the "Record" as the Crab Orchard paper was now called.

"Make sure no one enters the scene, Sheriff. Post a couple of men at the perimeter twenty four seven if you have to." Tip Tuck said this as he headed toward his cruiser not divulging to anyone where he was going. He sped away with his red light flashing and the siren blaring. The folks standing around the store could hear the siren as Trooper Tuck sped down the road toward Crab Orchard.

Lane Miller met the Trooper as he walked into his front yard at Paint Lick. He had been painting some lawn chairs in the backyard. The Trooper towered over the shorter man and stared him in the eyes. Lane knew something was wrong and nervously asked Tip Tuck why he was there? No one in Chapel Gap knew exactly where Lane Miller lived although they had known him for years. No attempt was made to call him because they weren't sure he had a phone.

"Where were you last night?" Tip asked.

"Why?" Lane responded curiously and nervously.

"There's been an accident. Babs Kirk is dead, burned up at her store sometime last evening."

Lane acted as if he would faint. He leaned up against a tree and steadied himself. "How?" He asked quietly.

"The store caught fire somehow, and Babs was in there when it happened. We found her this morning lying in the storeroom without her clothes. Where were you last night, Mr. Miller?"

"Do I need a lawyer?"

"Not unless you did something wrong. Now answer the question."

Lane Miller thought long and hard before he answered the inquiry, and after a few minutes of dead silence, he said, "I did nothing wrong. I love the woman."

Lane's wife was staring through the window trying to listen to the conversation. Lane motioned for Tip to follow him to the side of the house so that he could get out of the way from his wife's listening ears.

"I was with Babs just like every Saturday afternoon," he explained.

"What time did you leave?"

"About 8:00 PM. I stayed a little longer than usual."

"Was anyone else at the store?" Tip questioned while taking notes on a little pad of paper.

"I saw no one. The store was closed. People don't come to the store after she closes it."

Trooper Tuck had jurisdiction as a State Policeman all over the State of Kentucky even though his duty was in Lincoln County. Paint Lick was a Madison County town. He put his hand on his hip ready to draw his revolver in case Lane reacted to his next statement.

"Place your hands behind your back, Lane."

"What for? I didn't do nothing."

Tip carefully cuffed the man while he cussed and screamed that he had nothing to do with his lover's death. "I love the woman," he said while Mrs. Miller and all the neighbors standing in their yards and by the street heard his confession that he loved another woman.

Tip took Lane to the county jail in Richmond, Kentucky. Tip told him that he wasn't being charged for anything at the moment, but he was being held in custody for his own protection until the investigation was finished. On the way back to Paint Lick, Tip passed the Lincoln Town Car that Doug Morgan was driving. Tip thought once about turning around and stopping the attorney for speeding but didn't. He sped on toward Lancaster and Crab Orchard. There was no doubt in the Trooper's mind that Lane Miller called the attorney, and he would be out of jail within the hour.

"Brothers and sisters, we have had a terrible tragedy in our community with the death of this Godly woman," my dad was finishing his sermon at Babs Kirk's funeral. "We must all pray that her soul is in the arms of Jesus."

Babs' charred body lie in the coffin. Floyd had ordered the casket closed to protect the harmful image from the children, and a picture sat on the casket. She was young and beautiful, and this would be the remembrance that all her friends and family would have of her.

"She looks so natural," the mourners cried as they wailed and touched the coffin lying in front of the church. I couldn't help but think how they figured she looked "natural" when they couldn't see her body, and if they could, they would never recognize her.

No sooner had the casket been lowered into the ground of the Evergreen Baptist Cemetery than the gossips gathered in a circle. The sisterhood of tales. There was food on the wagons, and before the "blessing," the women had pronounced Lane Miller the killer. "He's covering up his affair," one said, "to save his own hide." They said these things in spite of the fact that Lane Miller had made no secret, nor did Babs Kirk, about their twenty years affair except to hide it from Birdie Miller. Many times when Lane would visit Babs on Sundays, he would be sitting in the parking lot of the church waiting on the services to end so that he could give Ms. Kirk a ride home.

Birdie Miller, Lane's wife, sat in the police station waiting room. She had watched Tip handcuff her husband and take him away in the Trooper's cruiser. She glanced up as Doug Morgan walked up to the desk and demanded to see Lane.

"I want to talk to him first," she said.

Morgan looked around and saw the little lady with blue hair and deep blue eyes. "Okay, that's not a problem," he replied.

Lane looked daunt as he came out of the prison chambers. He could not look at his wife or Doug Morgan, but instead, stared at his feet.

"You know," he said sorrowfully to Birdie.

"I've known for twenty years, Lane. How do you think you keep lying and lying, and I not know something was wrong?" She explained this as she wiped some tears from her cheeks and nose.

"Why didn't you say something?" He asked lugubriously. "Why didn't you try and put a stop to it?"

"I grew up with Babs Kirk, and I know her very well. She is a Christian woman, and I knew she would never violate the sanctity of marriage, even though I will never trust you the rest of my life. I figured you needed someone to talk to and have a relationship with. God knows you never had one with me, but as long as you treated me fairly, which you did, no violence or real trouble in our marriage, well, I made my bed, so I had to lie in it. Otherwise, my life was okay."

Lane still had his head down looking at the floor and asked, "Do you think I killed Babs?" Doug Morgan looked up from the papers he was shuffling eager to hear her answer.

"Of course not. You are incapable of that kind of violence. You're one great crime is indiscretion, and you've had plenty of it. And, the other thing is you're a coward. Too cowardly to face your real problems and do something about them."

Doug Morgan smiled now. He felt relieved. If Lane Miller's own wife had put up with an affair for twenty years, and knew her husband well enough that she would testify to his non-violent nature, there was no jury in the nation that would convict him of murder.

"Will you forgive me?" Lane asked remorsefully.

"Nope. Can't do that. In fact, I've already called my sister up in Lexington. I will be spending the rest of my life up there. No divorces, either. If you expect me to testify at your trial and save your rotten hide from being fried by telling the court what a great saint you are, then you'll have to agree in a contract that there will be no divorce."

This lady is good, Doug Morgan thought to himself. *She's going to make him suffer a life sentence worse than death.*

"Oh, another thing, Lane. If I ever hear so much as a word breathed that you have hooked up with another woman, I'll cut your part of the inheritance you've been living on for thirty years that my daddy left to me. So, if you are going to have another affair while still married to me, and you will be for the rest of your life, you pretty damn well make sure she's got money."

Lane Miller sat pale in Doug Morgan's car as he watched Birdie drive off in his Chevy. She turned on the Richmond Road that would eventually lead to Lexington, Kentucky. The car was packed with as much stuff as she could possibly carry, and Lane could barely make out the driver there were so many things piled up inside the car. She would send her nephew for the rest of her things as she needed them.

"Am I going to die?" Lane asked.

"Not unless you piss off your wife by breaking one of her rules," Doug reassured him.

The Evergreen Baptist Church had a far larger crowd than usual that Sunday morning after the funeral. Everyone knew that the Preacher was going to say something in his sermon about Babs' affair and the subsequent capture of her "killer." They weren't disappointed.

"Brothers and sisters hear me," he said. He had just stepped into the pulpit after old Sam Messer, Preacher Robert's wife's father, had sung "I'll Be A Friend To Jesus." The old man sang slowly, and this cut into valuable time the Preacher needed to satisfy his hungry congregation.

"Jesus said: If a man lusts after a woman, he has committed adultery in his heart already. Having an affair is lust. Anytime you take the emotions of love and transfer those to someone else other than your wife, you have violated the sanctity of marriage." The congregation nodded their approval of his wisdom; all were in agreement. There were some whispers, and Loretta Kirk said to one of the ladies sitting next to her: "Why did he take this long to preach about affairs?"

"Having an affair has nothing to do with sex," the Preacher explained.

My dad knew he had made a bad mistake that would cost him. He said S-E-X, and that word was never used in the Christian's conversation much less from a pulpit. A cold chill permeated the assembly like a bitter north wind. The tears that were always there when the Preacher preached dried up instantly, and acrid stares and leers pierced the Preacher's soul as he realized the impact this word had on his people. Several of the young people snickered because they thought what he said was neat. Fran stared at my dad, and when I punched him on the arm and made a gesture of "cool," thumbs up, he ignored me and frowned with worry.

"Drink water from your own well," my dad went on, "keep your eyes on the one you're married to. No man or woman has any business spending any time with a woman or man who isn't your husband or wife, especially if that person is not a Baptist." It was well known that Lane Miller was not a Baptist but a member of the Church of Christ; the people who believed musical instruments were sinful in their churches and believed you had to be baptized in water by a Church of Christ preacher in order to go to heaven. My dad preached about them many times calling them "Campbellites" because they split off the Baptists in 1826 and followed Alexander Campbell, a rogue Preacher from Pennsylvania who had split the Baptists right down the middle in the State of Kentucky. He hammered this point so hard that it was understood as if having an affair with a "Campbellite" was much worse than having an affair with a Baptist.

"Campbellites are a cult," he said in his message. "But, we are to forgive everyone of their sins as Jesus forgave us. Campbellites can be saved and go to heaven although it is harder for them to get saved than anybody from any other denomination."

It was getting a little hard to follow now because my dad did have a tendency to chase rabbits during his sermons now and then. I thought his change of pace might be a diversion. It seemed to be working because at the mention of the "Campbellites" people were now nodding their heads, and the icy congregation seemed to be thawing out; especially when Bro. Lord and Reuben Click broke the freeze by saying, "Amen."

The Preacher relaxed a little and left the subject of "affairs" in the Bible. He finished his message by thundering the evils of Alexander Campbell and how he led thousands of people to hell that believed his interpretation of the Bible. The diversion worked, it seemed. He even ended his sermon with a rare joke.

"The Baptist church was directly across the street from the Campbellite church," he said, "the Campbellites were singing the hymn, "Will There Be Any Stars In My Crown?," and at the same time the Baptists were singing the hymn, "No Not One." He laughed, I laughed, but no one else did. The church didn't like Preachers making jokes from the pulpit; especially, at invitation time. My dad bombed, big time.

The church had never seen one Sunday morning where there weren't people coming to the altar for salvation and re-dedication. That morning there was not one person standing in line, and it was weird. Fran later explained to me that if someone went for salvation or rededication, the members would think that person had committed adultery or was having an affair, and no one was going to risk that. This seemed plausible to me, and then I saw the sisterhood standing outside the church talking and whispering. Ever so often during the course of their gabbing, one or two of the sisters would glance at my dad shaking hands with the people as they coldly left the building. My dad noticed this as well.

"All right ladies, what's going on?" The Preacher asked as he boldly walked toward the group that he normally left to themselves. His suit was wet with perspiration from his preaching exercise.

"You have just given our children the right to use foul and lascivious language," Loretta Kirk said.

"I got their attention," he said, "and apparently yours."

This was a weak cover-up that wouldn't work, not with these women. "You keep preaching about the evils of tobacco," Loretta Kirk carried on, "but you grow it. You talk about the sin of movies and television and what they are doing to our kids, but you own one. You teach the children of the church not to cuss, but you used the foulest words possible in your own sermon!"

Loretta Kirk was the spokesperson for the Sisterhood, a position of influence she appointed herself to. She had the consensus of the group's members, and she knew it. The other women nodded in agreement with Loretta's rebuke, and one of them barked and gagged as if an evil spirit had entered her during the sermon. It was to become the most infamous sermon ever preached in Lincoln County.

"Sex is not a dirty word," my dad said although he knew it was.

"OH! OH MY!" Sophie Lord hailed as she fled toward her waiting husband in his new Ford pickup. My dad was in trouble.

That Sunday evening, there were fewer adults than anyone had ever seen since the day my dad took over the pastor ship of the Evergreen Baptist Church. However, the crowd was not diminished because there were more young people in the service than anyone had ever seen since he'd been there. Kids visited from Crab Orchard, Broughtontown, Pine Hall, Chestnut Ridge, and Copper Creek. The kids from the Baptist Churches in those areas heard instantly through the enormous grapevine that Preacher Smith had pulled a good one. They wanted to be a part of the coming out of the dark ages and experience the rebirth of the total effect modern preaching would have on the Christian world of the Knobs.

Kathy Friday was in the service that night, and the pain of having to watch her sitting across the auditorium from me was unbearable. I would have asked her if I could sit with her, but I was on restriction.

CHAPTER THIRTY-SIX

D o you give up your right to a speedy trial?" The Judge asked Lane Miller at his arraignment.

"He does not," Doug Morgan answered. "We want a trial as fast as we can. That's his right, your Honor."

"I know what his rights are, Mr. Morgan. Trial date is set in thirty days." The Judge hammered his gavel on the podium, and the noise echoed throughout the courtroom.

"Your client is going to the electric chair," Prosecutor Birdstein said. "He's guilty as sin itself," he mouthed to Attorney Morgan.

Birdie Miller had taken money out of her trust account and put up bail. No one except the Prosecutor thought he was a flight risk. He had lived in Madison County all his life and even though Paint Lick was in a remote area of the county, many people knew him and respected him. As far as anyone could recollect, he had never traveled outside Madison and Lincoln Counties in his entire life.

"The accused is a flight risk, your Honor. I recommend we hold him in custody until trial," the Prosecutor stated his opinion and motion.

"Shut up, Jack," the Judge said even though the two men were neighbors and friends. "Trial in thirty days," and then the Judge explained to Lane Miller what could happen to him if he didn't show up for his appointed day in court. The Judge swung his black robe over his chair and walked out of the courtroom.

The jury was selected of twelve men. No woman had ever served on a jury in Judge Williston's courtroom. He was a Democrat and perceived to be a liberal; the county was Republican, and he knew he could never be elected if he upset the Baptist Republicans.

Nearly the entire congregation of Evergreen Baptist Church was present in the courtroom the day the trial began. The Baptists sat on one side of the courtroom, and the Campbellite congregation from Lane Miller's church on the other. The trial had a lot of publicity in the local papers, so many curiosity seekers filled the aisle ways and stood against the walls as the trial began. Lane had been offered a plea bargain, but refused.

"They'll give you twenty years if you plead guilty," Doug Morgan told Lane. "You could get life imprisonment without the possibility of parole, or the Prosecutor could seek the death penalty if you go to trial."

"But I'm innocent," Lane cried in despair.

"Then we go to trial and the mercy of the court and jury," Doug replied.

Plea bargains were the beginning of the ruination of the Justice system in the United States. Prosecutors knew they couldn't win at trial against high-powered lawyers such as Doug Morgan. He had only lost one case. He chewed up the deficient prosecutors, who couldn't make a living in their own practices and hid behind the security of public money, like a corn picker spits out kernels on a hot summer day. The prosecutors ducked behind plea bargains, and they were doing it all over the country. They wore down innocent people with their threats of "conspiracy," leaving not guilty people who couldn't afford legal representation to lower court appointed attorneys who were in cahoots with the prosecutors and judges. Birdie Lane could afford Doug Morgan.

"It looks bad," Doug told his client after Birdstein ran through the investigation theories of the case after his opening statements.

"The prosecution will prove that Lane Miller murdered Babs Kirk and then set fire to the store to cover up his crime. He had motive, Mr. Juror, and he premeditatedly planned his crime," Birdstein explained to the jurors who were listening intently to his opening arguments.

"Lane Miller had been having an affair with Ms. Kirk for over twenty years.

"Objection!" Morgan yelled.

"Over ruled," the Judge said.

Birdstein went on. "His wife did not know about this affair. She never traveled up to Chapel Gap although she had known Babs Kirk for a long time, in fact, since they were little girls. This made matters worse and more heinous because Mr. Miller flaunted his affair in front of the Chapel Gap Community and the Evergreen Baptist Church."

The Campbellites stared at Lane. Apparently they didn't know about the affair although over the years many of them wondered why Birdie Miller was left alone on Saturdays and sometimes Sundays when Lane and Birdie didn't show up for church. The Campbellites glared across the aisle at the Baptists as if they were thinking, *You all didn't do anything about this situation and let the affair continue?* The facts were that the Baptists didn't know anything about Lane Miller except that he came to Chapel Gap in a black car for twenty years and sat with Babs Kirk.

"It's a known fact that Babs Kirk couldn't marry Lane Miller," the Prosecutor continued.

"Objection!"

"Over ruled," the Judge said and then motioned for Morgan to come to the podium. "Let the Prosecutor finish his statement and quit interrupting," the Judge said sternly and letting Doug Morgan know that be was not going to let the trial get out of hand.

Morgan sank low in his seat. He knew the Prosecuting Attorney would do everything in his power to discredit his client, and he was doing a good job.

"He murdered Ms. Kirk and tried to cover up his crime because Ms. Kirk refused to marry Lane Miller and demanded that he divorce his wife, or the affair was finished." The courtroom stirred with emotion, and people were talking. The Prosecutor threw this last tidbit of information out of the clear blue, and no one ever heard mention that Babs Kirk had placed a demand on the relationship.

Doug Morgan was about to lose his second case. The Prosecution had hammered Lane's credibility day after day, finding witnesses who testified that Lane was a living a secret life. Morgan was hard pressed to find anyone who knew much about Lane, but a few witnesses did testify to his competence and moral character, but that argument was shot down by the Prosecutor's reminding the Judge and Jury that it was Lane who did not have a very moral character because he was having an affair with a woman who was not his wife, and had deceived his own spouse as well as the Chapel Gap Community by leading them to think he was unmarried and was simply "dating" Ms. Kirk. Babs Kirk's credibility was never brought into question, except once. My dad testified that even though he was aware of this affair, he knew Ms. Kirk's values, and that she would never have an intimate relationship (he carefully avoided the word "sex") because she was a believer in Jesus Christ. He also told them that she attended the church but was not allowed to become a member because of her relationship with Lane Miller. He explained that he knew she was seeing a married man and had spoken with her on many occasions about all the indiscretions and sins she was committing.

"The testimony of her distinguished Pastor concerning Babs Kirk's moral values is even more reason for Lane Miller to murder his girlfriend." The use of the word "girlfriend" by the Prosecutor was a solid blow to the defense. "Girlfriend" made the situation sound even worse. "Imagine, men of the jury that you spend your whole life supporting a church. I have in my hand here the canceled checks of Babs Kirk's tithing practice for many years, and they will show that she was a most generous contributor to the Evergreen Baptist Church. I doubt anyone in this courtroom is giving, or has given, to the church with the compassion and consistency of Babs Kirk. No wonder the Pastor and congregation let this whole sordid affair slide. They helped murder Babs Kirk!"

Birdstein, a Catholic, had just attacked the Preacher and the entire congregation of Evergreen Baptist Church. As he spoke these words, the Campbellites sitting across from the Baptists stared at them with piercing eyes of contempt as the Prosecutor unfolded the Baptists diabolical scheme to further their financial prosperity and exposed it to the whole world. The Baptists to the Campbellites were the apostate church, and this proved it. Icy chills went up and down the spines as they thought of the sinful and wicked Evergreen Baptist Church, and their sneaky pastor that covered up illicit affairs for money.

"Babs Kirk did not any longer want to support a church and attend a church she was not a member of, and Lane Miller was standing in her way," the Prosecutor claimed. "She took to him an ultimatum that he either divorce and marry her or the affair was over. She needed to be baptized before she died and be a member of her church." Both the Baptists and the Cambellites were pleased with this part of the Prosecutor's argument. The Campbellites didn't think anyone could go to heaven without being baptized, and the Baptists believed in a "Baptist Bride" as the only church which would be assembled at the "Marriage Feast of the Lamb," and wear wedding garments as the Lord Himself took the Baptists as his "Bride" and lived with them forever in the Holy City.

"Lane Miller killed his girlfriend out of frustration and rage," and the Prosecutor was finished.

No one noticed Evel Martin sitting in the back of the courtroom day after day. He was careful to slip out just as the judge ended the arguments of the day and sent the jurors home. Lane Miller was the only one who knew he was at the store the same afternoon, but he had forgotten this, so Evel was not a suspect just as many who had bought things on credit, and the record that Babs kept by hand on a little notebook of the day's transactions, were not suspects.

On the last day of the trial, Doug Morgan and Lane Miller arrived a little late. The last witnesses would be called before the jury would be sent out by the Judge for deliberations. Doug Morgan was all out of witnesses. He couldn't call Lane's wife, Birdie, because she would be fatal with her testimony that she didn't know about the affair although she did. She would never testify to that fact because she wouldn't be embarrassed in front of all her friends and neighbors as to be so stupid as to not knowing the affair was going on. She wouldn't want to be judged as to why she put up with it either if the truth came out. The Prosecution could not make her testify because the law prohibited a wife from testifying against her own husband if she did not want to do so. Morgan wondered underneath his breath why he ever took the case in the first place, but Birdie had shelled out all the money he had asked for, and after all, he was a lawyer. He could do well with the money for a long, long time. He had only a weak witness or two, and that was it. Lane Miller was going to the electric chair and Kentucky executed, quickly. Doug didn't believe Lane was guilty, but he couldn't prove his innocence.

As Morgan and Lane entered the courtroom, Lane noticed Evel Martin sitting in the back pews. After all the investigation by Doug Morgan and his assistant up in Chapel Gap about who was in the store that day, Lane only remembered Uncle T. This was insignificant because Uncle T was blind. For some reason, his blindness kept the defense and the prosecution from examining him, and he was left alone. Lane had told them that Uncle T had left the store soon after he arrived, and that no one else had come. He completely forgot about Evel Martin until he saw his flaming red hair.

"He was in the store," Lane pointed out.

"Who is he?" Doug asked, "and why didn't you tell me this before?"

"I forgot, I don't know why. His name's Evel Martin from Broughtontown."

"Could he have done the murder? Does he have anything against Ms. Kirk?" Morgan quizzed his client trying to find any reason to postpone the jury deliberation while he checked out this Evel Martin.

"The Prosecution calls Evel Martin," Birdstein said. He had been saving this last trump card to finalize and seat Lane Miller's conviction solidly in the jury's minds.

Morgan watched with horror as the red headed freckled

Martin walked to take his place on the witness stand. Martin sheepishly climbed into the chair and looked over the church people who filled the room on this cloudy and windy day.

"Do you solemnly swear to tell the truth, the whole truth, and nothing but the truth so help you God?" The clerk recited as Evel Martin's freckles touched the Holy Bible. He swore to tell the truth although he never told the truth in his life about anything.

"Wait a minute, your Honor," Doug Morgan interjected. "This witness is not on the Prosecution's witness list." Everything happened so quickly that Morgan had forgotten to check the witness list.

"Court is recessed for thirty minutes," the Judge ordered. "You two attorneys meet me in my chamber."

"Court's in session," the Bailiff said as the Judge entered the courtroom, "the court calls Evel Martin."

Martin came back into the courtroom, his pants wet after he had dribbled on himself and took a seat. He had already been sworn in.

After the Prosecutor asked the fundamental questions about who Martin was, where he lived, he started the questioning.

"Mr. Martin, were you in the Kirk Store the day of Babs Kirk's murder?"

"Objection!" Doug Morgan cried, "there's no proof of a murder."

"Sustained," the Judge said.

"I was," Martin answered directly.

"Did you purchase anything?"

"Yes. A Clark bar and a RC Cola."

"Was anything unusual happening in the store between Lane Miller and Babs Kirk?"

"They were arguing."

"About what?"

"I'm not sure what it was all about, but I did hear Mr. Miller say that if she wouldn't marry him, he would kill her."

The courtroom stirred and then loud talking proceeded as the Campbellites yelled across the aisle at the Baptists. "This is a set up!" One of them yelled. "You Baptists have no morals, you'll all burn in hell!" Another screamed.

The Judge rapped heavily with his gavel on the podium and hollered, "Silence in the courtroom, or I'll clear it!" The courtroom's din died to a small whisper, and the Judge rapped his gavel again. All eyes focused on the witness stand where Martin grinned with pleasure.

"Did you hear or see anything else?" The Prosecutor asked.

"He was screaming at her that she had ruined his life and then he slapped her across the cheek really hard. You could hear it all the way outside, it was so violent." A tear fell from Evel Martin's eye and dripped off his nose.

"Would you describe this as excessively violent behavior?"

"I would," Martin said while wiping his eyes.

"How violent?"

"Ms. Kirk fell to the floor, and I helped her get on her feet."

"Anything else?"

"I paid for the stuff with a twenty." Martin caught himself, "a dollar, and she gave me change."

Fran and my dad looked at each other when Martin almost said that he paid for the candy and pop with a twenty-dollar bill. Morgan was debating whether he should put Lane Miller on the stand, but everyone knew that Lane was so passive that the Prosecutor would eat him up. That could be a fatal mistake.

GENTLEMEN OF THE JURY," Prosecutor Birdstein said loudly, "the Prosecution has proven beyond a shadow of a doubt that Lane Miller murdered in cold blood," he shivered and crossed his arms around his chest, "he had motive. He had a lascivious affair with a Godly woman. She was so Godly that she refused to have sex with Mr. Miller for twenty years." The Jury was shocked, as was the assembly listening intently to every word. There was a buzz of whispers at the use of the word "sex," but Birdstein knew exactly what he was doing. "He told her many times through the years that he was getting a divorce, and one time, he told her he wasn't even married!" Doug Morgan flinched at these statements since this was the first time he had heard anything about this. He wanted to object; he wanted to fly at the Prosecutor and shut his mouth for what he knew were figments of the Prosecutor's imagination and not ultimate truth.

"I did not! He's a liar!" Lane Miller cried from his chair behind the defense's table.

"The witness will restrain himself," the Judge ordered and Lane sank into his chair. Doug Morgan patted Lane gently on the arm because Morgan knew the Prosecutor was making things up.

"So, gentlemen, it would be a grave error to acquit a murderer and a liar. Do you see these people?" He pointed to the Campbellites on his left "Those fine Christian folks believed that Lane Miller was an upstanding and honorable man, but he is not. Instead, he is a conniving, manipulating, and pitiful excuse for a human being. Those Baptists?" He pointed to his right. "Those Baptists helped him cover up his sinful deeds by condoning his every action." They took Ms. Kirk's tithe money and hushed while she was having this affair with a married man; something they knew for twenty years. They helped murder Ms. Kirk. If they had done what they were supposed to do and exposed this affair, Ms. Kirk would still be alive today."

The Baptists were beside themselves, and especially my dad. There was fire in his eyes although he knew that the Prosecutor was making a small point by chastising his church in front of the Court. The Campbellites loved this even though they were there to support Lane Miller. Now, they had to make up their minds whether it was more important to help out one of their own or jump on the bandwagon of humiliating the Baptists.

"AMEN!" Several of the Campbellites shouted in agreement with what the Prosecutor said about the involvement in the murder of Babs Kirk. They made their choice. Lane Miller slinked down in his chair almost to his shoulders, and Doug Morgan buried his head in his hands.

Doug Morgan knew that his client was finished. Birdstein, the man who was Morgan's classmate in law school, had shocked the entire courtroom into submission with his brilliant oratory; Mr. Miller was indeed the murderer. This Prosecutor dressed in a double breasted suit that was so tight on him he could hardly get the jacket buttoned; his belly hanging over the thin cut above his belt, had condemned his client. He was going to lose this case. He once thought that this boldness of the Prosecutor, and how he handled the trial; especially, the bashing of the Baptists would be the Prosecutor's downfall in next year's election, but now he had doubts that anyone would oppose him.

"GENTLEMEN!" Doug Morgan began. "The Prosecution has proven nothing. He brings in a witness at the last minute, and he knew all along this witness had come forward." Morgan was on dangerous ground now as the Prosecutor sneered at him. *Did he just say I manipulated the court by holding a witness and didn't disclose that I would call him?* Birdstein thought.

"Evel Martin is a known liar," he pointed at my dad. "That preacher there was threatened by Martin one night during his church service. Martin was throwing beer cans on the parking lot!" The Baptists nodded, and the Campbellites shuddered at the thought of desecrating a church in such a manner. The Campbellites had another problem to decide. Should they keep their emotions focused on their innate hatred of the Baptists, or should they sympathize with them for having their church ransacked by a heathen that would do such a thing? They gasped.

"The Preacher had to straighten the man out, and he did. He whipped him right there in front of the whole church!"

"Yeah, brother!" One of the Campbellites yelled in support of the Preacher's decisive actions. Doug raised his voice; the passion echoing throughout the hollow chamber. "How could you, members of this most distinguished jury, convict a man of murder on the testimony of a liar, a moonshiner, a bootlegger, a gambler, and a church desecrater?"

This is brilliant, Birdstein thought. *He has taken my witness apart piece by piece.* Birdstein didn't bother to check into Martin's nefarious past to see if he was a credible witness before calling him to the stand. He looked at the Campbellites and then the Baptists, glancing behind him to see the reaction of the jury. They were nodding their heads in agreement with what the defense attorney was saying.

Evel Martin fled the courtroom. He was furious at the attack on his character, and he vowed once again to kill the Preacher, and now he added one more to that list. He would dismember Doug Morgan's body and rape his daughters. He found his car and left Stanford. As he sped down Main Street, completely unworried about cops because they were all in the courthouse, he saw Uncle T and Engel Barber walking with Sally Barber along the sidewalk. He watched them turn and enter the drugstore.

"In a few minutes, Gentlemen of the Jury, the Honorable Judge is going to ask you to make a decision. It may be the most important decision in your whole lives except your salvation." My dad was moved by this expression of Morgan's ability to even know what salvation was. He said, "amen," and the Campbellites turned their heads toward him. "That decision could or could not condemn a man to his death, who is innocent. Oh, I'm not condoning the activity for more than twenty years of my client. He was wrong, but it is not against the law for a man to have an affair. I will bet if we could look into the hearts of these Christian people here, they know what they have done, and many of them have led secret lives with the opposite gender whether it was for a long time or just a flash in the pan. There may even be one of these distinguished jurors here who had an affair." Doug knew that at least one juror had because he was the lawyer for the man's wife when she sued for divorce. "Having an affair is against God's law, but unfortunately, there is nothing against it in man's law. There ought to be, though, and we wouldn't be having these divorces that are going to break down our families and ruin this great nation. As the family goes, the nation goes!" Morgan was preaching and thundering his distaste, if he really had one, for the sordid and morbid ideal that extramarital affairs could affect this country to its complete demise.

"He's won this case," Birdstein quietly mused to his aide. "Plus, he will win the State Senate Seat he's seeking; he's insured his own election!"

Never in the history of Lincoln or Madison Counties had the Baptists and the Campbellites been in agreement about anything, but now they were. They were approving everything Doug Morgan said and were hanging suspended on every word.

"Gentlemen, I leave you with this one thought. Acquit this man of murder because he didn't kill anyone. He is incapable of that and many of these witnesses watching in this courtroom know that he is innocent and have testified about his good character. He is guilty of having an affair, and no good Christian will accept that as credible behavior. I ask you to consider this one thing: Acquit in this courtroom; find Lane Miller innocent, but leave the moral law and judgment to God. Lane Miller will have to face the Almighty Lord God in heaven one day at the Judgment Seat of Christ." The mention of Judgment Day brought tears on both sides of the aisle. "God will give Lane Miller what he deserves, but we must be responsible about taking a man's life that is innocent. I rest my case and leave it in the hands of this Jury and God."

The Judge had never seen a courtroom full of people jump to their feet and applaud. He was so moved by Morgan's speech himself that he could not find the strength to swing his gavel and stop the melee. Baptists and Campbellites shook hands as if this was the reunion in heaven itself.

"Quiet in the Courtroom," Judge Wilston ordered now regaining his composure and bringing things under control. He instructed the jury and they filed into the deliberating room to debate this monumental trial that had miraculously brought the Baptists and Campbellites back together since they split in 1826. They were not influenced by anyone on the outside, having obeyed the Judge's orders not to speak to anyone about the trial, and especially the "media." The only media present at the trial was Daphni Anderson, who took notes 'furiously throughout the trial for the Crab Orchard Reporter and some small time reporter from the Paint Lick paper.

It took only fifteen minutes for the jury to reach a verdict. The Judge was taking a sip of Jim Beam Bourbon when the Bailiff told him the Jury had reached a verdict. He had to hurry and put his robe hack on and hide the bottle behind some books.

"Gentlemen of the Jury, have you reached a verdict?"

"We have your honor," and the Foreman of the Jury handed the Clerk, Rosalee Baker, the decision. She handed it to the Judge who read it for more than fifteen minutes although it was only one count and two paragraphs. The Judge loved keeping his courtrooms in suspense and especially this one.

The Judge handed the verdict back to the clerk. "Please read the Jury's decision," he said.

The Clerk cleared his throat. "We the members of the Jury of Case Number 26407 of the trial of Lane Miller on One Count of Murder in the First Degree find the Defendant," she paused as the attendance in the room eased to the front edge of their pews, "NOT GUILTY!"

There were shouts and yells of joy. Lane Miller hugged Doug Morgan. The Christians united in shaking hands and forgiving one another although every one of them knew their Sunday morning message would be on "Baptismal Regeneration," and the fight would begin all over again.

"Congratulations, Doug," Prosecutor Birdstein said to Morgan.

"I thought you had me there for a while," Morgan responded. He was extremely grateful to my dad for informing him about how the jury could be brought to an acquittal decision. My dad basically wrote the notes during the Prosecutor's Close and handed them to Doug who sat directly in front of him. Doug Morgan had still only lost one case and that being the trial of Curt Kirk for moonshining.

CHAPTER THIRTY-SEVEN

W hat's all the fuss about?" Uncle T asked his brother
Engel Barber. He could hear a horde of folks filing out
of the Courthouse and walking past him.

"Lane Miller's trial," Engel answered.

"For what?" Uncle T was blind and often retreated into his
lair at home and shut himself up from the outside world for
weeks at a time. He occupied himself by eating peppermint
candy and making dancing men. "How could Lane Miller be
on trial for Babs Kirk's death?" He mused to himself.

Uncle T walked to the Kirk Store two or three times a week;
crossing the pastures that lie between the Barber farm and
the Kirk store. He sold his crafts at the store and used the
money to buy chewing tobacco and peppermint candy sticks.
He would never travel the main road. "Much too dangerous
for a seeing eye much less for a blind man," he said. "Those
beatnik kids will run you over." Uncle T was picking up his
new language from a TV show that was all the rage, and it was

his favorite besides Bonanza. "Dobie Gillis" and his sidekick, "Maynard" who was a genuine beatnik could keep Uncle T in stitches. There was a well-worn path that Uncle T had made for years as he walked to Babs' store. He knew every bump and every turn the path took beneath his size five-brogue boots.

"They set Mr. Miller free," Mr. Barber said, "the verdict was just rendered."

"How do you know that?" Uncle T said as the little man spat some tobacco juice on the street and being careful not to spit on the dress of the pretty young lady standing in front of him. Engel wondered how Uncle T could possibly know people were around him and what gender they were. He had never spat on anyone in all the years they had been shopping in Crab Orchard and Stanford.

Engel Barber looked at the crowd of people in the streets. He particularly noticed the Campbellites and the Baptists intermingling with casual conversation, mostly talking about the trial and Lane Miller's acquittal. He was not a religious man himself, but he did know the difference between the two groups' doctrines having heard Sally Barber explain it many times. He had never seen such a thing before, and he knew this truce wouldn't last.

"Bro. Lord told me. I went to the creamery to buy some cheese while you were sitting on the bench in front of the variety store," Engel explained. "Bro. Lord works at the creamery."

"I know where Bro. Lord works, but this means the killer is free," Uncle T replied.

"If there was a killer," Engel commented. "Most people think it was an accident and that will be the end of it."

"It was no accident."

"What are you talking about?"

"I know who did it, and if you had told me the cops thought Babs was murdered, I could have saved a lot of trouble."

Engel pulled his blind brother aside to talk to him privately. "What are you saying you foolish little man? How could you not know? You might have let an innocent man go to the electric chair." Engel, who was six feet two inches tall and towering over this little man, was also poking him in the chest of his bibbed overalls.

"It wasn't on Huntley and Brinkley, and stop poking me, dammit, or I'll slap your head with this dancing man paddle and knock it off."

Uncle T was feisty and did have a temper. Most of the time when he threatened people they had a good laugh, but everyone stayed out of his way.

"You didn't bother to ever tell me," Uncle T explained. "You guys do what you always do."

"What's that?" Engel asked.

"Keep information from me. If it ain't on Huntley and Brinkley, I don't know what's going on. You people think the whole world knows what's going on in this dinky little hick county."

Uncle T loved Chet Huntley and David Brinkley. He never missed one of their newscasts since the Barbers bought that old Crosley TV the whole neighborhood watched as they crowded into the Barber's living room on Saturday nights. Many times Uncle T would be lying in the bedroom of Sally and Engel Barber, where he slept, and just before they all fell asleep, he would say, "Good night, David," Engel Barber wishing to humor his funny little brother would say, "Good night, Chet."

"How do you know?" Engel said firmly while releasing his grip on his little sibling, and Uncle T told him.

State Trooper Tip Tuck was about to call Sheriff Crane when the call came from the Courthouse.

"Tip, get over here right away." It was Prosecutor Birdstein on the other end of the phone.

Engel Barber made a beeline for the Courthouse almost carrying Uncle T, who was screaming for him to slow down. They entered the Courthouse and went immediately to the second floor and went in unannounced and without knocking on the door of Judge Wilston's chambers. Doug Morgan was still in the building and was talking with the Judge and Birdstein. The Prosecutor was still rattled that he had missed an opportunity to put an innocent man to death. He would never stop believing that Lane Miller murdered Babs Kirk and felt her killer would never be brought to justice.

"My brother here knows who killed Babs Kirk," Engel said. The lawyers' eyes opened up with amazement at this strange statement coming at the conclusion of a very emotional and stressful trial.

"How could he possibly know?" The Judge asked as Tip Tuck made his way into the room and was surprised to see Engel Barber and Uncle T standing there. Sheriff Crane was almost back to Crab Orchard when he heard his radio call him from the base. Birdstein had called the Sheriff's office up in Chapel Gap, and his wife, Priscilla, called and told him to turn around and make beeline to the Stanford Courthouse. He was curious at this request, and all she could tell him was that the matter was urgent. Deputy Shanks had also heard the transmission and spun his pickup toward Stanford even though he wasn't invited. They all stood and looked at Uncle T as he swung his feet from the odd feeling wooden chair with the smooth arms and fluted back. He couldn't reach the floor, so he crossed his legs and swung them back and forth, pretending he was in a swing.

The Judge held his hand up and silenced the men. He would do the questioning. Something he always wanted to do since he had been elected Judge of Lincoln County was to question a witness.

"How do you know who murdered Babs Kirk?" The Judge asked.

"I saw him do it," Uncle T replied matter of factly.

"But, you're blind!" Doug Morgan interrupted as if he were going to defend whoever the killer was.

"Shut up, Doug," the Judge said which greatly pleased the Prosecutor.

"Sorry, Judge," Morgan said.

"You are blind Mr. Barber, so how could you possibly see the murderer?" The Judge gently raised this question to the nervous old man. The portly and graying Judge was mature, and he was about to show the uncouth Prosecutor some courtroom manners. Engel Barber considered how amazed they were going to be when they found out a blind man can see.

"I'm sorry," Engel said, "but the best way for you to see how Uncle T can see is to show you."

The assembled court of marshals, deputies, and lawyers grew quiet. Engel Barber drew some money from his small pocket on the front of his overalls. "What's this?" He asked as he handed the money to Mr. T.

"One dollar," Uncle T said proudly.

"And this?"

"Ten dollars."

"This?"

"A penny, a dime, and a silver dollar, 1922 minted in Denver."

"This is most impressive, but how could you possibly identify a murderer unless you did it yourself?" Everyone looked at Birdstein as if he were prosecuting Uncle T.

"Shut up, Jack," the Judge said to the Prosecutor.

"How could you know?" The Judge asked Uncle T who was swinging his legs above the carpet.

"Uncle T, does Judge Wilston have long or short hair?" Engel asked hardly being able to contain his excitement.

"Long hair," Uncle T replied without thinking.

"How do you know?"

"I can smell his Brylcream hair oil."

"How do you know it isn't someone else you smell?"

"He's there, and Homer Shanks is over there. There's only two people in this room with Brylcream Hair Oil." He pointed to each of the men. "The Judge and the Deputy. I know Shanks' smell, so that leaves only the Judge sitting in front of me. The rest of you aren't wearing hair oil except Tip, and he has on Butch to make his flat-top stand up."

Everyone sat in amazement. Although both Birdstein and Morgan wanted to question the witness further, they dared not open their mouths again and be berated so harshly.

"Who did it?" The Judge asked directly.

"There's a call for Trooper Tuck," the Judge's Secretary, Nancy Benton, said as she broke into the room. Tip left the chambers and walked into the Secretary's office. Even the Judge would not be allowed to intercept and listen in on this private phone call.

"Tip Tuck," he answered.

"Tip, this is Steve Hickman up in Lexington at the lab. I have the results of the fingerprint tests you wanted on that hundred-dollar bill. Sorry this took so long."

"Tell me," Tip said.

"One set is Blanton's, one Blanchard's, and the other is Evel Martin's."

"Are you sure?"

"Absolutely, no doubt about it. What do you want me to do with the hundred?"

"Keep it," Tip said as he hung up the phone and ran into the meeting where Uncle T demonstrated how he could tell how many feet a coin fell away from him when his brother tossed it and let it rattle around until it lay silent.

"Twenty-two feet," Uncle T described for the tenth time while the Judge hooped and hollered.

"Hot damn!" The Judge screamed as he had never seen anything like this in his life.

Whoever this murderer is, I'm not taking the case, Doug Morgan thought as he watched the demonstration.

Whoever this murderer is, I will fry him like chicken with this witness, Jack Birdstein thought.

"We have a positive ID on the thief who stole Doc Sinclair's money," Tip Tuck said.

"Who?" The Judge asked.

Before Tip answered the mysterious question he asked that Uncle T and Engel Barber to leave the room.

"Evel Martin," Tip replied as Homer Shanks and Houston Crane started for the door.

"Bring the Barbers back in here!" The Judge demanded. He leaned forward on his chair and half his body over the desk and asked quietly, "who did it, Mr. Barber?"

"Evel Martin," Uncle T said without one bit of hesitation, "don't ask me if I'm sure."

"Are you sure?" The Judge asked.

"I said don't ask me if I'm sure," Uncle T answered as if he were ready to take a swat at the Judge.

"Okay, Uncle, tell us how you know this for real." The Judge was careful not to upset Uncle T.

Uncle switched the wad of tobacco to his cheek so that he could be plainly understood. Doug Morgan put a spittoon by Uncle's chair.

"Evel Martin came into the store and bought a couple of things. I believe it was a Clark bar and an RC Cola. He had asked for a Zero candy bar, but Babs was out. I actually had bought the last one and was chewing on it when Martin came in the store. I heard Ms. Kirk walk to the back of the store where she kept money in a little wooden box I made her for one of her birthdays." Uncle T paused and spit in the spittoon hitting it perfectly in the center of the mouth without bending over. "I sat on the porch whittling and chewing my tobacco until Babs closed the store. I could tell by the way Evel walked that he was in a hurry and agitated by something."

"How did you know that?" The Judge questioned making sure that he didn't challenge Uncle T's ability to know anything.

"He walks a certain way when he's up to something. The same way he walked as a kid before he stole candy from her." Uncle T explained although agitated that his credibility may again be questioned.

"Then what?" The Judge asked while leaning further over his desk. Uncle T brushed the air letting the Judge know he could smell his breath.

"I decided to wait by the fence where I cross to go home. I sneaked into the weeds and waited. I was sure that Evel Martin was going to come back and steal something." Uncle T sounded so honest and so adamant that no one would interrupt his explanation.

"Sure nough, I heard Martin's car coming down the road from Broughtontown."

Uncle T had the same ability as Fran had and knew exactly which cars were which by the sound of the motor.

"What kind of car was he driving?"

"Shut up, Doug, or I'll throw you out of this court, eh, chamber," the Judge demanded.

"Go on Mr. T and don't anyone, and I mean anyone interrupt him. We're not interested in what you have to say, only him," the Judge directed.

Uncle T spat again and continued his story. "I heard Martin turn and go past the store. He stopped and backed his car into the drive that goes into Jack Brown's cornfield. He shut the door quietly so he wouldn't announce his presence like he usually does by slamming the door. I listened as he walked up to the store on the gravel. He was being especially quiet, but I could still hear the stones turning slowly under his tennis shoes."

"How do you know he was wearing tennis shoes?" The Judge asked.

Mr. T didn't bother to answer such a stupid question. "He sneaked on the porch and held the bell as he went into the store so that it wouldn't ring, and I heard the door close, so I knew he grabbed it and held it until he slithered sideways through the door undetected. Later, I heard Lane leave. He wanted to kiss Babs, but she wouldn't let him."

"Excuse me Uncle T," the Judge interrupted, "but were they fighting? Is that why she wouldn't let him kiss her?'

Uncle T hissed as if disgusted. Uncle T thought if a person is a judge, he should know everything, "She hasn't kissed him for twenty years. Says she had to be married first. Everybody knows that." The Judge turned a slight color of pink.

"Then what happened?" The Judge asked.

"She went back into the store. I waited but couldn't hear anything coming from inside the store. The next thing I heard was Martin fleeing. He didn't bother to hold the bell, so I knew she had caught him or something. He ran back to his car, backed out slowly, and then sped away."

"So you never heard them tussle or argue?" The Judge asked.

"Then how do you know Martin killed her?" Doug Morgan screamed.

"That's your last warning. Get out of here, now. You too, Jack!"

"What'd I do?" Jack pleaded. He certainly wanted to hear the rest of this.

"Get out!" The Judge demanded.

Uncle T cracked a faint smile at the Judge's order. He felt more important than he ever had in his whole life. This was real Perry Mason stuff, one of his other favorite TV shows. He never missed it.

"What about the fire, Uncle T?" Tip Tuck asked and the Judge said nothing to him for asking a question.

"I didn't know about the fire until the next day. I left. I figured the redheaded rat face had either been caught by Babs, or he maybe had the money. I took off. It was dark, and I didn't want to fall on my way home and hurt myself." Everyone left in the room had a puzzled look on their faces when he said this.

"Why didn't you say something before now?" The Judge asked.

"Am I on trial here, Judge? She died in a fire, and I never heard nothing about murder until this afternoon after the Verdict."

The Judge sat back in his chair and thought about the Bourbon hidden on the library shelf behind some law books. He sure wanted a drink. He ran his fingers through his gray hair and flipped a pen on his desk.

"Are we going to trial, Judge?" Uncle T asked like a little kid. He wanted to sit in front of a whole courtroom of people including the Judge, the clerks, the prosecutor, the defense attorney, and the jury. He would revel as he demonstrated how he could see, and the detail he could so explicitly explain. He would be on Huntley and Brinkley and would become famous.

"If we can catch the S.O.B," the Judge remarked. "Thank you Mr. Barber and Uncle T. You may have saved a man's life."

"Whose?" Uncle said while looking around as if the man he was going to save was standing in the room.

"Lane Miller's," the Judge replied, "he would go through his entire life time carrying the burden of whether he was guilty or innocent. He would be forever trying to prove his innocence, but perhaps he never would."

Uncle T and Engel Barber nodded as if they understood the Judge's explanation that one doesn't have to die or go to jail in order to have guilt placed on him. The tall handsome man and the short blind man left the Judge's chambers, walked down the steps of the Courthouse, and onto the street.

"You did well, T," Engel said as he patted his little brother on the back.

"I did, didn't I?" Uncle T spat out his wad of Day's Work and immediately drew his Case knife and cut another chew and placed it in his cheek.

"Do we have enough to charge him on the testimony of a blind witness?" The Judge asked the Sheriff and Trooper Tuck.

"We've got enough to charge him for the robbery of Doctor Sinclair, and the church's money," Tip said boldly. The Judge had forgotten about that.

"Here's a warrant for Martin's arrest," the Judge said, "pick him up!"

CHAPTER THIRTY-EIGHT

M en were gathered at the Evergreen Baptist Church on Saturday to dig the foundation for the new building. The Crab Orchard Bank decided not to loan any money to the church after my dad's confrontation with the Vice President. The issue of borrowing money was still a matter of contention within the church. Junior Cullen had argued that the Lord didn't want anyone in debt although he was paying for a new car. He and others said that paying interest was wrong, and the Bible taught against it. My dad had reasoned that interest payments were just part of the cost of doing business, and that the Bible said nothing about paying interest being wrong. He cited his argument that, "If the Bible says so much about lending, and the laws concerning lending were clearly stated in the Scripture, then why was it wrong to borrow?" He told them that Nehemiah made the evil men, who had charged interest to the people when they took their farms as collateral, was not interest, and he made them pay back the portion that was unfairly extracted. "Usury, usurious interest is what is wrong," he said, "the unfair extracting of interest. That's what's wrong. Even the state law allows a certain amount of interest on judgments and so forth, but the laws on Usury are very exact and stringent."

"The Bible says that it is wrong to borrow, and it is wicked," Junior Cullen proclaimed during the last business meeting.

"It doesn't say that," my dad explained, "it says, 'The wicked borrow and pay not again.' It means that it is wrong to not pay your debts, not that it is evil to borrow." When he said this, some of the people who had not or were not paying their debts lowered their heads. "Besides, Elijah told the Widow to BORROW pots from her neighbors so that she could make oil and pay the debts of her husband."

"The Bible says to 'Owe no man anything,' Cullen contested.

"It doesn't say that, either. Paul is not talking about money in the Book of Romans to the Roman Baptist Church. He's talking about the fruits of the Spirit. We're not to owe men those things. How many of you people pay your electric CO-OP bills in advance, or the phone company bills?" No one raised his or her hands. Then the whole church is sinning in this matter, Bro. Cullen, even you. You're borrowing from the utility companies and then paying them back after you have used their resources for three months."

My dad won this battle and sent the trouble making Junior Cullen packing once again with his tail between his legs. Even though he had won the battle, he did not go to another bank and borrow the money. He felt that sooner or later the money stolen from Doc Sinclair would be found, and he needed time for that to happen, or not happen, and let things settle down a bit. The church did have the money to buy some concrete for the footings, so they would get a head start.

Preacher Roberts and Henry May had brought their mules

to the church. The Preacher had an old scraper that had been used for years to dig out basements and crawl spaces. It was an odd contraption; a bucket that was shallow, approximately four feet in diameter by three feet, had wooden hickory handles, and a very sharp edge on the blade that would dig into the dirt and fill the bucket. The man behind the shovel guided the depth as the mules struggled to pull the sharp blade through the dirt. The contraption worked remarkably well. The dirt was then dumped into a wagon and hauled off to be dumped somewhere. Several of us boys were working on this project with the older men of the church.

Sheriff Crane and Deputy Shanks drove up to the church during this labor day of scraping the ground deep enough to get below the sixteen inch frost line in that part of Kentucky so that the footings could be dug. The cops were very official as they exited Sheriff Crane's pickup.

"Preacher, we have a warrant for Evel Martin's arrest." All the boys quieted down and Preacher Roberts brought the mules to a halt. Even though we were officially not supposed to hear this news, the Sheriff could not keep us from inching closer to the conversation so that we could hear what was being said.

"Why?" Was all my dad could think of saying. He didn't know what took place in the Courthouse the day before with Uncle T. He had no idea all that happened, and he wasn't privy to the conversation because the Judge had ordered all concerned to keep their mouths shut.

"He stole Doc Sinclair's money," Mr. Crane replied.

Praise the Lord my dad was thinking but never said aloud. "I knew that God told me to dig this foundation for some reason, and now I know why," my dad praised.

"I thought it would be good if you come along with us. Ethel Martin is real emotional, and we want someone to keep her calm while we pick him up."

My dad called a halt to the digging and told the men to go home. "We'll meet here again next week," he said. The men started loading up their tools in the pickups, and I thought about how much power my dad had. I had read about the priories in Old England run by the priests in the Middle Ages, and this was kind of like that. Chapel Gap was the Priory, and my dad was the Prior. He ran everything on top of that hill.

Deputy Shanks crawled in the back of Sheriff Crane's truck although my dad offered to sit back there. "I don't know what we'll find when we get to Martin's farm," the Sheriff said, "but I want you completely out of harm's way. You talk to Ethel and keep her calm while Homer and I take care of Martin."

"Did you call the State Police?" My dad asked.

"We're not going to involve them with this one, Preacher, we'll handle it ourselves."

My dad was uneasy about his instructions, and the fact that Tip Tuck, who was much more skilled in the use of firearms and other weaponry, wasn't involved. This was a county issue, but the Sheriff had always involved the Trooper in important matters such as this. Their kinship allowed them to bleed into each other's territory all the time. This time was different for the Sheriff for some reason; he decided to take care of the business of Martin himself, and this was frightening.

"I'm sure the money is in the barn," my dad commented, "I'm positive."

"So am I," the Sheriff said as Deputy Shanks put a gunnysack over his face to keep from breathing the dust as the Sheriff sped down the road.

The Sheriff kept the Judge's orders even though he knew if he did tell my dad about the murder of Babs Kirk, and the thought that Evel Martin may have done it, the Preacher would never tell a soul. He kept quiet. The Preacher had enough on his mind at this moment. The plan was to arrest Martin and find the money; the only crime by which he could be convicted at this juncture. They would then force a confession of murder out of him and try Martin in court for both crimes, using the Jury to hear the arguments and render a conviction.

Ethel Martin looked out the door of her house, peering behind her familiar spying place as she watched the pickup drive into the yard. She had a premonition the night before that Evel was in trouble. She knew about Doc Sinclair's robbery, and the fact that the money belonged to the church. She sat through the arguments about credit and actually voted for the building program by borrowing money from a bank. Her trepidations had started a long time ago because Evel was spending so much time in the barn. He had told her that if she so much as set a foot in the barn loft, he would beat her to death. She loved him, but she was deathly afraid of him. He used to be harmless and all mouth, but as of late, he had turned violent. He drank more than usual, cussed more, and he had completely thrown all his friends out of his life. She feared that he might be involved with the Doc Sinclair money. Her fears were about to be confirmed.

"Preacher, you go in and talk to Ethel, and Shanks and I will wait until you give us the okay sign that she is all right, and then we will go in." These were gentle instructions of a good man, the Sheriff. He was sensitive about the feelings of this criminal's mother and respected her as much for her concerns.

"The Sheriff has a warrant for Evel's arrest, Ethel," my dad broke the news as gently as he could.

"He stole that money, didn't he, Pastor?" She said sorrowfully.

"I believe he did. Tip Tuck has fingerprints on some of the money that Evel passed at various places with old Doc's mark on them."

"But that doesn't prove he did it?" She said quietly.

"He'll get a fair trial, Ethel."

Evel Martin was hiding in the barn looking from his vantage point as the two Sheriffs were waiting in the truck. He had seen the Preacher he hated more than life itself, and had vowed to settle up with some day, go into the house. He saw the Preacher come on the porch and give the sign to the cops that everything was all right in there. He wondered what his mother had told the Preacher, or if she was the one who called the law out there. Could they be out there because she had found the money and told on him? He wanted to kill her, too.

"Evel! We know you're up there. Now, you can come out peacefully, real quiet now, or we're going to come up there and bring you out. What will it be?" The Sheriff shouted.

For a moment there was no answer and then Evel screamed, "GO TO HELL, SHERIFF! What do you want anyway?"

"We've got a warrant for your arrest. You know what we want so come on down here!"

"Go to hell you pig screwing old farmer pretending to be a cop. Come and get me!"

Sheriff Crane grabbed Homer Shank's arm and tried to hold him from climbing the ladder to the loft. This was a situation that he now wished he had called Tip Tuck to help him with, but he didn't anticipate Martin resisting arrest. He thought Martin was a coward and would never face down a gun or the authority of the law. He also knew that he and Homer Shanks had never faced down a gun either except their fighting in the Korean War, but this was not the same situation. He had plenty of firepower to back him up over in Korea, but now there was only himself and this strong, tall Deputy who wasn't afraid enough.

"Evel, give yourself up," Shanks said as he slowly rose up the rungs of the ladder. "You better not have a gun." He wasn't worried about a gun; he was more worried that Martin would hit him with a pitchfork. That was more Martin's style. He drew his 38 Ruger and held it in front of him ready to shoot if Martin charged him.

Sheriff Crane did not have his gun in his hand. He had holstered it so that he could hold the ladder secure as Deputy Shanks made the climb to the loft some thirty feet above his head. He looked around and everything was familiar to him. Cow stalls, milking stools, hay hooks, an old bridle, straw strewn on the floor that had dropped from the loft on the dusty barn floor, and a couple of wagons, one of which was hitched up to an old Farmall tractor. Another thing that the Sheriff Crane noticed was the eerie silence that was almost uncanny; he feared for the Deputy's life.

Deputy Shanks slowly stuck his head into the opening of the trap door and looked below as Sheriff Crane stood retching his neck, looking straight up at him. He looked around but did not see Martin, and then he did. Standing in front of him as he laid his hand and his gun on the floor to get his balance; his face white with horror as he saw the twelve gauge shotgun in Martin's hands raised to his shoulder and taking dead aim. He flinched and tried to scream, but the sound wouldn't come and Martin squeezed the trigger. The buckshot tore through Shanks' face obliterating his eyes, nose, and mouth. Teeth shattered and nearly half of the Deputy's head lay on the other side of the loft. He fell straight down, releasing his strong grip on the ladder and fell on the Sheriff, who couldn't move being paralyzed with fear.

At first, the Sheriff thought that his Deputy fired the first shot, but the unmistakable boom of the shotgun made him realize his Deputy had been hit. He held the ladder as the Deputy fell thirty feet or so on top of him. The impact was like five hundred pounds had hit him, and his knees buckled under the load. He could feel the gory ooze from the brains and flesh mingled with blood exploding all over him. He lay under the massive pile of man and knew the Deputy was dead.

Martin dropped his shotgun as soon as he pulled the trigger. He had already stuffed as much money in his pockets, inside his shirt, and his underwear that he could carry when he saw the trio drive into his barnyard. His old .38 caliber Smith & Wesson pistol was stuck under his belt around his waist. He did not see the Deputy fall but instead leaped through the barn loft doors and grabbed the rope hanging from the tackle used to hoist hay bales into the loft from the wagons waiting below to be unloaded. As quick as a cat, he slid to the ground.

Sheriff Crane wiggled out from under the Deputy. There was no time, but he did know that Martin had escaped the barn loft when he heard a shot outside the barn. He took one look at the mutilated corpse and ran to the door and ducked behind the thick wooden planks of the front barn wall.

My dad was explaining to Ethel why the Sheriff was there and tried to keep her calm when they heard the explosion of the shotgun fired in the barn. My dad shuttered. Since World War Two, flying that dive-bomber, had nothing sent chills so vividly up and down his spine. He ran quickly to the door and saw Martin hanging outside the barn on the tackle and sliding to the ground. He instinctively yelled at Martin to stop, but Evel turned and pulled his gun and then fired it at my dad. Martin was not known for fine shooting with any gun. Many times farmers, who hunted squirrels and coons with him said, "Martin can't hit the side of a barn standing right next to it." The shot missed as it sped through the glass on the door and lodged in a picture hanging over Ethel's sofa. My dad fell to the floor of the porch as Evel fired another round, which went through the open door and hit his mother in the shoulder.

She went down clutching herself as the red liquid covered her fingers and then she fainted.

Sheriff Crane fired three shots at Martin as he was fleeing into the woods, but Evel was out of pistol range, and the aim was poor. The Sheriff's instinct was to run after Martin, but he thought better of it. *He'll hide behind a tree and ambush me like he did Homer,* he thought. That was a good choice because Martin was hiding behind a huge beech tree waiting to kill anyone who tried to follow him.

The Sheriff bent over the lifeless body of Deputy Shanks as my dad ran into the barn. "What in the world happened?" The Preacher screamed as he gasped in horror at the ghastly sight in front of him.

"Evel shot him in the face," the Sheriff sobbed, "he killed him in cold blood."

"Ethel's down," dad said, "she's bleeding pretty badly. Martin shot her while trying to kill me, and I don't know how badly she's hurt." The Sheriff called his wife and told her to get Floyd out there with an ambulance, but he was going to rush Ethel to the hospital down in Stanford. He explained to Priscilla that Ethel was hurt, but the wound was not fatal, and that they had stopped the bleeding.

"If she's not that bad, then why do you have to take her to the hospital?" Priscilla asked remembering the time Ethel tried to seduce her husband. The Sheriff clicked off the mike.

Within a half hour, there were a dozen State Police cruisers sitting in the Martin's barnyard. "Where's the Sheriff?" Tip Tuck asked as he looked at Homer Shanks' body.

"He took Ethel to the hospital. She got shot," my dad answered.

"Why didn't you take her, Preacher, what is he thinking? He needs to be here on the scene not running an ambulance service!"

"I don't know," my dad said, "he seems panicked. The Deputy fell on top of him, and he is covered with blood. Aren't we going after Martin? He's in the woods."

"Those woods go for miles, Preacher, and he knows them like the back of his hand. We'll catch him, though."

Floyd covered Deputy Shanks' body with a tarp he found in the barn and scratched his head as he watched two of the Kentucky State Police Troopers load the Deputy in the back of the hearse. "That Martin kid is a dangerous fellow," he mused, "I've always known it was just a matter of time before he killed somebody. I just don't know what Willow and all those kids will do without their daddy."

Floyd hardly ever shed a tear, at least not as any one had ever seen, but there was a trickle coming down his cheek. He was fond of the Deputy even though he couldn't read or write; he was a good Christian man, husband, and father. He was also considerably brave and loyal. This wasn't the first time Homer Shanks had faced down a criminal. He put himself in danger all the time chasing bootleggers and moonshiners back in the hills. He was a good tracker, but no more. He is dead. Floyd thought these things and pondered them grievously. He was calloused to death, and when bodies were brought to him from being mutilated in automobile accidents and such, he would not allow himself to get emotionally involved. He saw that as a professional weakness but not this death; this one really bothered him.

Tip Tuck kicked back some hay as he and my dad walked in the barn loft. "There's the money," Tip said as hundred dollar bills littered the loft's floor.

CHAPTER THIRTY-NINE

The preacher rang the church bell at the Evergreen Baptist Church forty one times; one for each year of Homer Shanks' life. By 9:00 AM on Saturday morning, the churchyard was already filling with trucks and tractors pulling wagons for the food that would take up every square inch of the flat beds. Floyd had already parked outside the church front entrance after being escorted to the church by a half dozen pickups with their red lights plugged into their cigarette lighters and flashing in unison as they brought Deputy Homer Shanks to the church. This would be his final resting place in the Evergreen Baptist Church Cemetery. By funeral time, the place was crawling with people; you could hardly stick a pin between them. The killing of Homer Shanks was noted as the worse crime in Lincoln County History. Evel Martin had killed two of Evergreen Baptist Church's members although it still needed to be proven that Martin had murdered Babs Kirk.

Willow Shanks and her thirteen children stood by the coffin. The sadness in the eyes of the children, who idolized their dad, showed the shock and grief at the loss of their beloved father. An American flag draped the casket and soldiers, some of who served with Homer Shanks in the Korean War, stood around the walls mingled with Houston Crane's deputies and Kentucky State Police.

"This killer is still at large," my dad preached, "but we will find him and bring him to justice. He'll get everything he deserves." The crowd stirred at this statement and wiped their eyes. Willow Shanks sobbed loudly and cried, "Oh, God, why did you take my husband!" Little Homer Shanks yelled, "I hate Evel Martin!" My dad reached over and hugged him in his arms trying to comfort the little redheaded kid.

The armed gunmen fired a twenty one-gun salute from over the hill by the cemetery having stationed themselves out of sight in the pasture of Sterling Deaton's farm. Garrard Anderson blew the bugle. No one had ever heard him play the bugle, and it was so beautiful that each mourner knew that Garrard was telling the truth for once in his life when he said, "I played the bugle for the Army in World War 2."

There were dozens of tributes spoken about Deputy Shanks, so the service was lasting for hours, but this was not uncommon in the Chapel Gap Area when one of their favorite sons or daughters died. One by one, the Deputy's children held their little hands above the grave and sprinkled dirt on their daddy's casket. Willow Shanks fell faint and had to be held up by a couple of the pallbearers.

"His soul is in Jesus' Hands," the Preacher said as he closed the meeting and prayed.

By mid-afternoon, there seemed to be no more grieving. The custom at Evergreen Baptist Church was to bury the dead and let them be buried. Children ran and played games of tag, running in and out of the ornate tombstones, while the men smoked and watched the women lay out enormous amounts of food prepared by each family and brought to the church to feed the multitude. Soon, the wagons swelled with victuals of every kind and imagination. The women always tried to outdo each other in order to gloat in the comments of how delicious their recipes were. The Shanks' kids ate like pigs, but it was enjoyable to watch. Tommy Shanks ate several pieces of blueberry pie and fell sick.

I looked at all the kids playing in the church yard and cemetery and thought, *It seems like yesterday that Fran and I were doing the same things these kids are having fun doing.* My little brother, Val Mark, and my little sister, Nila, were playing with the other kids running around and having a ball.

Fran and I were sitting under the "helicopter tree." We called it "the helicopter tree" because it was the largest tree on the Evergreen Baptist Church property. The tree bare large seeds which had a flange growing from one side of the seed, and when it was time to shed the seeds, the wind would whirl the seeds that looked like a helicopter coming in for a soft landing. Fran swatted one of the propellers falling beside him.

"Bud, we've got to find Martin," he said. "He's back in the woods at one of his stills. I found an old one a couple of days ago when I went looking for him."

"You went looking for Evel Martin?" I asked incredulously. "Are you crazy or something?"

"I'm not afraid of that hillbilly freak," Fran said as he swatted another helicopter.

"Okay, so you're not afraid. So what are you going to do if you do find him?"

"Kill em," Fran said matter of fact.

Sheriff Crane and Tip Tuck had led teams of men searching for Evel Martin, but he seemed to have disappeared in thin air. They kept a constant alert at every farm questioning people as to whether they had seen any signs of him. People locked their doors at night and stayed up late protecting their children. Kerosene lamps and electric lights, if you had them, burned late into the wee hours of the morning. Farmers carried their shotguns and rifles and searched their own woods several times a week looking for any sign of the murderer.

My dad loved to grill hamburgers, and we were enjoying his burgers while sitting under an elm tree. My whole family was enjoying the nice afternoon. Val Mark was pretending that he was shooting Evel Martin. "Stand still and don't move!" He yelled at the imaginary figure standing in front of him. "I'll have to kill you!" He then fired his tobacco stick and Martin fell to the ground.

Fran was deep in thought and we all noticed this. "What you thinking about, Fran?" my dad asked.

"Nothin'," he mumbled, but he was thinking something; I knew that for sure. My sister was sitting beside Fran eating a piece of watermelon, and Fran hardly paid any attention to her that was unusual for him. He was normally in third heaven when she was anywhere near him.

"You're staring in space," my sister commented, "I'm going to the outhouse."

Fran wasn't allowed to smoke around the family or church, so he and I headed back to the men's toilet and lit up. "What's bothering you, Fran?"

"I need to go home," he said as he threw half of his cigarette in the hole of the privy.

"For what?" I asked curiously, but he was already headed for the fence on the Hanover's farm and crossed it ignoring me as I called out to him. I thought once about following him home, but I knew he wouldn't like that because whatever he had on his mind, he had to take care of himself. We were almost sixteen now and things were changing between us. I blamed my sister for that. She was too young to make him wait forever, and I thought he was way too occupied with love to be wasting his life like this. It would never turn out anyway. She was using him, I thought, and as soon as she gets car dating age, she'll leave him like a hot potato.

Fran would go on "visitation" with my dad; something I hated to do. They would walk for miles sometimes, cutting through fields and entering milk barns and farmhouses, inviting people to come to church on Sunday. The Evergreen Baptist Church was the fastest growing church in Lincoln County, and my dad's reputation knew no bounds. The people loved him, dearly. The church was filling up with new people primarily because my dad and Fran spent every Saturday visiting. We would still go skating though we hardly ever saw Ming Morgan and her friend, Judy. I stayed out of their way whenever they came to Hall's Gap. Once in a while, Fran and I would go hunting, but those days were rare as we took up new interests, mainly, girls.

"I think you're too hard on Bud," Fran said one day as he and the Preacher were visiting.

"How's that?" My dad asked.

"You told him he couldn't get his driver's license, and you weren't going to let him have a car."

"Sonny needs to learn that he can't just go off doing whatever he wants and lie about it. The Kirk family was really hurt by what he did." My dad explained.

"Baloney," Fran challenged my dad which jolted him. Fran never questioned anything he ever said. "That whole Kirk family is squirrelly except for Gib and Stan. They deserved what they got. Ease up on Bud. If I were in trouble, he is one guy I'd want in my corner."

This seemed to trouble my dad, but he didn't comment. He steered the car into Nathan Smith's farm. This time he was seeking information about a rumor that some families were leaving the Evergreen Baptist Church, and the issue creating these problems was the money for the building campaign.

CHAPTER FORTY

Fran ran most of the way home after leaving me standing at the outhouse behind the church. He was clearly on a mission of some sort. Mandy stood by the old icebox in the kitchen. "Fran, what are you doing home?" She asked. "Yeah, what are you doing here?" June chided.

Fran didn't say a word, so everyone didn't push him. They had prior experience of how Fran didn't want to be bothered when he was "thinking."

"He's going hunting," Mandy exclaimed to June as Fran left the kitchen with his shotgun and rifle.

"He better not get caught," June commented, "this ain't hunting season."

Fran didn't take his well-worn path to the woods behind his house. Instead, he crossed the road at People's Corner, and Mandy watched him as he started crossing the wide-open fields that led to the Knob toward Pine Hall. He would eventually come to some cliffs that dropped sharply to the valley below. It was miles over there and impossible to see beyond the tall stands of Maple, Birch, and Hickory trees that guarded the way to no man's land.

Fran disappeared into the deep forest. He didn't know these woods, and he and I had never hunted there. Fran said long ago that a man could get lost in those woods and never be found. Jake Rickles' son got lost in there years ago, and they never found his body. Moonshiners were known to inhabit the abyss, and the only hope of catching them was to be stationed near a road or path where the cops and revenuers thought someone may exit.

Kentucky is cave country. There are more caves in the state than anywhere in the United States and maybe the world. The longest and largest cave on the planet is Mammoth Cave, and it is thought that perhaps its passageways reached for a thousand miles although one hundred fifty miles of it was all that had been explored. Fran felt the cool air coming from under one of the slate cliffs. He curiously explored where the mist of cool air was coming. He immediately noticed acorn hulls and walnuts where squirrels had cut them open with their sharp teeth. Deep green moss covered the face of the rock, and he felt the cool temperature drop drastically. He had lived there all his life, but no one had ever mentioned that there was a cave in the area of Chapel Gap. He knew of sinkholes. There were plenty of them and surely, he had thought many times, those holes led to caverns deep in the earth. He had even fanaticized about becoming a cave explorer or "spelunker" as they called it in Chapel Gap. He noticed paw prints of a larger animal and instinctively knew that bobcats or wildcats inhabited the space. *So that's where the little buggers hide out,* he thought.

The edge of the cliff hung precariously over the tiny pathway of slippery rock making it almost impossible for a person to climb over the mouth of the cave. He thought about the cave for hiding place but decided the way over was too treacherous. The rocks were wet and slippery; there were no handholds or ways to secure yourself while climbing over. One slip and a person would fall hundreds of feet to a certain death. There was a creek that poured its water out of the side of the mountain. "It must be Cedar Creek's origin," he reasoned to himself although talking out loud. It was a mystery where Cedar Creek began, but he doubted anyone in Chapel Gap or Pine Hall cared about it.

I'll come back with Bud and check this out, he thought. *We could bring ropes and let ourselves down over the edge. We could tie the ropes at the top of the hill.* The thought of doing these things excited him. The Knob dropped off sharply, and Fran had to be very cautious as he was carrying two guns. He knew if he slipped, there would be no way to find him as he would lay badly hurt or dead at the bottom of the cliffs, ever so carefully, he slowly made his way down the knob, kicking up rocks and watching them speed ahead of him until they echoed through the hollow as they landed far below.

I waited for Fran to show up at the church, so we could go over to Junebug's house and watch Bonanza. When he didn't show, I decided to go to his house and find out what the heck he was doing. Leah was frantic as well because she wanted to walk with Fran over to the Barbers through the field. When she would be safely out of sight of the church and my dad's spying eye, she could hold Fran's hand.

When I arrived at Fran's and found him gone, I asked where he went? "He took off with his guns," Mandy said.

"Both of them?" I asked.

"The fool headed for the Knob at Pine Hall," June chimed in. She was doing her hair. She had those big ugly curlers that made her look like some creature from Mars with the plastic pins sticking out of them.

"He went where?" I asked frantically.

"To the Knob over by Pine Hall," Mandy answered.

I wasted no time. I ran past Abe, who was now pretty much drunk and staggering toward his old car where he slept off his stupor.

"Slooow downnn," he mumbled.

I ran all the way to the church taking Fran's shortcut across the Hanover's pasture. I was out of breath when I screamed at my dad, "Fran's gone after Evel Martin!"

The Preacher was in his study at the back of the church, and I was standing in the room yelling at him. "How do you know that?" He asked, barely looking up from his Bible.

"He took both his guns and headed for the Pine Hall Knob!" I cried. "He'll get lost in there, and we'll never see him again! If Evel Martin sees him, he'll kill him!"

"Calm down, boy," he said grabbing my arm, "let's go find him."

We were closer to the Knob from the church than Fran was when he left his house. We ran to the back of the church property and swung ourselves over the fence by using a low hanging limb of the Sycamore tree standing by the outhouse. We waded across Hanover's strawberry patch carefully so as not to bruise the nearly ripe berries. At the far end of the patch, was where no man's land started, and the cliffs there were too steep to negotiate, so we walked along the edge of the woods until we found the place where Fran must have crossed into the dark forest.

"What if it gets dark, Preacher?" I amazed myself and my dad at this first reference to him as "Preacher."

"That's a good question. If we can't find him before then, we'll have to come back in the morning."

"But he'll be lost and besides tomorrow morning is church," I exclaimed stressfully.

"I forgot about that," the Preacher mused, "we'll come back after church and bring the Sheriff with us.

"That's not good enough for me, dad. I ain't going back until I find him."

"Don't say ain't," he commented.

We, too, felt the cool air from the cave. My dad stood and stared at it for a while. "I'll be darned," was all he said as we started down the steep Knob. Fran had been there because we could see easily all the disturbance where his feet had slid on the slick rocks.

Evel Martin was hold up in a small canyon by an old still where he and Curt Kirk used to make moonshine before Curt went to jail. The indentation in the forest was over grown with brush and almost impossible to get into, but once you were there; it was clearly one of the most secluded and secure still spots in the county. A creek flowed down through the vale, and the clear, clean water was good for making moonshine. Weeks ago, Evel had carried provisions to the hiding place in case he ever needed to escape and hide from the law. He never planned on killing anyone, but he was never going to get caught with the money and join his one or two friends in the Eddyville Prison. The wind was perfect in the canyon, drawing smoke from the small cooking fire he built and drafting it up the ridge like a well-placed flue.

Darkness came quickly in the valley as Fran began stumbling along. He could see the light of day through the tops of the trees, but daylight disappeared in the valley a couple of hours before the rest of the world turned dark. He was in limbo now; afraid to go forward, and scared to go backward, so he sat down beneath a large Oak tree and set his mind to pass the night away in the woods. *Why didn't I think?* He asked himself. *I started too late.* He knew what he was thinking. He could find Evel Martin long before nightfall, but he was wrong.

452 · SHERMAN SMITH

My dad pulled me along up the steep hill. It had taken us longer than we expected to get to the bottom of the Knob, and he determined that we better climb back up before we got stuck down there. I didn't want to go and resisted with all my strength. He was stronger than I thought as he took my arm and dragged me toward the base of the hill.

We were slipping and sliding while moving as fast as we could. We knew we could never make it after dark, but as we climbed higher, it got lighter making me wish all the more that I had run from my dad.

My sister was crying when we came back and dad told her we didn't find Fran, and where he was. "I'll never see him again," she sobbed, "he's gone forever!" My little sister, Nila, was crying with her although she was too little to understand what was happening.

My dad rang the bell on Sunday morning as usual, but he did something that had never happened before and has never happened since. Preacher Roberts took the pulpit that Sunday morning, and the congregation was shocked until Preacher Roberts told the half angry mob sitting in front of him that my dad had gone to find Fran Job, who was feared lost in the Pine Hall Knobs.

Sheriff Crane begged my dad, and so did Bro. Lord, not to go back down there without some help. The Sheriff tried to convince my father to wait until he could go down there with him. He said he would ask Tip Tuck to come also, but Tip was up in Lake Cumberland area looking for the murderer of the Sheriff of Pulaski County. Bro. Lord couldn't crawl over those cliffs with his bad legs, but he would try if necessary. The Preacher told the good brother that he needed to move fast so please take his family home after church and pray. "The church needs your presence and stability," he explained to Bro. Lord. Bro. Lord nodded in agreement, finally.

The whole church was unhappy about this preaching arrangement because they knew that Preacher Roberts might go on for hours preaching if someone didn't stop him. He was long winded although no one could remember a time when he didn't sleep during my dad's sermons. He led the singing at Evergreen Baptist Church after retiring from the ministry over in Copper Creek. One time my dad called out a chapter in the Bible he wanted everyone to turn to and read with him. Preacher Roberts stirred from his nap, and he thought my dad asked for the invitation song, so he jumped up in the middle of the service and yelled, PAGE NUMBER 11!" That was one time my dad had a hard time getting back to his serious sermon entitled, "The Ways of Evil Men." The congregation was still laughing as they filed out the door after the invitation.

Fran slept all night leaning against the Oak tree; his shotgun cradled in one arm, and his rifle in the other. He woke when a thin shimmer of light shone through the branches and leaves of the trees and cast a warm reflection on his face. The night was cool being mid-autumn, but the frost the farmers would wake to on the plateau didn't reach to the valley floor. He stretched and looked around trying to get his bearings of where he was. He had brought no food or other provisions, and he was hungry and thirsty. Fran could hear water flowing down the hillside, so he hiked up a ways and bent over the cool stream. *I better not lap the water like a dog,* he thought, *Gideon's men did that and out of thousands of men, he chose only three hundred who knelt and brought the water to their mouths with their hands. They were the only ones who would rout out the Midianites,* Fran thought, wanting God's protection. He knelt by the stream, cupped his hands, and brought the water to his lips and drank, all the while keeping one eye out for the enemy, Evel Martin.

My dad and I were standing at the foot of the Knob after

skipping the morning service. We could hear the groans of some of the people coming from the church as Preacher Roberts stepped into the pulpit. We made our way through the strawberry patch once again and found the route we had taken the afternoon before. As we made our way down the steep slopes, my dad told me to keep quiet and not to talk except in a whisper because the sound would carry through the hollow, and if Martin was in there, it would spook him. I knew for sure Fran wouldn't be heard, if he was still alive, because he was as quiet as an Indian creeping through the forest. Martin wouldn't make any noises because one of his defenses would be to listen for the rustling of dried leaves when someone would step on them. He would listen for casual conversation or the hidden flight of birds. In those hollows, you could hear the noises as if you were in a huge barrel.

Evel Martin made some coffee and pondered how long he could survive in the forest. He dare not go back home for fear that Sheriff Crane would have his deputies watching the place twenty four hours a day, which was the case. He had enough food for a couple of weeks and then as things died down, he would head for Tennessee and freedom. He wasn't sure how far Tennessee was because he had never been there. He did remember that Lester Bishop and Curt Kirk traveled there to buy fireworks and whiskey, and they were always back in a couple of days, so it couldn't be far.

Fran had walked for several miles and found no trace of Martin or any old moonshine still. He trekked along the ridges peering into the dark sinkholes and small canyons trying to spot any trace of the demon hiding out. Fran was lost, and he knew it. A bit of panic started entering his mind. *I'll never get out of here,* he thought. He came upon a patch of mountain tea growing in a shaded flat area. He took his pocketknife and cut through the stems of the plant and started stuffing leaves in his mouth. This would nourish him for a while, but if he was going to survive, he needed to find his way out of the forest. He didn't dare shoot a squirrel, quail, or dove for fear of tipping off Martin that somebody was in the woods. He tried to judge the time by the sun, but he wasn't very good at that. He carried his old railroad pocket watch given to him by his grandfather since he was a little boy, but it had run down over night and was useless. He judged it was now mid afternoon or later, and he dreaded the thought of spending another night in the woods. *Someone is probably looking for me,* he thought, *but they'll never find me.*

"We're way behind Fran," my dad whispered, "he probably got up early and started out. If he keeps moving, we won't catch him."

We had walked for miles and later in the day, we came to a narrow path deep in some brush at the base of another Knob. "Why would there be a path in this brush?" I whispered as quietly as I could.

"I don't know," my dad said, "but lets find out. Don't go fast," he cautioned, "keep from moving the brush and making noise."

We crept very slowly trying our best not to knock aside branches of thick weeds taller than our heads that would snap back and crack like a whip as it hit your legs or arms. The path was worn, and I figured that foxes used it to get back in the brush to their dens where they raised their babies. We almost crawled in some of the places so as not to make noise, and my knees were aching from crouching and moving along in that position.

Suddenly, we came to the end of the brush and stared into an open space that was about a quarter of an acre in size. The ground was lush with moss and heavy sweet grass. A creek was flowing through the middle of it, and we saw the remains of an old still rusting in the elements. Glass bottles were strewn around and then we noticed a lean-to resting against a tree. I had seen one of these before. It was exactly like the lean-tos that Martin and Curt Kirk slept in when they kidnapped Fran and me when we stumbled into his and Curt Kirk's still a few years back. We almost lost our lives that day, and the remembrance of Evel Martin's pleading for us to be killed sent cold chills up and down my spine. If it weren't for Curt Kirk, Fran and I would be dead. Curt Kirk wasn't here to save my life this time; he was in prison.

"He's here," I whispered to my dad who looked over the campsite from his crouched position.

"How do you know?" He asked with his index finger over his lips cautioning me not to whisper too loudly.

"That's the way he builds his camp," I said, "there's his blanket inside."

"Somebody's here," my dad said.

"Damn right, somebody's here," the voice coming from behind us said.

Evel Martin had heard us coming or saw us; I don't know which, but he had his pistol poked at the back of my dad's head. I shrieked. I couldn't help it.

"You can't take two of us," my dad demanded, "one of us will get you."

"That's the funniest thing I ever heard," Martin roared, "I'll kill you first and then beat the crap out of your little son, here."

What in the world is my dad thinking? I thought with horror, *I can't take Evel Martin!*

"You fellas move right over there," he pointed with his pistol and directed us against a rock face that rose at least two hundred feet straight up. We sat down as he stood over us.

"Lets see," he mused, "shall I kill you, Preacher, execution style or make you suffer?" His green teeth shown beneath his grisly moustache that covered his whole mouth and looked like he hadn't washed the food off his face for a year.

I was terrified beyond belief, but in that instant, I found out something about myself that I had never known before. I would die for someone I love, gladly.

"Kill me, Evel, and let my dad live." These words flew out of my mouth, and even though they didn't make any sense, my dad had the look of pride in his expression like I have never seen him look at me.

"Stupid idiot kid," Martin said, "I'm gonna kill you both. You first and then the Preacher so that he can watch his son die."

The hatred in Martin's eyes was Satanic, and he indeed looked like the demon he was. He despised the Preacher ever since he got whipped in front of his buddies and the whole church.

"You afraid of me?" My dad asked.

"Hell no!" Martin screamed.

"Then why don't you and I settle this little thing between us right here and now? I don't think you can take me. I whipped the crap out of you in the church parking lot, and I can do it again."

Martin was shaken, and you could see the temptation in his eyes. He paced back and forth like a wild man, hatred in his eyes. He stopped his pacing abruptly and stared at my dad.

"I can take you with no problem," he said quivering as he spoke. "The last time you had me at a disadvantage. I was drunk, and anybody can whip a drunk."

"Then put down your gun and winner takes all," my dad said. I prayed that Martin would fight my dad; I knew he couldn't take him and besides, I was as strong as Martin, I felt, maybe I could get an advantage over him and hit him with something or pile into the fight myself.

"All right," Martin said unexpectedly, "but I'm going to tie your kid up, and I'm going to kill him when you lose."

This caught my dad by surprise. Maybe Evel was smarter than he looked although it was somewhat foolish to offer your son as a challenge to a loving father.

"Tie him up," Martin instructed my dad as he threw a rope at his feet. My dad began tying me up all the while watching every move that Martin made. He didn't trust him for one second, and he expected Evel to shoot both of us at anytime. That was not to be, though, at least not yet. "Tie him up tighter and loop that knot behind his back," he said.

When Martin was sure that I was secure and no threat, he lowered his gun carefully and stuck it in his jeans behind his back.

"Put your gun down on the ground, Evel," my dad urged.

"This way, or no way," Martin replied as he lunged at my dad.

The first lick came from Martin as he hit my dad square on the forehead and jarred him backwards. Martin shrunk back quickly not allowing a counter punch. This was Evel's tactic. He had the gun, so he could stay reasonably out of reach of my dad's punches. He was taller and had longer arms, so he knew my dad would have to get inside his arms in order to land a punch. He hit my dad again hard on the face. I could see swelling under my dad's right eye, and I thought, *What's he doing?*

My dad took every punch to his head and body. Martin was swinging as hard as he possibly could throwing wild haymakers and roundhouses that my dad let land on him. Martin clinched his teeth and the veins popped out on his forehead as he mustered all the strength he had behind every punch. He was confident that my dad was beaten badly, and that the next punch would end it all. I feared for my dad's life. Evel pummeled him over and over; he surely was going to kill him. A trickle of blood seeped out of the wound Martin was making with his bare knuckles, and then I saw my dad look at me from his swollen eyes. There was no fear there, and I understood that he had no intention of losing this battle and his son's life. He was letting Martin wear himself out. My dad could take a punch; there was no glass jaw on this Preacher, and Evel was getting tired, breathing heavily now, half stumbling as his legs were giving way. My dad kept him in the fight by groaning and gasping in pain every time Martin hit him and acting like he was completely out of breath. Martin had no punch; the places he hit my dad should have knocked him unconscious but they did not. It was Martin who was fading quickly.

Evel Martin was spent, so my dad took the chance. He swung at Martin and hit him square on the jaw. Martin reeled backwards and fell on his butt, and as he did, my dad jumped on top of him. Just as he was about to finish Martin off, and before he could land the knockout punch to the side of Martin's face, the gun came out.

Dazed and wobbly, Evel put the nose of the gun to my dad's temple.

"Get up," he demanded. He was barely conscious.

"I thought this would be a fair fight?" My dad asked. He dared not taunt Martin or provoke him into pulling the trigger. The hammer was cocked and ready to shoot.

"There's nothing fair about going to prison," Martin answered. "Get over by that tree."

Martin pointed the gun at me and terrified me. I had never had a gun pointed directly at me before. "Get up," he said, "and stand over there by the Preacher."

Evel had made up his mind. He was going to murder us in cold blood, execution style. "I've changed my mind," he said, "I'm going to kill the Preacher first and then you," he looked at me. He pointed the gun at my dad and then at me again suggesting how he was going to dispose of us.

"You will never get away with this!" My dad yelled.

"HA!" Martin laughed.

Evel Martin stood about four feet away from my dad. His wild look was frightening, and it was obvious that after two murders, he had nothing to lose by one or two more.

"People are looking for us," my dad reasoned. "I can promise you that if you spare our lives that you won't go to the electric chair for the other killings."

Martin wasn't phased by this talk. He was smarting from the whipping my dad gave him the second time, humiliating him. "You can't promise jack," Martin said as he raised the nozzle of the gun and pointed it at my dad's head. I shut my eyes and squinted in prayer as hard as I could.

Please, Jesus, I mouthed, *is this how you want us to die?*

Ping! We heard the sound but didn't know what it was until we saw Martin's gun go up with his hand and arm toward the sky, and then a huge BOOM! He had fired the pistol into the air. Martin's eyes went wide open; more open than I had ever seen on a person, and the graphic look of surprise was in them. As he fell backwards, a gush of blood spurt from the tiny hole between his eyes. The pistol fell from his hand, and my dad grabbed it. Evel fell on his back with a thud. He instinctively put the back of his hand over the hole in his forehead and then it fell away from his body. Evel Martin was dead.

Fran had one bullet in his single shot twenty- two rifle. One bullet and one chance. He had been going in circles in the woods; lost in the abyss of trees and bush. He heard the screaming voices for a mile away and ran toward the sounds echoing around him. At first he couldn't get himself oriented because the echo confused him, so he decided to run in the direction he thought would take him towards Evel Martin's farm. He stumbled upon the group as my dad and Martin were fighting. He thought about rushing in, but then Martin may have killed us all, so he stood by a tree and took aim at the center of Evel Martin's forehead. He knew that if he hit Martin anywhere else, the tiny and underpowered 22 shot wouldn't make a dent in Martin or slow him down; he had to carefully place the bullet in the most vulnerable position; between the eyes where the bullet could penetrate the brain. The rifle had enough power to do this. He envisioned the bullet hitting Martin, and if it didn't go through his thick skull, it would at least knock him out, and the preacher could overpower him. When Martin raised his gun to my dad's head, Fran pulled the trigger. The bullet struck clean, and pieces of bone broke loose as the missile penetrated Evel's head. Fran hit the jackpot as the bullet found some soft tissue as if guided by God Himself and flew deep into the interior of Martin's brain.

"Glory to God in the highest," my dad exclaimed as he ran to Fran and grabbed him, while lifting him off the ground.

"Yes and Amen," I said, "Glory to God in the highest." Fran looked at me strangely when I said this. That was the most religious thing he had ever heard me say.

Only Ethel Martin, her arm hanging in a sling, attended the funeral of her son. The Preacher refused to preach the funeral of Evel Martin even though Ethel was a member of Evergreen Baptist Church, nor would the Preacher allow Evel to be buried in the church cemetery.

"That's it," Floyd said as he shoveled the last spade full of dirt on Evel Martin's casket. He conducted the funeral as part of his fee for the internment of Evel Martin. He charged her full price and threw in his other services as part of the deal. He got the funeral over with quickly, realizing that this was the most money he had ever made in such a short amount of time since he had been in the undertaking business. He was packing up before Ethel had a chance to grieve. She had no time to wail, and she had hardly sniffled into her handkerchief before Floyd said, "Amen."

Evel Martin came to a violent end. He was buried in the woods behind Ethel's house. To this day, there is no grave marker to honor him, and no one in Chapel Gap would ever speak his name again.

CHAPTER FORTY-ONE

was driving my 1960 Volkswagen that my dad bought me for my birthday. His talk with Fran worked in my favor as Fran convinced him he was punishing himself by not allowing me to have a car. "You'll have to haul him everywhere," Fran explained.

My heart was set on receiving a 1956 Ford Crown Victoria, red and white, preferably, but I misled myself. My dad had a friend over in Athens, Kentucky who bought the new little bug that was the rage. They were cheap to f ix and repair, and great on gas although gasoline was only thirteen cents per gallon, and the little puddle jumper held 10.6 gallons. The VW had a whopping 36 horsepower, and I could get it up to 80 miles per hour going down a long steep hill. The car was quite a novelty in Chapel Gap and Crab Orchard. I liked this special attention because I had the only VW in all of Lincoln County.

People turned their heads as I drove by, and some of the old timers didn't like the car; "Hitler's car," they called it. I had to endure some hardships owning a car like that when some-one would make fun of it as I drove by, "What's that got, a Singer Sewing Machine engine?" or "it looks like a long nose."

My dad made me suffer before I got the car just to let me know who was in control. He parked the car in the barn and wouldn't let me sit in it, drive it, or even touch it until I would get my driver's license a month later when I turned sixteen. It was torture getting up in the morning, and after chores, look-ing through the doors of the barn at the car I couldn't drive. That was a ritual I went through the whole month as the car sat in total confinement.

We had an evangelist in to preach a revival meeting that month. His name was Eugene Clark, and he was from all the way up in Michigan and the Metropolis of Detroit. For some reason, the people of Evergreen Baptist Church loved him. For two weeks, they listened to the man thunder from the pulpit. The crowds were large and many nights, there was no room in the building for the people, and so my dad put some speakers on the outside of the church so that people who couldn't get in could hear the messages. This upset those guys who skipped church and smoked because they had to listen to the preach-ing that made them feel guilty about their sins.

There never was a revival meeting quite like that one in Lincoln County. "Pastor Clark could call heaven down, or hell up," some of the people said about him. At the end of the sec-ond week, the members of the church decided in a vote that the meeting be extended another week. This was one time that none of us kids complained about extended meetings because we loved this kind of preaching that made people squirm in their seats. One night, it was so powerful that a woman grabbed the back of the seat in front of her and cried out loudly, "I'm such a sinner, Lord save me please!" It was Ethel Martin, but she wasn't the only church member that claimed to be saved but wasn't. Many of them said they thought they were going to heaven, but Mr. Clark preached the hell out them.

On the final night of the meeting, Clark preached about the Second Coming of Jesus Christ. He told us that we should "watch and wait because Jesus will come as a thief in the night and catch you sleeping. Does a thief announce when he is going to rob your house?" He asked this while pounding the pulpit with his large fist, "No sir, because you would be ready! That's the way Jesus is coming. He'll catch you off guard. You'll be smoking and chewing, and here He comes! You'll be drinking, and here He comes! You'll be gambling, and here He comes! You'll be in the picture show, and here he comes! You'll be lying, and here He comes! You'll be dancing, and here He comes! You women will be wearing men's clothing, and here he comes! You young people will be necking, and here He comes! What you going to do then? You better be watching, and what's more, you better be waiting and hope He don't catch you doing stuff you ain't sposed to be doing!"

Bro. Clark took a long swipe of his sweating forehead with his handkerchief and panted like he just ran ten miles. His shirt was wringing wet and his face was red as a beat. His voice became raspy as the members held on to their chairs. I thought about the smoking part and the picture show. I didn't want to be caught doing those things when Jesus came back, so I was up front rededicating my life and promised to stop those sinful practices. I wasn't the only one up there. Virtually every member of Evergreen Baptist Church stood in front of the church. It would be a while before this church settled back into its sinful ways after the Clark storm raged through town.

I felt guilty after that "Second Coming" message. I was standing outside the barn looking in at my chestnut colored little bug. *I want the Lord to come back,* I thought. *I want Him to come and pick me up and deliver me from this sin cursed world.*

I'm ready to meet Him; I'm not worried about that, but I sure hope He doesn't come before I get to drive my car.

I thought about all this stuff and how Eugene Clark left our church. There was no room anywhere the last night of the revival. He had to go home, and we were ready to stay forever. My dad had Bro. Clark stand in front of the church as was the custom after every revival meeting with every evangelist. People hugged him and cried. The line was coming from in the church and out of the church. Even those heathens who came to church, but didn't come to church were hugging and bawling over Mr. Clark.

My dad baptized fifty-six people at the end of the meeting, and the Evergreen Baptist Church had the biggest three-week growth of any church in the entire State of Kentucky. Pictures are still in the albums of some members as my dad stood in the cold Cedar Creek and baptized all those people with icicles hanging from the bridge.

I barely got my driver's license. I had been driving since I was ten years old, and I thought I knew everything. Driving in Stanford was different than motoring through the fields in a big truck on the farm. I failed my test four times. In Kentucky, you can only fail four times, and if you fail the fifth, you have to wait a year to try again. I was sweating bullets on my last try. I thought I was doing pretty well, and it was Trooper Tip Tuck who saved my life. He gave me all four tests, and when he failed me, he would sit there and shake his head.

On the final test, the fifth, he had allowed me to fix my taillight, which was not working. That was grounds for failure. Luckily, I had an extra bulb in the trunk, which in that car was on the front. As we approached the courthouse for the last time, he told me, "Sonny, if you don't run over that pedestrian crossing the street, you're going to pass this test." Wow! I didn't even see the little old man with a cane! I probably would never have stopped at the pedestrian walk anyway, which would have failed me, but killing a man on my driver's test was unimaginable.

"Learn to drive," Tip said as he handed me the okay and a barely passing grade.

I thought about these things as I happily drove my shiny little car down Main Street in Crab Orchard. I endured one snide remark coming from somewhere on the street. "Get some bug spray and kill that thing." I passed Jimmy Goodnight, the bank Vice President as he nailed up boards over the windows of the now defunct bank. Virtually every church in Lincoln County that did business with his bank withdrew their monies and closed their accounts. The memberships of those churches followed, and it was clear that the bank made a fatal error by refusing to loan Evergreen Baptist Church the money for its new building so badly needed.

The churches moved their accounts with their members to the bank in Stanford, which was very friendly about loaning churches money. In fact, they had sent out a letter to all the churches in the area asking them to come in and check out the great rates the bank would make for church mortgages. My dad deposited more than $300,000.00 into the bank in Stanford. This was done after a big fight at the church over what they were going to do with the money Doc Sinclair willed the Evergreen Baptist Church.

"We can't just let the Preacher have half this money," Junior Cullen argued, "it will ruin his ministry."

"How so?" My dad asked.

"Filthy lucre," Cullen responded, "the Bible says Preachers should not be guilty of "filthy lucre."

The Cullen family had more support on this point than my dad thought. Most of his congregation would never make that much money collectively in their entire life times. When he suggested that they not only pay for building the new building, which was going to cost five thousand dollars, but they should invest the rest of the money in missions and give it away, this stirred up a lot of people. He knew the church was going to split over the money, and it did. The Messers, Cullens, Smiths, and Clicks left the church saying that the Preacher had all those poor folks on his side that never had a penny. They viewed these people as too ignorant to make wise decisions as to how the money should be spent. The Messers eventually came back to church because they said the Preacher in Crab Orchard was boring, and they "weren't growing in the Lord." The others stayed away, but Nathan Smith told my dad not to sweat it because Junior Cullen was causing as much trouble for the Crab Orchard Baptist Church as he did at Evergreen Baptist.

My dad wanted to pay off the loans of all the Baptist churches in the Chapel Gap, Broughtontown, and Pine Hall areas. Evergreen Baptist didn't respect him on this, and he respected their opinions and viewpoints.

"Okay," my dad said during the meeting, "I'll donate my half of the money after my tithes to the church here to pay off those church loans and the rest to missions."

"Glory Hallelujah!" Someone cried from the congregation since no one ever heard of a Preacher giving all his money to a church.

"What do you expect us to do?" My mom whined. "We need a house, and you promised me a house. What now?"

"The Lord will provide," my dad told her, and He did.

The Preacher's reputation was sky high as the word spread throughout the county as to what he had done. He received cards and letters of appreciation from all the churches he helped, and the Louisville Courier Journal got hold of the story and did a big feature on my dad on the front page of the Sunday paper. He was famous, and his reputation knew no bounds as it spread to other areas of the state and nation. Had he not been more righteous, he would have accepted the movie contract that would have told his story to millions in the movie houses across America. "Can't do that," he told my mother who had already told every person she knew in the United States that a movie was going to be made about my dad.

He built her a house, and that made her happy. "Can't be too big," he cautioned, "the poor people don't even have their own houses, and the poor tenant farmers are lucky to have a roof over their heads."

The modest farmhouse was built some distance from the church and was nice. He built an inside toilet and put running water in the house, and we all thought we had died and gone to heaven after living in that cramped little trailer house for so many years and carrying all the water we used from the spring. Always enterprising with his church at heart, he used the trailer for Sunday School space.

Fran and I ran all over Lincoln County in my car. Fran loved it as his own, and I would allow him to drive it anywhere he wanted, but he hardly went anywhere except to our house to visit my sister, who couldn't car date yet.

As for me, I was planning and scheming how to get Kathy Friday in my car. She was unapproachable on the school grounds. We were making good grades, and she was at the top of our class. Her busyness kept her in the library most of the time, and at other times, she was walking around with her girlfriends, who were making eyes at all the boys. I was not a football player or basketball player; I was a baseball player and a good one. Some said as good as Crab Orchard High ever had, but baseball players were boring to girls, and that was against me. I got my genes from my grandpa of my same name.

My grandfather played shortstop for the Vine Creek, Kansas team in 1917 and 1918. In that day, many of the pro teams would travel around the country and play the local teams of America. The Cincinnati Reds traveled over there and played the Vine Creek farmers. The farmers whipped them soundly, so they hired my grandpa and my great Uncle Carl to play for them. Uncle Carl went on to play for the Kansas City Blues, which became the Kansas City A's and finally moved out to Oakland, California.

My grandfather didn't last. He was in love with my grandmother, Leona Claire Church. My grandfather was so homesick that when the train that carried the Reds across the country passed through Salina, Kansas, he literally jumped off the train and walked to Vine Creek and into the waiting arms of his lover, who he married and for sixty years after World War I, they never spent a night apart.

My heart jumped into my throat when I thought of this love story. He told me stories of being stationed in Manhattan, Kansas during the start of World War 1. My grandmother would travel once a month by buggy that she would drive all night just to get to see him for an hour. He told me of the times when she would arrive after driving all night in the rain, and she would be completely soaked in mud that fell on her from the horse's hooves as it plodded through the muddy trails. If only I could have a sweetheart like my grandmother, and no one would do but Kathy Friday. Every time I saw her, I would light up like a Christmas tree.

"Ask her out, Bud. She ain't going to know you love her until you tell her," Fran admonished during one of my more melancholy moments.

"What do you know, Fran? You've never asked a girl out."

"I asked your sister."

"She was ten years old!"

"Same thing," he said.

"No, it isn't. Kathy is sixteen and beautiful, I'm a stinking Preacher's kid and a baseball player."

"She likes your piano playing, and no one here can do that."

Fran's wisdom prevailed, and I got the nerve to ask Kathy Friday for a date. I decided to do it at her church over at Copper Creek and not on the schoolyard where people could see me. I drove the little bug over there and made an excuse why I wasn't in my own church on Wednesday evening Prayer Meeting. The churches called it "Prayer Meeting" although we never prayed on Wednesday evening. My excuse was that I had to stay late for school to help one of the teachers grade some papers. I told Fran to tell my dad this, so he would know where I was. "Really?" Fran asked me innocently. "Yeah, papers," I lied and then drove over to Copper Creek.

I pulled into the dusty parking lot of the Copper Creek Baptist Church about a half hour before services. The kids were standing and staring at my little orange Volkswagen. The men seem fascinated as well. "Sounds like a sewing machine to me," one man said making an old joke, and beneath the laughter, another shouted, "Hey Kid? Feel like a sardine in that can?" This was humiliating all right, but not as humiliating as when the service was over, and I discovered my car up against the outhouse where some boys had carried it and left it.

Kathy Friday noticed me when I came inside the church. It was rare to have visitors on Prayer Meeting nights, so everyone eyed the strange kid that walked in. She turned her head and looked at me as I sat down in the back. Everybody else was looking at me as well. My face turned red, and I wished I was somewhere else at the moment. I never did well in strange churches.

"We have a visitor," the Preacher said from the pulpit. His name was J. Otis Ledbetter, and his reputation was that he was a kind and gentle pastor and a good man. "What's your name, son?" The Preacher asked as I turned a scarlet shade of red. *What have I gotten myself into?* I thought as the sweat ran down my back.

"Bro. Smith," I said as the people chuckled.

"Bro. Smith, Bro. Smith," Pastor Ledbetter mused, "where you from, brother?"

"Chapel Gap, sir."

"Chapel Gap? Are you related to Pastor Jerry Smith?" I was shocked that he knew my dad, but why shouldn't I be? Everyone knew my dad.

"I'm his son."

"My, my," and the people turned and looked at me like I was the celebrity and not my dad. The Copper Creek church had no loans to pay off, but they looked at me as if they had, and my dad paid the bills. "I've never met your father, son, but I know he is a man of God." The members nodded their heads in agreement. "You should be very proud that you are Pastor Smith's son, and I will pray that you live up to his reputation."

"Amen," the men said in unison and a few women.

"Bro. Smith, does your father know that you are over here tonight? Shouldn't you be in your own church?" The pastor was inquisitive.

He caught me off guard, and unlike Fran, I didn't think well when put on the spot; especially, in front of a lot of people. I had to think quickly.

"Yes sir, he does. I had to run an errand over in Brodhead and couldn't get back to Chapel Gap in time, and I didn't want to miss church, so I knew of your great ministry here, and I wanted to hear you speak so much that I decided to be in your service tonight and not miss church. I haven't ever missed a Wednesday Prayer Meeting in my life." I said all this in one breath.

The Pastor cleared his throat obviously overcome at such

eloquence from a sixteen years old kid. "We welcome you in the name of Jesus Christ our Savior. I believe Pastor Smith has a good son."

"Amens" went up all over the church, and I suddenly felt at home.

"He plays 'Pearly White City'" Kathy Friday shouted.

I was stunned and looked for the reaction of the crowd. Evidentially, women were allowed to speak in this church; something I had never seen happen in a New Testament Baptist Church.

"You play the piano?" The Preacher asked. "Well, well, you'll have to come up here and play something."

I shook my head back and forth and shrank down in my seat.

"Amen," the men said, and a few of the women.

"Oh, do play the 'Pearly White City,'" Kathy Friday cried in the mixed company and usurping authority over the men.

There was nowhere for me to go, and Bob Miller, a kid I played baseball with and had no idea went to this church, pushed me on the back practically knocking me out of my seat. I reasoned quickly. *If I've a chance to ask Kathy Friday out and get accepted, it is right now at this moment.* The thoughts raced through my mind. I was suspended in space. If I refused, I had no chance. I got to my feet and headed toward the old piano that looked like it was on Noah's Ark one time.

I pulled the old piano bench out from under the ancient upright. The piano faced the wall, so I had my back to the congregation of eagerly waiting people, which was good. I found "Pearly White City" in the old Stamps Baxter Hymnbook; the same one we used over at Evergreen Baptist Church with the shaped notes that supposedly made it easier to sing by. I had only played through the first line when some old lady shouted, "The Pearly White City," and then she started wailing and crying "my poor mother, she's gone to be with the Lord!" By the time I got to the chorus,

In that bright City, Pearly White City,
I have a mansion, a harp, and a crown,
Now I am longing, longing and waiting,
For that bright City that's soon coming down.

There were so many people weeping and wailing that I thought I was at a funeral. I couldn't see behind me, and I was glad of that. I ended the song with a beautiful arpeggio, running my hands up the piano and crossing my left over my right, my fingers playing deftly the entire length of the keyboard, and then I ended the song with a soft E flat at the bass end of the piano.

No one clapped in the churches then, and I expected some "Amens," but there was dead silence as the stupefied group of worshippers didn't make a sound. I was afraid to turn around. Had I played that badly?

"Play the Old Rugged Cross," someone cried. I did.

"At The Cross," someone else requested. I played it.

"The Old Account Was Settled," the next person called out. I played it, too.

I played and played, and the more I did, the more they wanted to hear. I was wearing out, and I was happy when the Pastor Ledbetter said, "all right, Glory to God; we've been blessed from heaven itself, but we aren't here for entertainment although we're grateful to Bro. Smith here for blessing us tonight."

I played well past preaching time and expected to go home. I looked at my pocket watch, and it was past 9:00 PM, and the Pastor was still going to preach! I knew this already. The Lord's churches don't plan their services on music; they plan them on preaching, and it would be sacrilege to go home without hearing the Word of God. I didn't understand this rule because I believed that worship was worship, but I saw the people picking up their Bibles out of the racks on the backs of the pews where they had place them while singing from the old cloth hymnals.

Kathy Friday sat down in front, and I reveled in the fact that I could sit and watch her for a long period of time. I didn't care if the Preacher preached all night, and in fact, I hoped he would. I was already in trouble, so what did it matter? She turned and looked at me, and the other people saw this, too. She smiled beneath her sweet blue eyes, and her teeth were the whitest I'd ever seen. *My Lord, she's beautiful* I thought, and I couldn't keep my eyes off the back of her head. She must have subconsciously been aware that I was staring at her because now and then, she turned around and smiled. Every time she did, I almost fainted. She had no idea what I was doing over there.

"It's easier to get out of the Will of God when you're in it than get back into the Will of God when you're out of it," Pastor Otis exclaimed rather eloquently. Some of the women said, "Amen." I shuttered when the women spoke out as though the church would come falling in from an Archangel that God would send to destroy this little flock for violating God's Word.

The Pastor's statement impacted me. *He must be from California,* I reasoned. I heard Preacher Clark say during our revival that one of the reasons the Lord was coming soon is because out in California the women were talking out loud in church, and this would just spread across the nation just like all the other garbage that comes out of California." I felt like maybe I was out of the Will of God and could never get back in it.

Finally, the man quit preaching; The people knew exactly when he was going to finish because as soon as he shut his Bible, every single person in the congregation closed theirs and began shuffling. Some were putting their Bibles in little covers. Women in the churches would knit Bible covers of various colors and designs and almost every Bible carrying church member had one. No one was saved or rededicated as was expected on Wednesday Prayer Meeting night although I felt the need for rededication after lying in church to a whole congregation of people. Even though the people knew there would be no one coming forward during the invitation, the Preacher still stopped and talked between all five verses of the invitation song, exhorting sinners to repent of their sins and make it public. Finally, after the sixth verse, singing the first verse over again, the Preacher's wife, Gail, came and knelt at the front. They called this an "altar" but in our church it was forbidden to kneel at the front because the "Holy Rollers" did this and "prayed through." Baptists didn't believe in "praying through," so they would never want to be identified with the Holiness Pentecostals who had strange beliefs.

It was 10:30 PM when the service was finished. As the people filed out, I looked for Kathy Friday. She was standing by her dad's pickup talking to some guy I didn't know from high school. She pointed at me once, so she must have been talking about me. I was looking for my car at the same time, and then I saw it sitting way in back by the outhouse. No one could have driven the car through all the tombstones.

"We were just playing a little joke, Sonny." Bob Miller said. He then grabbed some boys and went back to the car and carried it gently across the cemetery.

Pastor Ledbetter and his wife detained me. "We sure got a blessing out of your playing, Bro. Smith. God has His Hand on you, son. You're going to be greater than your father."

I finally was able to tear myself away from them and ran to Kathy Friday's dad's pickup. She was getting in, and her dad already had started the pickup, letting the engine idle, while he waited for her mother and the other children.

"You were great," Kathy Friday said.

"Thanks, I didn't expect that."

"Let's go!" Mr. Friday yelled at his kids and wife.

"Come on!" Kathy Friday's brother, Donnie, screamed from the pickup where he sat in the back on a milking stool with his little sisters, Tammy and Robin.

"Would you go out with me?" These words suddenly came blurting out of my mouth.

Kathy Friday stared at me in disbelief and blushed. "Can I, daddy?" She asked to my disbelief.

"That boy can play the piano, and he is Godly. You need a Godly man to marry. Yep, it's all right." Mr. Friday said this while his darkly tanned arms and hands were on the steering wheel.

"Yes," she said and then climbed in the truck and left me standing unable to say a word.

I could hear the Friday children singing from the back of the pickup as they turned out of the church onto the dusty Copper Creek Road:

"Bro. Smith and Kathy, sitting in a tree, k-i-s-s-i-n-g!"

CHAPTER FORTY-TWO

I was elated and troubled at the same time. It was almost midnight as I started climbing the Chapel Gap Hill. I shifted the VW transmission down to second gear in order to make it up the hill. There was no telling what was going to happen to me. I told Fran to tell my dad that I had to stay after school; so I told Fran a lie because I knew he wouldn't tell my dad a lie, which he did anyway, but he didn't know better. I told a lie in church in front of all those strange people, who think I am a saint of God because I can play the piano, and they have never seen a boy play the piano except on television.

It was midnight as I pulled into the barn lot of our small farm. A faint ray of light shone through the window where my dad sat in his easy chair reading the Bible and waiting my return. I closed the barn door after parking my car inside and took the long walk toward the house and certain doom. I felt sick.

"Where've you been?" My dad asked as I came through the

door and carefully closed it behind me so that I wouldn't wake up the little kids.

I was in the deepest conundrum of my short life on earth. If I told him the truth, I was in trouble for lying to Fran, and he would check out my story by calling Pastor Ledbetter, who would tell him I lied to the whole church. My heart was in my throat, and I swallowed hard. I gulped a couple of times and then said nothing.

"Don't stand there, where have you been?"

I said nothing except "Just out."

"Out where?"

"Out there, somewhere."

I knew my dad was going to whip me for insubordination, but I felt the stings of the switch he used from the apple tree at the back of the house was better than getting whipped for lying to a church and preacher. He would surely cut the blood out of my back. He nearly did that as I danced around, but unlike other times when he punished me, I didn't make a sound. This took him by surprise, and I knew he was easing up while he struck me. He finished fairly quickly.

"Let that be a lesson," he said. He always said that, but this time he didn't know what the lesson was for. "Give me your keys," he demanded, and so I did. "And your driver's license. You're restricted until you tell me what you were doing tonight coming home after midnight and missing church."

I walked down to Fran's house and spent the night. I didn't have to ask permission to do this at any time because my parents knew that when they asked Fran if I was at his house, he would tell them the truth.

"We're walking again," I said to Fran as we lay on the big feather bed in the attic.

"What happened, Bud?"

I told Fran that I lied to him and about lying to the church at Copper Creek and about asking Kathy Friday for a date, and she said, "yes."

"God help you," Fran said lugubriously and then rolled over to sleep.

Fran would never tell where I really was in a million years. My dad knew that, so he never asked. We were walking everywhere unless Fran could get Abe's old 41 Chevy running and then we would drive that. Early in the punishment period, I thought about how screwed up this whole thing was. I had no car, so how in the world would I ever take Kathy Friday out? I saw her at school but was afraid to talk with her. The entire school was abuzz with gossip about my asking her out. She seemed proud of the fact that her dad gave her permission to date me. Was she in love? I doubted it. She was just curious, that's all and confused as to why I wouldn't talk to her. This was the most embarrassing thing that ever happened to me.

I had other problems. We were deep into competition in baseball, and I couldn't catch or hit. The coach told me that he would have to put me on the bench until my play got better, or I got over whatever was bothering me. I didn't feel like I would ever get over it, so I quit. I don't think anyone even noticed, or cared.

My grades were falling, too. My teachers sent home notes to my parents about how that I was going to fail the eleventh grade if something wasn't changed. "Sonny is smart," they wrote, "but he has no desire or direction." One teacher said, she thought I might be on drugs that were beginning to infiltrate Lincoln County. A couple of kids at Lancaster High were arrested for having some funny looking cigarettes in their possession. One of those kids was Ming Morgan.

"Problems, problems, problems all day long," I listened to the Everly Brothers sing their new hit and identified with the song completely. Stan Kirk, my old Booster Choir leader and kid that I admired more than any person except my dad and Fran, told me he was going to join the Navy. I watched Stan leave for the armed services that day, and the sorrow I felt was so heavy that I cried. No, I didn't cry, I sobbed. I watched his car all the way down the lane and didn't move until the dust from the wheels could be seen no more.

The night before Stan left, I stood in the middle of the road near our farm after taking a walk and was watching the lightning, "heat lightning" the farmers called it when no rain was involved. An inspiration hit me. I'm going to write a book all about this, I thought. I was sharing my dreams with Loretta Kirk and she said, "everybody wants to write a book. You'll never do it, you're not smart enough or talented. Besides, you're going to fail school and not graduate." Her words stuck in me like a dagger and then she went on and on about how Stan and Buster, her darling sons, were so smart and handsome. She thought her kids were perfect. They could do no wrong. When I heard these things, I almost hated Stan. I thought better of it, but I did despise Buster. "Carey is going to be just like his older brothers," she bragged, "he'll play football and get scholarships just like Stan. Stan's going to the Naval Academy, you know." Stan was not; he had a scholarship to Western Kentucky University over in Bowling Green, Kentucky, but he didn't take it. Bowling Green was too close to his mother, so he joined the Navy to get as far away from her as he could. I wanted so badly to tell her this because that's what I thought, but I didn't know this for sure.

Fran and I were fishing at the Macmillan pond over at Ottenheim. The pond was known as the best bluegill fishing in the area. Mr. Macmillan wouldn't let anyone fish there except Fran. Everyone loved Fran, and he could do things and get things done that no one else could touch, and fishing in the Macmillan pond was one of them.

CHRONICLES OF THE KNOBS · 483

"What's gonna happen to you, Bud?" Fran asked while landing a half-pound bluegill on the bank with his long cane pole.

"I'm in the deepest despair of my life, Fran."

"Listen," he said, "you're not in despair. To despair is to turn your back on God. You haven't done that, have you?"

"I feel I'm still a Christian, but not a very good one."

"You've never been a very good one," he said casually. This was the harshest thing he ever said to me, and the words hurt me, deeply. It cut to my heart, and I thought he was betraying me.

"You hate me, too, uh, Fran?"

"Shut up you fool!" He yelled. "What the hell is wrong with you? Of course I don't hate you and don't ever say that again! Good friends give good counsel if they love their brothers, and I love you!"

I was shocked! This was the first time in my life a man told me he loves me. We didn't use this word between boys for fear of becoming like those weird queer people living in San Francisco.

"Do you mean that, Fran?"

"Yep. Now shut up and knock it off, you're scaring the fish."

I smiled for the first time in over two months.

It was almost ninety days, and I still hadn't driven my car, or any car, because my dad had my driver's license. I had just finished milking the cows, the evening milking time, and I saw a strange car drive up in the barnyard. I recognized him immediately, and chills of fear and dread ran up and down my spine. *Pastor Otis Ledbetter!* I screamed in my mind.

I hid behind the chicken house where I couldn't be seen. I couldn't hear what the two preachers were saying, but after they were finished talking, they hugged each other, and the Pastor drove away.

"Pastor Smith, I recognize your picture from the paper," Ledbetter said as he met my dad coming from the house.

"I'm Pastor Ledbetter from Copper Creek Baptist Church."

"Oh, yes," my dad said, "I've heard a lot of good things about your ministry in the church over there. Come in for a cup of coffee or Postum?"

"No, no, I'm headed over to Chestnut Ridge to preach in a fellowship meeting. I've been invited to speak on Our Heritage; I'll be here only a moment or two."

"What brings you here?" My dad asked curiously.

"Your son," he said.

When I heard, "your son," I almost passed out.

"My son? What about my son?"

"He stopped by the church a couple of months ago or so on Wednesday Prayer Service. I thought it was strange that he was missing his own service to attend ours, but when I asked him about this, he said that he was on an errand for you in Brodhead, and it got late, and he didn't want to miss church, so he exited and drove over to Copper Creek."

"Copper Creek is a long way off 150," my dad commented, "he could have easily attended Brodhead Baptist Church, or for that matter, he had time to drive to Crab Orchard Baptist, perhaps."

"I asked him to play the piano after asking his name. He said his name was Bro. Smith," he laughed, and his round belly jellied, "and then he told us why he was there."

"Us? Where was he when you asked him these things?"

"He was sitting in church. I was welcoming visitors, although he was the only one, and I always talk to the visitors and ask them where they are from," Pastor Ledbetter explained.

"What if a visitor is a woman?" My dad changed the subject. He knew that Pastor Ledbetter had been sent from a seminary near Los Angeles, California, and he wanted to see if the

California preacher had brought the heresy of women speaking in church to Lincoln County.

Ledbetter avoided the question. "Let me tell you about your son."

"Oh, please tell me," my dad said sarcastically.

"He was asked to play the piano, The Pearly White City, I believe. Well, Pastor Smith, your son played that song so beautifully. The whole church was in tears, so they asked him to play some more. He played and played song after song, and the people were so blessed. I don't think I've ever seen Copper Creek Baptist Church that moved. They loved him and haven't stopped talking about his talents, and the way he uses himself for the Lord. We've never had a piano player in the church, so mothers are now making their children go to music school. The church hired a lady from Broughtontown Friendship Baptist Church, who teaches piano in the school at Brodhead. She comes to our church once a week, on Thursdays, and teaches several of the kids all at once. We pay her gas money, that's all she wants, and in fact, I'm learning to play myself, your son inspired me so much."

Gas money is fair, my dad thought.

"I'm afraid it's my fault that your son was maybe late getting home. I should have come over earlier in case he did get into trouble and explain that I didn't want to break the tradition of the church and not preach the gospel. I personally would have dismissed the entire congregation without the preaching, but they aren't quite ready for that step, yet."

This guy's a liberal, my dad thought.

"Thank you for coming and telling me this, Pastor." My dad cordially shook his hand, and the good Pastor Ledbetter drove on towards Chestnut Ridge.

My hands were buried in my face as I sat by the chicken house. I had already cut a switch from the apple tree. A big one this time, thick, and I was ready for the beating. My dad found me with my head leaning on my arms, which were on my knees, and my face in my hands.

"Here," I said as I handed him the switch. He threw it away. In fact, I didn't know it at the time, but this was the last time he ever had a switch in his hands to whip either of his kids. "But, I deserve the whipping!" I cried out.

"You deserve more than that," he commented harshly, "lying in the Lord's house and deceiving those people. You did that for a girl?"

Now, how did he know about Kathy Friday? I asked myself.

"The liberal Pastor from Copper Creek told me that a pretty girl in his church was talking to you after the service. Who is she anyway?"

"Kathy Friday."

"Don Friday's daughter? She is pretty." He was trying to put those words back into this mouth.

"What's going to happen to me, Preacher?" I asked sadly.

"What's going to happen to you? Happen to you? You're going over to Copper Creek Baptist Church on Sunday morning, sit on the front row, and then you're going to apologize to the whole church!"

This stunned me, and I couldn't get my thoughts for a moment. I had been punished this way in the past for smoking and stealing Sterling Deaton's gourds but never in front of another church!

"I can't do that, Preacher."

"You can, and you will if you ever want your driver's license again and your car, and if you don't, you'll never date that girl."

"But, I'll have to miss church!" I cried.

"So will Fran. He'll have to drive you over there. I'd do it myself, but missing church like that might ruin my ministry, that is, if you haven't ruined it already."

His words stung like a thousand bees, far worse than those bee stings I suffered crossing the dry creek bed at the Cullen farm following those boys to go swimming.

Fran and I didn't talk all the way to Copper Creek on Sunday morning. As we pulled into the parking lot, and I saw all the trucks and cars, people standing around, I thought that I would rather have a hundred whippings with an apple switch; my dad hitting me as hard as he could; that would be better than what I was facing now.

"Fran, you could tell him I did it," I said.

"You idiot. Don't you think he's going to find out?"

"He'll never question your word, Fran. Please save my life."

"That's exactly why you're going to tell him nothing but the truth."

"But you love me, you said that when we were fishing."

"That's another reason I'm going to tell the truth."

The church was packed, and people watched me walk to the front by myself. The end of Fran's involvement happened when he sat on the back row by Bob Miller. The people obviously thought I was going to play the piano because several of them said, "Amen" as I walked down the aisle. I saw Kathy Friday smile at me with a somewhat puzzled look in her eyes as I sat on the front row next to a little kid, who was holding a slingshot.

"Bro. Smith is back," the liberal Pastor Ledbetter announced. "Bro. Smith, come up here and play for us."

You would think the people would groan since they had to stay so long the last time I played here, and the Elder Ledbetter had preached afterwards. Maybe they forgot about this because one of the women said: "Yes, play the "Pearly White City." Fran startled when he heard this woman speak out and then frowned. I forgot to warn Fran that he might be shocked by the women in this Californian's church.

I wanted to get this over with; I wasn't going to wait until the invitation song and then come forward. That was useless, and the Pastor had given me an opportunity to stand and speak right now. I would stand, pretend I was going to the piano; no, I couldn't pretend in church, either. I would spill my guts out with deep emotion and then get the heck out of there. I wouldn't stop until I got home. I stood.

"Pastor Ledbetter? I have something to say."

The pastor looked somewhat stunned and then said, "speak what's on your mind, brother, give us your testimony."

I turned around and faced the congregation, and Kathy Friday was staring me down. "This ain't no testimony," I began, "this is a confession." The congregation gasped at these words.

What would he have to confess, and why isn't he doing it in his own church? Some were thinking.

"I came here a few months back and lied to the church." Kathy Friday's mouth flew open as did many others. "I told you people, and the great Pastor here that I was on an errand to Brodhead for my dad when in fact, I was here to ask Kathy Friday for a date." I didn't plan on saying anything about her, but the need to be completely honest was overtaking me at the moment. "I lied to you, and I'm sorry." Fran was sitting on his shoulders now, a familiar position for him when trouble was brewing or an embarrassing situation was at hand. I sat down red-faced and a sorry excuse for a human being. *Kathy Friday will never go out with me, and her father will refuse now that my nefarious past is out in the open,* I thought as I felt the daggers of stares piercing my back.

"Well, well," the Pastor said. "I want to apologize to Bro. Smith for something. I visited his dad last week on my way to the fellowship meeting at Chestnut Ridge Baptist Church. I told his dad about his son being here, and I know that is why Sonny is here this morning. I didn't mean to get him in trouble."

Maybe the liberal Pastor wasn't so bad after all. Maybe we needed some of his liberalness. He cared about people, and me.

"We should forgive Sonny," he told his flock, "and we should do it right now."

I had never seen anything like this. He surely wasn't going to get those people to forgive me on the spur of the moment; everyone knew that there was always a period of restoration before final forgiveness was made by the church, but Pastor Ledbetter's reputation was that he built caring churches.

Pastor Ledbetter took me by the hand and led me to the front of the church. He then asked the people row by row to come and forgive me. This was a different approach than Fran and me had seen. Normally, the people would just flood the aisles and crowd toward the rededication line.

He pointed to them row by row. "Those of you who won't forgive this man, stay in your seat. Those of you who will, come forward."

Row by row was emptied as the people filed out, and not one person stayed parked in his or her seat and wouldn't forgive. They took my hand and hugged me. They cried like they had known me all my life and said, "I forgive you, Bro. Smith." I was crying now. This was a joyful moment. I was being forgiven by the people. I never knew for sure in my own church when people forgave me. I was troubled by this at the moment. *A Prophet's without honor in his own country*, I reasoned.

My knees were weak when Kathy Friday came by, and I had to catch myself under the buckling of my knees to keep from falling to the floor. "I forgive you," she said softly, "and I love you." She then kissed me on the cheek and lingered there a little so that I could smell her sweet perfume that filled my nostrils. I sniffed strongly. The feeling of ecstasy ended when I caught Pastor Ledbetter's eye watching me. I knew he was going to chastise me and lash out at me for my lascivious basking in the redolence of Kathy Friday's hair. The outline of her ruby red lips must have been visible on my cheek. This may have been the kiss of death; such vileness in a church. He nodded his head and smiled while looking to heaven as if this were a divine moment, not an evil one.

I think the Friday family was like the Job family. The kids did what they wanted with little supervision, and I reasoned this when Mr. Friday shook my hand and told me he forgives me and then asked, "are you ever going to take my daughter on a date?"

I walked Kathy Friday to her dad's pickup, holding her hand. It was the most pleasurable moment in my short life. Her hands were soft like a rose petal, and her long blond curly hair bounced on her shoulders. I didn't want this moment to ever end. I would never wash my hand nor my cheek where her sweet lips touched my face. No, I would have to wash my face because my dad would know that I had been kissed. He had taught us young people of dating age to never kiss before the marriage altar. "You'll pierce yourselves with many sorrows," he said.

I glanced over my shoulder as Fran drove us away and waved a little goodbye. She blew a kiss. *Did this really happen,* I thought, *or am I in a dream? If it is a dream, I don't want to wake up.*

"Fran, can you believe all those people forgave me? I mean, my own church wouldn't do that."

"You're fixin to find out, Bud."

'What do you mean?"

"You're going to repent tonight and tell the truth in front of the Evergreen Baptist Church."

"My dad didn't say I had to do that!" I cried.

"No, but I did."

"Why, Fran?"

"One, because you have to clear your conscience in your own church in case this comes up in the future; you've already taken care of the confession and repentance. The church is bound to forgive you by Scriptural law whether they want to or not. Two, if you voluntarily do this when the Preacher has not specifically asked you to, you will have taken full charge of your sin, and he'll restore you more fully than the Prodigal son's dad did when he returned from the hog pen; he'll forgive every lie and every sin you've ever committed that he knows about."

Man, was Fran ever smart. I knew for sure that he loved me as a brother because he was still looking out for me that night at church. We both sat on the front row, so the people knew something was up. Before my dad preached, it was Fran who interrupted him and told him, "Sonny has something to say."

"Go ahead," my dad said to me, but I didn't go ahead, Fran did.

Fran stepped in front of me as I started to stand and pushed me down in the seat. *What's he up to?* I thought, and. my dad must have been thinking the same thing by the look on his face. This wasn't protocol; someone stepping in to speak for another member in a Baptist church.

"Sonny did a bad thing," he started. Most of the people had never seen Fran in front of the church except for a couple of times years ago when he was rededicating for something or the other. He then told them the whole story. "He is a brave man," Fran said, "I witnessed this myself, so I am standing here telling you that every single one of you should forgive him of what he did so that he can go to his maker in peace." I wasn't thinking about going to my maker at such an early age, but I did need to make my peace.

Fran has an ulterior motive, I was thinking as the people began filling the aisles haphazardly and coming to tell me they forgave me. He knew that if I repented, and especially he knew that for telling a lie in church, the members would want restoration and a period of "watch and care." That would bring on the gossip and things would never be right. He also knew that my feelings would be hurt if some of the people stayed in their seats, which some of them would have done, refusing to forgive me if he hadn't stood in my place.

Every single person came by, and not one stayed behind. They hugged me and cried, and it felt good.

CHAPTER FORTY-THREE

The first foreigner to move into the Chapel Gap Community created quite a stir. He was a twenty-nine years old Armenian by the name of Messiah Bardasian, and he moved down there from somewhere in northern Ohio. He bought the Rich farm, which was the largest farm in Lincoln County. The Rich brothers, kin to the famous Rich Ranch in Texas, sold the farm to Bardasian and moved back to Texas. Messiah bought the farm for an undisclosed amount of money.

The first thing he did was paint over the "Chew Mail Pouch Tobacco" sign painted on the giant roof of the farm's major silo. This upset the whole neighborhood because the sign was a landmark in the area. They were also upset because he called himself, "Messiah." "Why does he call himself, The Messiah?" The gossiping women asked each other over their phones.

Bardasian was small. He stood all of five feet two inches, or maybe less, but there was no doubt he was a rich and powerful man. "Where'd he get all that money?" Loretta Kirk asked

Sophie Lord one afternoon gossiping on the phone. "Probably stole it," she guessed.

My dad and Fran went on visitation one Saturday afternoon and decided to make a stop and visit "the Messiah" as everybody called him. He didn't farm, and some of the folks were upset because the farmland seemed to be wasting. "Why does he want a farm when he don't own any thing live except a cat?" They questioned. "He don't grow no crop." That was another reason they hated seeing the land wasted when there were so many poor people in the hollows.

This wasn't the main reason my dad went to see him. He wasn't only going to talk to the man about coming to church; he was there on a mission for Sheriff Crane. Messiah had been down at the pool hall in Crab Orchard, and some of the members of Evergreen Baptist Church, who weren't supposed to be playing cards in the poker tournaments Delbert Blanchard sponsored in his establishment, were complaining about the Messiah taking all their money.

There was also talk that Messiah wanted to open a brothel and gaming hall in Crab Orchard. "You let down the bars, and the goats get in," Bro. Lord prayed during one of his long conversations with God at the church. Everyone knew what he was talking about although he didn't mention Messiah by name. All the churches were in an uproar including the Churches of Christ, Lutherans, the tiny Catholic congregation at Ottenheim, and the largest churches in the Crab Orchard area, the Baptists. All these churches were filled with gossip about how to get rid of this man, who drove the shiny Packard Coupe with the huge chrome swan on the hood. Messiah liked to cruise through town sitting on two pillows so that he could see over the steering wheel while smoking a thick black stogie cigar on his way to take money from the boys at the pool hall.

Messiah was polishing his Packard when he saw the

Preacher and Fran drive into his property. As the Preacher came to a stop, Messiah yelled out, "Don't stir up so much dust when you come down my lane; can't you see I'm polishing my car?" He fanned away some of the dust before it settled on the mirror finish.

Fran walked over to the car and looked in the back seat. There were several stacks of money in plain view. More money that Fran had ever seen at one time.

"Mr. Bardasian?" My dad asked as he stuck out his hand.

"Messiah, you can call me, Messiah," Bardasian said.

"Okay, Mr. Bardasian," my dad made a point.

"What do you want?" He asked while keeping an eye on Fran as if he were going to steal his money.

"This here is Fran Job, and I'm Preacher Smith up on the ridge. Pastor of Evergreen Baptist Church."

"Job? That's a funny name," Bardasian commented.

Not as funny as your blasphemous name, Fran though.

Messiah was a handsome man. He had black flowing hair, and his skin was naturally tan; the only dark person living in Lincoln County. He was dressed to the nines even though it was the middle of the day, and he was polishing his black limousine. He wore gold bracelets on both wrists, a big diamond ring set in a solid gold cluster, and a gold necklace drooping down from his neck to his half buttoned shirt showing the hairs on his chest. Fran sized the little guy up and thought, *Real men don't wear necklaces and bracelets like women don't wear men's breeches; what a sissy!*

"We want to invite you to church this Sunday, Mr. Bardasian," my dad said.

"Now, Preacher, I can't go to your church."

"Why not?" My dad asked not understanding why anyone couldn't go to church.

"Well, I'd walk in there with all this gold, driving that big

Packard; everybody'd think I'm rich. They would fall all over me because they would be thinking about hitting me up for some money."

The Preacher didn't even respond although he had not heard this justification for excusing oneself from the Lord's house. He remembered the Scripture, though, in the Book of James where it said you weren't supposed to give space to people coming in the church with fine apparel and jewelry, so maybe it wasn't a good idea to tempt the flock like that.

My dad changed the subject and got down to the business of Sheriff Crane. "Talk is you're trying to open a whore house in Crab Orchard," he said.

"God knows there's plenty of whores over there," Messiah answered, "they might was well get themselves cleaned up and make some money. Oldest profession in the world."

"You know the Sheriff won't allow this."

"That chicken crap cop. I've eaten cops better than him for snacks. I wash down my beer with those menaces."

In the entire Preacher's ministry, he had never encountered a worse heathen than this, except maybe himself at one time. *Judge not lest ye be judged,* he thought.

"Judge Wiliston will shut you down as soon as you get your whorehouse open."

"Brothel!" Messiah screamed, "Stop calling a legitimate profession by a nasty name!" Messiah stood real close to my dad, who was nearly eight inches taller than him and twice his size. He was poking his finger in my dad's chest. "That crooked judge don't know his butt from a hole in the ground."

It was obvious that Messiah had no respect for preachers, *but neither did I at one time,* my dad thought as he was doing his best not to judge the man.

"There is also talk that you are going to try and get liquor legalized in Lincoln County," my dad said to the Messiah.

"I'll get it done with no trouble," he answered curtly.

"You gonna moonshine or something?" Dad quizzed.

"Don't need to. Get that kid away from my house!" He yelled. Fran looked through the windows in the front room of the big mansion.

"Let me show you something," Messiah said.

He then led my dad and Fran into the front room and on to the back of the huge home where he had his den. There were real stuffed animals everywhere. A lion with a huge mane and wild looking eyes, a few elk with large racks, a moose, a cougar fully stuffed, and the feature, a small giraffe.

"Don't touch my stuff!" Messiah yelled at Fran, and Fran shrank back pulling his hands away where he was rubbing the giraffe's neck like he just touched a hot stove.

"Sorry," Fran apologized.

There was a library that rivaled anything they had ever seen, and on one full wall of the room, was Messiah's stash of booze.

"See that Preacher and what's your name, Jock, Jerk or something? There is every kind of whiskey, bourbon, gin, wine, and fine spirits known to man in this room. I can drink all that I want in my own home, and nobody, no, not even the fartfaced Sheriff, can do anything about it. When I'm finished, this whole county will be able to buy all this booze from my liquor stores."

Lincoln County had always been dry since the State was founded in 1893, and as far as anyone thought, it always would be. No one in the history of Lincoln County had ever challenged the dryness of the county, but here stood a man who moved in the neighborhood, had seen an opportunity to make a lot of money, and was planning on capitalizing on it.

"He's dangerous," my dad told Fran as they pulled onto the Chapel Gap Road. "He wants to legalize prostitution, gambling, and booze. If he does this, and the bootleggers in the county don't kill him first, our whole lives will be ruined the way we know it now."

"What you gonna do?" Fran asked.

"Fight him."

"You can beat him up easily."

"Not that kind of fighting, Fran. I would never make a hero out of him by beating the devil out of him. That never stops a man like that. We'll fight by organizing the churches and forcing him out of our county."

My dad was worried because he knew this man was a real threat, and he wasn't afraid of anything. He started his campaign by purposely calling Loretta Kirk and told her what Messiah was planning. She was outraged, and my dad's plan was wise because if he didn't call her in on this, she would oppose my dad when he started the campaign by saying, "the Preacher ought to keep his nose out of other people's business."

The Preacher then enlisted Daphni Anderson to write an article in the "Recorder" exposing the devious plot. He also carefully used his tactics to include the idea that Messiah Bardasian thought the whole community was just a bunch of dumb hillbillies. He hit Messiah hard; harder than he'd ever been hit, and he enlisted the other pastors in the community, including Pastor Otis Ledbetter.

Pastor Ledbetter said, "We lived with alcohol and brothels in California, but the Lord still blessed." However shocking this rationale was didn't prevent Ledbetter from entering the battle. He did resolve the fight because he admitted that had the Christian communities out west have been stronger, California wouldn't be the den of iniquity it had become. He waged his own letter campaign urging other pastors around the state to join the war.

Messiah had backers as well. In fact, he had more of them than anyone thought. Every heathen slug in the county backed him. One day, during the War on Evil, hundreds of cars were seen in the barnyard of the Messiah place. Bardasian was standing on a wooden box on a wagon bed shouting about how it was high time that people who didn't believe all that Bible hokey baloney had some rights.

"We've got the right to have alcohol!" He shouted. "And we have the right to some entertainment with the ladies! We have the right to go to wherever we want, whenever we want and win some money!"

"Yeah, yeah!" The crowd of low life animals screamed, and you could hear them all the way to the top of Chapel Gap.

"We don't need self-righteous preachers telling us how to live; especially, that Preacher up there, and he pointed to the direction of Evergreen Baptist Church above Chapel Gap Hill, who thinks he owns the county and everything in it! His whole church are hypocrites. Why, I saw one of his deacon's bald head poking up under the tent watching the hoochy coochy girls at the Brodhead Fair!" This was true. Raymond Belcher was seen down on his knees by Fran and me while we were behind the tent smoking. His huge rear end was all that you could see as he snuck a peek at the nearly naked ladies. We never said anything about it, and Bro. Belcher was no more the wiser.

Messiah Bardasian was successful in getting a referendum on the ballot with the election of county officials and the judge. Judge Wiliston opposed the measures because he knew he couldn't get elected by upsetting the religious community who was fighting so hard. He was worried, though, because Messiah had brought a high-powered attorney down from Ohio, who moved in the county, just to oppose the judge. The County Attorney was being challenged as well. Some slick lawyer in silk suits, alligator shoes, and a lot of gold hanging on him moved down there to oppose Jack Birdstein for the prosecutor's job. Neither Judge Wilston nor Prosecutor Birdstein had ever been opposed.

There were three decisions to be made by the voters of Lincoln County.

The measures to be decided were ones that no one thought would ever be on a ballot in the County.

Legalizing gambling and prostitution were state issues, and no one could figure out how Bardasian manipulated the ballot even though if they passed, the issues would not hold up in court or the state, so everyone thought he must have been trying to send some kind of message for the future. This was not true of alcohol. Legalizing alcohol had been on the ballots of many counties in Kentucky's history, but this was the first time the Lincoln County voters had faced the issue of making their county wet. Reporters from the Lexington and Louisville newspapers were down there reporting on the outcome.

Messiah had his thugs dispersed on Election Day. He had them positioned in all the voting areas including the Chapel Gap School House which had been closed for years, but where the tiny community voted. The Ottenheim Store was another voting place, and the early word was that the small Catholic Community would not oppose changing Lincoln County from "dry" to "wet."

The thugs spread rumors about an affair the Judge had with his secretary that no one knew about and shocked them. More rumors circulated that Birdstein was taking bribes, and that is why so many bootleggers didn't get judgments against them when appearing in the Stanford Court. There was no doubt that these rumors were damaging both the Judge and the Prosecutor, but there was little they could do about it. My dad and Sheriff Crane were traveling as well, countering these rumors with the idea that if Messiah had his way, and one of those people running for office on his ticket got elected, Bardasian would rule the county and the graft and destruction of their moral values would know no bounds.

No one had ever seen a protest or picket before in Lincoln County. Sinful places like Los Angeles or New York were known for demonstrations but never in a small city such as Stanford.

Messiah Bardasian was demonstrating in front of the Stanford Courthouse where many voters from the city were filing in to their precinct. The little guy was running up and down the street, and sometimes in the middle of the street with a sign that said, JUDGE WILLSTON IS AN ADULTERER - PROSECUTOR BIRDSTEIN IS A CROOK! Now and then, he would change his protest tactics by replacing his sign that read, BAPTISTS ARE HYPOCRITES. STOP LETTING THEM RUN YOUR LIVES! Large crowds gathered on both sides of Main to watch the feisty Armenian run up and down the street in his white silk suit, patent leather shoes, and gold chains flopping around his neck.

In the evening of the Election Day, and after the polls had closed, runners from every little hamlet in the Knobs came to Stanford Courthouse where the votes would be counted.

"Praise the Lord," the Preacher said as the County Clerk read the results to the hundreds of people waiting with interest in the streets for the final tally. Not since John F. Kennedy got elected, and the entire Republican County opposed his election because he was a Catholic, had such a crowd gathered in Stanford. Sheriff Crane and Trooper Tuck had the street blocked off on each end of Main Street to contain the crowd.

Messiah lost every way. The prostitution issue only got a few votes as the voters didn't take it serious, and the voters soundly defeated the gambling part of the ballot which got hundreds of "no" votes even though it was not a serious debate either. Making Lincoln County "wet" barely got defeated, which surprised all the church leaders who campaigned heavily against the issue. In fact, the Sheriff and the Judge made the counters recount twice. Every minister except the more liberal ones was scared the vote would pass, and for the first time ever, they would have to deal with liquor stores and drunken parties.

Judge Wilston got reelected, but barely, and so did Prosecutor Birdstein. They rode to victory on the coattails of these controversial referendums, but the Judge's credibility was never the same and the same for Birdstein. The Prosecutor was brought up on charges of corruption in a public office by the State Attorney General and was forced to resign in disgrace. Judge Wilston got defeated in the next election. The Prosecutor was sent to prison to join those he had helped put there, and the Judge retired and moved himself and his girlfriend up to Ohio near where Messiah Bardasian was from.

"We must make sure that our county never is faced with these immoral issues," my dad told his congregation the Sunday morning after the election. To this day, it never has been.

Messiah Bardasian was in depression. Never had he been defeated by any election he tried to rig. He had put all the muscle and horsepower he could muster behind his efforts, but the so-called Christians in the Knobs were too much for him. His own county up in Ohio was "wet," had brothels, and gambling where he could clean out the pockets of all takers. No one saw him for a long time. One night he was listening to Billy Graham in his Louisville Crusade, and it would forever change his life. "God loves you,"

Billy Graham said, and the power of his message got Messiah's attention. *Now there's a guy who's comfortable in his own skin,* Messiah thought, *so is that Preacher up on the hill.*

He hated my dad but with a respectful hatred because the Preacher had stood up to him. "All the money in the world can't buy that man," he told one of his thugs. He had considered one time about having my dad's legs broken but decided that would only make a martyr out of him and strengthen him further. Now, here was a very powerful man on television telling the same message the Preacher told, "God loves you and died for your sins."

One Sunday night, Messiah drove up to Evergreen Baptist Church in his new 1963 Cadillac. He didn't come into the building and resisted anyone approaching his car and inviting him in. He sat on the outside of the building listening to the Preacher preach. As the congregation filed out, every eye noticing him, he waited until my dad finished shaking hands. Sheriff Crane wasn't budging his pickup until he knew that my dad was all right. He felt that maybe Messiah was up there to take revenge on the Preacher and kill him in cold blood at his own church.

"Hey, Preacher!" Messiah called out and ignoring everyone around him. "Can I speak with you?"

Fran heard this from down in the cemetery. He pretended to be going home, but he crouched behind a tombstone and watched for any action. He ran back to the church.

"Okay," my dad said keeping his distance and turning his body sideways so as to make himself harder to shoot. "What do you want?"

"Come over here," Messiah ordered, trying to be humble, which was hard for him.

"Don't do it, Preacher," Sheriff Crane warned.

"Shut up, you wannabe cop. I'm not gonna hurt him."

My dad approached Messiah's Cadillac moving sideways toward him at an odd angle, keeping his eyes keen for any sudden movement. Messiah sighed real hard and then put his empty hands outside his window and leaned on the door.

"Get in the car with me, lets take a ride," Messiah said.

Sheriff Crane shook his head "no" as my dad glanced over at him standing by his truck with his hand on his pistol grip.

"Well, I guess," my dad agreed as the Sheriff looked blank with surprise.

They drove off the property and headed toward Ottenheim, gravel kicking up behind the heavy Cadillac. *Smoother than a cloud,* my dad thought as the limousine took every washboard and chuckhole in the road as if they were riding on a super highway. Sheriff Crane was close behind them keeping a watch for anything unusual developing. The Sheriff slammed on his brakes and jumped from his pickup when Messiah, for no reason whatever, pulled into a dark alley that lead into the Macmillan's cornfield. The big read taillights lit up the entire area when Messiah pushed on the brake pedal.

Messiah put the Cadillac in park and leaned close to my dad. "Preacher, what do I need to do to go to heaven?" He asked lugubriously.

My dad caught his breath. He couldn't believe this question was coming out of such a vile and vulgar individual. My dad suddenly thought of an illustration he had heard once in Bible College. "Well, first of all, Mr. Bardasian, you have to get dressed up in that pretty silk suit of yours, all dolled up like you're going to a dance or something." Baptists didn't dance. "Then, you have to go down to your hog pen all full of slop and mud and filthy pig's dung."

"What else?" Messiah asked feeling the smoothness of his pants between his thumb and forefinger and noting this unusual method of getting to heaven. He couldn't imagine that every convert in the Evergreen Baptist Church was required to do this.

"Then you have to get down in that hog wallow on all fours, all dirty and muddy, and wet, and look up to heaven."

"Yes, yes?" Messiah asked.

"And then," my dad went on, "you have to look up toward heaven and say, Lord Jesus forgive me a dirty rotten sinner."

"But, I don't have any hogs," Messiah said.

"You can always do it at my farm, if you're serious." The Preacher figured the pig business would discourage Messiah. He would never do that in a million years.

Messiah ordered my dad out of his car, and then the Preacher slid into the Sheriff's pickup and watched Messiah speed toward Ottenheim.

"What'd he want?" The Sheriff was in a hurry to find out.

My dad told him the story, and the Sheriff said, "he's up to something, you'd better be careful with that man."

The Preacher never heard another word from Messiah Bardasian for two weeks. He was still tying to figure out what Messiah was up to the night he came to church. Good or bad, he didn't know, and then he found out.

The Preacher stirred in his sleep. Fran was spending the night at our house, and the noise woke us up. "Someone's yelling at the front door," my mom sleepily whispered to my dad. "Who is it, you think?" She asked.

"I don't know, but whoever the idiot is, he better have a very good excuse like somebody died or something for waking me up at this ungodly hour."

Fran and I were speechless as we watched from my bedroom window at the crazy little man on the front porch banging his fist on the screen door, screaming something incoherent, and dressed like a ballroom dancer.

Dad turned on the porch light and opened the door. In front of him stood a sight he never in his wildest imaginations thought he would ever behold. Messiah was dressed in his black patent leather shoes, his beautiful silk suit, and his gold rings and bracelets. His hair was cut and combed to perfection, not one of his hairs out of place, and my dad thought how impressive the man looked. The Preacher stood paralyzed for a moment and then asked, "what can I do for you, Mr. Bardasian?"

"Preacher, I want to do what that black man did in the story you were telling me. Show me the pig sty."

"I'll get my shoes," my dad replied.

Messiah was crawling through the fence. My dad held one strand of barbed wire with his hand and the other with his foot making a hole large enough for Messiah to crawl through. When Messiah was half way through the fence, and one shoe already in the thick muck on the pig's side, my dad said, "Mr. Bardasian, you don't have to crawl in there with your Sunday best clothes."

"What do you mean?" Messiah asked while looking up at the Preacher.

"Well, here's the rest of that story I was telling you in the car the other night. You only have to be willing to."

No one ever saw Messiah again. He left his farm although he didn't sell it. He paid to have it mowed and made a deal with one of the farmers. The contract stated that the farm's land remained free as long as the farmer stayed away from his house and took care of the property. He could give half the profits to himself, and the other half to the Evergreen Baptist church.

CHAPTER FORTY-FOUR

Missionary Night was one of our favorite times at the church. My dad would invite men to speak to the church who worked on the foreign fields giving their lives to the indoctrination and civilizing of peoples in far away lands. All the young people loved these special times because most of the missionaries would bring slides and show their work. I learned a lot by watching these most intriguing documentaries. I especially loved the slides of Brazil. I was fascinated with the country and its mystique. I fantasized about traveling up and down the rivers into the deepest unexplored jungles of wild animals and uncivilized natives.

My dad announced that Missionary Bob Crawford would be at our church that night and that he would have slides to show. When Fran and I got to the church, the parking lot was full and more cars and pickup trucks were arriving than we had seen at a Sunday night service for quite some time. It was not uncommon to have a hard time finding a seat during one of these events. In fact, my dad had stopped inviting missionaries in the winter months because as it would be this particular Sunday night, many people simply could not get inside the building. In the warm spring and summer months, the large windows of the church would be opened and men could stand on the outside and watch the show through the windows.

Missionary Crawford was serving deep in the jungles of the Acre Territory which at that time was not yet one of the States of Brazil. It was rumored that his post was only miles from known headhunters and he was blazing a trail for God in the most heathen and pagan world of unbelievers.

There were two people in the 1960 Ford Falcon as the missionary drove into the Evergreen Baptist Church parking lot. Mr. Crawford and his son. We watched with curiosity as the two started unloading their gear that would be used for the presentation that evening. A young, wiry, and handsome boy got out of the car. He was tanned and had platinum blond hair, crystal blue eyes, and almost haunting was their brilliance. "I'd kill for hair that color," one of the redheaded girls said. He was an inch or so taller than Fran and me and was dressed in blue jeans and a t-shirt.

We didn't like missionary kids much. They all seemed "holier than thou," my mother used to say. Most of the boys we considered sissies by the way they clung to their mothers. They always seemed afraid of us, or at least they acted this way, and it seemed they thought we boys from the Knobs were as wild and heathen as the natives they were ministering to in the jungles of the world. It was difficult to make any connection with these kids, so we didn't.

This kid in blue jeans seemed different. Mainly because he was wearing blue jeans and not store bought pants and a tie. He glanced at me, and behind those pale blue eyes, he seemed to be peering deep into my soul. I was intrigued by him and somewhat nervous about him. Little did I know that the boy would become a friend, and the friendship like mine with Fran, would be there for a lifetime.

There was plenty of time before the service on this warm summer evening, so as was our custom, all the boys were back at the outhouse smoking and yelling at the girls standing in line across the cemetery waiting for their turn in the ladies room.

I stood by the Sycamore tree puffing, hiding myself so as not to be seen by the Preacher. It was still the rule that virtually every member of the church knew I smoked, but no one ever mentioned it to my dad. Fran poked me on the arm and pointed to the path coming from the church. The kid was walking toward us. This was very unusual because we often thought of how those other missionary kids who came to our church could seem to get by without ever going to the outhouse. It was a known fact that most of the missionaries who brought their families to our church, told their children to stay away from the outhouses at Evergreen Baptist Church because the kids there were pagans. We thought the boy was either insane or very brave as he made his way toward us. We figured the kid didn't know the "missionary rule." One time after one of the missionaries came with his whole family, which contained a lot of kids, one of the guys saw him stop beside the road after he left the church and let his whole family, six kids in all, relieve themselves in the grader ditch beside his parked car. That was especially funny because the kid who said this, told us that the missionary's wife had a big fat rear end "white as a sheep's butt; it looked like a full moon shining in the dark," he said.

Buster Kirk hated every missionary kid that came to the church. Many times he tried to intimidate them and made fun of them until Bro. Lord, or one of the other men in the church, made him stop. When Buster saw the kid coming down the path he hustled around the outhouse and stood in his way.

"What's your name, boy?" Buster snidely asked.

"Mark," he answered respectfully.

"This here toilet's for church members, and you ain't no church member," Buster explained.

"I am too a church member. I'm a member of my church in Cruzeiro Do Sul Acre Do Brasil." This was the first time we had ever heard anyone speak a foreign language although Abe Job spoke German but kept it to himself.

"Cuckason chicken dung cazeel ain't Evergreen Baptist Church," Buster poked.

"I just want to use the toilet," he explained.

"Then do it the missionary way and pee on the road at the top of Chapel Gap Hill. That's what all the rest of em do," Buster shouted.

"That kid's going to fight," Fran said quietly in my ear.

"How do you know?" I asked curiously.

"He hasn't blinked his eyes once. That's what fighters do in the jungle when they are facing danger," he explained judiciously. I had no idea how Fran acquired this kind of information.

I watched the kid's eyes and he didn't blink. Instead, he looked at Buster Kirk square in his eye and stared at him. *Fran might be right,* I thought because I read once where ninety eight percent of the gunfighters of the Old West had piercing blue eyes and stared their opponents down. Bat Masterson said once that "Matt Dillon told me to put down my gun and hang it on the post outside of Dodge because no one carried a gun in Dodge. He was my friend, and I told him I couldn't do that, so he stared at me with those piercing deep blue eyes, and I hung up my gun."

The boy was calm, and Buster who was taller than him

stared down at him, but the kid never moved a muscle. He stood there staring back at Buster, not blinking once. I did notice that Buster seemed unnerved by this tactic and looked away a time or two only to come back with his eyes and finding the boy still fixated directly at him. They did look like two gunfighters facing each other down. The first one to make a move would lose.

Finally, Buster took a step closer to the boy and almost to his face. The missionary kid started to step around him, but Buster stuck his foot in the way, blocking his path. No threats were made by either man, but we all knew Buster. When this Mark Crawford didn't turn tail and run, it was an assault to Buster's nature as a bully. He would make the first move, and he would lose.

Mark stepped again to his side and again Buster quickly blocked his way. Then Buster made the mistake of his life; he hit the kid in the arm pretty hard to see what he would do. When Mark didn't react, Buster hit him again on the other arm. Again, Mark didn't flinch and then he did something that shocked us all. He turned his face sideways and told Buster to slap him on the cheek.

"That's girl fighting," Buster chided.

"Do it anyway and see what happens," Mark replied.

Buster thought about hitting with his fist, but the boy specifically asked him to slap him. He unfolded his knuckles and with his open hand, he slapped the missionary kid as hard as he could. The blow could be heard all the way to the church as he caught Mark Crawford, missionary kid, flush on the face with his calloused palm.

Buster stepped back waiting for the response, but there was none. The boys watching this weird way of fighting were laughing now. "Yep, he's a sissy," they exclaimed, "he's felt Buster's power and now he's scared."

Mark stuck out his face showing his other cheek as he turned his head. "Now, slap this one," he instructed.

"This is chickencrap," Buster said, "you gonna do nothin but run back in there to your daddy."

"Slap me and see," the boy said again standing in the same position. Buster look around him with a smirk on this face while some of the boys were nodding for him to go ahead. Buster hauled off and slapped the kid even harder on the other cheek. The kid's head went sideways with the blow, and his face contorted at the impact, but he didn't lose his footing. This made Buster even madder. He swung his fist, sending it flying toward the boy's jaw.

"I'll teach you a lesson, honey," Buster screamed.

We all knew that if Buster Kirk's fist connected, this kid was going to lalaland with a broken jaw or worse. That didn't happen. Just as Buster's blow was about to hit its target, the kid blocked his punch with his left arm. So rigid was the block that Buster's punch did not even move his arm a hair. At the same time, the kid raked his leg with lightning speed, catching Buster in the left calf and sending him reeling with both feet coming out from under him and landed him with a thud as his back hit the hard pack of the outhouse path.

We watched with wonder and awe at this demonstration of strength and unusual skill. We had never seen anyone fight like this before. Buster lay rubbing his calf muscle, quickly trying to ease the cramp that was setting in from the swift blow, and then jumped to his feet. The kid never made one aggressive move. He would stay on the defense and that would be the undoing of Buster Kirk and his big mouth.

Buster threw another punch, and this one was blocked easily, and the other leg of the missionary kid caught Buster behind his right calf sending him back down to the hard ground once again. Buster was now hurting in both calves, and he was slightly resisting the temptation to try again, the pain was so great, but he couldn't be embarrassed like this in front of all his peers.

Buster struggled up again, but this time he didn't throw a punch, he rushed the kid with all his power, but the boy stepped back calmly and caught both Kirk's arms between his in a circular motion, twisting Buster's hands out of position and horribly backwards, rendering him squealing and begging in agony. Then Mark Crawford slowly, methodically, released his grip, fell to his back on the ground, put his feet in Buster's belly, pulled with his own arms on Buster's hands, and kicked him at least six feet in the air and over the missionary kid's head, landing Buster ten feet away on his face.

No one moved as the boy strolled to the outhouse. He relieved himself and then walked coolly back to the church, acknowledging each one of us with a nod of his head as if nothing had ever happened.

Girls were giggling and pointing at Mark and making eyes at him all the way through the service. It was duly noted that the Preacher turned off the lights to make the slide show easier to see, and some pretty heavy making out took place in the Evergreen Baptist Church during these times of planned darkness. It was one time Fran and my sister could hold hands without being seen.

Most of the time when missionaries would come, the slide program consisted of picture after picture, showing people who had become converts and very boring, but this presentation by Missionary Crawford was different. I sat there thinking about how the jungle must look and feel. He showed pictures of trees of monkeys and wild beautiful birds such as the Macaw, parrot, and rare birds like the Japiim. I thought about how neat it would be to see that Toucan with the large beak flying over the jungle. He showed pictures of huge snakes. The Anaconda and Boa Constrictor were intimidating creatures to meet up with. One picture showed his son, Mark, holding a huge live Boa with perhaps ten feet of its thick body wrapped around his neck. This kid was no sissy.

The Crawfords were boat builders, and picture after picture showed how swift the speedboats Mr. Crawford built would go up and down the rivers. Those craft were the first the Acre natives had ever seen, and Crawford's reputation as being a God traveled far into the interior.

The town where the Crawfords lived was called Cruziero Do Sul, which means the "Cross of the South" and lies strategically under the great Southern Cross, a constellation seen only in the Southern Hemisphere from which this small jungle settlement took its name.

I thought about how isolated Chapel Gap was from the outside world, and in America where things were quickly changing, we were sheltered and caught in time warps that would not loosen their grips. For the first time, I wanted to be away from Chapel Gap. I wanted to explore my own country, see big cities with skyscrapers, and then travel to dangerous and remote areas of the earth.

I was intrigued beyond comfort, at least for me. Those areas in Brazil where the Crawfords lived was far more remote and dangerous than Chapel Gap with all its rough housing bootleggers. The missionary told of headhunters less than forty miles from his station, and he showed a picture of several shrunken heads in a dug out canoe that one of the native Brazilian missionaries under Mr. Crawford's tutorship had found on a trip into the interior. The missionary grabbed the canoe as it floated freely down the swift Japiim River; it occupants missing.

It was no wonder that Mark Crawford was so lean and muscled. The boy worked harder than we did on the tobacco farms. During this presentation, it was revealed how the Missionary's son found his fighting form and strong legs, strong enough to knock a big guy like Buster Kirk off his feet. Mark Crawford was a star soccer player. We had never been introduced to soccer, and I doubted we ever would. We knew about the game, but it was not seriously played in the United States and never in Chapel Gap. None of us were interested in the game or cared about it. Soccer would never be played by any serious athletes in the United States. We did believe; however, that this kid would make a great football player, and especially a kicker.

No one minded that the presentation took more than two hours. We were all fascinated and particularly myself. Buster Kirk stayed conspicuously away from Mark Crawford after the service. He was seen sitting behind the wheel of his mother's 1959 Ford waiting for her to quit gossiping so that he could get out of there.

"Mark, my name is Sonny, and this is Fran." I introduced Fran and me.

He stuck out his hand. We noticed how calloused his hand was; calloused as the two of us, and he had a very strong grip.

"I'm pleased to meet you," he greeted.

"Hey, where are you and your dad going from here?" I asked. "I'd like to see that show again."

"We're going to a little town called Mount Vernon, Kentucky."

"That's not very far, where you gonna sleep?" I asked.

"We'll sleep in our car; we do that a lot when back in this country."

"It's only thirty miles or so to Mount Vernon, so why don't we ask your dad to spend the night at our house?" Fran volunteered my family's house as his own.

"Far out," he said.

We rushed over to the Preacher who was talking with the Missionary.

516 · SHERMAN SMITH

"Hey, dad," I called. "These brethren here have no place to sleep tonight." I don't think my dad had ever heard me call any Christian bothers, "brethren." He looked pleased.

My dad made the formal invitation for the Crawfords to spend the night and make their way to Mount Vernon the next day. Later that night, Fran, Mark, and me, stood by the barn talking while Mark explained the Southern Cross and why his city of Cruzeiro Do Sul had such a name.

"Ever go giggin?" Fran asked out of nowhere as if he wasn't paying attention to the geography lesson.

"What's that?" The missionary's son asked.

"Bud and I wade the creeks and spear fish."

"Far out, he said. "We do that in the Jurura River with real spears." Fran and I couldn't fathom that. "It's too dangerous to be wading in the rivers and creeks with the Piranha, crocodile, and big snakes, so we spear from the banks."

"What's a Piranha?" Fran asked.

"Man eating fish with razor sharp teeth. Piranha's can eat a wild boar in seconds and reduce it to nothing but floating blood; they don't leave a scrap. They can kill a man in fewer seconds."

Fran and I looked at each other, and we were thinking the same thing. "Snakes, crocodiles, man-eating fish? This makes our trips to the creeks with some Copperheads, Cottonmouths, and Gars seem pretty tame.

Around midnight, we were walking through the woods to our favorite gigging spots. Mark had never seen a carbide light before and was quite fascinated with the small contraption that could put out so much light. He told us that in the jungle, they used torches that accomplished the same thing, but the carbide lamps would be more convenient. He also said they spot the red eyes of the crocodiles while drifting in a dugout canoe, and sometimes he or his dad would jump in the river and catch the crocs by hand. My little world of adventure was taking another step backwards as I listened to him talk about real adventure, and I wanted to experience that more than anything in the world.

We slipped carefully into the creek, and when Fran handed Mark a gig, he seemed to not know what to do with it. "I don't want one of those," he said, "it will tear up the fish."

"Then how you gonna catch one?" Fran asked disbelieving that Mark had ever gone fish hunting at night.

Mark said nothing until we came to the first riffle where a couple of bigmouth bass flopped in the shallows. "Stand in front of the fish with the carbide and hold it steady," he suddenly instructed. Fran and I always came to the fish from behind with our lights and stuck our gigs into the fish. I stepped in front of the fish and carefully shined the light directly into the face of the fish as I was told. Fran stood still and watched Mark sneak up to the fish, and with his bare hands, thrust his arms into the water without making a splash, and caught the fish.

"Don't tear up the fish," he said matter of fact.

This amazed us, so Fran and I quit gigging and for the rest of the night, we watched with wonder and awe at this agile Brazilian American teach us a lesson about catching fish. We tried it ourselves several times but couldn't quite get the hang of it. Fran finally did snag a small sucker using this method, and I knew that he would be trying this many times until he had perfected the method.

We built a fire after gigging, and Mark showed us how to roast fish on a makeshift spit over the fire. This may have been the most delicious meal I ever had, smoked fish. Who would ever think you could eat fish this way? Fish were made to be fried, not smoked. He told story after story about his adventures growing up in Brazil. He taught us how to say, "Bom Dia," good morning in Portuguese, and "Eu Amo Ti," I love you. I wanted to learn that important phrase so I could impress Kathy Friday.

Mark was so good at story telling that I felt myself standing in the steaming jungle watching the river banks for crocodile and man eating fish.

"I'd give anything to go to Brazil," I said longingly.

"Why don't you?" Mark said, and I laughed. "I'm serious, man," he reacted.

"How can I do that?"

"Come with us when we go back next year. You could come and stay on our boat for as long as you like."

"I have to go to college," I replied.

"Go down there," he said.

"I could do that?"

"Sure, apply for a foreign exchange program, and the Brazilian Government will send a student to the United States to live and go to school, and your education will be paid for. That's how I'm going to college here in the United States in a couple of years."

I had never heard of such a thing, but suddenly, I was filled with hope and enthusiasm that maybe this could happen.

"Your dad would be okay with this?" I asked doubtfully.

"More than okay, let's do it."

"How about you Fran? Would you go with me?"

"Not me, Bud, never, no way. I'm going to the Navy."

I was startled for a moment, and I stared at Fran in utter disbelief. How long had he been planning this? Why didn't he reveal his plot to me? I would ask him about it later.

My mom put some fish on ice to send over to Pastor Don Stayton at the Bible Baptist Church in Mount Vernon, and the Crawfords drove out of our farm lane and headed toward Crab Orchard.

"Fran? Why didn't you tell me about your plans to join the Navy?"

"Because, Bud, I knew it would upset you."

"You know I would rather go with you to the Navy than to Brazil."

"The Navy's not for you, Bud."

"Why not?"

"Discipline. You hate to take orders worse than anyone I've ever seen. I don't even know how you're going to work for somebody after you leave the farm; you hate other people bossing you around so badly."

"I don't understand," I said timidly.

Then he told me. "Remember a few weeks ago when Gib Kirk told you to come off the top rail of the barn where you had climbed assuming that was where you were going to hang the tobacco?"

"Yeah?"

"You told him to go to hell; that you weren't gonna hang on the bottom rail and that the top was where you always were. Do you understand why he fired you and told you, you could never work for him again?"

I was beginning to understand. "What's the point?" I asked.

"The point is, Bud, that the first Navy officer that gives you an order you don't like, you're gonna end up court marshaled."

Fran's wisdom was too high for me to fully comprehend, but he was right. I despised anyone telling me what to do. The only reason I wasn't in a reform school somewhere was because I respected my dad so much that I obeyed everything he told me to do.

Fran wasn't finished. "Do you know that I only suggest things to you instead of telling you this or that or the other? It's because you would hate me, and our friendship would never last a week."

"I would never hate you, Fran."

"If I started giving orders, you would."

CHAPTER FORTY-FIVE

I n our seventeenth year, after tobacco season was over and Fran and me could catch our breath, my dad called off the double date rule, which would make my sister wait until she was fifteen years old, and decided to let her date even though she was only fourteen. This made me sick because I knew every time I would want to date Kathy Friday alone, Leah would make a big deal out of it and insist that she and Fran be allowed to tag along. I argued about this with my dad and tried to convince him that she was only a mere child and shouldn't be permitted to date boys in a car double date or not. This was upsetting Fran, and when I suggested he find someone else to date, it almost ruined our friendship. I was stuck babysitting my sister on date nights.

"Is your sister coming with us again?" Kathy Friday asked when I picked her up at her farm. I knew she was getting tired of this. "Can't we just go to a movie or something? By ourselves?"

Taking a girl to a movie wasn't something I expected to be doing since Baptists weren't supposed to go to movies and when I went, I had to sneak. The Liberal Pastor Ledbetter didn't see anything wrong with movies, so his young people weren't forbidden to go as were the young people of Evergreen Baptist Church, who violated the rule anyway, but not officially. I didn't agree with the law either and accepted the opinion of the liberal Ledbetter that if it is wrong to attend movies, we shouldn't be watching television. The argument was that going to movies was supporting Hollywood and nothing good ever came out of Hollywood. Television was free, so we didn't directly support Hollywood. Pastor Ledbetter said that buying the products in the stores that advertised on television was the same thing. He argued that they had to get money somewhere, and the same studios that produced movies, produced TV shows. Even I could figure that out but for some reason, my dad couldn't. "Besides," Ledbetter explained one Sunday to his church, "They show the same movies on television after they have sold all the tickets they can sell in the movie houses." If I didn't love my dad so much, I would have gone over and joined Brother Ledbetter's church.

My dad about went berserk when Pastor Don Stayton at Mount Vernon told his young people that they could go to movies, and he let the women wear pants. He almost died when he found out that Pastor Ledbetter and Pastor Stayton were going to allow their high school seniors to attend the senior prom. When I heard this, I knew I was going to have some problems. Kathy Friday would expect me to take her to the prom, so how was I going to handle that situation?

"Damned if I do, and damned if I don't. If I don't take Kathy Friday to the prom, she'll dump me, and if I do, my dad will kick me out of the house." I complained to Fran.

I was having a slight problem with Kathy Friday, anyway.

I had dated her several times with my sister and Fran, and on the one and only occasion we could be alone and talk, she hurt me badly.

We were parked by a popular lake in Crab Orchard on a Saturday evening. We had tired of skating, and without much else to do, we became accustomed to driving out and parking at the lake. The girls didn't fish, or Fran and I would gladly have taken them fishing. The only restaurant around was the Dairy Queen over in Brodhead, and my dad wouldn't let Leah go that far. We couldn't go to the movies, couldn't dance, so we improvised. We found a spot by Scott's Lake, which was a popular place for late night lovers. We, of course, were not late night lovers, so we were gone when the heavy daters came in. We would sit and listen to the radio. Kathy Friday and I, nor Leah and Fran did much talking with so many people in the car. It was tight quarters in the little Volkswagen so privacy was forfeited. Once in a while, Fran and I would squeeze our girls' hands when some nice romantic song was being played, and that was about it.

That night Fran decided that he and Leah should take a walk "BY OURSELVES" he pointed out although he and Leah were the intruders and this was my car. Kathy Friday and I saw them walking over by the lake holding hands and shuffling along.

How could he care about a little kid like that? I thought and then I leaned over to kiss Kathy Friday. This was a bold move since there had been no kisses since the night I said I was sorry for lying to the church at Copper Creek.

Kathy Friday put her hands on my chest and pushed me off. "Whoa, Buster!"

She cried.

I managed to unmask my shock and asked, "What's the matter?"

"We're not going steady," she exclaimed, and I thought we were.

"I thought we were!" I cried.

"What made you think that?" She said while the Sherells were singing, "Soldier Boy."

" I well," I cleared my throat. "Well, you kissed me at the church that night and told me you love me."

"I didn't say, I LOVE you, I said, I love you."

"What's the difference? You said it."

"I said I love you like a brother in Christ, not I love you like a boyfriend."

"But your dad said it was okay to date you and maybe get married."

"Bull crap," she cussed, "he doesn't tell me who I'm going to marry, never. He was just running his mouth."

Was I was crushed? First because she cussed, and I never in my wildest imaginations would ever think she would cuss. Jane Pat cussed, and so did Rosalie Barker, but not Kathy Friday! Second, I assumed that because she said she loved me, she meant it romantically. I felt like a fool.

Then Kathy Friday delivered the dagger of daggers into my soul. She let it fly and twisted the blade until the agony was more than I could bear. I felt sick, and I wanted to die right then and there. I wanted to fling myself into Scott's Lake with a big rock tied around my neck and drown my troubles.

"Who?" Somehow I knew I shouldn't have asked this question.

"Charlie Bumgarten and Norris Wells."

My lips turned inside out, and I almost bit my tongue in two. Those were two of the worse enemies I'd ever had. They were making a fool out of me, and so was she. Charlie Bumgarten was one of the smartest boys in Lincoln County schools. He attended school at Brodhead High, and the paper had just announced that he received a Merit Scholarship because he scored higher on his ACT and SAT tests than anyone in the state. Norris Wells was the hot rod type. He went to school at Rockcastle High in Mount Vernon, and his dad was a State Senator. He cruised around Crab Orchard sometimes in his 1932 Ford Roadster all chopped down with flames running down the sides. Both of these guys made me sick.

She wasn't done. She stabbed me again. "Charlie's taking me to the Senior Prom next spring." She announced this like it was nothing; a nonchalant proclamation that was simply a matter of fact. She was ripping my guts out. I had feelings of anguish I never felt before. This was painful. I wrenched in agony; I couldn't get my breath as she was breaking my heart.

"What's wrong with him?" My sister asked as she climbed into the back seat of the Volkswagen.

"I don't know," Kathy Friday said, "he ain't talking to me."

We took Kathy Friday home first, which was required by my dad so that I didn't have to double back through Crab Orchard, waste gas, and be out too late. I didn't open the door for her, and I didn't walk her to the door. I would never open another door for her the rest of my life because I would never see her again.

On the way back to Chapel Gap, my sister kept bugging me about why I was so quiet and looked like "a calf in a dying snowstorm." She picked up this expression from my mother.

"You look like a calf in a dying snowstorm!" My mom said as I skipped spending the night with Fran and went straight to my room.

That night I was not going to sleep. I was angry, frustrated, heartsick, nervous, homesick, sweating, and sleep was not possible. If love was this hard, I never want to love anyone again. *I can't take this,* I thought, *how do people do it?* Then, I fell asleep from sheer exhaustion.

Kathy Friday shut the door behind her that opened to her room. She fell back against the door and took a deep breath. She was heartsick herself. "I really did say I love you to Sonny, and I really mean it. I would love to marry that boy, but I can't wait two or three years for him to get back from some god-forsaken jungle. He wants that trip more than he wants me," she whispered aloud to no one.

Kathy Friday decided to end our relationship before she got in deeper. She was sick of my sister tagging along on every date; not being able to do anything but listen to the stupid radio and look at a stupid lake. She knew our Pastors weren't in agreement and that in itself was causing problems. Yes, this was the best way, so she took me out at the knees and dropped kicked me through the goal posts of life. She cut me like a surgeon for my pride would never let me approach her again. She picked two of the most obnoxious boys she could find to obliterate my feelings and drive me into depression.

I did everything I could to rebel against all that my dad taught and preached. I went so far as to enroll in an experimental class at school that taught Evolution for the first time at Crab Orchard High. This was causing quite a stir among the Christian community, and I was even thinking about how much sense it made. This was so vile and so threatening to the Christian world that even liberals Pastor Otis Ledbetter and Pastor Don Stayton led their churches to the first protest by picket since Messiah Bardasian ran up and down the streets with his signs on election day. I was seen as on the side of the few that thought it was okay to teach that men evolved from monkeys, which evolved from one celled microscopic animals spontaneously generated in the seas billions of years ago.

"You've got to stop this, Bud," Fran warned, "you're ruining your Christian testimony."

"I've got no testimony," I said, "I don't need one."

I had never tasted alcohol. One night I threw in with Buster Kirk and a couple of other boys. Buster loved the fact that I got ditched by Kathy Friday. He didn't think I was ever a good Christian so to prove it; he invited me to go with him and the guys over to Buck Creek and buy some beer.

We drove over there and found Wendell Johnson selling booze out of his trunk by the creek. We paid for the beer, Pabst Blue Ribbon, and headed back to Chapel Gap to try it out.

On the way, Buster and I were drinking. I hated the taste of the stuff. To me, it tasted worse than buttermilk, and I hated buttermilk. I thought it was unfit for human consumption, and I wouldn't be near it. Beer tasted worse, but I kept drinking it, and it wasn't long before I felt really funny.

"He's drunk on one half pint of beer," Buster Kirk laughed although he was drunk himself on not much more. "He can't hold his liquor!" The others roared with the quip.

By 11:00 PM, and time for me to check into my house, we were all drunk. We were sitting in a stream that branched off Cedar Creek and where boys and men drove their cars to wash them. When Buster looked at his watch, it was midnight.

"Holy crap!" Buster screamed. He would have his own problems at home for being out this long.

I don't remember the driver of the car, but he tore out of the little lane and slid the car sideways in the gravel on Chapel Gap Road.

"Take me home first," Buster demanded even though it would be a much less punishment on him than me.

The car fishtailed wildly throwing rocks all over the sides of the road and kicking up a cloud of dust behind us. The driver could barely keep the car between the ditches, and he was going very fast. Then we saw a flashing light from the cop car behind us. "CRAP!" We all said at once.

"Hello boys," Tip Tuck said as he walked up to the window.

"Get out of the car." He looked at me and glared. I sobered up, quickly.

It turned out that the driver didn't have a license, had been arrested for driving under the influence a couple of times, and Tip charged him for contributing to the delinquency of a minor.

This is a mess, I thought as I sat in the jail cell in Stanford. Tip didn't say a word to me. It turned out that my dad had called Tip and told him to be on the lookout for Buster and me. My mom heard Loretta Kirk telling Sophie Lord on the phone that Buster was taking me out to make a man out of me.

The jailer came and got Buster first. I heard Loretta screaming at him after she paid his fine. It seemed to me that she was madder that she had to get up in the middle of the night than that her son was drinking. It wouldn't be that way with my dad. I waited all night. I jumped up and held onto the bars every time the door of the Sheriff's office opened. I hadn't seen Sheriff Crane either, but I figured I would sooner or later. I waited all day, and all day the next day and still no one came to get me. Then someone did. It was the jailer coming to take me across the street to court. He led me in the common area of the prison, and there stood my dad.

Of all the trouble I had ever been in, this was surely doomsday for me. My dad paid my bill, and I followed him to his car parked on the street. This was going to be a long ride home. We headed up the Chapel Gap Hill and then pulled into our yard. Fran was coming out of the house as I walked toward the barn. I had made the trip many times.

"He's messed up in the head," Fran told my dad. "No way he's himself right now."

"He has to be punished," my dad responded.

"Not the way you do it," and this statement startled my dad as Fran challenged his authority to discipline his own child.

"What do you mean?"

"You've whipped him way too much and way too hard," Fran explained. "You've only made him more careful not to get caught and calloused him. He'll take the beating and just keep on doing the same things except he'll get worse. My mom and dad never whipped me once in my life, never laid a finger on me, and I think I'm a good Christian. They taught me how to respect them, and they didn't need to punish me because of respect or beat it into me; I didn't do things that hurt them to get back at them. There has always been a mutual trust between them and me. Sonny's not doing things on purpose; he's getting back at you for all those severe whippings you've given him in his life."

"The Bible says that if you spare the rod, you spoil the child," Fran.

"Look at me, Preacher, do I look spoiled? My parents don't have a pot to pee in or a window to throw it out of and neither do I. Do you actually think the Bible means a ROD as in a literal ROD? If you're going to take that literal, then use a rod instead of a stick or belt. It's the ROD of discipline, Preacher, and there are many ways to discipline and correct a child without beating the kid half to death. You show me one place in the Bible where Jacob whipped his twelve boys with a stick, or better still, David was a good kid but nowhere in the Scripture does it say that his dad, Jesse, whipped him till the blood flowed from his back."

At first my dad thought that Fran must be studying some far out Psychology course at school, and it was messing him up, but he thought about it some more. What he was doing wasn't working so maybe he should listen to Fran. He took one look at the barn, and I shuttered as I stood in the open door, shirt off, and waiting for my discipline by the rod. The most astounding thing then happened. My dad took a long look at me and then walked toward the house. I thought he might be getting his gun.

"You better listen to me and listen well, Bud. You've got one chance now so don't mess it up. Get yourself straightened out. If you keep going the way you are now, nobody will know who you are. Remember this. What you are becoming right now is what you will be at age forty."

I couldn't comprehend being as old as forty, but I knew I was miserable and needed to do something with myself. *Get over Kathy Friday and move on,* I reasoned was the best answer to my dilemma.

"Okay, Fran, but is the coast clear?" I still didn't trust my dad to not beat me for drinking.

"It's clear, he won't do nothing, not this time."

I was so grateful even though Fran wouldn't tell me what he said to my dad. "Confidential is confidential," Fran explained.

I knew what I had to do, so would I do it? "Did the beer taste good?" My dad asked.

"Honestly dad, I hated it. It tasted worse than buttermilk."

That's all he said about the whole situation except that he wanted me to repay him for my bond, which was a whopping ten dollars, a lot of money for me. The judge never took us to court. My dad went down there and talked to him and told him I had learned my lesson. Out of respect of the Preacher, nothing more was said about the entire incident until Buster Kirk brought it up one day at church behind the outhouse.

"You should have seen him," Buster said, "his eyes were all crossed, and he looked real stupid. He can't hold an ounce of beer without getting drunk, and he said some crazy things." He told them some of the things I couldn't possibly have said. Vile things that I wouldn't say even if I were drunker than drunk. I'd had enough of him and his mouth.

"Hey pig breath," I called to him.

"What'd you say?" He asked surprised.

"I said you're a lying sack of pig crap."

Kirk had rage in his eyes. He didn't like me and never had. He was jealous of me, and the relationship I had with his dad, Gib. Even though Mr. Kirk said I couldn't ever work for him again, he still wanted me to come over and play their old piano. He would sit by the stove on winter nights and asked me to play "The Old Rugged Cross." One time when I was playing, Buster was sticking his finger in his throat acting like he wanted to throw up.

This fight was about to begin, and no one had seen me fight since I fought in the hay field with that kid years earlier. One of my friends, Junebug, started to get between me and the larger Kirk, but Fran held him back. "He'll take care of himself," Fran told Junebug, and he stepped back out of the way.

Buster Kirk stood taller than me by four or five inches. He faced me, and I said, "Slap this," as I stuck out my cheek. The boys laughed, but not Buster. His calves were still sore from the swift kicking by the missionary boy, who took him down.

"Oh, HA, no way you're going to kick me." He taunted me and then slapped me up side my head. The blow almost took my head off, but I didn't feel the pain as the open palm made my cheek numb.

I stuck out the other cheek. "Slap this," I said, and even Fran was curious as to what I was thinking.

"If he tries to fight like Mark Crawford," Fran commented, "Kirk will kill him."

"Sure," Buster said and then he slapped me on the other side of the face. That hurt me, and my cheeks felt like somebody had lit a fire to them. Kirk stepped back ready for the kick that didn't come. He made a mistake by readying himself for the kick and let down his guard. I stepped into him and punched as hard as I could on his nose. My uncle had taught me how to do that. "Guys who haven't fought many fights don't have grizzle built up by broken noses," he said. "The nose is one of the most vulnerable parts of the human anatomy. Hit a guy hard enough, and he'll grab his nose, his eyes will water, and his guard will come down. Quickly hit him on the jaw." He showed me exactly where to hit. "He'll go down with a broken jaw, or if he can take the punch, and his jaw isn't broken, he'll become disoriented and fall down, knocking himself out when he hits the ground." He pointed to the place, pinpointed the small area on the jawbone where to hit and accomplish this.

Kirk grabbed his nose as his eyes started to water, and a trickle of blood ran into his mouth. "I can't see!" He yelled and swung wildly, missing his target several times. I stepped inside his left foot and swung with an uppercut exactly to the spot my uncle told me to hit. Buster's eyes rolled into the back of his head as he was defenseless while wiping the blood from his nose, and the tears from his eyes. The hard blow caught him square on the jaw, and he reeled and went down, out cold.

"He's tall. that's all." I said to the boys watching.

"I told you guys not to mess with Sonny," Albert Payne warned. "He's tougher than a pine knot."

My dad came running from the church as soon as someone told him I was in a fight. He looked at Fran, who was grinning, and then at Buster Kirk lying on the ground, not moving. His mother, Loretta Kirk, was screaming from the church that I had killed her baby.

Fran knelt beside Kirk and took his pulse and then pulled his hand away. Seeing someone knocked out like that was unusual so there was some concern. As Fran stood up, satisfied that Buster was taking a little nap, Kirk opened his eyes and tried to focus on the activity around him. "What happened?" He asked not remembering for a moment where he was or how he got there.

"You'll be all right," my dad told him.

"Praise God!" Loretta Kirk shouted as she saw her two-faced son sitting up and breathing.

Buster was wobbly when he got up and still a little disoriented. His nose was broken and so was his jaw, so my dad told Sheriff Crane to run him to the hospital in Stanford.

I thought I was in serious trouble, but I wasn't. "It was a fair fight, Preacher," Fran said. "Kirk started the whole thing, and Bud even turned his other cheek when Buster slapped him, and Buster slapped him on that cheek as well."

"What was that all about?" The Preacher asked me.

"I figured it out, dad. Christians ain't supposed to fight, so Jesus said that when you are struck, turn the other cheek, so I did."

"But you turned the other cheek and let him hit you unchallenged," my dad expressed, "and then you hit him after that."

"Right. Jesus didn't say what to do after you got struck on both cheeks. That's what Mark Crawford did. He gave every opportunity for Buster Kirk to stop and cool off before he kicked the crap out of him. Then it became self defense, and that ain't no sin."

My dad was laughing so hard at this perfect logic that he had tears running down his face. All the way to the church you could hear him say, "Jesus didn't say what to do... ," and then he laughed harder. "That's some kind of Theology," he mused.

Buster Kirk was drinking from a straw for a couple of months. He couldn't get his mouth open to eat solid food because they had to wire his jowls. His nose had a funny little crook where the bone didn't heal properly. He complained about having a tough time breathing, but he never bothered anyone again. Those two whippings were more than he could take. His mother never spoke of the incident except one time when she was talking to my mother. "Sonny got lucky, that's all," she said.

CHAPTER FORTY-SIX

The fall of my seventeenth year was the year of tragedies. We were sitting in Psychology class one day when Mr. Lassiter, our school principal, announced over the PA system that our President, John Fitzgerald Kennedy, had been assassinated and school was canceled for the day. "The buses are outside to pick you students up and take you home," he announced, "this is a terrible day in the history of our nation."

I was watching the back of Kathy Friday's head, looking at the soft flowing waterfall of golden delicious hair that hung down to her waist, and daydreaming about the day we might get back together. Oddly, she had said that she was going to the Senior Prom with Charlie Bumgarden, but I never saw them together once, talking or anything, and Norman Harris always had other girls from our school in his hotrod when he came to town. The message about the President shocked me from my dreams, and the reality of what had happened hit me like a ton of bricks.

Lincoln County was no friend of John F. Kennedy and nearly ten to one, the voters voted against him. He had barely won the national election, and some say it was because that crooked Mayor up in Chicago had dumped voting booths in the Chicago River and fixed the election in Kennedy's favor. Lincoln County Republicans loved Richard Nixon because he was Dwight David Eisenhower's Vice President for eight years, and many of the homes in the Chapel Gap area had pictures of Ike and Nixon on the walls of their homes.

I noticed how the students of Crab Orchard High filed out of the building. Instead of running and screaming and loud talking as usual, the students had their heads bowed in disbelief and few were talking except to say, "I can't believe this happened." Fran and I drove through Crab Orchard, and we saw the window drapes drawn on the new bank, shops were closing, and the people were walking to their cars and pickups slowly and sadly.

JFK was a Catholic, so the Southern Baptist south broke its solidarity and many of the rock hard Democrat states voted Republican for the first time since the Civil War. No one knew at that time that the next election would be the downfall of the Democratic Party in the Southland. The south would vote solidly Republican from that time on, helping Republicans win in two landslides. Lincoln County voted against Kennedy because he was a Catholic, and they believed the Catholic Church to be the "Great Whore" in the Book of Revelation, and the Pope the "Beast" as described in that book of Holy Scripture. No real Christian would vote for a Catholic.

Politics aside, my heart was broken. Fran and I tuned in to NBC radio and listened as David Brinkley and Chet Huntley described the scenes unfolding in Dallas, Texas where the President was killed. The description of Jacqueline Kennedy, the First Lady, climbing on the trunk of the presidential limousine, with the brains and blood from her husband's head all over her, was an image that horrified me and made me angry.

Governor John Connelly was also shot, but he survived. Fran and I didn't speak until we drove into our farm. "I wonder how the Preacher is taking this?" Fran asked and then we found out.

My dad turned the TV on. This was something he never allowed in our house during the day. "Your mother will watch those stupid soap operas all day long," he complained. That's what she did most days when he wasn't around, which he usually wasn't.

"What do you think, Preacher?" I asked unsure of the answer.

"I think this is a sad day in America when somebody can kill our President just like that!" He snapped his fingers. "They took out a good man." Fran and I were shocked to hear him say this. "He was a Catholic, and I don't like him, but I believe he was a good person. I never put much stock in those rumors about JFK running around with other women and having an affair with Marilyn Monroe. What I hate the most is that we are going to get stuck with that crook, Lyndon Baines Johnson. He probably had the President killed," my dad reasoned and that was going to be the opinion of a lot of people around the country as they watched Jack Ruby kill Lee Harvey Oswald, the President's Assassinator, as he was being moved down a hallway by the authorities and then Johnson was sworn in. "He ain't sorry enough," my dad said.

Riley Pat and I were swimming together in the Cullen pond. We had a small rowboat in the middle of the clear lake. Riley wanted me to get on his shoulders. The idea was that the weight of our bodies would push us all the way to the bottom, quickly. There was much argument and debate how deep the lake was. The pond was a natural body of water fed by a spring coming from deep in the ground. It was clear enough to see almost to the bottom around the perimeter, but you could not see the bottom through the clear water in the middle of the lake. That was its deepest point. Many guys had tried to swim down, but when their ears started hurting, they were forced to the surface. Riley had read somewhere that if you blow out your ears when the pressure gets on them, it will equalize the pressure, and at each of those intervals, blow and you can safely get all the way down. He instructed me how to do this.

I climbed on Riley as he held onto the sides of the little skiff, and he locked his arms around my thighs. We both took a breath, and Riley let go. We went deep; so deep that my ears starting hurting. We both blew through our ears while holding our nose and tightly closed our lips. The pressure equalized and we sunk lower as the temperature of the water became very cold. I was wondering if I had enough breath to survive this adventure, and perhaps Riley thought that about himself because he made us sink faster by treading the water with his long arms.

The sunlight was barely visible in the deep water when we hit the bottom. Suddenly Riley let go of me, and I thought that he had lost all his breath, so I swam toward the boat and waited for him. Within seconds, he came up and was screaming at the top of his lungs. He screamed that he was hurt and needed help, but I could not understand what happened.

Blood came rising from the deep and surrounded Riley Pat's body. His blond hair was red from it, and the blood floated around his armpits. With horror, I watched as one half of Riley's left foot bobbed to the surface. I couldn't react very fast, but when I saw his foot floating toward me like a monster that would overtake me, I yelled for help but then realized no one could hear me, and then my attention turned immediately to Riley floundering in the water. With one hand I grabbed him, but he was bleeding so badly that my hand kept slipping in the warm blood, and I couldn't get a grip on him.

Finally, I pushed him to the boat and told him to hang on while I went for help. When Cecil Cullen reached the pond, Riley was barely conscious, and then he passed out. His chin was all that was holding him as the boat was drifting toward the rocks on the other side of the lake where we couldn't pull him out from the bank. Mr. Cullen told me to jump in and swim to the boat, and then he would ease the boat to the shore. It would be a miracle if we could save him now because it was evident by the trail of blood in the water following the little vessel that Riley had lost a substantial amount of blood.

We reached Riley Pat, and Mr. Cullen gently held his body against himself to keep Riley from drowning. I kicked the water and moved the boat to the opposite bank. Junior Cullen came running down to the pond, and Naomi Cullen brought a couple of quilts. Junior retrieved the piece of Riley's foot floating in the pond, and the three of us carried the boy while Naomi Cullen stopped the bleeding by a tourniquet she made from Junior Cullen's belt. Severed limbs are a gruesome sight, and I wondered how anyone could be a surgeon.

Riley Pat survived that day, and later Fran and I kept diving down to the spot where I went to the bottom sitting on Riley Pat's shoulders. Fran fished around in the muddy bottom until he felt the pieces of sheered glass. When he brought the glass to the surface, he revealed the deadly and dangerous shard that was a bleach bottle someone had thrown in the lake. From that time on, every boy was careful about wading in muddy ponds.

I was sitting in my Volkswagen parked in our barnyard and listening to the radio. I did that a lot because I could usually sneak a smoke or two. I was reminiscing about Riley's foot and how Riley had barely survived that day in the woods when

Benji McDuff tried to kill Fran and him. That happened, and three years ago Riley and I sunk to the bottom of the Cullen's pond where he lost his foot. I was thinking about how unlucky Riley had been when Fran came walking out of the woods at the back end of our property. He had just come from Riley Pat's mother's house, Donna Pat. Fran told me that he had just learned that Riley Pat had been killed in an automobile accident on Interstate 75 between Cincinnati and Dayton, Ohio. Riley had been working at the Chevrolet plant in Cincinnati and had been sent by the plant to Dayton on an errand.

This was the saddest thing to happen to one of our Knob boys. He had survived some tragic events in his life, including having to walk with a cane, but he did not survive the head on collision near Dayton, Ohio. The drunk driver was traveling eighty miles per hour on the wrong side of the freeway for over ten miles. Riley went to pass a car and pulled into his left lane just at the crest of a hill when the intoxicated sot hit him head on. Sadly, the drunken murderer survived, but Riley Pat's body had to be nearly peeled from the impact. The little 1963 Corvair with the rear engine he was driving could not withstand the impact at that speed after hitting a four thousand pound Oldsmobile Ninety-Eight that killed him.

Another tragedy took place that fall as well. June Job finally jilted Steve Green, the fat slob with the 1956 Thunderbird, no personality, peed a lot, and she was now married to Trooper Tip Tuck. The Kentucky State Police repositioned his family over in Cumberland County near Lake Cumberland, Kentucky. The good and honest Trooper was chasing a bank robber down the highway when a semi-truck pulled into the Trooper's lane ignoring the flashing lights of the cruiser and the siren.

Tip slammed on his brakes, but at the speed of over one hundred twenty miles per hour, he had no room to stop, and the cruiser slashed under the truck and sheered off the entire top of the Trooper's car including Tip Tuck's head. From that day on, I hated big rigs on the highways because as usual the driver of the truck that killed Tip was uninjured. The big rigs that intimidate and do what they please on the highways are responsible for deaths in America more than any other accident.

Sheriff Crane's wife, Priscilla, pressured the Sheriff to retire from his job. She convinced him that the job had become too dangerous, and there were more dangerous criminals in Lincoln County than he could keep up with. Most of them were transplants from out of state and made Evel Martin look like a Sunday School boy attending the Evergreen Baptist Church. "I want you around in my old age," she maintained, so Sheriff Crane hung up his gun and badge and retired to his little farm.

One of the worse things that happened that year was the disastrous battle that took place inside the walls of Evergreen Baptist Church. From its inception, the church had always been a member of the Southern Baptist Convention, and unlike so many Southern Baptist Churches, the powerful Convention did not finance the Evergreen Baptist Church building or own any of the property. They could not force the church to endow the Convention through the property, and there was no clause that stated that the church receiving loans had to always remain a Southern Baptist Church; therefore, the Convention had no jurisdiction of any kind over the church, and the church remained an autonomy.

My dad was disenchanted with the Convention for some time. First, because the Association Missionary kept poking his nose into the affairs of the church and was known to be traveling around the neighborhood inciting the members against my dad. He was burned up because my dad wouldn't yield the pulpit to him whenever he showed up at the church for one of the services. Also, Evergreen Baptist wasn't giving as much to the mission program of the Convention, but instead, was giving to several independent missionaries such as the Crawford's in Brazil. My dad felt men such as them did a much better job with missions than those under the authority and rule of the large Southern Baptist Convention bureaucracy.

Another reason the missionary was inciting Evergreen Baptist Church members to oppose my dad was that the Christmas before, the church gave nothing to the Lottie Moon Christmas Fund. Lottie Moon was some lady who served on a mission field somewhere. My dad didn't like the politics of this particular offering, and he was reasoning that a lot of money given by the churches didn't even get to the foreign field to save heathen sinners, so the church gave their Christmas offering that year to the Crawfords to help them buy the materials needed for a new house boat Missionary Crawford needed for his family living on the Jurura River deep in the Acre Territory in Brazil. My dad told the church on Christmas Sunday before the special offering that the Crawfords did more mission work than twenty Southern Baptist missionaries combined. That offering was the biggest mission outlay in the history of Evergreen Baptist Church.

All this upset the Association Missionary because Evergreen Baptist was the richest church in Lincoln County. Armed with the Doc Sinclair money, and the constant income from the Bardasian farm, the church could pretty much do what it pleased. When the large offerings stopped going to the Convention, the Association Missionary lost his prestige. He enjoyed his status as having one of the best giving Associations in the United States among Southern Baptists. My dad was fed up with all the politics and the wrong-headed professors at the Louisville Seminary. The Association Missionary was now so upset about my dad's lack of warmth toward the Convention, and his spurning of offers to become of some status himself, that the missionary was spending his days inciting the members of Evergreen Baptist Church to oppose the most important vote the members would ever face in their lives, and that was the defection out of the Southern Baptist Convention and declaring themselves Independent. The Missionary of the Association also had one other thing on his mind. My dad had a huge amount of influences on the other Baptist churches in the county especially after he paid off church loans and lent money to others. The Missionary could see a chain reaction, and he would be out of a job.

The main reason the Preacher wanted to be free of the Convention was because of doctrinal issues. The Convention was splitting in two. The word came from the Convention in Atlanta that the Southern Baptist's new leadership established themselves as no longer upholding "Closed Communion" and was no longer requiring members of other denominations who joined Southern Baptist Churches to be rebaptized. They would no longer require persons from other faiths to be a member of a Southern Baptist Church in order to take the Lord's Supper. "Alien Immersion" and "Open Communion" would become the standard of rule and practice in the formal Convention churches. For centuries the Anabaptists had held to their beliefs that no one could enter their churches without "Scriptural Baptism" which in their viewpoint was immersion by a proper administrator under the authority of a true New Testament Church. They also would not allow their churches to give communion to outsiders who wandered in off the street, but instead held the communion to be sacred and "Close." This meant that they wouldn't give the Lord's Supper to many of their own wayward members. Evergreen Baptist Church had cut its teeth on these ancient doctrines, and the Preacher wasn't about to give them up.

The Southern Baptist Convention leaders of the early nineteen sixties were going to change all this, so my dad got in the middle of the fight and stayed on the side of the ancient Anabaptists. The liberals Pastor Don Stayton and Pastor Otis Ledbetter took the side of my dad that repaired a lot of tension between them, and Pastor Ledbetter had already denounced the Southern Convention and led his church at Copper Creek out of the Association.

All of this upset the Lincoln County Association of Southern Baptists because my dad had the most influence. They worried about churches that were on the fence concerning these doctrinal changes and may fall off the fence over to the side of my dad. The fat Association Missionary was red-faced and tearing at his hair over all this. If very many of the higher giving churches such as Evergreen Baptist Church bailed out of the Southern Baptist Convention, it would mean the Convention would transfer him somewhere else or terminate his employment because there wouldn't be enough money coming from the county to justify keeping his employment.

The showdown came on a crisp, cool fall morning. The leaves had already turned to their most glorious colors, and as Fran and me drove up to the church, we could see the tall bell tower. white as flour, against the blue sky. "Helicopters" were falling from the tree beside the cemetery, and several of the children, including my brother Val Mark and my little sister, Nila, were running and trying to catch one.

There were cars and trucks everywhere and even some visitors from other Baptist churches, who came out of curiosity to see how the Evergreen Baptist Church and its famous pastor was going to handle this battle. There was so much smoke coming from the parking lot that it looked for a minute like the church was on fire, but soon the cigarettes, pipes, and cigars where extinguished by the steel toed shoes of the farmers.

Johnny Watson was the Association Missionary. He parked his 1959 Pontiac Bonneville Convertible with the top down even though the weather was cool. Several of the teenage boys were standing by the white car with the shiny chrome and bright red leather interior. They were admiring the huge dashboard and all the gadgets stretched across the front of the Pontiac from one side to the other. The Association Missionary smoothed down his thinning hair and clutched his big Bible under his arm. He was dressed in a black suit with a pearl tie tack that was real popular among the preachers. My dad had one. Mr. Watson stood around five feet ten inches tall and was extremely portly. In fact, we noticed that when he exited his car, he could barely get his belly from under the steering wheel. Fran said that was why he drove around on the dusty roads with his top down, the car's heater going full blast in the winter, the air conditioning on maximum in the summer; he couldn't get out from under the steering wheel and negotiate a roof without bumping his head. The convertible allowed him to stand almost straight up when he got out of his car. This made no sense to me until I saw it first hand.

The Evergreen Baptist Church building packed to the brim quickly. People were not lollygagging around at the outhouse or anywhere else on the property. As soon as they arrived at the church, they immediately entered the building to find a seat. My dad had assigned a couple of ushers to help keep order, but the people ignored them and rushed to sit where they wanted. The building was so full that extra chairs were brought in, and when they were filled, people began standing on the outside. My dad encouraged the men to allow the women to sit in the building and give up their seats. Practically the whole building was full of women, and even at that, some of the men didn't give up their seats as requested, so the remainder of the ladies were standing outside with men in the chilly autumn air.

Bro. Lord and former Sheriff Crane helped seat the folks filing in. There were people coming the members of the church
had never seen before, and my dad had been tipped off that
those people were members of Evergreen Baptist Church who
had never moved their memberships to other churches where
they had relocated. There were others, who were known
members, living in the vicinity of Chapel Gap but never came
to church. The sneaky Association Missionary had found a
membership list from records when the church used to report
to the Convention in previous years and had contacted every
single one of those folks, including many who worked and
lived up in Cincinnati and Louisville. Norwood, Ohio, which
is part of Metropolitan Cincinnati known as "Little Kentucky,"
and was a great source of information of Lincoln County Baptists who had moved up there to find jobs. The Missionary
had done a great deal of work locating the relatives of relatives
who were still on the membership rolls of Evergreen Baptist
Church. The only people not there to vote, it seemed, were the
members who were dead. Fran said that if Reverend Watson
could have gotten the dead there, he would have.

It irked my dad as Watson carted in. "Hello," he said, "I'm
Reverend Johnny Watson, Representative of the Association
here in Lincoln County." He greeted the people this way. My
dad hated the use of the term "reverend" as a title for preachers. "There is only one reference of the word "reverend" in the
Holy Scripture, and that is attributed to the Lord Himself in
the Book of Psalms. I'm not reverend, they aren't reverend,
only God Himself is reverend!" He preached this message
every time after the Association Missionary had visited our
church.

The Evergreen Baptist Booster Choir sang that morning
under the direction of Terry Kirk, who had taken over the job
after his brother, Stan, left for the Navy. After they sang the

same song they'd been singing for a hundred years, there were no customary "Amens." In fact, there was no festive mood at all in the church. There were so many people in the congregation that the members felt like they were in somebody else's church, and the new folks coming in that morning to worship hadn't been to church in so long they forgot what they were supposed to do.

The future of this church was up in the air. No one knew for sure how the vote would turn out, or who was going to vote for who. Loretta Kirk had taken a poll from eavesdropping on the phone for weeks and had told the Preacher that the vote would be close. "Anybody's call," she said.

"Brothers and sisters, we are here this morning on the Lord's Day to decide the doctrinal future of this church, and if indeed the church will remain one of the true Lord's churches as taught in the New Testament and held as sacred by our forefathers who died at the hands of the Roman Catholic Church. The Bible says that "The Gates of Hell shall not prevail against it, and the gates of Hell are open wide this morning trying to swallow up everything we've ever stood for, fought for, and held as our doctrinal position as our forefathers did down through the ages." This is how my dad began his powerful sermon that morning.

The crowd stirred at every descriptive word and metaphor, and the main body of believers stationed and fixated in their respective places knew and understood what he was saying. It was well known that the members of Evergreen Baptist Church, who were regular in attendance, were some of the most informed Baptists in Lincoln County and perhaps the entire State of Kentucky. They understood and believed the Word of God and most lived by it every day. Only those members present no one had seen for years, and some had never seen, knew nothing about what the Preacher was preaching.

They looked confused and kept trying to find things in their Bibles to contradict the teachings.

Many others had no Bibles, a dead give away that they weren't from this church.

"Our forefathers burned at the stake for our doctrinal position on Baptism and the Lord's Supper," he preached on, "and when the Roman Catholics tried to force us and suppress us to recant our position as truth in God's Word, they cut our eyes out, stretched us on a rack until our limbs tore off our bodies, cut off women's breasts, beat us mercifully, and finally burned millions of Baptists at the stake. They did these things to us, and we endured them so that today we have the freedom to worship as we please without interference from the government or a state church. We even suffered in this country in the early days of its settlement, and we thrived just as we are doing today. There were so many of us back then that founding fathers suggested to Roger Williams and John Clarke before the adoption of our country's Constitution that the Baptists become the State Church. We turned down this offer in the name of freedom and our distaste and detesting of state run religion is part of why we are free today. I am afraid now that the Southern Baptist Convention has overstepped its bounds and has imposed itself on the blood of our forefathers in trying to adopt doctrines that will be the ruination of our churches. This church simply cannot go the way of the Southern Baptist Seminary up in Louisville which has been filled with modernist professors of religion and don't have the backbone of jellyfish when it comes to defending God's Word. Here this morning sits a product of their heretical teachings," he pointed to Association Missionary Johnny Watson sweating on the front row having taken a seat from one of the women who gave it to him as if he were royalty, "and he wants to prevent us from joining thousands of other defecting Southern

Baptist Churches in America who aren't going to put up with this change in ancient truth. I'm telling you this is the start of the demise of the local church. The next thing you know, they'll try to ordain women deacons." No one in the church believed that was possible, but he threw it in anyway.

Never in the history of Evergreen Baptist Church had a message so clear and powerful been presented from that platform with the memory of James W. Bishop etched in the stain glass behind the pulpit. Many of the folks were wiping their eyes; especially, the women at the mention of what our forefathers had bled and died for. My dad shut his Bible after this short exhortation for the church to take a stand on the opposite side of the line drawn in the sand by the liberals, who wanted to ruin the Southern Baptist Convention and their churches.

Fran and I stood in the perimeter of bodies lined against the walls all the way around the interior of the church. "Either the Preacher's going to save the church, or he is going to meet his waterloo," Fran said to me as he silently pondered the situation.

The Association Missionary asked for the floor. My dad was not going to yield but thought the better of it. He already had some of the regular church members stirred up, and it would be chaos if he was viewed to be unfair. The Missionary had gotten hold of the church constitution and by-laws that were a century old and had not been changed, and he had them in convenient location nearby.

"Members of the Evergreen Baptist Church and distinguished guests in Christ," he began, "nothing this Pastor says is the truth. Instead, he has distorted the purposes of the great and mighty Southern Baptist Convention, the largest denomination in the United States. He would have you believe that our Catholic brothers were heretics; in fact, he said as much.

I wonder how Peter, the first Pope, is taking this up in heaven. Surely he is ashamed that this church is considering pulling away from the Southern Baptist Convention. This Pastor has distorted history. True Baptists have never denied the baptism of Catholics, Lutherans, Presbyterians, and Congregationalists, and never, ever have they refused to sit at the Lord's Table with these brothers and sisters in Christ, including the more modern Methodists, Churches of Christ, and Nazarenes."

"Is that what he's been taught up there?" Fran whispered to me.

The Association Missionary went on while some people were looking at my dad as if he had been lying to them about what Baptists believed. The whole discourse didn't make much sense, and he said in his closing remarks as people were looking at their watches, and one man took his off and shook it, "I admonish the members of this church to not only refuse to pull out of the Convention, but to dismiss this insidious and deceitful Pastor from the pulpit of this great church!"

There were so many whispers and buzzing that you would think you had just arrived at a busy hornet's nest hanging from a branch in the woods. My dad stood and looked at his flock. *I have labored with these people. I've been there when their children were sick with pneumonia, whooping cough, and measles. I helped them through births, prayed for them during their distresses, and buried their dead.* He was thinking these things while staring across the sea of bodies. *I love these people almost as much as I love my own children,* he thought.

My dad said, "we need to pray before we make this historic decision." He prayed but not for long. He asked the Lord's blessings on the meeting, and he was careful not to incite the folks during his talk with the Lord.

There was much discussion as to how the vote would be taken. Would they have a secret ballot, or would they have a show of hands? The Association Missionary argued that the Constitution of the church called for a secret ballot. He had forgotten that he had a copy of it in his suit jacket.

"Give me that copy," my dad demanded. The Missionary reluctantly handed dad the papers he had retrieved from the files at the Lincoln County Baptist Association Headquarters.

"Here it is right here," my dad read, "the members of Evergreen Baptist Church will receive votes by show of hands, and the counting of those hands will determine the vote by a simple majority."

"I thought it said, "secret," the Missionary mumbled.

"Bro. Lord, get the other deacons of the church, and you will be responsible for counting the votes and announcing the results. The six other deacons walked to the front of the church. One of the deacons, Bro. Nathan Smith, arrived late at the church, and he had to leave his family on the outside. Deacon James Lord, Deacon Nathan Smith, Deacon Houston Crane, Deacon Chris Stevens, Deacon Ron Wells, and Deacon Brad Jameson stood in front of the pulpit. It was already past noon, but no one cared. Sometimes when the service ran long on Sunday mornings the women, who had things on the stoves at home, would leave the service; especially, if it was the Sunday that the Preacher was coming to their home for Sunday dinner. The Preacher had preached long and hard about this practice, but they did it anyway. Today, however, the beans would just have to burn.

Preacher Jerry S. Smith was happy about the vote being a physical hand count and not a secret ballot. He wanted to see the "whites of their eyes" and know who his enemies were.

"Wait a minute!" Screamed Junior Cullen the fat redheaded one. The Cullens and the Messers were in attendance that morning. They had left the Evergreen Baptist Church because they didn't like my dad, and the fact that he was leading the church into debt before they found old Doc Sinclair's money Evel Martin had stolen. The two families had decided that they were going to move back into the church if the members voted that morning not to pull out of the Southern Baptist Convention. "I would like to say something," Cullen said, "if you please."

"You have nothing to do with this, Junior, so please sit down," my dad instructed sternly. He wasn't about to let this Moby Dick control another vote.

"I want the floor!" He cried.

No one ever saw Bro. Lord act like he did that Sunday. He was already irritated that the Messers and Cullens were there sticking their noses into the church business. *Half of the people here to vote aren't even born again,* he was thinking and then he turned toward Junior Cullen whose eyes were bulging from his head. He pointed his finger at Cullen.

"Sit your fat butt down, Junior," Bro. Lord said right there in the church, and the congregation gasped.

"Watch your language in God's house," my dad said which was the only thing he could think to say behind his grin.

When the fat sweating Cullen heard this, his face turned to rage; he started to speak when the other deacons turned and faced him and taking their positions beside Bro. Lord. Junior Cullen's mother, Naomi Cullen, realized that they were in no mood to put up with her son's self imposed candor, so she grabbed him by the coat tail and dragged him down into his seat.

When all was settled down, by dad began to call for the vote. "Bro, Lord, you and Bro. Stevens count the people on the outside. Bros. Smith and Wells, you count the folks sitting on my left, and Bros. Jameson and Crane, you count the folks sitting on my right. Also, Bro. Watson, you count with them."

When the crowd stirred at the appointment of Missionary Watson to count, my dad explained, "this Missionary has already lied once in this church this morning, and if we don't let him at least count some of the people, he'll accuse our deacons of falsifying the counting. In fact, I want the Missionary present for the entire count and take Junior Cullen with you. We'll start outside and announce the count section by section. Mrs. Anderson, will you add up the tally?"

"Do I hear a motion that the Evergreen Baptist Church here this morning come out of the Southern Baptist Convention and declare itself an Independent Baptist Church?"

"Motion!" Several of the men did this, but Elmo Kidd, who had made motions since he was seven years old, was not credited in the minutes.

"Do I hear a second?" My dad called.

Many "seconds" were heard and so many that Daphni Anderson, the Church Clerk and Lincoln County Recorder reporter, could not keep up with them, so she inserted, "Seconds by all."

"Brethren of the Deaconship, lets count. All others remain silent and pray that God's will be done."

Bro. Lord and former Sheriff Crane entered the building followed by Association Missionary Watson and Junior Cullen, "What's the count outside?" My dad asked Bro. Lord.

"Forty-seven for, and forty-seven against," he answered, and the others counting on the outside with them gave assent.

"How many on my left?" My dad had counted these because he could see the hands. Some of the people sitting there didn't vote because they were ashamed for my dad to see them. Deacon Wells answered, "sixty-one against and sixty four."

This is one of the most nerve-racking experiences I've ever had, I thought. *My dad is going to lose this vote.* That would bother me greatly because I would fear for my dad's ministry there. I didn't think he would survive if he lost this vote.

I vowed that if he didn't, I would remain in the community and haunt every last one of them. I watched as Fran seemed to be praying. He had his head bowed and his eyes shut. Missionary Watson and Junior Cullen followed the vote on the left and agreed it was even. It would now come down to the folks sitting on the right side of the congregation as my dad faced them from the pulpit. He was down by one vote. It was then that I thought about how stupid it was for the church to have a simple majority rule. It worked okay when Jewel Vance was reinstated into the church after her divorce and when the church voted to borrow money, but if this church lost its doctrinal position by one or two votes, that would be a tragedy.

Fran never lifted his eyes once, and you could cut the tension in the building with a knife. People were pressed against the windows and some had jammed the vestibule of the church pushing against one another in order to follow the drama like the common folk did when knights were jousting in battle for a king's daughter.

There were a lot of people sitting on the right side of the church. There were several sitting there that no one knew. "It's even, Bud, there are exactly the same number of visitors as there are attending members. If they all vote the way they are represented, the Preacher will lose this vote," Fran worried out loud.

"What's the count?" My dad asked Deacon Wells, who was standing with a little piece of paper in hand which had the outcome.

The Booster Choir seats were counted in the vote, which were perpendicular to the seats where the general congregation was sitting. Most all of the kids voted even though no one was more than twelve years old. Fran had calculated the kids, and this was one time that I agreed with the church on allowing all members to vote, even children. Without the voting kids today, there was no chance against all the rogues that the Association Missionary had planted in the assembly that Sunday.

"Seventy-two for, and seventy against," Ron Wells yelled although everyone could hear just fine.

The Preacher breathed a sigh of exasperation. He had not lost the vote, but it meant that the church may table the decision for some time which would give the Association Missionary and his allies more time to stack the deck before the vote came up again making it impossible to pull out of the Southern convention and make a statement to the liberal Seminary up in Louisville. The Preacher was in a conundrum as to what to do about this. The congregation was noisy. It was already mid-afternoon, and the people were restless. Hardly anyone had left the service and gone to the outhouse, but now there was a steady stream of ladies and men headed back there. The Preacher could either get this over with right now and yield, or take his chances on another vote.

He wasn't going to decide the vote either because according to Roberts Rules of Order, a system of organizational laws the church lived by, would not permit the moderator of a business meeting to vote, and my dad had chosen to be the moderator of the vote himself rather than entrust the stressful position to someone else to control a tense and stressful meeting that could easily get out of hand. He could step down and appoint another moderator like he had done a couple of times, but he thought that would affront the entire church who had gone to the outhouses and were now back in the building. My dad was just about to yield and table the motion when Loretta Kirk walked in. Because of the busy day and the crowd of people assembled there, no one had noticed Loretta missing from her regular seat. Nobody was sitting in his or her regular seat anyway and on any other day, there would have been hell to pay if one of the women caught someone in her seat where she had been worshipping for years.

Gib Kirk had trouble delivering a calf that morning, so he made Loretta stay home and help him deliver it so the boys, who needed church more than she did, could go. She had found out from Sophie Lord, who had gone home from fatigue and called Loretta on the phone to report the standings at the church. "The vote was tied when I left and my husband feared that the Preacher would yield to the Association Missionary and fat Junior Cullen. I just couldn't take it anymore." Sophie gossiped.

When Loretta Kirk heard this news, she didn't even hang up the phone. She left the receiver suspended on the end of its cord and rushed to her car in the barn. She quickly started the vehicle and spun her way in the direction of the church. She would have to drive quickly although she only lived ten minutes from the church. She spun into the church driveway and sped up the small hill leading to the building. When she got out of her car that was parked some distance away because of the traffic, she realized that someone had gotten her parking spot and that made her unhappy. "No one better have my seat," she said out loud to no one in particular when she entered the church. To her horror Missionary Watson was sitting in it. This was too bad for him; he had spent a lot of time with the gossiping women and Loretta, enlisting them for a campaign against the church and its plans to pull out of the Southern Baptist Convention.

Loretta Kirk did not want the church out of the Convention and had sided with the liberals on the doctrinal issues even though she knew better. The entire congregation held their breaths including my dad as Loretta stood in the aisle way, hands on hips, and on her way to tell the Missionary to get out of her seat, which she did. He got up making sure his one and only hope today was not mistreated. He even wiped the seat for her with the tie he had taken off that was choking the flab around his heavy neck.

"I haven't voted!" Loretta Kirk announced.

"Women can't speak in this church!" Junior Cullen yelled from his seat. "She's violated her right to vote by speaking out!" The Association Missionary scowled at Junior for his assault on his only voting ally left to sway the decision.

"Shut up, Junior, and sit down before I have you thrown out!" My dad screamed from the pulpit. The heavy Cullen sat down. "How do you vote, Sister Kirk?" She crossed her eyes a couple of times and seemed pleased that he referred to her as "sister."

"FOR!" She yelled at the top of her voice. "I'm against the Catholics and all her illegitimate children being taken into a New Testament Baptist Church without being rebaptized."

"Hallelujah, Praise the Lord!" People shouted and jumped-up and down and hugged one another. It was one time I was glad we had a simple majority rule for voting in the church. When I told Fran this, he rolled his eyes.

"Order! Order!" My dad cried trying to bring the crowd under some resemblance of controlled worship. When things settled back down, he followed Roberts Rules of Orders to the tee. "Any other business?" He asked.

"Yes," Bro. Lord said as he slowly stood and seemed exhausted. "I want to move that we change our constitution by-laws to state that anyone who misses church for a month is no longer eligible to vote on church business until they have attended for thirty days to have their voting rights reinstated."

This suggestion caused another stir. "Well, Bro. Lord has made the motion, is there a second?" Daphni Anderson had to report in the minutes, "Seconded by all, motion carried."

During the discussion time before the votes are taken, people can argue the pros and cons to the entire church and then vote. Some wanted to reduce the attendance rule to three consecutive services and make it constant church attendance for six months before a member could be reinstated and given the privilege to vote with the church. Others argued that this was excessive and would be hard on the older and more feeble church members and those who may be in the hospital by being Providentially hindered. The motion stood and it was ready for the vote.

"All in favor by the uplifted hand." My dad called. There was no need to count. Even the long lost crowd of Evergreen Baptist Church inexplicably voted for the motion.

"Any opposed by the same sign." No one opposed except Junior Cullen who raised his hand. "You can't vote, Junior, you're not a member," my dad said to him, and Junior Cullen quickly realized this and pulled his hand down, and everyone laughed.

"There will be no services tonight," my dad. announced even though Sunday night services had never been cancelled at Evergreen Baptist Church, but the members were happy.

There was fallout that my dad explained was natural. Many good people, who had been Southern Baptists all their lives, left the Evergreen Baptist Church and filtered into other Baptist churches in the county who remained in the Convention; even though, they had to drive long distances to worship. For the rest of us, my dad said that if the Southern Baptist Convention returned to its roots, the Evergreen Baptist Church would be right back where it was before all this happened. Many doubted that the Preacher would ever be happy again by doing that. He was enjoying the freedom of his newfound independence, and no Association Missionary ever bothered him again. The last one who did was seen driving down the road in a convertible.

CHAPTER FORTY-SEVEN

I n the spring of our senior year at Crab Orchard High, a strange car drove into our yard. My dad and I were sitting on the porch swing with Fran and talking about the weather, mostly nothing in particular, and sipping lemonade. The car had an official seal on the door, and a nice looking gentleman stepped out, grabbed his brief case from the back seat, stretched, and looked toward us.

"Which one of you is Sonny Smith?" He asked.

"I am."

"My name is Mark Blythe, and I am an official of the Foreign Exchange Student Program at the University of Kentucky."

I had submitted an application to the University and applied for an exchange with the University of Manaus, Brazil. We felt gratified that the University had taken this serious, and we knew that this man was here to deliver some exciting news, so we listened with anticipation.

"I have here an official document which says that you have

been accepted for the program of exchange. No university in the United States has ever exchanged a student from the University in Manaus, so I apologize for the delay and hope you are still interested."

"I am!" I yelled.

"Great! A student by the name of Silas Guedes de Oliveira will be coming to Lexington and live with a family there. This is a little different than the exchange usually operates. We normally bring a student in exact exchange where the families are swapped, but in your case, Crab Orchard is too far away to be practical for a student attending the University of Kentucky in Lexington, and the Oliveira family is too poor to take care of a student with fourteen mouths to feed. Robert Crawford has arranged for your housing in Manaus at the home of an American family living there, a Mr. John Hatfield. Do you have any problem with this?"

"I know John Hatfield," my dad said, "and there is no problem."

The official went over all the documentation in detail and asked my dad, who was making all the decisions, if he needed more time to digest the material before a final answer.

"We've already prayed about it," my dad explained, "and we've left it with the Lord. If Sonny here got approved, then that must be the Lord's Will. Otherwise, you wouldn't be here." The official looked at my dad as if he didn't quite comprehend this method of decision-making.

"Then that's it. The Oliveira family has already signed and submitted to the University of Manaus, so all you need to do is sign here." There were exes where my dad was to sign.

"What's the time frame?" I asked.

"Since the school year is different in the Country of Brazil than the United States, you will be scheduled to report to school the 19th of June, next year."

"That's two weeks after I graduate," I commented.

"Then you better start making arrangements," Mr. Blythe said.

Fran and I were walking down to the spring in the woods that rushed out of the hillside in the back of our farm. My head was spinning.

"Congratulations," Fran said softly. "Your whole life is about to change."

"I guess so, Fran. I'll still go with you to the Navy if you want."

"Naw, Bud, Stan Kirk went in on that buddy system thing, and his recruiter told him that he and Cris Johnson's brother would spend four years together. You can't trust them; they lie, Bud. They didn't even go to the same boot camp, and Stan hasn't seen Cris's brother since. You better go on to Brazil."

"Why don't you go to Brazil with me, Fran?"

"I don't think so."

"Why not?"

"Snakes and alligators ain't for me, and besides I leave for the Navy a month before you go to Brazil."

"What? When were you going to reveal that piece of information, and when did you do this? I'm with you all the time."

"The Preacher took me down to the Stanford Courthouse one day when we were on visitation. A recruiter from Louisville was going to be there and was traveling through this part of the state enlisting people for the Navy. He said I would get drafted since I am not going to college, and they would send me to Vietnam to be killed like Dallas Vance was, so I signed up."

Dallas Vance was the first and only casualty of the Vietnam War in the Chapel Gap area. "So that's why you're going to the Navy?"

"That's part of the reason. The other is that the Preacher was in the Navy."

"You're going to follow in his footsteps, aren't you, Fran?"

"Everything but preaching, Bud, ain't no way I'm going to be a preacher. He's looking for you to do that."

"No way," I said.

It didn't take long for the news to reach Kathy Friday's ears that Fran was going to the Navy, and that I was going to Brazil. Daphni Anderson had written an article that was on the front page of the Recorder that said, "Sonny Smith goes to Brazil, Life among the Amazone Natives." Her dad read the front-page news to her before dinner and then turned the page to read about Fran Job volunteering for the Navy.

Kathy Friday didn't eat dinner with her family after hearing the news that I was indeed going to Brazil. The paper spelled out the details of how the University of Kentucky had made this arrangement with the University of Manaus and told of how Manaus lies on the Amazon River one thousand miles inland.

"How can I fault him?" She said to herself as she grabbed a pail from the back porch and headed to the blackberry patch. "I'm the one who told him I didn't love him, and now he'll be gone forever."

"This is bullcrap," she said out loud as she threw the half-bucket of blackberries on the ground and watched as they spilled out. She then ran to the barn. Her dad stored an old pickup in there, and she found the keys in the ignition. She turned on the key of the 1950 Chevy and stepped on the starter. The truck fired up, and she "goosed" the accelerator a couple of times and pulled forward through the barn doors.

As she left the yard, her dad was standing and watching her, but she never made any attempt to slow down or tell him where she was going. He was trying to tell her that there was no gas in the truck, but she found that out when she started up the Chapel Gap Hill. Gravity caused the fuel to flow to the back of the truck, and being so empty, the manual fuel pump would not keep the engine running.

"Damn," she said. The fuel gauge had quit working on the truck several years ago, and Mr. Friday kept a watch on how much fuel was being used.

"Why doesn't he ever fix anything?" Kathy Friday said as she coasted over to the side of the road. Fortunately, there was enough room to stop, and she debated whether she should leave the truck on the hill where someone may run into it and cause a bad accident or coast down the hill. She opted to coast backwards because of the impending danger although going backwards down that steep hill would be no piece of cake, either.

Kathy Friday put the transmission in neutral and started coasting backwards toward the bottom of the hill. She put her arm on the back of the seat and let the truck roll. She didn't realize how steep the hill actually was, and the truck was picking up speed very quickly. She knew at this speed she would never be able to make the curve just below her, which was steep and treacherous. If another car or pickup was coming up the hill, somebody could get killed. Somebody was coming up the hill; it was my mother coming back from shopping for the week's groceries at the IGA Store in Stanford. My mom was driving her 1960 Mercury Station Wagon, which was the size of a tank, and my mother was not one for easing off the gas pedal when she was in a hurry or any other time for that matter.

My mom stepped on the gas to give the heavy machine enough energy to make the hill. The Mercury was powerful with a 428 cubic inch engine, and though it was a station wagon and heavy, it was very fast. The engine responded, and she could feel the surge of power as the transmission shifted into second gear. She loved to hear the gravel kicking out behind the wheels as they spun on the downshift.

Kathy Friday was approaching the curve from the upper side, and neither of the ladies could see each other. My mom was driving like a racecar daredevil when she hit the curve. She had driven this road hundreds of times, so she knew exactly how to counter steer when the big car's rear end started to fishtail.

Kathy Friday was barely keeping the old pickup on the road. The tie rod ends and bushings were worn, and the steering wheel had too much play to be safe. As she neared the curve and looking backwards, my mother had inched up on the wheel with a strong grip, peering over the huge steering wheel like she was drafting Fireball Roberts. She saw the tail end of the pickup coming right at her in the middle of the curve.

Kathy Friday was out of control. She had used the brakes so much that the old worn brake pads were smoking and when that happened, the brake shoes crystallized making it impossible to stop any vehicle in this condition. Kathy Friday could smell the smoke and then she saw the huge wrap around windshield coming at her with this little lady with both fists on the top of the wheel smiling like a Japanese Kamikaze fighter pilot. She slammed on the brake but to no avail. The pedal went all the way to the floor, and she knew instantly they were going to crash.

Shirlee Smith could drive. I found that out at an early age when I kicked my sister out of the car window and onto the dirt road one day in Kansas. She slammed on the brakes, put the car into a controlled skid, and moved the car in a perfect 180-degree turn that ended with the vehicle headed in the other direction. Now, her skills would be tested again. A split second before Kathy Friday's pickup plowed into my mom's front end, she swerved the big boat sideways, narrowly missing the rear end of the pickup. The car swung wildly but was soon brought under control by the swift thinking of my mom. She counter steered beautifully and was now in front of Kathy Friday. They were both headed down hill.

My mom sped up to catch the pickup. She realized there was nothing she could do now, and Kathy Friday was going so fast that the next curve, although not as dangerous as the first, would be impossible to negotiate. My mother's first thought was to speed around the truck and sacrifice her station wagon, but she thought that wasn't a good idea since she may slide into the truck, and they both could be killed.

Kathy Friday leaned over in the seat. There was nothing to do now but let the rest of the trip down the hill be left to God. "Oh, Jesus," she prayed, "if it is your will, let me live. If not, let me die in peace."

She put one arm between the bench part of the seat and the seatback. With her other arm she grabbed hold of the underside of the seat and held on.

Secured firmly with her stomach on the seat and holding on with her strong arms and hands which were made that way by milking cows and lifting bales of hay, she held on with all her might as the pickup started over the cliffs of Chapel Gap Hill.

My mother slammed on the brakes at the bottom of the hill and pulled her car across the road so that no one could get up the hill. She watched with horror as the pickup rolled over and over, crashing into treetops as it fell in open space after clearing the road and its slight grade.

Kathy Friday had the sensation of falling because that was what she was doing. The truck was in midair, and she felt the force and pressure as the flying vehicle was now right side up. She knew the speed of the falling truck would kill her when she hit those heavy hickory trees in the gorge below. Glass had crashed all around her, and the roof of the truck was almost on top of her. The pickup's roof could not withstand one more blow, or it would crush her under the sheer weight of the tangled mess of tin.

The pickup hit the top of a hickory tree and broke the limbs off the tree as easily as breaking toothpicks, but it was slowing the descent of the truck's fall.

"If this truck doesn't turn upside down again," she screamed, "I may get out of this alive!" The truck did start to turn over when it hit one of the heavier and thicker branches of a tall tree. When that happened, the force of the impact caused the door of the passenger side of the truck to pop off and sent it sailing into the woods. Kathy Friday could not hold on. Her grip was jarred loose as a big branch came through the windshield and took off the steering wheel like a razor cuts off a hair. The huge limb caught the truck, and with the help of the heavy branches below, the truck lie suspended twenty or more feet off the round.

When Kathy Friday lost her grip, the force of the sudden stop threw her out the odorless cab like a rifle shot, and she landed in another tree nearby. She was conscious until her head struck the tree; a glancing blow that caused her to fall helpless through the tree and towards the ground.

My mother watched in horror at this horrible accident. She didn't know this girl and had never see that pickup in the area. She watched as Kathy Friday bounced from limb to limb like a little rag doll.

The last ten feet left nothing but open space; nothing to break the fall, and it was hitting the rocks in the creek below that would kill her for sure if she wasn't dead from the ricocheting blows she was taking from the thick branches. She didn't hit the rocks; she landed in the water, and the cool shock of the cold creek revived her, or she would have drowned. She was floating, and the sensation made her think she was still in the truck soaring through the air, and then she felt water trying to suffocate her, and realized where she was.

"I'm alive!" She screamed out loud and so loud that my mother could hear her.

"Thank heavens!" My mother yelled to the family waiting to go up Chapel Gap Hill but had stopped to help if they could. My mom wasn't one to "praise God," but this was a great relief for her to hear Kathy Friday yelling from the creek. She and the farmer, Mr. Bledsoe, started running through the woods. Mike Hatten, who lived with his single sister Dot, heard the crash and was headed up the creek when my mom saw them.

Kathy Friday would drown if she could not swim less than fifteen feet to safety. She tried to swing her arms in a swimming motion, but they would not move. The pain in her side was so excruciating that she was cramping and beginning to paralyze. She tried to kick with her legs, but they wouldn't cooperate and lay limp less while both legs were dragging her into deeper water.

"I'm going to die!" Kathy Friday screamed again before her head fell below the surface of the cool creek water and things went black. Mike Hatten hit the creek diving headfirst boots and all. He swam under water and came up under Kathy Friday. He pushed her to the surface where she regained consciousness and coughed some water out of her lungs. Her breathing was raspy and hard, and each breath she took brought unbelievable pain and misery.

Dot Hatten and my mom were standing by a tree when Mike carried the little blond beauty out of the creek. Water ran off her clothes and hair, and Mike looked at her like she was the most beautiful thing he had ever seen. "This one here's a pretty one," he said.

Dot had stripped off her blouse and was standing in her

bra. My mom couldn't believe the size of her breasts for such a little woman. *Where'd she come up with those?* My mom was thinking. Dot wrapped Kathy Friday in her blouse which was too thin to do much help, so she took off her skirt and as she stood with almost nothing on, my mother motioned for Mr. Bledsoe to turn his head. That didn't help much because every time my mom would look away, he'd sneak a peek.

"Are you my angel?" Kathy Friday said to Mike Hatten.

"No, darling, but you could be mine," the old coot answered while hitting on my girlfriend.

By the time Floyd arrived with his ambulance, my dad was wondering where my mother was. I never saw him do this before, but he picked up the phone and carefully lifted the receiver so as not to disturb the other party. He wasn't for sure that anyone would be on there, but if something strange had happened to my mom, he could find out.

Loretta Kirk was talking to Sophie Lord. She had seen Floyd headed up toward Chapel Gap and said something about my mom being involved in an accident.

"What kind of accident?" My dad asked which startled the gossiping ladies.

"Hey!" Loretta Kirk yelled as she did not recognize my dad's voice over the phone. "Don't you know it's against the law to eavesdrop on other people's conversations, plus it's rude?"

"What happened to my wife?" My dad asked hurriedly.

"Why, Preacher! We never knew you to be listening in on conversations," Sophie Lord commented.

"I don't, now what happened?"

"All I know is that there's been an accident on Chapel Gap Hill and someone said they saw Shirlee driving towards there a little while ago," Loretta Kirk explained.

Dad yelled for me and Fran to bring the car from the barn. Fran drove and within minutes, we were going down Chapel

Gap Hill. As he drove down the steep grade, we saw a pickup hanging in a tree. The truck was unfamiliar to either of us.

"No way to survive that," my dad said.

We also saw several people down at the creek and knew that someone was either being treated in order to be taken to the hospital or was dead. It could be either of these things if Floyd and his Cadillac hearse were involved. We then saw Floyd leading the way as Mike Hatten and a couple of other guys were carrying a body out of the woods.

"Is that Dot Hatten in her panties and bra? What in the world?" My dad asked as Fran and I turned away although I sneaked another look and noticed that this old maid was pretty darn shapely. My dad caught my eye, so I coughed and rubbed my eye briskly.

"Who is it?" My dad asked as we got out of the truck and expected the Sheriff to be there, but he was off fishing. Of late, if you needed the law in Lincoln County, you had to take it into your own hands.

"Some girl we've never seen before around these parts," Mr. Bledsoe answered. "Real pretty girl, too."

"That has nothing to do with it. Find out who she is so that we can notify her next of kin," my dad ordered.

"I know who she is, dad." I looked at the body lying on the canvass stretcher and could not believe my eyes.

"That's Kathy Friday, dad."

"What? What's she doing all the way over here?"

My dad had never met Kathy Friday since she had never been to our church, and he rarely went to a ballgame since I quit baseball. On the few date nights that we had, I didn't have the time to take her up to Chapel Cap to meet my parents. Now that we had stopped seeing each other, there was no point.

Floyd lay Kathy Friday softly in the hearse. Her face was

bruised badly and swelling. By this time, I could barely recognize her. Her eyes were turning bloodshot, and the clear crystal azure was faded underneath the fluid filling her eyes. She was conscious.

"I love you," she whispered.

I thought I heard that, but did she say it as a brother in Christ, or did she mean that she really loves me? I knew the answer, and my heart jumped into my throat. I gulped a couple of times and asked, "Did you mean that?" She didn't hear me; she was gone again.

"Will she live?" I asked Floyd.

"She's badly beaten up, Sonny. She has internal bleeding, and I believe her ribs are broken as well as an arm and both legs. Why, do you know her?"

I wasn't sure how Floyd knew she had internal bleeding. "Yeah, I know her," I said sorrowfully.

CHAPTER FORTY-EIGHT

The Sheriff never did arrive to investigate the wreck, but the Kentucky State Police came just as Floyd was shutting the back door of the hearse. The new Trooper who took Tip Tuck's place wasn't from around Lincoln County. He had taken the job and moved from upstate New York. He had a funny accent, and he was known to operate strictly from the book. Most of the people living in the county didn't like him because he was writing tickets for driving without a license to the younger farm boys.

"Where you taking her?" The Trooper asked Floyd.

"Down to Fort Logan Hospital in Stanford," he answered.

Floyd moved quickly to get into the driver's seat and turn the light on that sat on top of his hearse.

"Hold on there a minute Mr. Undertaker," the Trooper said, "you're not moving the body until we get the paperwork done."

"The body is alive!" Floyd yelled at him, "and she needs to get to the hospital as soon as I can get her there."

"Not until I do my report," the Trooper demanded.

My dad heard this and walked up to the smart mouthed cop. The Trooper's uniform was perfectly pressed; the crease in his shirt and pants neatly done, and he kept bending over and wiping the dust off his black shoes so he could see the shine, "You better settle down, Barney Fife." my dad said as he stood facing him.

"What? Who are you? Back away, mister, and leave the scene, or I'll cuff you."

My dad walked straight past the Trooper and went to the front of the hearse. He reached in and pulled Floyd out of the driver's seat.

"Get in on the other side!" He screamed at Floyd. My dad started the Cadillac and put it into gear while the Trooper was pointing his pistol and demanding that my dad roll down the window. He beat on the window a couple of times before my dad scratched off in the gravel. The Trooper was in shooting position with his gun aimed at the hearse. He suddenly had the thought that shooting at a hearse might not be the smartest thing, so he holstered his gun and ran to his cruiser. He radioed something and then turned on his siren and lights and sped after the hearse.

My dad was driving like a maniac, and Floyd was holding on. I think my dad planned on driving anyway because he knew how cautious Floyd was with his own life even if someone were dying in the back. My dad glanced in his rear view mirror and saw the Trooper tailing him.

"That idiot's going to get somebody killed if someone don't stop him," my dad commented as Floyd was now down in the floor protecting himself from certain gunshots by the Trooper chasing them. My dad thought how badly he missed Tip Tuck.

The cars sped through Crab Orchard not stopping for the only traffic light and made the turn at the Crab Orchard Baptist Church and onto Highway 150 to Stanford. They whizzed by the William Whitley House, which was the first brick house in Kentucky and a State Shrine open to the public. Although the Shrine was only five miles from Crab Orchard, none of us had ever visited the place. My dad took a quick glance at the well-manicured state property upon which the estate was maintained, checked to see if anyone was leaving the park. When he saw no one, he remembered that in eight years he had never seen one car parked in the visitor's lot at the house; he gave the Cadillac the "goose."

The Trooper was having a hard time following the hearse and certainly couldn't pass him, but when the fast Cadillac approached the intersection of Highways 27 and 150 near Stanford, the Kentucky State Police had built a roadblock. My dad hauled the big machine to a stop. The new guy in the million-dollar uniform with the funny accent ran immediately to the hearse with his gun drawn.

"Preacher, Floyd, what in the world is going on?" The Kentucky State Police Lieutenant asked. The new Trooper had radioed that my dad had stolen the hearse and kidnapped the undertaker.

"We've got the body of a girl in here from Copper Creek, and she's dying if she's not dead. Have Gun Will Travel back there wouldn't let us leave unless he did his paperwork and has been chasing us all the way here."

"Get those cars out of the way!" The Lieutenant Dishon yelled. "Let these men pass. You! Harris! Get out in front and clear the traffic, and I'll call the hospital and get them alerted if they aren't already. Johnson! Follow up the rear!"

"Preacher, we'll get the details later," Lt. Dishon said as he leaned on the hearse. He glanced at Kathy Friday lying on the stretcher in the back and shook his head. "She's too young and pretty to be messed up like that."

Fran and I rode up with my mother to the farm from the accident site after my dad left with the hearse and the police cruiser chasing him. We drove the Volkswagen over to Stanford and were sitting in traffic waiting for the intersection to clear. We watched the Lieutenant grab the shirt of the trigger happy cop and shake him hard while yelling something about getting the hell out of Kentucky and back up to New York where fancy Yankees could kill each other up there.

Kathy, as I would now always call her, was in the emergency room when Fran and I walked in. I asked my dad how she was doing, and he said she was alive but barely. Soon, the doctor walked out of the emergency room and into the visiting lobby.

"Are you her father?" The uninformed doctor asked my dad. The intern was working in the emergency ward of the tiny Fort Logan Hospital, so he didn't know my dad.

"No. She's my son's girlfriend." Fran and I looked at each other.

Did he just say what I thought he said? I thought.

"You better notify her parents if she has any, or the next of kin. This girl's going to die before midnight," the doctor sternly explained.

The news shocked me, and I wanted to see her, but the new doc told me that only the nearest relative would be permitted in ICU but not until she was out of the recovery room.

"What's wrong with her?" I asked lugubriously.

"What isn't wrong with her is the better question," he said. "I cannot believe that anyone could survive an accident like that, if she does survive." He was being careful to not give us false hope. "She has a broken wrist and elbow, a broken arm, almost broken in two, both legs are broken in several places, and she has several broken ribs. In addition, her collarbone is broken, but miraculously, she has no cuts on her face and minor abrasions and cuts that aren't serious. All that won't kill her, but it may cripple her for life depending on how well the surgeon sets the bones. He's on his way from the Central Baptist Hospital in Lexington. The most life-threatening thing right now is a rib that has punctured her lung, and she is bleeding internally. We're trying to fix that but with the shock her body has taken, she may not have the strength to weather the operation. I've never seen anyone who can take pain like this girl can."

When dad, Fran, and I walked up on the porch of the Friday family's house, Don Friday met us at the door.

"What lies did he tell this time?" Mr. Friday kidded. "What can I do for you fellers?"

"Your daughter has been in a very serious accident, Mr. Friday," my dad said. I thought his answer was harsh, and I would have entered the conversation more gingerly, but the Preacher knew what he was doing. God knows he'd born bad news many times in his ministry.

"How serious?" Mr. Friday asked as Kathy's mother, Mary was standing nearby listening from the front room. She had her hand over her mouth to suppress the scream about to leave her lips.

"She went over Chapel Gap Hill in a pickup, and she's in the Fort Logan Hospital at Stanford. The doctors say you should get over there right away."

"Will she die?" Little Robin asked while feeding her baby doll.

"We'll pray to God, not," my dad said.

"That girl's not been herself lately, Preacher, she's been moping around like she's lost her best friend. She didn't have supper with us and took off in the pickup. I have a feeling your son here has something to do with all this."

Mary Friday drove over to Copper Creek Baptist Church

and told Pastor Ledbetter what happened to Kathy, and he took off for the hospital. Dad offered Mr. Friday a ride, but he declined, saying that he would feel like a sardine in the little orange car, and besides, he was claustrophobic. He thanked us, but he would wait for his wife and come over with her.

We drove back to the hospital and Kathy was in surgery. Pastor Ledbetter was standing in the waiting room area.

"How is she?" My dad asked.

"Very serious. They're operating on her lung now, and they have already set the broken bones. It is only God that will bring her through this," the Pastor said.

We waited all day for the results of the surgery. That evening, the doctor came into the waiting room.

"Is my daughter okay?" Don Friday asked the doctor.

"She will live. There wasn't as much damage to her insides as we first thought. She's out of recovery and in her room in ICU."

"Can we see her?" her dad asked.

"You may, but only for a few minutes."

When the doctor said this, Don Friday started toward the stairs leading up to intensive care. Pastor Ledbetter followed, and so did I.

"Hold on there, young man," the doc said, "you aren't going anywhere. Her Minister and her parents, that's all."

My dad restrained me, holding me back. "Why can't I go?" I pleaded "They should let me up there instead of Pastor Ledbetter!"

"Professional courtesy, Sonny, he's her Pastor."

This upset me very much. I wanted to ask her if she really loves me, or was she so delusional that she didn't know what she was saying, but I was relieved that she would live.

Kathy was recovering well through the winter of our senior year. Gone were the bruises and the swelling that was the aftermath of her tragedy, and she did say to me many times that she loves me. While she was in the hospital, I wanted to kiss her, but her lips were so swollen she couldn't pucker. Her legs were swinging from the tack that held the casts in the air, and one arm was completely covered with a cast leaving one free hand to function. She was a mess, but over the next few weeks and months, the casts came off and the wires out of her mouth from the broken jaw. It was amazing how good of shape this girl was in. She never complained once about pain, and I thought that she could take more pain than any person I had ever seen or met. The abrasions healed; there were no scars, and I realized that she was more beautiful than before. By spring, she had rejoined the girl's fast pitch softball team and took her old position at second base. She was something else. She could throw, hit, and catch better than most boys, and I admired her.

We had unfinished business. We dated every Saturday night. I ignored my teaching on the "picture show" and all its evils, and we had to sneak up to Somerset to the drive-in theater. It was amazing how many other Christians from the Baptist churches were sitting in the theater's parking area. I loved going to the drive-in even if it was an evil necking place. I liked sitting in my car in privacy, talking during a bad movie, and cuddling during a good one. We ate popcorn and hotdogs, and my favorite potato chips, Bachman Golden Delicious All Natural, made up in Reading, Pennsylvania. I could wolf down a couple of bags in no time. We had lots of fun together dating by ourselves. Fran was finally allowed to car date my sister, and once or twice we saw Fran's 1956 Pontiac Chief with the head of an Indian on the hood that lit up when the headlights came on. It was difficult for both of us to sneak to the drive-in with such conspicuous cars. I had the only VW in the whole three county area, and when Fran turned off his headlights, the Indian was still glowing as he slowly drove into the theater. We always pretended we didn't see each other, and my sister was forever lying over in the seat out of sight so that no one would see her until Fran got parked beside one of the speakers. Occasionally, we double dated, but that was getting rarer and rarer.

One Saturday in the spring, I drove to Kathy's farm to pick her up. I had planned on taking her over to the Dog Patch Zoo in London, Kentucky. I had been there a couple of times, but she never had. I planned on showing her some of the big snakes I would encounter on my journey in Brazil. One particular interesting feature of the zoo was a black man who lived in a snake pit during the day. He laid on the bare concrete floor of the den and allowed every kind of snake you could imagine crawl all over him, even poisonous ones. The crowd was delighted by his feature presentation. He would pick up a snake and bite the head off and spit it into a bucket. He would then hurl the torso of the creature out of the pit and into the crowd. This was entertainment for the hillbillies at its finest.

When I arrived at the farm, Kathy was dressed in blue jeans with one of her dad's large red bandannas wrapped around her head. She had her blouse rolled up and tied above her naval. I had never seen her stomach, but it was flat and tanned. I couldn't keep my eyes off her. The look in her eyes told me that this was not going to be an ordinary day. She had a couple of two gallon milk buckets sitting on the porch beside a table cloth and an apple basket.

"We're not going to the Dog Patch Zoo today; we're going picnicking and pick blackberries," she announced and not asking if that was okay with me.

I hated picking blackberries. I always got infested with chiggers and snakes inhabited blackberry patches. One time as a kid, I was picking blackberries with my grandmother who came to visit us. The next morning, I was covered from head to toe with swelling and itching from the chigger bites, and I was so sick I wanted to die. Ever since I got those horrible bee stings, I was allergic to anything that carried poison including those pesky little sweat bees that pestered us when we baled hay. These poisonous critters made me sick.

"I'm allergic to chiggers!" I said "They make me sick."

"I've already thought of that," and she had. "Put some of this pink lotion on you, and you won't get chiggers. It's Calamary and will kill the poison."

"What if a bee stings me?" I asked seriously.

"I'll keep them away."

"But, what if we see a snake?" It was well known that I was deathly afraid of snakes. I could let spiders crawl all over me, but if I saw a snake, I went into hysterics. Many times when I went to the smokehouse for canned jelly or vegetables, a snake would be coiled around one of the jars, and I would break out in cold chills and freeze in my tracks. More than once, I would go to my sister, Leah, and get her to get the jars. She was unafraid of the reptiles and would reach up and take a jar or two that a snake was coiled around without blinking an eye. I could never bear to watch her do this, so I would wait outside the smokehouse until she came out with a Ball jar my mother had used for canning.

"You're not afraid of snakes, too, are you?"

"Me? No way."

"Then let's go," she ordered.

We grabbed our buckets and started down the dirt path that led through the barnyard past the pigpen. I opened the "gap" which was a barbed wire gate used by the farmers. It had a loop of wire on the top and bottom of a wood stake that held the gate in place. I opened it, and we walked into the open field that led to Copper Creek.

"Why are you way over there?" Kathy asked while looking at me strangely.

"Uh, just looking," I replied nervously.

I saw the big black angus bull across the field and made my way immediately to fence and was walking along with one hand ready to jump over, just in case.

"That bull won't hurt you, he's friendly, here bully, bully, bull," she called, and I had one foot on the fence ready to go over.

I had never seen Copper Creek except crossing the bridge on the road that led to the church. I did notice as we approached the woods that hid the pretty rill that the hickory trees and beech trees were very large. Don Friday never touched these trees for firewood or sold them to the furniture manufacturers in Corbin, Kentucky as some farmers did with their hardwood trees. The leaves were full and the temperature dropped considerably as we approached the creek.

Kathy spread out the blanket on the creek bank, and I couldn't help but notice that the deep pool in front of us and the corresponding riffles, would be a good place for gigging. I would plan on asking Mr. Friday if Fran and me could gig the creek before I went off to Brazil in a few months.

"Me and daddy gig this creek every spring," Kathy said, "but he won't let anybody else gig here. He said if you start letting this person and that person gig then before you know it, they want to come here with their friends and before you can blink an eye, there's no more fish."

I listened to this. "You really go fish gigging?" I asked.

"Every year, many times, I love fried fish."

I had never heard of a girl wading a creek and gigging fish. Girls weren't supposed to wear pants, so that would keep them out of the creeks. It kept them from doing other man things as well. My grandmother said that when they started letting girls play sports, that's when their morals were compromised and girls put on men's breeches. There was no use asking Kathy what she wore when she gigged. This girl did exactly what she wanted, and I better get used to it.

"Donnie gigs with us, too," she commented, "but he's no good at it. He runs through the water scaring all the fish, and he can't hit the side of a barn. Sometimes daddy and me sneak away from him."

I was surprised that Donnie Friday, her brother, couldn't gig. He was a real good baseball player just like she was. He didn't attend Crab Orchard High because he wanted to play ball at Mount Vernon High in Rockcastle County where his grandma, MoMo, lived. He stayed with her most of the time while he was in school.

Kathy laid out the lunch. In the basket was fried chicken, Bachman Potato Chips, potato salad, and cherry cobbler, my favorite. My mom had told Kathy that I love cherry pie.

"Tammy made the potato salad," Kathy said. "MoMo taught her how to cook. I made the fried chicken. Your mom gave me the recipe; said it was passed down from your grandma's grandma. I hope you like it."

She had Coca Cola and a Pepsi Cola for us to drink. She liked Coke, and I drank Pepsi. One time we had a big argument about which was better, Coke or Pepsi. I was going to avoid another confrontation about the subject if at all possible. The last fight over the soft drinks ended up with me getting out of my car in the middle of nowhere and telling her to drive my car home, and I would pick it up sometime in the future. Unbelievably, she got behind the wheel of my VW and drove away. I watched her dust as she disappeared. *Oh, well, she'll come back for me,* I thought. I thought wrong. I had to walk sixteen miles to her house to get my car, and she wouldn't come out and talk to me.

We lay on the blanket sipping our drinks through a paper straw. I thought there could be no better heaven than I was in right then. I put my arm around her and drew her close to me. This was the first time that we had been that close. Whenever we kissed goodbye, she always pulled a little away from me not allowing our bodies to touch below the neck. Not today. She scooted near me, and I felt her warm body against me, and I had feelings I never had before. *This is true love,* I thought.

Kathy looked deep into my eyes. "You have beautiful blue eyes," she said softly, "what's behind them? What are you thinking?"

I couldn't tell her what I was really thinking because it wouldn't be proper. I was perspiring with desire and embarrassed for her to see me like this.

"Don't worry," she said, "it's natural."

Holy cow! I thought.

"I was thinking have you ever been with a boy?"

"What kind of question is that?" She said curtly. "I'm a virgin if that's what you mean. I'm a virgin, and I'll stay a virgin, so if you have any big ideas, forget it."

I don't know how she knew what I was thinking, but now I felt guilty. I became quiet and Kathy noticed this.

"Temptation is no sin," she said, "yielding to temptation is sin."

"Have you ever been tempted, I mean, in that way?"

"What do you think I am, a zombie? Of course I've been tempted."

I knew better than ask any more questions. These kinds of things needed to be left unasked and unanswered. I drew her close for she had scooted away from me. I put my arms around her once again and her body pressed against mine. This was torture, so I touched her bare belly while I kissed her. She grabbed my hand without breaking our embrace and kiss.

"You can't touch me there," she said, "I don't want no baby."

As soon as she finished her kiss, she rolled away. "Let's get those berries," she said.

The blackberry patch was on a section of the creek bank a hundred yards away from our picnic spot. Kathy explained to me that blackberries are the sweetest when they have some cool air and afternoon shade. I didn't know anything about blackberries except they were black, grew on thorny bushes, and harbored snakes and chiggers, so I couldn't argue with her.

"Put some lotion on to protect yourself," she said, "here, I'll do it for you."

She put the lotion in her palms and rubbed them together. I thought I would die as she spread the smooth and slick gel over my arms, face, and neck.

"Take off your shirt," she demanded.

I took off my shirt all the time when I was working in the tobacco barns, patches, and hay fields, but I never took off my shirt and showed my chest to a girl. Timidly, I unbuttoned the shirt and let it fall on the ground. She immediately picked it up.

"You can't leave your shirt on the ground, silly, the chiggers will climb in there and bite you the rest of the day."

So that's what does it, I thought. I laid my shirt in the grass by the blackberry patches all the time while I was picking.

Kathy looked at my chest and at the golden tan and well defined muscles developed while working in the crops and lifting heavy alfalfa bales.

"I like hairy chests," she said while rubbing her hands over my heart. "Your heart's beating pretty fast, you all right?"

How does she know she likes hairy chests? I thought, but I wasn't going to ask.

Her smooth hands rubbed my chest and back, and even

though her hands were calloused, they still felt soft as a baby's bottom. No good farm girl wore gloves when they worked; that would be considered "sissy." Never mind, this was feeling real good, so I put my arms around her and drew her against me again. I kissed her and those same feelings came rushing through me.

"Let's pick berries," she said as she gently pushed me away. "Now, stuff your pant legs inside your socks. That will keep the chiggers from crawling up your legs."

I was sure glad she didn't ask me to take off my pants, so she could rub my legs, or we would have been in trouble for sure. My legs were white as lamb's wool, and that would have been embarrassing.

We each took a bucket and started picking berries. It wouldn't take very long to fill the pales for the berries were plump and ripe. I loved the sweet berries, and as my personal custom was, I picked one and ate one. I had never gotten sick doing this although I would eat an entire two gallons of blackberries before the day was done.

Kathy was silent as she stood some distance away from me picking her portion of the tasty berries. I tried to pick toward her, but she kept her distance. I didn't know if she was doing this on purpose, so I didn't let it bother me.

"What's on your mind?" I finally asked.

"You," she said.

"What does that mean?"

While I was waiting for her answer, I looked down at my feet. My whole body froze solid with fear. I could feel the goose pimples rising in my chilly state of dread and running up and down my whole body. I screamed, a deadly cry, because directly below me and almost to my feet, was a big thick blacksnake; one of the biggest I had ever seen. It had to be six or seven feet long, and it was staring me dead in the eyes. It flicked its tongue several times, smelling the flesh that had invaded its territory. Blacksnakes aren't poisonous, but I knew if this beast bit me, I would die anyway. I would have to have a tetanus shot to prevent disease and some psychological counseling, and the shot would be worse than the snake bite not to speak of spending the rest of my years in a mental hospital. Yes, a snakebite would be bad for me.

"It means that we have some unsolved things to talk about concerning our future together," Kathy said while she was casually walking over to where I was standing afraid to move a muscle. In fact, I couldn't move if I wanted to.

When she was within reach, the snake had already wrapped around my feet and its head was exploring my knees. "Stand still," she said, "you'll scare the snake."

Hello? I was thinking.

"You know that day I wrecked the truck? Do you know that I was headed toward your house to see you?" She said this while she bent down and grabbed the vicious and demonic reptile by the back of the neck and unwrapped it from my ankles.

"Why?" I said nervously as she took the snake away from me. The snake was coiling itself around her arm, and I was growing faint. I might do that any second, faint.

"I wanted to apologize to you for telling you those lies about going to the prom with Charlie Bumgarden and Norris Wells. I can't stand either of those creeps."

Kathy untangled the snake from her arm while still holding it firmly; the neck and head pinched between her thumb and index finger.

I breathed a sigh of relief that the snake was no longer going to attack me. "I didn't think you cared," I said while the snake was now partly stretched out, two thirds of its body being held away from Kathy and one third of it on the ground.

586 · SHERMAN SMITH

"What I wanted to tell you was that I was being selfish. I didn't think I could get in deep with you while you were off to some foreign country."

Kathy grabbed the snake by the tail and let go its head. It thrashed wildly; its mouth open and showing a row of teeth. Its tongue flicked and its piercing deep ebony eyes were raging in anger at what this person was doing to it. It struck several times at her but was unable to get its head close enough to bite her.

"I was going to let you go, but you are a mean rascal. If you try to bite me one more time, I'm going to take your head off!" She yelled and instructed the snake like she knew it personally, and it could understand what she was saying.

"That's it!" She warned loudly as the snake struck not once, but twice in succession.

She swung the snake round and round several times, turning in a circle and slowly raising the dizzy snake over her head. The snake was no longer trying to strike but resigned itself to let gravity have its way as she spun round and round, and the centrifugal force which she controlled took every single curve out of the snake's body as it was swinging around her head straight as a stick.

Suddenly, she stopped spinning, and the snake didn't move. She took its tail and whipped it like a bullwhip as hard as she could. She cracked the snake, and the resulting sound of the snake's head popping off its body echoed through the hollow, and the head flew thirty feet and landed in the creek. She discarded the carcass and kept on talking. She threw the corpse in the creek near where the head was now floating with its tongue still flicking.

I was through picking blackberries. Once or twice during Kathy's demonstration of snake handling, I thought that she should be the one going to Brazil.

"Lets talk about this," I said while trying to lead the way back to the picnic area where our drinks were cooling in the creek, and cherry cobbler made by Tammy Friday, were waiting.

"Just a couple more, and I'll join you," she replied while continuing to throw berries into her pail.

I waited well away from the briars of the blackberry patch and watched this amazing girl from a distance. Now and then I glanced at my feet to make sure the snake didn't have a partner and then I heard Kathy speaking to the ground.

"Come over here, and you will meet the same fate your brother or mother or whatever got," and the snake slithered away into the briars.

I could have watched Kathy work forever. She seemed to never stop the steady pace she kept except to wipe the sweat from her forehead and her forearm. She was as regal in that blackberry patch of thorns as a queen sitting on a throne. I was deeply in love with this girl, but how was I going to be away from her for two whole years? The thought depressed me.

"I know you need to go to the jungle, sweetie." This was the first time she ever called me anything except my real name. This wasn't going to work. "Who am I to stand in your way?"

"If I had known that you were on your way to tell me all this when you wrecked the truck, I wouldn't have let the Preacher sign the last set of papers sealing the fact that I have to go down there. My dad won't let me out of it now for any reason. Says that I need the discipline, and I need to get away from all the temptations out there that will ruin my Christian life. He's got Fran's assent on this as well, and that's too much horsepower to deal with and fight."

"Your dad's right." She sided with Fran and dad? "I'm going to college anyway, sweetie. I need a couple of years at least."

"Where?"

"Dad's got some money. He' s been running that little garage over in Brodhead and saving money for college for all us kids. I'm thinking Campbellsville College. That's a real good Baptist school, or maybe Georgetown College, that's another, I'm not sure."

"What do you want to do?"

"I want to work for Child Protective Services in a big city, do juvenile work and learn sign language, work with deaf people. Do you have any idea how mistreated colored children are in a big city?"

"Have you ever seen a colored child?"

"No, I haven't, but I've seen a Negro man. He tried to get a drink at the water fountain at the Dairy Queen in Brodhead, and they almost killed him. Said no niggers were allowed in Lincoln County. I hate that word. I started reading up on the culture of Negro people, and that's how I found out that so many of their children are growing up without fathers."

This was too deep for me. I had only seen one colored person myself, and that was over at Dog Patch Zoo in the snake pit. I did remember reading when I was in the fifth grade the story in our "Weekly Reader" of that Negro girl who went to Central High School way out in Little Rock, Arkansas. I remember well the impact of that story when I saw the picture of Governor Faubus and some self-righteous preacher, M.L. Moser, Jr. standing on the Central High School steps and blocking the entrance of this poor little colored girl to get an education. I couldn't stand this treatment of human beings.

"You know," I said to Kathy, "I think this is the most honorable thing I've ever heard, and I love you for it."

We talked it all out that day, and it was decided that I would go on to Brazil, and Kathy would attend college over in Campbellsville, Kentucky. It would be a long time to be apart, but we could write each other and that would have to be sufficient.

It was almost dark as we stepped on the back porch and parked our berries. I felt a little embarrassed about having only a bucket full, and Kathy promised that she would never tell the snake story.

CHAPTER FORTY-NINE

E vergreen Baptist Church had a huge rift the spring of my
eighteenth year. For years, the church held to the doctrine
concerning church members who were guilty of committing "Spiritual Adultery." This rule was strictly enforced, and
many old-fashioned historical Baptist churches adhered to
the law religiously. If any member worshipped in any other
church except a Baptist church or received communion from
any other church, it was considered a sin; especially, if a member was caught worshipping and attending a Catholic church.
The member would be expelled from the membership of the
church until that person recanted his fornicating ways and
was reinstated after rededication. This law was indefatigable;
no use for excuses, the law's the law.

One of the "sister" churches in the community had disciplined a member for this crime against the Lord's church. The
member had been thrown out of the church, but the majority
of her family still attended. This family had so much influence

in the body that the church split over this, and some of the dissenting faction, who were family members of the diseased one, were coming to the Evergreen Baptist Church and joining up. Many of the members felt these new people were going to infect Evergreen Baptist and compromise their doctrinal position although no one had ever been excluded from the church for "Spiritual Adultery or Fornication."

The famous business meeting at the church that would forever change the Preacher's life happened one Wednesday night in April before my eighteenth birthday. The showdown came when word got out that some of the members of Evergreen Baptist Church were attending churches of other denominations; especially, those members who lived too far away to come to Sunday night services at the church. For convenience sake, some of them who did not want to miss a Sunday night service, did not think it was a sin to worship with another denomination, and so they did.

The Preacher knew about these sins for some time and never denied those folks their rights to worship nor confirmed those rights. When all this was found out, people started blaming my dad for compromising the church's doctrines. My dad was so sick of the gossip that he wanted to put an end to the problem once and for all. For once, Loretta Kirk wasn't part of the problem. She actually supported the rule against Spiritual Adultery even though she was known to sneak into the Campbellite services once in a while. She did have a tasty appetite to find out who all the culprits were, so she made it her business to inform my dad by picking up some of the names of the sinful church members on the phone.

The Preacher called for a business meeting to discuss the church position on Spiritual Fornication. As always on business meeting nights, the church was packed, and the building more completely saturated with bodies than usual because there were members of other Baptist churches attending in order to witness this historic occasion that could define how Baptists were going to believe and practice in the Crab Orchard area concerning this teaching. "Call this meeting to order," my dad said and everyone got quiet.

"Let's have the reading of the minutes of the last meeting." Daphni Anderson didn't get elected in the annual voting of teachers and officers of the church, and for the first time in thirty-nine years, the church had a new clerk. The members felt that Daphni had served well but was too old to take the minutes anymore. Her demise happened a few months before when she mistakenly read a note she had made to herself during one of my dad's sermons. She jotted down that she felt my dad's sermon that night had too much "sexual content that wasn't good for the children." She didn't realize that the Preacher was teaching from the "Song of Solomon" a book of the Old Testament. She read this note as part of the minutes that completely discombobulated the entire church. So in the annual election of teachers and officers, she was voted out for no good clerk could make such a mistake. She was in tears when someone said, "that could be read in a hundred years and ruin the church's reputation and the pastor's ministry." This was what the minutes recorded officially from that meeting concerning the vote taken to elect a new church clerk.

Rhea Ford, a nineteen-year-old daughter of Preacher Lam Ford, who had joined the church after retiring from the pastorate at Science Hill, Kentucky and moved his family over to Chapel Gap and joined the Evergreen Baptist Church, was nominated as the new Church Clerk replacing Mrs. Daphnia Anderson. Rhea had been elected church clerk even though she was attending Berea College in Berea, Kentucky studying to become a nurse. She came home every weekend to attend church and drove over after school one Wednesday night a month so that she could take the minutes of the business meetings. She was a very pretty and attractive girl but was untouchable by any boys living around Chapel Gap.

"The reading of the last business meeting minutes are:

Mrs. Maggie Pat requested that paint be bought for her classroom. She would do the work herself. Motion made by Bro. Lord and seconded by Jerry Gaston. Motion carried by the church. Bro. Burns mentioned the need to clean out the outhouses' privies and to hire it done. Motion made by David Blythe and seconded by Jerry Gaston. Motion denied by the church. Motion made by Bob Turner to buy new Sunday School material needed by the Junior Sunday School Class. Motion seconded by Jerry Gaston. Motion tabled until the next business meeting in order for the deacons to review the new literature. Motion made by Hugh Connell that Jerry Gaston stop making motions and give somebody else a chance. Motion seconded by everyone. The church discussed buying new hymnals to replace the old Stamp Baxter hymnals. There was much discussion on this after Elmo Kidd made the motion to buy the new "Baptist Hymnal" from the Southern Baptist Book Store in Nashville, Tennessee. This motion was tabled until it could be decided if the church wanted to buy hymnals from the Southern Baptists. Motion made to adjourn by Fran Job and seconded by Sonny Smith. Motion carried."

Everyone was pleased at how well Rhea Ford took the notes and read the minutes for such a young lady. I always wondered what would happen if the church denied the last motion of every business meeting and that was to adjourn.

"Do I have a motion that we accept the reading of the last meeting's minutes?" My dad asked as the moderator.

"Motion!" Bro. Houston Crane said.

"Second!" Bro. Wells said.

"All in favor by the uplifted hand. Any opposed by the

same sign." Rhea Ford recorded in her book that the motion had carried.

"Any old business?" The Preacher asked and Bro. Lord rose to his feet.

"Yes," Bro. Lord announced. "The deacons have reviewed the new Sunday School literature for the Junior Class and found it is better than what we are using at the present."

"Any discussion?" The Preacher asked.

Deacon Ron Wells stood. "I think we can trust the deacons and the Pastor on their judgment, so I move that we purchase the new material for the Juniors."

"I second that," John Baxter said.

"All in favor? Lift those hands." The motion carried.

"Any other old business?" My dad asked again.

"I think we ought to buy those new hymnals," ten-year-old Elmo Kidd squeaked.

"Any discussion?" The Preacher asked.

Surprisingly, there was none because nobody cared whether the church bought hymnals from the Southern Baptist Book Store or not. The motion carried.

Another point of contention in the church was the speaking out of women in the church assemblies. Although this was not a planned part of the business meeting that night, my dad was sure it would come up. He held strictly to the Biblical teaching that women are not to "speak nor usurp authority over the man in the church." There were more and more Baptist churches allowing women to testify and pray in the public assemblies. There was even talk of Baptist churches over in North Carolina ordaining women as deaconesses.

The Preacher was having a problem with all this. He knew that if the women were allowed to speak, his business meetings would never be the same, and the church would be run by women like they were at the liberal churches who compromised the Scripture for worldly gain. Women in those church-es could speak their minds in public and that was one reason the Messers and the Cullens left the Evergreen Baptist Church and joined down at the Crab Orchard Baptist Church.

No woman could speak out in Evergreen Baptist Church for any reason, and the occasions where that happened were very rare. The women could not pray in a mixed assembly, speak in any public matter, or teach the men. They could not make motions, or discuss business during one of the business meetings. They could, however, sing in mixed assembly, sing solos in mixed assembly, teach children of mixed company to age twelve, and read the minutes out loud by themselves in the business meetings. Evergreen Baptist Church was not alone in this teaching and belief. For centuries, this doctrine had been practiced by Baptists.

Another problem the Preacher may face that night was the issue of women wearing a "covering" in the church dur-ing worship. Many Baptist churches held to the practice of the Catholics that women should have their heads covered when entering the sanctuary of a Baptist church. He had faced down the contention once before. Was the Bible talking about two coverings in the Book of First Corinthians? The woman's hair should not be cut because that was her glory for her husband, and the woman should cover her head when in worship be-cause that would honor God and show her subjection to her husband. You should have been there that business meeting night.

The fight was long and loud. A motion almost carried that women should wear a veil over their heads since the word for "covering" in First Corinthians was actually the Greek word for "veil." After a long discourse of doctrinal discussion of who said what and who meant what, it was decided that the women could wear a veil if they wanted, but it would look like the Catholics. The consensus was that it wouldn't be a sin not to wear a veil and a hat would be just fine on the heads of the worshipping women at Evergreen Baptist Church. Having their heads "covered" was the important thing.

The women began wearing hats. The church was so full of hats that you couldn't see the Preacher or anyone around you. There were all kinds of hats of various colors. There were hats with feathers; big feathers like peacock feathers; hats with wide brims that bothered the person next to them and sometimes, two women couldn't sit beside each other their hats were so large. All this pomp disturbed the Preacher.

"How can I lead the church when I can't rule my own family?" My dad reasoned with my mother. She refused to wear a hat because she thought it was ridiculous, and this was a problem for him because the members noticed this blatant act of rebellion on the part of the Preacher's wife.

All the hat business threatened to tear up the church because some of the church leaders were complaining that their wives wouldn't any longer wear hats because Shirlee Smith wouldn't, and the entire church was in an uproar.

What to do? My dad thought while sitting in his study one afternoon preparing his message for Sunday morning.

"Brothers and sisters in Christ," he began. "We have come to a time for decision making." He looked out across his congregation of hats, "After much prayer and supplication, I have come to the conclusion that women in this church no longer are required to have their heads covered in order to honor God." There were whispers of concern as this news traveled from seat to seat. "Look at you people." Everyone looked at the person next to him or her. "Is anything wrong here? Let me tell you what's wrong. You women are dishonoring God by wearing those hats. How so? Well, let me tell you how so. This hat business has gotten out of hand. Sunday mornings are like a fashion show. You women are more concerned about outdoing each other with your hat wearing than you are honoring God or your husbands."

Loretta Kirk and my mom were sitting in their familiar places, next to each other where they sat every service, and both were not wearing a hat. Loretta said she wouldn't wear a hat because she wasn't in subjection to her husband or any man, so what was the point?

"This is Scriptural Counter production," and no one had ever heard that doctrine before. Several folks were seen trying to find the words in their concordances in the back of their Bible so that they could look up the Scripture where this doctrine was found.

"I'm telling you right now, throw away those sinful materialistic coverings."

This was the reason there were no hats in this business meeting, or the services of Evergreen Baptist Church any longer. Gone were the colorful and fancy coverings that honored each lady's husband and God. Oh, some of the old women still pulled their shawls over their heads during worship, but they had always done that.

With all the business out of the way, he was now faced with the most important decision of his ministry at Evergreen Baptist Church. He was sitting on a powder keg with a short fuse, and he knew it. The tension in the meeting that night was so thick you could cut it with a knife. Not since the church voted to disunify itself with the Southern Baptist Convention had so volatile a decision threatened the well being of his church.

The Preacher looked over the list of sinful members that Loretta Kirk had given him, and the list included her; his archenemy. Of all the people on the list, he was most grieved about Loretta Kirk. Sure she had caused some problems, but she had been there for him several times when she realized he was being harmed unfairly. She came through for him the day of the vote to leave the Southern Baptist Convention and many other times he could count on her. If the church decided to vote out all these members who committed Spiritual fornication, she would have to go, and this grieved him; the thought of it. *What will happen to her?* He thought. In all the years that he had preached at the Evergreen Baptist Church, Loretta Kirk attended nearly every service, and besides the times she committed Spiritual adultery was not on the church's regular meeting days; she attended other denominational services when those meetings didn't interfere with her attendance at her own church. This was true of many on the list as well. Loretta had kept her word to quit smoking as he had quit drinking coffee and switched to Postum on the agreement between the two of them years before.

"Brothers and sisters," he said, "we are faced here tonight in this historic business meeting of the Evergreen Baptist Church a decision that will define the future of our good church and quite possibly the future of many Baptist churches in Lincoln County, or maybe the whole state for that matter."

The crowd stirred uncomfortably at these solemn comments. "I have here in front of me a list of members, who are present this very night, who have become guilty of the sin of Spiritual Adultery." Every head turned and looked at Loretta Kirk.

"The doctrine of discipline this church has established and practiced has included such sin, but we have never as a church supposed ourselves to ever have to deal with it in a public manner. Part of this is my fault for not informing the church about the Scriptural teaching of such a doctrine. Now, we are faced with defining what we believe about this and making that decision part of our by-laws and creed. Do we exclude our friends on this list from fellowship with this church? If we do not, are we violating Scriptural principles and saying that the doctrines of the false churches are no longer false? This church has believed and practiced that the Scripture teaches salvation by faith through Jesus Christ our Lord, and that alone is how we get to heaven. Are we now going to say that it doesn't matter? You tell me. This morning, I got up before dawn and prayed about all this seeking God and His wisdom. How will I present this, Lord? The decision lies with the church; not me alone. I don't know how to advise this church, Lord, and I know we need to be very careful how we approach this delicate issue. First, we must decide if our church constitution is going to continue to read that members are to be disciplined for Spiritual Adultery and Fornication, and we need to define what Spiritual Adultery is. Are we going to allow church members to worship with other denominations, or aren't we?"

It was very difficult to understand where the Preacher stood on this difficult matter. This was the first time the church had heard this doctrine put in these exact terms, and there was an uneasiness among the congregation when faced with this poisonous serpent that was about to attack them. Many began to consider how delicate this business meeting had become. They began to take sides.

"Do I hear a motion that we exclude the members on this list for Spiritual Adultery and Fornication?" No one made a move.

"Pastor, do we fellowship with these other churches as a church body?" Bro. Lord asked.

"No, we don't," my dad answered.

"If we don't, how can we place our blessing on individual members doing this?"

The Preacher rubbed his five o'clock shadow. "I really don't think we can. I believe we need a motion as to whether our constitution should be amended to strike the rule out, or keep it. Then we can decide what to do with the members."

"Wait!" Ten years old Elmo Kidd said. "You can't get into a Catholic church if you aren't baptized a Catholic. Just try it. If you marry a Catholic, and the person is not a Catholic who you marry, that person who is the Catholic will be excommunicated. Their churches don't seem to fall apart by this doctrine. You can go to their masses, but you can't take their Holy Communion unless you are a confessed and confirmed Catholic. So why should this church worry about excluding its own members when we are doing nothing more than protecting our faith like the Catholics do theirs?"

No one could believe the wisdom of this Kidd kid. They whispered among themselves and reasoned about what he said. Elmo sat down with his plump round freckled face, shining. He had baby fat all over him, and his round belly rose as he breathed a deep sigh. No one could understand where this boy got his wisdom, but surely the hand of God was upon him.

"The kid is right," my dad said, "every denomination protects itself through its own baptism. You can't become a Methodist by attending one of their services. You have to be baptized a Methodist. The same goes for the Churches of Christ, Lutherans, Episcopalians, Presbyterians, Nazarenes, and cult Pentecostals. Otherwise, we would just be one big happy family with no set doctrines to preach and protect like the Holy Roller churches." Then, my dad said something unbelievable to his confused congregation.

"Elmo, what do you think this church should do?"

"He's asking a child?" Loretta Kirk whispered to my mother who just shook her head as though she couldn't believe this herself.

Elmo Kidd was baptized when he was seven years old. He grew up in the church having been dedicated by my dad when he was born. He held little Elmo in his arms as the infant cried and then prayed that God would have His hand on the child and that he would grow up arid become a mighty warrior for the Gospel of Jesus Christ.

The Kidd family lived up a creek in the woods on the Pine Hall Road. They were too poor to have a car or truck, so the church Jeep Station Wagon picked up the entire family of thirteen and brought them to church. Later, there were others on the road that wanted to attend church but had no rides, so the church purchased a couple of buses from the school district and drove bus routes to the church every service. This allowed many families to attend the Evergreen Baptist Church who otherwise would never come to the church. Fran and the Preacher spent hours walking up these creeks and finding poor people living in the woods and talked with them about their salvation. The Kidd family was one of these poor clans who rode to the church every service on one of the buses.

Every member of the Kidd family had been baptized. First, the oldest daughter, Pam, and then Beatrice, the mother, after which Elmer the father, and then the other children. Elmo was the youngest and was baptized when he was seven years old and began making motions in the business meetings as soon as he was baptized and became a member.

The Kidds walked down the dirt path that led through the woods and followed the creek nearly one half mile from where their log house covered with tarpaper sat surrounded by hardwood trees. In the winter of 1959, Kentucky had its worse snowstorm in history, and when the bus came for them, they were all huddled together waiting for the ride to church. The bus was late that day because of the ice and snow on Chapel Gap Hill, and the family was nearly frozen to death.

My dad believed that the round redhead with big freckles was special because of an event that happened to Elmo when he was two years old. Beatrice had a very sick family that winter, and there was no way to get treatment for her children's illnesses except those homemade recipes that sustained them medically through the years. The children had whooping cough, and little Elmo had pneumonia. My mom had been down there helping to keep the children warm by bringing many quilts she had collected from the ladies in the church.

One of Beatrice Kidd's remedies, and not exclusive to her for they all used it when needed, was to put some "coal oil" as they called it in the Knobs, which was kerosene into a tin cup that had been heated to a boiling temperature, and then given to the sick child to drink. They used kerosene or "coal oil" for many things such as sore throats, colic, colds, and whooping cough.

Beatrice gave little Elmo a teaspoon of coal oil for a sore throat. Later that day when the family was out cutting and gathering firewood, Elmo found the cup with only a teaspoon missing and drank the whole thing. When they found him, he was lying on the floor, the tin cup near him where he had dropped it when he passed out, and he was already turned blue. Beatrice picked up the cute little boy and held him, but he was barely breathing, and his breath and heartbeat were getting fainter by the minute. Elmer, Mr. Kidd, ran out the door and down the path to the main road as fast as he could.

It was Ethel Martin who lived up the road from the Kidds' who first saw Elmer frantically waving his arms and standing in the middle of the road just hoping and praying that someone would come along before his little boy died. She stopped and asked the frantic man what was wrong and then sent him packing back up the creek to bring the child to her car.

Elmer Kidd carried his son, who was lifeless and limp in his arms. He told Ethel Martin he thought the boy was dead, but she rushed him to old Doe Sinclair's office in Crab Orchard, hoping and praying that the Doc was there.

The Doc told Mr. Kidd that his son would soon be dead if they could not get the coal oil out of his stomach. Doc Sinclair had a remedy for every thing. He had no stomach pump like the hospitals used, so he fed Elmo mustard and water. "Better than a pump," he said, "works every time."

The Preacher arrived soon because Ethel had yelled to Sophie Lord as she went by her house to call the Preacher and tell him to get down to Doe Sinclair's office. When the Preacher arrived, he the found out what had happened.

Elmo gagged a couple of times, which was a good sign, and then began throwing up the coal oil which was now black with the disgusting fluid that was poisoning him. After a while, he was through throwing up the liquid, and the Doc explained that Elmo would have dry heaves for some time and then would be all right.

"He may have brain damage," the Doe said, "but he'll live."

In a few hours, Elmo stirred and then opened his eyes. "I want to be a preacher like Preacher Smith," he yawned.

Elmo didn't have brain damage. In fact, his brothers and sisters said he was smarter after drinking the coal oil and almost dying than he was before.

Elmo Kidd was larger than his ten years of life and smart way beyond those ten years. He heard his name called by the Preacher and the question. He took a quick glance at the people whispering to one another and thought he heard Loretta Kirk ask my mother why was the Preacher calling on a child for advice? This didn't bother him so much because he was used to people complaining because he made a lot of important motions in the business meetings.

Elmo stood up in the face of a somewhat hostile congregation anxious to hear what wisdom a ten year old child could impart about Spiritual Adultery to saints many times his elder. He wasn't old enough to commit adultery, much less know anything about how the term applied to church people. He hiked up his bibbed overalls and looked at the Preacher carefully and keeping his own eyes from being distracted by the din of whispers in the background.

"Order!" My dad screamed, and the noise quietened as people wanted to hear.

"Preacher, I don't see how we can protect the purity and integrity of our church if our members are going to fraternize with the people of other denominations who don't believe and practice what we believe. If we don't have some way of checking our faith and make a statement, there will come a time when Baptist churches will be ashamed of their name because they won't have the stomach to stand up for what they believe. They'll even change their name from Baptist to some generic name so that they won't offend people. We have the largest group of believers in the United States of America, and we have more missionaries on the field than any other sect or denomination. Just look at what has already happened to us. We're ordaining women, women are speaking out in mixed assemblies, and every Tom, Dick, and Harry can take the Lord's Supper with us. We accept the baptisms of other denominations that don't even believe in Salvation by Grace through Faith or the Virgin Birth or Deity of Christ. Now, we're going to send our own members over to coddle these unbelievers? All of you should be ashamed to even think about killing this motion and putting your approval for worship with those who don't believe the Scripture as we do. If we don't take a stand right now, those doctrines we hold dear, and our forefathers held true, will be compromised. We'll take on the robes of social disgrace. Even now in the big cities, the prison dress codes are stricter than some Baptist churches."

Elmo sat down after he picked up his Bible and a very thick and heavy commentary he carried around with him all the time. We all knew he had to be a genius and was a voracious reader, but no one thought he had this much wisdom and could argue his beliefs at such a young age. Those whispers of discontent over what he said came from those who couldn't understand his big words.

"Any discussion?" My dad asked.

"Bro. Moderator," Francis Jenkins said. "I listened carefully to what this Kidd kid said, and I don't for one minute believe there will ever be a time when Baptist churches take the name "Baptist" off their signs."

What's this have to do with anything? my dad was thinking, *but Elmo brought it up.*

"Thank you, Bro. Jenkins, any other discussion?"

"Yes," Elmo Kidd said. "The Catholic Church will not let you come into their assembly and take communion with them or go to confession unless you're a Catholic. You can't just walk in off the street and say, "Here am I priest, bless me." They ain't afraid of public opinion. You know what else? They will excommunicate anyone who goes knocking on any other door but a Catholic church. I've heard the priest up in Ottenheim tell one of my friends at school to stop coming to Evergreen Baptist Church, or he would die and go to hell." Elmo Kidd had the attention of the members sitting in this business meeting. All eyes and ears were tuned into the larger than life boy who lived in the woods with thirteen people.

"Is the term, Spiritual Adultery" in the Bible?" Elmo asked.

"No, it isn't," my dad answered not really knowing where Elmo was going with this question.

"All right, it isn't. So, why don't we quit naming doctrines and giving them definitions that ain't in the Bible? The Catholics don't call it Spiritual Adultery or fornication because the term ain't in the Bible. Why should we? Change the language but not the conviction."

He sat down while the entire congregation was pondering this latest flash of wisdom from the redheaded kid. I personally never thought redheads could be that smart.

"Any other discussion?" The Preacher asked.

There was much discussion about what to call the doctrine that no one could prove was really a doctrine. The principle would mean that no member of the church could participate in the ordinances of other denominations, and if they did they would be excluded from their church, but those folks who simply wanted to attend a church of another denomination would not be excluded if they didn't miss their own church services in order to do so. It was also brought up that it might be a good idea that if a member of Evergreen Baptist Church attended a church of another faith, that member could exchange places with one of those members of the false church. The reasoning behind this part of the discussion was that if you went to a false church, your friend who invited you to attend his/her church would come to your church and get the truth. This was getting really complicated, and it looked like it would take a major church police force to enforce these rules.

Elmo Kidd shook his head through all this discussion and warned the crowd. "You don't go to bars and dances in order to get the drunks to come to church with you, or to a whorehouse in order to get the whore to church." Elmo knew this language in church; especially from a kid would shock all of them, and it did. "What do we have here? Five, ten members at the most who practice Spiritual Adultery? I'm telling you that if you do not take a stand, it is going to tear up our church; it will split right down the middle because you don't want to hurt the feelings of a minority of folks."

"I believe we ought to exclude Elmo Kidd for using filthy language in church!" One of the men yelled from the back of the church.

"The word, "Whore," is in the Bible," my dad answered.

"So is piss!" Someone yelled, and the young people snickered.

Things were getting out of hand, so the Preacher brought the discussion to a conclusion. He now had another problem, and that was to vote on those people who had sinned and exclude them from the church. After that, he would deal with the problem of Spiritual Adultery, and the name change Elmo Kidd suggested.

"We certainly have some things to consider," the Preacher said. "We'll begin by deciding on a doctrinal name change." He suddenly changed his mind about how to approach the trouble. "Do I hear a motion that we change the name of the doctrine?"

"Motion!" Jerry Gaston gestured. "Let's call it Church Attendance at Another Denomination."

This was simple enough and when the Preacher called for discussion, there was none.

"Second?"

"Second!" Bro. Roundtree, a new member, yelled from the back of the auditorium.

"Motion carried to change Spiritual Adultery and Fornication to "Church Attendance at Another Denomination" were the words that Rhea Ford wrote in her book of minutes.

"I have a list of people that have been guilty in the past of Church Attendance at Another Denomination," my dad said. "Now we have to decide what the penalty for going to another church is going to be."

When my dad called for discussion, there was a lot of debate. If the church decided that these members should be excluded, this meant there were a lot of friends on the list that would no longer be members of his church. He had baptized every one of them in the Cedar Creek by the bridge, and some of them in the wintertime. It was finally decided that guilty members would not be allowed to vote in the regular business meetings until they rededicated their lives in front of the church and asked forgiveness.

This meant Loretta Kirk. "Hell," she said to my mom, "I re-dedicate every once in a while anyway. They won't know what I'm up in front of the church for."

"What do I do with this list?" My dad asked the busy crowd.

"I make a motion we do nothing to these people. To make it retroactive would not be right. We start fresh, right now, and give these people a chance to forsake their sin." This motion was made by Nathan Smith who had come back to the church after leaving with the Messers and Cullens for pulling out of the Southern Baptist Convention.

"Second." I motioned quickly just to move things along.

The motion carried, the business meeting was voted to adjourn, and the members of the Evergreen Baptist Church left the building. That should have been the end of all things controversial, but it wasn't.

The old timers in the church did not like the doctrinal "twist" as they called it, and the young lions in the church, who wanted to see the church progress out of the Dark Ages and into more modern times thought the rules were ridiculous, and they would do whatever they pleased and never repent before the church.

Money got involved. If the Preacher alienated the old folks, who had the money, his church could not survive financially. If he alienated the young people, he would have no one to raise families in the church and continue its posterity.

Fran and the Preacher were on visitation one Saturday afternoon. I had gone to see Kathy.

"I don't know what to do, Fran," my dad said lugubriously. "I feel like I'm losing my people. Ever since the business meeting last month, they have been fighting like cats and dogs. They're choosing sides."

Fran pondered the Preacher's feelings on the matter, but he had been thinking. "You know, dad," and then Fran caught himself. He would call the Preacher "dad" if he ever married my sister. My dad noticed this and was pleased for he wanted more than anything in the world to have Fran Job as his son-in-law. "When it gets right down to it, people are going to do what they do, and there ain't much anybody can do about it. You can't legislate Spirituality. They are either Godly, or they ain't."

Fran would be leaving for the Navy in a few weeks, and I would be going to Brazil. The Preacher's older folks were getting older and with the war in Vietnam, he was going to lose some of his boys to battle. The business meeting quickly changed everything in his ministry. It happened when he was unprepared. He was kicking himself for his lack of understanding that things were changing, and he had no ability to adjust because he was a victim of his own preaching.

My dad walked around the church one Sunday morning. Sally Barber and Junebug had finished cleaning the building and put the new Baptist Hymnals, purchased from the Southern Baptist Book Store in Nashville, in the book racks on the back of the seats. He was using visiting cards now and asking all the new visitors who were first time attendees to fill out the cards and place them in the offering plate. Even this change caused a riffle throughout the church membership because some felt that the Preacher was getting too modern.

The Preacher was thinking about the special business meeting he called to suggest that members of the church under sixteen years of age should not be allowed to vote or make motions. They overwhelmingly shot that down saying that you may as well quit baptizing children. Only Elmo Kidd, who had been making motions since he was seven years old, Fran, myself, and Bro. Lord sided with him. My mom voted against it. Even a passionate display of oratory by the young Kidd kid, who had persuaded the church before, made no difference. When Elmo reasoned with the church that too much pressure was put on the children with motion and voting rights, it was to no avail. The Preacher lost a battle he was sure would be no problem to win.

This church is lost in time. He was deep in thought as he looked at the stain glass window behind the pulpit dedicated to James W. Bishop. *Part of this whole scene is my fault for trying to hang on to so many traditions. The entire world is changing, and as soon as they blacktop that gravel road over there, there will be no more Evergreen Baptist Church as I know it now.* The thoughts were flying through his brain ninety miles an hour.

He walked around the cemetery. This was something he had not done in eleven years of preaching at the church. He looked at all the people he had buried. Some he knew well, and some he didn't. He looked at Benji McDuff's grave and remembered what a rascal he was. When he came to Riley Pat's grave, he broke down in tears. He touched the tombstone of old Doc Sinclair and rubbed the monument the Evergreen Baptist Church had erected to this man who gave the church all his money. He thought about the Doc and how that no one really knew what religion he was or if he was born again. "Rest well, old friend," he whispered while tears fell from his handsome face. He walked passed Sterling Deaton, and remembered the night Fran and me stole the man's gourds, and he had to whip me in front of the entire church, and he smiled. He touched Simon Gastner's gravestone and remembered how his old coon dog howled in bitter grief at the passing of his beloved master. He bowed his head as he looked at John and Meg Frazier lying side-by-side resting in peace and then he came to Tip Tuck's grave. He stood there staring at the tombstone until his whole shirt was wet with tears. "I loved this man," he agonized, and the memory of the accident of this most gentle man whose life had been snuffed out prematurely, tore out his insides.

He finished the tour passing little babies and children, passing old folks, whose time had come to die and depart the world, and then he came face to face with the burial resting place of Homer Shanks; the good Deputy who couldn't read and write. On his stone it said, "He loved his Lord, his Preacher, and his family."

"That's it," my dad said to himself out loud. He walked to the long rope hanging in the vestibule of the church and rang the bell to call his people to worship at the Evergreen Baptist Church for the last time.

CHAPTER FIFTY

P eople dressed in their Sunday best could be seen walking across the fields and along the road that leads to the
church. As had been for years, cars and pickups began to
arrive in time for Sunday service and Sunday School. The bell
was rung exactly thirty minutes before service time and once
more at five minutes until 10:00 AM. The atmosphere in the
church seemed to note that people had forgiven each other
for harsh words and strong gossip. The old ladies were in their
regular seats, and the old men were sitting by the windows,
spitting tobacco juice at an occasional "wasper" that flew down
from the nests in the eaves of the building The young people
nearly filled one side of the auditorium. The attendance of
many youth was a change that had taken place over the years
at Evergreen Baptist Church. There were so many youth sitting in one section that the people called it "youth acres." Except for the Preacher, all seemed normal and busy as usual.
My dad didn't look at all happy and didn't seem to be himself.

"Something's up, Bud," Fran said to me.

I knew better than to ask Fran how he knows anything anymore. He just knows, so I kept my mouth shut.

"What's up?" I asked him casually.

"I'm not sure, but the Preacher don't look right."

"Maybe he's sick," I said although I hadn't heard he was. He was never sick, but I did notice that things weren't quite right about him.

I watched my mother. She kept looking at her husband and then looking down. Whatever this reaction of his to what something was, she knew about it, too. It was all good and normal until the Preacher stepped behind his pulpit after the last congregational song. Preacher Roundtree's family had sung a special, and April May and her son, Chuck May who was down from Cincinnati visiting his mom for her birthday, had just finished their song, "Jesus Savior Pilot Me."

The crowd said "Amen" in unison after the song, and even the women were now saying "amen" when the whole congregation said it. This was a change in the church worship that the Preacher was powerless to stop. Chuck May had a whiny country voice and never fully pronounced his words. He trailed off, "Jesu Savio Pilo Me," while his mother, April, sang in a slightly off key alto, which she had been singing for more years than anyone could remember. This duet was loved by the Knob people and many would wipe the tears from their eyes as the loud, off key duet echoed off the walls of the church.

My dad stepped behind the pulpit without acknowledging the special music as being "wonderful" or "heavenly." He usually went on and on about how lovely it was to see a mother and son praising the Lord in song, or a whole family like the Roundtrees dedicating their voices to God. If the special singers were waiting for those compliments this Sunday morning, they were disappointed.

The Preacher always opened his Bible before he said anything. His habit was to stand there in silence until he found the Scripture and then he would ask the congregation to raise their Bibles if they had one, and let him see them when they had found the text from which he was going to preach. This was his method of getting every single member and visitor of Evergreen Baptist church coming to worship to carry his or her Bibles to church. Not holding up your Bible wasn't good. He did none of this. He never opened his Bible, and the whole crowd knew something was wrong with him. Even the smallest children recognized everything was out of sync. He didn't say, "Brothers and Sisters in Christ," either. He said, "Ladies and Gentlemen of Evergreen Baptist Church." This was bad, real, real, bad. I felt a sickness in my stomach, and I was hoping he would say, "just kidding," but there was no evidence of a smile on his face.

"I've been praying about some things heavy on my heart," he began, and we listened as you could hear the proverbial pin drop in that place. There were some men on the outside that crowded toward the open windows, and some of the women bit their shawls.

"I have prayed diligently about what I am going to say this morning. I say it with the most humble but heavy heart. I was thinking about waiting until the end of the service to tell you what's on my mind, but I can't see that the Holy Spirit would ever bless this message with all these things weighing on me."

When he said these things, Loretta Kirk sank low in her seat. She was thinking that he might be going to throw her out of the church for causing him all the grief she had through the years, and she wasn't the only one thinking this. Ever since that first night when he stepped in the pulpit and began his ministry at Evergreen Baptist Church and then whipped Evel Martin, the people never doubted that he meant business. He was faithful and loyal to them, but sometimes they took him for granted, and there wasn't one person in the assembly that morning that wasn't thinking about that.

The Evergreen Baptist Church had many pastors over the years since its organization at the top of the little knob a hundred years before, but no one could remember a pastor like this one. The man who many said looked like Gregory Peck had left his wheat farm in Kansas and moved his wife and two children to take up a pastorate of this little known and obscure congregation of "Knob dwellers." No one had been in all their church lives more loyal, more faithful, more loving, and less self-serving than this Preacher. He had built this congregation to one of the largest of any church in Lincoln County, but today they were afraid of what some had gossiped was the inevitable. No shepherd stayed with the flock forever.

My mom was crying because of all the memories, and I could only guess that a dark day was about to dawn on unsuspecting members of this good church. "People, I feel that God is through with my ministry at Evergreen Baptist Church. I don't say this lightly, but I do say it. This morning, I am resigning my position as Pastor of the Evergreen Baptist Church."

"NO!" Someone cried and soon there was weeping and wailing throughout the entire congregation inside and out. Grown men who were tough and rugged were weeping at this announcement. Those men, who stood on the outside of the building and smoked during the services, were crying. Floods of tears were saturating the clothing of these startled and grieving people.

"I've grown up here," he said, "as a man of God, and I doubt in my lifetime I shall ever encounter more wonderful people. It would be difficult for any pastor to love his membership and community as much. But, God has called me just as he called me to salvation that day in the Sun Valley School House in

Vine Creek, Kansas. Now, I must answer His call once again. This next Lord's Day, I will be the new Pastor of the Northside Baptist Church in Lexington, Kentucky. The Scripture says that when you quit, "Quit ye like men." And then, he wept, unable to speak as the tears of sorrow flowed from his eyes before his whole body of believers.

"Did you know this, Fran?" I asked while we were both crying.

"No, but I knew something was up when he went over to Lexington last week and wouldn't tell me about it."

No one could sing without breaking down. Preacher Roberts picked the worse song in the whole world for the congregation to sing at invitation time. "Blest Be The Tie That Binds Our Hearts In Christian Love." We could barely sing this song, and if you had just walked in the church, you would think we were speaking in tongues or something because the syllables were not understandable. The Preacher wailed through the whole song, wiping his eyes and blowing his nose. We sang all the verses not remembering what the message of the song was, but every word triggered more weeping. The song was finished. My dad stood in his usual place at the door. Sometimes, when he did this ritual of hand shaking, some would slip past him because the women could go on and on about how great his sermon was that morning even though many of them slept through the whole exhortation.

No one sneaked out that morning of resignation. Every person in the church waited in line to touch the man of God. They fell on his neck and kissed him, men and women, wiping their tears on the side of his face and shoulders. Little kids, who sensed the sadness of it all, hugged him around the knees, and he would lift them to his chest and hug them for the last time. Young adults, who knew no other preacher than him, cried and begged him to stay. A couple of the members said they would ask the church to change anything he was un-happy with if he would reconsider.

Loretta Kirk came to her place in the line of grievers. My dad looked at her, and she looked at him. She was a large woman, not fat, but tall and big boned; taller than him. She held her place for a moment and then rushed him. She hugged him, raising him off the floor and kissed his face over and over while tears fell from her eyes, and his did the same. She told him again and again how sorry she was and that if it weren't for him, she would be dying and going to hell. "You saved me," she said.

Bro. Lord hugged my dad, and former Sheriff Crane; all the deacons took their turns and their wives. Fran and I were last. My mom had taken my two sisters, Leah and Nila, and my brother Val Mark, to the farm to get them away from all the grief. My mother could stand it no longer, and she would miss Chapel Gap and the Evergreen Baptist Church as much as my dad.

Fran cried worse than I had ever seen him cry. He sobbed and sobbed, and he knew this was going to be the scene he would face with his parents and friends when he left for Navy Boot Camp. My dad held him, and then it came my turn.

I looked at my dad while shaking my head in disbelief. I could say nothing except, "Dad, you're not going to be my Pastor anymore!" This solemn thought hit me right between the eyes. I had never thought about that in my whole life. Few kids have the privilege of their fathers being their dad and their pastor. The preacher's kids I knew, except for Mark Crawford, almost hated their parents and their ministries. Most of them turned out to be terrible people, resentful, but not me. I loved and respected my dad both as a father and a pastor. I would miss Chapel Gap and the fiery preacher who boldly told the folks how the Lord wanted them to live.

Loretta Kirk stood on the parking lot waving at all the women. She would not allow one of them to escape, and she started shouting orders.

"Sophie, Gertie, Halley, Sharon, you make pies. Becky, Sally, Margaret, Ethel, April, you all kill chickens and fry them. Shirley Messer, Joyce, Lizzie, Mandy, June, Juanita, Agnus, you all make corn on the cob and settle between you what vegetables and casseroles to bring. I'll bring hot rolls and mashed potatoes and gravy. You other ladies there, make plenty of Kool-Aid. The Preacher likes cherry. All you men standing there doing nothing but smoking and chewing, bring your wagons and meet me here at 6:oo PM!"

Thus, Loretta Kirk repaid my dad in one afternoon all that she had done to make his life miserable. She took charge and orchestrated my dad's last Sunday at the church.

"There'll be no preaching," she ordered. "Preaching is finished for this man. Lots of music and good food is what we'll have! Jess, you and Burl round up some guys and bring your banjos and fiddles."

She interrupted Burl.

"I don't care what the Preacher don't like. It's high time those good musicians got to play songs in church rather than the bars. The devil's had them long enough, and besides, he ain't in charge here no more!"

People left the church in a hurry because there was much to do. I told Fran that I wasn't going home with him; and instead, I was going to Kathy's house and bring her up for the evening festivities.

I drove over to Kathy's and found her in the hay barn raking some straw from the loft to the cribs below.

"Hey, girly."

"What are you doing here? Why are your eyes so bloodshot?"

"I need to talk to you."

"Come up here and help me finish this," she instructed, "then we'll talk." I climbed the ladder to the loft, and as soon as I got to the top and stuck my head through the trap door, she kicked straw all over me. I jumped up and chased the little bugger all over the hayloft and then we both dropped on some soft straw and kissed.

"My dad resigned the church," I said.

"You're kidding?"

"I wish I were; the people are a mess."

Kathy was sad and lay there for a few minutes as we both stared at the mud dobbers building nests on the barn rafters.

"The church is having a big shindig tonight for my dad's last service. I want you to come with me."

"Did they know about this, and you didn't tell me?"

"We all found out about two hours ago during his morning message."

"Then how can they have dinner on the grounds with no notice?"

"Loretta Kirk, Kathy, you should have seen her screaming at everybody and telling them what to bring tonight."

"Do you need to tell Pastor Ledbetter that you won't be in services tonight?"

"What? I don't ask him where I go or don't go. He's got no control over who does what. I do what I want. No problem," she said. Maybe this is what Elmo Kidd was talking about concerning the changes coming; preachers losing control of their churches.

When Kathy and I got to the church, there were more people than I had ever seen including old Doc Sinclair's funeral. Wagons were loaded with food of every sort, and the ladies of the church had hustled wonderfully to get all those victuals fixed. Chestnut Ridge Baptist Church dismissed their Sunday night services as many of the ladies called around the area to tell their relatives and Christian friends from other churches the news. Several folks came to the festivals that were members of the Mount Olive Church of Christ, and a couple of Catholics.

"You know we're going through this same thing, don't you?" Kathy said as the VW pulled into the church drive off the gravel road. "In about a month."

"I don't want to talk about it right now," I said, "I've got enough on my mind." She squeezed my hand.

There wasn't the sadness like the morning goodbyes. These people had a way of accepting things quickly and then moving on. They reasoned with each other that this event should be a parting celebration of the good man's ministry and not a death dirge.

"Quiet, quiet!" Bro. Lord said as he beat a spoon on a gallon jug of sweet tea. "Gather round here." We all gathered and pushed closely to the wagon where Bro. Lord was standing above the crowd. "I'm calling a business meeting!" He yelled. "Do I hear a motion that Bro. Smith can't go to Lexington to another church and leave us?"

"Motion," Elmo Kidd shrieked.

"Second?" Bro. Lord asked.

"Second!" Loretta Kirk yelled.

"All in favor? Raise your right hands."

All hands were raised, and then they laughed, and then they cried.

CHAPTER FIFTY-ONE

W e stayed on the farm at Chapel Gap while my dad went back and forth to Lexington to preach on Sundays and Wednesdays at his new church. He and my mom went to find a house, and while they were in Lexington, they stayed at my dad's friend's house, Carlo Sandlin. I was leaving soon and so was Fran, so my dad decided not to sell the farm until we were gone.

The church hired a new Pastor from the Lexington Baptist College where my dad graduated with his degree in Theology and Ministry. His name was Donnie Asher, and the people liked him. He was unmarried, young, and fresh in the ministry, but my dad knew him and trusted that he could perform his pastoral duties even though it was never a good idea for a pastor to be single. I thought Pastor Asher was a little weak, and that if he ever ran into somebody like Evel Martin, he wouldn't last a week. He would have his hands full with the likes of Loretta Kirk, but she would probably give him the best education of anyone in the ways of leading a flock. The church trusted him because he was from the same college that molded my dad, and besides, the church was grounded enough in the faith that they wouldn't be sidetracked by the mistakes he was bound to make. There was one thing that Pastor Donnie Asher, or anyone else who stepped into that pulpit must realize, and that was one step out of line with Pastor Jerry Smith's preaching and method of doing business, would end with the guy's neck on the chopping block. The young Pastor's first sermon on "Moses Thy Servant Is Dead," almost got him kicked out of the church his first Sunday morning. He also wasn't strong enough to ring the bell before services, which wasn't good. Loretta Kirk suggested that he go out and work for her husband, Gib, on the farm to get himself "toughened up."

My whole family went down to Stanford to meet Fran's recruiter who would drive Fran to Louisville where he would catch the bus that would take him to the Naval Base in Chicago for Boot Camp.

I stood by myself as Fran kissed my mom and dad goodbye and hugged Leah.

"This is the time, Bud," Fran said as he walked over to me.

"I guess so," I said sadly. Memories had been plaguing me all that week as I thought about all that Fran and me had been through. We were "joined at the hip" as some of the farmers used to say when they would watch us work in the fields and tobacco crops.

We were going to become "unjoined," and it was time to grow up and become men. We both dreaded this day, but I knew Fran could handle anything thrown at him no matter what it was.

"Don't sink any ships," I said.

"Don't get eaten by a crocodile," he said and then we hugged each other but refused to cry.

We watched as Fran looked out the rear window of the recruiter's car and waved goodbye. I wouldn't see him for a very long time. I drove down to Stanford by myself because I planned on going up to Kathy's and eat fried chicken dinner with her family that evening. It was Donnie Friday's birthday, and this family was big on birthdays. Kathy refused to come with me to see Fran off. She said she couldn't stand any more sad farewells.

All the way to her house, I thought about our graduation. Fran, Kathy, and a host of other kids growing up in the Knobs, graduated that year, including myself. In fact, it was the most graduates of all the schools combined that the Knobs had ever seen. The average grade of school that the Knob people completed was seven.

It was a solemn day, that graduation. I wasn't going to have time to enjoy it all. I was leaving two weeks afterwards, and Fran left today. My dad was the speaker for the graduation service. He told us how our lives were about to change, and that we would never be the same. He said, "Many of you will waste your lives. You'll sit in front of a television set until your brain becomes the size of a pea."

None of us could fathom anyone watching television for any length of time; especially, kids who had so much energy and so many places to play. Television would never take the place of playing in the streets or old sand lot baseball fields.

I thought about how wonderful and beautiful Kathy looked as she accepted her award as Valedictorian of Crab Orchard High School. The sun shown off her hair making her look like she was wearing a halo, *I'm so in love with that girl, I can't stand it,* I thought. *I can't bear the thoughts of leaving her.*

We graduated, and the boys were looking at working full time on their dad's farms. Very few would go to college; only a handful of us if that many. Most of the kids that had grown up

626 · SHERMAN SMITH

in Chapel Gap would be there for the rest of their lives while the world tried its best to capture them.

The Saturday before my dad would drive me to Cincinnati, Ohio to catch the plane bound for Brazil, Kathy and I spent the entire day together. Her dad wanted her to at least do some chores, but she snuffed him off. I knew the day would go very fast, and it did. Too fast. We drove up to Cumberland Falls, Kentucky, the largest falls in America besides the Niagara Falls up in New York State. We walked along the trails of the falls and watched the spray and let it hit our faces, cooling us in the heat of the hot sun. We drove over to Cumberland Lake and then back to Copper Creek. We were both sad when the day ended, and when I kissed her goodbye, it would be the last time we would date for a very long time.

I quit going to Evergreen Baptist Church and attended with Kathy at the Copper Creek Baptist Church. The Preacher told our family that we should get out of the church at Evergreen Baptist and stay out of the new Pastor's way. That was okay with me because I didn't like his preaching anyway. I did like Pastor Otis Ledbetter. He didn't seem much older than me, and he liked to play ball and fish. He couldn't stand the cold water in the springtime, so he didn't gig. He was a good man.

My family was in Lexington at the new church. My dad bought a house on Lane Allen Road, and they were staying there while I stayed at the farm. After church on Sunday, I ate dinner with the Fridays, and I would have to leave in mid-afternoon and drive to our house in Lexington. Kathy and I took a walk to the creek where we went often to talk.

"What am I going to do without you for two and a half years?" She asked quietly.

"And what will I do without you?" I asked. Two years seemed like a lifetime, and I was already losing my appetite for the jungles and adventures of Brazil.

"This will test our love," she said.

I thought I knew what she meant, but I laid off asking any questions. I held her close in my arms while she and I both sobbed. We loved each other, and we would be soul mates for sure. I would see Kathy Friday again, but it would be a very long time from that day we said goodbye standing by the blackberry patch on Copper Creek.

EPILOGUE

I could see the Knobs as I flew toward Brazil. I looked down on the region I loved and wondered how long could the place be so lost in time?

I had seen these big jets fly over our mountains hundreds of times, but it never registered to me just how I could ever be one of those people so high in the sky looking down on my world.

I knew that I was going into a country that was even more remote and infinitely more dangerous, but those people living in the jungles of Brazil that I would get to know, weren't supposed to know all that we do in America. The Knob folks resisted the modernization and philosophies of the world rather than embrace them. They were happy living their lives without the interference and intrusions that threatened to change the way they lived and thought. Little did I know that I would wonder the same things about those isolated natives living in a distant jungle. Were they as happy and content as the Knob people? Would we spoil their world? If so, then why didn't we just leave them alone?

I thought I saw Kathy Friday's farm after I had looked down on the Evergreen Baptist Church surrounded by a well-kept cemetery. Way up high, I was so far from her, yet she was only a few thousand feet below me, and I couldn't touch her one more time. Like a dream, she may have seen the plane and waved to me, knowing at that same instant I was looking at her out of the small window and blowing a kiss.

I was already homesick. I wished I hadn't gotten on that plane, but it was too late. What would happen in this life to come? Would I be singing, or would I be crying? Would the years roll by with happiness and peace, or would they move on in solitude and sorrow?

The Preacher did not know the first day he walked into the pulpit of the Northside Baptist Church in Lexington, Kentucky that he would begin another love affair with a group of people that would last for thirty years. For decades, he would preach all the funerals and marry more people who grew up with him at the Evergreen Baptist Church. They would never allow another pastor to take his place so long as he lived. He would always be the Preacher in Lincoln County. When he died, the funeral procession and line waiting to view his body was so extended that it was a block long of steadily passing folks paying their respects to a good and decent man. Many of those folks were from the Knobs.

Fran Job went to the Navy. He spent four years on an aircraft carrier somewhere in the Mediterranean Sea. When he married my sister, Leah, he still had never looked at another girl. He became the head and eventual owner of the family business and is a successful businessman today. He never left the Preacher's side after coming back from the Navy, and was a deacon in the Preacher's church until the Preacher died.

My little brother, Val Mark, is a Pastor in California and was before his surrender to the ministry and following in his father's footsteps, a successful businessman himself.

Nila, my little sister, married a good man and travels extensively as a publicist for the giant Toyota Corporation and meets stars and superstars as she raises thousands of dollars for Toyota's benevolent programs and projects.

Loretta Kirk lives in the Knobs as do most of those whose stories are told in this book.

The Evergreen Baptist Church functions well and still sits on the little hill surrounded by the cemetery. The stained glass window dedicated to the memory of James W. Bishop is still behind the pulpit.

As for those fictional characters in this book, they just went away to make room for the Amish people who have moved into the area and have changed the landscape. Perhaps they are trying to bring back another world gone by.

As for me, I married Kathy Ann Friday thirty-three years later.